The Crystal Contract

There were, just as there had to be, two black nylon shoulder-bags, identical save for the telltale chalk mark near the lock on one of them. For a moment the temptation to take the other, to take the one that was hers, was a biological imperative, but something in her had set, she was committed to see this through, get it right, and she took the one with the chalk mark.

Now it was like the walk to the scaffold, an interminable trek into the second bottleneck. Green channel, nothing to declare. Red. She faltered, took the green. It divided. Long benches to the left, long benches to the right, surely reassuringly understaffed, only two Customs officers behind each. She hesitated, went left, behind a gang of skins, including the couple she had spoken to. The customs would be ready for them, would expect them to be loaded with speed, dope, and crack – whatever that was.

And it was working. Three of them were called over, and that appeared to take care of all available officers. Somewhere in her brain brass bands began to play, scarlet tulips opened in spring sunshine, she did not even see him as she made for the exit, yet he came from somewhere, came from behind and tapped her on the shoulder.

'Good morning, miss. I should like you to accompany me over to the bench for a moment.'

Books by Julian Rathbone

JULIAN RATHBONE

The
Crystal Contract

A Mandarin Paperback

THE CRYSTAL CONTRACT

First published in Great Britain 1988
by William Heinemann Ltd
This edition published 1989
by Mandarin Paperbacks
an imprints of Reed Consumer Books Ltd
Michelin House, 81 Fulham Road, London SW3 6RB
and Auckland, Melbourne, Singapore and Toronto

Reprinted 1989 (twice), 1990, 1994

Copyright © Julian Rathbone 1988

A CIP catalogue record for this title
is available from the British Library

ISBN 0 7493 0076 0

Printed and bound in Great Britain
by HarperCollins Manufacturing, Glasgow

Contents

Part One

Dramatis Personae

1

It was one of those clear, bright mornings you get in the early spring in California before the high fog sets in: the foothills green, snow still flashes from the peaks, and the jacaranda trees are just beginning to bloom.

A Dodge Monaco, sapphire blue, black vinyl top, wire wheels, pumped white dust through orange groves. The Sierra on the far edge of the valley hung above them in the east, violet shading to lavender beneath a cerulean sky.

The road took a sudden turn towards the mountains, and Lili Brel, cradled in black leather, with her feet on cashmere carpets, caught her first sight of Villa Mendoza. Near the foot of the mountains, like a headland off a cliff-bound coast, a rocky hill rose abruptly, in places almost precipitously, from the plain. Along the crest but spreading out from it was a linked complex of white buildings with red-tiled roofs, mostly low, though those built into the hillside had three or four storeys. Much of it was shielded from below by poplars, cypresses, and more exotic trees, some in lavish bloom with swags of falling yellow and purple.

Still five circuitous miles to go. She took off her shades, unfolded gold-framed half-lenses from a slim red leather wallet, looped the silk cord over her head. A long finger, perfectly manicured but no longer young, ran over a three-sheet CV of the man she had come to see.

Don Pedro Mendoza y La Cerda, duque de Pastrana y príncipe de Eboli, born in the la Paz clinic, Madrid, 10.2.53, she read, *was privately educated at Monte Cielo, the Mendoza home near Granada, Spain . . . In 1976 he was invited to represent Spain at the Olympic Games in the foil and dressage but declined. He knew he could not win either event and Mendozas do not lose in public . . . Principal residences: Villa Mendoza in California and Monte Cielo, Granada, Spain, but also has homes in New York, Madrid and Rome with* pieds-à-terre *in London and Paris . . .*

For the last six years his overriding interest has been scientific breeding, and genetics. He has created a small but impressive stud of thoroughbreds and has donated large sums to research establishments specialising in selective breeding in many fields: from roses, orchids and seed corn, to dogs, and even higher primates . . .

His only marriage, to Doña Octavia Arias de Quesada, of Barranquilla and Bogotá, Colombia, ended after six months when she was killed in a car crash . . .

The basis of the Mendoza fortune is land in Andalusia, mainly devoted to producing quality olive oil and manzanilla sherry. But the conglomerate known collectively as Mendoza Holdings also owns a large slice of the Spanish nuclear industry, has holdings in South African minerals and metals, international agri-business, and US sunrise industries. Excluding a large and very valuable art collection Don Pedro's personal fortune is estimated conservatively at one billion dollars . . .

Brel took off her spectacles, tapped the gold rim on even but slightly protrusive teeth and let her mind dwell for a moment on Mendoza Holdings: not quite in the top hundred, but not far off it, a manageable size, a size she could manage. She gave a little shudder which expressed a lot. Lili Brel was a woman who rarely let her feelings show. She folded away the spectacles, slipped the document back into its wallet.

A signposted turning, and the Dodge, which had met her at LA airport, swung on to a private road. It climbed through more orchards, of grapefruit now, many of them rotting on the ground beneath the trees, to a white arched gateway with the sixteen quarters of the Mendoza arms on the posts, done in a nicely curlicued rococo style. While the chauffeur offered plastic to scanning devices Brel, fiscal consultant to the superrich, noted amongst the arms the lion of Léon, the castle of Castille, the vertical stripes of Aragon, all to be found on the achievement of Juan Carlos I himself.

The usual notices warned of guard dogs. These turned out to be not the conventional Dobermans but a cross between Anatolian Shepherds and Arctic wolves. She noted them too, guessed that they must be a product of Mendoza's obsession with breeding, heredity – the obsession which had made her visit possible. Bigger than wolves and shaggier, they lay,

4

tongues out, in the shade of the ilex and cork trees amongst daisies, wild lavender and broom, but they looked lean, hungry. Brel zipped the document back into her case, folded back her glasses.

A second set of gates, less forbidding than the first, opened into a circle at the foot of the craggy hill. There was stabling beneath giant cedars, and presumably a garage. At any rate the big car slid to a stop, and the Mex chauffeur opened the door. Lili Brel refused his hand, swung thin legs elegantly shod in tan snakeskin court shoes to the soft surface of cork granules, straightened, smoothed the skirt of her Liberty paisley silk, done in muted shades of beige, accepted the jacket from the chauffeur and her slim pigskin document case.

She was the sort of woman who appears taller than she is: thin, a head always held high with short hair cut like a cap and tinted to suggest that gilded silver was silvered gold. She had a long thin nose, lilac eyes, a thin mouth, and her pose, twisted as she took in her surroundings, with her shell-framed shades dangling from long, perfectly manicured fingers, expressed alertness, confidence. She was fifty years old, and even in the harsh Californian sunlight looked no more than forty.

A tall man dressed in a tweed cap, white shirt, leather waistcoat and jodhpurs, came towards her from the stables. He had a brown, lined, out-of-door face, strong hands. 'Miss Brel? My name is Jean-Luc Cazenove, and I am Pedro's stud manager. He has just phoned down his apologies. He will not be through with Signor Vasari for half an hour or so, and he suggested you might be interested in seeing something of the stud.'

She shrugged, smiled. 'If half what one has heard is true, it would be silly to miss the opportunity.'

He understood her correctly and led her directly across a cobbled, scrubbed yard to a loosebox larger than the rest, roomy and airy, lit by skylights ten feet from the ground.

The stallion was big, eighteen hands at least, a very dark bay, almost black, with a white flash on his forehead and one white sock. He had a narrow head which, at seven years old, looked small on top of his strong arching neck. His quarters were heavy and strong, his chest deep, his balls like purple fruit, ovoid aubergines. He was sweating slightly, clearly excited, restless, rolling dark eyes that occasionally flashed white. A smell came off him that was acrid, electric, the smell you get after lightning has struck uncomfortably close. Occasionally he neighed, and it was high and clear, sharp and peremptory.

Cazenove explained: 'We have two brood mares on the other side of the yard, just coming into heat, and he can smell them. We expect him to cover at least one later in the afternoon. If you're still around it's worth seeing.'

'He never raced, is that right?' Brel spoke in a soft voice that trapped people into paying attention.

'Oh yes. Sherpa came under orders twice as a two-year-old. Both times in Ireland. The first time he took a class field by four lengths over six furlongs. The second time he killed his jock in the starting stall. After that there was no question of racing him again. Clearly he might injure himself and that would have been the end of an investment worth several million dollars.'

The merest hint of a smile lifted a corner of Brel's mouth. 'But how do you get stud fees on a record as limited as that?'

The stallion had come to the front of the box, tossing his head up and down over the long high sill which ran the whole width. Jean-Luc let him nuzzle into his shoulder for a second, gave him some small treat taken from his waistcoat pocket.

'You've heard the story they tell about him then.'

'Of course.'

He gave Sherpa a good heavy pat on his glossy neck, pushed the narrow but intelligent head away. 'Let me say this. If it had happened it would have happened like they tell it.'

'So?'

Cazenove laughed. The stallion came back to him, ears pushed forward, nuzzled again at his shoulder, then curvetted away, tail in the air like a black panache.

'He knows the story, likes to hear you tell it.'

'Maybe. Okay. Dawn, end of June, three weeks after the English Derby he would have run in if we had let him, we got together a field of eight. One five-year-old and two four-year-olds including a third in a previous Derby and horses placed in the previous Oaks and St Leger. I won't say more, wouldn't do their owners, trainers, or jocks any good if they were identified. Used the old tapes for a start instead of stalls . . .'

6

'So what happened?'

'What they say happened is this. He came into Tattenham Corner fifth and took it wide. The grass had grown a bit, and the top was quite hard. One thing we could not do was go over the course, get it ready the way they do before a big meeting. So no chances of damage or as few as possible. He came round wide on the outside and almost lost touch with the leader, the four-year-old, dropping back to sixth. But then the jock dropped his hands and he lengthened his stride and came back well. He held him there, about four lengths from the front, in the middle of the course, to the first furlong marker, changed his hands, let him see the whip, and he came away like Concorde . . .' Enthusiasm lifted Jean-Luc's voice, his eyes had a distant look, as if he really was on playback, seeing it all. 'He took them by three lengths, only one second outside the record. The jock said it was the best ride he'd had over the course, and he'd had a few. That's what they say happened. On Epsom Downs, one day in June, nearly four years ago.'

'And they say,' said Brel, 'you can see it on video, but only if you're booking his services, and seeing it on video puts a quarter of a million on the price.'

'That's what they say,' said Jean-Luc, coming back to earth. 'And of course that would be fair. You know, if he really had run in this alternative Derby, it would have cost a lot of money to set up, a lot of money to get the other horses to run, a lot of money to make sure no one could ever put a case in front of the Jockey Club such that they would have to believe it and do something about it. A lot of money.'

'But it's paying off. I don't suppose those mares waiting across the yard for his lordship's services are rubbish.'

Jean-Luc came off the wall he had been leaning against, and spoke a little more slowly than before, with even more care. 'They are the best. And Sherpa is better than the best. And that's really the point, you know? What Pedro wants is to make sure the best breeds with the best. For all Sherpa has the right blood, the very best might still not have been made available for him, without . . . without the legend. And for Pedro that would have been tragic. For him, in every generation the best must breed with the best, at any cost. That's what he believes, that's what he sees is his duty and responsibility, the responsibility that justifies his position and privilege.

Maybe I sound, how do you say, over the top. No matter. It's the truth.'

A bleeper burbled in his waistcoat pocket.

'There, he's ready for you now, I think.'

He led her back out of the stables and pointed up the hill. 'He'll be waiting for you at the house. Five minutes' walk, just follow the path.'

The main building lay across the top of an escarpment. The rocky slopes below had been landscaped into lawns, gardens, terraces and grottoes, planted with camellias, azaleas, brooms and heathers. Through it all a small stream tumbled over artfully natural waterfalls into still, deep pools above whose lotuses and purple flags jewelled dragonflies darted and hovered. The air was heavy with almondy scents but spiced with the brightness of citrus. There was sculpture too: a Calder mobile turned imperceptibly beneath a sequoia, a bronze nude by Elisabeth Frink rode his pony out of a shrubbery of oleanders. Brel, who was not easily impressed, was . . . impressed.

At the top, a long colonnade of plain semicircular white arches behind a narrow parterre fronted the main building. A small flight of lichen-covered stone steps dropped into a rose arbour. The balustrades at the top were punctuated with two terracotta urns, and between them, and nicely placed just off-centre, stood the man Brel had come to see: Don Pedro Mendoza y La Cerda, Duke of Pastrana and Prince of Eboli.

He was thirty-three years old, five feet eight inches tall, slim but well-built, athletic. He had blond to brown hair, slightly wavy, and worn a little longer than one would expect, so it just rested on his collar, which was cut high. His good looks were spoilt by the fact that his pale blue eyes, habitually sulky in expression, were set rather close together. He was wearing a dark blue light-weight suit, waisted, with two vents at the back, a shirt that was almost white, just tinged with lilac, and a Cardin tie, lilac polka dots on very dark blue silk.

They had met three times before, though always at large, formal gatherings.

Brel paused at the foot of the steps. Pedro used a thumbnail to lever the cigarette he was smoking from a small holder, checked the buttons of his jacket and the zip of his trousers with an apparently careless gesture of his right hand and came down to meet her, but waited where one step was wider than the rest, made her climb towards him. He shook hands briefly and without pressure, made sure she ascended the remaining stairs just very slightly in front of him.

'I am sure Jean-Luc has looked after you splendidly,' he said. 'He is a fascinating man is he not? Did he tell you the wildest stories about Sherpa? Of course. Do go straight ahead. Through the glass doors. I am so sorry I had to keep you waiting. Vasari was tedious, wanted his pound of flesh. My flesh, you know? But we agreed in the end.' He did not sound like a Spaniard speaking English, more like a German, a very well-educated German with vowels too perfect for a native speaker. 'Anyway, come and have lunch with him before he goes.'

Lunch was served in a conservatory at the end of the building, a glazed semicircular bay closing off the end of the house. It faced east and was cool. The views, which took in the snow-capped southern end of the Sierra, were magnificent.

Brel had also met Giorgio Vasari on several occasions, done business with and through him. Balding, middle-aged, fat, in a crumpled grey suit and open-work two-tone shoes, his eyes, deep-sunk in purple sockets, suggested he was terminally ill, but he survived. He operated out of the law practice he led in Milan but had a global reputation for drawing up contracts that held water anywhere. He acknowledged her presence with a brief nod while Mendoza introduced her to the second person there.

This was Jana Pensión. She was about twenty-five, as tall as Pedro, with fluffed or fluffy dyed-straw hair held in place with an elasticated blue band, large brown eyes, and a button of a nose that was just a little too small even in a face that was thin. She was dressed in a blue Puma tracksuit. It wasn't immediately clear what her function in the household was.

The meal was simple and slight: oysters Florentine with hot fresh French bread, a green salad which Pedro himself turned, and wild strawberries to follow. They drank good Californian Chablis – Inglenook.

Brel quizzed the lawyer. 'You've agreed terms then?"

Vasari shrugged hugely. 'In principle, yes. The marriage settlement has been no problem, there are conventions, precedents. But the bride price is another matter: if we were Zulus and he was paying in head of cattle, I could no doubt tie him up.' His voice was gravelly, perhaps through fatigue and jet-lag. He gestured at Pedro with a fork from which spinach dropped back on to his plate. 'But in our society we are more used to negotiating dowries than the other way round.' He reached for a black-pepper grinder, twisted away furiously at the top. 'And the sums of money involved are . . . large. I understand you are arranging how they will be paid to my client.'

'That's right.' Said drily, indicating that it was not a subject she wished to discuss.

The big, tired man shook his head, chased a shelled, steamed oyster on to his fork with a large piece of bread, drank deeply.

Brel turned to the girl. 'And you? You are from . . . ?'

'Tulsa, Oklahoma.' Her accent, a near Southern drawl but sharper, not so lazy as the Deep South, confirmed it. Brel, with the impertinence of the superior middle-aged probing the young, asked her what she did at the Villa, was she a secretary, receptionist, housekeeper, that sort of thing?

Jana's eyes widened, a little colour came into her cheeks. Brel felt rewarded: the question had worked like an oyster knife. The words she had used, applied to a personable girl working for an immensely rich, single duke, had suggested living-in mistress.

'I'm a certified physiotician. I help maintain Pedro's phys-ico-mental equilibrium and efficiency.'

'Keep-fit? Aerobics? That sort of thing?'

Again she was finding the 'wrong' words.

'It's a technology that goes way beyond aerobics.'

Brel turned to Pedro at the head of the table in a chair larger than the rest. Carved, high-backed, with arms, it suggested a throne. 'Surely, señor, that cannot be a full-time job. You look pretty fit to me.'

He offered his plate a frown. 'We work out for two hours each day.'

The American girl added: 'Each day I plan the workouts according to the results I've had from checking out the data I get from monitoring his physical functions. I use a computer. Okay, so I have some spare time, but not as much as you might think.'

Vasari asked: 'To what end? We're all going to die anyway. Might as well get some fun out of life first.' He looked round, clearly hoped that someone would refill his glass.

Pedro looked up, his eyes dark now with anger or some deeper emotion. His voice took on the tone of reverence used by those who claim to have been vouchsafed by some deity a truly religious experience.

'We may die but our genes need not. And the fact is I now, more than ever, have good reason for maintaining myself, both body and mind, at peak condition. A woman's ova are all inside her when she is born, their quality already decided for good or for ill. Only large doses of radiation can alter them, can affect the outcome. But a man's sperm are constantly remade after each emission and the quality, health of each batch is conditioned by his general health at the time. If I am to carry out my duties properly, I must take proper care of myself.'

Vasari shrugged as petulantly as a large man can, looked at his watch, announced that he would have to go. A little later, a small Sikorsky took off from somewhere behind the Villa, and clattered away south west, back towards town.

In a gallery that faced north, with starker views of *páramo* uplands climbing to snowy peaks, Brel unzipped her document case and pulled out a sheaf of papers. Sitting in a cane chair opposite her was Pedro, and beside him a dark man whom he introduced as Teseo Feijoo. Feijoo was small, with thinning greyish hair, brown eyes widely spaced, a sallow face pitted with pockmarks. Although Brel had not met him before, she knew he looked after Mendoza's financial interests in the New World, was a Guatemalan by birth, educated at Harvard Business School. He had a nervous twitch which jerked his head upwards and to the side quite frequently. Brel knew his reputation: in ten years he had doubled the real value of Pedro's American interests.

'Right,' she began. 'As I understand it you have agreed a . . . what did Vasari call it? A bride price. Of six hundred million dollars to be paid over the next three years. What we now have to do is agree the means by which these moneys shall be transferred to the accounts to which your future grandfather-in-law has access. Since the origin of these funds will be . . . problematic, I don't need to emphasise that this will have to be done with some finesse. Now. What I am proposing in the first instance is that we set up a company, let's call it Mendoza Holdings (BVI) for the moment, in Tortola, in the British Virgin Islands . . .'

'Why? Why there?' Feijoo's grey mask of a face twitched, and Brel wondered if he was in need of a fix. If that was the case then she wished he would go and get it.

Pedro stretched out his legs, lit a cigarette. 'Uncle Toñi has a bank there, doesn't he?' He yawned. 'I've had enough of figures for one day, you know? There are more important things in life. I am sure you won't mind if I leave you to sort out the details with Teseo. He can give me a digest later.'

'All right, señor. But I will require your signature on a few documents . . .'

'If Teseo approves, I'll sign.' The cane of his chair creaked as he stood up. He nodded, paused at the door to glance at the framed pencil drawings of Dante's descent into Hell done by Rauschenburg that hung there, and then was gone.

Brel immediately leaned forward towards Feijoo, smoothing the silk of her skirt down her thighs as she did so. 'Listen, before we go any further there is one important matter that has to be cleared up. Has he . . .' – she gestured back to the door which had closed behind Pedro – 'has he agreed to go with you to Colombia? Because we've heard that he is most reluctant to do so.' With her small chin supported on her right hand she waited for his reply.

Feijoo's head did its sideways twitch, more a lurch than a twitch this time, then he smirked. 'He's agreed. But you are right. He was very, very reluctant, but finally agreed when I made it clear that a satisfactory deal with the Arias family depended on his presence . . .'

An hour later she had the signatures she wanted, and Pedro offered to come some of the way with her back down to the stables and her car.

He led her through a square windowless lobby. In the middle were two small, high-backed gilt rococo seats set back to back, and in two of the corners large jasperware vases of madonna lilies. On opposing walls, facing each other and the seats, two large pictures both covered by velvet drapes whose colour matched the vases.

Pedro touched a button by the door, and the drapes opened over the left-hand painting.

'Doña Octavia Arias de Quesada. My first duchess.'

Lili Brel took her time, pondering the painting for at least two minutes with her right hand again beneath her chin and her elbow on her left hand. Four years earlier she had been part of a large group that had gone to the Met to hear Placido Domingo in *Rigoletto*: it was one of the formal occasions on which she had previously met Pedro. She remembered Doña Octavia as a dark, petite, vivacious person. She was then only seventeen, had been delighted to hear and recognise 'La Donna è Mobile' and was making fun of Pedro by singing it. Woman is faithless. Not a song to endear her to her grandee lover with the gift of a name nine hundred years old.

In the painting she was dressed in black lace with a black mantilla, very stiffly posed. In fact she looked like, was intended to look like, a Goya duchess, and that part of the painting was a competent pastiche. The background was much bolder, *fauve*, jungly with parrots and macaws, and included naked Indians in feathered headdresses and armlets of Chibcha gold. Slick, competent kitsch.

'Octavia was a lovely person,' said Pedro. His voice was now cool, emotionless, as if he were reciting a lesson learnt by rote and repeated too often. 'She came from one of the very oldest South American families. Her ancestors were Viceroys of New Granada. In many ways it was a most suitable match. Of course she had a very lively temperament, and was not always biddable. Nevertheless . . . I regret her.' He sighed. 'But time moves on, and she died leaving me without an heir.'

'Died,' Brel recalled, was a euphemism. Octavia's 1958 250 GTS Ferrari, a wedding present, had been crushed between two tankers on the San Bernardino Highway. The petrol tanker blevvied. The other, filled with some noxious gas, also exploded, and an area five miles in radius had to be evacuated. It was never really explained why she was driving alone, at one hundred and sixty miles an hour, nor who was in the helicopter that had been flying low above her, apparently buzzing her, when she ran into the back of the petrol tanker.

She was only nineteen then, had been married to Pedro for four months. He had been distraught.

'Time moves on and . . .' he gestured around him, and a shy, almost awkward smile appeared fleetingly on his face, as if he were a child seeking approval – 'you have seen something of what I have, what has come to me, a little of what I am. I must ensure that when I pass on, there is someone suitable to . . . take over.' He lit a cigarette, making something of a business of it – the gold case, the lighter, the small holder. He snapped out the flame, breathed acrid blue smoke into the cool but close atmosphere of the small, closed-in room, became brisk. 'In fact it is . . . a duty. Civilisation depends on breeding. It always has. It is not fashionable now to say so, but the scientific truth is clear and unequivocal. I am not immortal. This frame, this box' – he tapped his chest – 'is no more than that. A transitory object, a suitcase, a package for . . . the genes. They are what makes us worthy custodians not only of themselves but of all . . .' – again he gestured – 'all this.'

Briskly he tapped a second button, and the second set of drapes slipped open.

Again a full-length canvas, and again the work of a fashion-able technician, but as different in style from the other picture as the subject was different. This girl was tall and fair, with a fragile shy beauty quite different from that of Octavia, which was more a matter of Latin energy than classic line or proportion. But here was the face of Botticelli's Primavera, and much of its mysterious expression or lack of expression. It was a resemblance the painter had been aware of. She was posed standing, but twisting towards the onlooker from a crimson rose she had been about to smell or pick. She wore a white and fluted cotton dress, which, with her pale blondness, contrasted with the garden of dark shrubs and evergreen trees in which she had been set. At her feet there were more flowers. The artist was a good draughtsman in the way such painters are, and as eclectic as the first, though here the imitated master was Raphael rather than Goya. There was one moment of drama, if not of originality. Behind the still, cool beauty of the face lightning flashed from a thundercloud that might have been painted by Giorgione.

'Well, you must know who she is, though she has been brought up in seclusion and not many people have seen her.

Europa Malatesta, the daughter of Federico Malatesta and Princess Theodosia of Thessalonika, both dead. The Malatestas trace a direct line back to one of the oldest Roman senatorial families, one connected with the Julian clan, the Caesars, through a daughter who was raped by Alaric the Hun and bore his child. Princess Theodosia claimed descent from the last Byzantine emperors. Europa's genes therefore demand to be allied to those of the Habsburgs and Bourbons and those of the royal Goths who took Spain from the Moors, all of which I carry. The result will be the most perfectly bred creature ever to have existed. But first like a knight from the age of chivalry I have to pass the tests set by her wicked guardian. Eh? And that is why you are here.' This was said with a sort of flippant bitterness. He levered out his half-smoked cigarette, stubbed it into a gold and silver art deco ashtray that stood on a waist-high pedestal by the door. 'I cannot say I am looking forward to this Colombian trip.'

'But you will go.'

He shrugged. 'Oh yes. I'll go. The first of my ordeals. There we are, then. That is what I wanted you to see.' He looked at this watch. 'Did Jean-Luc tell you that Sherpa has an appointment this afternoon? I like to see that these things are done properly, so I will come down with you.'

Out on the parterre again he paused to look out and down the tiny landscaped valley, across the fortifications and the parkland patrolled by his new breed of wolfish guard-dogs, to the citrus groves and Sierras beyond. A musty smell of rotten grapefruit came for a moment on a breath of air from the west.

'You know, one cannot overemphasise the overwhelming importance of good breeding, of improving the blood-line. If the European dynasties had taken more care in this respect, had on one side avoided the dangers of inbreeding, and, on the other, kept their lines pure of plebeian traces, emperors would still be on their thrones, and monarchs would hold real sway.'

He descended the lichen-covered steps, to the rose arbour, and drew her attention to a fine-looking standard, with velvety crimson just showing through sepals of an especially deep and glowing green.

'This is the rose in the painting of Europa. It is called Royalty. It is a concept that is the summation of my philosophy. Royalty is the principle of genetic excellence. The science of genetically controlled breeding becomes an art, is perhaps most pure when one aims for beauty alone and use is not a consideration. Thus it is with a rose. It is the result of the most delicate engineering, the old principles of grafting taken into the laboratory. No need any longer for consummation through physical union – the chances and mistakes of passion are eradicated. Unfortunately we do not yet have the techniques perfected with higher forms of life. But they can be rigorously controlled.'

They walked on down past the still, silent pool through shrubberies of radiant azaleas.

'Do please note the Rider and Horse, a bronze by Marini, I am told it is one of his best.'

They were looking at the Elizabeth Frink. Brel judged it would not be wise to point out the error. It was becoming clear to her that Pedro was not only manically obsessive, arrogant, and spoiled, but, like many of his kind who have a veneer of high culture, ignorant. That this was so caused an intense satisfaction suddenly to blossom in the recesses of her soul – a satisfaction she kept entirely to herself. The feeling was inspired by a blunt English proverb, a maxim by which she often operated: a fool and his money are soon parted.

They were almost back at the stables and now had a clear view of the yard framed between two tall mimosas in bloom. Activity was building up. Grooms, directed by Jean-Luc Casenove, were placing straw bales around the corners and across the gate, two new cars had arrived and two men in white coats stood near Jean-Luc.

Brel asked: 'Don't you want to go down?'

'No. They are professionals. There is no need to interfere.'

The mare was also a bay, lively, glossy, in the peak of condition. She was blinkered but not hooded, and held only by a nose halter. Her tail had been bound with a bandage. One of the white coats inspected her vulva, was satisfied with what he saw, did not touch her.

A clatter of hooves, stomping, scuttering on the cobbles, and again that shrill neigh, something between a bugle-call and a scream: Sherpa. He looked even bigger now with four men holding him by a nose halter and two neck halters. He was sweating, twisting and turning. Although he was hooded his pizzle was already out, mottled black and pink, about half distended. They got him behind her so his head was thrashing about just behind her quarters, then at a signal from Jean-Luc one of the grooms whipped off the hood.

His neck arched, his teeth flashed, his eyes rolled. Nothing could have held him then. He was up on his back legs, pawing the air towards her with his front hooves. He gripped her mane in his teeth, her shoulders with his knees, and found his own way in.

In fifteen seconds it was over. He came off her and out of her, his front hooves clattered on the cobbles, and he gave a brief whinny before turning away, almost docile now, back to his stall. She gave a long shudder which ran from her rump to her ears, finished with a shake of her head.

Brel allowed herself a disdainful shiver, turned away, and then in spite of everything her attention was caught again. On a natural outcrop, partly hidden from them by a cedar, Pedro's laid-back physiotician, Jana Pensión, was leaning forward: there was a spot of colour in her cheeks, her fists were clenched and pressed into her thighs, and she was breathing heavily. Then, just like the mare, she threw up her head and shuddered.

Pedro had not seen her. He tapped a cigarette on his thumb, lit it, blew smoke in the air, and smirked. 'Worth seeing, eh?' He held out his hand, 'Are you going straight back to Madrid?'

'Yes.'

'My regards then to Uncle Toñi when you see him.'

2

Harriet Jones woke to a grey drizzly dawn that did nothing for the small bedroom, for the brown damp-stains up near the ceiling, for the patch where the white vinyl paint she had slapped on three years ago had begun to shed angular shards with the texture and thickness of photographic paper. It did nothing for the unevenness of the wooden floor that tipped a degree or two down towards the window and made cupboard doors flop open. Above all it did nothing for the creature in bed with her.

He was a warmth she found oppressive even in a damp cold

English March. In bed he was thin, bony and greedy – greedy in love-making and greedy with the baggy duvet in its Habitat cover printed to look like graph paper. At twenty-four he was eight years younger than her, but in the grey light looked as old, with grey patches round his eyes, and his designer stubble looked like stubble, and his feet smelled, and . . .

'You'll have to go.' Harriet said it aloud, but he did not hear.

She swung a long, thin, ivory-coloured leg off the bed, pulled a cotton wrap from the brass hook on the back of the door, padded downstairs on large but shapely feet. She paused briefly at a narrow sash window and looked out at the backs of Victorian cottages: ochre brick stained black, narrow gardens, crocuses flopping, daffodils still only showing etiolated spears. A thin mist of acid rain softened the edges, enough to make the cats that infested the area cringe in sulky low profile beneath the leaning walls.

In a bathroom she had wanted to make sybaritic with mahogany and gold-plated taps but which had become tatty with untidy use and cluttered with intruders like the washing machine, she began to wash: face first, then stopped. The eyes, a pale yellowish green flecked with hazel, gazed back from the mirror in a long, cool expressionless stare of appraisal. They took in a good brow beneath reddish-brown hair tinted to a rich chestnut, cut well and swept back from her temples, a thin but high-bridged nose above a generous but not overfull mouth, and a chin that was well-shaped, but small enough to be called weak on a man. Lurking freckles threatened the texture of a fresh complexion. It was, she knew, a face younger than she deserved – ageing was not the problem. What was wrong was the sour expression that spoke of chronic if mild disappointment, an expression that said: all right, things are not too bad, but they are not what I hoped for.

'Which,' said Harriet, 'will not do.' She straightened and her mouth tightened into a grimace of decision. 'Time to break a mould or two.'

'Oh yes. I'll do it.'
  'Good girl. Goooood girl. I knew you would.'
  'But not for two grand. Five.'
  'Five!' Paul Roget, big, plump, jolly, and, in Harriet's

estimation, 'one of us', somebody who had the breeding and nerve to go for what he wanted and bugger the world, gave the short high crow of laughter that was a habit, and a trademark. 'My dear girl, two is the rate. The rate. No one gets more.'

He twirled the stem of his glass. The heavy plain conical bowl of it caught light from the spot above the small table, and he reached for the bottle of Sancerre blanc de blanc that had gone so well with the monkfish roasted with garlic that he had cooked for her. 'Shall I open another?'

'Not for me.' Harriet covered the top of her glass.

'No one gets more than two grand. That's the rate. Market forces and all that. Honestly. It would be smashing my profit margins to go anywhere near five . . .'

'Bull. You can't really have thought I'd do this for a measly two thousand.'

He raised one heavy grey brow and lowered the other, a trick that could be as irritating as his laugh since, like it, it was cultivated, learnt, and always put to the same use: it was a rebuke to the innocent from the worldly-wise.

'Frankly, sweetie, it had not occurred to me that you were doing it for the money. You're not short of a bob or two. I assume you'll be in it for kicks.'

Certainly she did not look like a pauper. For Roget, who was fifteen years older than her and who had last been her lover ten years ago, she had dressed with care, achieving an under-announced style in an off-white shirt, generously cut, and a full cinnamon skirt. What made it buzz was the belt and the shoes: both were a light tan snakeskin, not quite a match, and the shoes, which could have been old, were certainly not cheap. Perfectly shaped court style, they looked as if they had been unostentatiously dusted with gold.

Harriet avoided his eye, ran her finger round the thin edge of her empty glass. 'I've done my homework, you know. I've done the sums. If it's a three-kilo run you stand to make a hundred grand. Profit. So. I am not going to let you rip me off. If I'm to mule for you, you pay me the five I need . . .'

'Harriet, sweetie, you do not need five. Nobody *needs* five grand. Two is fun. A hundred is what one needs. What do you need *five* grand for?'

She looked up and smiled, a smile that packed a sting.

'I'm going to chuck Jeremy out. And it's going to cost me

that to do it. I'm going to say to him, "Piss off Jeremy," and he is going to say "What about the Zanussi cooker, what about Blanca?" and I am going to say, "Jeremy, here is five grand, now piss off."'

Paul Roget's crow was unchecked. 'A good cause. Yes. He demeaned you. A nice girl like you does not need a stud. Who's Blanca?'

'Le car. Five?'

'All right. Five. Because it's you.'

'Five because you're in a hole, you can't find anyone else. And because it's me and you trust me, and because I want to make getting rid of Jeremy quick and surgical. Paul?'

'Yes?'

'Five now. Cash.'

Again the laugh. 'Dear Harriet. You can't think I was going to pay you with an invoiced cheque.'

'No. But I want it now. The banks are still open.'

'Half now and half when it's all over.'

'Paul. I've been trying to get you to understand something.' She picked up an apple, sniffed at it and gnawed squirrel-like. Her pale green eyes searched his face. 'You're asking me to do something crazy. Something horrendously illegal, and just possibly immoral too. But you've hit me at very precisely the right moment, and next Monday or whenever will be too late. I leave you this afternoon with five grand, cash, or I don't do it. Right?' She took a deep breath, and her eyes flinched away before coming back to his. 'And you needn't worry. I won't let you down. If we agree, if I take the money, I'll go through with it.'

'Come on, Harriet. Come on.' He drew it out . . . o-o-o-n. An American inflexion. Roget's childhood had been spent in New York, a refugee from the France of Laval and Pétain. In '45 his parents, art dealers, had come back not to Paris but to London. He traded privately in Islamic art but the profit margins could no longer support a lifestyle he liked to think was gracious. 'You could chicken out, and just walk away from the stuff. Or you could hijack it and flog it yourself. Either way I lose my investment and my profit.'

She grimaced, felt a spasm of relief as well as disappointment. Then she pushed back her chair and paused before rising, hands on the edge of the polished cherrywood table.

'Right, then, no deal. Do you want me to wash up before I go?'

Paul chewed his thumbnail, chucked his napkin on the table as if it were a boxer's towel. 'You always were too tough by half. But honest with it, so I suppose I shall have to trust you . . .'

'I should think so too.'

He stood up. 'Come on then.'

But not to the bank. The surprise was theatrical, delightful and finally ensnared her. Reverently he lifted an eighteenth-century Persian prayer-rug from the wall by the fireplace. It was quilted and embroidered with silk flowers, white, red, green, yellow, blue, simple but lovely. He unlocked the small Chubb safe which lay behind it and counted five thousand pounds in used fives, tens and twenties.

'One of the problems with this line of business is the flow of cash. Rather than the cash flow. If you see what I mean. Neither buyers nor sellers like cheques. Anyway I always have rather more of the stuff lying around than is really sensible. Lord knows how the big league manage.' He packed the notes into a black nylon bag. It had two large compartments and several smaller pockets. Roget demonstrated: one long zip circled it, enclosing the larger compartment and half the pockets. Its tag then clipped into a locking slot.

'Make this yours. Forensically yours. Take it home, fill it with dirty clothes, put the combings from your pretty little head in it for a day or two, shake them about before tipping them out. Blow your nose and leave the Kleenex there, that sort of thing. Handle it a lot. You get the idea? What size clothes do you wear now? Twelve? Ten? That's fine. Let me think a moment.'

He got up and bounced round his small but split-level and beautiful fully furnished sitting-room. The house was smaller even than Harriet's, but he had converted it into a nest of interlocking caves, Aladdin's caves, filled with Islamic treasures. There were Persian miniatures on the walls and prayer-rugs from Ispahan, Turkish ceramics inspired by tuli-pomania, copperwork from the Yemen and kilims woven in the tents of the Kurds.

'You still buy most of your underwear plain at Marks, but occasionally good-quality fancy at Harrods or in South Molton

Street, yes? Clothes of course basically ditto, either sensible and plain or the very best. So what would you not be seen dead in? I think I've got it. Chelsea Girl, Miss Selfridge and cheerful prints. An orange or cadmium boilersuit, T-shirts with jokey inscriptions. Right? Am I right? Don't look so puzzled . . . All will become clear in due course.'

'It will?'

'It will. You see, I promised you there would be no risk for you, and now you've agreed I'll tell you how it's done . . .'

An hour later she stood on the doorstep of Roget's Bloomsbury cottage and let him kiss her solemnly but chastely on the cheek. A large man in a donkey jacket and white safety helmet gave them a wink as he went by, dropping heavy plastic orange bollards in a row behind him, all the way down Purbeck Street.

She climbed the five stone steps to her narrow front door and let herself in. As was usually the case these days the unassertive but inescapable tattiness of her home immediately oppressed her. Part of the trouble was that the rooms were too small to support the lifestyle that had been imposed on them: the 'good' furniture, the pair of oriental vases, the paintings whose handsome frames were, inevitably, chipped, had been made for more generous environments. In the tiny bathroom and kitchen that jutted out at the back, one on top of the other, the washing machine, bidet, dishwasher, fridge and freezer, microwave and food-processor, coffee machine, and all the rest of it jostled for space to the extent that in some corners she had to open doors in the right order to keep them from getting in each other's way.

The whole scene announced things about her which no longer mattered. It no longer mattered that her father had been a prosperous county-town solicitor whose clientele included the local gentry – one of whose younger daughters had been her mother. She no longer gave a fig for the fact that she had been expensively educated and could be presumed to have taste. There seemed no longer any point in being an independent, intelligent, talented woman who made a good living as a freelance portrait photographer specialising in successful businessmen. She'd built up a practice on her own, hiring out pictures from her library to the media, until it brought in three or four hundred pounds a week and nicely topped up the small private income she got from a family trust. She had worked hard to set it up and keep it going, and it had been fun for a lot of the time. But after ten years it had gone rancid on her.

She wanted . . . a cup of tea? Was Jeremy in? Should she give him a shout, get him to go down to the tiny, overcrowded kitchen which smelt of garbage and leaking gas, get him to brew up a pot of two of Darjeeling to one of Earl Grey before she chucked him out? No. She'd refused a brandy at Roget's but she'd have one now, a socking big one.

What did she want? Her married sister had an answer: a decent, old-fashioned bloke, properly large and not skinny like Jeremy, who'd knock her about a bit and make sure she had children before it was too late. But that precisely was not it. Most of the females in her family, of her caste, enjoyed a brief or even quite long fling of independence, but then they all married successful businessmen, bankers, top professionals and sank back into dull lives, dull loves, servicing males and children. But not Harriet.

Lifting the glass, peering through dark topaz liquor already half gone and twisting it so the grapes and vine tendrils engraved on it spiralled before her eyes, she knew that that was what was really wrong: she was bored. Roget's trip would help. For a few days it would set the adrenalin flowing again, no doubt of that. But then what? Chucking out Jeremy would help: but after him . . . ?

The door clicked, stuck, and burst open. Tall, very thin, with black hair cut short up the sides but left thick on top, with stubble and an ear-ring, wearing a collarless striped shirt above baggy cotton trousers tucked into purple suede bootees, Jeremy looked down at her.

She was spread on the sofa like a land of milk and honey waiting to be plundered, one shoe kicked off, and totally relaxed so the small roundness of her tummy rose below the belt and he could make out the presence of her nipples beneath the pockets of her cheesecloth shirt. She looked up at him from under a quiff of rich chestnut hair. He smelt the brandy and felt the warmth from the popping gas-fire. The rain outside had become more serious, streaked the windows. He knew she was against sudden sex in sitting-rooms, but he detected sulphur in the air, animal electricity.

'I didn't hear you come in.'

'Nooo.' She pursed her lips, drew out the words with anticipatory relish, which he continued to misinterpret.

'Where have you been?'

'To London. To see the Queen.'

'Oh, right! I say, if you're swigging brandy, can I have some?' For all his punkish appearance he had been to Rugby and was in the process of becoming a small objects expert (nineteenth century) for Sotheby's.

'If you must.' She waggled her tumbler on the chintzy arm of the sofa. 'Top me up.'

'I say, coming on a bit, aren't we? You didn't say where you've been.' He poured brandy.

'Don't stint yourself. You may need it. Paul Roget cooked lunch for me.'

Youthful male arrogance masked from him the unspoken threat – indeed, to his ears there was still promise in her voice.

'In that dinky little bijou residence? He's a mean sod. Never buys a chap a meal if he can avoid it. What did he want?'

'He gave me five grand.' Then sardonically using Jeremy's slang: 'Five thousand sheets. I'm going to give them to you.'

'Oh, I say!'

'Yes. So if you'd like to go upstairs and pack up your stuff, then, um, I suppose you'll be off.'

'I say, listen, Harry. I'm really not with you.'

'That's right, Jeremy. You're no longer with me. Shall I spell it out? I want you to go now. No messing, no recriminations, no tears, and above all no debts. I think if you tot it up and I keep the car and the other odds and ends we've put in here since you arrived, five thousand will not leave you out of pocket.'

She was still lying back on the sofa, forcing herself to keep cool, calm, to sound indifferent. But she could feel the pulse in her neck and he could see the pinkness rising towards her ears. The blood was beginning to pound in his head too.

'You really do mean this, don't you? I think at least we ought to sit down and have a proper talk.'

'No.' Almost she shouted. 'That's one thing we will not do. That's the form, isn't it? Part of the accepted ritual, the steps in the anti-courtship dance. Endless proper talks, whose main purpose will be to let you persuade yourself that you're not to blame, that it's all my fault.'

She was sitting up now, bolt upright. She felt he might hit her if she stood, was far less likely to if she stayed sitting.

'But, Harry, I can't just go. I mean, damn it, where to? I say, isn't it possible this is just a touch of the old PMTs. I mean, aren't you about due?'

There was enough truth in this to make her even more angry. The little sod could, just for once, leave her body chemistry out of it.

She went on, forcing her voice to remain quiet, but unable to prevent the pitch from rising. 'Jeremy, you really are a wimp. In that bag you have five thousand pounds and you are telling me you have nowhere to go. Now, for Christ's sake, just piss of, and we'll take the proper talking as read. And premenstrual tension has its uses. Without it I might not have screwed myself up to do what I should have done months ago.'

He tried as hard as he could to bang the door, but, as usual, it stuck. Through the thin ceiling she could hear him stamping about and slamming the cupboards. He did not take long. He had a lot of clothes but not much else, and a very large suitcase with straps to put them in. He came back in and picked up the black nylon travelling-bag.

'Are there really five thousand sheets in here? Oh, all right, I'll take your word for it. I'm not going to count it here and now. But I hope you checked it when Roget gave it to you . . .'

'Shit.'

'What's the matter?'

'Tip it out.'

'Why?'

'I've just remembered. I'm meant to keep the bag.'

'Jesus, Harry. How mean can you get?'

3

Five o'clock in the afternoon, but five hours later and five thousand miles away, James Mulligan looked at the wall-clock, gritted his teeth and nodded briefly to himself, expressing the satisfaction one feels when the moment has come to put in train a course of action one had agonised over for a long time, when one implements at last a decision that has cost a lot to make but which you know is the right one. He expanded the hinged jaws of an old-fashioned briefcase and began methodically to go through the entire office, starting with the desk drawers, moving on to the filing cabinet, packing into the bag files, papers, objects which were his, papers for his eyes only, the things his successor should not see, would not want to see. Although he was a big man in a small room, his movements were neat, precise.

The process did not take long, but while it lasted Mulligan was ambushed by the effect it had on the tiny environment he had made his own for over four years: each object removed, each sheaf of papers slipped away, contributed to the room's relapse into the stale anonymity it had had when he first entered it. He had not liked it then: at this irrevocable moment it was pleasing to find the distaste creeping back. He would feel no regrets when finally he put out the lights, locked the door behind him.

By the window he paused. The large rubber plant would stay, of course. But what about the four small cacti in Hopi Indian pots decorated with snake patterns? They were a present from his son, then eight, now twelve, whom he saw for perhaps three months a year if he was lucky, would see even more rarely now he had decided on this move. Suddenly the pain was back, spiced though it was with an ironic edge of self-awareness: yes, the briefcase would accommodate them easily enough back to his apartment, but then what? Box them up and air-freight them to Europe? Empty out and chuck the domed, doomed succulents with their geometric arcs of spines, keep the pots? But they went together. All right, they were made for tourists, said as much about real Hopi culture as a cuckoo clock made in Taiwan says about the Swiss, but the pots were there for the cacti, for these cacti . . .

Postponing the decision he let his gaze dwell for a moment on the spaces beyond the high windows, a sky already lilac with impending dusk, bisected by a vapour trail that glowed with white luminosity above a sun he could not see, though the glass walls of office towers, many of them bronzed against its glare, threw back its reflection a thousand times. Sheets of gold. One block, when the light on it was less intense, often mirrored for him the marble silhouettes of the Hill, the Capitol, the Library of Congress.

'You'll miss the view. The Interpol building can't match it.'

Mulligan gritted his teeth. Neither the voice nor the smell of pipe that came with it was welcome.

'You're wrong. The Bois de Bologne and the Eiffel Tower beat this.'

'Come on, James. I've been there. Rue Armengaud overlooks a crummy apartment block and a railway line. Be a man, admit you're wrong, stay. It's not too late. Okay, in five weeks we put up the shutters here for the last time, but you can take your pick of desks in the FBI or the DEA. You know that. Okay, okay. The ground's been gone over too often already. You really are on your way and you're wondering what to do with those dinky little plants. I'll take them off your hands. Myra'll put them with her African violets, you know? She has a controlled environment, a micro-climate for her collection. Maybe for her they'll flower.'

'The hell she will.' Mulligan scooped them up, two in each large palm, and carried them back to his desk, signalling with body language his distaste for the intruder.

Fat, tweedy 'Spider' Dayton read the signs and ignored them. Never a prepossessing person, he had learned the language forty years ago at grade school. He had discovered then that loud bonhomie backed up where necessary by downright bullying generally overrode the message, jammed the signals. Puffing at his noisome pipe, he watched while

Mulligan lowered the pots into the bag, thought better of it, retrieved them, put them back on the desk.

'So you really are going. Okay. So now tell me why. I mean, really why. Not the shit about this new outfit in Interpol, what's it called . . . ?'

'Eurac.'

'Eurac. Fucking nerve. They even copy our name. The shit about Eurac carrying on where Centac has been forced to leave off. Cut all that out and tell me the real reason.'

Mulligan felt hostility rise like bile, fought to master it. It was not an easy fight: today was already yesterday – the need to accommodate Dayton had gone. Why bother? But he did.

'But it's true. The methods Centac put together over – what? – nearly a decade, work. Better than anything else. I've been in drug enforcement for nearly twenty years. It's my job. I want to do it well. The Centac way is the best way. The bastards here are closing us down. Over there they're opening up. An agency with Centac's philosophy. Eurac . . .'

'I said cut the shit. The real reason. What is it? Gay Paree? Why not? But it's not your style. I mean, I don't suppose you'll spend too much time at the Moulin Rouge or whatever. And the smart food and smart wines – well they're all here too. Put space between you and Daphne? And the kids? But they already did that for you, moving out to the Coast. I suppose she has another feller by now, and they call him Dad . . .'

'Fuck off, Spider. Go fuck yourself.'

'So that could be it.' Dayton put his ass on the desk, rapped the bowl of his pipe on the edge of the ashtray, pulled out a pipe-smoker's tool, scraped clinker.

Mulligan slammed shut a metal drawer, made it sound like a hand-grenade. His strength matched his size. 'You want it straight, without the jargon, the newspeak? You know, I know, there's only one methodology that works. The Centac way. For the rest, it's just kick a few doors down, get some powder on the table and put a few guys – middlemen if you're very lucky, otherwise street traders, ouncers, mules – in the slammer for ten to life and see them out on parole in five years maximum. It all does about as much good as aspirin for secondary cancer.'

'And you want to find the cure. You want to wrap the whole

thing up so there's no more drug abuse anywhere, ever again. I mean, who the fuck do you think you are? St George? Jesus?' As he grew older, and higher up the ladder of his profession, Dayton cut the doses of bonhomie to smaller and smaller amounts, moved on to bullying with more and more readiness.

Mulligan slumped into his big office chair, let his weight tip it back, pushed a big palm across the short grey pelt of hair that covered his big round head. 'You know it's not that. The only cure for drug abuse, the only way the problem will go away, is legalise the whole caboodle . . .'

'What? Even the real killers? Smack, crack . . .'

'And pop.' They both laughed at the reference to an in-joke, and the tension between them ebbed a little.

Mulligan went on: 'I think so. Listen. The Legalise Pot campaigners have come up with an interesting new theory . . .'

'Shitheads. They're full of it.'

'Listen. It goes like this. The more you repress, the more you criminalise a drug, the more you stimulate production of more and more concentrated and dangerous hits. No one bothered with heroin when opium was legal. Prohibition converted beer and wine drinkers to spirits in droves. Crack hits your system quicker and harder than an old-fashioned snort. And nobody snorted when you could buy cocaine in solution over the counter wrapped up as a patent medicine or a soft drink. Legalise the lot and the damage done by the killer varieties would drop by ninety per cent overnight, and a whole raft of other problems would disappear too . . .'

'Like our jobs.'

'Sure. Like the whole industry of drug enforcement across the globe. Think of it. A cataclysm. Police, agents, social workers, researchers, prison warders, the list is endless. It could cut ten per cent off the price of office space right here in Washington, DC. It would smash the economies of at least six countries and push them that bit more quickly towards revolution and socialism, many of them right here in what the Big White Chief so lovingly calls our own backyard. So it won't happen. On all sorts of grounds it's the rational solution, but it won't happen. And not because men are innately irrational. They're not. Just selfish, greedy and frightened. Too many jobs would be lost, too many structures would crumble. The first imperative for any organisation is survival.

No organisation is going to campaign to remove its *raison d'être*
. . .' Mulligan was smiling now like a happy Buddha, at ease
with himself, pleased with his fantasy, pleased because he
knew this sort of talk infuriated Dayton – it challenged too
many assumptions, too much received wisdom, it was, as he
would say, too fucking intellectual.

For six months the tweedy fat man had been Mulligan's
immediate superior, seconded from the FBI during the transition period during which Centac, the Central Tactical Unit,
was scheduled to cease functioning as an agency independent
of the FBI and the Drug Enforcement Administration. Clearly
none of the Old Centac hands who still hung on liked him –
but equally he found them difficult to take too. They were all
a fucking sight too clever, or worse, too idealistic. A policeman
with a sense of mission was, in Dayton's book, a bad policeman. Now he countered Mulligan's genial flight of reason with
a smokescreen: huge sucking breaths dragged the flame of his
flaring lighter into the large bowl of his pipe, and soon he was
swathed in swirling clouds. Mulligan reluctantly reached for
his pack of Marlboro. He was trying to give up, but if he was
going to smoke at all he preferred to use his own rather than
someone else's.

'Okay,' said Dayton. 'Not the crusader, not the dragon-
slayer. And the problem stays, no solution because according
to you the only solution is the one that no one is going to
implement. So why stay in the business at all? A guy with your
gifts, background' (said sarcastically: Dayton was concious
that there was Ivy League, old money behind Mulligan; he
didn't like that) 'could start a new career easily enough. You'd
make more money as a consultant. You may be fifty but you
look forty . . .'

'It's what I've learnt to do. Too old a dog for new tricks.'

'Then stay. Stay here with the FBI, the DEA.'

'No.'

'Where we came in. Why not? For a rational man, James,
you're fucking full of contradictions.'

Mulligan grimaced, forcing his well-shaped mouth into a
snarl. He pushed the cigarette back into its pack. He stood up
again, resumed packing, but talked too. 'Job satisfaction.
That's what it comes down to. There's no job satisfaction in
putting the pushers, the dealers, the smugglers away. None at

all in organising the destruction of say half a ton of top-grade snow. That doesn't do anyone any good at all. Four and a half years in Centac has got me used to taking out the big guys. People like Alberto Sicilia-Falcon. Only the strategies Centac developed can get that high up the chain, and since I've tasted that sort of meat I won't be satisfied with anything less. Eurac offers that possibility. It no longer exists here.'

'But does it? Does it really? As I understand it, Eurac is very much a pilot scheme, hardly funded at all in real terms, and monitored every inch of the way by Big Daddy, Interpol proper.'

'That's part of the challenge, Spider. It's got to be made to work, it's got to be seen to work. It's part of the job satisfaction. A goal, a recognisable goal worth achieving, instead of just moving from one batch of low-grade hoods to the next.' The case was nearly full. Carefully he put the four Hopi pots on the top of the stacked files, experimentally closed the top to check the cacti were not about to be crushed. From the bottom drawer of the filing cabinet he produced a three-quarter-full bottle of Southern Comfort and a shot glass.

'Drink?'

Dayton barked, the nearest he could manage to a laugh. 'Never knew a cop that didn't have a whisky habit.' He knocked back the offered dose in one gulp, wiped his pipe-slack mouth on the back of his hand, and went on, to Mulligan's back now, for he was again at the window, savouring the deepening sky, the first star-punched hole in it. 'Do I have to spell it out, the scenario that follows? Either you fail. Or you succeed. And if you succeed, if you really get to the top or near it, then Eurac will run into the jaws of the same fucking monster that screwed Centac. You get that high, you hit politics. You hit politics, you run into the CIA. Or whatever front the CIA has over there. Troisième Bureau. SIS. That's what killed Centac. If Eurac works it'll kill Eurac too. The folk in pairs like Mormons, dressed like Mormons in pin-striped vests, and like Mormons fucking sure that they are right and everyone else is wrong. May I?'

'My guest.'

'Aren't you having one?'

'No. Not yet.'

Spider Dayton poured another shot, put it away, coughed

on it, stuffed his pipe back in his mouth. 'They'll screw you. The moment you point a finger at some warlord who fights Commies with arms bought with heroin, they'll screw you. The moment some Southern Cone president says "My democratically elected government will crumble and let the reds in if you go further down this track," they'll shaft you. You know that. Better dead than red . . . fine, I go along with that. Better shot to hell with nose candy or smack, I'm not so sure about. Why aren't you drinking?'

Mulligan, still at the window, reflected. Dayton was a redneck, a plebian, a democrat. Probably he supposed that he, Mulligan, Ivy League, old money, instinctively preferred a nation of hopheads to a nation of reds. He could not have been more wrong. But there was no way he would ever convince him this was so. The chasms of misunderstanding between them would never be bridged. He sighed. 'It's too sweet. I don't like my booze sweet. I found that bottle when I moved in. Keep it if you like.'

'Go fuck yourself, Mulligan, for the toffee-nosed bastard you always were. And turn the lights out afterwards, right?'

But he took the bottle.

4

The coach thundered down straight roads chasing the sun but not quickly enough: night would soon catch up. Black poplars flashed by in stroboscopic rhythms, rulered dykes as white as mirrors perspectived out across green meadows, occasional windmills offered ghostly gestures, not waving but sailing. The curved glass of the windows became opaque with the dimly lit reflections of the interior, and Harriet gave up trying to make sense of the darkening landscape.

Across the narrow gangway a Canadian girl sat with her feet pulled up under her, her back against the window facing out across the empty seat next to her. Her hair was thick straw-blonde cut short at the neck but swelling up into a thatch. She had tough blue eyes, a mean mouth, wore a blue T-shirt and flowered trousers that looked to Harriet as if they had been run up out of curtain material. She was drinking 7-Up out of a litre-sized plastic bottle which she offered to a youth who sat in front of Harriet, whom she could not see, and apparently he refused.

'You just cannot believe how expensive T-shirts are in Amsterdam. Nothing under ten dollars Canadian, but those like fast food bars with savoury pastries were okay, you know?'

She rattled on to a perfect stranger with a cool ease that made no allowance for personality, age, nationality, background or sex. Certainly not his sex. Harriet sighed, turned back to the now black glass of the window, and wished that she was not alone. She had never felt so alone in her life. The top of her chest felt tight, her stomach felt cold, her bowels felt loose, and the coach thundered on through the darkness like an armed missile irrevocably doomed to explode on impact.

Desperately she played through her mind, as if on the Walkman whose phones now rested on her collar-bones, Roget's endless reassurances: they came through in fragments and confused and with the staleness of things remembered too often; they no longer convinced.

'In the first place only one passenger in four hundred who goes through the green channel is ever challenged . . .'

'Who gets challenged? Why?'

'Those who stand out. Not because they're drawing attention to themselves through clothes or behaviour or anything like that, but because they're acting in a way that is clearly odd for them, out of character. Carrying the wrong piece of luggage: too expensive or too cheap for the rest of their appearance, that sort of thing . . .'

'Like going to Amsterdam by the very cheapest route, when clearly I could afford something better?'

'Precisely, sweetie, why I told you to wear your most ordinary denims. Listen. Invent an occupation that fits. You're a primary-school teacher, a social worker . . .'

'My passport says Freelance Photographer.'

'Right. So you're on an assignment for *Tulip Importers Monthly*. Or you're doing a feature for the *Sunday Times* on how the ordinary Brit swings in Amsterdam over a spring weekend. Seriously, you look just right. You know you do. Coming over you didn't feel conspicuous or odd or different, did you?'

'Coming over I was not carrying a bag filled with three kilos of cocaine.'

'Nor will you be coming back. Just the same travelling-bag you've been carrying all through the trip. The bag you carry through Customs is that bag, no other. You have to make yourself believe that.'

'Oh dear. Paul. Are all your mules such wimps? I bet they're not.'

'One in four hundred. But that's an average. Our chances, your chances, are going to be better than that.'

'Why?'

'Because, sweetie, the Pensioners have a friendly against Ajax on Sunday, warm-up for Ajax's Euro-Cup Final, and not only will there be the usual thousand or so daffodil fanciers piling through Customs with their booty, there will also be a few hundred skins, punks and whatever celebrating their team's success at, pardon the vernacular, kicking the shite out of a load of Dutch wankers. Police and Customs are going to have their hands very full indeed on that Monday morning . . .'

'All right, Paul. Okay. They are not going to stop me. But what do I do if they do?'

'Keep your head, sweetie. You've been good at that all your life. No problem.' But his small, hard eyes had flinched away, and he had made a business of stubbing out one cigarette and lighting another. They had been in her room at the hotel, a small place, not expensive, near Rembrandtsplein. He had insisted that they share the same hotel, but not the same room. He wanted her close, he wanted to have an eye on her, but it must not be possible to tie them together, so he had come the day before, taken a room on the floor below. But now she was there he kept close, did not want to go out, stayed with her all day, smoking, reading, listening to tapes on her Walkman, which had two outlets. It had given the trip an uncomfortable intimacy that recalled their affair of ten, twelve years ago, exciting her a little at times so she wondered if they would make love, and what she would do if he suggested it, and then realised that the idea was growing out of boredom, like a white plant forced on in darkness.

'Paul. Tell me. What shall I do?'

'I can't tell you that. How you play it must come from you, out of your own personality.' He swung his legs back on to the

other single bed, lay back, pushed smoke at the low ceiling.
'Imagine what you, being you, would do if you genuinely
found that someone had stuck you with a suitcase filled with
Lady . . .'

'Lady? Is that what you call it?'

'Some people call it that.'

'Why?'

'It makes you feel sexy. Girls especially. Good aphrodisiac.
Haven't you ever tried it?'

'Yes. Seven or eight years ago. The boyfriend who came
after you used it occasionally. He called it "toot". It didn't do
a lot for me.'

'Probably been stepped on too often.'

'Stepped on?'

'Every time you cut it half-and-half with something harmless
that's stepping on it and you obviously dilute the effect, and if
you're selling it doubling your profit. Pure stepped on once
only is okay. You know you've had a toot. It's okay. Though
since I've been trading it I tend to keep off it. Stepped on more
than once it's not worth the hassle or the money. Anyway. I'm
not going to write you a script. You'll do it better if it comes
out of you. But I should imagine you'd be angry. You'd do the
"Come on, officer, I'm a toff" bit. And if they didn't back off
then you'd go for the full "I know my legal rights, where's my
solicitor?" routine. Christ, Harriet, I don't know. You have to
put it together yourself. But it's not going to happen.'

But there had been something – she didn't know what. She
had known Roget for a long time, knew him well. His style
was relaxed bonhomie, suave self-confidence, but there, then,
in the small crowded room, with its twin beds and TV set
perched on a shelf by the door, he had been grey and nervy,
and, worst of all and most uncharacteristic, willing to eat fast
food brought in from lightning excursions down Amstel Strass.

Gent on the illuminated road signs. She read it as short for
Gentlemen, then remembered. Ghent. Where the good news
starts. *I sprang to the stirrup, and Joris, and he; I galloped, Dirck
galloped, we galloped all three . . .* and the bus thundered on.
Zeebrugge, forty-six. Forty-six kilometres, forty-six minutes,
less, oh SHIT. But it was going to be all right. Wasn't it? In
the end Roget had given his high tumbling laugh – about

35

midday on Saturday, yesterday, that had been – and had said: 'Okay. What you lack is a good reason for being here. Right. We'll give you one. I'll find you a nice plump Dutch business- man, he's a diamond merchant but very strictly legit, they almost all are in Amsterdam, not in the smuggling scene at all, and you can take his pictures, you'll have a camera full of film exactly the way it is when you've been on a proper job. Do you think that will help?'

He spent a couple of minutes on the phone, sitting on the edge of the bed, one plump leg across the other, gestured cigarette circling the air, speaking a language Harriet could not understand. He hung up. 'That's fine.' Again the laugh. 'And he'll give us lunch too, how about that? We're to pick him up at his shop in fifteen minutes. It's just off Spui, we can walk.'

Zeebrugge, twenty-four. The Canadian girl woke with a start, rubbed her neck, looked round; her hard blue eyes searched the narrow spaces for contact. Harriet's flinched away, found their reflection in the black glass. They looked as if they belonged to someone with a bad conscience on the Day of Judgement, staring huge and luminous from black shadows. At the back of the coach a beer tin rattled aimlessly across the floor and a voice squawked: 'Keep your fucking hands to yourself, you fucking pervert.'

Lunch had been a gas, the best part of the trip. Vincent Van Willet turned out to be a large untidy man with a mop of dark hair streaked with grey, kind eyes, and a large stomach which made everything near his waistline look untidy. He had decided that Harriet was Roget's mistress and that he could have some fun at Roget's expense by flirting with her in good if accented English.

In his shop the lighting in the sales area was theatrical, seductive, in planned contrast to the horseshoe of workbenches where three men in blue overalls wielded precision machines that clasped diamonds in weirdly shaped tungsten steel claws mounted in teak. Wheels span at thousands of revolutions a second, splitting, cutting, grinding, polishing. Each workplace was surrounded by a clutter of dirty coffee-cups and full ashtrays and was lit harshly by lamps whose purpose was truth rather than seduction.

Van Willet tipped uncut grey stones into his broad palm and chatted away to Harriet about their size, probable quality, how they would be cut. Then he took a lady's gold watch from one of the display cases and insisted on fitting it round her wrist. It was a delicate object in two different colours of gold, with a bracelet made from thousands of tiny chain links. The round dial was circled with diamond chips with more substantial stones at the quarters. Its weight on her thin wrist was a surprise, a substantial presence, though it was delicate and small enough not to look like a manacle. Harriet could not help liking it.

'How much?' Paul asked.

Vincent shrugged and pouted. 'What a question to ask! It is a thing of beauty. An adornment for a beautiful wrist, for a lovely lady. You cannot set a value on such things.'

'Come on, Vincent. How much?' The thick eyebrow comically raised.

'More than you can afford. Unless you intend to make an honest woman of her and keep it in the family. Twenty thousand. Sterling.'

Harriet twisted her wrist beneath the spot Vincent had directed towards her, relished the play of fire, then turned it over to unclasp the watch bracelet.

'Keep it on if you like. Wear it to lunch. A loan. Perhaps this mean bastard will be persuaded to buy it for you.'

She laughed, but insisted on taking it off.

She used up her film, thirty-six Tri X, working briskly mixing posed shots with less formal ones, and rather liked the way things were going. This was nothing like her usual routine, which involved a Canon with a motor, and on formal occasions a Hasselblad, lights, and an assistant. She had brought the lightweight Pentax because she felt naked without a camera, but had not expected to use it professionally.

When she had finished, Van Willet took them down Spui to a small, dark Indonesian restaurant. Following his advice the main dish she had consisted of shreds of spice-coated meat fried crisp with tiny slivers of chili. It was hotter than any curry she had ever had, but if she avoided the chili she discovered aromatic flavours that were quite new to her.

It appeared that Vincent Van Willet was, like Roget, an amateur and collector of Islamic art. 'But Paul's collection is

37

much finer than mine, though I have one or two Moorish pieces from fourteenth-century Spain which I know he covets. Lord knows, Miss Jones – all right, Harriet – just how he can afford it all. Simply by unscrupulous dealing, one imagines.'

'Actually he smuggles cocaine,' Harriet had almost said, but remembering the various stages of fear and panic Roget had exhibited during the previous twenty-four hours she bit the words back. And of course, now, Zeebrugge thirteen, she realised just how untrue it was. Roget did not smuggle cocaine. His poor sodding mules did it for him.

On the way back to Rembrandtsplein they had been followed, though it had not seemed like it at the time. When they crossed to the middle of the square with its small plane trees and beds of sprouting but not yet flowering bulbs a small man, dark-skinned but Polynesian rather than African or Indian, dressed in a black coat, approached them with a broad and meaning-less grin on his face, but walked past without speaking. They realised he was looking at someone behind them, and turning they came into full-face close-up on a miniature Sony video camera, held by a small dark woman, also dressed mainly in black, but memorable because of the apparently premature ageing in her face. Her eyes were large and the whites yellowed, there were crowsfeet round her mouth, and her cheeks were sunken. She smiled at them as she lowered the view finder, and white metal, not gold, gleamed in her teeth, which were long and discoloured. Beneath her furs she was very thin.

Roget threw up his hands, frightened and angry.

'Come on, Paul, what's the matter? They're tourists. Taking moving pictures of each other to show the folks back home in Manila or wherever.'

'Nevertheless, that's the last time I'm going out with you. Really, Harriet, we must stay indoors, not be seen outside together again.'

This had irritated her, especially since, thanks to the Van Willet assignment, she had felt she could face the Customs with a really good and professional reason for being in Amsterdam on her own. She was ready to enjoy what was left of the trip, and she did not intend to spend the rest of it watching Roget smoke in her room while she agonised about how to react if he made a pass at her. She locked him out, had a rest, a shower and went out on her own into the chill March evening.

Her outing started pleasantly enough with a gin and tonic in a 'brown bar'. She enjoyed looking out through the wide windows at the pleasure boats and barges on the Amstel canal, listening to the sounds – music, hurrying feet, distant traffic, the bells of the trams as Amsterdam wound itself up for a Saturday night. She ordered another, took her time, and of course it was almost dark when she left. She found now that the streets were not as brightly lit as she thought they should be. There were too many dark corners, gloomy black patches of cold canal water, and tiny alleys between the tall houses. There was music certainly, and plenty of people, but all in pairs or larger groups, apart from single ragged men of all ages from sixteen to sixty who were at the very best pot pedlars, but more probably muggers, rapists, white slavers.

So she dined on pizza with a half-carafe of red in a small Italian restaurant, then slipped back to her room without speaking to Roget. There she put on the TV and was mildly interested to find that the programme was satellite-beamed by a company called Star Charge, and in English, though clearly directed at a cosmopolitan audience of rock fans. A famous British performer, whom even she recognised though she had paid little attention to pop during the last fifteen years, was being interviewed. Blond, epicene and fit, he earnestly expounded what he said was the central philosophy of his life. This seemed to be a personal brand of right-wing anarchy: he could do as he liked, because he was beautiful, talented and rich. Less fortunate people should do as they are told. Harriet agreed but felt such things should not be said too often, too loud.

She turned it off after a bit, drank duty-free Scotch until she was ready to sleep. As she turned out the light she was conscious of mild chagrin that Roget had not at least checked that she was safely in.

During the next day she did the canal trip twice and the Rijksmuseum too well. Rembrandt's old people filled her with heavy sadness, *The Night Watch* turned out to be a bore. A load of self-congratulatory, overdressed men who were clearly taking themselves far too seriously: it was too like the sort of pictures that made her her living.

The moment of truth came at last – a long moment of truth, for she got back to the Dam at seven and she had to wait for twenty-five minutes before moving. She drifted round the big brown and grey square, forcing herself to see, to notice, to be, for Christ's sake, a photographer.

She snapped the Buddhist monks with their saffron robes, turquoise-blue bongo drum, finger bells, and crimson banner – *Hare Krishna, Hare Krishna, hare hare, hare Rama* . . . and tried it out. Nirvana failed to flood her agitated soul. On the far corner from Holland International, at the opening into Rokin and the most notorious part of the town, not one, not two, but three pedlars offered her hash. A joint. Not a bad idea. Do more for her than *Hare Krishna*. But perhaps forensically not a good idea. One sniff from a sniffer dog and they'd do her over for sure . . .

She picked up her bag, the black nylon bag she had used for days and made her own, and took it out to the coach. The leering driver – was he really conspiratorial, or was it just her imagination? – hoisted it up and dropped it, plop, exactly next to an identical one already there. Identical apart from a small chalk mark by the lock, the small chalk mark Roget had told her would be there.

Floodlit docks, barriers, queues of lorries, coaches and cars, again no police or customs checks of any sort. The two-funnelled boat, sister ship to the *Herald of Free Enterprise*, was a ghostly presence in bluish green, white and red looming beyond a trellis of cranes.

The driver stood up and out of the dim light made his announcements – time of arrival, the routine with the baggage, and, dear Lord, Customs – and his thick glasses seemed to pick her out. He dumped himself back in his seat, and beyond, through the curved glass of the windscreen, she could see an officer with a walkie-talkie guiding him up a ramp. The bow of a boat had been raised to suck them into its maw. It looked like the jaw of a horrendously enormous shark.

5

Roget had checked out of the hotel near Rembrandtsplein at half past eight the previous morning. He carried a small green holdall containing his night things, a change of clothing, and the documents he did not expect to use during the day, and a black nylon shoulder-bag identical to the one he had given Harriet. This he held on to tightly at all times. Beneath a selection of clothing and toiletries he had bought from the married daughter of his cleaning lady, it held five thick manila envelopes containing an assortment of used British notes, amounting to one hundred and twenty thousand pounds.

Clutching the black bag fiercely and with the green holdall held more casually, he jogged across the tramlines and swung himself on to a number five tram. He stood, although there were plenty of empty seats, and watched the Amstel, the Hotel Europe, and the Dam, already littered with football louts dazed with booze and dope, slip by. He got out in the wide airy square in front of the Central Station. You could sense the port here, the distant sea. Terns flickered, vicious beaks poised, then swooped for sprats above the Oosterdok, and gulls mewed against the cold sea mist.

The 9.40 inter-city to Rotterdam was almost empty and he sat back in a first-class compartment determined to make himself relax. The line sank beneath bleak suburbs with their empty allotments hazed with frost into the station for Schiphol airport, re-emerged into a web of motorways, then sliced across canals with their windmills, the fens with heavy-uddered Friesians, and prairies of tulips and daffodils – buds spiky but unopened. Slate-grey herons flapped lazily over the occasional patches of watery woodland: poplar, willow, whitebeam. Tidy Dutch towns flew by, Leyden and Delft, recalling the jolliness of Brueghel, the peace of Vermeer.

Then the huge tower blocks of Rotterdam, and the Eurotower on the horizon.

Robert San was a very fat man indeed, who made Roget realise that his own podginess was not the depressing problem he sometimes allowed it to become. He also enjoyed San's tastes in food and drink, which were as refined as his own but based on a particular expertise Roget lacked. Sitting now in one of the dimmer recesses of the Floating Paradise surrounded by gilded dragons cavorting across red lacquer and lit by a tasselled lamp, San guided him to the right choices amongst the bewildering variety of snacks on the Dim Sum trolley. Beyond the windows and the pagoda eaves a huge container carrier obeyed the promptings of three tugs, slipped down the deep water channel of the Maas.

San was Chinese, certainly, but had Dutch nationality and thought of himself as Dutch. He wore heavy black suits, smoked thin Java cigars, drank *oude jenever* neat by the shot glass. He spoke Dutch without an accent and English like a Dutchman. But he spoke Cantonese too, and almost all his trade, in London, New York, as well as in Paramaribo, Barranquilla and Colombian Cartagena, was carried on through Chinese. His suits may have reassured Dutch port officials, but the gold rings with solitaire diamonds and the solid gold belt-buckle in the shape of a dragon's head impressed his associates.

They also impressed Roget, or rather filled him with nervous awe: San was very, very alien, belonged to a cruel world of cut-throat commerce that knew no sanctions but expediency, had no frontiers that could not be breached by telexed bribes or threats. Yet, five years earlier, they had come together through the world of Islamic art. San was no connoisseur, but he traded in anything that could be bought and sold, and through him Roget had engaged to buy two jewelled *chenangkas*, scimitars forged for a fifteenth-century Sumatran sultan.

Roget thought he could find a buyer before he would have to pay. The end of it all was that he was stuck with two articles for which he owed sixteen thousand pounds which he could not raise. San had a solution: a Volkswagen van filled with Santa Marta Gold, at that time the dope of choice in London NW. He never discovered whether San had set him up in the first place or had opportunely exploited a situation he had not created.

Eighteen months later they met again and San suggested a similar arrangement, but this time with cocaine. He had a buyer in London who could be contacted through Scapino, a hard-rock coffee bar off Covent Garden. The profits were better by a factor of ten, and a suitcase was easier to handle than a Volkswagen. Within two years Roget was importing three kilos every six months, selling two to Ricardo, the manager of Scapino, and breaking the third into ounces which he sold on to a circle of ten friends and acquaintances who distributed them through the Bloomsbury world of academics, publishers, literary agents, media folk.

And now San was telling him that the show was over. His voice was surprisingly soft and light considering his size and the bleak toughness of his hooded eyes. Neatly he indicated mushrooms, resting like coracles on their caps, each crewed by a large shrimp, and glazed with a deep red-brown sauce. He tapped the edge of the porcelain bowl with his chopsticks, then went on: 'I must not say too much, you understand that . . .'

'Of course.'

'But I would not like you to think that there is anything personal in this. You should try these next, I think. They are chicken coated in sesame seed. I have the highest regard for you, for your professional approach to our association, it is not because of you that I choose now to terminate it.'

'Acutally I planned to make this the last trip.'

'I think that's wise. Wise in any case, forgetting this . . . intervention.' San dabbed at his thickish lips, passed the napkin along the silky line of a moustache trimmed with micro-exactness. The yellow diamond on his podgy little finger, half a carat at least, winked beneath the lamp. 'No one survives at your point in the trade for ever. You are too exposed. For me it is a sideline, just one of many very different operations. It is easy for me to cover myself, to set up fall-guys if the police get close. As you know, I never handle the stuff. At the end of this meal I shall be as near to it as I ever am, and if anyone dares to kick in the door here, it will be in your possession not mine . . .'

He was referring to the procedure they always followed. Paul arrived carrying a bag filled with notes which he would leave in the cloakroom. When he collected it on leaving, the notes were gone and in their place the appropriate amount of cocaine: always in kilos sealed in flat polythene bags. Early on Roget had objected that this exposed him to too much risk: the cocaine could be rubbish, stepped on, or there could be nothing there at all. San had replied with chilly seriousness: 'You take me for a gangster, a crook? I am a merchant. I buy and sell. If I try a trick like that on you you do not buy from me again. What would be the point?' 'But,' Roget had insisted, 'I bet you have the money counted before changing it for the coke.' San had turned his very heavy hands so the palms were exposed in a gesture that seemed to say it all: 'I am a merchant but you are a crook.'

'Wise to get out,' he went on. 'You should try these dumplings, they have a filling of spiced ground pork. Wise to withdraw intact and with money in the bank.'

'But there has been too . . . an intervention?'

'Yes. I repeat, I cannot say too much. Enough I hope to make you realise this is not my wish and does not reflect my opinion of you. But the fact is, my suppliers have asked me to give a guarantee that nothing they pass on will find its way to Scapino in London. And you deal with Scapino. I have other outlets. My firm and its associates trade along the coast to Hamburg, the Baltic. I can go upstream to Köln, Frankfurt, Basel . . . I don't need Scapino. I don't need London.' He shrugged. 'I think now we are ready for some tea. What do you say?'

At the cloakroom he stood back, a large, watchful presence behind Roget as the attendant passed over the black nylon bag. It weighed about the same, but he knew the clothes, those he had bought from his cleaning lady's daughter, would be folded far more neatly now than they had been. He turned, hand stretched out to say goodbye.

San smiled. 'For old times' sake, I'll give you a lift to the station.'

He drove the big black Merc himself, not aggressively but with quiet skill. He parked on the station forecourt, helped Roget out and into the lofty modern concourse with its grey, granite-tiled floor and huge glass wall. Beneath gigantic photographic negatives, hung to advertise film or an exhibition or both, he shook hands and then held on. For a moment Roget sensed his physical presence more strongly than ever before: the dry warmth of the huge hand, with the brutal hardness of gold nestling in its heart, the huge stomach crowned with the dragon's head belt, the smells of strange foods and sour tobacco, the small dark hooded eyes that never lost their watchfulness but were suprisingly touched with warmth.

'We shall not meet again. At least not in this line of business. You are right to pull out now. In Europe so far it has not been the same sort of scene as in America. There I would not get involved for a million a year. Though it's easy enough to make as much. But it is a dangerous business over there, and it is going to get like that on this side of the water. It will cease to be an occupation for merchants, or indeed for anyone who values their health. Paul, take care.'

The huge Chinaman padded back through the glass doors, paused on the kerb, lit one of his greenish-black cigars before getting back into the big black car.

Roget bought a packet of Camels, then checked the time. Only five minutes before his train, the 2.55, was due, so he set off down the subways and up on to the correct platform. He flipped up the lid of the packet, shook one out, and put his green holdall on the floor to light it. The black bag, of course, was securely hung from his shoulder and clutched beneath his arm. The big, yellow round-nosed diesel rumbled into view, the long line of yellow and brown carriages snaking behind it, coming out of the watery sunshine and in beneath the glass canopy. And then it happened. He hardly felt a thing: scarcely more than the removal of a presence from between his feet. An urchin – literally, from the colour of his skin, a street Arab – had snatched the green holdall and bolted, was already no more than a tousled black head of hair disappearing down the subway steps.

Roget had to think very fast, but the thought that shrieked at him louder than anything else was: I must not go to the police with four kilos of cocaine under my arm. Yet he dithered in mind-twisting panic while passengers pushed around him and hydraulic doors hissed shut. At last, just in time, he hoisted himself up into the train and found a corner seat. He lit another Camel, he had chucked the first getting in, and tried to force himself to take stock. What had he lost? His

British Caledonian return air ticket Schiphol to Gatwick, Euro-cheques, one hundred and twenty gulden and about five hundred and thirty pounds sterling. Plastic: American Express, Visa, Euro-cheque card, British Library reader's card. Passport. Right, he reckoned, as the grey suburbs slipped by with glimpses of distant docks and the Telecommunications Tower behind three enormous blocks of flats, he had the hour before the train reached Amsterdam in which to decide what to do about it, but once there he'd have to move fast and decisively and get it right.

Back in Amsterdam, with only three hours in which to retrieve the operation from disaster, with fingers crossed and in a mental state as close to prayer as anything he had achieved since adolescence, he rang Van Willet.

His luck held, or at least showed signs of returning to normal: Van Willet was at home, answered the phone himself.

'Vincent. I've been robbed. Can you help me?'

'Oh my God. Of course, yes, Paul, anything I can do, what have you lost?'

Roget listed: passport, return ticket, plastic, money.

'And of course today is Sunday, everything is closed . . .' Van Willet's *o* sounds had just a trace of an *a* in them, especially when emphasised, drawn out, 'claosed'.

'And really, it is important I don't miss the plane tonight.'

'All right. We will do what we can. Where are you?'

'At the Central Station.'

'I can be there in twenty minutes. Now, I shall bring some money – how much?'

'That is the point, Vincent, the crunch. You see, I still have unfinished business to conclude here and I need five hundred pounds sterling, notes. Can you do that? And say, another fifty just to help me get home.'

'And your ticket. Really, you British are so incompetent. But okay. I can fix this for you, but I shall have to go to the shop. On a Sunday I just do not happen to have sterling notes about my person. I'll meet you there in twenty minutes.'

At his shop Van Willet, bearish, untidier than ever in his weekend gear of too tight Lacoste sweatshirt, floppy trousers and sneakers, continued to tease as he unlocked doors, disengaged alarms, fiddled open the safe.

'I'm sorry to see you have lost your delightful companion,

46

Harriet. A lovely girl, and so professional with her camera. One thing is certain. She was not with you when your bag went for a walk. British men are incompetent for one very good reason: with such competent women to clear up behind them they can afford to be so slovenly. Never mind. Here we are. You are lucky I have so much sterling unbanked. It's not a currency one likes to stay in for too long these days.' His podgy fingers riffled through the notes, mostly tens, stacked them in hundreds and folded the outer note over each sheaf, in the continental way. 'There we are. And another fifty for loose change. You can send me a banker's draft as soon as you get back. I cannot help asking myself, Paul, just what business it is you still have unfinished on a Sunday afternoon in Amsterdam. Something to do with that black bag you are refusing so well to put down? If it's naughty, don't tell me. We are friends, so I can help you, but more easily if I have a clear conscience about it.'

Sharp bastard, thought Roget, but hopefully he suspects nothing worse than smuggling Islamic *objets* duty-free.

'Now the next thing is the piece of paper you will need from the police attesting you have lost your passport. You did not stay the night in Rotterdam?'

'No.'

'Then you are resident here. Where was your hotel?'

'Rembrandtsplein.'

'Then we must go to the Leidesplein Police Station.'

In town Van Willet drove a neat Citroen Visa with more bravado than Roget really enjoyed: he was grateful that the streets were almost traffic-free. The police station was awful – a foretaste, it seemed probable, of the shape of things to come. It was a harsh, depressing place. Behind the duty counter five policemen, two uniformed, with truncheons and guns, indulged in loud camaraderie and horseplay, and it took some time to get their attention. When they did, it was all done brusquely and with routine, offhand efficiency. One of the policemen took them upstairs in a lift and into a small waiting area, where he brought them a sheaf of carbonned forms. The walls were painted in thick cream gloss but everywhere was just slightly grubby, old, chipped. Some of the blotches could have been blood, indeed probably were: the only other two people there were British punks, wrapped in Union Jacks. One

47

of them had his head tilted back while the other dabbed at his bleeding nose with a corner of one of the flags. Roget hoped that they would not realise he was British.

The form was simple enough. Where did it happen, list of lost or stolen objects, address at home, in Amsterdam and so on. The policeman countersigned the form, tore the pad carefully into its separate sheets, gave Roget a yellow one.

Outside again Roget breathed in deeply, and Van Willet slapped his shoulder. 'Right. What next?'

'Well, I have this business to conclude . . .'

'And you don't want me to be there for that. All right. How long will it take?'

'Five minutes, no more. The appointment is not until a quarter to seven. But we still have my air ticket to fix up.'

British Caledonian ('We always remember you have a choice') was open, and the girl behind the counter in her tartan uniform was efficient and helpful. She took the details of Roget's lost ticket as far as he could remember them, told him to return at seven o'clock. By then she would have confirmed by telex with the London office that it was in order for her to issue a replacement.

Van Willet shook his hand warmly, turned aside his gratitude. 'I was, you knaow, maowing the lawn. This has been much more fun.'

Roget strolled the short distance to the Dam, then more deliberately into Rokin. He did not have far to go. The Jolly Jack Tar is a pub patronised by British gays, but it is seedy, down-market, a place where the middle-aged, or even elderly, the unchic and unattached, can make contacts that lead to brief liaisons in even tattier houseboats not far away.

Ron Smith was in his shirt-sleeves sitting beneath a framed poster advertising Capstan cigarettes, showing two bell-bottomed British tars with their inner arms round each other's shoulders and their free hands clutching the gaspers. In the background a Dreadnought steamed confidently past white cliffs.

Ron too had a cigarette clenched between his nicotine-stained fingers and a half-litre glass of lager in front of him. He squinted up at Roget through thick spectacles, and tilted back his bentwood chair from which hung his bus-driver's jacket. His peaked hat was on the table beside him.

'Nice evening, Mr Roget. I see you have the package there ready for me.'

Always he was like this: seeming to take over, seeming to be in charge. Roget suppressed his irritation, put the bag down by the peaked cap.

'That's right, Ron. All present and correct. And I think you'll find this correct too.' He pushed across the envelope into which Van Willet had folded the five hundred pounds. 'The lady is tall, fair, dressed in denims, rather good-looking . . .'

'They always are.'

'Yes, well she's a bit older than the last, mid-thirties. I'm sure you'll keep an eye on her for me. Make sure she gets on the boat.'

Ron Smith touched his nose, a pasty object with tiny blackheads. 'You can rely on me, Mr Roget, you know that. I foresee no trouble for us – they'll have their hands full with these here football hooligans. And I'll see you at Gatwick in the morning, as per usual?'

'That's the idea, Ron.'

6

Harriet wandered up and down companionways, across narrow halls filled with video games and ten-button bandits, considered booking a bunk in a cabin but found they were all taken, considered going to the video lounge to see an old Clint Eastwood film, but found that full too. Eventually she ordered a large gin and tonic in the bar, resisting an upbringing that she had never quite bucked which said nice girls do not drink on their own. The barman – gay, she supposed, weren't they all on ships? – sympathised, was friendly, uncensorious, and offered her a second before she had quite finished the first. She accepted.

Then the duty-frees – but first, she had Dutch guilders to change. In the queue she was chatted up by a skin – savage, rough, tired, but surprisingly tender with his girl, who was in worse shape than he. Beneath the hedgehog hair and the creaky leather, she was just a plump, pale, tearful teenager, who clung to her bloke, refused to be left alone, and could not, without assistance, remain upright.

'It's the crack, see,' said her man, who was big, big-shouldered, big-limbed, and had no need of the slogans studded across his back: he was frightening enough without them.

'Crack?'

'Yer, Crack. They give it her in this caff, see. Bar. They took a tenner off me and gave her this crack – crack they call it.'

'What is crack?'

'Well, it's like crack, innit. I mean crack's crack.'

'I suppose so.'

'I mean like speed's speed, and crack's crack. They're okay. I don't hold with the Chinaman though. I mean I don't drop nothing, no way. But I hadda ged er off the Chinaman, it weren't doing her no good, see? I just booze. Booze killed my Dad and that's good enough for me. But she don't like booze, see? Makes her puke.'

'What . . . did it do to her? The crack, I mean.'

'Well, it like gave her the hots it did. That was all right. Didn't mind that.' He didn't leer when he said this, but a wistful, nostalgic note was there. 'Then after, she come down like a lead balloon. Well, you always do, don' you? But she like said this was the worst and she'll top herself if she don't get some more.'

The leather creaked again as the girl pulled herself into him, dragging at him with her nails and whimpering.

Next – the duty-frees. Paul had said she should. That like everyone else she should come through Customs clutching her clinking carrier. For a few minutes she grappled with the rules posted on the window outside the shop. Goods bought in the EEC. Goods bought duty-free in the EEC. Goods bought outside the EEC, whether duty-free or with duty charged on them . . . Lord, what a load of garbage, could she handle it? She was tired, very tired, and almost paralysed with fear.

She had not felt like this since she was thirteen years old. Then she had hated and feared the dentist more than God or her father. Somehow she had evaded two appointments through the hols so that her father had sent her back to school with a note requesting that Sister fix her up to see the school dentist. She had destroyed the note . . .

The long queue slowly threaded round the stacked shelves. Choices had to be made. Two hundred Marlboro. She was trying to give up. One day she would. This just did not seem the right time. A bar of Toblerone. A socking big bar. Milk chocolate, honey and nuts, so many calories, but what comfort! She realised that anxiety was driving her back into childhood. Thumb-sucking would be next, whimpering for Nanny. Come on, Harriet, take a grip. A bottle of Beefeater's. Fine. Can't remember what else I'm allowed, so that will have to do.

She settled into a dark glassy area filled with reclining seats with an empty place right up by the windows. It was quiet and warm but not stuffy. There were even blankets. She ate her chocolate, fiddled with her Walkman, set it going. Pav in *Trav*. He sang of the bliss of carefree love and only the trombones threatened the arrival of his father. She slept.

The coach rumbled down the ramp. She had a brief glimpse of pearly mist over Dover harbour, of white and grey buildings girdling a bay beneath a hill with a castle on it. Then the swift succession of bends took them beneath cliffs and even it seemed through them, and the harbour was gone, just walls of grubby chalk and long sheds.

'Hey, it really is white rock,' cried the Canadian girl.

They toppled out of the coach they had been in a scant ten minutes and joined the huge queues that filtered through the doors. Signs directed them like rats into different channels – holders of this sort of passport, holders of that – which pushed them through garishly lit bottlenecks, tiled in cream with crimson lines. And at Passport Control she was held. She should not have been. Her passport was valid, her appearance entirely unexceptionable, but the official, a pale sandy-haired young man, held on to her and her thin blue book for . . . half a minute?

She had been spotted, she knew she had, and the message had gone on.

She went with the crowd into a bigger, wider hall. Hundreds milled around. Children cried fractiously, men grunted offensively at their spouses, and somewhere a German Shepherd dog barked. Or bayed. Over at the far end, by the two twin channels, red and green, a policeman held him in check, but only just, as the punks and skins gathered together. Clearly this dog knew as well what he was after as the ones trained to sniff out coke and dope: at the sight of Doc Marten boots and spiky hairdos he was already slavering.

There was only one carousel and it was not heavily laden, not the way such things are in airports. Only the heavy baggage of coach users was on it: rucksacks, cases, bags, carriers. Most of the people who pushed and shoved to get at them were young, many of them American, Australian, or Canadian. In Harriet's book, colonials. There were, just as there had to be, two black nylon shoulder-bags, identical save for the telltale chalk mark near the lock on one of them. For a moment the temptation to take the other, to take the one that was hers, was a biological imperative, but something in her had set, she was committed to see this through, get it right, and she took the one with the chalk mark.

Now it was like the walk to the scaffold, an interminable trek into the second bottleneck. Green channel, nothing to declare. Red. She faltered, took the green. It divided. Long benches to the left, long benches to the right, surely reassuringly understaffed, only two Customs officers behind each. She hesitated, went left, behind a gang of skins, including the couple she had spoken to. The customs would be ready for them, would expect them to be loaded with speed, dope, and crack – whatever that was.

And it was working. Three of them were called over, and that appeared to take care of all available officers. Somewhere in her brain brass bands began to play, scarlet tulips opened in spring sunshine, she did not even see him as she made for the exit, yet he came from somewhere, came from behind and tapped her on the shoulder.

'Good morning, miss. I should like you to accompany me over to the bench for a moment.'

He was a pale thin man, with dark lank hair and pock-marked skin. Yet beneath the tiredness, the sourness, the probable ill health and encroaching middle age, he had authority, carried weight. He was not in uniform, a fact that signalled seniority, wore a double-breasted navy-blue jacket with brass anchor buttons over charcoal trousers.

She said: 'I've been through Customs and I'm going home.'

He took her elbow. She could smell the fatigue on him, but sensed in his grip an excitement too. Through an eight-hour night-shift he had been waiting for this. The bag weighed like lead, slipped absurdly off her shoulder. There was not much she could do to stop it with her camera, lens, handbag all also looped round her, and the duty-frees swinging against her knees. Suddenly too she wanted to pee, remembered how she had refused the need when she woke up to find they were already penetrating the harbour moles of Dover. She had been afraid that if she got herself into a loo she'd stay there.

There were almost no other clients, if that was the word, at the benches. Four skins listlessly watched as two uniformed officers unloaded one large kitbag which appeared to hold everything all four had taken with them, and two small dark-skinned people, neatly dressed in black, who had the latest miniaturised video equipment which they intended to use during their holiday in Britain, and, yes, of course, if you please it is our earnest intention to take it back home with us . . .

The lady, small, yellowish beneath the brown skin, actually raised the camera and panned slowly on to Harriet's face. She was very close, and her white metal teeth flashed in a crooked smile half hidden by the camera. Why? Who was she? But things were moving too quickly, too badly, to worry about that now.

'Please put everything you are carrying on the bench.'

Two uniformed men moved in on her, though the low counter stood between her and them. The older man remained behind her, at her shoulder.

'You have read the notices relating to the different channels?'

'Yes.'

'And you are not carrying any of the prohibited articles or substances?'

'No.'

'Please give the key to the black bag to the officer.'

'It's in my handbag.'

She reached for it. The older of the two uniformed officers, a fat man whose studied impassiveness was betrayed by a very slight hand tremor, got there first, undid the clasp, tipped it out, found a bunch of keys. She picked one out for him: small, brassy.

It did not fit.

'Are you sure this is the right key, miss.'

A sudden rush of excited determination almost swept aside the fear. The routine was working. It was under way. All she had to do was keep her head. She took a deep breath, and shook the auburn quiff of hair back off her forehead.

'Quite sure.'

'And you have no other.'

'Not with me. The spare is at home.'

'Perhaps you'd like to try.'

She shrugged, again flicked back her hair. Her fingertips were slightly sweaty, but they did not shake. She had to put the bag on its side, resisted the temptation to say it felt too heavy, let all that scene come naturally, at the right moment.

'No. It doesn't seem to fit.'

She sensed a sudden stillness, a boredom, almost a despair, settling over the three men.

'It wouldn't, would it, miss?'

Her heart jumped. They knew. Their only hope now was to trap her into showing that she knew they knew.

'I don't know what you mean. It should. I mean, it is the right key.'

'But it doesn't fit.' The un-uniformed man, still behind her, sighed. 'Well, miss, it is our opinion that it is our duty to examine the contents of this bag. If you cannot provide a means to open it without damaging it, we shall have to force it. Some damage will inevitably ensue.'

'Which I imagine you will make good.'

He refused to rise to this, nodded at the younger of the officers, not much more than a boy, with spots. From a shelf below the counter he produced a small pair of metal-cutting shears. One snip was enough. The released zip tracked round the bag and the top part of it fell open. The older man began to unpack: a nylon nightdress, pink, short; a T-shirt, inscribed 'Guinness is Better for You, It Makes You Blind But It Does Not Give You Hairy Palms'; another inscribed 'Bognor Regis, The Last Resort' . . .

Harriet began to laugh. She heard it, and some detached corner of her mind relished how unforced it sounded: Roget had done well.

She spluttered: 'Really, you know, as far as I'm concerned you need not bother about the damage you've done . . .'

54

Four plastic bags containing a white crystalline substance . . . *Four!* The bastard. He had said there would be three.

'. . . because, quite simply, that is not my bag.'

The tall man behind her sounded tired, very tired. 'Your bag, miss, I suppose is still on the carousel.'

'Well, really I suppose it must be. Indeed, I hope it is. It's got in it the film I went to Amsterdam to shoot. My whole trip will have been wasted if that's gone.' She said 'gawn'. Let the bastards know who's who. 'And if you let me get it you can check it out, and if we're very quick I suppose there's just a chance my coach will still be waiting.'

'No, miss. Prima facie we have enough evidence to charge you with substantive importation of a substance contrary to Section 3, para 1, of the Misuse of Drugs Act 1971 and I must ask you to come along with me.'

'The coach will go without me and I'll be late back. This is very inconvenient and will probably cost . . . And you'll have to let me have a pee first, I'm bursting.'

The swapped-suitcase scam, invented and perfected by an American cocaine smuggler, semi-fictionalised under the name Zachary Swan in the book *Snow Blind* by Robert Sabbag, is, as Swan says, foolproof in any country where the Rules of Evidence apply – so long as the mule keeps her head. It is used a lot by smugglers who value the freedom of their mules and are prepared to take on a slightly increased risk of losing their coke in return for guaranteeing their mules' safety.

The set-up is familiar to Customs officers: they call it the 'double-shuffle', and their first reaction when they hit it is deep irritation, approaching anger. They know their only hope of a conviction depends on breaking the mule down. And even that is not enough. In court the forensic evidence will be solidly against them, and a good barrister will make it clear to the jury that any statement the mule made was frightened out of her. So they not only have to break her, they have to break her good – good enough for her to reveal the identity of the man who is running her, and all she knows of his whole operation, enough for them to get him in the can as well as her.

Harriet had declared a need to pee. So they kept her waiting, standing in a narrow tiled corridor, for forty-five minutes, guarded by one male and one female officer. She held on, reiterating her request at five-minute intervals, though the discomfort came close to pain and she began to wonder whether or not she was doing herself an injury. After twenty minutes the tiled walls billowed in on her and then receded like the sides of a tent on a windy day.

At last the tall, tired man in the blazer returned.

'Miss Jones, I have to tell you that tests have now shown that the chemical you were carrying . . .'

'I was not carrying it.'

'Miss Jones, you were carrying it.' Said firmly, the voice raised. 'The chemical in question is crystals of cocaine hydrochloride. We are now holding you under Section 170, para 2, of the Customs and Excise Act of 1979. You do not have to say anything unless you wish to, but what you say may be given in evidence.'

'Are you charging me?'

'You will be told very clearly when you are actually charged. Now please go with the officer – '

'I want to pee. Not until I have a pee.'

He turned to the woman officer. 'Miss Sands, kindly take Miss Jones and observe the full toilet routine.' He paused, looked Harriet up and down very slowly, with a cold, black expression that nevertheless very clearly spoke of his consciousness of her sex, of her appeal. 'And then a full rubdown please. I'll send in Dr Bahjee.'

First they took her to an open latrine, where Miss Sands, a carrotty-topped buxom lady of about forty years old, with a white, tired face that almost sang of emotional deprivation and brutalised feelings, was joined by a shorter, darker lady, ethnically dark in fact, whose long black and rather greasy hair was scraped back into a tight bun. This was Dr Bahjee. She wore a white overall and carried a black bag. Harriet silently named her Onion Bahjee.

Dr Bahjee told her to sit on a white porcelain bowl, no seat, and with a sealed outlet. And they stood in front of her and watched her. In spite of the near agony she was in, it was a full two minutes before she could relax her sphincter, and then only because Onion Bahjee muttered to Carrot-top in the exaggeratedly cultured accents of an educated Hindu: 'She doesn't want to micturate; she is just wasting our time.' This made her so angry she was momentarily distracted and let go.

Onion Bahjee, using a pipette and a small flask, took a specimen of her urine, released it.

Then they took her to a small cubicle with nothing but a plain, high surgical couch in it. It was unheated, cold.

'Take all your clothes off, Miss Jones.'

'What if I refuse?'

Onion Bahjee looked at her, and a tip of pink tongue ran across her full, dark top lip. 'Then Miss Sands will take them off for you, Miss Jones.'

Harriet undressed. She put her clothes on the couch and stood at the end of it, shivering fiercely, arms clutched over her breasts. Miss Sands, Carrot-top, went slowly, meticulously, minutely over every scrap of clothing. Her knickers were very slightly stained – the period she had been expecting had just offered a show. When she discovered this Carrot-top made a slight but very clear clicking noise with her tongue, and stirred Harriet's anger and sense of outrage alive again just when it was fading into self-pity.

'On the couch, please. On your side . . .' Dr Bahjee's voice suddenly hardened, took on a vicious edge. 'Facing the other way. Flex your top knee.' The snap of surgical gloves, then cold penetration, mercifully eased with petroleum jelly, deep into her vagina and then past the sphincter of her anus. 'Nothing there. Yet. It can take thirty-six hours to come down though, you know. And we can hold you that long if we have a mind to.'

Harriet exploded, swung her long legs off the couch with such suddenness and force that both doctor and officer were surprised, stepped back. 'You fucking bitches! With four kilos in my bag I'm hardly likely to be stuffed with the muck as well, am I?'

Carrot-top's eyes narrowed. 'That's abusive and threatening behaviour, dear. And if my ear did not deceive me, and Doctor heard it too, an admission you were carrying drugs . . .'

'It seems that after all you have admitted to being in possession of drugs.' In another plain tiled room, but with desk, filing cabinet, three chairs, and a telephone, the arresting officer began his interrogation. It was all done, Harriet noted sardonically, in the approved fashion. His head was in shadow, hers lit. The chair she was offered was hard and plain; his allowed

57

him to recline and swivel. He had warned her that he was legally permitted to tape the interview, had activated a machine.

'No.'

'"With four kilos in my bag, I'm hardly likely to be stuffed with the muck,"' he quoted, looking for confirmation beyond her shoulder to the door, where Carrot-top now sat on a chair as uncomfortable, she had been pleased to note, as her own. His voice was not loud, but it grated, as though there was a presence in his throat, a growth perhaps. 'Let's start with you telling us where those kilos came from.'

'No. I have not admitted to being, as you put it, in possession. I was, in error, thinking it was mine, carrying a bag which transpired to contain those four bags of whatever you said it was . . .' Her voice trailed off. Was 'transpired' really the right word? Didn't it have something to do with breathing? She was very tired, and was aware now of a familiar dragging feeling between her legs. At any rate, nice to be sure that prick Jeremy had not left her in the club. 'And I want my bag. My real bag. It was on the carousel . . .'

'You are sure of that, aren't you, Miss Jones?'

'Yes . . .' she saw the mistake and her insides shrivelled, for a moment she thought she might cry.

He stood – all she could see of him was his trousers and waistband in the brightness of the light – then he moved away, became a shadow beyond the light.

'You are sure of that, Miss Jones, because you made bloody sure your other bag was there before you picked this one up.' Suddenly he was at her shoulder, leaning over it, so she caught the heat of his breath on her cheek. 'Listen. You are in a mess. Let me be very blunt, Miss Jones, and I know I won't shock you because you used similar language to Dr Bahjee and Miss Sands, you are . . . in . . . the . . . fucking . . . SHIT.' He swung away again, round, faced her, jabbed a pencil at her. 'You are in line for a life sentence. As of this year that is the maximum. Life. Right? Now. The best thing you can do is tell me all about it. Two bags. Both of them yours. One left on the carousel – you have told us you knew it was there – and one in your hand. Come on now, Miss Jones. Let's start right at the beginning, shall we? How did you get into this? Eh? Where did it all begin?'

Harriet dug her nails into the palm of her hand, bit her lip. Then: 'My period has just started. There is a Tampax in my handbag. I demand to have it, and decent privacy to put it to use.'

He banged the desk with the flat of his hand. It sounded like a pistol shot. 'Answer my question. Where did it all begin?'

She shouted back: 'Not until you've done what I've asked.'

He slumped back into his chair. His fist came into the light on the table, his fingers slid down his pencil, reversed it and slid down again.

'Your sanitary tampons were shredded to make sure they were not being used to carry more illegal substances.' Harriet felt tears form, then spill. He went on: 'Miss Sands will fix you up with something when I choose to end this interview. Now. Let's start again. Miss Jones, you are in the shit. You must be very well aware that your unreserved co-operation at this point will be taken into consideration when you are sentenced. The street value of the cocaine hydrochloride you were carrying is not far off a million pounds. The usual rate for your role in this business is one thousand pounds per kilo. Miss Jones, someone was making a fortune out of you, and on top of that you are now going to go to prison for him. Nothing you can do is going to stop you from going to prison. Nothing I can do is going to stop you from going to prison. But there are prisons and prisons. An educated lady like you, I am sure, is well aware of the difference between Holloway and a nice converted stately home out in the country somewhere. And believe me, to anyone – but particularly to a nice girl like you, with a lot of the best part of her life ahead of her, the chance still to marry, settle down after all, and have children – the difference between ten years which will be seven with remission, and life, is going to be . . . well, I don't have to spell it out, do I? Do you smoke? We shouldn't, should we? I've been trying to give it up, but . . .'

He shrugged, came round the table again, sat close to her on the edge. His shins almost brushed her knees. He offered her a man-size Kleenex, and she sniffed, blew her nose, dabbed her eyes. Then he shook out a cigarette, a Silk Cut, a brand she hated, lit it for her in his own mouth, handed it to her.

'Would you care now to start at the beginning?'

She looked up at him with eyes that burned with anger spiced with hate. On top of everything else the bastard was a patronising male chauvinist pig. Well, he would be, wouldn't he? Settle down and have children. Give the poor girl a nice big hankie and let her have a good cry. And rip up her Tampax. She inhaled deeply, gagged, nearly retched, then reached forward and stubbed out the offensive cigarette in a tin ashtray by his side. That brought her very close and his eyes, brown, slit against the smoke or because he was trying to paste a smile into them, met hers. And it was his that flinched away: perhaps after all he knew she had his number.

'Mr . . . I don't know what your name is.'

'Price.'

'Mr Price. I am a professional photographer. I specialise in portraits of businessmen, bankers, financiers, for trade papers, the national media, company reports, and so on. I am now expanding into Europe. I am just returning from a trip on which I took pictures of an Amsterdam businessman, Vincent Van Willet, a diamond merchant. If you develop the film in the bag I left in error on the carousel you will find pictures of him, and his card too with his telephone number . . .'

An hour later he called a halt. Miss Sands took her away to a small but clean, bright and warm room which was in effect a cell, though it tried to pretend it wasn't. She was given a full British breakfast, which she demolished down to the last smear of cakey lard congealing with the eggyolk on the plate, and machine coffee sweet enough to be bearable. A little later Miss Sands brought her an adhesive sanitary pad.

She knew she had, for the time being at any rate, pulled it off, won.

7

At half past seven that same morning, Smith parked his coach at the set-down point at Gatwick, clambered out of his seat, and plodded across tarmac and concrete through the early morning sunshine to the nearby gents' toilets. A 747 thundered low overhead. Roget – pale, indeed haggard, after a night of hanging around airports with a brief flight between, not long enough to snatch a nap in – was waiting for him.

Smith nudged up close to him at the urinal and unbuttoned. 'It's gone wrong, Mr Roget. She's not on the coach.'

'Christ, Ron.' Roget could smell the man's tiredness, the tobacco smells and the urine mingling with cheap disinfectant coming off the yellow chemical spheres that lay in the trough. The bus-driver was pissing on them, chasing them up and down the channel. Roget moistened his lips. 'What happened, Ron.'

'They bust her. That's what happened.'

'Did she get the second bag? I mean did she tell them . . .?'

'Honest, Mr Roget, I don't know nothing else. Last I saw they were opening the bag you give me. I waited a bit for her, then checked back, and they told me like she was being held, and if I had a schedule I should stick to it. So that's what I done and here I am.' He shook his peg, shrugged it away, zipped. 'Shame really, Mr Roget. She seemed a nice girl.'

Roget took the shuttle train to Victoria, the tube to King's Cross, where he rang Harriet's number from a public call box. No answer. He went on trying at half-hourly intervals throughout the rest of the morning and the early part of the afternoon. When he wasn't ringing he sat in the station buffets, working his way through all of them, and those next door in St Pancras too.

At four-thirty, just as the rush-hour was beginning to pick up, again, she answered.

'Harriet?'

'Yes?'

'You're home. Listen, just answer yes and no. Am I right in thinking you really are home? I mean, they are not expecting you back, next week?'

'Yes, you are right. No, they are not expecting me back.'

'Phew. Jolly well done. You see? I told you it would work. So I take it you didn't have to reveal, um, the provenance of the goods?'

'No. I did not.'

'But . . . I take it that the goods are all irretrievably overboard.'

'That is entirely correct.'

'Right. They're not going to be as easily shaken off as you

might think. So keep a cool head if they come back. In the meantime, I think we had better keep a distance between us. I'll think of a safe way of calling you in a week or so, and perhaps we'll have a bite somewhere and you can tell me all about it.'

'What you're saying is: "Don't call me, I'll call you".'

'Right.'

And she rang off sharply – perhaps, for all he could tell, slamming the receiver down. At any rate she was gone.

With pork pies, Cornish pasties, station coffee, station tea and station beer swilling about in his bloated stomach like so much cement in a mixer, he trundled himself back to Purbeck Street, now almost entirely ripped up on one side by the water company. He tried to check out that his house wasn't being watched, saw no one more menacing than a meter maid who obviously could not cope with the problems left by the road works.

Lamps lit up his cluster of Aladdin's caves. His treasures – miniatures framed in thin gold beading, pots in burnished copper and faience, his small but very expensive collection of silk prayer-rugs – caressed his tired and lacerated senses with a welcome more innocent of all ambivalence than any friend or lover could offer. Within seconds he was sitting in his chintz-covered armchair, in front of his gas-fire, and cradling in his podgy, still tremulous hands a large cut-crystal tumbler of gin and tonic. It was good to be home.

Slowly, he assessed the damage, much as a worsted tom-cat, back from scrapping with half the street, will sit in its favourite armchair and slowly, inch by inch, examine, clean out and lick smooth the scratches, torn fur and possibly poisoned bites. He was down – down a lot. Not in prison, for which Harriet and guardian angels must be thanked, but that, at the end of the day, was the blessing to be counted. The rest was all debit. He was down one hundred and twenty thousand pounds, the money he had paid to San. He was down five hundred stolen, and five hundred paid to Ron Smith. He was down five grand paid to Harriet. He was down all the other expenses of the trip. At the end of the day, we are, he said to himself, talking about, worst case, bottom line, one hundred and thirty thousand pounds.

He held his glass to the light and watched the pale gold

bubbles soaring to freedom or gathering trapped round the twist of lemon that floated at the top. He dabbed it with a finger, released some, watched more form. He muttered to himself: 'Someone is to blame. No doubt of it. I was set up. But who by? And why? Well, why is clear enough. Only one reason. Someone somewhere wants me off the street, wants me out.'

And, dear Christ, they had succeeded. He was done, through, washed up. He knew, right then, he had made his last move, he would never again dare to put himself on the line. He had felt on his cheek the very breath, sharp and acrid, of Nemesis, and that was it.

Above the mantel-piece the Name of God calligraphically compressed into a dynamic swirl of black ink and raised gold throbbed in his eye, refusing him the tranquillity its abstract perfection usually offered. The game had turned nasty, had become the sort of thing drug trading was always meant to be about; no doubt he'd been lucky so far that that side of it had not touched him, but now it had that was it. Paul Roget, collector, epicure, man of taste, was not a gangster: in a world suddenly agonisingly uncertain, that at least was incontrovertible.

He pottered down the narrow stairs to his bijou kitchen, poured another, sipped, quite suddenly sniggered, then let the laugh come, his high crowing laugh. When all was said and done, and the chips were down and had to be counted, this was it: it was a relief to be out. All right, he'd have to sell a few pieces, he'd have to live a bit carefully for a few months until something else turned up, but in the meantime, yes, it was a relief.

A month or so later he was not so sure. Both terror and euphoria had subsided and he was left with the cold reality of bank statements and bills and a future in which he would have to struggle to make thousands a year out of consultancy fees and trading in Islamic *objets*, instead of the tens of thousands that had become such a pleasant habit.

He had also had quite nasty confrontations with two of his ouncers, retail traders in cocaine. They had been expecting him to supply them, knowing that he had a shipment lined up. One of them, a student in tropical medicine from Sierra Leone whose family had got on the wrong side of the government there and who could no longer pay his fees at the London School of Hygiene and Tropical Medicine, threatened by turns suicide and murder, both by disembowelling.

The second was a publisher who financed a serious cocaine habit of his own by retailing Roget's ounces amongst his associates in the book trade. By June he was down to his last ten grams and he assured Roget that his career would be doomed if he did not get topped up soon: without coke he was a wreck, and certainly he could not afford to buy his own. He had a wife, two children at private schools, a mistress who was looking forward to a fortnight in Mauritius, and a mortgage of one hundred and eighty thousand pounds still outstanding on his Regent's Square house.

Both of these were close neighbours, as indeed were most of Roget's clients, and they made him feel harassed, at risk, and even, in the case of the black medical student, guilty.

It was not surprising therefore that in the end he responded, albeit reluctantly, resentfully and fearfully, when the summons came.

The first intimation was a frightener: one Thursday morning late in July the postman delivered a strong brown envelope containing his stolen passport. There was no note, no explanation, but there it was. It said a lot. It said: the snatch on Rotterdam station had been no accident; someone knew a lot about him – his address for starters. How much more, remained to be seen.

Another month passed. This time the postman brought a stiffie, an invitation – gilt-edged, deckled pasteboard: *Leisure for the Discerning requests the company of* Paul Roget *at a weekend of formal and informal reorientation and skill enhancement. September 26–28, at Skrape, Coombe Bissett, Hampshire. Personal Reception for* Mr Roget *at 3.45 p.m. 'Meet and Greet' Session, 5 p.m. (Tea and Biscuits), followed by Course Induction.* And in the top left-hand corner a long number that looked familiar. It took only a moment to check that it was the number on the passport.

8

Four o'clock in the morning, and the light was already seeping along the north horizon towards the east, heralding a March dawn; an iron-grey sea ran in front of a chill breeze that scarred its crests with white. With the most southerly tip of the Isle of Wight, St Catherine's Point, a bare smudge and a winking light ten miles to the north, it was an inhospitable place to be if you were alone in a twenty-four-foot offshore powerboat with no crew.

Worst than inhospitable if you had just received a drop of ten kilos of virgin Lady from a Panamanian banana freighter, which was already hull-down on your beam heading for Rotterdam, while on your lee the dipping swell showed you a solidness in the sea that matched the blip on your radar that had been bothering you for ten minutes or more.

He's shadowing you, that's now certain. And he'd rather you weren't too sure about that, because, like you, he's wearing no lights. And that could mean that he's an illegal too. And now you've actually spotted him, visually, you can see he's quite a bit bigger, looks like a Princess 38, and that means two things. He's got a five-knot edge on you, and he almost certainly must be crewed.

He doesn't have to be an illegal. He could be Customs, shadowing you, hoping to see you make a drop that will lead them on up the chain to Mr Big, but if that's the case he's being clumsy about it. They must know that you've spotted them. And if you've spotted them then the moment they make a hostile move you're going to drop the whole caboodle, plop, plop, plop, overboard. So. On balance, he's not Customs. And that means he's a pirate. Only one way to deal with pirates . . .

Thus reasoned the lean, tough young man perched up in the open cockpit of the Sunseeker 24. He spun the wheel, watched the railed prow in front of him shift across ninety degrees, felt the heave of the swell running straight now from stem to stern. Each action was done with practised assurance, a precision that seemed to flow naturally from his dark, intelligent, hard eyes, his long, strong fingers. He throttled back, programmed the auto-pilot to keep her on the new bearing, and reaching behind him found his Fujinon SX marine binoculars. With ninety-five per cent light transmission they brought the alien presence, now a mere couple of hundred yards away, perhaps three, into ghostly but quite sharp detail. Yes, a Princess all right, and still showing no lights at all, and, now he had her whole length briefly in view before she turned to echo his turn, no flag either. There was not even a glow behind the black glass of her raked windscreen, which in this dull light gave an oddly sharkish look to her, a black mouth between the cockpit canopy and the hull.

And she's coming closer. Right. Suddenly brisk, decisive, he put down the glasses and, moving with the same practised precision, lifted the side seating, heaved into view the three components of a Kapp-Duxbury Nutcracker rocket launcher. It took him less than ten seconds to assemble them, to load the shuttle-shaped missile, swing the whole thing on to his shoulder and aim. Hang on, give the bastards a chance, one across the bows first, let them see what they're up against. He switched off the infra-red beam which would have guaranteed ninety per cent accuracy, aimed visually, and fired.

The missile looped and twisted, self-correcting its flight, its cone of fire reflected from the slate-coloured waves like a sabre slash. It flashed across the bow of the Princess and detonated with a satisfying thud a hundred yards or so beyond her. But before the breeze could snatch the propellant exhaust away from the open cockpit, certainly well before he could reload, the response came, swift and uncompromised by the sort of consideration he had shown.

The bigger boat surged forward as if a leash had been slipped, her prow came up and the bow wave sheeted like a diving fulmar's wings. At a hundred yards covered in five seconds, she showed her beam again and two black figures, black-masked, in the open cockpit in the stern. The cold dawn air shattered with noise, the darkness parted like a wound beneath a scalpel of light, and the hull of the Sunseeker split along the waterline beneath a blast of heavy tracer.

They pulled him out of the water two minutes later, unharmed apart from a cheek gashed by a flying splinter, hustled him over the stern sheets, down the companionway, through the galley and into the forward berth. Shaking with rage and shock he banged on the veneered door, and bellowed: 'Who the fuck are you? What the devil do you think you're doing,' but got no answer. Then the craft lurched, tipped him off balance on to the big double bunk shaped to fit the prow, and he heard the whine of throttled-up engines, felt their vibration and the sudden push of their power. There was a huge hooded bathrobe on the bed. He pulled off his sodden Guernsey and jeans, wrapped himself in it, realised he was bleeding into it and on to the bunk too. Serve the bastards right.

Presently the door opened again. The man who came in was still in a wetsuit, but the mask had gone, revealing a blotched face, fair straight hair, a fair moustache above a thin, hard mouth which, nevertheless, offered a smile. 'Hot drink sir. What you need after an experience like that. And a dressing for your face.'

He leant over him, swabbed the wound, sprayed it with an aerosol, pressed the lips of the gash together and snapped on a field dressing – the sort whose adhesives are as efficient as old-fashioned stitching. 'Looks nastier than it is.'

Strong tea, spiked with dark rum. He took it, drank, got the shuddering shiver that had gripped him as soon as he halfway relaxed under control.

'I know you, don't I?'

'We have met, sir. Port Stanley, four years ago.'

'Christ, yes. I remember. Special Boat Squadron. Can't remember your name though. Are you still with the SBS? I mean, is that what all this is about?'

'Drink up, sir. Then, when you're ready, the man, er, in charge, would like a word with you.'

Two steep flights of steps this time, and they shepherded him on to the low-roofed bridge. Stooping, he could see through tinted glass a coastline of white cliffs and bays, and almost dead ahead the lighthouse that marks the last of the Needles. Dawn had broken, but grey: no sun yet. Two men in the swivel bucket seats up front. One of them swung round to him and a pair of big round spectacles flashed up at him from a pale, very ordinary sort of face which the young man nevertheless recognised.

'Shit. I might have guessed.'

'Yes. I suppose you might.'

'What do you want?'

'We want you to work for us again. Of course. And after what we've just seen, quite frankly, I don't think you have a lot of choice in the matter.'

The young man grimaced, winced at the jab of pain he felt in his cheek, sat down on the leather bench that ran along the side. He sighed, tightened the belt of the bathrobe. 'No. I suppose you're right.' Then he grinned, flashed even teeth, and there was quite a lot of charm there – in the spontaneity of it. 'Well, things could be worse. You'd better tell me what you want.'

On the same day, which was also the day Harriet was busted at Dover, Pedro's uncle, Antonio Pérez y Mendizábal, Marqués de Boltana, met Lili Brel, financial fixer to the mega-rich, to exchange progress reports in his office in the Banco de Corpus Cristi, Madrid. Handsome, robust, a well-kept fifty or so, still poised on a pinnacle of corseted good health, he welcomed her at the huge mahogany door that was the last barrier between the president of the bank and the outside world. He took her Chanel gaberdine and scarf, handed them to his male private secretary whom he then dismissed with the tiniest of nods. He kissed the fingertips of both her hands, took her elbow, and directed her across an acre or so of Aubusson, past the Goya portrait of the ancestor who had founded the bank, to the huge desk that filled the window at the end of the long, oak-lined room. There he placed her in a high-backed carved chair upholstered in lilac watered silk.

They drank coffee and exchanged murmured banalities for a moment or two before he pushed across to her three sheets of A4 onionskin paper. He made a church of his fingers beneath his spreading but not flabby chin and watched while she folded out half-lenses from the soft leather purse she carried, and placed them carefully across her long, thin nose. She did not pick up the pages, but turned them with a perfect fingernail lacquered in a soft but not weak rose that matched the thin lips of her small mouth. The desk was high, so her back was held straight with her head a little tilted – a pose that expressed an alertness and confidence that went well with the restrained glamour of the styles she affected.

The Marqués sighed. A long time ago and for a brief moment they had been lovers. They had been working together to tie up Spanish Moroccan oil reserves before the multinationals could get to them. A time to remember with gratitude – ecstasies shared, and untrammelled by contract: neither those emotional and financial ones that lurk beneath the marriage bed, nor the more vulgar variety that buy a rut with spoiled flesh.

Caught by this longing for last year's snows, and annoyed with himself for it, the big polished man swivelled his throne and gazed through the high window at what was left of this year's: a few discoloured rags caught in the sunless gutters above the Plaza de España.

Presently he heard the dry thin paper rustle and knew she had moved to the second page. Recruitment of personnel in London. She sighed, tapped her fingernail on the desk's polished marquetry.

'This must be managed with the greatest discretion,' she murmured.

'My dear Lili. Everything is being managed with discretion.' Boltana's voice cracked on phlegm. He cleared his throat, restored his voice to its usual organlike boom. 'As I understand it Hector has arranged a most thorough screening process. Employees are selected first because of their success in the trade. That already means they are discreet. Then they are vetted very, very thoroughly. It is a long process, can take as much as six months. Finally they will be invited, induced, to attend very carefully planned induction courses, followed by practical training. Hector, you know, is very thorough. Very, very thorough. At this stage most of the people he's looking at are not aware at all of what is happening to them.'

She pursed her lips, signifying a certain scepticism, if not downright doubt. Her fingernail tracked on.

'He's not cheap.'

'Hector is very thorough. Very competent. He likes to do things on a big scale, but he watches every detail too. It's silly to pretend an operation like this is unattended by risk, but I am sure that Hector is the right person for the job . . .'

'He's a crook – '

Boltana interrupted, allowed his irritation to show. 'My dear Lili, of course he's a crook.' He grunted. 'It could hardly be otherwise, could it? But few men, honest or otherwise, have his financial gifts, organisational ability, above all vision. The vision to do the big thing and do it well.'

Lili fixed him over the top of her spectacles. It was the sort of look one might imagine a particularly severe and astute mother superior using to rebuke an erring novice. 'Toñi, it is not Hector Myklades' criminal nature I object to. It is the fact that he was caught . . .'

'He was unlucky and he was not prosecuted. The London Department of Trade merely found that he was not a suitable person to exercise proper stewardship of a publicly quoted company. He is by no means alone in that. The episode in question was, as you very well know, a function of the very breadth of vision, the um, Napoleonic scale on which he likes to do things.'

'Nevertheless, I shall want to feel sure that nothing similar is likely to happen. Quite clearly another Department of Trade enquiry even into the purely financial side of things could bring with it quite disastrous consequences.' She took off her spectacles, wound the silk cord round them, tapped the frame on her teeth. 'I shall want to see him. I shall want to assure myself that things are being done properly before he actually passes any funds into areas where I might be associated with them. My reputation is unblemished and I intend it should remain so.' She pushed the papers across to him, settled herself back in the high-backed chair.

'Well, that can be arranged, I'm sure. Perhaps in Paris, once the Colombian thing is settled.'

'All right. But in the meantime, as I said, he wants a lot.' She shrugged. 'At any rate too quickly. I can get him five million sterling by the end of May, and thirty or so by the end of August. After that he should be on the way to being self-financing.'

Boltana stood up, looked down into the canyon of the plaza below. Already the flowersellers were touting daffodils from the south, and mimosa too. They arrived earlier every year.

'We should be running profitably by then. But a lot depends on how well Feijoo does in Colombia. Did he say anything about that when you met him?'

'Not a lot. And there are aspects of all that that I'm not entirely happy with.'

'Yes?'

'The whole relationship between your nephew and the Arias family seems . . . problematic.'

'Yes.' Boltana's tone now suggested he was trying to close doors.

Brel persisted. 'Frankly, Don Pedro expressed extreme distaste about the whole idea. Yet Feijoo insists that his presence is essential. Why?'

Boltana shrugged. 'They are snobs. They liked the idea of a real duke, a real prince in the family. Now they like the idea of doing business with one.'

'I think there is more to it than that. The Colombians are notoriously dangerous, tricky people. There is something going on there I don't understand. I shall have to look into it. I suspect Pedro did not like his first wife. He certainly hates her family. I hope he is capable of concealing these feelings.'

'I'm sure he is, But you know, Lili, the Colombia end really is not your concern. Feijoo can handle it. And the Pensión girl can handle Pedro. She'll keep him in line.'

Brel smiled. 'Yes, she impressed. What the Americans call a tough cookie.' She thought for a moment. 'Well, we'll see. How it turns out. Meanwhile, things went much as I hoped in California. I already have Pedro's signature on a lot of documents. But a limited power of attorney, internationally viable, will save time. After all, your nephew is not the most businesslike of people. His man, Feijoo, seems capable, but I don't want him interfering on the European side.'

'I'll see to that. But don't leave my nephew overexposed.'

She injected a note of no-nonsense realism into her voice and her eyes searched for and found his again. 'Exposed he has to be. You know that. He's not your safety net if he's not.' Then she smiled. 'But if they ever get that close you know how it will be: the playboy millionaire owner of Mendoza Holdings will claim ignorance of the drug trade carried on in his name. And Feijoo. Certainly he's competent, but how far can we trust him to do what we want? I mean if the worst happened

71

would he mind retiring into anonymity with a very handsome pension?'

'No.'

'That's how we'll do it then.' She smoothed her Chanel skirt, picked a fleck of dust from one of the two pleats. 'Now there's the other side of it. We need something I can pass the profits across to.'

'Is that necessary?' Boltana tapped a thin gold pencil on the blotter in front of him. It made no noise. He reversed it, began to doodle.

'Yes, I'm not a clerk. I'm not going to sit at a desk all day with Pedro's chequebook and pay out every time Malatesta wants a million or two. What I have in mind is a charity. A charity devoted to the sort of things Malatesta believes in, and with its offices in Switzerland. You already have the Margeli-bank of Zug. That could be useful. And I could keep a close eye from my office in Bern.'

Boltana's pencil sketched three groups of concentric circles whose outer circumferences cut across each other and from whose centres lines radiated and intersected with each other.

He said: 'Mendoza Holdings, the British Virgin Isles branch, buys cocaine. Finances its movement on to Hector Myklades in London. The starter capital you are going to generate in the next three months finances Myklades' operation, right?'

'Yes.'

'Myklades sets up his organisation in London, passes the take back to Mendoza Holdings (BVI). And Mendoza feeds it to this charity you are going to set up for Malatesta.'

'Yes.'

'And you can make the cutouts between watertight?'

'Yes.'

He put down the pencil, and this time it was he who caught her eye and she who flinched off.

'It's not possible,' he said.

She shrugged. 'All right. Always there has to be a thread that is unbroken. Energy can become a spark and cross a gap: money can't. From Mendoza to Myklades and back there will not be much problem. We can keep it all very fluid, very liquid, close and open avenues as we see fit. The same between the charitable organisation and Malatesta's projects . . . What shall we call this . . . charity?'

Boltana, at the window, shrugged, laughed. 'Jonquil? Mimosa?'

She wrinkled her nose, stood up, joined him, looked down with him across the big plaza. A flurry of snow whirled by, dry small flakes. One landed on the pane in front of her. Slowly it dissolved. She smiled. 'How about . . . Crystal?'

'Crystal. Why not.' He laughed too.

She went on: 'But the problem remains – the interface between Mendoza and Crystal. We have to have a membrane between them that looks impermeable: they must be insulated from each other. And yet the money must cross. Well, I can set that up. As you say, it is nonsense to claim I can do it so no one anywhere ever will crack how it is done. But I can make the probability very high that no one ever will.' She nodded her head, a gesture expressing both certainty and self-confidence.

For a moment, standing there together, an intimacy stirred between them. Acknowledging and fearing it, they went back to their seats.

Another silence lengthened between them, then brusquely she straightened. 'That's it then. My fee is a retainer of a million dollars. After that I shall divert a half of one per cent of what passes between Mendoza and Crystal.'

Boltana's fingers froze on the pencil, his eyes widened, his cheeks inflated, and breath exploded minutely between pouting lips.

She smiled, stood again, smoothed her skirt. 'That way you can be sure of my loyalty to the whole enterprise.'

He dropped the pencil, laughed. 'I never doubted it.'

Together they crossed the huge Aubusson towards the big mahogany door. His hand rested lightly on her thin shoulder and they paused for a moment in front of the Goya. At the door he helped her back into the silky gaberdine and watched as she tied the scarf.

'You know, Toñi, there is finally something rather stupid, wilful, about this whole business. If I had Mendoza Holdings to run just as I wanted, I could generate this sort of spare cash. It would take five times as long, but I'd do it more or less legitimately and with no messing about with drugs.'

73

'Lili, I know you could. But can you imagine Pedro letting a woman run his affairs? And anyway he won't wait fifteen years for Europa, and the whole point for Malatesta is that with the money now he might just achieve something before he dies. He is eighty, you know?' He cupped her small chin on the first two fingers and thumb of his right hand and kissed her on her lips.

'Adiós, Lili.'

'Adiós, Marqués.' Head on one side she let a little warmth into her smile. 'Nevertheless, I do like the name. Crystal.'

And she was gone.

Part Two

The Barranquilla Contract

9

Two o'clock. Two silver Cadillacs slid out of the passenger pick-up bays at Barranquilla airport, out beneath a vibrant sky filled with blinding sunlight, swung beneath immobile palms and past dusty banks of municipal flowers and cactuses set in huge concrete tubs, and so into the relentless stream of trucks, taxis, buses, minibuses and private cars on the freeways. The brief passage across the searing heat of the narrow strip of concrete broke sweat on Pedro's neck and back. In the front, next to the black chauffeur, Jorge Aguirre, Pedro's cousin by his first marriage, noted his discomfort, prodded buttons on the dashboard console and created icy draughts.

He leaned over the seat to offer Pedro a cigarette from a case made of mother-of-pearl mounted in what looked like pewter or nineteeth-century gunmetal. He was a big, strong-looking man, dark, with a large, bushy and glossy moustache, and hands that looked as if they could bend iron bars. His coat drifted open to reveal a sprung holster and the butt of an Astra .357 Magnum. Pedro, who liked to believe he knew about such things, approved the leather, which looked old as well as tough, tanned to a Cordoba red, and tooled with a carnation pattern.

'Five years, is it?' Jorge's smile was as open as a small child's, both innocent and shy.

'Five years?' Pedro was deliberately offhand, breathed out smoke, fingered at his lip as though he thought there might be tobacco there even though the cigarette was filtered and he was using his holder.

'Since . . . you were here last.'

'Since the funeral?'

Jorge nodded silently, and his dark brown eyes filled with deeply felt sympathy. 'We met. Briefly. I don't suppose you remember. There were a lot of us.'

'I was upset.' Pedro twisted away, looked out at the barrios of the working classes, the bleak high-rises gaunt against the tropical sky, standing in their bulldozed wastelands. A wave of disgust suddenly rose like bile out of the pit of his stomach, and he ground out the cigarette. He hated this. All this. He hated coming back to Colombia, he hated his slaughtered wife's snobbish, pretentious, very large and very wealthy family. He hated . . . and feared them too.

Jorge was relentless. 'Of course. Of course you were upset. Doña Octavia was a lovely person. A lovely person. I remember her very well. As children we played together. Often. At my uncle's house. We were kissing cousins.' Jorge laughed, a fond, gentle laugh, at the memory of the slight, lively girl, the tomboy of fifteen years past. Then he sighed. 'What a tragedy! Like a Greek play. To have so much and lose it so young. Of course you were upset.' He turned back, faced forward.

Settling into the car behind, Jana Pensión asked her chauffeur to open a window. He refused in a Spanish rendered incomprehensible to her by glottal stops and a plethora of *s*'s and sh's that made him sound like a suddenly switched on kitchen tap. Feijoo, sitting in the other corner of the huge back seat, interpreted for her.

'Arias won't allow him to drive with open windows.'

'Why not?'

'Too easy to lob a bomb in, or stick us up with a handgun at the lights.'

Jana shrugged, shifted her small tight buttocks on the soft leather, and swung her long legs diagonally towards Feijoo's small feet. He was wearing crocodile shoes, white and dark blue. Twisted thus away from him she looked through the glass, tinted, toughened . . . and fixed. Beyond concrete ramparts, a wasteland of shanties replaced the bleak swathes of dusty baked earth from which an earlier generation of shanties had been bulldozed.

'Why are we here?'

Feijoo's head gave its characteristic twitch. His lips curled back over yellow teeth, and a gold molar momentarily flashed in the dim, shifting light of the interior.

'Pedro holds the family of Doña Octavia in the highest esteem.'

Jana looked at him for a moment. Her eyes, large-pupilled, the dark amber irises flecked with gold, became disdainfully expressionless.

Feijoo's, which were rarely still, flickered away. 'It's true.'

'Like fuck.'

He felt in his jacket pocket, shook out a Chesterfield, snapped a tiny gold electronic lighter at it. He knew the smoke in the relatively small area would infuriate her. Feijoo and Pensión barely tolerated each other: a week after her arrival in Pedro's entourage he had attempted first seduction then rape. She had seen him off with a dislocated finger; now she countered his cigarette by taking a packet of Chiclets from the pleated breast pocket of her combat-fatigue-style shirt. Leaning on the back of the front seat she offered a wafer to the mestizo driver. Taking both hands off the wheel he took it with broad brown fingers, oil-stained, with broken nails. His Indian face cracked in a gold-mounted smile.

'Business too,' Feijoo offered. 'The Arias family are very well connected.'

'I bet.' She popped gum at him, and he turned away in disgust.

The freeway divided. They passed beneath giant signs, one of which indicated Santa Marta, sixty kilometres. A memory six, seven years old stirred into focus in Jana's mind: a high-school senior in T-shirt, crewcut and sneakers who had tried to buy her ass with grass he said was the best – Santa Marta Gold.

The two cars cruised down a slipway, swung under the freeway, began a climb into gentle hills, leaving behind the seething, hot, unfinished concrete sprawl of docks, slums, sweatshops, and wealth that makes up one of the Caribbean's largest ports. The road climbed through banana plantations set behind low walls built of breeze blocks. Huge, obscenely phallic flowers alternated with giant green bunches supported on crutches like the dropsies of the poor. With the thicker vegetation came a steaming mist. Palms like giants floated above it. A Plymouth convertible swung round the hairpin bend next above them, its headlights four perfect discs of silver in the vapour that was shot with lilac and gold. They blinked in salute just before the cars crossed.

A little later a barrier garrisoned with private security guards armed with Beretta sub-machine-guns admitted them to the ghetto of the rich. The road, no longer pitted concrete but tarmacked with purple velvet, climbed above the mist. They stopped in front of gates trimmed with gold leaf. An old man with a bandolier over his shoulder, a machete on one scrawny buttock and a huge revolver on the other, heaved them open. A drive circled up through a tropical park, an ornamental orchard of citrus, guava, mamey, tamarind and almond. The ocean, as white as wood ash, flashed in the distance below.

An ostentatiously modernistic house appeared. It rambled like a crazy wall, turning in on itself and then unravelling across the uneven hillside, never a straight line in it, the windows and doors bowed, bayed and arched, even the perpendicular walls bulging or bending in, the roofs sweeping in concave curves like pagodas or swollen outwards like giant onions. Generally it was finished in pale ochre rough-cast but much of it was inset with ceramics and gleaming mosaics.

Pedro hated it. He had been here twice before: to be married, and to immure the scrapings from the San Bernardino highway that the Coroner had declared were his wife. And now he was here to lay the foundations of a fortune that would buy him a second and altogether more suitable mate. And that, the maggot of fear murmured, is something the Arias clan had better not find out about.

10

The following morning started for Pedro with a brief visit to the cemetery, where he placed a wreath of fast-wilting lilies in front of the slab which marked where his wife had been immured. Then he and Jorge took rich, smooth, aromatic coffee on a lawned terrace surrounded by exotic blooms and filled with huge butterflies and hummingbirds. Below them mist fondled the trunks of forest giants, lay in sheets across the lower plantations. In the distance sunlight flinked from the ocean. A small group of white-faced monkeys swung about the nearer trees, and occasionally the braver ones came close, begged for sugar or macaroons. On the silver tray amongst the cups and a jug a small gold cocaine kit glinted: burnished mirror, small cellar, and tiny gold spoon, which held, levelled off, precisely one-twentieth of a gram of pure, a thin gold straw, and a tiny gold-mounted knife whose blade had been fashioned out of polished agate. Jorge divided a tiny pyramid of white crystalline powder into two lines. Gratefully Pedro snorted up one of them. He leant back in the deep, high-winged cane chair, spread his legs and arms, let the rush take over until he felt he was coasting above the crazy Guadíesque roofs and treetops. It was the first moment of ease he had felt in Colombia, in the home of his dead wife.

Sunlight was suddenly blocked off his face and he opened his eyes. Jana Pensión stood above him, legs astride, hands on hips, head on one side and thrust down at him, like an inquisitive but angry bird, a small hawk perhaps. She wore a headband and a tight, skimpy leotard made from some glossy pale blue material which set off the coffee creaminess of her skin. A towel was slung round her neck.

'Workout time, señor.' Her voice was husky, lingered on the last word, made it scoff.

Pedro was petulant, squinted up at her, shaded his eyes from the brazen sky. 'You can see. I'm not dressed for it.'

He was still in the clothes he had worn to the cemetery: charcoal suit, white shirt, black silk knitted tie, though he had taken off the jacket and folded back the shirt-sleeves.

She shrugged, pouted, did not move.

'Okay,' cried Jorge, 'I'll join you. Let's do it. I could certainly use the exercise.' His huge hairy hands smacked his robust stomach.

Pedro remained reluctant. 'Where? Where can we work out? And I really cannot be bothered, you know? To change and everything.'

Perhaps it was the way the coke had got to Jorge. Perhaps his enthusiasm was more calculated. 'Here. What's wrong with here?' He swung an arm over the lawn. It was soft and deep, a blend of clovers and camomile. 'And who needs clothes? I mean what is this, some sort of aerobics?' He began to pull his shirt out of his waistband.

Jana was laconic. 'All right. This will do. Keep your shorts or whatever on. Otherwise you'll bang yourselves about.'

She had brought her Hitachi stereo-cassette player with her, and tapes – Springsteen and old Stones numbers. She set these up on the table while the men stripped to pants: Pedro tight briefs, and Jorge a baggy pair of boxer shorts. Beneath a mat of black hair, Jorge's body was fat but large-boned and well-muscled. Pedro's was lean, fit, but pallid.

To the fast heavy beat of 'Born in the USA', Jana swung away from them across the sward, head high, long arms swinging, buttocks taut above legs that did not have an ounce of surplus flesh or an inch of slack skin.

'Right. Walk. Fast. Faster. On your toes, on your heels, knees bent, stretch up. Lift your knees, clasp them, like this. On your toes again, on your heels, knees bent, turn . . . Okay. Feet together. Knees up, left, right, swing them out, across, now straight, one, two, three . . . Feet apart. Lunge to the left, weight change, lunge to the right, now do it with a karate chop, to the left, to the right, one, two, three, four, on five swing back and up, and circle round, weight changing and brushing the floor with your hand . . .' 'Get Off of My Cloud.'

Over half an hour she strung together a sequence of six exercises, and then made them go through the whole sequence eight times. The two men were soon sheeted with sweat, and Jorge's hairy dark skin became blotched with crimson patches. The scent of trampled camomile drifted around them, mingled with frangipani fragrances from the flowers. She took them over to the edge of the lawn, scavenging for shade beneath the oaks as the sun soared above them. A huge toucan with chestnut and yellow mandibles flapped down out of the crown of a giant almendro, scattered porcelain, silver and gold around the wrought-iron table, spilt sugar and cocaine, made off with the last of the macaroons. Jorge faltered to a gasping standstill. 'Don't just stop, bad for the heart – if you can't keep with it, jog.' Doggedly Pedro mirrored her movements but she did not stop until he too was jogging on the spot. Then she went through the routine once more on her own. 'Okay. Elbows on your knees, head down, breathe in and stretch . . .'

From a leaded window pierced in a bulbous tower Doña Serena, mother of the dead Octavia, watched. Her hennaed hair was scraped back from her temples and held in place with small platinum and emerald clips. She wore a kaftan made from wild cotton. She drank through a straw a long, frozen daiquiri, almost neat rum but decorated with tiny blue star-shaped flowers, and she watched: the slim long-legged girl whose thighs were like beech saplings, her gross cousin wallowing like a white manatee in the floor exercises Jana now had them doing, and the neat, virtually unblemished body of her son-in-law. In gestures that were baroque he twisted his thighs and buttocks away from his torso and chest, and in her mind's eye she painted his taut muscles with streaks of scarlet.

Meanwhile down in Barranquilla Feijoo let himself into a small conference suite he had rented on the fourth floor of the Cadebia Hotel. First he went to the windows and closed the shutters in front of them and then the heavy drapes across them, excluding the roar of the traffic, the smirched sunlight, the smog and stench of a tropical port where European standards of pollution control are dismissed as pointless extravagance. He also shut out some of the possibility of external surveillance. To counter the gloom he had induced, he adjusted the rheostats, increasing the power of the spots above the table, but dimmed down the lighting concealed in the cornices. He turned up the air-conditioning.

He checked the main table: an extended rectangle with narrowing ends and rounded corners, with three chairs on each side and blotters, ashtrays, small bottles of mineral water, glasses, and a thermidor filled with fresh ice; then a sideboard with small cups and saucers, a coffee machine full of very black coffee, and coloured sugar chips in a porcelain bowl. Between the centre table and the window there were two smaller tables with telephones, a small computer with a modem, and a video-tape-player.

The only other room was the bathroom, which he also checked out, looking for bugs. He had a pee, combed his wiry, receding hair, straightened his dull but expensive tie, adjusted the amount of handkerchief that peeped from his top pocket. Finally he dosed himself with one-tenth of a gram of cocaine, carefully measured, and his preparations were complete. At precisely ten o'clock Reception rang and told him that his guests had arrived.

The formalities were untidy and took too long. The other side had sent two principals instead of the one he had expected. He was annoyed too when they insisted not only on a second careful check for bugs, but on keeping two of the four bodyguards they had brought with them actually in the room. But by 10.35 they were ready to begin.

Feijoo, small, intense, nearly dapper but looking tired and a little seedy, took his place with his back to the windows. In front of him – the opposition: fat Felipe Cortazar in a dark blue suit and a lot of gold. ID bracelet, signet rings, cuff-links, all heavy, chunky, his voice fluting, unbroken; and Desiderio Rapal, a cinema idol and pop singer gone savagely to seed, his face pasty and pockmarked, his eyes bloodshot, in black tailored jeans and a black silk shirt left open to show a gold St Christopher nestling in grey, wiry hair. His voice had a harsh resonance. The bodyguards were bodyguards, large men of mixed race, beetle-browed, who sat in chairs on either side of the double door and filed their nails.

As soon as they were settled Feijoo delved in his top pocket and brought out a pair of black-rimmed half-lenses, opened the document in front of him and began his presentation. He spoke quickly, in monotone. His left hand remained on the page, usually with a Chesterfield clamped between index and middle fingers, and at times followed the course of what he had to say with the middle finger. The right constantly fidgeted with his slim gold pencil, sliding down the barrel to the table, reversing it, and sliding down again.

'The consortium I represent has registered offices on Tortola, in the British Virgin Isles, and in the canton of Zug, Switzerland. I have here letters of credit from banks in those places, and also documents from lawyers prepared to hold substantial sums in escrow. The necessary anonymity of my principals need therefore in no way prejudice your readiness to do business . . .' Without looking up he pushed a sheaf of letters and other documents across the table.

Fat Felipe poked at them with a nicotine-stained finger. 'We'll take time out later to check these through, and we will decide then how much weight they carry. In the meantime I must emphasise that in matters of this sort personal contact counts for a great deal more than mere documentation . . .'

Feijoo tapped the table quite smartly with his pencil. 'You already know that a principal member of the consortium is Señor Don Pedro Mendoza y La Cerda. He is by marriage a kinsman of more than one of the people whom you represent.

He is a man of substance and honour. With his name before you and the financial guarantees these documents represent, there is no point in asking who else is involved. Pointless too, because, quite simply, this is not a matter on which I am empowered to negotiate. It is non-negotiable.'

He sat back and let the silence he had produced lengthen. A flush spread up Desiderio's bullish neck. He pushed back his chair, gave his fat colleague a look that said, with a third-rate actor's hamminess, come on, let's go, what have we to do with people like this?

But Felipe touched the back of his hand, and leaned sideways to mutter in his ear. Then he looked up at Feijoo and nodded, suddenly benign. Leather creaked beneath them all as they shifted and relaxed.

Feijoo cupped his slim gold lighter and drew in smoke from another Chesterfield. What he really wanted was another tenth of a gram, but he felt a quick trip to the bathroom so soon would look weak, even suspicious. He looked round the dull room with its expensive but anonymous hotel furniture and back to the avaricious and unhealthy faces which were now composed into expressions of wary expectancy. He was deeply aware that what lay ahead was not going to be easy – basically he was there to persuade them to sell in a market they had sewn up at a price substantially below what other buyers were prepared to pay. He gave a tiny, almost unnoticeable shudder, and began again.

'Basically, what the consortium I represent proposes is this: that we will buy from you substantial amounts of product . . .'

'*¿Producto? ¿Qué?*' Desi Rapal was puzzled.

Fat Felipe explained: '*Perica. El mejor.*'

'. . . at agreed prices, at agreed intervals, spread over a significant period of time. We will guarantee to buy, you will guarantee to supply. The first aim of the proposal is therefore to remove from trade in product a large element of the uncertainty that afflicts producers and buyers alike. I should say now, the parameters of the deal I am about to suggest, the amounts involved, the period of the initial contract, options on future contracts, guarantees, penalties, are, as far as we are concerned, quite firmly drawn. We have arrived at them as a result of extensive market analysis, analysis of forward trends, projections regarding such factors as law enforcement in the areas where we propose to sell on, and the costing we have done on setting up or expanding the necessary infrastructures. These factors dictate the price we are prepared to pay. However, we are open to reasonable negotiation.'

He paused, put down his pencil, reached for the glass of water. Through some combination of lighting and the deep crimson of the leather on which it stood, it had a very faint bluish tinge. Bubbles ghosted their way to the surface, glowing like seed pearls. Opposite him Felipe shifted his enormous bulk, and a slight whiff of gas, mashy, rotten, escaped.

The voice dropped a register, fluked reedily like a badly played clarinet. 'Come on, Feijoo. How much? Per gram, how much?'

Feijoo allowed himself the smallest of smiles, enough to show a glimpse of yellow teeth to the men opposite. 'In fixing on a price,' he said, 'we have also given some consideration to the vicissitudes you have had to face in the past, and the state of the market as it exists today.'

He picked up his pencil again, let his half-lenses drop a millimetre or two down the slope of his nose, and embarked on a concise history of the Colombian cocaine trade tailored to show that his consortium was bargaining from strength and knew it . . .

When the workout was over Jana took Pedro to her small servant's room. She spread a rubber sheet over the narrow bed and had him strip off his briefs and lay himself flat upon it. She tied a crackling celluloid apron on over her leotard, and pulled on latex gloves, skin thin. Using the equipment she had unpacked the day before she made a minute examination of his physical condition, and fed the information she gathered into her computer. The green light from its screen, mixed with the glow filtered through the shifting fronds of a pepper tree, lent a cool subaqueous ambience to her ministrations.

'Your pulse rate's still up . . . and your blood pressure. Not much, but they should come down quicker than that. Heart sounds okay. Your respiration's still not quite back to normal, you know?' She went over every inch of him, kneading, touching, smoothing, lifting, stretching with clinical firmness. 'I can still palpate that liver, you know? It's not AOK, just yet, though it is one hell of a lot better, and not bad considering . . .'

Her expressionless amber eyes frequently met and held his in unblinking, unwavering gaze, and his flinched away only when she found something she did not approve. 'Open wide.' Her face was now very close to his as she came round into the narrow space she had created behind the bed. Almost she cradled his head in the crook of her arm, as she expertly went round his mouth with probes and a dentist's mirror. 'Some plaque between the bottom ones. Just a scrape now. We'll have a more thorough session on them in a day or so. And some nicotine staining. Have a rinse.' He spat into a kidney bowl she held for him, and she wiped his mouth on a napkin.

Instruments chimed as she put them down, then she straightened and looked down at him. Again her eyes, coolly expressionless as ever, met and held his. 'You've gone over the top with cigarettes and booze. By how much? Four, five cigarettes? You tell me. If it's not alcohol something else has got at your blood pressure. Fat George giving you coke? I thought I saw it out there with the coffee.' She moved away. 'Now the fluids. Got any pee? Fine. Too much colour there. Drink more mineral water, you need it in this climate. No albumen, fine.'

Instruments clinked again. 'Still, I'd like to check out your blood count. Just a tiny jab.' With unhurried precision she prepared a slide and put it on one side. 'On your back again, knees flexed a little, spread them and we'll see if we can get a sperm count.'

Lying back on his elbows, legs splayed, head hanging, he could see upside down a small Daliesque painting of the Temptations of St Jerome in the desert. Three blonde maidens, small-breasted, round-tummied in the Flemish fashion, representing not simple carnality but the lure of pagan literature and philosophy, could not distract the ancient scholar from his translation of the Bible into Vulgar Latin. Worms emerged from holes in their breasts and from other orifices. The desert was bare apart from scattered rocks that resembled disintegrating furniture, and was drawn in steeply receding perspective.

Jana passed her left hand under his raised thigh and pushed her gloved middle finger, baptised now with K-Y Jelly, into his anus. For a second or two the sphincter almost burned then settled into a warm glow and his prick rose to a strong erection. She eased out her finger, rolled on a condom to catch the seminal fluid, eased her fingers back in, and with her right thumb and forefinger formed into a ring caressed the tumescent glans with a swift but gentle milking movement. The finger inside him searched up towards the front of his pelvic cavity and suddenly the spasm was there, felt more inside him than elsewhere as the muscle clamped compulsively round the intrusion.

'There.' His prick flopped and she eased off the condom, handed him another small napkin. 'Wipe yourself.' She snapped off the latex gloves, binned them, pulled on another pair. 'You know that took fifteen seconds longer than last time, and there was, I'd guess, some three or four millilitres less fluid. I'll check the quality later. But you've been up to something, haven't you? Well, okay. But if you've been sodomising the help, watch it. You don't know who's been there before, and you don't want AIDS, right?'

The last part of the process he liked best of all, even more than the sperm collection. Still in her apron and gloves but standing in the stall with him, she went over every inch of his body with the hand-held shower head turned to full pressure and alternating icy with hot. Then she took a silver wire brush and skilfully stimulated his skin to a deep red, but without ever actually breaking it. She followed this with gels compounded from rare plants and the secretions of endangered cats, essences extracted from the livers of fish and monkeys. She smoothed them in and washed them off with a Red Sea sponge as soft as the caress of an affectionate mermaid. Then she wrapped him in a big white towel with a hood.

'Okay, back to your room and rest. And one glass of wine only at lunch. All right. It's the big meal of the day and you're the honoured guest, so you can have two. Stick to the salads and the fish, lay off the meat. With your blood pressure up you can do without the cholesterol. Run along, Duke. Be good.'

11

Feijoo's voice droned on, its resonance deadened by velvet drapes. Faulty air-conditioning provided a rhythmic backing, Cortazar and Rapal intervened occasionally with sighs, squeaking leather, as they shifted and fidgeted, wondered how this sallow, twitching Guatemalan had found the nerve to tell them what they already knew far better than he.

Through the sixties and seventies the syndicates had traded in marijuana harvested from huge plantations spread across the north of Colombia, but especially on the slopes of the Sierra de Santa Marta, and huge fortunes had been made. However, by the late seventies the market had drifted away from them: Mexico, Jamaica, Belize made *Cannabis sativa* their principal cash crops, street prices tumbled. There was the added problem that their rivals, with the overland routes across the Rio Grande open to them, were less vulnerable to detection and confiscation than the Colombian freighters off-loading at sea on to speedboats and dodging Customs launches from Fort Lauderdale to Cape Cod.

It was against this background of a falling market in dope that they had diversified to cocaine, expanding hugely what had already been a small but profitable operation. The trouble was that the profits remained very largely in the hands of the Mafia, which controlled distribution and sales throughout the States.

'At that time, ten years ago' – Feijoo's voice became insistent – 'the price of product, ex-processing plant in Bogotá, was six dollars a gram, and on the street in New York one hundred and seventy-five dollars a gram. Clearly the distribution and marketing organisations were taking a disproportionately large amount of the profit. Furthermore they refused to handle more than a tiny fraction of the potential supply, simply because they saw any increase as a threat to their chief import, heroin.'

Cortazar was dismissive. 'We saw them off. Wops.'

'Quite. But at very considerable expense.' Feijoo fingered out a stapled sheaf of papers from the pile in front of him, leaned forward to peer down at it. 'The war that followed cost you a billion, and the bills are still coming in. All right, it paid off. After all, you had won. For several years you maintained the street price, New York, at or around one hundred dollars per gram. By manipulating the market skilfully you were able to get the price even higher for short periods, and of course, albeit offset against the expenses of that war, this was now your money, no one else's.'

Fat Felipe suddenly yawned. It began as an accident which he tried to conceal, but when he realised it was too big to be hidden he brought it right out into the open and allowed it to expand like a vast and sonorous balloon.

Feijoo took a deep breath, and suddenly the longing for another snort was imperious. He fought it, won. 'Clearly a market that was now making such huge profits stimulated production first of processed product, over which you did have fairly complete control, then of unprocessed product, and at this point I must remind you that you do not control the initial stages of manufacture, you buy the raw material processed at or near the point of harvest into a transportable paste. You do not control how much of that raw material is produced. And the producers, aware of the enormous profits you are making, produce more and more.

'For a time this overproduction or increased production was not a problem. Indeed, and naturally enough, you welcomed it. With considerable skill you enlarged the United States market by a factor of ten, and your profits became astronomical. It is a well-known fact that you offered to pay off Colombia's national debt if President Bétancur would desist from persecuting you. When he refused you shot his justice minister. But . . .' – and he tapped the blotter with his pencil, and paused, very much aware that he was about to make the first substantial point in his argument – 'this market does finally have a limit. With over four million regular users and a further fifteen to twenty million casual users the United States has reached saturation point . . .' – the pencil-tapping became more insistent – 'and you are now faced with a crisis. Across the eastern jungles of Bolivia, Peru, and of this country too, thousands of growers are harvesting enormous amounts of leaf, producing enormous quantities of pasta, more than you can handle. You are faced with three choices. You can buy, and destroy what you cannot sell. This will slash your profits. You can refuse to buy and so they will sell elsewhere, and a price war at street level will result. All wars make inroads into profit, but price wars are the worst, eh?' This time his yellow smile exposed his flashing gold molar. 'Your third choice? You can find, open up, and exploit entirely new markets.'

He spread his hands, palms up, and the smile was now tinged with sympathy. He was beginning to enjoy himself: the two men in front of him sat slumped or slouched, but a brightness in their eyes, their very immobility, indicated he had their attention.

'This you are trying to do. But there are – are there not? – problems. Europe is not America. For a start it is not one nation but twelve, fifteen. Everything is so much more complicated. The banking, the finance. The fiscal laws. They vary so much from country to country. And, as was the case in the States, much of the trade in product that already exists is in the hands of the Mafia, and you don't want a second war with them, neither a price war nor a shooting one. In short, while an operation as large as your American one looks feasible, and although the markets, potential consumers with plenty of spare cash, are certainly there, it cannot be done in the same way, using the same strategies and techniques.' Again he offered them the sad smile of a sensitive wolf approaching a staked goat.

'You have tried. We have a very good idea of how you have tried. And always the same story. Once your operation has reached a certain level it has either stopped expanding or crashed. Only in Spain, where at least the language is on your side, have you achieved any significant enlargement of the market. And what happened? Precisely the one thing you have been able to avoid in your American operation. Product went down-market with pushers literally on the street selling heavily cut, one could say polluted product to maintain their own habit. The trade became heroinised. It functioned like the heroin trade.

'And that is bad news. Heroinisation means you lose control of the market. You are put in the place of suppliers only, you are at the mercy of market forces, competition, because inevitably the market becomes fragmented, it's not properly run, but is taken over by small-time crooks and unorganised pedlars, students, the jobless, punks, people you can't keep a hold on, people you can't rely on. Product is reprocessed into cheaper, nastier hits like crack, it loses its cachet as the fun drug of choice, and the spiral of falling prices takes a further twist. Now you could not prevent that happening in Spain where you speak the language. It will happen inevitably as you try to expand the market anywhere else in Europe.

'Let me put your problem in a nutshell: there is a huge, rich market waiting to drop, as good as the one you developed in America. In France, Germany, and in the United Kingdom in particular where the alcohol taxes have conditioned people to pay for their highs, there is a vast stratum of society with substantial spare cash. You made product a leisure industry in America, for just that class. It's waiting to happen in Europe. But only French, Germans and British can do it. And those you do not have. That in a nutshell is your problem. The consortium I represent is going to go a long way towards solving that problem for you, but before I tell you how, we can have some coffee, I think, and you can look at some of the detailed data I have prepared for you.'

They shrugged, shifted, reluctantly accepted tiny cups of *tinto*, the very black coffee Colombians hit themselves with throughout the day. Feijoo smiled again for a moment, masking the sudden anxiety he felt: he knew that if he failed to get the arguments across as forcefully as possible the final offer he was going to make would be deemed at best a joke, more probably an insult. He waited until he was sure that they had accepted the break, then, with teeth clenched, walked briskly back to the bathroom. He was less precise about measurement this time, took nearly half a gram, knew immediately he had taken too much. For a moment he felt as if his head was expanding to fill the small room, that his temples were pressing against the tiled walls. The feeling subsided and was overtaken by something much worse, a sudden wave of terrible loneliness, of panic. He felt like a three-year-old separated from its mother in a crowd.

The feeling faded, the euphoria returned, the potency, the conviction that he could do anything, master anything. Briskly he washed his hands, rinsed his face, looked in the mirror. With some difficulty he adjusted the inane grin to something more urbane.

Again it took longer than he wanted to get them into their places. For all their experience as hardened negotiators neither Cortazar nor Rapal could resist the computer and video: they fingered up the latest prices from Wall Street, how the London markets were closing. But at last they let Feijoo use the machines to run analyses of how trade in product had moved in Europe during the previous ten years, with projections of what could be expected in the next five. He doubted whether the Colombians were taken in much by this, but the trickle of flow charts, sliced cake charts, and graphs were pretty, had a mesmerising, soothing effect.

Back at the table he found that once again he could speak clearly, to the point, and with conviction. That, at any rate, is what it felt like. The high he was still on had sharpened his senses: the muted colours outside the spots seemed to pulse gently, the brighter ones under the lights sang. The interplay between the coffee fragrance and harshness of Rapal's cheap Piel Roja cigarettes was like neo-classical polyphony. He was aware too of a near-erection that helped his general feeling of wellbeing and potency.

'To recapitulate. The root of your problem is that you have too much pasta. You can't not buy it, it will go elsewhere and blow apart the markets you have. You can't just destroy it – too expensive. You can't open up the markets that exist in Europe – you don't have the expertise and you don't have the infrastructures. We propose – the consortium I am here to represent proposes – to make a very significant inroad into.this problem for you.'

He paused, palms again turned up on the table in the gesture that was expansive, generous.

'We propose to start with one hundred and fifty kilos a month, gradually increasing until at the end of a three-year period we will have bought twelve US tonnes. According to our best information that is equivalent to about one-quarter of the surplus you will be stuck with if you buy enough pasta from the prime producers to ensure you maintain control of the market.'

A silence had fallen over the room, and Feijoo's high

expanded. He had them now, at last, in the palms of those spread hands. Felipe was leaning back with one podgy arm spread across the back of his chair and his head thrown back on the palm of his hand. Thus he could give the ceiling and the far wall his full attention. Desiderio watched Feijoo with intent but carefully expressionless eyes. However, the fingers of his right hand drummed lightly on the soft leather: a Salsa rhythm. Probably they had been expecting a quarter, even a tenth of this. They knew now that he was serious.

'I don't have to add that one enormous benefit you will reap from this deal is that a large sector of your operation will be regularised. As far as you are concerned all the vicissitudes of a market that is, however lucrative, shot through with uncertainty, will be removed. All you have to do is supply product and bank the money. And you will be receiving that money on a completely regular basis. Our guarantees of that will be watertight. That certainty alone, which you would not get if we were broking oil even, and certainly not, say, coffee or copper, just about doubles for you the value of the offer.'

Feijoo poured more mineral water, sipped, turned a page or two in the folio in front of him.

'In return we will require certain very specific undertakings. We'll work out the details later, but these are they, in broad outline. We have already cleared the fact that throughout we are talking about pure product, uncut. The next is this. For the first three years, for the span of the initial agreement, we intend to supply one particular market. We will guarantee not to sell on outside that market, and we will expect you to do everything you possibly can to make sure that that market is not penetrated by you or by other producers outside this agreement. Only by maintaining a reasonable street price can we guarantee to maintain the price we propose to pay you.'

He paused, aware that he was about to drop to the hungry jackals the second piece of real meat. 'The market we wish to take over, which will become ours alone, is that of Great Britain. All right, a big market, one with a lot of potential. But we are proposing to put into it something like five times more product than you are actually selling there now, and we propose to do this without dropping the street price by more than ten per cent. And of course we guarantee not to sell elsewhere.' Again he paused, reached behind and his long fingers tapped in a request. An expensive printer purred and spewed a slip of paper into his waiting hand. He adjusted his spectacles. 'Street price last night on Leicester Square, specifically in a nightclub called Rage, was sixty pounds sterling a gram cut fifty-fifty with glucose. That's an up-market outlet; over the whole country we are probably talking about a mean figure of fifty sterling, seventy-five dollars, cut product, double that pure.'

He was moving at last towards the climax of his presentation. They all knew it. Whenever he paused the sounds in the room filled the gap with exaggerated clarity: the air-conditioning, the bleeps and buzzes from the hardware behind him, the rasp and fall of Desi Rapal's emphysemic breath.

'We are taking off your hands product you cannot sell and a market you have not been able to expand. We intend to sell at prices comparable to those currently prevailing, so you will not suffer a global fall in price because of our operation. We are removing from you all the attendant risks, all the overheads, all the day-to-day costs of that market . . .'

He looked around at the waiting faces, and the gold in his molars flashed. Even the bodyguards stopped manicuring their nails, and were waiting, heads on one side, expectant in the stillness.

'And there is one other factor too I must emphasise before I table our offer. Throughout this morning I have spoken of you, the Colombian processors and sellers of product, as if you were one entity, one firm. And of course you are not. You represent Arias, and he controls through a loose network of alliances a substantial part of the Colombian end of the business. But it is a loose network, and there are two families outside it. Do I need to spell it out? If you don't like the offer my consortium has chosen to make first to you, because of Don Pedro's family relationship . . . well, we have alternatives.'

This time Cortazar's response was visible. His fat fist clenched, the knuckles showed white, the muscles beneath his flabby jowls tightened. He was angry. The scarcely veiled threat had needled him. Feijoo felt a tremor of fear: perhaps he had gone too far. He hurried to his conclusion.

'To produce one gram of product, ex-factory in Bogotá, costs you eight dollars. Taking everything into consideration, the whole scenario as I have put it to you, we propose to pay you eleven. Eleven dollars a gram, plus a shipping fee of two dollars a gram to a collection point we will agree later. Thirteen dollars a gram is our offer.'

The reaction was precisely as he expected; it was what would have happened if he had offered twenty or even twenty-five. But no doubt the price he had placed on the table enabled the actors to go through the motions with genuine sincerity. As Feijoo shuffled his papers into neatness Felipe banged the table with two fat palms and pushed back his chair so it toppled as he stood.

His squeak was almost a screech. 'Come on. We are dealing with clowns. Jokers. Double that offer would have been merely insolent. But this is . . . *loco*.' And folding down all the fingers of his right hand except the middle one, which now stuck up from his fist like an erect chipolata, he leaned across the table and jerked it up under Feijoo's nose.

Within a minute they had gone. Feijoo slumped back in his seat, drained of energy, a cold sweat glistening on his forehead. Only the erection remained, more potent now than ever. He looked at his watch. One o'clock. He was not expected back at the Arias mansion: the arrangement was that he should meet up with them all at the bullfight in the evening. Plenty of time to find the whore he now wanted, needed more than anything, have a meal and a few drinks, get her back to a hotel room, either here in the Cadebia or wherever.

Outside, a sudden crackle of fireworks announced that with lunchtime work in Barranquilla had stopped: the festivities of the last day of Carnival were about to begin.

12

The *agasajo*, a welcoming reception, took place on the lawns where Pedro and Jorge had struggled through Jana's workout. Beneath awnings erected for the occasion, tables whose white linen billowed like the sails of privateers were laden with silver and gilt dishes: there were two sucking pigs, glazed and sliced but retaining their shapes; fresh tuna, its meat as dense as lamb and as pink; guinea fowl, and wild duck from the swamps to the east. At the furthest point from the house two huge braziers emitted clouds of blue smoke: on one, half-kilo slabs of steak were briefly burnt; on the other, skewers laden with cubed swordfish and slices of lime. There were paw-paws, medlars, sapodillas, ugly guanabanas, mamey fruit, and wild strawberry sherbets flown in from the high hills above Bogotá. There were traditional local dishes too: *mogollas* (whole-wheat muffins with raisin centres), *almojabanas* (rolls made from maize and filled with a salty white cheese), and tiny creole potatoes with yellow flesh, served in their skins like wizened walnuts with a coriander dip made fiery with cayenne.

There were wines, Colombian and French, and iced mineral waters, but the waiters in their white T-shirts and ducks circulated with trays laden with rum punches and whisky-sodas, and most of the guests drank these.

There were nearly a hundred, if one included the quite large number of children. The gravelled forecourt and the top of the drive were filled with Mercedes, Volvos, Cadillacs, the larger Toyotas, and there was a sprinkling of Porsches, Lamborghinis, and two Ferraris. There was also a cream-coloured Hispano Suiza coupé from 1935 that Pedro coveted as he looked down from his window and smoked a second cigarette before making his entrance.

He was the honoured guest, the reason for the occasion. Dressed in a dark mocha lightweight suit put together by his Roman tailor from the material woven from yarns that included a fair amount of Thai silk and cost half a million lire a metre, he stood between Don Octavio and Doña Serena and shook hands with the elders, the heads of families and their spouses, but briefly, in the manner of royalty. Octavio was a big, bullish man, whose skin was tanned to the colour of best calf's liver, and clearly, like his ancestors, he ruled. Like theirs his power base was the gun, the boot and the whip, but while their wealth had come from Chibcha gold, his derived from cocaine.

The people he welcomed personally were dressed with a standard Western formality, though with more variety, style and expense than one would find at a similar occasion in, say, the London of the mid-eighties. Although the men all wore suits each contrived some stylish and differentiating extravagance in material, cut, jewellery, tie or shoes; similarly their women went for the simple elegance of line that only the best couturiers can achieve, but in materials that dazzled with textured waves and shimmering colours. Their jewellery alone, costume size but none of it paste, justified the presence of the small army of bodyguards who patrolled the peripheries of the party with repeater shotguns slung casually from their shoulders.

The younger men were dressed for Carnival, for it was Shrove Tuesday and Carnival in Barranquilla rivals Rio's for excess and exuberance though not for style. They affected flamboyant weirdnesses from the *ateliers* of Barcelona and Milan, while their companions were clothed, partly clothed, in plastics and leathers, slashed and torn, chained and fastened to make the most of long tanned limbs, offering glimpses of breasts like gourds and buttocks as smooth and sweet as dark tropical honey. Two ocelots on jewelled leads arrived but were upstaged by a black-phase jaguar. In the dappled sunlight beneath the giant oaks its shadowy mariposa spots seemed to float beneath the surface of its fur. It snarled quite viciously at the children that wanted to stroke it, but quietened when a waiter brought it a slab of raw steak. Later it slept in spite of the noise.

There was plenty. The end of the formal part of the occasion was signalled when a Salsa band struck up and Octavio led Pedro down from the terrace where they had been welcoming the senior guests. Doña Serena, with emerald clips and wild-cotton kaftan, floated proudly away, stumbling only slightly on the last step through the glass doors, and was not seen again. The onslaught on the food tables began.

Jana had dulled the leading edge of lust, and Pedro soon found the attentions, persistent and explicit, of the girls variously claiming to have been cousins or best friends of his darling dead wife, as appealing as Port Said fellahin selling carpets or their sisters, and as obstinate. With some determination, he dragged a motley retinue towards the one person there who offered magic: the girl with the black-phase jaguar.

She was dressed in slashed black plastic: it had the suppleness of thin latex and the strength of skin. Her own skin, a lot of which was visible, was chalky white but the muscle tone was good. Not much of her face was visible above her mouth which was full and painted with plum-coloured cosmetic: the rest lay behind a close-fitting mask. The eyeholes were trimmed with emerald chips and sprays of feathers swept up from her temples to meet above and behind but quite close to the back of her head. These too were black and had once carried a condor above the chasms of the Andes. She sat, very upright, with legs pulled in and crossed at the ankles, in a white wrought-iron chair with a high heart-shaped back that framed her head.

Her jaguar lay alongside her, asleep with its chin on its front paws. Occasionally its very red tongue flickered like flame. *La Loca*, the hot wind that drives people mad, gusted and blue smoke laden with the smell of charred flesh swirled around them.

Several men paid court, but one – short, middle-aged, with a brown weathered monkey face – Pedro recognised. He was wearing the informal uniform of the bullfighter that resembles the costume of a flamenco dancer. He looked fit and nimble but the cummerbund of his *traje andaluz* drew attention to his stomach. He carried a short, silver-mounted cane. Pedro touched him on the shoulder.

'¿Chico?'

'¿Señor? ¡Señor Pedro! ¿Qué tal?'

He took Pedro's hand in a firm, brief handshake, holding him very close.

'I'm fine, Chico. You look fit. We're all looking forward to this evening. Don Octavio says the bulls are good.'

The matador shrugged. 'Of course. He paid for them. But it's always the same. There are some fine animals on the ranches here, but these people must show off. Because it is the last corrida of Carnival we have to have Miuras brought from Sevilla. They are never reliable, the voyage has left them dull, at least one is a sure manso.' He shrugged. 'We'll do our best, but I can't speak for the bulls.'

Pedro felt that was enough in the way of courtesy.

'Chico, who is the lady?'

'The lady, señor, is a model. Immaculada Dalfinger.'

Pedro breathed out a swift sort of sigh. 'Of course. I did not recognise her with the mask.'

'Do you know her? Shall I introduce you?'

'No, no. I believe we have met.' This was a lie, but Pedro did not want to make Dalfinger's acquaintance through the offices of a torero, albeit the best of his generation.

Chico shrugged, looked at his watch. 'It's time I went. The preparations, you know?' He stooped, bending his knees in a gentle, unhurried movement, and placed his hand under the jaguar's right ear. Silence and stillness spread out from them as the people around realised what he was doing.

He looked up at the model. 'What do you call him?' he asked.

No one could see her expression, but the hand that held the chain tightened its grip.

'Napoleón.'

With his face barely two feet from the big cat's he appeared to be mesmerising it, holding its now wide topaz eyes with his own in a fixed, still trance. Slowly the warm black cheek nuzzled into his palm, and in spite of the remorseless Salsa beat they all heard the throaty purr. But as Chico straightened, the right paw flashed at his receding hand, and for a second they thought he had been struck. But the matador had been quicker. His right hand swept over his shoulder and flashing down placed the point of his cane right on the tip of the cat's nose. Although the movement was as swift as a snake's strike the touch at the end of it was as light as a fly alighting. Yet the jaguar cringed beneath it, snarled up at the cane, sabrelike feline teeth exposed by drawn-back jowls, ears flattened against the sides of his anvil-shaped skull.

'*Sólo es un gatito.*' He's only a kitten. He took off his straight-brimmed, low-crowned black Andalusian hat and held it briefly in front of his stomach. '*Adiós, señorita, señores.*'

Someone muttered: '*Suerte, señor,*' wishing him luck for the corrida.

The dark lips beneath the mask snarled, not unlike the cat. *¡Idiota!*' Then they softened to a smile and she held out her free hand. 'I am Immaculada.'

Pedro took it and briefly touched it to his mouth. It was icy. Their eyes met. The ones behind the mask were green, though not as vividly so as the emerald chips that framed them. They had fine blonde lashes, unpainted. Pedro released the pale cold hand and straightened above her.

'I am Pedro Mendoza y La Cerda.' His voice sounded hoarse in his own ears, pushed past a sudden constriction in his throat.

*

Up on the terrace behind him a late arrival, fat with a thin moustache, gripped Don Octavio's fist and, standing close, spoke quietly in a high-pitched fluting voice. Don Octavio's face darkened from brick to plum. Both men looked down across the lawns at Pedro and Dalfinger. Octavio spoke brusquely, decisively. Felipe Cortazar, reporting back from his conference with Feijoo, nodded emphatically, accepted orders.

Dalfinger sat up with her back straight against the white heart-shaped chair, and her hands gripped its arms, which were cast like the heads of dragons. She spread her knees. In her crotch the black plastic narrowed to less than half an inch and a curl of blonde hair peeped round it. Pedro felt his blood begin to pound. At her feet Napoleón flapped his long lazy tail. The other men around them apart from Jorge, drifted away and there was nothing but the smoke and the beat of the Salsa music between them.

13

Her name was Filomena. She was a big woman, dressed formally in a silk suit, but showing deep cleavage between dark mottled breasts, dimpled knees. She had luxuriant dark hair, a haze of moustache on her top lip, and she was altogether what Feijoo had been looking for. He found her quickly too – in the cocktail bar of the Cadebia. He bought her a drink and presently the warm dry palm of her hand was resting on top of his. With her other hand she smoothed her silk suit over her ample thighs. Soon she caught in his eyes an expression of dull appeal.

'I should like you to have lunch with me. Here?'

'I like Chinese,' she said.

An alarm bell sounded in his head – it would be foolish to leave the hotel – but he ignored it.

They went to Los Jardines de Confusio, the Gardens of Confucius. On a terrace from which they could see some of the port, but which was protected by fans and screens from its smell, they ate crisp seaweeds, soy-flavoured salads with fresh coriander, baked sea-bass with fresh ginger. Feijoo drank a lot of rice wine – the after-effects of cocaine and the tension of the conference began to fade. Fear, however, remained: there would be a reaction to the price he had offered – not a downright refusal, but a clear signal that it was far too low, insultingly low. He could not help wondering how and when this reaction would come.

Filomena was quiet, reserved, but not out of shyness. She lacked curiosity or she did not wish to appear to pry: perhaps both. At all events, she did not try to make conversation by asking him about his past, his work, his family. They talked quietly about the food, about the restaurant, about the Carnival that would reach its climax as afternoon faded into evening and night. She declared that nothing would tempt her on to the streets after dusk. He said he was to meet Pedro and Don Octavio in the Presidente's box at the corrida, she declared that she did not like bullfighting, and he agreed. Nevertheless that was the arrangement and he would have to stick to it.

On the way to her apartment they stopped at a *confisería*, bought a selection of dark chocolates and a small bottle of Tía María. The sidewalks were hot, dusty, deserted. An old white Falcon with white-wall tyres cruised behind them for a hundred yards or so and Feijoo thought it was following them, but it turned up a wide street when Filomena stopped to fiddle a bunch of keys out of her handbag.

Her apartment was small, untidy, dirty, The living-room, into which he did no more than glance, was a mess of bookshelves, papers, posters and unwatered plants. She took him straight to the larger of the two bedrooms. The lightweight duvet had not been straightened, the pillows, several of them, were rumpled and askew. The drawers in the chests were open, clothes spilled out. There were pictures on the walls, a Sacred Heart, and Chinese brush and ink: flowers, prancing ponies.

She put a plain silk wrap across the end of the bed. 'You should rest, you know. Undress, put this on, lie down. All right?'

He did as he was told. She brought in the liqueur and tiny glasses shaped like eggcups each with a red ring below the rim. She filled them carefully to the ring with the brown sweet drink and undid the elaborate wrapping on the chocolates. 'They're delicious. Quite the best.' They were very dark and some were crowned with crystallised violets, real flowers. She sensed his wariness, his unasked questions. 'My son lives with me. He's at medical school, and since they are occupying part of it and planning to have a demonstration later today there's no chance he'll come in. His father and I separated . . . ten years ago. Medical school is very expensive. I'm going to have a shower now.'

She peeled off the dark blue polka-dot suit and threw it over the end of the bed. Under it she was wearing a brownish yellow slip which almost exactly matched her skin, and stockings supported by a small girdle. She put her foot on the bed to unroll the first over her knee and he could see that she wore no pants. The discovery caused a throb of excitement in his diaphragm. She wriggled out of the girdle but left on the slip. Her breasts were large but no longer full, dimpled but shapely still.

Feijoo drank another glass of liquid chocolate, ate a candy and savoured the contrasts between sweetness and bitterness, between the softness of praline and the brittleness of crystal. Then he slipped a hundred-dollar bill under the chocolate box but let it show. He lay back and listened to the sounds: traffic, still very little of it in the hottest part of the day, the lazy chirp of a sparrow, the hiss of the shower.

She came to him moist and cool and smelling freshly of orange blossom.

The large soft bed dipped beside him and with arms that were stronger and harder than he had expected she pulled him on top of her. He felt the nails of her hands scratching down the small of his back towards the crack between his buttocks, remembered their immaculate scarlet lacquer, and presently let himself go. It felt like the release of ripe fruit from a large paper bag whose bottom, weakened by leaking juice, has burst at last.

It was well past five o'clock, the time of the corrida, when she woke him, and he was annoyed. He began to pull on his clothes. She was already dressed – in shirt and jeans which he did not think suited her, were not comely. His mouth was filled with stale sweetness, he had a headache, longed for cocaine.

'But you were sleeping so heavily. You needed it. At least have a shower. It will freshen you.'

'No.'

'Coffee then. I can have some coffee ready very quickly.'

'Listen. They are important people. I should have been there for the start, before the start.' Feijoo was bailiff, agent, broker, and a good one. He believed that the people who employed him to look after their interests in the markets of the world were intrinsically and exceptionally important, as important as the huge sums of money they paid him to handle on their behalf.

'There were disturbances. In the streets. I turned on the radio and the police were breaking up a demonstration. Between here and the bullring. So . . .' – she shrugged again – 'I let you sleep.'

He knotted his dull but expensive tie.

'How will you get there?' she asked. 'I can run you there.'

'Is it far?'

'Five minutes if I take you. Fifteen if you walk. It would be no trouble for me. I have a Fiat Uno.'

She drove skilfully through streets that were busy again. A fiesta *paseo* had started: crowds, often in families and dressed in their best clothes, ambled along the sidewalks and often into the street itself, music everywhere, Salsa – spicy, beaty Afro-Latin, Caribbean. Cars sped by, horns blared, people in weird, fantastic and occasionally beautiful costumes hurried to rendezvous for the processions. They crossed a major intersection, a square where riot police still stood in groups round water cannon. Broken placards and banners littered the gutters. When they stopped at traffic lights a small boy kicked a used CS gas canister so it clattered against the side of the car and Filomena tossed her head and swore.

The bullring came in sight at the end of a small avenue of palms. Its battlements were decked with flags and the large open space around it was filled with parked cars and coaches. She slowed to a standstill at a lowered pole barrier, began to explain to the guard that she did not want to park, just to take her passenger to the main entrance, he was an important person, a guest of the Presidente. But Feijoo said he preferred to walk, let himself out.

She called after him: 'Ciao,' and he ignored her, hurried

across the carpark. She pressed the horn derisively, slammed the gear into reverse and backed sharply – into the Falcon that had come up behind her.

Feijoo heard the clang, half turned, and saw two men launching themselves after him. Buttoning his jacket he broke into a run. Although the worst of the heat was over, the temperature was still in the low nineties and it was very humid. Within yards he was almost blinded by his own sweat, but he had a good start and knew where he was going: the President's box would be on the first floor and its door would be above the porticoed main entrance. Above the clatter of his feet and the roar of his breath and the blood in his ears he could hear a storm of booing and shouting, rising and falling, and rising again to a terrible climax, then gunfire.

Inside, the noise from the spectators' terraces rolled up the short corridors, echoed and crashed around the galleries beneath. A squad of paramilitary guards jogged by, their boots a new rhythm in the general pandemonium. Feijoo leapt out of their way, put them between him and the two men behind. He stormed up on to the first-floor gallery. The President's loggia was clear enough. Two suited men, large and clearly armed, stood outside, and crossed flags had been placed above it.

Feijoo felt sure he had made it, was safe. He fell against the high, wooden, carved door, reached for the handles, cursed the guards who would not open it for him. At least though, he thought, nothing will happen to me in front of them, and he turned to them, gasping for breath, struggling for the explanations that would get him past the door, or anyway a message to the people on the other side. But instead they grabbed his arms, pinned and held him, back to the door, to face his pursuers, who now broke out on to the landing five yards away.

They paused, like him struggling for breath, then the larger of the two, a completely bald man in a dark suit, straightened his jacket, and wound a short length of brass chain round the knuckles of his right hand. He glanced at the men who were holding Feijoo and they pulled slightly apart, exposing his face and torso. As he twisted hopelessly and ineffectually away from the first blow one thought carried with it a crumb of comfort: it was not to be a killing – there would be knives if they meant to kill him.

The demonstration had delayed the arrival of the President's party, and so the start of the corrida. Driving down from the hills into the steamy town the small convoy – paramilitary outriders on motorbikes, two Cadillacs and six more cars belonging to Don Octavio's most important guests – had been held up at the point where their route crossed the stagnant canal that snakes beneath a skin of green slime through downtown Barranquilla.

A couple of hundred students streamed across the bridge towards the cars. The sloping hulls of Cadillac Gage Commando vehicles, three of them in line abreast, trundled in pursuit. The Arias outriders, protected by the thick windscreens of their bikes, metal leg-guards and visored helmets, stood their ground in front of the lead car in which Don Octavio and Doña Serena sat with two bodyguards. The students hesitated, thinking they had been trapped between two separate forces. Firearms cracked, and RAGs, ring airfoil grenades that spew out CS powder when they hit their targets, smacked into the crowd. A thick jet of white water from a Mercedes water cannon followed the RAGs aimed to fix the CS powder and activate it on the skins and faces of the demonstrators.

They broke, and from the second car Jana saw their anguished faces, the pain and panic, the streaming clothes. A girl, not much younger than her, T-shirt clinging to her braless breasts, turned to scream at the advancing police. Head thrown back, throat exposed, long dark hair streamed down her back. Then one of the hollow cylinders, spinning at eighty revs a second, caught her full in the face, and blood transformed it as instantly as if it had been hit with a custard pie laden with scarlet filling. Jorge leaned across Jana to get a better view, gave a crow of delight, squeezed her thigh. She pushed him off.

Pedro twisted to look behind. Immaculada Dalfinger sat high and upright next to the goggled chauffeur of her Hispano Suiza. In the hot hazy sunlight the emerald chips round the eyeholes of her mask glittered like fairy dust. Napoleón suddenly appeared out of the rear seat where he had been lying.

He leapt up on to the back of it, using the full length of his chain, snarled and spat at the students as they fled past.

The bikes of the outriders roared, spewed exhaust, slid forward again, but slowly, a touch unsteadily, and the convoy moved on to the bridge. Twenty riot police, with heavy shields and long batons, trotted past in open order, pausing to beat those who had been cut down by the scything missiles or overcome by water and gas. Two of them heaved up the girl who had been hit in the face and bundled her through the lines, moving past the cars again, so Jana could see how the blood had mixed blackly with the water in her hair and how thick red welts were already forming from the blows she had taken across her bare shoulders. Above her a boy suddenly leapt on to the parapet of the bridge and, comically, took hold of his nose, jumped feet first and body straight into the fetid water below.

'Why were they demonstrating?' Pedro asked.

Jorge shrugged. 'Who knows? Freedom to do this, the right to do that. Fundamentally for money.' He smiled, flashed large even teeth. 'That's what it always come down to, eh? Money. If the things they want did not cost we would let them have them, it's as simple as that.'

The bullring was packed for the last corrida of Carnival and the crowd was raucously impatient. Bullfights are expected to start on time even in countries where nothing ever does. Firecrackers were let off, a blue haze of smoke drifted over the orange sand. The cheaper seats in the sun resounded to a slow handclap which steadily speeded up into a roar, subsided and started again. Big bass drums thudded in heavy rhythms. Much beer had been sold during the wait and cans clattered down the aisles. A roar, part derision, part relief, swelled up when Don Octavio and Doña Serena (dressed now in Andalusian *maja* gear – black lace, mantilla cascading from an enormous comb) appeared in the box. But Don Octavio refused to be hurried. He saw to it that his guests were properly comfortable in upholstered gilt chairs, that the others in the party had arrived in the neighbouring loggias. At last he took his seat in the middle, spread his knees, placed his large hands on them. His right hand lifted a white handkerchief no more than an inch – enough to bring things to order, set things in motion. A huge Coca-Cola bottle that had been set in the middle of the spirally raked sand for over an hour suddenly rose up, revealed feet, and trotted off, swaying ridiculously. A trumpet brayed, high and clear, and the three espadas with their cuadrillas formed behind them entered the ring.

Chico, as senior matador, took the first bull. It was large, with fat heavy shoulders, but came through the toril with genuine *alegría*. One of his peónes held a magenta cape aloft and let loose the high mocking call 'To-o-o-rrr-o-o, to-o-o-rrr-o-o.' The bull wheeled, charged, hooked at the flapping cape, and then came round far more quickly than the peón had expected, scything after the flashing thigh as it disappeared into the gap, embedded itself into the wood. The bull struggled, heaved, twisted, and the horn snapped at the root.

The crowd began to clap again, to hoot, whistle, scream. They wanted a new bull – not something a presidente grants easily, and certainly not until he is convinced that the animal is too damaged to fight. Chico came away from the barrier, tried to attract the demented animal with more calls, more flapping of the cape, and it came at him bravely, but tossed its head in the air and bellowed as it came out of the cape, refused to turn. Firecrackers went off and beer cans cut parabolas through the air. The storm of protest rose even further as Octavio signalled that the lidia should continue, that the picadors should come on, and the rolling slow handclap began to reverberate again across the terraces.

The first into the ring was a tall thin man, with unshaven stubble, a bald patch, dressed in carnival costume like a clown. He ran in front of the picador's horse, waved his arms. More men and even some young women followed him, spilled into the ring. The bull twisted away from Chico's cape and, scything with his one good horn, caught a youth in the midriff, transfixing him, tried to heave him up but found the weight too much, stumbled to his knees with the man still impaled. A squad of police trotted into the ring, loosed their carbines into the air.

Jorge shook Jana's shoulder, screamed with frenzied glee, '*Loca, loca, Barranquilla en carnival es una cuidad loca*,' Barranquilla is a crazy city. Behind them the door on to the gallery outside flapped open and, unnoticed, Feijoo lurched through it. Blood streamed from his face. He staggered towards Pedro's back, hand outstretched, and slumped to the floor. Only Jana noticed him.

Pedro, standing erect, face pale, fists clenched, looked out over the seething terraces, storm-tossed with rage and fear, let the pulsing roar beat about his ears, saw the smoke rise into the darkening sky, the flash of guns and crackers below. There was electricity in the dusty, smoke-filled air, sharp in the nostrils and on the tongue like the taste of charged copper. He glanced along the curving sweep of loggias, and saw across the vertiginous maelstrom of the riot the tall figure of Dalfinger. Her long white arm, partially covered in clinging black, came up and moving from behind peeled off the feather, gem-studded mask. She shook out white hair, cut straight across the nape of her neck, breathed slowly in, head high, nostrils flared beneath her kestrel nose, inhaled the incense offered by the madness below.

Down in the ring the bull collapsed at last beneath the weight of twenty people. Chico cut its throat, spilled black blood as if from a bucket on to the churned-up sand. Jana Pensión cradled Feijoo's battered head in the crook of her arm, screamed for attention, but no one heard her.

14

A full moon, circled twice with a double nimbus, tugged the monstrous spread of flat water up the shingle, like a child dragging on a carpet. After each heave the sea slipped back with a rustling sigh, and phosphorus flashed like sheet lightning along the crest of each long ruck. Twenty yards from the beach a whitewashed adobe cabin, thatched with palm and cane leaves, marked the end of a long ribbon of concrete road. In front of it two cars, the Hispano Suiza and a modern Cadillac, lay askew, slewed against the sun-bleached, sea-smoothed limbs of fallen trees which glowed in the moonlight like the skeletons of dinosaurs. A rusty Coca-Cola sign, pock-marked with bullet holes, announced El Bar de los Ruiseñores – the Bar of the Nightingales.

It had a veranda with a board floor and two old metal

collapsible round tables and slatted chairs. A single bare light bulb rocked in the breeze. It heralded a dawn crouched beneath the horizon like a striped cat waiting to spring. There was a doorway but no door, spaces for windows but no windows.

Massive Jorge Aguirre sat on one of the chairs, tilted so the back of his head rested against the door jamb. His knees were spread and his huge hands hung between them. Although he was asleep a rictus etched lines as broad as zebra-stripes on either side of his big black moustache. Above his head, above the lintel of the door, the horns of a giant bull, black-tipped and curved like Apollo's lyre, had been fixed to frame the entrance.

A girl appeared in the doorway. She was dressed for Carnival in fetishist gear – a cut-away black brassière that forced her full breasts together, thin black suspender belt, lace knickers and black fishnet stockings, one of which was drifting down her long white thigh. She held, wrapped round herself, a torero's capea, magenta silk, with a cadmium-yellow lining. She sighed, made a clumsy attempt to sit on Jorge's knees, curled up with her arms round his neck. He grunted, the chair fell forward and tipped her on to the boards. She grabbed at the limp, stained table-cloth as she went and a small coffee-cup clattered after her. She yawned, curled up inside the cape, went to sleep at his feet.

Pedro sat inside but draped across one of the window-sills. His eyes were open but empty, mesmerised by the moonlight on the water which shifted like slowly seething gold snakes. His mocha suit was stained, and his tie had gone.

Behind him Immàculada Dalfinger sat on the bar in the lotus position, her head pushed back so the straight white hair fell almost to the vertebrae between her shoulder blades. She was still dressed in her black plastic but it was more slashed than before. One small flat breast was fully exposed and a gash, shaped like a hook, almost circled the nipple, gaped a little and oozed a little blood. Her jaguar lay at her feet in a litter of paper serviettes, mussel shells, chicken bones and cigarette ends. Diminished by death, his lazy litheness had dissipated, his gorgeous fur with its submarine mariposa markings was sad. He had been shot below one ear, in the cheek Chico had fondled nearly eighteen hours before.

Chico himself sat on a stool at the bar, talked quietly with the half-black, half-Indian bartender, drank rum. The snub-nosed black pistol that he had used on Napoleón still lay at his elbow.

Slowly, delicately, Immaculada shrugged herself out of her pose, stretched out a long pale arm, and, without hunger, began to murder a small bunch of purple grapes.

The moonlight faded. The sky turned to nacre, the gold-laced black of the heaving sea to the colour of the grapes, and a glaucous haze began to form, like the yeasty bloom upon the fruit. A cock crowed, swaggered out from the canes behind the cabin. With a flap of his stunted wings he lurched up to the veranda. The dawn pounced and the cock shook new sunlight from his jewelled plumes. A russet harem scratched and scavenged in his wake.

A big open Chevvy trundled round the shallow bay, rocked over the potholes in the concrete, sighed to a standstill behind the Cadillac. Alone behind the wheel Jana Pensión took off shades, pushed back her streaked-straw hair. She was weary, but alert and wary too. She checked the small purse-shaped shoulder-bag on the seat beside her, checked that the flap was undone, that the pistol she sometimes carried was ready to fire, then swung her long legs out. She was dressed in a short denim skirt, with a plain blue T-shirt, espadrilles. She stood for a moment on the veranda, tapped her tiny teeth with her sunglasses and looked down at Jorge, at the girl in the cape, at Pedro. Then she walked between the horns and took in the scene beyond. She went back to Jorge and suddenly, with venom, kicked him on the shin. Again the front legs of his chair crashed to the boards.

'*¡Coño!* You did not have to do that.'

He blinked up at her, rubbed his leg.

She jerked her head at Pedro. 'What's the matter with him?'

Jorge shrugged, leant back, his jacket fell open over the Astra Magnum. He grinned now, screwing his eyes against the horizontal sunlight.

'Tired? I guess the señorito's tired.'

'Like fuck.'

She returned to the bar, stood in front of Immaculada, her

feet apart, her hand resting on the flap of her purse. Again she jerked her head towards Pedro.

'What's got into him? What's he had?'

No one spoke. A big fly buzzed, making the most of the early coolness. The half-caste barman, as inscrutable as a Chinaman, polished a glass. Chico shook out a cigarette, offered it to him. They seemed to be in league. Jana thought: none of them speaks English. Wilfully, to mock, they would refuse to understand her Spanish. With one finger she tracked the curving gash on Immaculada's breast. She said: 'I'm sorry about your cat,' and turned back to the veranda. Immaculada spat out a grape pip, simply to be rid of it, not as a gesture.

Jana brushed past Jorge. As she passed she said: 'Put him in the back of the Chevvy.' She got back into the driving seat and waited, carefully concealing the fear she felt that she might not be obeyed. Jorge hesitated, then went in. He reappeared a moment later, carrying Pedro in his arms. He placed him in the back seat gently, almost with reverence, much as Joseph of Arimathaea might have laid Jesus in the tomb. Pedro's eyes remained open but expressionless. At the junction boxes of his brain images were scrambled into rich fantasies and the life he lived there remained locked in.

Jana said again: 'What has he had? Come on. I have to detox him.'

Jorge shrugged, smiled sheepishly. 'A few rums. *Perica.*'

'Yes?'

'A little peyote. Not much. Listen. I should stay with him. Don Octavio said I should stay with him.'

'Okay. You follow in the Caddy if you want. But don't mess with me. Don't try anything on.' She pressed the starter, swung the big car round in a neat three-pointer.

The white concrete ribbon widened into a dual carriageway divided by desiccated oleander-like bushes and then palms. Small white villas stood in plots which even in that tropical climate had not had time to become gardens. Crystal clear at this early hour and not many miles away the snows on the Sierra Nevada de Santa Marta floated nineteen thousand feet above banks of gold-edged mist and then were shut out by blocks of apartments, hotels, shops. Hoses played already over beds filled with strelizia, the bird of paradise flower, and giant poinsettias with scarlet heads as big as small umbrellas.

Jana cruised with her eye half on the Cadillac behind, half on the wide sidewalk at her elbow. The road became a boulevard, a promenade with cafés and clustered complexes of boutiques, *supermercados*, kiosks and at last she saw what she was looking for: a bank of three shiny new perspex and stainless steel telephone blisters. Fifty metres on there was a space big enough for two large cars and she pulled in. Jorge slotted the Cadillac behind her. She switched the engine off, became conscious of the monotonous boom of a nearby churchbell calling the faithful to Mass on the first day of Lent.

She looked at her watch. Seven-sixteen. In Madrid? She wasn't sure. Twelve-sixteen? Probably. Anyway not yet 1.30. She checked her purse, found the one-hundred-peso pieces she would need.

Five thousand miles away Antonio Pérez Mendizábal, Marqués de Boltana, high up in his suite in the Banco de Corpus Cristi building, watched tiny flakes of dry snow gust like bubbles of polystyrene foam across the grey spaces above the Cervantes monument. A buzzer sounded and he watched the brisk progress of his eager young personal secretary over the enormous Aubusson carpet, past the Goya portrait. He took a slip of paper from him, glanced at it.

'All right. Make the connection from here. On the grey phone.'

The secretary dabbed out the long sequence of digits and waited.

'Jana Pensión? The Marqués will speak to you now.' He passed the handset to his thickset, silver-haired boss.

'Leave us.'

Dutifully, and brisk as ever, the secretary made the long trek back across the carpet, and the Marqués watched him all the way, not speaking until the huge mahogany door had clicked behind him.

'*Aquí Boltana. ¿Qué quiere?*'

'Marqués. May we speak English?'

'As you wish.'

'Right. Listen. I think right now I should give you an update situationwise as it pertains here as of now.'

'Señorita, I thought we were going to speak English.'

Go fuck yourself, thought Jana, and her lips pulled back in a tiny snarl. She took off her shades, wiped her forehead on the back of her brown hand.

'Anyway, where's Teseo? Señor Feijoo. Why can't he report to me?'

She breathed in, took a grip on herself. It was twenty-four hours since she had slept.

'Feijoo has been hospitalised in a private clinic. I reckon he's okay. The doctor said so. But he's not about to get to a place where he can contact you privately.'

'And Don Pedro?'

'Pedro is in poor shape too. They dosed him up with coke and mesc, and right now he's on cloud nine. No saying when he'll drop in on us again, or what sort of shape he'll be in when he does.'

'All right, Miss Pensión, I think you'd better tell me the whole story, as briefly as you can, but don't leave out anything important.'

'Yessir. Yesterday morning, Feijoo went into town, made his pitch . . .'

Far away in Madrid, Boltana suddenly frowned, began to tap the fine inlay representing Raphael's *Triumph of Galatea* on the top of his desk.

'Just one moment. How much do you know of what he was meant to be doing?'

'I know. Not the details. Just the outline scenario.'

'Yes?'

'Sure. Pedro gets lonely, likes to talk to me. Okay? So I know we're here to take a load of snow off the hands of the Colombian drug barons headed by ex-father-in-law Don Octavio, and that Feijoo is handling the business angle. Right?'

'Go on, Miss Pensión.'

Was it just the distance, some quirk in the pulses bounding off the satellite, or had his voice gone cold, like that of an articulate robot? Shit. Who cares? She was too tired to care, and suddenly wanted desperately to pee, consequence of dropping Filon tablets.

'I'll try.' Briefly, panting slightly, she described what had happened to Feijoo. She concluded: 'Before I left him in the clinic he said I was to tell Pedro to tell you that they were angry at the offer he'd made and this might be their way of saying so. And to try to get you before half one Madrid time. But I have to add this. Don Octavio said Feijoo should never have gone out in the streets alone – probably he was just mugged, or a rival clan did it, people who don't want the Arias group to make this deal. Probably a family called Welser. Okay? Does that make sense?'

'Go on.'

'Just a minute.'

Sweat was pouring off her now, she had begun to shake, her bladder felt like a ball of fire. She looked round. The telephones were between a palm and a patch of tall shrubs with large red trumpet-shaped flowers. She stooped one way then the other, pulled off her pants, hitched her short skirt up an inch or two, sank into a half-crouch, legs apart, and let go. It seemed to go on for hours and sounded like Niagara. Luckily most of it sluiced on to the dry earth beneath the shrub and sank away almost instantly. When it was finished, she felt a whole lot better, indeed lightheaded the way you feel when you've gotten away with something really cool, that you had no right to take so easy. But her rope soles were wet, and she shucked them off.

'Marqués, you still there?'

'Yes, but what – ?'

'Never mind. Where was I? Pedro. Well, like I said, he's in no shape to call you the way Feijoo said, so I thought I'd better. That's it. Did I do okay?'

There was quite a long pause, meters clicked in both their ears, then his voice came again, somehow nearer and warmer than before.

'Yes. Yes, you did. You've really done quite well.'

Bastard, she thought, I didn't ask you to patronise.

'Listen. Here is what I want you to do now. It's not going to be easy, but I think you're up to it. Listen carefully . . .'

They looked as if they were in mourning. Dressed in black or near-black they stood and sat at a semicircular banquette in the middle of the departure area Terminal Two of the airport. Four or five articles of hand luggage were stacked about them, the rest had already been checked in. Pedro never went to the departure lounge until he had to, remained in the outer larger spaces until the 'boarding now' sign flashed up. Jana removed her shades, tapped her teeth with them, looked up and down the wide hall, glanced back to the displays. Avianca 168 for Miami flashed off and on. They were into the last five minutes. She glanced at Feijoo, and his bruised lips stretched thinly into a grimace.

Pedro was not bothered. Pneumatic drills were taking up the freeways of his mind and he tried to defeat them with an uninterrupted and largely unnoticed monologue.

'I think,' he was saying, 'for the time being we have had enough of the New World. We will go back to Monte Cielo and take stock, refresh ourselves. We have been on this side of the Atlantic for too long.' He looked at his watch, shook his head with fleeting embarrassment, looked up at Jana. 'Nine months is it?'

'Almost a year,' she said. 'You just got back stateside when you took me on.'

'Odd to think you have never been to Monte Cielo.' His voice took on a musing tone, irritatingly didactic. 'It is the most perfect home in Europe. Being there elevates the mind, purges the soul, puts one back in touch with the unchanging verities. It is not surprising it can do this. It has been there for a millennium, and some of the most cultivated minds of two great civilisations have devoted their gifts to it. These things matter.'

His lean pale fingers dipped into his jacket pocket for his cigarette case, then he remembered that Jana had emptied it. He threw her a look of pure but infantile spite. 'The New World, of course . . . has its excitements. Energy. Heat. But there is too much turmoil. Too much . . . corruption. It is still the melting-pot, and the dross is still there, often really rather too near the top. I did not expect you to enjoy this trip but I went along with it because you' – he indicated Feijoo – 'and Tío Antonio felt I would be useful. It has all been a waste of time. And it could have turned out worse. You know, at times I felt there was real danger. I am not, as you know, a coward, but these people are basically, for all some of them are very well bred indeed, simply ruffians. Teseo. I seem to have no cigarettes. Will you please either give me one of yours or go and find some for me.'

Carefully he kept his eyes well away from Jana as he cupped his hand round Feijoo's lighter, sucked in smoke.

'It won't help,' she said. Avianca 168 for Miami, now boarding. She checked her purse, her Harold Robbins.

He coughed and the purple shadows round his eyes darkened.

'How can you be so sure? I don't know how you can be so sure of that.' He pulled back from Feijoo, then his back straightened, and in almost one movement he stood, stubbed out the freshly lit Chesterfield, took off his shades. A small group of people was surging down the long hall. Travellers and porters got out of their way to watch as they went by.

At the front was Immaculada Dalfinger. She was dressed, partly, in white, a full tunic with a neckline cut almost to her waist, and a fluted miniskirt. Her sandals were white too, thonged to just below her knee. But her skin, which, three days ago, had been corpse white, was now a rich reddish gold. Her long thighs rippled majestically, her head was thrown back and her white straight hair swung behind her. She looked fit, athletic, like the Goddess Diana loping through coverts in pursuit of Actaeon, and behind her came her dogs: fat Felipe Cortazar, wheezing flutily in the struggle to keep up with her; Desiderio Rapal, dressed this time in a linen jacket and wearing a wide-brimmed black fedora.

'*Querido, mi querido*, what are you doing? How can you think of leaving us?' Immaculada placed her long arms on either side of Pedro's neck, and looked long, longingly into his eyes. Her head came forward and their lips touched. He felt her tongue, the tip small and urgent and with a taste on it, both fragrant and bitter. Recollections of paradisial visions, of panic and despair, of passions whose imagined consummations had been like the coupling of titans, came flooding back.

Behind them fat Felipe caught Feijoo in an embrace that was almost as close. 'Let us,' he murmured, 'say . . . eighteen dollars a gram.'

Feijoo broke backwards, took off his shades. His eyes glinted coldly through puffed yellow lids. 'Fourteen,' he said.

Felipe was genial: 'About sixteen we can talk.'

Immaculada released Pedro, spread her arms to enfold everyone. 'We are,' she cried, 'invited. Don Desiderio has a *finca* on the Guajiro. And his own plane is waiting to take us there.'

Rapal doffed his fedora. 'You will be my most honoured guests.'

'You see,' said Felipe, 'it may take a few days to sort out all the details.'

'Probably,' said Jana, as Avianca 168 disappeared from the display, 'our luggage is on its way to Miami.'

'No problem.' Jorge Aguirre, his presence a new warmth in the air behind her. 'It is all stowed in Desi's plane already. No problem.' With him was the dark girl who had worn a torero's cape through Carnival, who had been with him at the Bar of the Nightingales. Jana wondered who she was, where she fitted in.

Part Three

The Web

15

Stately, plump Buck Mulligan came from the stairhead ... this, the opening phrase of Joyce's *Ulysses*, had come to Dayton's predecessor at Centac the first time he had set eyes on Mulligan five years earlier in Washington. A man of some culture, he was also a perfectionist. When compromise had become the name of the game in Washington he left, and took the very particular *esprit de corps* he had built with him. Inevitably the people who were closest to him followed suit.

Plump, Mulligan was not, stately he could be, and he had not objected to the nickname, which had travelled with him to Paris. Stately he was, as he stopped at his front door and checked his locks before swinging away, down the steps, through a tiny vestibule and out on to Rue Lamarck. He wore a dark grey pin-striped suit, his head was bare, his short-cropped grey hair smooth like a pelt over his round head. His fresh, healthy face shone from a close shave done with a cut-throat razor.

Coming out into the steep monochrome street he turned left and climbed the last few yards of the hill that dominates the city north of the river. He made the half-circle round the cluster of pillars, arches and domes piled like children's bricks to make a shrine for the Sacred Heart, traversed the belvedere that exposes almost the whole of Paris. For a moment he savoured it, enjoying the huge expanse of greys and whites, tinged with the same French blues that glow in Impressionist urban painting. It came, he thought, from the ultramarine quality of the slate roofs, filtered through the smoke of a million Gauloises.

Banks of low cloud rolled in from the west, on a stiff but warm June breeze that swept through the pollarded acacias, filling the air with a snowstorm of fluff. Squalls rinsed the huge new blocks of flats on the skyline towards Orly, while in the other direction the wind shafted golden sunbeams across the wooded hills towards Versailles.

Spirits lifted – it really was great to be working in Paris – Mulligan skipped on down to the funicular. The ratchets clanked and rumbled as the roofs and canyons rose to meet him, the terraced gardens disappeared behind. He crossed Place St-Pierre, head and shoulders above the housewives and seamstresses, dropped through the bazaar-like chain of haberdashery and fabric shops. He crossed Boul' Rochechouart with its centre section of plane trees and gravel where the old men and the young *en chômage* would play boules later in the day, where on that day in June the green cast-iron pagodas carried posters advertising a Rod Stewart concert at the Palais Omnisport, and a rally of the National Front at a local cinema against further immigration of Moroccans. At last his grey round head dipped through the art nouveau arch of the Anvers Métro.

He surfaced at St-Lazare to find the rain had blown in hot dark splashes that laid the summer dust and he came as near to scurrying as a big and sometimes stately man can. He crossed the forecourt, offered a curse at the absurd modern sculpture of piled suitcases cast in bronze that insults the Second Empire elegance of the station's façade, bought a ticket at one of the large metal-box machines on the concourse. He had timed it all to slip on to a seat in the suburban shuttle just as the warning bleep sounded and the doors slid shut.

The man on the orange bench opposite was reading the middle pages of *France-Soir*: Mulligan stole his headlines – *EXPULSION EN MASSE DES CLANDESTINS*. Twenty-four policemen had put a hundred blacks from Mali on a specially chartered DC8; they were handcuffed to the aeroplane seats, and some had been beaten . . . Chirac's new law had been invoked. If you don't have the right papers you're out, straight out, no appeal allowed, especially if your skin is black. The National Front had approved that one, but to tell the truth most right-thinking Frenchmen had too. Weather: *Sortez aux parapluies* – well, they'd got that one right.

The train rattled across the oxbowing Seine, began the long sweep south. Between the huge glass palaces of La Défense, pyramids and ziggurats, part of it recently blown up by an Arab bomb, he caught glimpses of the Eiffel Tower and the

Bois de Boulogne. Sometimes Mulligan felt that his new life swung round that monstrous metal phallus as if it had some sort of pull, kept him in orbit. From the top of Montmartre he could see it, on this train journey it was almost always there, and of course from the office they had given him in Rue Armengaud there it was again, in spite of what Dayton had said, sticking up like the prick of some metal monster lying on his back behind the distant beeches and chestnuts.

At St-Cloud he ignored the short escalator, took the steps two at a time, turned sharp right into Rue Armengaud, a narrow leafy street running parallel to the railway and sixty feet above it. Trees sheltered mouldering shuttered houses set in gardens that sloped too steeply to make any effort worth while. Halfway along it, hoops of steel set in the tarmac blocked off the building where he worked.

A drab grey shoebox set on its side, it is about sixty yards long, set back off the road and below it, but on concrete stilts so there are spaces beneath it and the ground floor is level with the street. It is fortified, no other word for it. The stilts, the slope of the hill give it a deep dry moat. There is a high wall of square steel railings in front of it, and in front of them the hoops set in the road. The railings are pierced by a gate at the far end made out of the same steel, and the slipway drops steeply down from it to the trees and parking places below.

And it has a garrison. Permanently outside that gate a CRS van squats, and six guards armed with automatic rifles, truncheons, pistols and CS gas and equipped with radios loiter around it. Above the gate and along the front CCTV cameras, white and hooded, record every passer-by. It's plain enough what the building is for. The flag, a white globe on a blue background, of L'Organisation Internationale de la Police Criminelle – Interpol – droops from a flagpole just inside the railings and six tall aerials soar above the roof, as tall again as the four storeys.

A CRS guard in forage cap with gold beading, badged with a grenade, black anorak above dark blue trousers and boots, scrutinised Mulligan's pass, pushed open the heavy gate. It annoyed them that almost alone out of all the men who worked there, the tall American came on foot: but Mulligan had his reasons. Cars are traps. They can be identified, their numbers taken, descriptions noted and normally you only have one. A car you use can be followed, ambushed, bugged and bombed.

A corridor on the third floor led to a double door blocking off a section from the rest of the building. EURAC. European Action Against Drugs. *Entrée non autorisée interdite.*On the other side Anton Suk was already waiting for him. Suk was tall, intense, originally Czech, now naturalised French, newly appointed to be in charge of Research and Resources. Mulligan judged him to be one of the cleverest men he had ever met. To his department the larger, umbrella organisation passed everything that came into the building relating to drugs. His team then sifted, collated, stored it in a Pathfinder database, ran constant scans through it searching for patterns, repetitions, the telltale clues that point to the presence of networks, syndicates.

When Suk felt confident that a structure was emerging, he indicated that a committee should be formed to analyse and evaluate the evidence. If the committee found he had a case, a small task force was formed inside the organisation and given a number, and an operational officer to head it.

The next stage was the one it was hoped would break moulds. Eurac's first function was as an intelligence-gathering and -evaluating unit, but, since it was not answerable to any particular Home Office or Minister of Justice, it was tacitly understood that it would use covert and even illegal means of gaining information which are generally closed to police forces in democratic countries. The two channels of intelligence open to Eurac but closed to most police forces were to be the use of undercover agents (UCAs), and electronic hacking. The first would be Mulligan's chief avenue into the heart of whatever organisation Suk might locate, the second would be Suk's concern, working secretly within the walls of the Eurac floor in Rue Armengaud. The ultimate aim of all this, and its justification in the mind of its supporters, was to take out drug synidicates right through to the very top, to implicate and indict the men and women who ultimately bank the profits of a trade whose turnover puts it in the top ten industries in the West, whose profits expressed in percentages of turnover and return on investment outstrip all others.

Once the evidence was there, sufficient to convince hard-bitten and cynical policemen if not judges and juries, then

Eurac would move into its second role. Requests would be sent out asking national police forces to liaise in using the clandestine evidence as a basis for getting facts that judges and juries would accept, and then to combine in a final co-ordinated operation in which the Eurac officer, the one man with all the threads in his hands, would be accepted as the linchpin.

Suk – tall, lanky, with dangling arms and wrists, with a round Slavonic head, not much of a nose – took Mulligan by the elbow, immediately urged him out across the corridor and into the sealed computer room which was his empire. With banks of VDUs, keyboards, telephones with modems, it could have been the communication and information centre of an up-to-date business anywhere in the world – there was nothing to indicate that it was not, say, the editing area of a modern newspaper, the stock analysis sector of a middle-sized chain of supermarkets, or the nerve-centre of a dealer in financial futures. Nothing, that is, unless you had the entry codes that would send the information it was programmed to deal with scrolling across its screens.

'Buck, how are you, did you sleep well, I'm so glad, because, you know, I have to say I think we're getting there, getting through in such a way that the gentlemen upstairs will have to take a lot of notice.' Suk's accent was exuberantly Middle European, his mannerisms almost always flowing, generous. Almost always – Mulligan had already discovered that Suk was vulnerable to depressions that he blamed on constipation: they came suddenly, left him confused, indecisive for up to a week, but eventually he would breeze into the building and announce that he had 'been', had shifted a stone or more of what he called 'blockage', which he was quite capable of describing in analytic detail in order to reassure everyone that all was now well again and that the fight against crime could be resumed.

Suk's CV revealed that he had actually been born in a Nazi extermination camp, that his mother, not a Jew but a Party member, had survived and ensured his survival, but had committed suicide in 1948.

'I can show you if you like two hundred metres of printout, and because you are a mathematical genius you will instantly perceive the patterns that are there and interpret their significance. Of course.' The irony was heavy. In Suk's book

Mulligan was innumerate. 'But maybe it's better if I show you the pretty little digests these lovely machines have run up for us instead.' His fingers flickered over the nearest keyboard. 'Cocaine busts in Great Britain first quarter of last year in red, first quarter of previous year in green. Expressed in terms of cocaine confiscated, in terms of convictions secured, expressed in terms of actual incidents. Virtually identical. Now the first quarter of this year in blue. Nearly a ton more. Twenty-five more convictions. Right?' Undulating graphs swooped and climbed across the screen. 'Now this. Price paid per ounce, per gram by street dealers over the same periods.' Block charts mounted and fell like a child's building bricks. 'You see? Over the first two periods little change. Over the third period little change, but what shift there has been has been down. The British drug squads are confiscating far more, putting away far more smugglers, mules, dealers, so what would you expect? Here is what the computer suggests: a market responding with an increase in price of 37½ per cent. But what happened? A drop in price of 6.2 per cent. Why? Don't answer.'

'Where did you get all this information?'

'Off the British Police National Computer for the most part. The facts, that is. As far as I know, they haven't yet produced the same analyses.'

'Do they know you've been in their knickers?'

'Oh my God, Buck. What do you think? Of course not. Nearly all of this they sent to Daddy anyway as a matter of routine.' 'Daddy' was Interpol.

'So they're not going to wonder where the hell we got all this from when we send it back to them.'

'Certainly not. I cover my tracks, you know? No one knows where I've been. Let's move on ... Incidence of related medical problems actually reported. Incidence of social problems ranging from break-up of families where a cocaine user is involved to bankruptcies. The same pattern. What do you make of it?'

'I know what I'd like to make of it.' Mulligan's voice was dry, laconic, concealed deliberately the excitement he felt. 'I'd say – '

'Wait. There's more yet. If there's something big happening in one sector of the coke market it will make ripples elsewhere – waves even. Look at this.' Again the intense Czech's fingers flickered. Glenn Gould playing a Bach two-part invention would not have been more exact. 'This represents the flow of Mob money through their Marseilles accounts, the ones we know they launder their coke money through. You see, over the same period a significant drop, fifteen per cent. Now they run, used to run, a very good slice of the UK market, mainly through a man called Ricardo whose front is a fashionable coffee place called Scapino – '

'Yeah. I know about Scapino. Close to the Covent Garden shopping precinct.'

'That's the one. They were believed to have two principal sources of supply. The Arnolfini set-up in Turin, using models as mules. And a Chinese merchant called San whose main house is in Rotterdam. There were others. The National Drug Intelligence Unit in Scotland Yard managed three relatively minor busts in the past, but Ricardo always kept clear. They'd like to get him . . . Anyway. That's by the way. Get back to my original question. What do you make of it?'

Mulligan pulled in a deep breath. 'I'd say – '

'You'd be right.' Suk slapped his shoulders with broad hands and his dark eyes gleamed. 'A quantum shift in cocaine dealing in the UK. My guess is a new outfit is on the scene. A very big one. It's closing down rival networks hence the sudden rise in successful busts acting on information received, or it's absorbing them. And it's pumping a hell of a lot more coke into the UK, so the price holds steady or drops when it ought to rise. Buck, there's something out there, there really is.'

For Mulligan the moment when a seemingly random agglomeration of drug-related data in a particular area takes on a shape that can be explained only by postulating the existence of an organising intelligence had always been a moment of mystery filled with spiky but thrilling angst, a sort of annunciation. He imagined that radio astonomers might feel like this when the evidence begins to pattern itself to suggest a new quasar.

'Buck. Go for it. We have to go for it, you know?'

'Anton, I know. Sure. We'll go for it.' Their eyes met for a moment, excited, grinning – urchins planning a jape.

Anton slapped his shoulder again. 'That's my boy, then. Go for it.'

16

Nightmare receded, satisfaction remained. Harriet was pleased with herself: she had not cracked at Dover; she had not let Roget down – he had lost his coke and a lot of money but he was not in prison for life. She reckoned she'd earned her five thousand, and pushing Jeremy out with it had been a gas. In retrospect, she enjoyed the thrill, the excitement, even the terror.

Handling Price had not been so difficult. She had reserves to draw on conferred by a privileged background and an independent lifestyle: her mother was an Austen, related by birth to the Earls of Oxford and by marriage to the Earls of Riversdale; her father was the senior partner in a firm of solicitors whose main office was in Jewry, Winchester, but who kept a *pied-à-terre* in Lincoln's Inn; she had been a professional, freelance, independent businesswoman for eight years, albeit cushioned by ten thousand a year (1986) paid from a family trust. When the crunch came, especially if it boiled down to a matter of holding out against a man bullying in the name of a despised authority, she coped.

Harriet's psyche was motored by a cheerful hedonism that had very little to do with morality. She believed in loyalty – to friends, family, her caste, 'people like us'. She believed they should stand together against the masses, the ignorant and unwashed, who remained an abstract idea received from her background. When she actually had dealings with the lower classes – the punks on the boat, for instance, or her favoured photographic assistant, a toy-boy called Steve – she generally got on well enough with them, even perceived they had a common enemy: the tedious regulators, the Little Hitlers. She believed with fervour in personal freedom, in the right of people, especially 'people like us', to do what they like. Above all she believed in her right not to be bored, and in a life that had become a sight too flat and 'samey' the Amsterdam trip stood out like a fairy castle on a hill above a dreary plain.

Routine settled back over her like a thick fog. The compensations of independence and self-esteem no longer justified the vain but generally podgy faces squared off in her viewfinder, the endless repetition of boasting and banter, of deep-voiced flirtation with occasional determined passes. She had a brief affair with a barrister, but although he was a renowned bully in the courts, he was wimpishly scared of his wife, and she put a swift end to it.

She was, then, ready for something new when, five months later, the phone rang one Wednesday afternoon, though there was nothing in the conversation to suggest anything other than a routine commission.

'Miss Harriet Jones? The photographer? *THAT* magazine here.' The voice was female, brisk, but with an artificial ingratiating jokiness built in, that sometimes foregrounded as a giggle. 'Upper-case italic, *THAT*, geddit? The way people say it's *that* magazine when the freebie hits the mat. You won't have heard of us yet, so I'll fill you in. Basically we're a freesheet, but with a difference. Glossy and covering a very select area, initially Belgravia, Kensington and Chelsea, but expanding to Hampstead and out into Surrey if it goes well. We plan for each issue to carry an in-depth interview, with picture, of a prominent resident in the profiled area, including a bit about which shops he uses, which restaurants, even which taxi-service. With me?'

'Yes, I'm with you. Nifty way of getting retailers to buy display space.'

'That's it, I mean that is what it's all about, isn't it? Anyway, we aim to kick off with Hector Myklades, the financier. Mr Myklades is aware of your work, and he has agreed.'

'When? Where? I don't do studio work.'

'Tomorrow at half eleven. He is very busy but he has a half-hour spare about then. He'll be at the offices of one of his companies, Ambrose Finance, which is on the first floor of Union House in Moorgate, just before you get into Finsbury Square.'

'On a job like this I use an assistant so it's going to cost you two fifty. With a further hundred for each repeat. I expect to be paid promptly, preferably before you print.'

She rang round: a journalist who worked on the business section of *The Times*, a headhunter who worked out of an office in Baker Street. Neither knew a lot about Myklades; both acknowledged they would like to know more. He was thought to be of Armenian extraction, about fifty. Some time ago he had been rapped over the knuckles by the Department of Trade for running a publicly quoted company as if it were his own private fief. Now he was thought to have a good slice of electronic leisure, computer and video games, that sort of thing. Not really an 'in' sort of person. More than a touch fringy, iffy.

Thus the journalist. The headhunter said much the same, but was more forthcoming about Ambrose Finance.

'I didn't know Myklades was behind that. They've had a facelift, aim to be high-powered in post-Big Bang finance. They've been looking for market-makers, jobbers, commodity dealers. It's a seller's market right now, but Ambrose Finance are going for the best and paying over the odds. Golden hallos and a hundred grand a year with perks. As I read it it's not going to be huge, Ambrose Finance isn't going to be a second Barclays de Zoete Wedd or anything like that, they're looking for four or five guys at the top, no more. Also the best in back-up staff, top secretaries, settling clerks, that sort of thing.'

Boring. Even the 'iffyness' was routine in the City of the eighties.

Nevertheless, on a Thursday morning in early September, she checked her camera bag: one Hasselblad with two magazines of 6 cm x 6 cm daylight balanced Ektachrome 64, and two of tungsten-balanced 50, and two Canon F1 bodies preloaded with the same in 35 mm. The tripod, ball and socket head, lenses 35 mm to 200 mm, a can of Dust-Off, filters, were always there.

Steve arrived. Although pretty, camp, sexually ambivalent, he knew his stuff. He carried her lighting box and her soft camera-bag to the cab for her, perched on the fold-down seat opposite her. He was dressed in a powder-blue sweater which claimed that Cardin had had something to do with it, grey trousers that bunched stylishly at the waist and smart soft leather moccasins. His hair was cut sub-punk but not overtly coloured.

'Who's the lucky guy today then?'

'Hector Myklades. Mean anything to you?'

Steve frowned, looked out at the Imperial War Museum, at the huge gun-barrel mounted on a plinth in front of the colonnaded doors. 'Nasty big gun goes bang, bang. No never heard of him. Should I?'

But Harriet felt the name had caused a tremor, which was interesting. Steve lived on the edge of one of London's nastier underworlds: male prostitution and designer drugs. Once she had come to his rescue, got him to Charing Cross Hospital in a hurry, luding-out on Methaqualone and suffering from anal bleeding. Was the client part of that scene?

They crossed the river – the elegant dome holding its own amongst the walls of glass and stone – passed Monument, Exchange, the Bank and all the other banks. In a way it was her patch: canyons of hard-edged Portland, dark alleys smelling of beer and meat, narrow streets where taxis fight the buses that fight the Mercs, Porsches, BMWs and the not infrequent Rollers. Leathered couriers on noisy bikes bomb through the lot like angry wasps. And on the pavements and in the offices the men in suits, with shiny confident faces, fight each other and the other men in New York, Tokyo and Hong Kong (which they always refer to as 'Honkers') for half a per cent here, a point there, trading paper they don't own with money that is not theirs. Often there were faces she knew – in ten years she had photographed perhaps as many as one in ten of the older ones – faces, pale and hard like Portland stone in rain, faces that light with charm and bonhomie like Portland stone in sunshine if there's a bob to be made or a pretty face that might give. The trick was to get the shifty look out of their eyes, straighten the snarl that compromised the grin. No easy matter – but generally she managed, they liked her for it, and paid.

Into Moorgate and the mix gets less fatty – there are cafés as well as champagne bars, snack counters as well as chophouses, souvenir ashtrays for a quid in the gift shops as well as those touted by Hermés for a ton. Across London Wall the rents drop from thirty-five pounds a square foot to a mere thirty: Ambrose Finance was going for the quieter image, but only just – with Merrill Lynch round the corner they were hardly down-market. An ageing bull with campaign ribbons across the breast of his military-style jacket checked through her bags in the foyer: not a Little Hitler but a large one, the sort that service their employers' self-esteem more effectively than they guard property or lives.

Behind her a lift door purred.

'Miss Jones? Miss Harriet Jones?' He was young, suited, smart, fit, and instantly forgettable. His welcome was as sunny as the free offer on a cereal packet, worth less. He showed her into the lift. Steve, carrying the bags, only just squeezed through in time.

'Mr Myklades is busy just at the moment, but I'm sure he'll be free shortly.' The smile softened into a conspiratorial leer that acknowledged the intimacy of the lift. The sexual harassment was as real as if he had touched her up. He dodged round her as the lift door opened, threaded a plastic card down a black matt slit and stood aside as the heavy panelled door clicked open. 'Welcome to Ambrose. I'll get one of the girls to fetch you a coffee.'

The long, high-ceilinged room, perhaps a hundred feet long and forty wide, had clearly once been a suite of perhaps six rooms with a corridor down the middle: the walls between every second window were scarred where the dividers had been torn out. Immediately inside, there was a reception area that was almost finished – a shell within the shell. With a false ceiling only half the height of the real ceiling and one wall not yet in place it looked like a luxury cave set down in the middle of chaos.

A young woman dressed in a black skirt with a pearly-white silk blouse and chunky gilt costume jewellery put a small tray on the marble-topped table. There was one small cup with a coffee filter on top of it, a tiny jug of cream, a porcelain bowl filled with chips of coloured sugar.

'I'm sure Mr Myklades won't keep you a moment. Just now, though, he is in conference with the man from Data-stream, the man from Stratus Computers, and the architect.' She laughed, an inane little tinkle. 'Poor things can't agree about where to lay their cables.'

Harriet smiled inanely back, sat upright, resisted the seductive embrace of a soft blue leather sofa. Steve dumped the cases beside her, sprawled in the single chair nearby, grinned.

'Lot of dust about,' he said. 'Could be a problem.'

'Yes. But there has to be a private office or boardroom, doesn't there?'

Beyond ferns and rubber plants a lot of the floor was up, exposing a cat's cradle of cables and coloured wires; more hung in swags from the ceiling like jungle creepers. There were stacks of wrapped panels – the housings for video terminals and switchboards; someone was sawing and someone was drilling; a smell of pine sawdust and organic, bone-based glue mounted an assault on the coffee aroma, settled for coexistence. She could not have imagined a worse milieu in which to take portrait photographs.

She looked at her watch. Five minutes of the precious half-hour already gone.

'I'm afraid the snarl-up remains unresolved.' Mr Forgettable was back. He sat beside her and the leather dipped as if a wave had passed. 'We've ordered Reuter, Telerate, SEAQ TOPIC, and NASDAQ as well as in-house research and databases, so you see it really is quite a tangle to fit it all in a properly functional way. Mr Myklades will be here in a moment. Trouble is he likes to keep an eye on absolutely everything.'

'Not too good at delegation?'

'Oh, he delegates. I mean, you won't actually catch him with a paintbrush in his hand. But he'll make sure it's going on smoothly.'

'Just what is Ambrose Finance?'

The winsome grin. 'As of now, a mess? No, really. Ambrose will optimise deregulation, the twenty-four-hour market and the new technology to provide a tailored financial service to a small group of companies. Mr Myklades has an interest in several of them . . .'

She looked past him and down the long, echoing cavern to where a group of men, lit by a stray shaft of sunlight which picked out the motes of dancing dust above their heads, pored over a large sheet of quality tracing paper. She tried to guess which of them was Myklades.

Mr Forgettable burbled on. '. . . serviced by a central technical infrastructure, including voice and data networks, with compatible systems handling information distribution, risk management, accounting control and so on – '

'Good gracious!'

'Left you behind, have I?'

She delivered a severe glance straight from the top drawer. 'Certainly not. No. But I do think I can spy, with my little eye, my cousin Rupert.'

'That would be the Honourable Rupert Bridge?'

'That's right.'

'He's Mr Myklades' personal assistant. I believe he's very well connected.'

'That's right,' said drily. 'But he's a shocking rogue too.' Cousin Rupert, second cousin once removed actually, was tall, with curly black hair that touched his collar. A scar he had not had when she had seen him last added bravura to his good looks. He was three years younger than Harriet and she did not know him well, had met him occasionally at large family gatherings, weddings, funerals.

Behind him the group was dominated by two men: one tall with yellow hair, the other dark, plump, glossy. She presumed the latter was Myklades, but she was wrong, for it was the plump glossy man who now shrugged, rolled up the paper and struggled ineffectually to get it back into its cardboard tube. The rest, headed by the tall man and followed by Cousin Rupert, picked their way towards her through the debris.

'Hi, Harry.'

'Hi, Rupe.'

'Harriet, this is Hector Myklades. Hector, Harriet Jones.'

She had supposed Armenians to be Mediterranean or Semitic. Myklades was neither. He was tall, had wide shoulders and overlong arms: that was the first impression as he came towards her with the light from all the windows fierce behind him. His hair was thick on top, but cut short at the back and sides, a deep cadmium yellow, surely dyed. He was dressed informally – the only man there not in a suit apart from the workmen – but expensively. A dark blazer, cavalry twills, shoes hand-made by Lobb, Turnbull and Asser shirt and tie. Harriet was expert in the field, clothes were a clue to a man's self-image, and understanding a man's self-image led to pictures he was glad to have.

He offered her a hand that was pale, bony, manicured, cold, just the fingers in a brief, shallow grip. There was a ring with a small diamond on the little finger of his right hand.

'Miss Jones. Enchanted.' There was awkwardness here, almost gaucherie. Surprised, she looked up at his pale blue eyes, distanced by tinted Christian Dior glasses. They carried no expression, no glitter, no response. Tall though she was, their gaze shifted on to something apparently beyond and above her. 'I imagine a few snaps will not take long. How much time do I have, Rupert?' His accent was not perfect. There was a guttural sound behind the *h*'s, and the *r* was very slightly rolled.

'Ten minutes, Hector. Perhaps fifteen.'

Harriet felt her colour rise. 'I shall need more than fifteen minutes.'

'How long?'

'An absolute minimum of half an hour.'

His mauve lips set in a thin line. 'The days of long exposures are past. Perhaps you should update your technology.'

He's winding me up. She adopted a nursery tone of voice, the one nannies reserve for precocious little boys who insist on knowing why. 'Mr Myklades, if you go to a studio you will find lights already set up, a camera on a tripod, and a technician to press a button. At a cost of five minutes of your time and maybe twenty guineas you will have a portrait which will make even you look like everyone else who has passed through ahead of you. However, if *I* take your picture *THAT* magazine will get pictures that say something personal, and possibly impressive about you. I need the time to find the right poses, the right backgrounds, and the right light. You need to relate to me in a way that will produce an image of yourself you might want people not lucky enough to share your actual presence to have. Shall we start?'

He looked down at her across the distance he had kept between them, legs slightly splayed, feet turned out, one arm parallel to the line of his square-cut double-breasted blazer, the other elbow supported on it so he could chew briefly at a thumbnail.

'Rupert?'

'Not more than twenty minutes, Hector. Your appointment at the Bank is at twelve.'

One pale eyebrow lifted above the gold rim of the glasses. 'Enough?'

'Not enough.' She was firm. 'And I don't see a suitable background here anyway. Come on, Steve.'

Myklades shrugged. 'See Miss Jones is properly compensated for time wasted. Miss Jones, I am impressed by your professionalism. Rupert will tell you I very rarely have as much as an hour free at one time. It may, however, be possible to come to an arrangement early next week. My secretary will be in touch. Good day.'

Thus he got out ahead of her. She felt that that was important to him: he had to terminate the confrontation, for that is what it had become, on his terms. An arrangement? Stuff that. And why was he coming on as if he had commissioned her? She was there for *THAT*, not for Myklades.

Back at Witham Square she paid off Steve, thirty in notes. He said, as he took them, pushing back the artfully constructed lock of hair that nodded on to his forehead: 'Harry, that Myklades. Watch him. Turn your back and he'll shaft you. Okay?'

At tea-time a courier on a motorbike arrived with a cheque for one hundred and fifty pounds, drawn on an Ambrose Finance account at the Finsbury Square branch of the City and Wessex Bank and signed by Rupert. An hour later her cousin was on the phone.

'You got your cheque? Good. Listen, what do you think of Hector?'

'A cold fish. Quite impressive too. But he needn't think he can bully me.'

'No one bullies you, Harry.'

'That's right. You tried once and I had to spank you.'

'A treasured memory. Harry, listen. Hector too was impressed. With you. And he remains very keen that you should do some pics of him. He wants you to spend Tuesday with him, just following us around, grabbing chances when you can and squeezing in a more structured session towards the end. He'll pay you three hundred.'

'For a whole day, four hundred.'

Rupert laughed. 'Right. That's what he said you'd say. Listen. He wants you to meet us at Southampton, the Vauban Hotel at ten o'clock. He's spending the day at the Boat Show. And one other thing. No toy-boy, no assistant. Just you.'

'No Steve, no lights. I'm not carting my lighting kit about on my own. Rupe, tell me about Myklades.'

Silence at the other end. Then, 'He's a businessman.'

'Oh, right. What do you do for him?'

'Harry. You don't ask questions about Hector or of Hector. Just let him tell you what he wants to tell you and leave it at that. Questions make him nervy, and when he's nervy he's about as safe as an angry scorpion. See you Tuesday.' And he rang off.

Rupert was nervy and dangerous too. She remembered Christmas at Scales, the Bridge family mansion in County Wicklow, eighteen years ago. So long. Rupert had persuaded the younger children to play Roman Slave Markets. Tipped off, Harriet had found her kid sister in an attic, with prepubertal puppy fat, naked and goosefleshed in the cold, tied by the wrists to the end of an ancient four-poster bedstead. Rupert, eating stolen hothouse grapes and dressed in a sheet, was contemplating the possibilities of the situation.

Since then, Sandhurst and the Royal Buff Caps, the amalgamated Rifle Brigade whose antecedents included the regiment the Bridge family had created for Marlborough's campaigns. His army career included a raid behind Argie lines with an SAS troop and he had been decorated: for what he called 'savagery beyond the call of duty'. He resigned his commission: the Falklands had given him what he wanted from the army, and a similar chance would not come again. For a time he traded on the floor of the London Mineral Market before being barred for racial remarks about the 'Jewboys, who,' he claimed, 'have the market sewn up'; he sold arms for Kapp-Duxbury, the makers of the Kapp submachine-gun and the Nutcracker Rocket Launcher; and he had been disqualified for dangerous conduct in the Isle of Wight Powerboat Race. His boat had been called *Snowstorm*, bought, he openly boasted, from the profits of a year spent broking cocaine.

That Myklades should employ him as a personal and confidential assistant said things about Myklades and Ambrose Finance which Harriet estimated not to be all pluses. Nevertheless she went: and not just for the money, but out of curiosity and with a sense that the excitement she craved might lie ahead. For Harriet – anything, once.

137

17

The train was awful: it was noisy, and the movement as they
neared Basingstoke so violent that the coffee slopped from the
nasty little polystyrene mug that the buffet provided, spilled it
on to the knee of her jeans. Glad that she had not worn
anything more vulnerable, Harriet bought a Scotch and ginger
instead, feeling that she needed to be steadied and that not
even BR would be able to mess that up. She was wrong. The
surly steward sold her a miniature of White Horse, and a tiny
can of ginger ale with a ring-pull top. Back in her seat she cut
her finger on the can: a hairline only, but it bled and was sore.

Around her, sharp men with what she called grammar
school accents swapped self-congratulatory stories about boats
they had broked, punters they had swindled, and the horsepower generated by the latest marine engines. They manufactured excuses to pass and repass her, to stretch above her for
coats or beneath her for document cases, and of course always
touched her. 'Sorry, love.' 'Ooops, was that you?'

At Southampton station they told her the Vauban Hotel
was less than five minutes' walk away, but omitted to say that
a steep hill had to be climbed to get there. It was a windy,
blustery day with intermittent sunshine, and she arrived on
the hotel forecourt dishevelled and flushed and only just in
time. Rupert, wearing a grey checked suit and the brown
derby that he usually kept for racing, opened the door of a
large *café au lait* Mercedes 500 SEL before taking her bag
round to the other side and getting in beside the chauffeur.
She found she was sitting next to – or, since there was a good
yard between them, with – Hector Myklades.

He did not offer her his hand, barely nodded.

She attempted cheerfulness as the car slipped out through
the narrow entrance. 'I'm not late, am I? Sorry if I am.' She

looked at her watch, then up at the clock on the grey campanile of the Civic Centre. 'No. Still only two minutes to ten.'

'Not late.' The mauve lips narrowed into something a shark might have recognised as a smile, but the eyes behind the violet-tinted lenses shifted away, found something interesting in the Lawcourts and Central Police Station.

She found she was staring at the pale, mottled hand that rested on the soft yellow hide beside her. The diamond ring had been replaced with a large onyx seal. The design cut in the stone looked intricate, possibly Arabic: Roget (goodness, she had not given the poor man a thought since that one brief and nervy phone call – how was he?) might have been able to say what significance it had. It said something about Myklades that he did not always, as most men do, wear the same ring.

The big car surged and stopped and effortlessly surged again through a couple of roundabouts filled with red roses that tossed and shuddered in the breeze but held on, then dropped on to Western Esplanade. Here, beneath the grey city walls, the traffic congealed.

'This is a bloody nuisance.' Myklades pronounced it 'bloddy'. 'They should have arranged a facility for those whose cars will drop them. We don't need their bloddy carparks.'

'Well,' cried Harriet, still determined to be bright, 'at least it gives me time to establish some ground rules.'

'Ground rules?'

'I mean about how and when I can take pictures.'

Myklades shrugged. 'As and when you like. I have nothing to hide, and any I do not like are destroyed. Yes?'

'That's right. But can you give me an idea of what the schedule is, so I have some idea of how long we are likely to be in any given situation?'

Myklades' hand lifted an inch or two from the seat and dropped again. It was a signal that Rupert should take over. He did so, leaning back over the thick upholstery that separated them.

'Hector is considering purchasing a firm that specialises in shortlease and charter packages for wealthy visitors. It includes boats and a lot of the things that go with boats. So this morning we are checking out what's on offer. That will take us to half twelve. Hector has an engagement for lunch that runs on into the afternoon, but we will be back at the Boat Show to meet the people he is dealing with at six o'clock.'

'You mentioned a structured session at some point.'

Myklades turned back from the window. 'That will be at half past four. If you still think it necessary. We want Gate A. On the right.'

As they got out Rupert handed her her bag. Though heavy, it was part of her, once on as much a part of her as the hands that manipulated it or the hip-bone it rested against. As they walked through the gate she unzipped, slung the Hasselblad round her neck, checked the magazine for daylight-balanced film – she did not expect to be able to ask Myklades to hold a pose – and zipped up again.

Rupert, with a guide to the show as thick as a paperback, led the way into a huge marquee filled with stands displaying a haphazard collection of goods and services from yacht charters in the British Virgin Islands to the Salvation Army, from apartments at Brighton marina to Southampton Sea Cadets. He carried a large document case and paused to pick up free sheets and brochures but refused the advances of salesmen. At each stop Myklades hung back behind him, feet splayed, hands in pockets.

He was wearing a pink padded topcoat with toggled strings at the neck and an anchor embroidered on the zip-up breast pocket, white ducks, blue and white casual shoes, and, worst of all, a blue sailing cap with a black braided peak. In a crowd where most people had perhaps self-consciously refused the obviously nautical, he stood out. It was not just the clothes that made him incongruous. His pale skin was a stranger to wind and sun, his gold-rimmed glasses with their hothouse tint suggested boardrooms, conferences, video terminals, not sea spray or squalls.

These brief halts in their progress gave Harriet a chance to stand back and take a few preliminary shots. The light was a nice mix: cool and even through the canvas of the marquee, warmed and strengthened by the glow from the stands. There was very little strip about, the colour should hold. Seeing him now in her viewfinder, distanced by prisms yet concentrated and singled out by sharp focus, she began to get a hold of the face. This was one of the excitements of portrait photography: the power it conferred over a personality in the space of a few minutes. But it was an odd mix, the face she was scrutinising now: the pallor of the skin, the bright unnatural yellow of the hair, the gleam of gold and that creepy inelasticity in the skin. Then Myklades moved, and behind him she saw, for the second time, a sharp, hard face, the face of a big man in a dark blue mac.

Rupert hurried on down the aisles and she pieced out the pattern of his stops: yacht charters, marinas, accommodation near marinas were what drew him, then suddenly they were out in the blowy sunshine again and surrounded by caravans and mobile stalls, flags and, beyond, another marquee. For a moment the two men conferred and she took the opportunity to switch cameras – with the Hasselbad on her chest the image had been too often obscured by passing bodies, she would do better at eye level with a Canon. The change took her barely twenty seconds but almost she missed them. It was the big man in the raincoat who gave her the clue: she saw his back disappear into the marquee entrance.

This brought her into a wide and uncluttered space: a stage, collapsible chairs in the middle, set between a display for Jaguar cars and UniqueAir Cellular Communications at one end and a champagne bar at the other. The large man in the mac had taken a seat at the end of the third row nearest to the Jaguar, and beyond she could see Myklades and Rupert already in earnest conversation with a rep from UniqueAir. As she came up with them, pausing to frame them in the viewfinder, Rupert turned and grinned at her. She snapped him.

'I doubt if I'd buy even a new Jag from you, and certainly not a second-hand one,' she said. 'I suppose you know you're being followed.'

'I seriously hope not.' His eyes, suddenly anxious, flickered over the whole hall. It was a professional glance, a soldier's checking out the ground. 'Bert's meant to tell us if that happens.'

'Bert?'

'Down there. Third row. Big chap.'

'That's who I meant.'

'Bert? He's not following us. He's part of us.'

'Minding?'

'Not exactly. Minding is one of my functions when I'm

around. Bert's our sweeper. Counter-surveillance. He's an ex-copper and knows what he's doing. Look, why don't you sit down too and watch the show. Hector's going to be here for some time. He thinks there might be something he can use in cellular communication but first the salesman has to convince him it can't be penetrated.'

'Nautical fashions? Rupe, it's going to be as tacky as fly-paper.'

'Yes. Well. Problem is Hector has a thing about models and there's a couple here he's interested in.'

'He's a touch weird . . . isn't he?'

'He flays little girls who say things like that.'

'I'm not frightened of him.'

'No? You should be. Don't mess with Hector. Nobody does.'

He turned back to his boss, and Harriet settled her back against a tent-pole, with most of the chairs in a shallow crescent to one side, and the Jaguar and UniqueAir areas to the other. Almost idly she swung the Canon about, searching for compositions, watching the metred display shift, twisting the image in and pushing it away again.

Under her smart gilet Bonnie has a heavy hundred per cent cotton T-shirt. The neat little cap can be adjusted to fit even the biggest head . . . Here we see a college-style cardigan – if you want to look like one of the British Challenge crew, this is what you need. Jill's shorts are in cotton twill, available in red, white and navy, with a smart little Challenge logo on the right leg . . .

Jill and Bonnie were okay: not more than twenty but both had class, a class way at odds with the ambience. Jill had short dark hair cut to a flat-top, large brown eyes, a straight narrow nose, full well-shaped mouth, good but slightly uneven teeth, good chin, long neck. She bounced back personality from reactive features which responded to the commentary whimsically, gaily and occasionally with unrehearsed disdain. Perhaps at five seven, five eight she would be too small to reach the top, but Harriet felt she might go close.

Bonnie was fairer, taller, had a very slightly protuberant lower jaw, was at first sight less obviously a looker, but she moved like an athlete, a dancer, a thoroughbred. It was clear that they were friends and that they were enjoying themselves. Harriet wondered if that would still come across at the end of the week.

All Speedo costumes are available at Mermaid Pleasure boutiques here at Stand Y 32 and at all prominent South Coast marinas, as is too the fabulous Rich Bits designer jewellery worn by Bonnie and Jill . . . and neither should be worn while bouncing huge red and yellow beach balls. The music – a bland mix of Gospel and Caribbean with a heavy beat – was climaxing and the girls, with the two men they had been sharing the show with, surged back, staggering and rolling in contrived and gawky foolery to bring it all to an embarrassing close.

'We're just about through here. And I've got you a glass of bubbly, compliments of UniqueAir.'

'Rupe! Where's your upbringing, your breeding? That is not a glass, it's a flute. A fl-o-o-o-t.'

'Dash it, of course. You're right. A fl-o-o-o-t. Wasn't that awful?'

'But Mr Money-bags I suppose enjoyed it.'

'The models, you mean. Well, why not? The two girls were okay, you know?'

Harriet experienced a blighting touch of sadness, like the first frost. They might do well. They could make a lot of gelt. But they would have to cope with the Ruperts and Hectors – cope, and worse.

'Where now then?' She drank off the fizzy wine and found it better than she had expected, but less: that's flutes for you.

'Boats, of course. What else?'

The procession re-formed. Rupert in the front, a herald, a guide; then his master – tall, grotesque Mr Myklades. Behind them, Harriet contrived to catch his profile of gold-wire-framed glasses pinkly reflecting the clouds and enough blue to make if not a sailor's suit then at least a bikini bottom for a popsy. The nose was a little larger than she had thought, more prominent anyway, if pinched. He was like nothing so much as a big old flamingo, an exotic stranded in an English pond. And behind her Bert paused and his heavy head swung on his thick neck like the turret of a tank, searching out followers, spies, assassins.

Thirty-fours, Sadlers and Westerly SeaHawks seemed to be the ones of choice, though Harriet, who was not a boat person, could see little reason why or noticeable difference between them. Below she bumped on unexpected corners; her bag got in the way and the zoom lens too. The salespersons insisted that eight friendly people could be accommodated. Harriet doubted she had ever been that friendly with anyone, let alone seven other people at once. And where was the bath?

Myklades seemed as ill at ease as she was. He knocked off his cap climbing up out of the galley of the first, and after that refused to go below decks. In each boat he checked out a very limited range of data: price, range under power, bulk storage facilities, and he noted the details in a leather-bound pocket-book. Rupert was more thorough.

On the third boat, a SeaHawk, she remained in the cockpit with Myklades. He sat in the stern sheets behind a large wheel, with his cap perched quite rakishly over one glinting lens. A small boy wanted him to move so he could hold the wheel, peer at the gimbled compass and play pirates. Myklades looked as if he might eat him.

Harriet unzipped her bag, unfastened the cumbersome zoom, packed away the Canon and got out the Hasselblad again. She slotted in the dark slide, changed the magazine for one with slower stock, and thought about ways of reducing the untidy forest of masts and rigging to a blur, but a blur with some depth. The large wheel might be useful: A Captain of Industry on Course for Bigger Profits. Or something.

'No more pictures.'

'Not at all?'

'Not now.'

'Why not now? The light's good. I can make something of the situation.'

'And make me look a bloddy fool in these clothes. A bloddy fool.'

The instinct that saves the cleverer sparrow in front of an irritable python suppressed the grin she felt coming.

'Always I get the bloddy clothes wrong.'

'If you have a change of clothes at the hotel, perhaps we can try again after lunch.'

He brightened, and a little later, when they went down to the pontoon, an improvised complex of piers where boats actually floated, he became almost cheerful. On a Princess 45 with twin Volvo TAMD70E diesels, and a host of extras including air-conditioning, echo-sounder, ship-to-shore radio, freezer, the latest in microwaves and even a small hipbath as well as the inevitable shower stall, he got into a fast and enthusiastic conversation with an Italian couple. His Italian was, as far as Harriet could tell, immaculate, Tuscan, and a lot of the conversation was about the overbearing airs the English continue to give themselves.

He turned to Rupert. 'This is a proper boat. This acknowledges the twentieth century and turns it back on your focking Nelson. Do Mermaid Pleasure have a boat like this?'

'Yes, actually they do. A couple, actually.'

'Good. Good. I'm glad to hear it.' Myklades looked at his watch. 'Tell Bert to call Pablo. We'll be at the gate in ten minutes.'

As they passed the Volvo exhibit, there was a sudden commotion. Two girls, caught by the elbows, were trying to get free of Bert, who'd dropped his radio to catch them.

'Ge' tha' filthy hands off of me, yer fat old goat,' called the smaller, darker one, while the taller, with fair hair, tried to kick him in the shins. Rupert, his right hand sliding towards his left armpit, moved in to help, and so did a Burns security guard, a long-haired lout in slate-blue jacket and ill-fitting American-cop-style cap. Harriet had recognised the girls, felt sure they meant no harm.

'It's yoo, hen, we wanna talk wit, noo the gent. Tell yon ape to le' goo a uz, or I'll ca' a cawper.'

'I'm sure they mean no harm. It's just the girls from the fashion show.'

'Wha' should we wanna harm? Wa's the marrer wi' you all?' The accents were broad Geordie, not easy to follow when they were excited.

'All right, all right. But Hector's not always utterly popular in that area.' Rupert muttered this for Harriet only, then, louder, 'But if it's you they want to talk to . . .' His head lifted in question to Myklades, who nodded minutely. 'Okay, Bert, let them go.'

'We saw you takin' pictures o' uz at yon show.' This was the lovely dark one, dressed now in worn jeans and a threadbare black sweater. She rubbed her arm, and pulled a wicked face at the bullish Bert.

'And Carl said you is Harriet Jones.' The fairer one was smarter: she wore buttercup-yellow stretch pants to her shins and neat slippers. Now she was off the walk she wore glasses: round grannies in gold frames.

'Miss, is tha' reet? It is? Hey, that's brill, reel greet. Bonnie, she is th' reel Harriet Jones.'

'Yes, but I'm here working for Mr Myklades. He is my client. I mean it's him I'm here to take pictures of.'

'Oh, sure, that's a' reet. We onnerstan tha-at. But if ye could let us ha' prints o' the pics y' took o' the two o' us we can pu' um in ooor por'fol-i-os, y'know, could we do that'. . .? I mean tha' wo' be reel greet. An' we'll like peah for them, y'ken that'.'

'Weel, we'll look a' thum feerst.' The fair one was more cautious.

'Give me your cards and I'll see what I can do.'

'Bonnie, gi' Miss Jones ah cards, y'greet hen.'

Bonnie, the quieter one – there's always a quiet one and a lively one, thought Harriet – also carried a tiny shoulder-purse. She took two slivers of pasteboard from it: *Jill Jack and Bonnie Day. Orlando Gardens, Clapham.*

She laughed. Jill Jack and Bonnie Day. Which of course signalled French – *Bonne Idée.* Good idea! Well, it had a sort of style, and they had a lot going for them, no doubt of that.

Back in the foyer of the Vauban Hotel Myklades touched Harriet's elbow.

'I should like you to come to my room for a few moments.'

Doubt in her eyes.

'For a few moments only. I have your advice to ask.'

Rupert muttered: 'Go on. He means it. He won't rape you. I'll meet you in the bar.'

Myklades' room was second floor front, above the conference suites. As soon as they were through the door he pulled open the big wardrobes, drew out two drawers from a chest, then began to take off his clothes, the peaked cap, the pink padded topcoat, even the white trousers and two-tone sneakers.

'Always I get the bloddy clothes wrong. So you choose.'

Quite without embarrassment he went the whole way, removing silk underclothes. His body was thin, very white, the white of lead, but with freckles and harsh red pimples. His pubic hair was bright red, his genitals, at that moment, small. He found a long silk dressing-gown, peacock blue, put it on, and at last sat in the upright easy chair in front of the dressing-table. He offered her a cigarette from a slim gold case. It was untipped, genuine Turkish, Yeni Harman, and very good, not scented, not harsh like Virginia, not overflavoured like Balkan tobacco.

'Well, all right. But what are you doing this afternoon?'

He looked at his watch.

'In twenty minutes I am having lunch with the West Country Military Club. They meet here. It is a collection of retired soldiers, police, officials, even historians, some of whom are war-gamers. They meet to listen to a guest speaker riding a military hobbyhorse. After lunch I am addressing them on the Mystery of Waterloo. It sounds like a detective story, yes?'

'Not at all.' Harriet's father was an amateur of Napoleonic warfare, in so far as Wellington was involved in it, and it did not need any great intelligence to work out where, for Myklades, the mystery of Waterloo lay. 'I imagine you will try to explain just why Napoleon failed to win.'

He laughed, pushing the sound past his thin lips. 'Not exactly. It cannot be explained. The stomach trouble – exaggerated. His age . . . but that was the same as his adversary. Marshals who chose not to obey orders – it always happened. But I will tell them what they do not like to hear. That Wellington should have bloddy well lost.' He drew in smoke and his pink nostrils flared as he let it out. 'At four o'clock Rupert briefs me for the meeting with Mermaid Pleasure, and at six or half past, I shall not mind to keep them waiting, we go back to the show and I do a deal with them. So. What do I wear? Not this stuff. Not the uniform of the man who hires out pedalos on the Serpentine.'

She moved to the wardrobe, pushed suits and jackets, perhaps ten or more, along the runner. How long was he here for? A day. Two at the most. The number of outfits was an index of his insecurity, and judging by the mistakes he made it was an insecurity he was right to feel. Especially as it seemed to matter to him.

'Well. Both functions call for a suit. But not too formal. A light check, maybe. Or this?'

. *This* was a rich brown, with the softness of exotic wool, but not too heavy. The back was pleated and belted in recollection of old-fashioned shooting jackets.

'I think you are joking.'

'No, I am not.'

'It's French.'

'So? You are not English. And it doesn't matter if you're not English.' She thought for a moment, of her father, of Rupert, of county towns, of 'good' regiments, and the right clubs. She smiled. 'It does not matter much. They will forgive you for being a foreigner. It is not your fault. What they will not excuse is any pretension on your part to be English. So, if you want my advice – be foreign. It's what they expect.'

She peered into the drawers and picked out an eau-de-nil silk shirt – it even had a monogram: H and M intertwined. Finally she found a rich Liberty tie, red and gold and brown in woven acanthus-leaf patterns.

'All right?'

She waited. He brooded over it all, now spread on the bed in front of them. At last he reached towards an ashtray. Fuck him, she thought, he expects me to fetch it for him. But she did, a heavy glass one off the dressing-table.

'And it'll look good in *THAT* magazine.'

'What have they got to do with it?'

'I'm meant to be taking your picture for them. Remember?'

'Your Myklades is weird.'

'Yes.'

The bar downstairs was crowded. She sat on a leather-topped stool in the corner where the counter circled into the wall, with Rupert next to her and close. All around was the jabber and bray of British business. Men mostly in navy blazers swapped tales whose point was always the same: to demonstrate the wit and acumen of the teller.

Harriet bobbed down the lemon twist in her gin and tonic. 'Yet he has a sort of class too.'

'A lot of class.'

'And underneath it all . . . evil.'

'That's a bit strong, isn't it? Why do you say that?'

'Because, dear Rupe, he's caught you. And you're evil.'

It was already her second double and they were going to her head after the Scotch on the train, the flute of bubbly, the wind and fresh air. She felt exhilarated too: possibilities were in the air, new experiences, adventures. She liked the feeling:

psychically she was wading off a sandy beach into treacherous surf, the sort you get in places like Hossegor or St-Giron between Bordeaux and Biarritz, when the great waves break and surge up to you and burst around your body and there are vicious undertows that can pull your feet from under you, feet whose sandy footing is being undermined by the sweeping water.

'I'm evil?' Elbows on the bar, glass held beneath his chin, he glanced quizzically over his shoulder at her. His knee touched her thigh, not assertively, but with confidence.

'Certainly you're evil. It's not just that you're a bit of a blood. You don't *care*. You don't care at all. And you don't want *things*.'

'What do I want?'

'I'm not sure. Excitement. Risk. But more than that. If it was just that you'd go rock-climbing, *ski extrème*, hang-gliding. You'd gamble.'

'Well, I've done all that.' Said dismissively, with irritation too.

'Rupert Bridge could go far but he lacks application.'

'Actually, that's wrong. I apply myself. I learn trades. Skills. Properly. I'd be dead now if I didn't.'

'You learnt how to kill.'

'Of course.' He grinned. 'Load of Argies.'

She put her hand on his. 'Don't.'

'Oh, come on!'

She straightened her back, regretted the moment of softness, drank. 'So what does Myklades give you?'

'Hector? Difficult to say in a few words. A framework, an area to work in. Not exactly an aim or a purpose, but space.' He paused for a moment, chin in the air, challenging. He finished his drink in a gulp. 'Lunch?'

She looked around at the blazers and the brass buttons, felt on the air the heavy flavour of used fats, of warmed-over vol-au-vents, of Margaux served too warm and Chablis too cold. 'Here?'

'No. Not here.'

They walked through tired backstreets of Edwardian villas converted into flats or guesthouses, then up a wider street which ended with a stuccoed terrace of older cottages. The road that crossed the end was suddenly lively with restaurants, pubs, and an odd mixture of shops: amongst hardware and greengrocers, petfood supplies and a launderette, there was a classy photography shop, a couple of good antique dealers, and a shoe shop that would have attracted custom in Bond Street. In the centre, on a corner, was Pizza Pan, a window of Italian wines and another of stuffed clams, squid, bass, and oysters. Inside, it was airy and busy.

Rupert took the waiter by the elbow and walked him over to an aquarium where ten sleek black fish with pairs of whiskers beneath their puggish jaws twisted and weaved in hectic if graceful arabesques. He signed the death warrant of two of them.

Harriet was momentarily repulsed: she did not want so obviously to be the cause of death. But she knew she had been challenged, that exhibiting irrational squeamishness would drop her out of the category of people like us that she sensed Rupert had placed her in, albeit provisionally. The fish were very good, and so was the Frascati that came with them.

She had no reservations about bed – indeed, would have been disappointed if he had not suggested it. His room in the Vauban was smaller than Myklades', but it was comfortable and filled with a cool light filtered through the big plane trees outside. She stood in the window, looked out at the chestnuts beyond, and the wind-tossed rose beds. Always, she thought, rather an awkward moment, this. There ought to be some etiquette, some convention . . . She sensed his presence behind her, expected a hand round her waist, on her breast, a not too overtly sexy kiss for starters.

'Try this.'

She turned. He held his palm twisted over in the manner of a stage waiter supporting a tray, the little finger and heel of his hand quite close to her nose. In the hollow below his ring finger (a gold signet with the crest of the Bridge family) a tiny pyramid of white powder glittered, as much as you might get from the smallest of levelled salt spoons.

'Goodness. I thought you were meant to cut it into lines and use a twenty-pound note.' Nevertheless her heart had lurched, and somewhere a small voice said: Get out. Now.

Harriet did not like small voices.

'Definitely last month's flavour. First because it's ugly. Snorting. This is sniffing. Second because it's middle-class, conceals a certain meanness. The main reason for all that was to avoid wasting any. And third because it is actually a touch dangerous. I mean if Mr Plod calls and finds all that gear around he just knows he's come to the right place. Press one nostril shut, and have a good, deep sniff. Go on. It's quality snow.'

She pushed her hair back, held it, then released one lock to bring a finger back down to press on the side of her nose, aquiline but not large, dipped her face into his palm, and sniffed deeply. The first sensation was not particularly pleasant, dusty, cutting, but then suddenly cool and clearing through her sinuses to the back of her throat. She let her forehead drop forward on to his large, lean, but strong hand. It was as steady as an altar.

18

She waited, eyes closed, in a world of crimson velvet. Quite quickly the colour energised, became scarlet, vermilion, she felt her heartbeat rise and waves of warmth pulsed out across her body and found loci to collect at, like iron fillings, in her breasts, the palms of her hands, the soles of her feet, round her groin, her anus.

'Oh dear,' she murmured. 'That is nice.' Then lifting her head: 'Have you had some?'

'Of course.'

'Gosh. Hey. Roget was right. I really do think I'd like to go to bed. Rather soon.' She put her long arms round his neck, pulled his face down. He kissed her, but gently, just letting his tongue tickle her lips as he pulled back.

'Ah yes. The splendid Roget. What did he say?'

'That it makes you feel sexy.'

'Don't tell me this is the first time.'

'Only once before. It made my nose numb and did about as much for me as a large G and T.'

'Ah. Inferior stuff. Well, what you've just had is fifty per cent pure, and the very best in town.'

He pushed her gently away from him, sat her on the edge of the bed and took off his jacket. She stripped off her jumper, unzipped her jeans, then saw he was wearing a small shoulder holster in his left armpit.

'God. What's that?'

'Toy really.' Almost miraculously it appeared in his hand.

'Hey, that was quick.'

'Sprung holster.'

'Let me see.' He sat beside her, twisted the revolver so it lay on its back in his large palm, and released the chamber. A shake and the shells fell into his other hand, then he handed her the empty gun.

'Very ordinary. Snub-nose Smith and Wesson, .32. Almost a lady's gun, though lots of police still carry them routinely, more for decoration than anything else. Took it off an Argie subaltern who had no further use for it. I'd just knocked his head off with something bigger.'

She hefted it, then whipped it up, steadying her wrist with the left hand, squeezed the trigger three times. Click, click, click.

'Do you always carry it?'

'Lord no. Spoil the shape of my suit. But with Hector in a public area. He likes to know it's there. *Are* you going to drop them or not?'

She giggled. 'Oh yes. And this thing had better not be some sort of manhood surrogate.' She handed it back, swung her legs on to the bed and let him peel off the jeans.

Jeremy had been skinny and not robust, a presence that invited and later demanded coddling, care, mothering. He had caught Harriet when she wanted to be needed: that moment, too long prolonged, had passed. In twenty minutes or so she now rediscovered with Rupert that the softnesses of her body were charged not with the comforts she had wanted to press on Jeremy but with vulnerability – to pain as well as pleasure. Not that Rupert hurt her. But she sensed the skills he was using included a deliberate restraint: they did not exclude the possibility of pain.

The moment, when it happened, was the climax of something that had started with the cocaine, and it was as powerful as any she had ever experienced, a sudden release of tension, a shedding of burdens, a breakthrough out of ennui.

She dragged in breath, and then gently but firmly pushed him away.

'God, that was nice,' she murmured. 'Bridge's acquired skills go beyond the battlefield.'

He sighed, a deep heave of achievement. 'You know, I've wanted that for a long time.'

'You should have asked.'

'When you were still of an age to spank me?'

'Why not?' She giggled, stroked his cheek with her finger. 'This scar, it's new, isn't it? Another souvenir of Goose Green?'

'No, actually. Much more recent. Pranged my tub on a piece of driftwood practising for this year's Round the Island Race. Lucky to be picked up, since I was on my own and – '

But men talking of sporting exploits bored Harriet. 'How long have we got? I'd like a bath.'

'Hector won't finish with Wellington for at least another hour. And Mermaid Pleasure aren't expecting us until six. So. Have a bath.'

'You can scrub my back.'

He did. And there was intimacy in it, something from the nursery, something not a hundred miles from incest, that had not been there when they were making love. Then, wrapped in a towel, he sat on the loo.

'He's weird,' she repeated. 'Your Myklades. Is he really going to carry on about Waterloo for a couple of hours?'

'He really is. He's a Napoleon freak. Probably knows just about everything there is to know about the Little Corporal. And he's obsessed with Waterloo. He's even got a house there. Well, I think he has.'

'What do you mean, *think*?'

'Well, I'm not sure if it's he who owns it or someone else. Lili Brel.'

'Christ. Is he in with her?'

'I think so. What do you know about Lili Brel?'

'Not a lot. But she's a crook. A top-class, financial twister.' She soaped her breasts. 'Why's Myklades so insecure? About clothes and things.'

'The British. He hates us, fears us, and the particular operation he's developing at the moment is to be British-based. And always he feels he's going to come unstuck here. Once he did. Quite badly.'

'Yes. I heard. Department of Trade inquiry. The works.'

'That's right. They threw the book at him and he damn near did time for it. And he can't understand what went wrong. As far as he was concerned he did nothing that ten, twenty other people he or I could name have done. A bit of inside trading. A bit of overmanipulation of public companies. And he's convinced they went for him because he's an outsider, not one of us, an intruder. And he's afraid it will happen again. That's why he wants you.'

'What?' She sat up suddenly so the water slopped. 'What do you mean?'

He grinned. 'That's what all this is about, you know?'

'What do you mean, *wants me?*'

'Well, not like that. Or not primarily or in the first place.' The grin widened. 'Though I would be surprised if it didn't come to that.'

'Well?'

'It's not easy to explain, but it's real enough. You know how a certain sort of businessman, operator, especially at the dodgy end of things, likes to have a model in tow, a bit of glamour, a pretty face and a nice pair of legs? Not for sex, but to impress. Like the Gucci shoes, the customised Merc. He can hang a few rocks on her, wrap her in a nice fur, show he's worth a bob or two. It tells the opposition that he's to be reckoned with. Right? Well, in a vastly more up-market sort of way Hector wants you to be like that for him. It's not glamour he wants, and he certainly doesn't need to show he's got money. What he thinks he needs is class. The class that doesn't give a fuck.'

As if to make the point he got off the lavatory seat, dropped the towel, turned, peed. The sight of his bottom, lean, hard as polished rocks, tanned precisely to the same level as the rest of his body, provoked another wave of pleasure. She lay back in the hot water, hair piled and loosely pinned on top of her head, and let her neck rest on the rim of the bath. He shook himself, pressed the flush, sat down again.

'Listen. Hector needs really good bankers' references and commercial ones if he's to run Ambrose Finance the way he wants to. I'm trying to persuade Uncle Geoffrey to fix him up with a quiet weekend chatting to Sam Dorf, Jimmie Lennox, Alec Greene, you know? In the first place I'm not sure Uncle Geoffrey will do it for me, but he will for you. And in the second place Hector's very worried about it. He's terrified his clip-on bow tie might fall in the soup. He's terrified he'll pop off his Purdey too early or too late, wing a dog or a beater.'

'But none of that matters. It doesn't matter a hoot. And especially not with Uncle Geoff.'

'You see? That's why you are precisely what he needs. The fact you can say that proves it.'

She stood up, slicing the water off her long arms and thighs. Her normally white skin had a pinkish glow from the bath, perhaps from a deeper excitement too. 'Pass me a towel.'

He did.

'So what is all this about? Just what do you want me to do?'

'I want you to use your wiles on Uncle Geoff and get him to agree. Almost he has, but you'll tip the scales. And then I want you to hold Hector's hand there, at Wrykin Heath. Advise him on the social side of it, chat up the ladies for him, generally give that touch of solid class to the entourage that he thinks it needs. It's pretty indefinable really, but if you're there, in his corner, he'll have that bit more confidence. He'll get across the feeling that if they don't provide what he wants he'll damn well get it elsewhere.'

She went back into the bedroom, sat on the edge of the bed and lit a cigarette.

'They'll think I'm his mistress.'

'No they won't. You'll be billed as his personal assistant. Or maybe a court photographer. Anyway, that doesn't matter a lot these days, does it?'

'Well, I think it does.' She breathed out smoke, patted it away from her face. 'If I come, and it still is *if*, I'm there on a proper basis, not as his popsy. And another thing. This has all been set up, hasn't it? I mean the THAT magazine thing, taking his photograph. It's just been an excuse for him to check me out. Hasn't it?'

'Sort of.'

'Don't bullshit me, Rupe. Not any more. But where did the idea come from? Why me? And it's a pretty crazy idea anyway. Where did it start?'

He walked over to the window, kept his back to her. 'I knew what he wanted. I know you. Uncle Geoff looked good, and Uncle Geoff likes you. Simple as that really.'

He was not telling the truth – she was sure of it. 'Well, I'm not at all sure I like it. I'm certainly not at all sure I like him. I've more than a half a mind to go back to town. Now.'

His voice hardened. 'You've been commissioned for the day, you're a professional and you'll fulfil your part of the contract.'

She shrugged. 'A contract I entered without being properly aware of the facts. I really do have a mind to tell you all to piss off. Have your got a hairbrush?'

'Be my guest.'

She stubbed out the cigarette, sat in front of his dressing-table, pushed the brush through her hair. 'It's a big thing then, this operation Myklades is setting up?'

'Bloody big. Multi-million big.'

There was a throatiness in his voice that quite took her by surprise, though she was aware too that she had tightened pelvic-floor muscles in excited response to it. She ran the tip of her tongue along her top lip.

'What's it all for?'

'Crystal. Name mean anything?'

'Actually it does. Client the other day asked me if he should give it money. It's the sort of thing they do – try to make me feel big by asking my advice on unimportant matters, you know? I asked him what it was and he said a Swiss charity that supported projects that would preserve the best of European civilisation that promote security. I gathered there was more to it than that.'

'There is. I'm not saying more now, partly because I don't know much more. But Crystal needs a lot of money, and it's going to do exciting things with it. Ambrose is just one of many fund-raising projects serving it. Exciting things, big things' – he pressed her shoulder – 'and it's going to be a marvellous thing to be in on at the beginning, I promise you.'

Again the throatiness. Almost it frightened her. If Rupert was excited then it was exciting, probably wicked, certainly dangerous. She shivered, went on brushing. 'I'll let you know'

She dressed, went for a walk. She crossed the Isaac Watts Park with its rose-beds and chestnut trees, already turning patchily yellow, already with small boys tossing up sticks and empty cans to dislodge the conkers. A clock chimed, the big city clock in its tall campanile, four o'clock, then a carillon played the first lines of Watts' most famous hymn: 'O God Our Help in Ages Past'. Harriet's mind put to it the words the boys of Cheltenham school had sung. Why was I born so beautiful? Why was I born at all? Good question. Not to spend a working life massaging the already inflated egos of pompous businessmen – there had to be more to it than that. Not for relationships with wimps like Jeremy.

She sat on a bench, could not stay still, got up and walked briskly to and fro between the rose beds, kicking at the litter of conker shells, and the tune that can sound so majestical, booming out down the aisles of St Paul's on one of those huge, inflated City occasions, so full of self-congratulation and flatulent hypocrisy, a funeral perhaps, a memorial service, trickled back into her mind, but jaunty, taunting. Why was I born so beautiful? Why was I born at all? I'm no bloody use to anyone, I've only got one ball.

Once, years ago, she'd given a hunt saboteur a ferocious cut across the cheek with her crop. The silly little runt had given her mare, which was a dear with a lot of Arab, quite a nasty fright. Anyway, on that occasion the commodity broker who later married her sister, whom he regularly knocked up, and occasionally about, had said: 'Old Harry's got balls, all right. That's her trouble.'

Had she? She wasn't too sure what Crystal meant, but if she had it right, if the whispers in the City had it right, then balls and a lot more would be needed – if one got really into it, became part of it. Again she shivered, but she turned her face into the breeze, let it blow back her hair, and she looked out, across railway lines, past warehouses, timber yards, container parks, huge hoists and the gleaming water, across to the other side, the woods climbing a long crest a mile or more away, suddenly gold-dusted with rolling sunlight.

> *Sweet fields beyond the swelling flood*
> *Stand dressed in living green*
> *So to the Jews old Canaan stood*
> *While Jordan rolled between*

> *But tim'rous mortals start and shrink*
> *To cross this narrow sea*
> *And linger shiv'ring on the brink*
> *And fear to launch away*

The words were by Watts, engraved on her memory by years of school chapel, the view in front of her the one that had inspired him. Was she a tim'rous mortal, was she one to start and shrink . . .? Certainly not, Austens never were.

19

'I am impressed. You have done well.' Lili Brel's voice carried no warmth as she said this: it was a clinical assessment of the situation, not intended to confer personal approval.

Nevertheless Hector Myklades was pleased and relieved. He cleared this throat. 'Of course it has not been cheap. But as you see, the main aim has been achieved. Not only is each part of the operation sealed from every other, but we have, I think, solved the chief problem that has bedevilled ventures of this sort on this scale in the past. Movement of product is sealed from movement of money. No matter where the opposition penetrate they will immediately meet cutouts. May I?'

He poured Perrier, drank. At times of tension, insecurity, his body played unpleasant tricks on him: a dry throat could be a prelude to severe itching, often in places embarrassing to scratch. Social unease was worse than anything and with Brel that was a problem. Myklades' whole personality rebelled against women in overt positions of power: while he conceded they could often wield considerable influence from within the recesses of the harem, he could not tolerate them out there in front.

Brel remained in the high window for a moment, framed by old-gold velvet, apparently watching the glossy traffic in the Rue de Rivoli. Here and there amongst the green of the chestnut trees in the Tuileries beyond, a leaf was edged with yellow, a reminder. She sighed, but inwardly, inaudibly. 'I particularly like the way you are restructuring Ambrose Finance.'

'Yes. The arrangements are watertight. Every penny that passes to the offshore companies and banks will be accounted for as the proceeds of legitimate market operations. By the time it reaches Mendoza Holdings (Tortola) it will be clean.'

'But this does depend on getting the references you need. Is Rupert Bridge being helpful?'

'Not directly. When I suggested to him that he might be, he said that his reputation in the City was not up to it. However, he identified a woman we were already vetting as a possible distributor as a relation of his and very well connected. I think she will be useful ... If you can deliver Sir Alec, as you promised, I am sure the rest will fall in place.'

'So. On the financial side everything is going well, according to plan and on schedule. But in other respects things are not so good . . .?'

Myklades leant back, fingered a Turkish cigarette from an orange packet. The inquisition was over; it was his turn to move from the defensive. Almost arrogantly he drew in smoke, exhaled.

'No. Frankly the supply side is a mess. The Arnolfini-Scapino set-up is a typical Mob-based botch-up, quite out of keeping with the scale of what we are attempting. At the very least there is no reason why their long history of product lost, minor couriers arrested, and intermittent gang warfare with rival groups should not continue. At the worst they threaten the whole enterprise – '

'Yes, yes.' Brel was irritated, and showed it. 'We've been over this before. But Boltana decided that you would need an infrastucture in place if we were to get things moving quickly, if only to give you a breathing space in which to set up your own. And then there was the problem of the Mob itself. We can't afford to alienate them, they have to be in on the act at some level . . .'

'Very well. But I shall replace them in due course and I already have something in mind. But the problems of supply go far deeper. You know the details of the Colombian deal with the Arias clan and I do not. But what I do know is not satisfactory. As I understand it we are guaranteed only five hundred kilos now, and there is no certainty that the rest will follow. Yet because of this deal the other Colombian syndicates are refusing to deal with us – '

'How do you know that?' Brel was abrupt, swung away from the window, thrust her immaculate head towards him, bottom lip pushed out.

Myklades felt his skin prickle, pushed his freckled hand

across his head. 'Apart from Arnolfini, who never handled more than ten kilos a month, Scapino also took deliveries from San in Rotterdam. San buys from the Welser clan, the people Arias says beat up Feijoo. San now refuses to deal with Scapino.'

'You approached him?' The anger still there.

'No. But Ricardo did. And that was the answer he got. I did not tell him to. I know quite well that you would prefer it if I did not involve myself with that side of things. Nevertheless . . .'

Brel said nothing for nearly three minutes, appeared to be contemplating again the first signs of a Paris autumn with the melancholy one might expect from a woman turned fifty, who knows that time is no longer on her side and that if she is to make a place for herself in a world where she has always been a servant, she must be decisive and opportunist, grasp every chance as it comes.

Myklades was careful not to intrude on her reverie. At last she turned back again. 'We need to know more about this. We need to know how much the Welsers know. What I should like you to do is this. Approach San. Make him believe you have nothing to do with Scapino, but let him know who you are. And if he refuses to sell to you try to find out why . . .'

'All right. I'll do that. But I must emphasise: we have made a very heavy investment on the financial side to guarantee safe transference of very considerable sums of money; but also distribution, marketing and sales, tied into an elaborate and skilful promotional campaign, are all almost ready and in place, and the whole operation is keyed up to handling four tons a year by next spring. You know, Lili, how much this has cost, and will continue to cost. Very substantial amounts indeed. But with a projected turnover of six hundred million pounds a year, the investment is justified. But your backers are not going to get anything like the return they expect if we end up trading only half a ton a year. The whole operation depends on steady, reliable supply of product in the volumes we have been led to expect. If this cannot be guaranteed, then I think we, you, should look about for alternative sources.'

He reached forward, dabbed ash, drank Perrier. Beyond the double-glazed windows the traffic purred.

Lili Brel looked down at him, at the reflections in his rose-tinted spectacles, at his pale blotched hands, at the inelastic skin below his chin. Her face was a mask; nevertheless, when her head lifted back to the chestnuts in the Tuileries the movement was sudden, unstudied. Almost she had flinched. 'You're right. Of course you're right. But half a ton between now and the New Year . . .?'

'That's fine. But I must be sure there's more to follow. I can shift that much, no problem. But I need to know if I have to hold some back. This trade is no different from any other. We have gone a long way towards eliminating or absorbing our competitors, but if we suddenly find we can no longer supply they will return, they will fill the vacuum we have ourselves created and we will be back to square one.'

'Yes, yes, Hector. I do take the point. Listen. The full board is meeting at Plancenoît in early November. The case you are making will come better from you than from me. They will suspect my motives. I think you should be there, and I shall put it on the agenda that we talk through the whole problem of supply, from the bottom up. Now. What else is there to discuss?'

'Security.'

'At what level?'

Myklades shrugged. 'At all levels.'

'You should concern yourself only with the British end. From import, through distribution and sales. Back to Ambrose. From what you have told me I think you are doing it very well. Albert Burke and Rupert Bridge seem ideally suited to the tasks you have given them. It has cost a lot, and I shall have to defend the expense to my associates, but beyond that I don't see that your security is part of my brief. And my security and that of Crystal and Mendoza (Tortola) is certainly not yours.'

'But supposing the connection could be made, and made to hold water – '

'It's not possible.' Brel was irritated again. She did not like to be corrected, she did not like to be pressed on points where she was sure she was right. 'But even supposing the very worst happened, it would be embarrassing merely. A London finance house that has been making charitable subventions directly to Crystal is shown to be laundering coke money . . . so that? On paper it will be only one of many private individuals and companies making donations – '

'It would look less good if the chain linking Ambrose to Mendoza to Crystal was also established. All right. I'm sure you are covered against prosecution, even litigation – nevertheless, even a whisper that Crystal was heavily financed by cocaine would be severely damaging . . .'

Again the silence lengthened. Brel tapped her thumb-nail on her teeth, then she sighed again. 'Hector. I am getting the message that you know something that I don't. You had better tell me what it is.'

His lips lengthened into a tight smile. At last he was almost enjoying himself, enjoying the moment – which would be transitory, he knew – when he was in charge, in control. He cleared his throat. 'As you know, Albert Burke can arrange access to the PNC at level ten. Not as high as we would like. But high enough. And what he has discovered is this. The Interpol drug department has a new section. It's called Eurac. At the moment it is a pilot scheme but equipped with the very latest technology and unofficially empowered to use undercover agents. And there are signs that they are already looking in directions which could be of importance to us . . .'

'Well, clearly we must find out more. Find out more and devise a counter-attack.'

'Exactly. Now Rupert Bridge has come up with a strategy. But in itself it is not unattended by risk. And so I felt I should discuss it with you first . . .' He lit another cigarette, leant back, let the smoke hang like a question mark between them.

Lili watched as one spearlike leaf, eighteen carat, detached itself from an ebony branch and floated down to the still unlittered gravel. The first. 'Go on,' she said, and sighed again. 'You had better go on . . .'

20

Behind her a row of six farmworkers' cottages had been knocked together into one long house; in front roughly cut lawns and autumn-shaggy flowerbeds dropped steeply to hawthorn bushes pimpled with scarlet haws. A guelder rose with clusters of shiny red berries hung across a stile. On the far side of a sour-looking field with reeds sticking up through the grass, furze and heather climbed to pinewoods on a distant crest. To the left, coverts of birch, willow and larch stretched along the ridge to the side of the house. Hazy sunlight rolled back a frosty mist and the sharp smell of bonfire cut across the fainting fragrance of a hedge of dying sweet peas.

A line of five shooters emerged below the pond, with a couple of springers, liver and white, frisking but obedient at their heels. They were all dressed in Barbours with flat cloth caps, except the tallest, who wore a deerstalker hat and a cape whose arm slits were set too low so it lifted like a bell tent in a wind when he raised his arms. It got in the way as he hoisted himself over the stile, exposing plus-fours and ankle boots. The rest were in cords and green wellies.

Harriet sighed. 'Oh Lord.'

The old man beside her grunted. 'Silly ass. Why's he wearing gear like that?' Then he shivered. 'Damn chilly,' and turned, stumped away up cracked paving, through french windows into an oak-panelled library.

He headed for the log fire that already blazed freshly in a polished granite fireplace. Harriet followed, reflecting that he was not the man he had been – what? three years ago? – when he retired. The cheeks that had shone with health and the precision shaving of a dandy were stubbly, the barrel chest had caved between stooping shoulders, the voice that had sounded like a cello played with panache now rasped. Yet Geoffrey Slaker was one of the few businessmen whose charm and style still attracted her. In his middle years he had achieved what almost no other British industrialist had managed: the adaptation of a family business which had made succeeding generations of Slakers fortunes in slavery, cotton, railways, and finally precision engineering, into a market leader in tailored computer systems. To the world he was Lord Slaker. To her, by the family tradition that confers a closer sanguinity on the remotely related but rich and powerful, he was Uncle Geoff.

'Damned if I'll stay as late as this another year.' He was thinking of Capri.

Harriet was thinking of Myklades. 'He thought it was going

to be a drive, shooting from a peg, I don't think he expected to have to walk.'

'Haven't had a proper shoot at Wrykin Heath since I sold the Slaker 3000 MB to Fujippon.' He looked up at her, small, hard blue eyes narrowed, swollen knuckles tensing on the broad chintz armrest of the chair he had sunk into. 'Look here, young Harry. I've done you proud, you and young Rupert. Getting Sam, and James, and that bully Alec Greene here with his awful wife. I didn't have to lay on a ruddy shoot as well. What's he want from them anyway?'

'I told you. References from Lennox and Greene, and an in into the Mineral Market from Dorf.'

'What's he up to?'

'I told you. Ambrose Finance.'

'And what's Ambrose for?'

'It's handling the surplus cash from several companies he has an interest in. The idea is to use the new set-up in the City to move it about the markets, instead of just letting it sit around until it's needed.'

'What companies?'

'A loose network selling leisure and leisure-related services. Advice, book clubs, computer games, travel, holidays – much of it passes through Designer Living Card.'

'Ah.' Slaker showed grudging respect. 'He has a slice of that?'

'Owns it, according to Rupe. And this is how Rupe told me it's all meant to work. Say a Designer Living Card retailer sells a Turkish rug for fifty thousand pounds. He takes his chit to DLC's bank, which is Alec Greene's City and Wessex. City and Wessex pay the retailer and debit the DLC account. DLC are now owed fifty thousand pounds by the purchaser, card-holder, and one thousand pounds by the retailer, and though the money won't be in the bank for a month, you've got good paper saying it's on the way. DLC notify Ambrose, who put it around the 'changes and markets. DLC notifies Ambrose daily of total new credits, so Ambrose knows what sort of leverage it has available. Often too there's a lot of money in hand covering bills that haven't fallen due like bookings in advance on holidays, that sort of thing. Not worth doing in small amounts for each separate company, because of commissions and so on, but worth doing when Ambrose can lump it together. But to move credits, not actual money in the bank, Ambrose needs a good banker's reference, something that will say they're good for a million or so and no questions so their market makers can move as soon as they see promising positions. And the obvious choice is DLC's own banker, Sir Alec Greene, City and Wessex. And as well as that Myklades wants seats in two or three of the faster commodity or money markets, or anyway dealers he can trust to move fast when he asks them to.' She paused. 'I'm sure you understand it all a lot better than I do.'

Guns popped. Lord Slaker put his head on one side, listened. 'Woodies. They've raised the woodies down the bottom. Pigeon pie if any of them are any good. What's he got? What's he using out there?'

'Beretta over-under.'

'I'd have thought he'd have something a bit more flash than that.'

'Well, yes. But he couldn't get a "best" that suited in time. Not off the peg.'

'I suppose he knows what he's doing.'

'Rupe's been coaching him for a fortnight.'

'Lord! They'd better keep behind him, then. Won't help the cause if he fills their backsides full of shot.'

'Uncle Geoff, do *you* think he'll get what he's after? I mean, he has a past, in the City.'

'Shouldn't stand in the way. Chaps like Jimmie Lennox and Sam Dorf like a whiff of iffiness. That sort of smell generally means a couple of points here, half a point there over the odds. It all adds up when you're trading several hundred grand a day. They'll want a slice of the action too, though. And of course Dorf can offer Ambrose something even more valuable than just a seat in a market.'

'What's that then?'

'Well, I'm not going to speculate about just where the iffiness of Ambrose lies. But one thing I'm pretty sure about is that Myklades will want to operate in places where the VAT man can't see what's going on. Vatman has draconian powers, you know. If he knocks on the door you open up. Everything. But of course only if the transactions are liable to VAT. And on the commodity markets, like LMM, this is not so. The dealers deal with each other, as principals, not as agents. So, no VAT. It's called the Black Box, and neither the fraud squads nor Vatman can get in without a warrant and a prima facie case that something's wrong. Keep a low profile and you can get away with a hell of a lot once you're inside the Black Box. So that's what your man wants from Dorf. And Dorf will (a) make him pay, and (b) do his evil bidding in return. Because poor Sam wants out. He's had enough. But he owes too much to get out that easily.'

He reached forward and prodded the fire with a poker.

'I have to say it, Harry – your man knows who to go for, who he can get. Not so sure about Greene though. City and Wessex don't underwrite every Johnny-come-lately who knocks on the door.'

'I don't think he's worried about Greene.'

'Oh?'

'No. You see, it's a question of what Ambrose is for.'

'And?'

'Well – ' She took a deep breath. 'Rupert reckons Hector's going to tell him Ambrose is working for Crystal.'

The old man breathed deeply for a few minutes, rheumy eyes peering into the fire, splayed fingers rubbing his knuckles.

'So that's it. If that's true, Greene will cough up – Crystal is precisely the sort of nastiness that appeals to people like Greene. But if it's true I don't see why he needs the City and Wessex at all. That lot has got, well, the Banco de Corpus Cristi for one. And that may not be the BNP or City-Corp, but it's big enough.' He let the fire crackle for a bit. 'Pass me the paper, will you? And my specs. He'd better not tell Sam Dorf that he's running for Crystal.'

She did as she was told, knew that she had been dismissed. She felt too that she had annoyed or offended him.

'It's really not anything to do with me. I just take photographs.'

'So you say, my dear. But you set up this weekend, and Myklades recruited you because he knew you could. Rupert couldn't have done it on his own.' He gave a short bark. 'Rupe's all right, good for a laugh, but I don't do him favours.'

She put the paper down on the arm of the chair and he caught her hand.

'But for me you do, eh, Uncle Geoff? I appreciate it. I really do.'

More distantly gunfire popped again.

'Might not have done if I'd known what I know now.' He patted her hand, let it drop. 'Take care, Harry. You and Rupe are in with a pretty rum lot, and you'll have to look out for yourself a bit. And don't expect Rupert to do that for you.' He unfolded his spectacles, shook out the paper. 'Lord knows where this Guinness thing will end . . .'

An hour or so later she heard them coming back. She had spent the last half-hour with Lady Greene, a fat, blowsy, overdressed woman, pretentious and empty-headed. As Phyllis Steed she had been a Rank starlet, had appeared as the *ingénue* in a Margaret Lockwood film before netting young Alec Greene, a.k.a. Alexei Gorodny, who had just made his first half-million on the bullion market and needed a wife with RADA vowels. Not that she ever mentioned this distant past – she might have been worth listening to if she had – the drift of her unconnected chat was the burden she was under as chair of various charities. 'Of course they should kick me upstairs,' she said, 'make me President. Let someone else do the donkey-work. But they can't, you see?'

Harriet obliged. 'Why not?'

'Because it would mean asking HRH to step down.'

The sound of a dog barking, and then the pop of guns again, much closer, felt like the relief of Mafeking. Harriet remembered that Myklades had asked for a photograph of their return, of the bag. She presumed this was to supply some excuse for her presence: what had Rupert said her position should be? Personal assistant, court photographer? Not, after all, mistress. Why not? She was sure she would have said no, but was a touch miffed not to have been asked. But that was it. Whatever else, Hector was clever, percipient. And he would never ask for something he might fail to get. She went to her room and collected the Hasselblad, daylight stock, not fast, and her Pentax with Ilford XP1.

Back out on the terrace she snapped them with the Pentax as they wound down the path that skirted a truly Alpine-looking rockery: Myklades in front, gun perched unbroken over his shoulder, head swinging, deerstalker slightly awry. Some way behind, and with a wary eye on the muzzle of the Beretta, came a young man called Donald: Slaker's estate manager at Wrykin Heath – part gamekeeper, smallholder, forester. Then the dogs, and finally the other three guests: banker Sir Alec Greene, big, deep-voiced, swollen cheeks the colour of crushed blackberries from the exercise and the nip in the air; James Lennox, tall, thin, lantern-jawed, senior partner in a firm of shipbrokers; and Sam Dorf.

Dorf was the most genial of the trio, smooth-faced, angel-lipped, with dark eyes that could be cruel but for the most part beamed with a happier hedonism than the other two ever achieved. He had lost a lot in the bauxite crash – money and credibility – and, for all his air of unpunctured confidence, had been heard to admit that at times he felt tired and would get out as soon as he was once more fairly ahead of the game.

Myklades swung his gun off his shoulder, handed it to Harriet. She broke it and let it rest over her forearm.

'How did it go?'

'I did not expect to have to walk so far.'

'Did you get much?'

Donald tipped out the game. Several pigeons, three rabbits, a cock pheasant and one small brown bird that had been blasted almost to pieces. Snipe or woodcock, it was impossible to be sure. Indeed, now she looked more closely Harriet could see that most of the game was more damaged than it should be, that there was too much plum-coloured blood congealed in the feathers and fur.

Donald offered explanation, advice, in a carefully expressionless tone warmed by Hampshire vowels. 'The combination could have been improved. Mr Myklades was using too little choke, too much shot, and too large.'

'And that way I hit what I aimed for and killed it.'

Dorf laughed throatily. 'You certainly managed that, Hector.'

Dorf's wife, a pale thin woman who clutched dark furs about her, and was making her first appearance of the morning, drifted in closer. 'How did you do, Sam?'

'Oh, we didn't do too much. After the first pigeons we tended to hang back and let Hector get on with it. Really, he was doing all that needed to be done.' And he laughed again.

Myklades looked around: the faces he saw were, in turn, amused, expressionless and, in Greene's case, annoyed, even angry.

With his left hand he rubbed his right shoulder. Harriet

read the signs: Magnum cartridges, too much recoil. And then she noticed that since he had gone out a very nasty red rash had appeared between the collar of his cape and his left ear.

'I had good sport,' he said. 'Let's have a picture. Let's make it like those old ones. A line of gunners . . .'

'Shooters.' Greene sounded as if he were in pain.

'Shooters. And the game laid out in front of them. Come on.'

Dutifully they lined up facing Harriet's tripoded 'Blad, then suddenly Dorf frowned, backed away.

'Fly in my eye,' he said. And was lost from the group portrait, for there was no chance that she'd line them up again in front of the display of mutilated game. She was a little suprised: she did not think Dorf was short on vanity, rather expected he would have held things up until he was ready. She was even more surprised to see Myklades looking at him with definite admiration.

Slaker joined them in the scene. 'Time for a sherry or whatever, I should say. Donald, this afternoon we'll have a drive, after all. Out of Brooker's Wood. There should be plenty of pheasants just about ready there. Get a couple of the Cooper lads to help beat and set out pegs for as many guns as want to come.'

Myklades turned up towards the house, his mauve lips set now in a grin. As Harriet came up beside him he said, quite audibly: 'You know I should have expected a man of Lord Slaker's standing to have had a bigger place than this.'

Harriet went out with them after lunch; sat on a stick in her scarf and sheepskin jacket behind Myklades, offered quiet warnings and advice, and was rewarded by hearing Lennox on the next peg say to Dorf beyond him: 'Well, who would have thought it? Chap next to me can shoot like a gentleman after all.'

She wasn't sure whether Myklades had heard, and waited for a breathless moment, chewing her bottom lip, to see if he would respond. He did: he loaded the magnum again, knocked a high hen pheasant out of the sky at a good forty yards. In another ten she would almost certainly have been Lennox's.

'Hey. That was rather a good shot. But you could have waited.'

Myklades offered her his tight, sour grin. 'Oh, I can shoot all right. But I'm not too good about the rules, you know?'

On the way back, winding down the narrow gravelly paths cut through the brown heather by the russet ponies, they raised a small bird of prey out of the top of a tall solitary pine. They all stopped, watched its neat swooping sharp-winged flight skimming low over gorse, swinging occasionally like a swallow.

Behind Harriet, Lennox boomed: 'Kestrel. Lovely little chaps, aren't they?'

In front of her Myklades turned, and tall, heron-like, peered across the top of her head. '*Falco vespertinus*.'

'Really, old chap?' Lennox was accommodating. If the strange, gangling Armenian wanted to show off pointless erudition, well, that was all right with him. 'I'm sure you're right. But to me he's a kestrel. Good old English name for a good old English bird.'

It swung nearer, climbed to a pitch above ground below them so in fact it was not that far above them, and there it hovered.

Myklades sniffed, 'Even about their beloved wildlife the English are bloody ignorant.' More loudly, indicating that this time Lennox could understand that he expected to be heard: 'The mail, that is the breast, is slate-coloured, the pounces are red' – the *r* was more guttural, swallowed back than ever – 'that is *Falco vespertinus*, I don't know what you call it in England.'

Donald knew. 'It's a red-footed falcon. We've had three pairs all through the summer. I'm surprised he's still around. He should be back in Egypt by now. As you saw, they're primarily insect-feeders. Oops, there he goes.'

Myklades nodded appreciatively: 'A fine *yarak*. Stoops well. When the rodents hibernate he'll move on.'

He grinned again, pleased to have appropriated a slim slice of English culture, strode on down the slope; his long gangling gait made even more heron- or flamingo-like by the unevenness of the ground. From behind and above Harriet could see how the pimples had crept up out of his collar and into the thin yellow hairs in the nape of his neck. They looked as angry as the poisonous yew berries on the tree by the garden gate they

170

presently turned through, and, like them, bled little drops of clear but viscous ichor.

'Psoriasis. Guttate psoriasis. You need not conceal from me that you find it repulsive.'

'But I don't.'

'You do not object that I have asked you to do this?'

'Of course not.'

'It is important, because of the cortisone, that the ointment goes only on the spots, and nowhere else. That is the problem. That is why I have to depend on someone else to anoint the places I cannot see to reach.'

He was standing naked, bent over the bed, with his elbows on the silk bedspread. Squeezing tiny smears of brownish ointment from a tube on to the little finger of her right hand she continued to dab each red spot on his back, working down from his shoulders. There were literally hundreds of them, small, except where several came together in one patch, raised, and most of them weeping.

'You have nothing to fear. It cannot be caught. It is an affliction of the skin with a genetic origin, and it recurs for no apparent reason, at ever-decreasing intervals. This is the first outbreak in six months.'

'Isn't stress a factor?'

'That has not been proved. I am under no stress. Things have gone well here.'

'Good.'

'Yes. More easily than I expected. These are dull people, you know. If you can make them think they have pulled a fast one from under you, they will do anything. Anything at all.'

'No problems then.'

'No. And of course we are guests of Lord Slaker. *Uncle* Geoff. Then once Lennox and Dorf knew that old Billings was on board on the legal side' – he began to mimic, broadly, with some disgust in his voice – 'and Arbuthnot and Sebourg were in tow as auditing accountants, things went swimmingly. "If Billings, and Arbuthnot and Sebourg, are in your corner, then count me in, old chap, say no more . . ." Pah!'

The *p* was explosive, made the sound spit.

A tiny giggle bubbled in her throat. He looked up, caught her eye in a mirror, saw the smile.

'It does not annoy you I speak of your people like this?'

'Indeed it doesn't. Pompous pricks. I know a darn sight too well what they're like.' She dabbed on down the long, thin white blemished back. The skin had a cold, dead feel to it, but she had not lied. 'This stuff has an odd smell. It reminds me of something . . .'

'Coal-tar, as well as cortisone.'

'Yes, that's it. And Greene? I imagine he's not quite so susceptible to that sort of window-dressing.'

'Ah. You know about him. The Ukrainian background. The story that he bribed his way west after the war, brought the right papers and so on with gold fillings from the camps . . . No, you are right. With him other tactics were necessary.'

'Crystal?'

He swung right round, rising as he did, knocked her raised arms aside, and slapped her – not hard, but not playfully either.

'Jesus! What did you do that for?' Scorn and anger rinsed out whatever warmth she had begun to feel, then, as the sting flooded into her cheek, humiliation. He had not hurt her at all but she realised she had been smacked – smacked in the way adults of her caste smack their children. 'At least one can trust English gentlemen not to behave like *that*.'

'Oh really? I understand it was quite usual, though perhaps only in wedlock. What do you know about Crystal?'

'Nothing at all damn you.'

'Come!'

'Rupert mentioned it once. Twice. Said that Greene would be impressed if you told him Ambrose was working for Crystal. That is all. Now I'd like you to tell me why you hit me, and what makes you think you can.'

'I did not hit you. I did what I did so that I may, might, may – fock your stupid language – engage your attention. Convince you that what I have to say next has gravity.'

She looked up at him. She realised he had adopted precisely the stance he had taken when he dismissed her from the offices of Ambrose without having had his photograph taken: feet slightly apart, left forearm exactly horizontal across his stomach, right elbow resting on the knuckles of his left hand, right cheek nestling in his right palm. The difference was that he was naked now. But nudity did not bother him. Come to that it did not bother her either. There he was: white as lead, pimpled with hundreds of red spots and his tiny prick nestling in a bush of foxy fur. The shock of the slap, and really it had not hurt at all, had receded and she felt suddenly . . . touched.

'Crystal is important. Very . . . sensitive. Maybe soon you will meet Crystal . . .' The grimace shifted into a shy grin. 'You think I look absurd?'

'No.' Suddenly she was close to laughing.

'I'll put on my dressing gown.'

'No. Don't bother. Go on. Tell me about Crystal. And I'll finish doing your spots.' She didn't know why she wanted to laugh: probably the sudden tension created by the slap, followed by its equally quick detumescence, had left her lightheaded. She made an effort to inject hardness into her voice, tried to make it sound like a command not a plea. 'But don't hit me again. Ever. Not if you want me to stay around.'

He didn't answer but was obedient about returning to his former position stooped over the bed.

'Crystal is, on the face of it, a charity, promoted by a group of powerful, wealthy people who intend to influence events, history, without being seen to do so. But charity is not enough. Ambrose is in place to fuel Crystal. And that appeals very much to the vanity of men like Greene. *Sir* Alec is Chairman of one of the big six banks of Britain, but he knows that even such eminence does not give him immortality. It does not even justify his past.'

Impressed, she dabbed on. Eventually: 'Isn't it sore at all?'

'No. It doesn't even itch much unless I get too hot. Which is why I wear as few clothes as possible.'

'It looks sore here.' She had reached the top of his natal cleft. 'Very raw.'

'So it repels you.'

'No.'

'Why not?'

'I've seen you without it. You say it comes. Then goes.' She smiled to herself. 'Believe me, I prefer it to the horrid corpulence of most of the men I have to photograph.'

'Really? You can stop now you are reaching places I can reach for myself. And if you are trying to stimulate me in other ways, then I have to say for that sort of thing I hire professionals. Always I like to use professionals.'

She was furious at the implication, put down the tube, found a tissue and wiped her finger. 'In that case you should have got a nurse to do this job for you.' The tension was back.

'Perhaps.' He looked at his watch. 'Dinner. Do I wear black tie or white?'

'A nurse. And a valet.' But at the door she relented. 'Black.'

At dinner Myklades was ebullient. Over the vichyssoise Lady Slaker – a tall, toothy lady, much younger than Lord Slaker, who actually maintained her independence as a physiotherapist with a private and exclusive practice and was out much of the day – asked him how the shoot had been.

'As good as these things ever are. But it is a barbaric way to hunt. Noisy and unnatural. The best way to hunt, Lady Slaker, was shown to us by a red-footed falcon as we came over the heath. Once you have tried falconry you will never want to handle a gun again.'

'And you have?'

'Oh yes. It was the tradition of my ancestors, who owned land near Tbilis, and before that were nomads. My father kept a mews in Egypt. And I now fly hawks when I have the time from Pedro Mendoza's place in Granada – '

Greene boomed: 'Mendoza. Is that the Duke of Pastrana?'

'The same – '

'I believe I met him at – '

But Lady Slaker would have none of that. 'Tell us, Mr Myklades, you must need a most frightful amount of patience to train up a hawk. Do you start at birth?'

'You can. Eyases taken from the nest are certainly more reliable, but they do not hunt as well as passage hawks, as haggards. And that is where the excitement, the pleasure, lie: to train a haggard until she – they are always the females, never the males – waits on in style, is a wonderful experience.'

'Waits on?'

'Keeps her station close above her master without raking on until the quarry is sprung, and then she goes, and there is always that moment . . . will she come back? For a hawk that is trained from the wild, is always wild. She can always come and go as she pleases . . .' He stopped, put down his spoon, and raised his glass to drink, sat back, glanced round the long candle-lit table, pleased that almost everyone there was listening to him with unsimulated interest. His eyes reached Harriet's, and he touched the glass to his lips. 'The first season or two with a new bird are almost painful because of that. But by the third, you can usually feel sure of her.'

'What quarry will such a falcon take?'

'Almost anything these people would choose to shoot, Lady Slaker. From herons to rooks . . .'

He kept it up right through the jugged hare and the water ices, almost to the end of the meal.

21

They left at half past nine the next morning, in the big beige Mercedes, driven by Pablo, the Italian chauffeur. Pablo had had to spend two nights in the local pub – not a pleasant experience. Saturday rowdiness followed by Sunday closing at 10 p.m. had been shocks; and a supper of one warmed-over steak pie filled with glutinous brown muck, a deep insult.

'Really,' Hector commented, 'it is ridiculous of Slaker to maintain such a small establishment, scarcely more than a *pied-à-terre*, so one has to make resorts of this sort. I am not sure where we are going yet, Pablo, so please turn off at the next junction while I make some calls.'

Harriet, beside him, said: 'Still, you got what you wanted.'

'Oh yes. Thanks to you, in part.'

'In part?'

'Well, I took some shares off his hands too. Kapp-Duxbury. Private deal, a put-through, his price.'

'The people who make the Kapp gun? That Rupert worked for?'

'That's right.'

The big car swung across a dual carriageway, past a filling station, and slid into a wide lay-by a hundred yards down a minor road. The view was magnificent. New Forest heath, woods, then the Avon valley shrouded in mist and to the west the Dorset downs. The sea glinted five miles away, yellow through the lilac haze beyond the thick black ribbon of

Christchurch, Bournemouth, Poole. An oil-rig sat on it like a motionless spider suspended between sea and sky.

Myklades pulled out a small memo book. Harriet, at the other end of the long, soft leather seat, the colour of rich butter, with the thick arm pulled down between them, nibbled her little finger then tossed back her hair.

'I'll get out while you make your calls.'

'Certainly not. In fact you can get the first one for me.' He nodded to the handset, set on a raised console above the floor between them. She picked it up, turned it over, dabbed out the sequence he gave her, handed it to him. The conversation that followed was one-sided: whoever was at the other end was obviously reporting – what? Movements on the world markets? He replied monosyllabically and Harriet sensed that he was not pleased with everything he was told.

At last he concluded: 'Patch me in to Rupert Bridge. He's at Skrape.'

There was a moment or two of silence, broken only by the burble and click of electronic gates as connections were re-established across the Racal-Vodafone networks, and the trickling song of a lark outside. Neither lasted for long: with autumn the lark was losing interest in territorial claims, and the latest in mobile communications systems was as quick as it claimed to be.

This time it was Myklades who did most of the talking.

'The news from Amsterdam has been confirmed. San will definitely not deal with us or Scapino in future, will not in fact export to Britain any more. Number one: I want to know why. Number two: depending on the answer to number one, though I doubt it will materially alter my perception of the situation, I want San taken out. I don't think it will be necessary to dump him physically in the Meuse, but I don't see what harm can come of it if Bert passes over to the Dutch police what we know of his operation. Since he has never dealt directly with Scapino, but always through intermediaries, I don't see that he can do us much harm. Which reminds me. One of those intermediaries is at Skrape now, I think. It is this week, is it not, that you are processing the second batch of Designer Living operatives? Right. I think I'll come over and see the man myself.

'Yes. Things went well at Wrykin Heath, though I have to

say I was impressed with neither the appointments nor the facilities. Yes the shooting went quite well. In the morning I bagged more than anyone else on a rough shoot, walking up the game. Are those the right expressions? Absurd. In the afternoon we had a more formal business with beaters and so on and Harriet had to reprimand me for taking my neighbour's quarry . . .' He smiled across at her as he said this, quite impishly she thought. 'Yes. She did very well. She is a true *yarak*. Yes. We got what we wanted. We should be at Skrape in . . . half an hour Pablo tells me.'

He replaced the handset, turned to Harriet. 'I don't know what your plans are. I have to go to Skrape. You know Skrape? You can come with me if you like. Or if you have to get back we'll use that thing to get you a car.'

'They're expecting me at the lab at two to talk them through some tricky printing I have lined up. Will we be in town by then?'

'No.'

'I can put them off. May I?'

She reached for the Vodaphone. 'How do I get an ordinary Telecom subscriber?'

He told her.

Skrape is a Queen Anne house set in gently undulating parkland about ten miles north-west of Southampton and on the northern edge of the New Forest. Coombe Bissett, the nearest village, is a mile away. The third Baron Riversdale built the house in 1710 on an estate given to him by a monarch grateful for the significant part he had played in the Duke of Marlborough's campaigns. Using money from his Irish estates he had raised a regiment of foot which for a short time he led himself, though not actually into battle. Not only did he get the Skrape estate, he was made an earl as well. The present Lord Riversdale, Rupert's elder brother, offers it on short lets to individuals and organisations who require a small conference centre with guaranteed security as well as all the usual facilities.

Myklades made two more calls on the way – international ones presumably since he used first Italian then Spanish, neither of which Harriet could follow – then he turned to her again.

'The man I wish to interview at Skrape is your friend Paul Roget. But it occurs to me I do not wish him to see me, to be able at a later date to identify me. Also he may be frightened of me. He is not likely to tell me the truth as he knows it. He will embroider it to please me, conceal it to avoid angering me. You might do better – he trusts you.'

Harriet felt a sudden surge of fear, but before she could frame any of the questions that stormed through her head, Myklades went on.

'Roget bought cocaine from a Chinese Dutchman called Robert San, and sold it on to a man called Ricardo, at the Scapino Coffee House near Covent Garden. I want to know the full history of his relationship with San, and, most important, what he knows, if anything, of why San will no longer do business with Scapino. All right?'

'I suppose so.'

'I see no reason why not.'

He turned away, and she felt the icy dead coldness that seemed to lie at the root of his being, a coldness she suspected no one would ever be able to thaw, since he would never allow anyone to approach its source. Certainly, at that awful moment, when questions were tumbling through her mind, and panic was melting her bowels, it had become an impenetrable barrier – he had closed the conversation. To ram home the point he snapped on the radio. Radio 3, a Mozart quintet. They slipped through a small red-brick village nestling beneath a down and then followed a long, high grey stone wall for a mile before it was broken by a pair of high gates.

These were hung from posts that were crowned with carved lions holding the Bridge arms. The points on the spikes gleamed – not with the usual gold leaf but with what looked like razor-sharp stainless steel. Clearly they were secure, and there was no one around to open them. One stone in the right-hand gatepost had been replaced with a grill that suggested an intercom. Myklades snapped Mozart into silence and let himself out. As he did, Harriet was conscious of a small movement high up behind one of the stone lions. A grey hooded camera had tracked to keep him in view. He muttered into the intercom, and the gates swung back.

There was a second pair which would not open until the first had been secured: the reason became clear moments later.

The drive was unfenced tarmac and it wound gently through a grassy park, which was shaggy and unkempt since it had not been grazed by cows or deer. Beneath the oily darkness of a substantial evergreen oak a small pride of lions raised their heads as they passed. A touch more stylish than Dobermans or Rotweilers, and probably just as effective as a deterrent. The black-maned male yawned hugely but the two females showed an interest that was more alert. They had two pairs of cubs to feed.

The front of the house was plain: a classically pillared double front door set between tall windows, three on each side, echoed by slightly smaller ones above and then dormer windows in the roof. Large ornamental urns stood at the two corners. Autumn sunlight drew a warm glow out of the mellow brick.

Their feet crunched briefly on gravel; Harriet, still shaking, followed Myklades up the stone steps to the doors, which were opened by a small, compact man, hard-looking like teak, possibly an ex-Gurkha. He was dressed in a black boiler suit that looked like prison uniform, but his belt supported a gun holster on one side and a large brass-mounted curved knife on the other.

Behind him Rupert came forward, hand out to welcome them. Myklades ignored it, said brusquely: 'Is the man Roget available?'

Rupert, a tiny frown creasing his brow, said: 'He's just gone into Dr Lovejoy's lecture. I can get him out.'

Myklades, right elbow on left fist, tapped his teeth with his knuckles.

'No. He shouldn't miss that. And indeed it would be a good idea for Harriet to hear it too. Take her to the lecture theatre, and then come and see me in the library.' He turned his back, strode away.

Rupert took Harriet's elbow, offered her a grin, led her across a high white semicircular hall with two life-sized, full-length portraits of periwigged Bridges and a good chandelier, through the green baize door behind the graceful and cantilevered staircase. A narrow passage took them out into the yard.

'What's wrong with God? He seems huffy.'

'You should not have mentioned Crystal to me. Or at least you should have sealed my lips after you had.'

'Oh Lord. Well, I hardly said a thing.'

She stopped suddenly, in spite of the urgent pressure on her elbow, and looked round her. Cobbles, stables, a few late martins swooped after a few late midges, their white bums bright against a massive black cedar that towered above a low modern building, hexagonal, big tinted windows, drawn hessian curtains.

'Rupe, what is going on here? Why is Roget here? What does he' – she meant Myklades – 'know about me and Roget?'

'Too many questions at once. Answer to your first: what's going on here is a special course for new recruits. Mostly known dealers and importers of cocaine on a small scale, being inducted into the service of, well, Crystal. Good idea you should hear Dr Lovejoy. He's only just got under way. And he's rather reassuring.' Rupert grinned, held open a large glass door for her, led her across noiseless black rubber flooring, through another door, and into a circular room, dark apart from a brightly lit dais on the far side. 'And it would appear,' he whispered, 'that Hector is using the opportunity to complete your induction. Welcome aboard.'

About fifteen people sat scattered in tubular chairs with swinging rests for notebooks attached to the right arms. Rupert found her an empty one at the back, and she slipped into it without interrupting the flow of the speaker on the dais. She looked around for Roget, identified his sleek greying hair and his plump shoulders quite near the front, but then, still quaking, surrendered her attention to the speaker, who was – and one felt the effect had been self-consciously sought for – charismatic. The name – Lovejoy – had struck a chord; the man confirmed it. From a surgery off Harley Street he wrote prescriptions that other doctors are reticent about, but only for the super-rich. He fulfilled other 'medical' needs too, including cosmetic surgery. She had once heard a Marchioness braying across the Green Room at Covent Garden: 'Why go to Rio de Janeiro when you've got Lovejoy on your doorstep?'

He was tall, wore a roll-neck cashmere sweater, Harris tweed jacket, cavalry twills and sound brogues. His hair was silver, waved into rococo patterns like the beading round a Victorian salver, his voice brown honey, and he smiled a lot revealing un-English orthodonty. But his eyes were cold, chips of uncut amethyst, and his hands were strong, broad, with squared-off finger-ends. Firm and precise they could be, even delicate; gentle, never. He had a very slight accent: one part European, one part transatlantic, both parts well polished. Sitting under a spotlight in the otherwise darkened hall, with one ankle across one knee, he spoke for nearly an hour.

As Harriet strove to calm herself down she realised he was telling them about cocaine: how it is a white, crystalline alkaloid derived from the leaf of the coca bush, *Erythroxylon coca*, which grows on the tropical and equatorial Andean highlands of northern South America. How the chewed leaf is nutritious, rich in Vitamin C, how it is a mild, non-habit forming stimulant. It alleviates altitude sickness, tones the digestive tract, promotes good teeth. Early in the nineteenth century it recommended itself for these qualities to the attention of doctors on both sides of the Atlantic. In 1855 a German scientist named Gaedcke isolated the active principle in an alkaloid he called Erythroxyline, from which another German called Niemann derived a purer form in 1860 which he called cocaine. Cocaine is an organic compound, $C_{17}H_{21}NO_4$ – benzoylmethylecgonine, an ester of ecgonine, an amino alcohol base, and benzoic acid. Its white crystals are long and prism-shaped. It is a complex alkaloid, bitter to the taste, carbo-hydrate, no protein or fat.

'The first doctor to take a close look at it,' Dr Lovejoy said, 'was none other than Mr Shrink himself. Dr Sigmund Freud wrote six papers on it between 1884 and 1887. He found it to be a beneficial stimulant, giving a sense of lively euphoria and suspending lassitude. He himself took oral doses in liquid solution and found it lifted depression, steadied the mind, suppressed the appetite and strengthened his hand. For some years he hoped it would cure neurosis, but finally he got round to inventing psychoanalysis instead.'

Dr Lovejoy recrossed his legs, grinned out at them with shiny bonhomie.

'Cocaine now took off in America – this is from the 1880s through to 1906. You could drink it in bars in solutions such as Freud had used, it became the basic and often the only active ingredient in hundreds of patent medicines curing anything from indigestion to chronic catarrh. It was sold freely and openly in such preparations and no form of prescriptions was necessary. Early in this period a certain soft drink firm stole a march on its competitors which has left it to this day the market leader, by spiking its cola extract with coke, and calling it Coca-Cola. In 1903 it took the cocaine out of the drink but left it in the brand name.

'Why did it do this? Well my friends, we have to blame the honoured profession of which I am a member. As you are no doubt aware we have maintained, since we came out of the barber's shop and the herbalist's kitchen, a privileged position in society by a complicated system of restrictive practices, and by generating a mystique around ourselves that would excite the admiration of any Amazonian shaman. Thus we convince ordinary mortals that when they believe themselves to be ill they need a doctor and they need to pay a doctor, and pay him well, before they will feel better. But, ladies and gentlemen, what the frontier-minded, individualistic people of the still young United States had discovered was that, for a tiny fraction of what a doctor and his lackey the pharmacist charged, they could buy a cocaine-based medicine off the shelf which made them feel as well as anything the doctor could offer. Not only that – in a few cases it actually cured the complaint, which the doctors almost never did.

'Naturally my colleagues of the past mounted an extended, powerful campaign against the miracle drug, insisting that it be classified erroneously as a hard narcotic, and they encouraged the myth that cocaine-crazed blacks were raping white women everywhere south of the Mason-Dixon line. The police forces in those areas used this as an excuse to change their .32s for .38s and thereby also put a lot more work in the way of my colleagues. In 1914 the Harrison Narcotic Act drove cocaine underground in the States, and Europe soon followed suit. Patent medicines lost their efficacy, and people deserted the drugstores where they had bought them, returning again to the doctors' surgeries for prescriptions which could only be made up by the pharmacists.

'Friends . . .' – the orthodonty flashed becomingly – 'this may seem jokey to you, but it is the only explanation that historically and medically fits the suppression and criminalising of cocaine.' With one Harris-tweeded elbow on one cavalry-twilled knee, and the hand raised with finger spread, he now tapped off with the index finger of the other hand the points he was making. A large gold seal-ring added to the light display. 'It is not a narcotic. Narcotics induce drowsiness, sleep, coma, death. That is what the word means. Opium and its derivatives are narcotics. Barbiturates are narcotics. Alcohol is a narcotic. Cocaine is not a narcotic. Nor is it addictive. Deprivation for the habitual user does not, in itself, promote a craving that can only be satisfied by the drug itself. Withdrawal does not lead to physically or mentally painful states. All opium derivatives are addictive in this sense. Alcohol can become addictive in this sense if the intake is large and habitual. Cocaine is not addictive in this sense . . .'

'Hey, man!'

It was like an interruption in church. Several people looked round, someone said 'Shush.' Harriet craned to see who had perpetrated the outrage. He was a big black, dressed in a royal-blue jacket shot with silver lurex. The smile on Dr Lovejoy's face dissolved.

'Hey, man. What you say about crack? What you say about free basing? What you been saying about coke don't fit no way with crack and free-basing. Man, I quote to you: crack is the most addictive substance known to man.' The deep voice fluked, ended on a high whine.

Lovejoy's voice sharpened, honey spiked with vinegar. 'Naturally the authorities have been at great pains in recent months to exaggerate or invent dangers related to cocaine. Not even crack is addictive, if we are using that word with any sort of precision . . . I understand too that the crack problem will be raised at a later session.' He flung an arm across his brow to shield his eyes from the light, peered out into the darkness. 'And I must also insist that we have no more interruptions.'

Perhaps because he had been unsettled, Lovejoy now rattled on at a steadier lick. He described how cocaine works – in much the same way, he said, as most clinically approved antidepressants. Stimulated nerve-endings release norepinephrine, which causes the blood pressure to rise. Normally, the nerve endings reabsorb it almost instantly. Cocaine inhibits this reabsorption. Blood pressure and body temperature rise, and the experience known as a high is achieved. This does not last long: the body metabolises cocaine very quickly, and no lasting ill-effects are perceived. It is not, he said, habit-forming, let alone addictive, except in the same way anything which gives pleasure is habit forming. It is not aphrodisiac, nor does it improve sexual performance except as a function of its effect as a mood elevator. Of course, if you are feeling more at ease with the world than usual, more breezily active, you will do better in the sack and enjoy it more. You will also perform better at the piano or on the floor of a City commodity market.

'There are, of course,' he admitted with becoming frankness, 'contraindications: because of its effect on blood pressure it is not suitable for people with cardio-vascular problems. Nor is alcohol. Because like the local anaesthetics to which it is chemically allied it is broken down by the liver, it is not advised for people with diseased livers. But an awful lot of everyday substances are kept from people with diseased livers. Snorting . . . ugly word, *sniffing* sounds a little nicer? Anyway ingestion of crystals through the nasal passages, if practised excessively over a long period of time, will damage the tissue of the nose, especially the nasal septum, that is the membrane that separates your nostrils. It does this because it causes the vessels that secrete mucus to constrict and the protective mucus is thus sloughed. The medicaments we use to ease the systems of the common cold have the same effect. It's not a serious problem, since it is possible to come off cocaine without withdrawal symptoms, and nasal tissue, left to itself, heals rapidly.

'Of course there is a lethal dose. There is a lethal dose to everything. Like everything else it varies from individual to individual. But it's a lot easier and cheaper to produce and take a lethal dose of, say, Paracetamol than it is of cocaine. Certainly asprin has killed more people than cocaine has.

'Right.' He smiled, and spread his hands on either side of his face, in what looked like a valedictory blessing. 'That is just about all there is to say about the physiological aspects of cocaine. Of course, there is much to be said about the psychological and social aspects too. But they are not really my province. I would say this, though. There is no doubt that it can, like alcohol, become a crutch for people who either live under constant and considerable stress, or who suffer from personality deficiencies, a crutch which after a time they would really rather not have to do without. Such people will always find a crutch, and they will always suffer to some extent as a result, especially in a society that is not sympathetic to such problems. In some ways it is a pity that it is occasionally cocaine that such people turn to. It gives it, and us, a bad name. Yet, I have to say this. To everything except their pockets they will do less damage if they stay with cocaine than if they use alcohol in the same way. And, of course, they will kill themselves with heroin or any of its allies, and they will go mad if they use amphetamines or hallucinogens to that level of excess. Yes, all in all, your trade is a clean one, and on medical grounds I cannot condemn it.'

It was clear that applause was in order. Sheepishly they obliged.

22

Lights came on, still not bright, and in a shuffly way the audience got to their feet. They were a mixed bunch, many of them quite elderly and well dressed, almost as many women as men. They avoided each other's eyes, kept away from each other. Harriet guessed: they were all in one way or another traffickers in cocaine, and, in spite of Lovejoy's persuasive lecture, still very nervy about it. Probably gatherings of the persecuted or guilt-ridden are always like this to begin with: support groups for compulsive eaters, for instance, or of the men who are beaten by their wives. The black stood out: more for his size, loud clothes and stridency than for his colour.

Harriet stood in Roget's way, waited for him to recognise her.

'Good Lord, it's Harry!' And he gave her a big, warm hug. 'Don't tell me they've hijacked you too. But of course. They were following us, you know. All through Amsterdam. But it's great to see you.' He looked round, suddenly wary, weighing up the situation. 'Look, there's meant to be coffee and biscuits now. Half an hour. Not my scene at all. Why not come up to my room and have something more sensible?'

'Count me in, feller.' It was the big black.

'Well, no actually, Earl, if you don't mind. Harry here is an old personal friend, and we have a lot to talk about. Another time, okay?'

As they climbed the sweeping stairs in the main house Roget muttered, *sotto voce*: 'Earl is a lovely guy, I mean that. But, you know, you heard him interrupt. And he keeps doing things like that. And these people don't like it. It'll end badly for him, I'm sure of it.'

He took her up two floors to a small room with dormer windows. It had flowered wallpaper, a washstand, a TV and a VTR, a narrow-bed.

'Maid's quarters, eh? Never mind.' He let off his crowing laugh. 'Here's my comfort.' And he opened the little cupboard beneath the washstand, took out a bottle of Gordon's and a litre of Sainsbury's low-calorie tonic. 'I'm afraid we'll have to share the glass. Okay. How come you arrived late? But, my, it is good to see you . . .'

Harriet was overcome by conflicting emotions. She was still in shock from the revelation – almost casually made, she now realised – that Myklades, Rupert, Ambrose, the whole thing, was a front, a laundry, whatever, for cocaine dealing. During Lovejoy's lecture she had begun to put together how she had been recruited, why she had been chosen: they had been watching Roger and had stumbled on her . . . and now, they were, in a sense, asking her to spy on Roget. It was all too much. She reached for the gin and tonic, drank deeply.

'Paul. You won't believe this. But until just before I got into that hall I'd no idea I'd been recruited by a drug syndicate.' She paused, for quite a long time, and the angry emotion that comes when one feels one has been a fool, been made a fool of, produced an angry flush that slowly climbed her neck. 'But I should have guessed. I should have guessed.'

The silence lengthened between them, then he shrugged. 'Yes. I know how you feel.'

'And that's not all.' Roget was an old pal, one of us, one of those we stick together with, even if he was an Israelite. She resorted to a typical tactic of people faced with this situation – a show of utter frankness, however unpalatable. Sitting on the bed, with the glass cradled above her knees, occasionally flicking back her auburn locks, she now admitted that she had been told to find out all he knew about San.

At first he was angry – 'You've been planted on me!' Sudden suspicion – 'Right from the start you were.'

'Come on!' She threw the anger back at him. 'Just remember

you got me into this. Not the other way round. You set it up that I should mule for you. The idea certainly was not mine. Look, I've been straight with you. You can tell me if you want, or not if you want. If you don't they'll find other ways to get to you.'

Suddenly he shuddered, reached for the glass, drank it off and poured another. 'Yes. Certainly they will. Well, okay . . .'

He repeated the story of San and the Malay scimitars, how he had been inveigled into smuggling first cannabis, then cocaine, how it had become a career.

'And why has San dropped out now?'

Roget could only repeat what San had said to him in the Floating Paradise in Rotterdam. San had been told not to sell to people who dealt with Scapino, and that was it. No indication of why, but the implication was that big syndicates were fighting over the UK market.

Roget concluded: 'He told me to get out. That it was all getting too dangerous, too big. I wanted to.' He shrugged. 'If you . . . if that shipment had got through I would have done. But it didn't. We were shopped. By . . . by these people, I suppose.' He shrugged. 'They're very big, you know. It's a huge organisation. Frightening resources. Do you know, they actually had a video on that thing – ' he pointed to the VTR – 'that showed me dealing with Scapino, the two of us in Amsterdam, and Lord knows what else . . . all there to convince me I should stay in step. They're a big bunch, Harry. But I'm sure you know that already.' He finished the second tumbler. 'And we're going to be late for the next lecture . . . Are you coming?'

They were indeed almost late. As they took their places – together this time, and near the front – a small dark man trotted lithely up on to the dais out of the shadows where he had been waiting. He was slim with the middle-aged slimness that says – once, I was fat. He was energetic, enthusiastic, almost manic, but older than he wanted to be. Silver wings of hair folded up from his temples into a darker thatch that might have been a transplant, and when he took off the heavily black-framed, tinted spectacles his eyes were set in deep, purplish-brown sockets that did not look healthy. He was dressed in a black turtle-neck sweater embroidered in scarlet and silver with an abstract design which announced that the industrial process that might mass-produce this garment had not yet been invented. His trousers were crimson velvet cord and his scarlet shoes had silver buckles.

'Right, let's not waste time. Client approached me six months ago. Simple target in view. Expand the UK product market tenfold in twelve months, maintaining current retail price levels. I'm calling IT' – heavy emphasis – 'product, because that's the word lies easiest on an ad-man's lips.'

His hybrid accent was a coarser version of Lovejoy's: there was Vienna in it, and Brooklyn, but cut with something grand in an Anglo-Saxon sort of way, East Coast honk, Oxford drawl.

'So I set up a new outfit tailored for this contract. We called it Good Life Promotions. And the first thing we handle is a mail order firm client has acquired. This operates through and in conjunction with the Designer Living Card, which, as I understand it, is going to provide a lot of the infrastructure through which you will be paid.

'Right. You know what I'm talking about. The Designer Living Card specialises in retailers of objects of distinction and taste, and services too. You want a top decorator to do out your recently acquired cottage in Royal Berkshire – a DLC card will put you at the top of his waiting list and let you pay by instalments. Every month each cardholder gets an updated copy of the Good Life Mail Order Catalogue, which specialises in rare and personalised items, limited editions, luxury objects with a difference. Right. This set-up accesses us straight into the area we need. Analysis of DLC accounts targets a thousand people whose consumer profiles indicate potential product users, so the next thing we had to do is approach these people with a questionnaire. For this we use VALS techniques, Value and Lifestyles Research, the greatest thing to hit the promotional industry since Dr Gallup.'

At this point the speaker snatched up a remote-control unit, and the screen of a large video back-projection unit behind him came alive with sliced cake charts, block charts, conventional graphs.

'First of all we applied VALS techniques to our sample to obtain our psychographic segmentation. This fell out much as we expected. Remember, this is no cross-section we are talking of, the DLC, Good Life Mail Order Accounts have already done a screening job. There are no need-driven consumers in our sample at all . . .'

The ad-man's jargon, Roget's gin and tonic, the mesmerising visuals on the screen, post-shock euphoria – all combined to produce a drowsy, mind-wandering state behind Harriet's suddenly heavy lids. A lot was falling into place, many half-framed doubts and questions were finding answers. Rupert's suppressed excitement at being involved in what appeared to be a fairly normal business venture had not been, she now realised, characteristic. Financiers, however iffy, do not normally have armed minders about them unless they are thought to be likely targets for kidnappers. And it was big, very very big: Ambrose, Designer Living, Mermaid Pleasure, and now his crazy induction course for dealers and pushers . . . this aim to – what had the ad-man said? – to increase cocaine use by a factor of ten, and presumably supply all the new customers through this one organisation. Harriet found her mind was suddenly unable to cope with the noughts that trickled through her head following the simple fact that one gram of uncut cocaine can cost the user one hundred and fifty pounds. That means one kilo is worth one hundred and fifty thousand pounds. One ton one hundred and fifty million pounds . . .

'. . .Our next target was a scale of response to product from negative response minus ten to positive response plus ten, but with reasons. And this we got.' His long white fingers often hovered on either side of his face, like the white wing-tips of a black, frenetic bird. 'On the plus side response singled out that product is clean, natural, cool, fashionable. In the middle, expensive, chic, over the top. On the negative side, dangerous, dirty, illegal, and – and this is inneressing – old hat, unfashionable, and . . . natural. Clearly we had to follow up just how it could be good natural and bad natural, fashionable and old hat. We'll shift through the spectrum from the negative end first.'

She heard again Rupert's sly murmur: Welcome aboard. Well, was she? And what did it mean? Would she have to *do* anything? And if she were not aboard, then what? Go straight to the police, tell all? No, clearly not. At least, not just like that. If *they* felt there was the slightest chance that she even had it in mind they would kill her: Rupert's pistol said that, the Gurkha's kukri, the lions in the park . . . she shuddered. So, not the police, not yet. And, tell the truth, there was no real urge to, no imperative at all . . . A sudden flash of self-knowledge revealed to her that the only motive for going to the police would be fear – fear that the consequences of not doing so would be worse than if she did.

The ad-man, coincidentally, seemed now to be talking precisely about people who felt the same. '. . . The moral angle hardly exists in the group and sub-groups we're talking about. They see nothing wrong in itself with having a toot when they feel like it, and they know it's not much of a hassle to be busted for having a gram or two about the place for personal use. Good lawyer, first offence, and you get off with a suspended, maybe just a fine. No sweat. A lot of inner-directed people, those who live their lives according to inner drives and values rather than those derived and received from others, collect a lot of parking tickets and speeding busts – they're not unused to that scene.

'Unchic phased us until further analysis showed resistance to snorting from the aesthetic angle and a general feeling that the old mirror, razorblade, lines and rolled banknote ritual is more than a touch *passé*, no longer the flavour of the month. We're working on this but could use some help. The trouble is that the nose remains the way in of choice. Sure you can mainline coke in solution but needles are now bad news, but everywhere. Smoking too is bad news in the areas we are talking of, and not just because of cigarettes. These people no longer want to identify or remember the good old days of passing around the turd-like joint with other guys' spit all over it. And certainly not smoked as crack. That reeks of high-rises and council estates, inner-city decay and all that scene. Crack goes with smack and is not indicated. You can drink it like good old Doctor Psycho himself did back in 1885, and you'll get euphoria, enhanced mental ability, but what you don't get is a rush, a high. And at a eighty sovs a gram, stepped on the once only, you want something that has the edge over a large g and t.

'So we're back to the nose, the conk. Trouble is that unless you're an Eskimo whose culture has erogenised the conk, or Nefertiti whose nasal cartilage was a thing of beauty and a joy for ever, people tend to not want to think about their noses and certainly not foreground them in a way that puts them in a high-profile situation. Which is precisely what snorting does.

'We're looking at sniffing or snuffing, like Jeanne Moreau way back in *Touchez-pas au Grisbi* does off the back of her hand. We're looking at snuffboxes, back to Beau Brummell and all that scene, we're looking at ways of giving it an update. Trouble here is again the mechanical angle. For full value you need to get the stuff right up your nose, not trapped in the hairs and the snot but way back into the nasal cavity. Hence the straw. We're looking right now at nasal sprays and they may be the answer. They can be chic, nice things in themselves – Good Life Promotions could flog them to Designer Living cardholders.

'Right. Where was I?' Where, indeed? The video still showed a cartoon of an Eskimo touching up Nefertiti's nose. Fast-forward went too far, rewind took him back to a photo of a very large-nosed person snorting cocaine with his eyes crossed. 'Ah. Here we are.' Double-axis graph with a line swooping into a cross-over and out again and the area in the middle shaded. 'The crucial response area that said chic, expensive, OTT – crucial because it can be pushed either way into a definite negative response, a definite positive response. Well, the secret here is to demystify product without deglamourising. Because what lay behind this response seems to be it's okay for mega-rockstars, it's okay for millionaire brain surgeons and the girl on the cover of *Vogue*, and while ordinary we ain't, we're not in that league.

'So following on from that, what we have to do is to get product into family and neighbourhood situations. At the moment it's the drug of choice in the workplace, and out-of-home leisure situations: the club, the casino, the disco, the yacht and so on. We see this process of shifting the emphasis to the hearth, and especially the yuppie hearth, to be also part of the demystifying process and they can go hand in hand. So, you will find, hopefully, if all goes well, as each of your mini networks comes on line in a particular area, that your local media, the *Evening Echo*, local radio and telly and above all the freebie promotional rag that goes through every letterbox, will carry coke stories carrying the angle we aim to foreground.

'The basic thrust will be on these lines. Quote. There is rising concern in Emmerdale and Brookside that the coke epidemic has reached even our peaceful corner of a green and pleasant land. Reports indicate that the coke is available to all who can pay and who know where to get it. Young professionals and no-so-young seem to be finding it easy to obtain. It's been reported that middle-class mothers are turning to coke for that mid-morning lift once the children are at school and all those consumer durables are churning around doing the housework. And, taken moderately, a local GP says it could do less harm than the half-bottle of sherry many get under their belts between eleven and four. Certainly less fattening. Unquote. That sort of thing. Of course there will always be the pay-off about the dangers, but played down. The general effect should be: everyone else round here is getting their toot, why the hell aren't I? Where's it at?

'We're also getting a hook-up with the most up-market producer of soft porn video films. Now, if you're not into this scene you may not readily believe this, but it's true. They are a very skilful and well-rationalised operation. The ambience aimed for is always one of glamour, adventure, but never way out, never too glossy. And of course they are always upbeat. Along with the bums and the tits and the half-dressed ladies see-sawing on top of the fellers, there's always some relaxed laughs, never anything heavy. Right, a feature of these up-market skinflicks from now is going to be sniffing. Nothing heavy, you understand, but enough to suggest that a good time with coke has an edge over a good time without it. And they'll be hitting your local video libraries just as and when you get your own acts together . . .'

'Finally, friends, and briefly, because I'll have to burn rubber if I'm to stay on schedule' – the black wristband of his sweater pushed back allowed the spot to highlight a chunky Rolex Presidential – 'finally the positive response gleaned from our survey of cross-cultural consumer characteristics. Here, you remember, what we found was the image of coke as clean, cool and . . . natural. Take that last one first because it gives a clue to the positive strategy we are developing. First of all we thought that when folk talked of coke as natural they meant in contrast to synthetics from Qua-aludes to speed and acid, the designer drugs and all that scene. Well, certainly that is there. But what we also found, with in-depth probing and a back-up survey of those who had particularly developed this line of response, was that for them nature stroke good meant unadulterated, additive-free, simple. You see, what we are discovering, and I think we are ahead of the field in this, is that perceptions of the natural are shifting away from fibre and the floating turd towards spring water, simple salads, and *nouvelle cuisine*.

'We kicked this idea around a bit. Someone said how about "better-natured", but that didn't sound right and our big US rivals N. W. Ayer used it for Sunrise Coffee, and finally we came up with "the better side of Nature".

'One thing too was now very much still in the air and that was what should we call product? Or rather, which of the many current names it goes under should we home in on and foreground? Coke – the Real Thing. Tempting. Charlie, the royal as well as the common touch? Lady, Girl? No, we don't want to overplay the aphrodisiacal angle. Chanel? Too esoteric. Star-dust, Mood-dust? No, that's putting it back in the mystified ghetto we're at pains to carve it free from. Nose candy – but we want to play down the nose. Toot. Toot got a lot of support. It feels friendly, relaxed, unproblematical. Having a tooting good time, why don't you? Of course, I don't have to tell you what won. But just watch this . . . and before you say we'll never see it on commerical TV, just let me tell you this. This piece of film will be run with no comment as an interlude on a satellite TV network your organisation has accessed, and already we're piloting it amongst the trailers on home videos. Why not? It's an attractive clip. Above all, it has . . . Yuppie Appeal.'

The screen brightened. Film header with numbers on their sides flashed by. Pearl grey slowly deepened to a deep, pure cerulean blue. A band of lilac deepened across the bottom third and became distant snow-clad mountains. Slowly at first but then accelerating faster and faster these rushed in closer and closer as though the camera was mounted on the nose cone of a supersonic Mirage. Which it might have been. And in the crenellated wall of Alpine peaks a snowfield gradually centred itself and, as the vehicle rushed headlong at it, it filled the screen until there was nothing but pure, unbroken white, and only now, as silence flooded back, did you realise that the last seconds had been filled with the screaming thunder of a jet, crescendoing to the double boom, multiplied by echoing rock faces, of the sound barrier.

Hold on the whiteness, and the silence. Then a tiny red dot on the top right-hand corner detaches itself and begins a slow weaving descent across those immaculate slopes in a perfect ballet of stem christies and parallel turns, pumping out white powder behind, scything up sheets of it on the tighter turns, giving space and perspective to the blank whiteness. And again the rush, the swift filling of the screen with red as he homes in on you and the crescendoing sibilant hiss of his skis until you feel sure he'll smash into you but at the last moment he surges past, the goggles momentarily reflecting the peaks and the blue skies, and the camera swoops around with him through one hundred and eighty degrees to catch him as he flies up to a crest of snow drawn across the picture like the waist and hip of a virgin, and he's gone but he's carried you up into the blue again to hold on a hang-glider, scarlet and gold against the blue, and again the silence of the hiss of the skis but out of the silence the rippling thrum of the trailing edge of the hang-glider's wings trembling in the breeze that also sings in its wires, and, reflected in the pilot's goggles, a last image of the skier, launched into a jump that arrows him like a different sort of bird over an abyss that poses him no threat. And at last a voice, epicene but sexy, with a throb in it too: 'Clean. Cool. Snow. The Better Side of Nature.'

23

Rupert took Harriet back to town in a new yellow Lotus Esprit Turbo HC. It was not, he claimed, the performance car of choice – not at any rate of his choice. 'It's a bugger to get in and out of, as you've just discovered,, and once you're in it, you practically have to lie down in it. The windscreen' – he rapped it with his knuckles – 'is so raked you have to peer through the reflection of the top of the dash.' He flicked back from fourth into third, achieved fifty to seventy-five and back again in the three seconds it took him to get past a huge Mitsui container on the Winchester bypass. 'It's a mover. No doubt of that. But I'd rather have had a second-hand Ferrari for the money.'

'Why didn't you get a Ferrari, then, if that's what you wanted?'

'Sir gave me this. Not my place to argue.'

He seemed preoccupied, worried even, drove aggressively. Harriet broke the lengthening silence. 'Don't you want to know what Roget told me?'

The restricted by-pass became motorway and she felt pressure on her shoulder-blades as he accelerated. Without taking his eyes off the fast lane and the cars hurtling towards them on the other side of the barrier at a collision speed exceeding two hundred miles an hour, he answered: 'We know. You were bugged. Nervy character your Roget. Hector rates him a bit of a risk.'

Harriet felt the chill again. 'What are you asking him to do?'

Rupert attempted to stretch in the leather cocoon, drummed on the small black leather wheel, wriggled his buttocks. 'I hate driving this bugger. You've got no real freedom, it makes you feel like you're just the soft part of the machine. The answer is, not a lot. His value to us is his team of retailers. A good one. Bloomsbury, book-trade, telly people. He'll be asked to receive keys from us, break them up, and pass them on. That's all. And keep that circle of retailers intact. Anyway. How do you feel about it, now that you know all?'

'I'm still in shock, you know? And rather frightened. Well – petrified, actually.'

'No need to be. Apart from the odd toot when you feel like it, you'll never see the stuff – you'll not be asked to do anything specifically illegal. Hector wants you to help in other ways. You'll see. Meanwhile, the security is elaborate and efficient, but even if the unthinkable happened no one would be able to pin anything on you. Honestly, just now security is not a worry except in so far as the cowboys who are running it in for us are a risk. It's as if a tiny importer of tomato paste was being asked to handle the Heinz account. They used to shift ten keys a month, we're asking them to handle a hundred and fifty.'

'Where does it come from?'

'As I understand it, it all starts with a crappy old oil-rig, out in the Caribbean somewhere, now converted to a shrimp-processing factory; it trickles into Genoa, and they try to pass it on a kilo at a time using models as couriers.' His laugh was harsh, sardonic. 'Two thousand keys a year gift-wrapped in condoms and stuffed into popsies. It's not on. It's just not on.'

He gritted his teeth, gunned up the revs, and, hand punching the horn, herded an XJ6 into the middle lane. 'Just not on.'

Seven thousand miles away a long slow swell bent the surface of the ocean, and the downward-facing slope of it caught the dying sun, bounced sheets of shocking pink across the darkness that mirrored the deepening sky. Four pelicans oared their way through the thickening air and above them a planet glowed like a hole punched by a knitting needle in the fabric of the sky.

Danny turned, attention caught by the distant throb of engines heard through the hum of the generators beneath him and the never quite regular slosh of the swell breaking against corroded and limpet-encrusted piers. He pushed his hands down the thighs of his stained and greasy jeans – it was not possible to touch any surface without picking up smears of rust, decaying paint, or oil – and moved along the iron catwalk. Facing west now he could see four small fishing boats chugging towards him. Their masthead lights bobbed above the blackness, a geometry of angled booms and lines flickered across the sun, a red half-plate sinking into the cut-out line of the far horizon.

He watched them for a moment, then turned between heavy sprung doors permanently fastened back unless a falling barometer promised storms or worse, stepped into the large glassed-in area that had once been the oil-rig's control room. Where there had been dials and visual display screens, there were now black holes. Loose wires protruded like antennae of giant insects. A new set of electrics had been screwed into place but from an older technology: Bakelite switches that sparked when thrown; gauges and clocks that would not have looked out of place in the cab of a steam engine; skeins of plastic-covered wires that snaked in and out of junction boxes and disappeared into unneatened holes sliced through steel walls and floors.

Danny threw four switches. Huge pools of light blossomed

on the oily swell below; the throb of the generators rose in pitch and volume and a tiny vibration tingled the soles of his sneaker-shod feet; a klaxon boomed mournfully and briefly.

In rusting, evil-smelling warrens below, four black women tied up their coarse hair with headscarves, pulled on wellingtons, striped aprons and heavy-duty rubber gloves. Two Mexicans, small, compact and tough, and four Guajiro Indians from Colombia, thin, stringily built with muscles and tendons as hard as the thin bones that anchored them, manned the hoists and tackle above the landing stages, pulled hoppers of crushed ice out of giant air-blast freezers.

The first of the boats came alongside. It was small, sixteen metres, with sheer prow and stubby stem. Sturdy but weatherworn, at least twenty years old, two men and a boy were enough to work it: blacks, Mexicans, anyone who could scrape together a deposit and mortgage the catch for half a decade, anyone content to sell off the shrimps for five per cent less than the big boats charged.

It had to be done at night. In the heat of the day the shrimps could turn and spoil, and in daylight too clouds of voracious sea birds would swoop and swirl about them, miring the catch with droppings, threatening to lay open cheeks or hands with bills as vicious as cutlasses.

From each boat a thousand pounds' weight of shrimp was hoisted up into the belly of the rig, where one of the Mexicans weighed and agreed the weight with the boat's master. Each boat then took on twenty tons of crushed ice. Finally the master took his chit up on to the bridge, where Danny entered the catch into a ledger and paid him in US dollar-bills, sealing the transaction with half a tumbler of sweet, oily rum.

The fourth boat had no crew, and no shrimps, and it hung back, its engine idling, a hundred yards off. When the other boats were cleared the big black man behind the wheel brought it in, nudging the jute fenders, and holding it against them with a boathook in one hand while he looped a line round one of the piles with the other.

He wore a short-sleeved shirt on which Disneyesque monkeys chased through gaudy splashes of green, yellow, and red. It was unbuttoned because the buttons would not do up over his massive chest and stomach. Somewhere under the latter the top of a pair of once white shorts had been fastened, it was impossible to tell how – a fold of flesh nine inches thick hid the waistband.

He ducked back into the deckhouse and reappeared carrying six cylindrical airplane bags, white, new, nylon, emblazoned with the logo of the Mexico '86 World Cup, slung by their straps over his shoulders, three on each side. By the time he reached the top his face and chest were sheeted with sweat and he was gasping from the effort of hauling them up flights of iron steps almost as steep as ladders.

Danny took him through a spacious mess-room. The carpets had been taken up, and the furniture apart from banquettes had gone. Their vinyl had been slashed, and flocking basically white but stained with reds and browns pushed through the wounds. When he had too much rum in him they reminded Danny of his one tour on a Norwegian whaler four years before.

Danny was big too, as tall as the black. Both had to stoop beneath the transom that separated the mess from his cabin. In here everything was neat. Danny had worked boats all round the world for ten years, had the tidy habits of a fo'c'sle sailor. It had taken him two days to clear and clean the place out to his satisfaction. All that remained of the slum left by the Guatemalan ladino who had been sole caretaker of the abandoned oil-rig for two years, was a pile of Mexican pornographic magazines stacked in the storage space beneath the narrow bunk. They featured pubescent mestizas and Indians: plump, unformed, with faces whose racial characteristics were utterly unlike the prettiness of similarly aged Western girls. Nevertheless, Danny kept them.

The black, panting like a stranded walrus, swung his bags on to the bunk, where they lay like overfilled bolsters. His big mouth split into a wide grin. Gold and ivory flashed. He took the tumbler of white, ice-cold rum Danny had poured for him, Nicaraguan Flor de Caña, the best, not the oily poison he had given the other three skippers. He sat back in a wooden office chair beneath the open porthole. The chair cracked but took the strain. He wiped his face with the corner of his flamboyant shirt and let out a long noisy sigh.

'Shit, man. I needed that.'

He reached out his huge arm, thick like the trunk on a bull elephant, and took a lime from a bowl on the far side of the table. In his huge fist it glowed like a green walnut. Using a small sharp knife he sliced the fruit in two, sucked one half, squeezed the other into his glass, then topped it up from the bottle.

Danny muttered: 'Be my guest.'

'You bet.' His breathing was almost back to normal. He leant back, the chair creaked again. Spread in front of him his legs glistened like monstrously huge slugs.

Danny spun the dials on a large wall safe and hauled open the heavy door. From the top shelf inside he took a second ledger and a set of electronic scales. He took a polythene pack filled with fine white crystals from one of the bags. Using the thumbs and first fingers of his strong hands he eased open the heat-seal, dabbed with one finger and placed a few tiny grains on the tip of his tongue. It went cold, then numb, and quickly he spat. He took a little more on the edge of a spoon, dropped in into a glass of water, and stirred. The powder disappeared, leaving no sediment or discolouration.

'The best,' said the black. 'Virgin girl.'

Danny shrugged. 'Perhaps.'

Using clear tape he resealed the opening he had made, then put the whole package on the tray of the scales. Exactly one kilo.

There were eight packets in each of the nylon bags, forty-eight kilos, nearly half a hundredweight.

'And that's not all, man.'

'What do you mean?'

'There's twice that still down there in my boat. And I'm not bringing it all up on my own. You gotta help me, see.'

'Jesus. Another hundred kilos!'

'That's right, man. From now on we have to handle three times the amount. Look. It's all here.' From a hip-pocket located somewhere behind his vast rear he pulled out a grey, sweat-stained piece of paper. Danny unfolded it, smoothed it across the table – a telexed instruction asking him to accept one hundred and forty-four kilos of preserving salt from the bearer, instead of the usual forty-eight, and pay him pro rata.

'Shit.'

'You gonna help me, then?'

'I suppose.'

They carried the empty bags down the long steep stairs,

down to where the black's small boat swung against the fenders. The floor of the tiny deckhouse was covered with nearly a hundred more of the white plastic packs. They refilled the nylon bags but made two trips of it, each time carrying only three bags each.

When at last it was all up, Danny went back to the safe and added a thousand dollars to the five he had already put on one side. He swung the door shut and spun the locking wheels. At this point he felt some relief. There was just a chance the black might jump him, try to take both money and cocaine. Danny was tough and big, knew he could handle the black but preferred not to have to. He counted out the fifteen hundred dollars into the oil-seamed greyness of the black's huge palm.

'Make you rich, eh?'

The black shrugged. 'Leaves me shit-scared, man.' His deep voice rumbled on. 'Too much to carry at one time. You know what that's worth?'

'I'd rather not think about it.'

'Me neither. It's temptation. Any those mother-suckers down there know I'm carrying that much, they'll take up piracy.'

Danny watched him cast off. Diesel fumes swirled in the floods and the small boat's nose swung towards him. From the deck house, set forward in front of the mast and booms, the glow of a cigar marked the track of the black's farewell. Danny returned to his bridge, killed the floods. Out of the darkness above, the Caribbean constellations swung closer.

On the deck above the landing stages the largest of the Jamaican women was abusing the Mexican foreman. Behind her, beneath bare unshaded bulbs, the heavy red rubber gloves of her companions flickered over the piles of brown chilled shrimps, scattered weed, fragments of shell, the occasional tiny squid or crab on to the iron floor, spread the shrimps across a slowly moving belt. There was a rich sweet smell of shellfish mixed with hot steam, and somewhere at the back of it all the pungency of ammonia from the freezing plant.

Work went on for most of the night. Using equipment salvaged from a hurricane-stricken processing vessel, the shrimps went under steam jets which cleaned, sterilised and part cooked them, then through a cold air blast. On the other side the other two Jamaican women, together with the Guajiro

Indians, shucked off the loosened shells and stacked the now pink torsos in the freezer trays. These were divided into rectangular sections so the shrimps came out four hours later in solid one-kilo blocks which the women then packed into cartons.

And Danny worked in his cabin, coaxing the kilo bags of white powder into similar cartons, folding and sealing them, packing them into cardboard boxes. To keep the books straight he had to discard filled cartons taken from stock already processed, and in the hipbath in his private head the pile slowly grew and, as they defrosted, glazing fluid seeped out of the corners, staining the bright smiling face of Signor Prezz' Spezz' . . . It was, Danny realised, too much, more than he could handle in the time, more than he would be able to pack away in the freezers below before the crew started again on the next shift. It occurred to him too that by trebling the ratio of cocaine against shrimps, the risk of discovery was probably increasing ninefold. It was all too much. More than the system could handle.

'This is crazy, you know? You are behaving like a mother whose daughter is about to have her first baby. You know what I think? I think anything goes wrong with this it will be your fault. Your fault. Everything is normal. Completely normal. Only you are not normal. Listen. A traffic cop sees you like this – a traffic cop, let alone the criminal bureau or the port police – he'll want to know why. So do us all a favour. Stay indoors, out of the way, until it's over, right?'

Giann' Arnolfini turned away from his older brother and the picture window which framed as fine a man-made view as the Mediterranean can offer. Below them steep hillsides covered with villas, cypresses, gardens dropped away to an indigo bay polka-dotted with tiny sails. A long mole pushed an arm out to embrace it, an arm with a white finger, a lighthouse, Capo Faro. Inside the arm the coast swept on in a huge semicircle, edged with docks, elevators, container hoists, warehouses; tree-lined avenues threaded together the Stazione Marittima, the marinas and the yacht clubs.

Behind the curve of the bay the *carugi* of the medieval quarter climbed the steep hills to the cathedral of San Lorenzo and the palace of the Doges of Genoa. Funiculars linked them to the new commercial quarter where glass skyscrapers punctuated the wide stone-faced boulevards.

Giann', nearly forty, tall, well-built, in a classy grey suit that set off his permanent ski-tan, took a *grissini*-stick from the silver dispenser on the sideboard, snapped it, crushed it, and let the fine crumbs trickle from his clenched fist into an ashtray. In the window Ernesto, ten years older but looking fifteen, fat, pasty-faced lowered the bulky 20 × 50 Zeiss binoculars he was using, pulled out a huge white silk handkerchief and wiped his bloodhound cheeks, his heavy mouth. It was a face recognisable throughout Liguria and Lombardy, a face whose stylised representation beamed with well-fed joviality, with Olympian benevolence, from the signs above a hundred supermarkets, off the packets of a score or more of branded products, the face of Signor Prezz' Spezz', Mr Cut-Price himself. But now it did not smile. Now it was the face of a man haunted by fear. Giann' doubted if even their mother would recognise it.

'She's docked. She's in. The Customs are going on board.' Ernesto's voice was deeper than Giann's, rougher, corroded with nicotine and alcohol. He too turned to the huge sideboard, supposedly Quattrocento, and poured himself mineral water from a Pellegrina bottle. Giann' felt he could smell the fear, moved away in disgust, took his brother's place at the window, picked up the binoculars.

'Okay, then, so where is she?'

'Take the spire of Sant' Agostino. Track straight down to the quays. Move to the left. Fifth boat in.'

All but the superstructures were hidden behind the port buildings. Giann' could just make out the flag hanging limp at the stern, which he knew must be that of Panama, tracked back and could read clearly the intertwined PS on the squat ventilator stack that sat behind the bridge.

'Hey. This you should see. Three carabinieri on the bridge. They're handcuffing the master. Now, they're sealing the hatches . . .' He laughed.

'You're making jokes. Where's your upbringing, Giann'? Some things you don't joke about, you know?'

'Jesus, Ernesto! It's not as if your boats never smuggled in coke before. It's not as if you're not a criminal already, maybe a hundred times over . . .'

Ernesto sighed, heavy hands gripped the table edge, podgy knuckles whitened with the strain. 'Never, Giann', never before more than a dozen kilo or so, tucked away here and there. We could blame the crew, the ship's cook, the cabin-boy, some Lascar idiot couldn't even speak Italiano. But you know on that boat is one quarter of a ton, and in packets with my name on, my picture . . . Once it was a nice little earner, all in the family, we knew everyone, could trust everyone . . .' He scooped up a tiny long-haired terrier which had begun to yap at his ankles. 'See, little Eyck don't like it either.'

The phone bleeped. Ernesto's pallor deepened. He croaked: 'You take it.'

Giann' moved towards the cordless handset on the ormolu-mounted inlaid table by the door. He shrugged as it bleeped again, tried a grin at his brother, but it twisted off his face like a snake.

'Si. Si. Bene. Ciao.' His second attempt at a smile was more successful. 'It's okay. Fine. They've gone, routine check, nothing opened. They start unloading in half an hour.'

With air-brakes exploding and hissing the Fiat articulated truck squeezed round the nineteenth-century brick and stucco posts of Dock Gate Six, thudded spongily over the cobble and rails that separated the quays from the Sottoripa, picked up speed as it found a place in the stream of traffic threading up through the town to the Torino autostrada. A silver Mercedes 380 SEL slipped in behind.

Giann' drove, Ernesto sat behind him, with Eyck asleep on his knees. His lugubrious face peered up at its clownish representation stencilled on the back of the cube container in front of him. Signor Prezz' Spezz'. Mr Cut-Price. Scampi de Qualità. A wet finger writing in the dust had added 'is a fascist bastard who fucks his mother.' They separated in front of the toll gates but fell in behind again as the long curling ribbon of the motorway unwound up into the Ligurian Apennines. Vineyards fought for space with new factories, with truck parks and estates filled with warehousing, and the vineyards lost. The smoke of autumn, burning stubble and vine prunings, softened the bite of diesel fumes and factory emissions, drifted over the roaring torrent of traffic.

The valley narrowed, the motorway became part of an untidy plait woven by an imbecile giant, lapped in and out and around the railway which snaked beneath its own mesh of electric power and the old main road. Giann' gritted his teeth, scowled, and his fingers began to drum on the chamois-gloved wheel as the whoosh of cars zipping by in the fast lane settled into a predictable rhythm.

'This is crazy, you know? What are you afraid of? You gave your instructions. You have the most reliable driver in the pool in that cab. Listen. The Polizia Stradale come by. They see me cruising behind that container. They know me. They know us. Five times they give me speeding tickets this year already. They ask themselves so what's so special about this load Mr Cut-Price himself has to watch it all the way from Genova to Torino. Maybe we should look. Maybe we should check it out . . .' At last Ernesto raised his left hand and motioned him on with a quick backhanded wave much as if he was smashing a weak return at table tennis. Giann' nodded emphatically, looked over his shoulder, and with horn blaring swung out into the first half-gap that appeared.

The truck pounded on, no different from thousands like it spilling over the mountains into the Lombardy Plain, the Po valley, feeding the factories of Milan and Turin with raw materials. With good reason such roads are described as arterial. The land flattened into hot, humid fertile fields, market gardens, orchards; slip roads served small towns each behind its screen of identical poplars. This is not countryside: it is all industry, whether it is maize, pears, or grapes for Asti wine, or whether it is isolated factories and plants belching effluent too noxious for the great cities – like that at Seveso, where Wojtyla's church still refuses women the right to abort foetuses deformed by Dioxin.

The buildings thickened. Acres of square, ochre-painted, tight-shuttered, red-roofed apartments, high-rises with patches of yellow grass where children play and dogs defecate, and, just beyond the motorway's terminal toll-booths, huge low shops specialising in mass-produced furniture and cheap shoes. The highway narrowed, sad acacias heavy with friable pods screened older houses painted in umbers and the red of dried blood, hung with road signs and festooned with wires. An ancient track with modern trams clogged the traffic as the lines switched from the side of the road to the middle and back again. A huge concrete football stadium dominated a suburb. Along its battlements a garrison of spindly metal insects with batteries of floodlights for eyes kept watch.

The best driver from Mr Cut-Price's pool swung the truck off the main road beneath a winking traffic light. Air-brakes exploded and hissed. Five minutes later a second turn threaded him through a narrow gate, and up a ramp into a grid of concrete lanes serving a small estate of warehouses. He pulled into a bay and the facsimile of his employer beamed down at him with benign approval: *Signor Prezz' Spezz' keeps the world's best food fresh for you.*

Two hours later Giann' Arnolfini led a Deputy Sub-Inspector from the municipal health department to locker six. Outside, Ernesto sweated wretchedly in the Mercedes, which was parked in front of a Fiat van with the Turin arms painted on the door. Two young men dressed in leather and denim leant against the folding doors and smoked. Black swifts swirled and mewled down the narrow corridors between the warehouses, chasing the midges that hung in clouds above trapped pools of oily water.

Inside, a brass key released a heavy padlock, a steel beam was swung, the heavy door eased open. Icy air tumbled about their feet. Vapour formed around their knees. Both had clipboards. Giann' identified thirty-six large cardboard boxes that had been set aside from a larger stack.

'These are the spoilt ones,' he said.

The Deputy Sub-Inspector squatted, peered through thick-ish spectacles, checked off the stencilled numbers. He straightened, attempted a twisted grin. 'They smell terrible,' he offered.

Giann' declined to be amused. Using the flat plastic tape that corded them he hoisted the first pair of six-kilo boxes. The Deputy Sub-Inspector helped him and soon all thirty-six were outside. Giann' closed the door, swung the beam into place, refastened the padlock. A slight haze of vapour came off them, drifted into the warmer air.

'If they don't smell enough, you just leave them lying around until they do. Right?' he paused. 'Those really are good scampi, you know that? And they do have to be destroyed?'

'It's checked at the incinerator. I can't get you a certificate saying these boxes have been destroyed unless they actually do turn up there. It's to make sure spoiled food doesn't get to the street markets.'

They moved back into the warm evening sunlight. The two young men in leather and denims tensed but kept their gaze fixed on the corrugated roofs above them. Giann' laughed, caught the fist of the other man in a handshake that drew them together so that their stomachs almost touched. His left hand groped for the other man's pocket, slipped a wad of paper money into it. He slapped him on the shoulder.

The Deputy Sub-Inspector scuttled to the door of his van. 'You'll get a copy of the certificate tomorrow. Maybe the day after. There are procedures . . .'

Giann' banged the door. 'Tomorrow. Right?' He got into the back of the Mercedes, next to his brother, and grinned again.

'Okay. It's done. It's okay.'

Mr Cut-Price let out a long slow sigh, reached for the radiophone, dabbed out numbers. The little dog called Eyck began to yap and he had to hold its tiny mouth shut with his big hand. 'Message for Signor Malatesta,' he murmured. 'Tell him two hundred and sixteen kilos of first-grade scampi have been certified spoiled and are off our books. Right?' He turned back to Giann'. 'This really is crazy, you know that? You tell me now how we shift an amount like that through to London before the next lot is due? And for why? Giann', I'm rich. I don't need this sort of money any more, you know?'

'Don't worry. I have a nice coupla girls lined up tomorrow, already, and after that a very good plan for taking out seventy-five kilos in one go, and after that . . . Something will turn up.'

Nevertheless he bit his nail as he turned away.

24

Bonnie Day was having trouble with the make-up person. 'Listen, weel ya? ah canna take Leichner, aw reet, it's the' best, burr Ah'm allergic, and tomorrer you'll be peeantin' ou' a fearcefu' o' spaw's. It's patherric, they just don' onnerstan plee-an English.'

Studio Two at Super, Turin, reverberated with misunderstandings. The big gym-like room was white, cluttered with lamps on stands, redheads and blondes, reflector boards on magic arms for directing the light, and French flags for cutting it off. From a roll fifteen feet off the ground and thirty feet long a huge sheet of red paper wound down and out, and in the centre of it Jill Jack, pert and dark, dressed in sable and knickers, twisted and turned. Lighting technicians adjusted lamps, snoots and barndoors, changed gels, an assistant squirted Dust-Off at lenses. The photographer, lean, bald, dressed in black cashmere and cords, leant against a wall, tried not to listen to the Client, a thin Englishman in radiant blue suit and buttercup-coloured shantung tie. Around them scuttled dressers, make-up people, hair-stylists, and long racks of clothes which seemed, so often were they shunted, as mobile as the people.

An attention-pulling commotion at the big steel doors, and three leather-clad security men, two armed with light carbines and truncheons, the third with heavy steel cases locked to his wrists, stormed through. Forms were signed, counter-signed, exchanged, chains unlocked and locks unfastened. Treasure blazed on velvet trays filled with gold: coins and medals, hung as pendants, suspended from bracelets, mounted on snakeskin belts with gold clasps. The Client lifted one heavy medallion on a chain from the top tray and dropped it over Jill Jack's head. The photographer slipped in a quick toot, taken from a gunmetal pill-box.

Making the chunky medal swing, Jill Jack jaunted back to the colourama, shrugged the sable off her shoulders, pouted her painted lips. The gold sun winked evilly from just below her collar-bones.

'Corny,' remarked Bonnie Day. She was standing off the colourama, finger on her chin. Tall and slinky in an Armani dress, with a chain of smaller gold coins round her waist, she looked wildly chic apart from her pink-framed granny spectacles.

'I like it, I like it. Sexy, isn't gold sexy? Don't you think gold is sexy?' cried the Client. 'But it's got to look real, authentic. That's the effect we're aiming for.'

'It sair'nly fee's like gol'. Reel wee-ah'y.'

'"Wee-ah'y"? No capisco. What does she mean?'

'Weeah'y. 'Evvy.'

'Okay, let's have the two of them on together.' The photographer, feeling better, motioned Bonnie to the huge swathe of red paper, next to Jill. 'And I don't like that fur. Someone find her a rag that's at least halfway classy. And we'll need makeup on the gold. Damp down the glare . . .'

'But it's got to look REAL,' the Client wailed.

'Someone look after me specs for me. Please?'

'All right, darlings. Now let's try you side by side, and the blonde one, Sunny . . .?'

'Bonnie. It's patherric. Th' hool worrrl' want to ca' me Sunny.'

'Okay, Sunny, you put your arm over your friend's shoulder, that's right, let the fingers drop the medal, not too obvious, yes, yes, si, si bene, bene. I like it. That's great . . . Roberto! Roberto? You call yourself a lighting technician, but it's bouncing off the gold. Santissima Maria! Look. I take a coupla Polaroids, you see this is crazy, quite crazy . . . We have to do something. Okay, break. Take five, take ten, while we worka something out, all right?'

'But it's got to look real, we're marketing them as authentic reproductions, limited edition, numbered, hallmarked eighteen carat. Listen, girls, one thing I wanted to tell you. I want you to meet Giann' Arnolfini, he really knows the scene here and he's invited us out to a late lunch, early supper, and then he's got this heavenly shack like up in the mountains – what do you say? I promised we'd show up, so don't let me down, eh? There's good girls.'

'I've had a brill idea. Why don' we have me with me chin up like this, and Bonnie can hold the medallion unner it, like we did with burrercups when we was kids . . . That way use the reflection.'

'Caption. "And she likes butter too." Or "This won't melt in her mouth." We'll try it. But you are okay for this evening? You'll love Giann', great guy, awash with the stuff, drives a Lamborghini Miura . . .'

'Aw reet. But tell him noo hanky-panky. We're goo' gurr'ls, an' we ee-ahm t' stee-ah tha' wee-ah.'

Two days later the assignment for Good Life Promotions, modelling sets of gold jewellery based on reproductions of Renaissance coins and medals, available only to holders of Designer Living Cards, was over. In their room in the Bristol, Bonnie and Jill had almost finished packing when the Client arrived with four parcels.

Cool light filtered past closed shutters, mingled with a warmer glow from a dull bedside lamp shaded by flower-shaped glass. Outside, the roar of Turin's traffic, blaring horns, clanging trams, shrill whistles from the white-helmeted police, but all, like the light, muted by the shutters.

'We woan' do i'. An' tha's tha'.'

Bonnie Day sat on one side of the large bed, actually two iron-bedsteaded beds pushed together, Jill Jack on the other.

The Client looked down at them, at the four gift-wrapped parcels on the woven, textured counterpane between them. Galeria 90, Torino.

'Why not? They're chocolates. Two of them really are chocolates.'

'An' the other two?'

'Best not to ask. Best if you don't know. Presents you were asked to bring back. Simple as that. Look, he's even had messages put on them. To Divine Rosa with Love from Eco.'

'His name's Giann'. Wee-ah noo tuchin' 'm, and thaa's an en' to i'.'

'What about you, Jill? Giann' was awfully kind to you. You owe him. You really do.'

Jill straightened her back. Both girls were now dressed for

travelling in black woollen dresses, very short, black tights, and their faces were scrubbed, shiny. Jill's was pale too, with heavy shadows round the eyes.

She grinned though, bright blue eyes, startling beneath her black hair, wide with mischief. 'Giann's a pawpet, reet enuff. The wee-ah he drives that car was a reel thrill in itsel'. Brill . . .'

'Fine. So you'll do it. Now get your friend to do it too.'

'Ah dinna see-ah ah would. Wha's innit, enny wee-ah? Toot? It's sair'nly somethin' yon Giann's into.'

The Client chewed his bottom lip, turned away from them. His heel squeaked on the tiled floor. Then he swung back, grasped the iron bedstead and leaned over it. He spoke more quietly now, but with venom.

'Okay. You've had a good run but a short one. You can piss off back to Tyneside and tell your friends all about it. You'll have time for that. What's the unemployment level for school-leavers up there? Girls? Fifty per cent? More? But of course there is the Youth Opportunity Scheme.'

Bonnie flared. 'Wha yer on aboot?'

'This is what I'm on about. You take those two parcels, and you get a grand each. You also stay on the books of Clouds. And I remember you. And that means Good Life Promotions remembers you. And that means work, commissions, travel, loot.'

'An' more wee parcels to carry?'

'Perhaps. But forget that angle just now. Just concentrate your pea-sized brains on what I'm telling you. You are at the bottom of a very competitive profession. You're bloody lucky to have got so far. But you do not go one step further in it unless you carry those parcels.'

'Aw, cum on, wi'ya? Ther's other eahj'ncies. You're no' such a big shot ye can cut us off fro' wurrk. It's a big wurrl', an' there's plen'y more like you innit. We've Tok-ee-o nex' week, an' we' can jus' stay theah or go on to the Wes' Coas'. We don' need yer. Here, hen, pass me me make-up bag and ask the gen'lman to leave, will yer?'

The Client straightened, went to the marble-topped table by the window, opened a document case. 'What's your biggest asset in this game, would you say, Bonnie? Your laid-back charm? Your cool? And feisty Jill? The way she communicates life is fun? Okay. You both have style. But that's no fucking use if you're not lookers too, am I right?'

And he dropped two glossy black and white half-plates on to the counterpane.

'Kerry Gold, remember her?'

The face that looked up at them might once have been beautiful. It was difficult to be sure. Frightened eyes caught in a flash stared out from a lattice of scars, scabs and stitches.

Jill gasped, caught her breath and choked on it so it was almost a sob. Bonnie swore. 'Shit. Yurra wurrm. Yurra a patherric wurrm. Sod y'.'

In the silence, foregrounded by the distant traffic, water dripped from the brass tap in the basin, then the bed twanged as the Client took his weight off the bedstead again. His face was twisted in an ugly but triumphant grin.

'Right. That's settled then. You'll be met at Heathrow. The Clouds car that took you there, the red Scirocco, remember? It'll take you to Scapino, off Covent Garden, and you drop the parcels in the ladies in the basement. Have a coffee or two and leave. The same driver will take you to Orlando Gardens, and the money will be on the back seat. Okay? Be good. Ciao.'

The youth, not long out of school, had red hair, cut short up the sides, almost a shave, to a flat doormat across the top. His hair really was gingery red, not dyed. He wore large, nearly round spectacles with thin gold frames. A long black plastic coat trailed to his black, pointed suede boots above a collarless shirt and dark grey baggy pantaloons with tight ankles. The button-sized muffs on his Walkman were orange. He was carrying a bright green Virgin Megastore plastic carrier out of which a French stick protruded.

A busking conjuror on the forecourt of the church opposite the old market defied the laws of matter and made a chain out of four solidly round chrome hoops. A small child howled as her silvered balloon shaped like Tom in the Tom and Jerry cartoons broke free and soared over the roofs and into the grey sky. The youth watched it until it was a black dot lost in the cellular images reflected from the retinae of his own eyes. The clock set in the entablature above Doric columns struck twelve.

The youth walked down the north side of the Market,

turned a couple of corners, and halted with studied casualness at the window of Scapino. It was framed in a border of purple, green and cerise stripes. Inside he could see purple leatherette banquettes, a lot of chrome, globe lights, ferns, brutal lithographs of rock stars and motorbikes – BMWs and Harley Davidsons. The youth went in.

It was a long narrow room with more tables and chairs than it could comfortably hold. At the back there was a self-service counter with a coffee machine, glass cases offering large sticky cakes, ice-creams, milk-shakes, Pepsi. The till was managed by a plump, pasty-faced adolescent girl, but behind her stood a large, heavily built man with very short black hair and a black roll-neck sweater beneath a grey suit. A jukebox, self-consciously old-fashioned with domed top and rows and rows of buttons, belted Heavy Metal through a modern sound-system.

The youth bought a cappuccino, sat at a table near the stairs to the toilets, took off his Walkman. There was a mirror on the lintel above the stairs and he could see his reflection in it, a ghostly silhouette against the brightness of the street. There were not many other customers – two girls who looked as if they might be models, one blonde with granny specs, the other pert and dark, both dressed in black, and a group of four skins in check shirts and Doc Martens. The youth sipped his coffee, mimicked distaste, carried it back to the counter.

'I've decided I'd rather have a Coke. If all you've got is Pepsi I suppose I'll have to make do with that.'

It was what he had been told to say. The girl took back the coffee, opened a Pepsi bottle, using an opener fastened to the counter with a chain. Behind her the large man in the grey suit went on probing the nails of his left hand with a wooden toothpick. But as the youth sat down again he broke the toothpick between thumb and finger, dropped it in an ashtray and walked down the room, almost up to the youth, but turned, went down the stairs into the basement. For one second their eyes met in the mirror above the stairs, and the youth felt a moment of terror.

He drank half his Pepsi, picked up the bright green Virgin Megastore carrier with the stick of French bread, went down the shabby stairs to the basement. One strip of neon lit a closed bar decorated with fairy lights not lit and plastic vines.

There were green tables with green bentwood chairs upturned on them beneath an imitation Venetian glass light-fitting, also dead. He left his carrier on the counter of the bar, looked around for the gents.

The door was marked with a plastic top-hatted, monocled cut-out head. On the other side, a cracked urinal and two doors. He began to use the urinal, but then – he was frightened – felt a deeper need which, suddenly and with panic, he knew had to be met. He turned and yanked blindly at the nearest door. It resisted, he pulled harder and it flew open sending him backwards against the other door, which also opened as his weight fell against it, and dumped him on a wet floor of cracked tiles. Behind him an ancient toilet bowl. In front a broom cupboard.

He just had time to register the flattish white polythene bags, twenty of them, each the size of a kilo of cooking salt, stacked against the wall of the broom closet, a much larger black bag, tagged, and the dry scuttling of cockroaches shifting away from the sudden noise: then the door to the basement bar burst open again.

The man in the black roll-neck and grey suit stooped, used one ham-sized fist to pick him up by the loose folds of his collarless shirt, and with the other slapped him forehand and backhand across the face. His round glasses slithered away, miraculously unbroken.

The youth screamed: 'All I wanted was a crap, I must have a crap, please, please.' There was no doubting his sincerity.

An hour later he was in a toilet again, but this time on the Inter-City to Oxford. The French stick had lost one of its crusty ends and a tunnel had been hollowed into it. In the tunnel nestled a knotted condom filled with fine white crystals. The red-headed youth sat on the swaying pedestal and struggled with the knot. With nails chewed to the quick this proved difficult and almost he gave up, but then the knot in the smooth, talced latex began to slip. Again he was terrified. He might spill the powder in the swaying train. The consequences were beyond thinking of. But that made what he was doing all the more necessary. It's the way certain minds work at a certain age: they need highs that come not from drugs but recklessness.

Not that the chemical high was not worth having. The youth took two pinches, one in each nostril, sniffed deeply, quickly reknotted the condom. He sat there and two minutes later felt an irresistible urge to sing. He banged the door of the tiny room and the frosted window, as the train roared and rattled on, and sang not music from the tapes of progressive rock he played on his Walkman but the only song whose words he recalled from school: 'The Lay of the Last Minstrel.' Ribald puns on the word 'lay' scuttled back into his mind and he began to giggle helplessly. Then, swaying and shaken with the motion of the train, he masturbated, with his baggy trousers round his ankles and standing so he could see his prick in the mirror above the basin. It was altogether the greatest high he'd ever had from just two tiny sniffs of the stuff. It did not occur to him to wonder why this should be so: if it had he could have doubled the profit he was about to make.

A dinner party had been arranged at 12 Lithgow Street, Oxford. The caterers, an enterprising gay couple who provided a quality dial-a-dinner service, had already delivered a meal, *nouvelle cuisine*, wrapped in tinfoil, which Miranda Payne put in the Zanussi oven to keep warm; Archie Payne had mixed a large jug of his famous special, eighty-proof vodka just flavoured, just tinted with Angostura Bitters, and put it in the freezer; the cleaning lady had done her best with the motley collection of furniture and ornaments.

12 Lithgow Street, once a small red-brick corner shop, had been converted by a post-doc psychometrician and his wife in 1970. They had been into the new ruralism, had put in a cast-iron spiral staircase, and wallpaper much like that later popularised by Laura Ashley but in those days clumsily block-printed by hand. The curtains and rugs had also been made by dedicated amateurs and had, with time, dropped or frayed. In 1986 the psychometrician finally gave up hope of a chair at Oxford and took one at Hume, Christbourne. They left most of the furniture and fittings to the Paynes.

Miranda had not had time to do anything about all this although she and Archie had been there for six months. But they had brought their chrome and black leather furniture with them and had got rid of the cottage chairs and rough-hewn tables. And an aunt of Archie's had left him a huge

Victorian sideboard and some quite good silver and glass. So Miranda felt they were ready for their first major dinner party. She was keen to make a go of it, wanted Archie's clever friends to feel – not impressed by it all, that was the wrong approach – but comfortable with them.

Archie was anxious too. His first six months with Varsity Specials had not been easy. It was a high-powered outfit, a co-operative of post-doc technologists who pooled their resources and their capital and advertised themselves as able to solve any technical problem industry or government might throw at them. The trouble was he knew he was not bright enough for the job, and Miranda did not get on with the other wives.

Dark, intense and almost beautiful she got on well enough with the husbands. Sometimes too well. At an al fresco party in the summer she had been found fucking one of them in a potting shed. Archie had not minded the infidelity, much. Miranda had been a dancer with a contemporary group whose routines were both severely artistic and overtly erotic. But he knew that this was only the most obvious social gaffe she had committed: the wives, who were either top-drawer unreconstructed Sloanes, or scientists as brainy as their husbands, had decided Miranda was not knowable.

So Archie, tall, strongly built, with a boyish mop of curly auburn hair that remained unruly although he had just celebrated his thirtieth birthday, and who spoke with the slight stammer, a hesitation really, that his 'good' public school conferred on most of its alumni, Archie whose grandfather had been a world-class mathematician and whose reputation and money placed Archie in situations he was never quite up to coping with, was anxious to impress. He spent the afternoon polishing the silver salver until it shone ferociously and rolling new ten-pound notes into thin tubes. At six o'clock he crossed Oxford in his Morgan Plus Eight to a squalid set of digs in an Edwardian cottage on the Osney road, and there paid three hundred and seventy-five pounds for five grams of cocaine. He took with him his electronic scales and disconcerted the red-haired youth by insisting on the right amount, right down to the last scruple, the last milligram.

The party started well enough. Only one of the couples had backed out at the last moment and only one of the wives, leaving unattached an engineer from Bradford who looked and sounded like a youthful David Hockney. Over the consommé and with the drinkers already tipsy on Archie's special, which he was able to serve well below sub-zero temperature because it was so strong, the conversation became quite scintillating.

'I adore your spiral staircase,' said one of the wives, striving to be nice to Miranda. She was a plump blonde, Sloane not clever, wore flowered cotton cut low to reveal a lot of creamy bosom and full to mitigate a large behind that had spread on the backs of horses. She was called Rowena, and Archie craved for her.

'Oh, really?' Miranda replied in her harsh, high-pitched voice. 'I can't wait to get rid of it – they're so *vieux jeu* now, aren't they? But I can't think what to put in its place.'

The bright lad from Bradford suggested a lift, a cage big enough to hold two – it would be original, a feature. With a topic they could be clever about the men vied with each other suggesting ways of overcoming the technical and structural problems. The wives discussed styles and finishes.

Undercooked breasts of wild duck garnished with sculpted beetroot and watercress followed the consommé. The men turned to shop: Varsity Specials at that point in time had been asked by the Home Office to develop an aerosol spray that would induce panic but no after-effects in crowds or mobs. They were to look at the possibility of making it ethnically selective, especially efficacious on West Indians and Ulstermen. Archie was almost certain that they were on to a non-starter, but did not like to press the point in case he was proved wrong. 'I-I-I mean, actually,' he said, 'I do know the work has been done on this one, and the state of the art is just not . . .' He escaped by serving the dry white which was the Wine Society's recommendation of the month.

Archie did not trust his own taste in areas where he had not 'done the work:' he belonged to clubs and societies that chose his fiction for him, his drink, which records to buy. One of these clubs, called Leisure for the Discerning, an offshoot of Good Life Promotions, ran a monthly magazine, and it was an article in this about the spread of cocaine abuse that had captured his interest in the stuff. Of course the article had emphasised the dangers and the illegality; nevertheless it had also dwelt on the social cachet as well as the high which, it appeared, often promoted intense sexual activity. Miranda mentioned that they had used it in Carnival Ballet and she rather missed it. A week later she gave him a number she had got from one of the girls in the troupe whom she still occasionally talked to on the phone, and that led to his trip to the seedy digs in Osney.

Of course as he poured out the wine he realised he was now sinking into a desperate funk about the whole thing. Were his guests, people whose social ease and intellectual brilliance overwhelmed him at the best of times, really going to hail him as the new messiah when he brought out snow with the After-Eights? Or was it not far more likely that they would disapprove, be stricken with horror, or just ignore it as yet one more example of poor Archie's incorrigible callowness, of his wife's dreadful vulgarity.

Ignorant of the social dilemma Archie was about to force upon them his guests prattled on. The wholesomeness of the duck prompted one of the wives, a dietician by trade, to ride her hobbyhorse about upward mobility – that it was all down to what you ate. A diet of sliced white bread, orange squashes whose basic component was tartrazine, chips fried in animal fats and so on, made working-class children morose, unbiddable, and moronic. That was why comprehensive schools had not worked, could not work. The Bradford lad laughingly admitted that his mother, although almost working-class, had been a feminist single parent and deeply into wholefood.

The sociobiologist, Rowena's boorish husband, took issue, being a firm believer in the selfish gene as the ultimate determiner of all human behaviour, and others joined in with well-worn arguments drawn from their own disciplines. Miranda closed the discussion with cunningly marbled water-ices and the blunt assertion that, no question, the genes had it. Her mother was deeply gifted though misunderstood and she, Miranda, was every inch her mother's daughter.

Aware of raised pulse and sweating hands, Archie set about trying to create an atmosphere that would be conducive to acceptance. Using the dimmer switches he lowered the lighting, spun the Stockhausen tape off his Bang and Olufsen and replaced it with the Modern Jazz Quartet. Miranda intervened.

'I can't stand that tinkling crap, it makes me go all edgy.'

She turned to the Hockney look-alike. 'Neil, see if you can't find something jollier for us to listen to.'

Not easy when the only records he could find had been chosen by the maestros of the Keyboard Club. He rejected Brendel playing the Prometheus Variations (February's choice) and Lipatti's Chopin waltzes (the introductory offer), settled for Scott Joplin, remarking as he loaded the CD that at least he couldn't scratch the record or ruin the stylus.

The physicist was grateful for the cue and announced, as he had at every opportunity since April, that some of the laser technology that had enabled the Americans to pinpoint their targets in Tripoli so terribly accurately, give or take a residential area or two, had been based on research done by the firm he worked for before he came to Varsity Specials. It was indeed a well-worn track, but three or four of the others allowed their trains of thought to be shunted on to it and each in turn revealed yet again the inside knowledge they just happened to have on the higher technologies that had been brought into play on that occasion. Rowena, who had children as well as horses, looked at her watch, concealed a yawn, and wondered if the au pair had got at the Armagnac.

This galvanised Archie. He had been fantasising that if an orgy developed she would drop into his palms like a plump ripe peach.

'Coffee,' he called, and it sounded like a bugle. 'Coffee, and we do have some liqueurs, and well, y-y-you know . . .' He stammered to a halt.

'Perhaps,' said Miranda, 'our guests would like to disport themselves in the comfier end of the room while I get the doings.'

'Gentlemen, we may smoke,' said the pompous physicist, and proceeded to do so.

'Let me help,' said Neil. 'I'm really quite domesticated, you know.'

Archie pushed chairs round the simulated log fire, arranged occasional tables, dimmed the lights yet more. He was sure they could hear his heart thumping, and he tripped in the unravelling end of a folk-weave rug. He and Miranda had carefully prepared the next moment. It was to be done nonchalantly, without fuss – a hint they had picked up from the article in the Leisure for the Discerning magazine. It would come in just as another tray amongst the coffee, chocs, liqueurs.

'Ya-ta-ta-taa!' bugled Neil from the kitchen door. 'Just look at what the lovely Paynes have set up for us. Charlie! You know, the last time I had Charlie was before my last finals paper six years ago.' And he carried the gleaming tray with its little open salt-cellar and spoon and stainless steel razorblade and its tightly rolled tenners at shoulder height, swung it in an arc so the lights bounced off it. It came to rest on the largest table where the coffee was supposed to go, instead of discreetly to the side on the little gate-leg.

Bright red, head on one side with his unruly lock banging in his eye, huge hands twisting in front of him, Archie loudly stammered: 'And I shall be c-c-counting the sheets before anyone leaves.' Sheets meant ten-pound notes. Rehearsed as a joke, it came out like a threat.

Immediately, without pretending politeness, the physicist and his dietician wife were off. Rowena and the sociobiologist stayed for coffee and mints, but brayed about how the police make a point of harassing Range Rovers.

Archie overdid it, took two snorts, and drank off what was left in his jug of Burke special. He felt very happy blundering about the place and didn't mind about Neil and Miranda. They were in the kitchen. She had one foot up on a chair, with her little black party dress hitched up over her thigh so the gusset of her black tights was exposed. Neil was telling her all about the latest thinking concerning fast-breeder reactors, massaging her through the nylon.

Later – he was not sure how much later – Miranda took off her clothes and did a number remembered from her days with the Carnival Ballet, to a tape of Bach solo violin partita, which meant it was art not porn. Not long after that Archie closed the musical side of the evening by falling heavily into the Bang and Olufsen, causing it terminal damage. When he woke up it was broad daylight and Neil was letting himself out of the front door.

Both Miranda and he had dreadful hangovers, and he was sick. They blamed the nearly raw duck.

In fact the cocaine was more to blame than they realised. Back at Scapino's, Rupert Bridge listened impassively while

Ricardo, still in his black roll-neck and grey suit, stormed up and down the little basement bar, knocking the bentwood chairs over, smacking his forehead, waving an index finger as brutal as a gun muzzle beneath Rupert's nose.

The anger, fury even, was not genuine: it was simulated to cover feelings of shame, inadequacy. Ricardo was in a mess and he knew it, suspected it was partly his fault but wanted Rupert to share the blame. The gist was that there was too much cocaine coming into Scapino's. They could no longer handle the flow, they couldn't shift it quickly enough. It was piling up in all sorts of unlikely places. (He did not actually mention the broom closet.)

'And the cashflow too, it is right out of hand. Look. Just look at this.'

He stormed into the gents, came back with the big black bag, a dustbin liner, that the youth had seen there. With a dramatic gesture he upended it and shook. A cascade of paper, some in bundles, some loose, flowed out over the floor ... fivers, tens, twenties, even some fifties.

'All this waiting to be processed, just lying around.' He flung his arms in the air above his head and the mock-Venetian light fitting rattled and chimed as he hit it. 'And that's not all. We have no space, no time. One day we sell off three bags of lactose, no coke at all in it, and we have some very angry people back, you can believe me, so then we check back and find that yesterday we sent out a kilo of pure, totally unhit, so a lot of people have been having a real ball. Okay. Okay. So, what you going to do? That's what I want to know. What you going to do?'

Rupert thought: Ged rid of you, old son, for starters. Aloud: 'Well, obviously something has to be done. But you must understand this is only a passing phase. Mr Myklades is working on his own distribution network and it is almost in place. I think you'll find it all falls away quite sharply from now on. Meanwhile we'd like you to store spare coke at Lowndes Square, the top flat, for a few days. As for the money, if you'd like to count it, do, and when you have I'll give you a chit for it. Now for God's sake try to pull yourself together. Two, three weeks and we'll have it under control. Right?'

Ricardo swung back, put his big hands on the table, dipped his face so it was scarcely more than a foot away from Rupert's.

'I get it,' he growled. 'I understand. You use us now, while you need us. But soon it will be all over – you'll be through with us. Is that it?'

'Oh, no old chum. You'll stay in place. We need a fall-guy. If things do get just a bit warm we need someone to throw to Mr Plod to keep him quiet. So there'll always be plenty coming through here, even if it's only a small proportion of the whole.'

Their eyes met, cold, hostile. Then Ricardo straightened, grinned, finally forced a laugh. 'Fucking British bastard. I never know when your sort are joking or serious.'

But the truth of the matter was that he knew Rupert was not joking. He also knew Rupert was a killer, and that he, for all his bravado, was not.

Back outside, Rupert glanced up and down the narrow street, registered the receding presence of a policeman and -woman, helmet and chequered hat moving as if on wheels above the heads of the crowd, before folding himself back into the seat of his Lotus.

'Fucking wop cowboy.' He grinned across at Harriet. She was pale – paler than when he had left her ten minutes earlier. 'You all right?'

'Not really.'

'Why not?'

'Suddenly I'm frightened when I see Mr and Mrs Plod go by.'

'No need to be. No need at all.'

'Come on. They must be on to you. Someone, somewhere, is burrowing away at you. And they won't tell you they are. They'll just come out of the blue one day, the hand on the coat-collar and the clang of the cell-door.' She was trying to sound bright, send up what she was saying, but the anxiety was plain.

He patted her knee. 'Don't worry, Harry. We've got it all in hand. We know precisely what the opposition are up to, and I'm organising a little jape right now which is going to leave them with a lot of egg on their faces. Come to think of it, you could lend a hand. Alec Greene. Sir Alec. What would be nice would be if you could engineer an invitation to dinner with him and Lady Greene at their Lowndes Square pad some time next week. Do you think you could manage that? Say you want to take pics of their lovely decor for a colour supplement. You know. Appeal to their vanity.' He turned the ignition, started the engine. 'Get them to ask me along too if you can . . . It'll be a laugh, I promise you.'

Part Four

The Lowndes Square Fiasco

25

Light sources, coloured, moving, flashing, blobbed and threaded through sheets of glass, black with night, streaked with rain. A steady hum intermittently wound itself up to a distant mechanical scream not loud enough to compromise the acoustically adjusted noise: it merged with the background. Mulligan sat back in a high, armless chair and waited while his companion, a tall blond man with a neat moustache, pronounced cheek-bones and prominent front teeth, switched channels on the video terminal in front of him, scanned the data he was receiving. Mulligan looked around at the control centre they were in – the filing cabinets, the communications systems, the chipped corners, the scuffed doors and walls. It was a room used by transients who took no care of it: not even a rubber plant or a girlie calendar had been left to cheer it.

Philip Seton, a Senior Investigation Officer at Heathrow, swung his swivel chair round from the screen, and excitement forced a grin even after twenty years in the service.

'They're on board. SN611 is rolling. ETA one hour away.'

The urge for both of them to check their watches was irresistible.

'And the water containers?'

'In the hold. Checked in at baggage, no sweat. And Rex Tyler is on his way too. He'll be here in twenty minutes.'

'He's meeting us here?'

'Yes.'

'Well, I'll have another Coke.'

Mulligan wound himself up to his feet and loped across to the machine, punched buttons.

Seton grinned after him. 'Difficult, isn't it? I mean when you've got a big one set up and running and there's nothing left to do.'

'Sure. Coffee for you?'

'Please. No sugar.'

Mulligan returned to the table, leaned over it, fiddled with a pack of Marlboro, his lighter. Already he had had one more than the ten a day he allowed himself. 'You've worked with Tyler before?'

'Oh yes.'

'And that works out all right?'

'On the whole. But he's a nervy bastard, takes the job very seriously.'

'Yes?'

Phil Seton gave a short laugh. 'Yes. Silly bugger packed the whole thing in for a couple of years. Got pissed off about Operation Snowstorm – we all did, but you've got to learn to live with it. Joined a security outfit, but when he found that was even more bent than the Met he came back in. So, he's straight, you can say that for him, and thorough, but . . .'

'But?'

'Well, like I said. Over-anxious. And once he's decided some guy's a villain then he goes for it and nothing will make him change his mind. And like all of us, he can be wrong. Or . . .'

'Or?'

Seton cradled the plastic beaker, peered across the room, but his eyes flinched away from Mulligan's.

'He's over-keen to pull down the big one. Takes risks. And then loses not only the big one but the little ones he could have been sure of.'

'And you think he may be doing that now?'

Seton shrugged. 'Could be. Four kilos is not huge. But it's more than a hundred grams in a condom. If we let it run and then lose it, we'll all be in the shit. Not just Customs. Everyone.'

Mulligan nodded, and gave in. His strong fingers flickered over the pack, and the cigarette arrived between his lips with the smoothness of a conjuror's transition. His gold Zippo flared, he breathed out smoke. 'We've been putting this together for some weeks. I think I know him quite well. And I think he's done it properly. Although I've had some of your doubts, now it's running I want it to work.'

'I can guess what you mean.' Seton's uneasy laugh came again. 'Eurac needs friends, and the only way you can win friends is by proving that the philosophy behind your methods works.'

'We're not liked?' Mulligan pushed smoke through his nostrils. 'Why not? Because we interfere, trespass on other people's patches?'

'Not exactly. But because you're allowed to do the things we've always wanted to do but never been allowed to.'

'Running undercover agents, hacking into finance networks?'

'That sort of thing. Yes.'

Mulligan shrugged, frowned, and stubbed out the cigarette. He was angry with himself for having lit it in the first place. Then his head came up, and his actor's mouth widened in a smile, conscious of his role as ambassador for Eurac. 'There are good reasons for what we're doing. We aim to identify the big set-up and then take it out, all of it, from the top down. We're dedicated to that: I don't mean spiritually, I mean dedicated like a purpose-built piece of machinery is dedicated. And because that's the way we're tooled up we get results. Hopefully. It's early days yet. It's only just over six months since we were in place and rolling. Anyway. Here comes Tyler.' His big handsome head nodded at a point beyond Seton's shoulder. He pulled in his legs and got to his feet again.

The first impression one had of Tyler was of energy. He threaded the furniture like a skier on a slalom course, his long black mac swung dangerously near coffee-cups, threatened to sweep piles of paper to the floor. He dropped his narrow-brimmed cheesecutter cap on the table with one hand while the other flashed between the two men in quick, hard hand-shakes. His face was round, moonish, with small glittering eyes and a hard thin mouth, but the body beneath was lean. He looked more like a newsman than a policeman.

'Hi. Mulligan. Seton. Good to see you. No coffee. I'm so bloody high on this thing I need something to calm me down. Let me tell you, Buck' – his head switched briefly to Seton – 'did you know they call him Buck where he comes from? Let me tell you, Buck, this is all coming together beautifully, since we last spoke there's a whole new raft of stuff come in, I can't tell you all, but how's this for starters? On the Milland family. You know this Milland woman has a sister in Plancenoît, south of Brussels? Well, you know how this sister supplements her pension? No? I'll tell you. She's caretaker of a big house, very private, only opened up for a few weeks every year, and it's owned by Tulip. Phil, you need to know about Tulip: well, it's a property company in Brussels owned by Iris, and Iris is tied in to all the things our Mr Big, codename Spiderman, has his fingers in.

'Incidentally' – he swung back to Mulligan – 'I sent an officer down to Companies House just as soon as we knew the name of the company that owns the Lowndes Square property, he pulled the fiche on it, and sure enough the articles were drawn up by the same solicitors who handled the purchase of Scapino six months ago. So that's another tie-in. Right. So what's the state of play at this end, fill me in.'

Seton, the Customs man, leant forward. 'The Millands are on Sabena 611. ETA forty minutes. They've got the coke in solution in – wait for it – four five-litre containers purporting to hold holy water from Lourdes . . .'

'Hey, hey, I like it, the bastards!' Tyler slapped his thigh, put on an Irish accent. 'Jasus, Mary and Joseph, it's another murruc'l!'

Seton smiled. Years ago, as an Assistant Preventive Officer on the baggage bench at Holyhead, he had had the temerity to pull a nun off the early morning Dublin car ferry. Those had been her words when her eight bottles of holy water had turned out to be eight bottles of Gordon's gin.

'We're not sure how they plan to leave the airport, but since Charles Milland has this progressive bone disease and is tied to a wheelchair . . .'

'And that is genuine, that disease,' Tyler interrupted again. 'We had that checked out – not easy, professional codes in the medical profession and all that crap – but we checked it out. Poor bastard needs treatment only available in Sweden and it costs, so maybe that's why he got into this caper . . . Sorry, go on.'

'Anyway he's not going to leap to his feet and run – we reckon probably they'll be met or it will be a taxi. Either way, we have a full surveillance team lined up, parked round the back of Terminal Three all ready to roll. First-class team. Only thing is, they don't have shooters, and I don't want to expose them unnecessarily.'

'I've laid on all that. I said I would. Thing is it's been such a rush putting the act together since we got your telex' – he nodded at Mulligan – 'but all the real priorities are properly in place, I can promise you that. We've got a D11, tactical unit, laid on, boys who really know their stuff. Your lads won't have to go near the place until we're sure it's secure.' He smacked his hands together. 'Hey, I am really wound up, you know? Do you really think we'll bring down Spiderman?'

Mulligan nodded his big head. His eyes glowed, intense, serious. 'I think there's a chance. Even if he's not there, and my sources indicate he could be – his weakness is that he likes to be on the spot, he likes to be sure his people are doing their jobs properly – but even if he's not there we've got him tied in so many ways, he's going to have some pretty tough questions to answer. And at the very least we're going to knock off a sizeable shipment, we're going to knock off some of the people who handle it in bulk, not just the distributors or retailers, but the warehousemen. And that's getting very close indeed to the top.'

Seton gave the slightest of shrugs, registered for the other two men the fact that he doubted still, then looked at his watch. 'Right. Twenty minutes.'

'That all! Must have a leak then. Wise man when he can, fool when he must.' Tyler caught up his hat, swept out into the corridor.

Seton waited until he had gone. 'Tell the truth I do feel jumpy about this.'

'Why?'

'Because it's been put together by you and Tyler. You: the gear coming from Turin via Lourdes, the pick-up by this Milland couple. Tyler: Scapino and the Lowndes Square distribution point, and the connections to this Mr Big he calls Spiderman. Yet if we lose four kilos of gear, I'm the one who carries the can. Normally I wouldn't mind too much. I mean if I had made the decision on an opo I had put together myself, one in which my boys had been directly involved, I'd feel better. I just feel I'm taking a bit too much on trust.'

Mulligan suppressed a twinge of irritation, kept his voice even. 'You've seen all the reports. We've got a lot to go on. It's all pretty solid.'

'Oh yes. It *looks* solid. I just haven't touched any of it. Yet.'

Tyler bounced back in and his coat brushed a tin of paperclips on to the floor. He stooped to pick them up.

Seaton said: 'That's what we'll all be doing if this blows up in our faces. Senior Investigation Officer in Charge of Paperfasteners, Victoria Station. That's what I'll be.'

Again Mulligan pushed back the irritation he felt. 'Rex, what's your plan? Are you staying with us all through?'

'No. I'll see the containers landside, get a look at the Millands, then I'll go on ahead to Lowndes Square, make sure the boys are ready that end, that there's been no hitches.'

'Can't you make radio contact now and check it out?'

'No. We have strict radio silence except in emergency. One of the many things we know about this mob is they have three ex-coppers in tow, bent ones, so they are up to date on all our surveillance techniques and ahead of us in anti-surveillance. Let me tell you: the biggest kick I'm going to get out of this is nailing that particular trio of bastards.'

Mulligan looked at a wall-clock – twenty to eight – sensed the antagonism between his companions. Customs and drug squads . . . but was there more to it than that?

Seton dabbed at a keyboard. Displays tumbled into new patterns. 'SN611 is zoning. It'll be on finals in a couple of minutes, touchdown at 19.44.' His voice throbbed with returning excitement.

They moved to the windows, Seton killed reflections by turning out the light. Through a radiophone he murmured warning and confirmation to four different points. Beyond the streaked glass, pools of light splashed against the darkness in the cargo bays. Tugs, forklift trucks and fuelling tankers lazily circled and serviced the aircraft already there. Runway lights receded in steep perspectives and above them moving lights floated, some steady, some flashing. They counted in a 747 and a DC10.

'Next one,' breathed Seton. 'Here she comes.' And suddenly they could see the long cigar-shape of the white and red 737, its nose tilted for landing, then dropping horizontal to hurtle forward through the serried lights. 'Right, lads, let's see what we've got.'

Corridors, a steel door that clanged, and suddenly Mulligan felt again the sharp coldness of the wet air. Seton took them on to a steel gallery twenty feet or so above concrete beneath a cantilevered canopy. Fifty yards away the torpedo nose of the 737 was just swinging to a standstill, swept with the rain, the white and red plastic paint gleamed in the lights like tight wet skin. The high-pitched scream of its engines rose and then died, but made little difference to the general level of noise, which was high: the rumbling of trucks, shunting of metal trolleys, the whirr and clank of other machinery, and always in the background the roar and scream of approaching and receding aircraft. It made Mulligan realise just how sanitised the indoor areas are from the real business of transport by air – and it was not only the noise the glass and acoustic panelling kept out, but the fumes too: of petrol, diesel, and kerosene unused and volatile, or used and giving off a warm stench.

Only one concertinaed port was used, attached to the rear door just below the point where the tail fin began to rise, but beneath the belly of the aircraft baggage doors sliced open and almost instantly the weird miscellany of luggage that a hundred people or more had found necessary to take with them or had been unable to resist acquiring on their travels dropped on to the waiting trolleys – cardboard boxes, and tanned hide cases, metal containers and canvas bags, a bag of golf-clubs – and four plastic jerry cans.

A man in uniform, with a radio at his cheek, the aerial brushing his peaked cap, turned and raised his thumb. Seton spoke back, snapped down his own aerial, and turned.

'Right. We're in business. come on.'

Tyler slapped his thigh. 'W'hay,' he cried. 'Oh boy, oh boy.'

Almost they ran now, down steep metal stairs, across concrete, in and out of shadows, swerving out of the way of forklifts and tugs pulling short chains of wagons, their coats flapping about their thighs, hats and cases clutched awkwardly to them. Another flight of steps took them up again alongside a wide belt made from jointed metal that was already hoisting the baggage from the tarmac where the handlers heaved it off the trolleys below. Catching his breath at the top, waiting for Tyler to catch up, Mulligan momentarily reflected that they were behaving like kids, whooping and cavorting about the place as if up to some traditional jape like ringing the bells on old people's doors and scampering off. Then he pushed through another steel door behind Seton and found he was in a room that was long, not wide, and not big enough for the action it contained.

It was little more than a corridor of rough concrete walls painted with the inevitable gloss cream. At the end through which they had entered the belt pushed the luggage through a heavy pair of leather or rubberised flaps on to a second belt which carried it the length of the room, a short thirty feet or so before dropping it on to a third belt, this one tilted so the baggage tipped slightly towards the outside edge, and following a flattened semicircular track that brought it through one pair of flaps and took it out through another. Mulligan realised he was on the inside portion of one of the baggage carousels that take the stuff out into the baggage reclaim area that lies between Passport Control and Customs. Handlers stood at the two points where the baggage trundled from one belt to another, but most of it shunted along without their intervention – only occasionally did they have to right a toppled case or move on golf-clubs or whatever that had jammed.

What made the place cramped was the presence of four Customs and Excise officers in uniform, a man with a video camera on his back, a bank of four CCTV monitors, and now Seton, Mulligan and Tyler, who had to squeeze and jostle their way into the centre. They were just ahead of the jerry cans.

'Where are the fucking dogs?' cried Tyler.

'No use,' Seton snapped back. 'They can't smell it in solution. Let the camera in, give him a good look, I want that tape to show those jerry cans in close detail, right?' He had one of them between his knees. Like all the others it was a five-litre container, just a little bigger than a gallon, made out of white, opaque plastic with a moulded handle in the top and a black screw cap. Baggage retrieval tags had been threaded through the handles. Seton noted the numbers, called in the video for a close-up, since they would already be tied on the computer to the Millands' tickets.

The sides were decorated with large glossy decals, part metallised, depicting the Virgin in her grotto, and Bernadette Soubirou on her knees with her sheep around her. *I am the Immaculate Conception*. They stooped over it almost reverently: after all, they were looking at a quarter of a million pounds, a million, may be a million and a half, all together.

Tyler cleared his throat – of phlegm if not emotion.

'What's that round the cap?'

'Black tape.'

'They're sealed then.'

'Easy enough to replace.'

'Come on!'

Mulligan thought: Tyler's right. There could be the very simplest sort of device beneath the tape – a piece of coloured thread exactly positioned, anything that would show that the tape had been lifted if it was not precisely replaced. No doubt an expert could do it accurately but it would take time. Too much time.

Seton's voice fluked up. 'Rex. I want a sample. I want to run the test on it . . .'

'For Christ's sake! You've got them on video. The test? You're talking about undoing one of those caps, and a delay of what? Twenty minutes? The Millands'll walk off if they're kept waiting that long. They'll sure as hell walk off if they see one of the caps has been lifted.'

'From a million?'

'Come on, Phil. They're walking away from ten grand at the most, and ten years' porridge if we nick them. Jesus. I thought we had this all sorted. We're going to let it run, right? Right to the distribution point and pull in the big guys. Now for Christ's sake let it run.'

'I don't like it.' Seton's mouth pulled back exposing his rabbit teeth. 'Look. We've got good grounds for turning them out at the bench, rubbing them down while the tests are done on these, and then running them up the road on a substantive importation charge they can't possibly dodge. They'll grass. People of this sort always do. And on their evidence we'll get a Bankers' Book Evidence Act summons on your Mr Big, and after first January we can lob the Drug Trafficking Offences Act at him too and get to him that way. We've got a million-quid haul, the press will love the Lourdes water bit and an invalid. Everyone's going to be happy, pats on the back all round. But if we let it run . . .'

A spot of colour had appeared on Tyler's forehead, just below the brim of the cheesecutter which he had pushed to the back of his head in exasperation. They were all standing very close to each other, chests almost touching. Anger and anxiety, doubt and frustration beat about their heads like invisible bats. Tyler smashed one heavy fist into the palm of his other hand. 'Balls, Philip. You're talking balls. We'll be going for the board with conspiracy charges at best. They have millions, millions behind them. Look at these, dozens like this have gone through.' He kicked one of the containers. 'I don't have to spell it out. They have the best lawyers, unlimited bail money, and a million or two over for juries. But run it my way and we have them cold, right near the top, on substantive charges, actual possession, the stuff on their property, the sort of evidence juries can't buck, not paper and statements. Christ, we've talked it through a dozen times – why chicken out now?'

'It just doesn't have the right feel.'

'Oh shit.' Tyler took a half-turn away. Behind them the other officers straightened, watched with serious faces, waited.

Mulligan murmured: 'Go on.'

'Oh, I don't know.' Seton pressed his palms into his face, dragged them down to form a prayer beneath his chin, then dropped them. 'It feels . . . scripted.' Tyler banged a fist against the wall. Seton rushed on. 'Look. An invalid. A wheelchair. Holy water from Lourdes. Right. It feels like something written, composed. Fine . . . if it works out. But that guy really is an invalid. And if that turns out to be water, just water – '

A bleep. One of the officers handed a radio to Seton, and he gestured up to the monitors. 'Here they come.'

Grey, underexposed, and seen from above, the wheelchair trundled across the hall through a scattered crowd of travellers funnelled into queues. The man wore a tweed hat and a coat whose tails he clutched about his knees. His face had once been handsome, was now deeply lined, the eyes bright beneath the brim of the hat. The woman who pushed him was tall, thin but well-built, dressed in slacks beneath a short sheepskin jacket. Her hair was grey, conventionally permed.

The smile Mrs Milland gave the immigration officer, over whose shoulder they were looking, was shy, a touch nervous, but no more so than the smile most people offer when they encounter anonymous officialdom. Although there was no sound Mulligan felt he could hear the flip of stiff paper as the officer, a woman, riffled through the pages. The smile again, and another camera picked them up, distanced them as they entered the angled corridor which would take them into the baggage reclaim area. A buzz, and a light flashed above the monitors.

'Action "O",' Seton murmured. 'Discreet point-out to Customs. She did it right for once. Some of them might just as well blow a whistle for all the discretion they're capable of.'

A third camera watched the wheelchair glide into view again. The woman put on the brake, a yard or so behind the carousel, squeezed her way into position amongst the other travellers.

Tyler spoke through clenched teeth. 'So. There they are and wondering why the fuck their coke hasn't come through.' He looked at his watch. 'I'll give her three minutes. Then ten will get you thirty she buggers off just as fast as she can push that chair out of there.'

Seton sighed, stooped, picked up the nearest container and swung it back on to the belt.

'Right. Let it roll. Let it travel up the chain. But I just hope we're doing the right thing.'

The belt tightened, the baggage on it jolted, and then slipped forward. Seton and Mulligan put the three remaining containers on, amongst the rest. Tyler beamed, pulled the brim of his cap back over his eyes and slapped Seton's arm. 'That's my boy then. Right. I'll be away. See you at Lowndes Square, right?' and he threw a mock punch at Mulligan's chin.

26

Cromwell Road: plane trees shedding silver rain through orange light, tall hotels behind stuccoed porticoes, and a chain of linked traffic lights, all red. Mulligan on the middle bench of a Volvo Estate, twisted uneasily, wrinkled his nose against the smell of wet cloth drying on human bodies, looked over Seton's shoulder. The Customs man's eyes flicked over a small screen on which green lines and blobs weaved and shifted to plot the movements of the target car and the lead car of his team, a silver-grey Honda. The target car was a big Ford Executive driven by a black chauffeur smartly uniformed in pale grey.

There had been some awkwardness in the Customs Hall at Heathrow. Mrs Milland had not been able to manage two nylon zip-up airline bags, four water containers and her chair-bound husband. In the end she had pushed her husband and the bags through the Nothing to Declare channel and had then sought permission to go back for the containers, which she put on a wire trolley. 'Stupid, I know,' she said, 'just water when all's said and done, but it means a lot to the poor souls of the St Luke's Hospice for Incurables.' Her accent was almost too good: Kensington royal articulated with a precise perfection native speakers rarely achieve.

The Executive, protected by Disabled Person stickers, was parked on the no-waiting set-down area outside the terminal. The black chauffeur, a tubby short man with pockmarked cheeks, helped Mr Milland out of the chair and into the back of the large car. He put the bags on the front seat, folded the chair and put it in the boot with the water containers. Mrs Milland watched all this, and then got in the back with her husband. They drove off, and the caravan fell in behind them, six mobiles in all.

Four of them took turns in the 'eyeball' position; the Volvo control with Seton, Mulligan, and two more officers as well as a driver remained two cars behind the Executive; the sixth remained out of sight on a parallel course, a street or so away.

At the Hogarth Roundabout their link with CEDRIC, the Customs computer, told them that the target car was owned by Mansion Car Rentals, a City firm with an EC address.

Now, as they slipped past the floodlit extravaganza of polychrome brick and terracotta moulding that makes a cathedral to knowledge of the Natural History Museum, Seton suddenly swore. 'Fuck Tyler. Fuck him for the stupid bastard he is.'

Mulligan leaned forward. 'Why?'

'Because this stinks. It's getting worse and worse. Either between you you've cocked this up and there's no gear around at all or . . .'

'Or what?'

'Oh, the alternative is just too crazy and awful to think about. Either way, we're on a hiding to nothing.'

'There's been no cock-up. Yet. The coke's there all right. It must be.'

'We should have checked. And turned them out then.'

A bleep, then a voice. 'Right, right, right.'

'Where's he going now?'

'He's dropping into South Ken.'

'Why, for Christ's sake? That's not the way to Lowndes Square.'

One of the officers in the back seat behind Mulligan murmured: 'But it's right for Fennimore Gardens, where the Millands have their flat.'

'Christ, you're right.' Seton unclipped the mike with its spiral lead from the console and broke what so far had been radio silence all the way from Heathrow. 'Bravo one . . . Control. Receive. Target likely to pull in. Observe procedure if he does. Bravo four . . . Control. Receive. Proceed to grid ref 85–42, 36–28 ahead of Target. I want an exact record of who and what goes into premises. Right. Everyone clear? Driver. Drive past 83 then put us round the corner at the east end out of sight. Shit. You know, if there's any more upsets we're going to run out of mobiles.'

Mulligan said: 'Tyler must have at least one spare up at Lowndes Square.'

'No. We'll manage.'

Mulligan guessed what was in Seton's mind. If there was a cock-up, the Customs man would not want Tyler bleating that he had lost a mobile just before he needed it.

With the Honda in front they slipped round two corners into a quiet crescent with a thin patch of fenced-off garden running down the middle. The brake lights on the back of the Honda glowed briefly, then it pulled over to the right, passed the Executive, already parked against the kerb.

'Where's that fucking Rover?'

'On the other side, sir. He arrived just as we made the turn.'

'Can he see what's happening?'

'Very well placed. The trees give him cover.'

They passed the Executive and accelerated away to avoid giving any impression that they were interested in it, but Mulligan snatched a brief glimpse of Mrs Milland standing on the kerb under an umbrella. The chauffeur was helping her husband out. The boot was still shut.

Round the corner they pulled in behind the Honda.

'Bravo four . . . control. Commentary please.'

'Control . . . Bravo four. Ten-four. All parties have now entered premises. Chauffeur helping the elderly gentleman, the lady behind carrying one cloth-type bag. Chauffeur has returned. Has opened the boot . . .'

Seton breathed: 'If he takes out the containers I'm going in.'

'. . . he's carrying in the wheelchair. He has closed the lid of the boot. The lady has come back out and has collected the second bag. The chauffeur is now back out too, the lady is talking to him, she has given him something, money I suppose . . .'

'Bravo two . . . Control. State ten-two.'

'Control . . . Bravo two. My ten-two is eighty-five, forty-five; thirty-six, twenty-eight.'

Seton covered the mouthpiece. 'Right. All mobiles . . . Control. Receive. Bravo two listen to Bravo three, when he tells you come into the Gardens and take over Eyeball. Bravo one, stand by to fall in as back-up. Bravo two, talk Bravo three through then stay and maintain surveillance on the flat, following anyone who leaves. Call up support from the Chelsea nick if that happens, but somehow I think they'll stay put. Here he comes. Easy, everybody. Easy, please. We look like a fucking cortège – use your skills, for Christ's sake. Bravo three . . . Control. Receive. Did anything leave Target apart from the two passengers, the bags and the wheelchair?'

'That's all, Chief.'

Seton sat back, let out a long slow sigh. For a moment it almost seemed that he was allowing the sweeping wipers to mesmerise him into sleep. Then he sat up again. 'Well. It seems we're still in business, and back on course for Lowndes Square?'

The driver answered: 'That's right, sir. Turning into Brompton Road, I caught a glimpse of Target level with Harrods.'

'Back on course, so we follow agreed procedure. Head for Motcomb Street, where Tyler should be waiting for us.'

Less than five minutes later they turned into the narrow side street which used to be a linking lane between the long rectangular square and the service mews behind. The Volvo pulled in behind Tyler's red Sierra, which in turn was parked behind a big black police van with caged windows.

Tyler, cheesecutter pulled down over his eyes, coat swinging, strode down from the corner on Lowndes Square, pushing down the aerial of his handset as he came. He ducked into the Volvo next to Mulligan and pulled himself forward, using the back of the front seat so his mouth was by Seton's ear.

'Okay, boyo, how's it going? I tell you this end could not be more perfect. Ricardo Carracci arrived an hour ago with three hoods from Scapino. But better still Rupert Bridge and that Harriet Jones are there too. Now, they are so close to Spiderman, I really do believe we'll get him.'

'Target dropped the Millands at Fennimore Gardens, but he's still got the containers in the boot. He should be here by now.'

'Right. My OP can talk us through.' He fiddled with his handset, used call-up codes, but got nothing back but screaming white noise with a human burble at the back of it. 'Shit.' Without asking he reached over the seat back, dabbed buttons on the console, turned a knob.

Mulligan checked. 'OP – Observation Post?'

'Static Observation Post. OP . . . Control. Receive. Commentary please.'

The voice they heard was soft, had a Welsh lilt. 'Ford Exec, black, reg number B230OPR, has just parked outside target house. Chauffeur, grey uniform, Afro, opens boot. Takes out two plastic water containers, gallon size. Closes boot, takes them up steps. Rings bell. Can't see which. Speaks on intercom. Door opens. He's gone.'

Seton: 'How many bells?'

Tyler: 'Five.'

'Chauffeur back again. He's reopened the boot. Takes two more containers. Closes boot. He's left the door open. Goes straight in . . . back out again, almost straight away this time, straight into car, he's off, heading north up towards Park Tower Hotel, signalling left, he's turned, gone. Yes. Gone down the ramp into the private carpark. He must have a pass – can't get in without one . . .'

Seton yelled: 'God damn it all!'

Tyler: 'Hey, what's the matter?'

'For Christ's sake get someone in there now, quick, into that carpark, before . . . Oh Jesus!' Seton slapped his forehead with his gloved hand. He snatched the microphone, dabbed the buttons, went wrong, had to try again. 'Bravo two, leave the crap out and listen. Tango has just entered private underground carpark with access to Park Tower Hotel. Get in there after him and turn him out. NOW!'

'Will do, Chief.'

Tyler was livid with anger. 'Seton, you've fucking flipped! You heard my man. The gear's in the house, the chauffeur handed it in.'

'I hope you're right. For all our sakes, I hope that's right.'

'Of course it bloody is.' But there was a note of doubt in Tyler's hoarse voice. 'Will you let me retune to my OP?'

'Not until my boys report from the carpark.'

Tyler slammed his backside into the back of the seat, reached forward again, but this time for the door catch, thought better of it, slumped, groped in his pockets. He came up with a pack of Embassy, and his Ronson rasped behind a cupped hand, throwing chiaroscuro light across his tired face, making his small dark eyes glint behind puffy lids. The sudden rasp of Virginian on the wet musty air made the back of Mulligan's throat burn. He took out his own pack, lit the thirteenth of the day, cleared his throat of the sudden rise of tarry phlegm and asked: 'This Bridge and the girl . . . Who are they?'

'The Hon. Rupert Bridge has been part of Spiderman's entourage for the last three months, almost since we first began to get an inkling that he was into coke. He's a smart arse, smart background, county and city-slicker. The girl is a sort of cousin of his. Photographer. We reckon she joined the board a month or so ago. What's interesting is that a month or so before that Customs at Dover turned her out, and lost her. She pulled a double shuffle on them and got away with it. Here we go.'

The radio had bleeped.

'Bravo two here, Chief. No luck in the carpark. The barrier is unmanned and you need plastic to operate it. I sent in Jimmy on foot, and it's taken him till now to locate Target. He's just radioed back to me that it's empty and locked. Instructions, please.'

'Maintain surveillance on Target and follow if he comes out again – one of you will have to stay in the carpark. I'll send in support, but if that chauffeur comes back and tries to get anything from the boot you turn him out straight away.' He snapped off the microphone, turned his head. 'In you go, Jones.' One of the two officers behind Mulligan climbed out through the tailgate. They could see him turning up his collar against the rain, pulling his hat down as he turned into the square.

Rain drummed on the roof. Seton rubbed the balls of his hands into his eye sockets, pressed a button; his window sank, rain gusted in; he wound it up again. 'Tyler, before you smoke in a mobile of mine, fucking ask me first. What do we do now?'

Tyler looked at his watch. 'Give my men four minutes to seal the area, and the villains time to look at the gear, handle it, then in we go.'

'Kick the doors down.'

Tyler was brusque. 'That's right.' He felt for a handle to operate his window; there wasn't one, so he opened the rear door and tossed out his cigarette. Mulligan sought an ashtray, couldn't find one, tried pinching his out between finger and thumb, created a tiny firework display. Tyler went on: 'I take your point. There could have been a switch. He could have had duplicate containers in the boot, and he's handed in those, and the ones with the gear are now lost in the hotel. It's possible. But we've come this far. We have to go through with it now. If we don't we're in the shit. At least, I am. The OP is a penthouse across the square and it's costing us a ton a day. If the DAC doesn't see a return for that I'm on the carpet anyway. And Carracci is in there, and his boys. We have to move. We have to.'

Seton sighed again. More rain on the roof. Then: 'Okay. Send them in.'

The watch again. 'Three minutes.'

'Well, why not fill in the time by telling us about the target house.'

Tyler sighed. 'Top-floor maisonette. Access by stairs, lift, and fire escape at back – we'll be using all three. Two reception rooms, two bedrooms in the roof, kitchen, bathroom. Present occupants Carracci, two Italian waiters from Scapino and a third who we think is a Colombian illegal. Bridge and Jones. Carracci is the leaseholder from Citeecon Properties, which is owned by Mr Hector Myklades, alias Spiderman.'

'And the rest?'

'Irrelevant, but I'll tell you. Two middle floors, large

maisonette leased to Sir Alec Greene, tonight hosting a dinner party which I hope we won't disturb too much – he's a very big noise in the City, Chairman of the City and Wessex Bank. Ground floor split into three offices: a firm called Montebello Consultants, something to do with promotion and the media, I believe, the editorial office of a local free sheet called *THAT* magazine, and the registered office of an RC charity that gives spiritual support to wealthy incurables in the area. Vicars with AIDS, that sort of thing. All three locked up and empty as of now. Your three minutes are up. In we go.' He reached forward, picked up the mike. 'Delta One One, Delta One One, you have clearance. Go.'

The back doors of the big black van swung open and spewed men, much the way the Trojan horse must have done. Mulligan counted ten out – all dressed in dark or black clothing heavily padded on the torso and chest, and all clutching weapons across their chests: Kapp machine-pistols they looked like, and Browning 9mm automatics. Black balaclavas masked their faces. They were lithe, catlike, in the way they came over the rear fender and dropped to the ground, and totally certain in the way they divided and melted away into the rainy blackness. A casual passer-by would hardly have had time to take them in, might easily have been persuaded that the momentary apparition was a hallucination bred from inner-city paranoia. But no one saw them go: blocks had covered all entrances to the square for four minutes and it was now deserted.

Tyler swung his legs out, straightened, ducked his head back in. 'Four more to make the place secure, then we go in and arrest as planned. Right?' They saw him cross the road, skipping up on the the pavement with his coat flapping about him, then he was gone.

Mulligan waited a moment, then asked: 'As planned?'

'We take them down the Lane and do them for substantive importation, and conspiracy to do same. Then they're lodged in the cells at Holborn nick. Tyler notifies the beak in the morning that he'll be hanging in with possession with intent to distribute as well, and we oppose bail.'

'The Lane being . . . ?'

'Customs and Excise Investigation HQ, New Fetter Lane. But I'm pretty sure it's not going to work out like that.'

'Why? Why are you so sure?'

'I'm not going to bad-mouth Tyler's op, but you have a close look at the name of that charity on the ground floor as we go in.'

Mulligan did so. Sheltered by a stuccoed porch supported on Corinthian capitals the brass plate gleamed: *St Luke's Hospice for Incurables*. His heart sank. He was beginning to understand what Seton feared, and beginning to believe he might be right. Inside the hall a staircase swept down from above with some grandeur, half circling a lift cage. An officer of D11, the special tactical unit, saluted briskly by slapping the magazine of the Kapp machine-pistol which he held across his chest. The balaclava had gone, and apart from the gun much of the menace and mystery. He was tall, tough, but dressed in an ordinary Guernsey with a bullet-proof raid jacket, sleeveless and quilted. His trousers and boots looked very normal: just a copper after all.

'The lift is working, sir.'

Mulligan just had time to take in the three solid doors with ormolu fittings, before Seton clashed the lift gates behind them. Seton pressed the button for the top maisonette, but as they passed the first landing they saw through the cage a small group standing outside an open door, Tyler amongst them, heard voices raised in anger. Seton pressed the lower button and down they went again.

They emerged from the lift on to a thickly carpeted landing, hung with gilt-framed oil paintings and furnished with an occasional table. A very large man, who would have been imposing if he had not also been fat, dominated the scene. He was dressed in a dinner jacket with watered-silk reveres and a low-cut waistcoat across which was strung a very fine gold chain. He had corrugated white hair, receding, a very red face that shone with the charisma of good living, thick lips that shook. His voice was deep and bell-like, but the bronze cracked.

'There is, Mr Taylor, no aspect of this dismal affair which I intend to overlook. My solicitor will make that abundantly clear to your superiors in the morning. Meanwhile unless you can produce an enabling document that might entitle you to question my guests, I shall have no option but to call the

Assistant Commissioner and request him to send over someone with the authority to have you removed.'

Tyler, well aware that the mistake with his name was insultingly intentional, stood his ground. His black coat still glistened with the rain, his hat was again pushed back from his broad high forehead and the anger spot glowed. Beneath it his face was pale, tired. The energy and excitement that had animated it throughout the evening had drained away. He spoke reasonably, but with an edge to his voice that showed he was not yet ready to give in.

'Sir Alec, I am investigating a very serious crime. I have a warrant to enter and search the premises above these. As I have tried to explain to you two of the persons I expected to find in those premises and interview, having good reason to believe they would be able to help me with my enquiries, are in fact not upstairs where I expected them to be, but in your company. Furthermore, this building has been under surveillance and certain articles were seen to be delivered here fifteen minutes ago. Since these are not to be found on the premises above yours, and since these persons who you say are your guests – '

'God damn you, sir, this is the very grossest impertinence . . .'

But Mulligan's attention had gone, first, but only momentarily, to the younger man who stood slightly behind and to the side of the banker. He was tall, had the upright bearing of a soldier, but his black hair rested on the collar of his dinner jacket and his lips were twisted into a grin that was sardonic and malicious. He had a small scar on one cheek. Then, and it seemed for the time being irreversibly, his gaze shifted to the girl, woman, who completed the trio apparently ranged against Tyler.

She was tall, but not exceptionally so. Her hair, which was swept back in a full but stylish cut, was basically chestnut but tinted with red gold. She was sheathed in deep-blue silk, cut high to enhance an ivory neck that was circled with a string of fine small pearls. And she smiled. The corners of a full but not large mouth were very slightly lifted, and her large green eyes flecked with gold were clearly amused and somehow involved, but out of curiosity, Olympian curiosity, rather than out of concern. For a moment they met Mulligan's and narrowed very slightly, as if with a deeper interest than before, and the smile broadened momentarily before they flitted away, back to Sir Alec and the wretched Tyler.

Into Mulligan's mind a thread of verse was spun, a memory of a poem he had come across as an adolescent in St Louis, and which he had always retained because it made out of the quotidian ordinariness of his environment an image of discovery and desire: *O my America! my new-found-land.*

Tyler's voice, very angry now, brought him back to reality, or a lower plane of it. 'Nevertheless, the articles were seen to be brought into this building, and since they are not in the residence where we expected to find them, I am going to go through the rest of the building until I find them.'

'Kicking down doors, I suppose.'

'If doors are not opened as requested my men will have no option but to kick them down.'

Quietly Seton intervened. 'Rex, I should, if I were you, start with the offices of the St Luke Hospice for Incurables on the ground floor. That's where you'll find the containers.'

He was right. There was no one there so they did have to kick the doors down. Actually they used fire-axes and a huge cast-iron mallet. The doors were well-made, securely locked, and a lot of old oak had to be noisily splintered before they got in. The containers were there, in a tiny vestibule, unopened, and apparently exactly the same as the ones they had examined, alas too briefly, at Heathrow. Tests later confirmed Seton's suspicions. They were filled with spring water, pure, uncontaminated.

27

'We were well had over. It was deliberate. We were set up. And stroked.' Tyler's voice sounded hoarse, tired.

'I guess you're right.' Mulligan's deep drawl was solicitous, sympathetic. He let sugar slip on to the frothy roof of his cappuccino, stirred it in. His eyes, solemn as if he were supporting a friend at the funeral of a loved one, held Tyler's.

'I'm right. Here. Before I forget.' Tyler unzipped his document wallet, pushed an A4 card folder on to the table. It was unmarked. 'The file you asked for. And it wasn't easy to get. That's how bad it's been.' He squared his elbows, cut a slice off the Danish pastry in front of him. Behind his back, seen through plate glass, the traffic in Leicester Square thickened and congealed as last shoppers and first commuters filtered through.

'Many thanks. But why was it so difficult to get?' Mulligan lifted the cover, saw three sheets of computer printout, well-filled, closed it again. 'Because of this business?'

'Too right. It's off the PNC. Police National Computer. Access level fifteen which is just where I used to be. Not any more. Back to level ten for Joe Muggins. Source of much mirth on Floor Five, I can tell you, but I still have friends and one of them pulled this for me. I would have had to ask him anyway, even if my level had not been dropped.'

'Why is that?'

'Because every access to the PNC is logged. And the DAC has warned me off Spiderman and anything to do with him, so accessing this for you would have dropped me back in it, just as I was heaving myself clear. Anyway, the nub of the problem is we were stroked.'

'But looked at one way it has its pleasing side.'

'It proves we're right.' Tyler's fork prodded the air between them. 'On the right lines. Fair enough. And it also proves these bastards have a lot of leverage, and some of it a sight too close to home for comfort.'

'Someone inside. Someone on Floor Five?'

'It has to be. And it has to be someone near the top.'

'You'll have to explain.'

'In a way I just did. All the time we were setting this up I was using the PNC. That is, I was using it to access data and I was feeding it everything I got, from you and elsewhere, and every input and every extraction I made was logged with my ID. Now given someone with clearance at level twenty, all they have to do is run a scan on Scapino and Spiderman, and they surface at the same time the history of who on the Floor, and when, has made a put-in or a retrieval. Soon the name of yours truly will become very evident. They'd only have to do it once. That would be enough to show them how close I am, how well I'm doing, enough to give them a motive for shafting us.'

He drank off the rest of his tea in one big swallow, wiped his mouth on the serviette before bunching it and tossing it on to the plate from which the pastry had vanished. Inevitably he burped.

'But the fact someone has run that sort of check must be logged too.'

'I put that to the DAC. He just got angrier. You see, this was put together so well no one there believes I was stroked. They all think I made a monumental cock-up. So he's not going to order that sort of scan anyway. But even if he did, they'll have it covered somehow. I mean they could make it look as if it was me that had run the check. And I'd have no way at all of proving otherwise. I'd be the only person who knew for certain that it wasn't me. And unless I can prove I wasn't in the building when it happened, then I don't stand a snowball's chance in hell.'

'There is, of course, an alternative.'

'There is?'

'It could have been me, or Seton, or even yourself.'

Tyler choked, spluttered. 'You're bloody joking.'

'But it is a possibility. A theoretical possibility.'

'Bloody theoretical. No. It has to be the way I see it. And you see they could monitor it the whole way. And because they knew precisely where we were and when, they were probably listening to us as well. Christ.' He slapped the table and his cake fork hopped to the floor. He retrieved it. 'I still feel very angry about it, you know? Stroked. Every bent copper in the Met is going to hear of it, and every one of them is going to piss himself when he does. And the ones bigger than me won't bother to hide the smirk when they see me coming.'

'So. What are you going to do about it?'

'I'm going to bust them. All of them. It's going to be bloody difficult, more difficult than it already was, but I'm going to do it.' Emotion throbbed in his throat, his mouth twisted almost as if there were a sob to be bitten back.

'But you've been taken off it.'

'And do you know what they've found for me? Not paperfasteners. I'm in charge of home-grown pot. Busting the piss-artists, students, schoolteachers, out-of-work darkies who grow a plant or two in their window boxes. But time I will have. Plenty of spare time.'

Mulligan's finger touched a pool of the tea Tyler had spilled, drew it out in a thin loop. 'Have you worked out a strategy?'

'Oh yes. The first thing is to winkle out the supersnake who set this up from the inside. It's not going to be easy, because he will have covered his tracks very well. But not impossible either. I've got good friends there, good blokes, and they want this sorted as much as I do. We're working on the marked fiver routine for starters. We'll get there. And when I can show the DAC this was set up, we were stroked, then I reckon we'll be sailing. But until that happens it's not going to be easy.' He sighed, peered into his empty cup. 'And what about you? You're still there. You wouldn't have asked for that file otherwise.'

Mulligan pushed back his chair and his open, unforced grin blessed Tyler like sunshine. 'Oh, I'm right in there. This has been a hiccup only, a very temporary setback in one sector of a very ongoing routine.'

'Well, good on you. But there's one thing you ought to know.' He pushed and pulled at his clothes, extracted folded sheets of a photocopied document. He passed them across the table. 'Read it later. Memo from the AC. This is the gist. The earlier guidelines have been scrapped. From now on Eurac is a piece of Interpol, nothing more. Any request for information you make, let alone action, will go through the National Central Bureau. They will assess it, just as they do all Interpol requests, issue directives and requests according to their assessment. That is they will pass it on to Floor Five. Now there, I can tell you, anything from you personally will be spiked. Anything from elsewhere in Eurac will be given a very close going-over, before being rated action-worthy, as per that memo. But you will be spiked.'

'How long is this going to last?'

'An enquiry has been set up into the Lowndes Square operation. Its brief is to assess the extent to which the balls-up was the result of earlier policy decisions to give Eurac what amounted to a free hand in setting up operations here. To what extent Eurac's criteria for this sort of action fall short of ours. And so on.'

'And when will it report?'

'A month. Maybe more. Then a couple of committees will consider its recommendations. And the Home Office will look at their findings. And then . . .' he barked – a sort of laugh, but bitter.

'What excuse is there for being so bloody-minded?' Mulligan himself sounded unusually petulant.

'You saw the newspapers. That turd Greene threatening criminal proceedings because we scratched his Chippendale. The wop Carracci telling the *Sun* it was a poor thing he couldn't invite friends round for a game of cards without the police kicking the doors in. And the Public Analyst issuing a statement that he didn't rate Lourdes water alongside Vichy or Evian, but on the basis of what was in those four containers he couldn't see anything wrong with it. With the Home Secretary, not to mention Maggie herself, being all pi and high-minded about drugs at the moment, this was just the wrong moment for the drug squads to be caught with egg on their faces. *She* was upset.'

Mulligan chewed a knuckle, stared out at the tatty crowded square. A pedlar selling metallic balloons filled with helium was being hassled by a pair of coppers. One of the balloons, shaped like Tom in the Tom and Jerry cartoons, broke free and soared into the purple sky.

'All right. I get the message. As of now there is no way I'm going to be able to operate in the UK with anything like a free hand. No more access to the PNC, no more questioning suspects myself or sitting in on interrogations. Nothing any more of any of that. And obviously no more working with you or whoever to put together actual busts.'

'That's it. For the time being, over here, you have about as much clout as a private eye.'

'Then it's as a private eye I'll function.'

'That's my boy.' Tyler stood up, forced a grin on to his tired, angry face, pulled on his coat, smashed his cheesecutter cap on to his head. 'This is my home address. Stay in touch, right? And take care.' He went.

Alone, Mulligan turned back the cover of the folder Tyler had given him. Across the top of the first sheet, various numbers and coded entries, a date and a time, then the heading: Harriet Jones. Report from H M Customs, Dover Collection.

Back in his hotel he read it through a couple of times and spotted, as someone coming cold and fresh to a new file often can, the one lead the Customs had not checked out. Either they had failed to see its potential, or, just possibly, Tyler's supersnake had had the power, rank, to stop it dead. It took Mulligan to Amsterdam, and Van Willet.

For weeks after Skrape nightmare stained every moment of Roget's waking life, severed him from the normal, everyday world he had inhabited before. Certainly this had been sharp and competitive when he was dealing in Islamic *objets*, and had included shifting, spiky personal relationships which often flared into quite traumatic rows, but all cushioned by modest wealth, predictable routines, and the beauty of the objects he traded. Above all, this normal life out of which he had only occasionally ventured into drug-running had been a shell within which he could function and forget the brutal realities that lay beyond. But now he felt like a hermit crab deprived of a carapace, continually on the scuttle for refuge, constantly aware of the raw vulnerability of his flesh to casual predators.

The last lesson he had learned at Skrape had been dramatic and nasty – indeed, so nasty he often told himself it had been staged. On his second night there the West Indian, who had been identified as a session musician with a coke network based in Tin-Pan Alley, had another, and this time major row with management. In the morning, when Roget left, he, and presumably all the other distributors on the 'course', passed an ancient Thunderbird crashed against an oak tree in the park surrounding the house. The lions gnawed lazily on fresh dark meat, and the cubs fought playfully over a large woolly hat in the Rastafarian colours of black, yellow and green. The message, staged or not, had been clear.

The Firm had been presented to its new employees as a large enterprise with all the resources of information, communication and organisation technology can provide, as an enterprise clearly well capitalised and run by managers with state-of-the-art expertise, with an annual turnover comparable with some of the largest corporations in the country. And all of that was true. But also it was a gang – a gang of ruthless thugs. A significant amount of its huge resources was devoted to monitoring every relevant moment of its operatives' lives, and the message was clear, the message provided by the lions of Skrape: they need not fear the slow degradation of personality in one of Her Majesty's jails – a swifter, but no less unpleasant death would intervene.

But if time and routine do not heal, they are analgesic, and so is money, a lot of money. He was paid one thousand pounds for every kilo he shifted, and a lump sum of ten grand when he upgraded two of his pushers to distributors with their own networks. Following the methodology of pyramid selling, he was paid an extra two hundred pounds for each kilo handled by these new distributors, who now occupied a lower level in the pyramid than his. In the first fully operative ten weeks he had been paid a total of twenty-four thousand pounds, and was on his way to a second big bonus.

Clearly the PR campaigns vaunted at Skrape were paying off. Out there there were a lot of punters willing to pay twenty-five pounds for a snort, for a sudden rush of joy and an hour of euphoria, their seventy-five pounds for a guaranteed stepped-on-the-once-only gram of pure cool snow, the better side of nature.

Contact with supply was rigorously controlled by procedures whose details were never the same. A phone call from a public phone box would direct him first to a place where he would find coded instructions which directed him to the cocaine. The point was that the instructions could be placed before he received the phone call, and the cocaine placed before he reached the instructions. Thus, even if he had been turned by the Law, or was under close surveillance, there was no way he could lead them to whoever it was who was placing the instructions or dropping the cocaine. The most the Firm risked was loss of a kilo: the personnel above Roget in the distribution chain were undetectable through him.

On two occasions the instructions simply consisted of the key to a left-luggage locker some miles away. On other occasions they directed him to the cistern of a public lavatory, to a carrier bag placed in a litter bin in one of the remoter corners of Kew Gardens, and once to a discreetly marked packet of Tate and Lyle icing sugar placed at the very back of the shelf in the Brunswick Centre supermarket. The fact that the cocaine was obviously at risk in some of these places led him to assume that he was under constant surveillance, at least during the short trip from message to cocaine, but he was never at pains to see how. He knew that looking about too curiously would anger his employers – and deep at third man prowled the lions of Skrape.

Having got the cocaine safely back to Purbeck Street the next job was to parcel it up into twenty-five-gram bindles, thin transparent plastic envelopes which he bought in bulk from a discount package store at the untidy end of Finchley Road. The job was laborious, and he did it in the spare bedroom at the back of his cottage. First he checked the weight of the kilo on his Ohaus three-posted equal-arm pharmaceutical balance. Then, using a polished square of slate as a base, from which any spillage could be retrieved, he spooned it into the bindles, with a spoon specially constructed to hold precisely twenty-five grams of levelled snow. Even so he had to check the weight on the balance before heat-sealing the bindle.

The temptation to treat himself to an occasional snort was easily resisted. He had used cocaine in the past. If he took minute quantities, he got little more than a cool, numbed sensation in his nose, and a slight and transitory raising of the spirits. But if he took more, say three lines, a third of a gram of coke that had only been stepped on once, good quality stuff fifty per cent pure, then the rush was too much, his blood pressure soared, and while his pleasure nodes buzzed and jumped, a rational corner of his soul took fright at the loss of control. Once this had even equalled the sudden and bootless panic one experiences in the last seconds before going under a general anaesthetic. Roget preferred his Beefeater's and slim-line tonic.

As well as recruiting and maintaining his pushers he was also responsible for what his Director, a smooth young man who had been his last contact at Skrape and who had spent two more sessions with him on one of the windier parts of Hampstead Heath, called pastoral care. This meant meeting them regularly, so he could monitor any dissatisfactions they might have, encourage them to develop their own circles of pushers, and allay their fears. Cocaine never changed hands on these occasions. Usually the bindles were passed on by drops, but less elaborately organised than the ones he received it by, since there was no point in concealing his identity from them. Most were social acquaintances, even friends, and one of the things that kept him awake at night was the knowledge

252

that he was expected to report them if he felt that they in any way endangered the operation. Particular evils he was to be on the lookout for, apart from the obvious ones of cold feet and grassing, were adultering the cocaine he passed on to them, converting it to crack, charging more than the going rate, or, like unprofessional publicans who drink their profits, overindulgence in the commodity itself. He also of course had to keep rigorous accounts of exactly how much each pusher received from him.

This was essential, since without it one of the cornerstones of the whole operation would crumble: the fact that the money travelled by routes quite separate from the cocaine. Roget's pushers did not pay him. They kept one-third of their take and passed the other two-thirds back to the Firm by means that were never revealed to Roget. However, if one of them fell behind in these payments then Roget was instructed to administer warnings and threats. If these failed it was understood the reneging pusher would suffer an uncomfortable loss: a hand, say, or a leg. So far nothing so disagreeable had occurred.

Roget himself discovered that he had become the Eastern art consultant to Good Life Promotions, who paid him a retaining fee, and lump sums for specific (but spurious) commissions, including a freebie to Paris to look at a set of erotic Persian miniatures, reproductions of which were to be offered to Designer Living cardholders at very inflated prices. When he upgraded his first two pushers to the distributing level he was asked to place ten thousand pounds on account with a firm called Ambrose Finance. Two weeks later he learnt that speculative but unimpeachably legal dealing in stocks and commodities had turned the ten thousand into twenty. A cheque for that sum would be posted immediately following the next settlement day, and so it was. As far as he could tell all these transactions were properly documented and he suspected that it would be very difficult indeed to show that they had any connection at all with trading in cocaine.

He began to worry about tax and the Vatman. The message came back that, yes, he would have to pay tax, but it was suggested that he place his affairs in the hands of accountants who would do his returns for him and minimise his liability. He was given a name: Arbuthnot and Sebourg.

His time, however, was no longer his own. Indeed, he was working perhaps as hard as he ever had done in his life, but he was making very good money too. While he did not expect to maintain a rate that could finally net him well over a hundred grand a year, he did expect to be a lot better off than ever before, and – or insidiously so it began to seem – his income was certain and regular and since he had turned fifty, that was a comfort. He signed up with a legitimate personal pension fund and began to look forward to a well-cushioned old age.

So, the analgesia of work for a regular and handsome income dulled the daily fears and the nightly panics, and bit by bit he brought the drinking back under control. Then, just as he had begun to feel he might be able after all to live with it, Van Willet rang.

The line was clear but had that dead quality international calls often have. Van Willet's voice, disembodied from his considerable and genial presence, seemed cold and his accent more pronounced than usual.

'Paul. How are you? Listen, Paul, this afternoon, I had a disturbing visit from the police. One was an agent from the Lijnbaansgracht Station at Leidesplein, you know, where we reported your stolen bag and passport back in March? The other was I think from Interpol.'

Roget felt a sudden cold constriction in the middle of his chest, a distillation of the chronic anxiety he had suffered since that moment when his bag had been stolen on Rotterdam station.

'Initially they were interested only in Miss Jones, you know? Apparently she was caught at Dover on her return from Amsterdam, with four kilos of cocaine in a black nylon bag, but managed to convince the Customs it had been planted on her – '

In spite of the sweating palms and jellied knees that compounded the constriction in his chest, Roget managed to think swiftly and sound unbothered. 'Yes, Vincent, Harriet told me all about her adventure. An uncomfortable experience for her, but one on which she still dines out, I believe. But why did they get in touch with you?'

'They wanted to know if I had had any sense that she was followed during the time she spent with me. I answered of course no. Unfortunately, perhaps, I mentioned that she was in Amsterdam with you and gave your name and mentioned the stealing of your bag the next day and so on. I thought you should know this.'

Roget raised his eyes to the calligraphed name of God above his mantelpiece, and wiped his brow with his free hand. 'Oh, really? I can't see why.'

There was a pause, then the Dutchman cleared his throat. 'Well, I'll be frank with you. Two things bother me. First, I was surprised that the police had no awareness of your presence with Miss Jones in Amsterdam, no awareness that you travelled together.'

'But we did not. I went back on the plane, she returned on the boat.' Roget contrived to sound testy. It was as well Van Willet could not see him. 'And the second thing that bothers you?'

'Paul, you spent the day in Rotterdam. I don't know why. You lost one bag, but you had a second when I met you. You kept a very tight hold on it. Paul, it was a black nylon bag.'

'Good God, Vincent. You can't imagine I had anything to do with the stuff that was planted on Harriet!' That sounded false. Positively theatrical. Roget dug the nails of his free hand into the palm until it hurt. I must do better than this, he thought.

'Well, I'm sorry. I am sorry. But it did cross my mind. You see the coincidences, the black bags and so on. At the time I thought you were up to no good. A small prayer-rug perhaps. Something you would prefer not to declare. I remembered of course that you have done business of this sort with Robert San in the past . . .'

'And so have you.'

'Yes. But I should add that San is now under investigation by the Dutch drug squad and our national Central Bureau of Interpol following seizure of cocaine in one of his warehouses. I am sorry but it adds up. At least it seemed to, while I was talking with this man Mulligan.'

'Mulligan! Not French or Dutch then. English?'

'No. He is an American, I understand.'

'But working for Interpol. And you left him with the impression that I had something to do with the cocaine that was planted on poor Harriet?'

'I am afraid I might have done. Given that impression, I mean.'

'Just one moment.' Roget picked up the entire phone, disentangled the lead from a lamp standard, and contrived to get himself into a chair. Standing was no longer viable. Also he wanted to get away from the window: a noisy diesel road-roller had started up outside, flattening new tarmac over the relaid water main.

Through it Van Willet's voice rattled in his ear. 'Paul, are you still there?'

'Yes, I'm still here. So. I suppose I am now to expect a visit from this policeman or some British opposite number.'

'Yes. I have to say that is possible. That is why I rang . . .'

'Good of you to take the trouble.' Roget managed the sarcasm with ease. 'At least it won't come as an entire shock to discover international police forces think I'm a drug smuggler.'

'I thought you should know. But there is another aspect. It's possible, because they know I assisted you in Amsterdam, after you had lost your other bag, that they may think I am somewhat implicated . . .'

'Vincent. There is nothing to be implicated in. Not even a prayer rug.'

'Fine, fine. But the suspicion is there. And, frankly, in my position, as a dealer in gems, with the opportunities that provides of moving large sums of money, I can do without that sort of – '

'And that's why you rang. Oh, piss off, Vincent, why don't you?' At last Roget had an excuse to put down the receiver, end the conversation, and give himself time to think. And for Christ's sake a stiff G and T to help the process.

It took time for the enormity of it all to sink in. Supposing Mulligan turned up, interrogated him, and he got away with it, talked himself out of it, as he felt sure he could – there was no real evidence against him apart from the fact he had stayed in the same hotel as Harriet and spent some time with her in Amsterdam – supposing all that, then surely he was still all right, in the clear?

No. He remembered the stolen bag, the passport returned in the post, the video left in his room at Skrape. The Firm's resources surveillance-wise, its ability to oversee and record his every move without his knowing it had already proved formidable, apparently limitless, and could not be ignored. It was possible that they already knew of Van Willet's call, that as a matter of routine they had his phone tapped, every conversation on it recorded.

He remembered the lions of Skrape.

Roget paced and padded about his small but treasure-filled cave, lost one tumbler, poured another, found the first, drank both, decided that to gamble on the Firm not discovering that he was under investigation was unthinkable. That left just two possible courses of action. Either he activated the emergency procedure they had told him to follow the moment he suspected he was under any sort of surveillance, or he went straight to jail, did not pass Go, and offered to turn Queen's evidence in return for cast-iron permanent protection.

Outside the road-roller ground to a halt. What a dismal object it was. Green sheet-metal bodywork, two big steel-clad wheels at the back, one smaller roller at the front. It spewed black fumes, and the poor driver had to wear earmuffs against the noise. Sharply he recalled the glorious monsters of his childhood, driven by steam, gleaming with brass, with prancing horses on their boilers and the blazon: *Invicta*.

He doubted his ability to survive even a year in jail, he doubted the ability of the police, prison officers, whoever, to save him from the lions of Skrape. He turned away from the window, reached for the phone, activated the emergency procedure.

28

Mulligan hired an agency to investigate Roget. Forty-eight hours later the proprietor phoned him at his hotel, which was large, unchic, and close to Roget's Bloomsbury address, to say they no longer wished to handle the assignment. They had discovered that Roget was distributing cocaine in ounce packets to at least two pushers in Bloomsbury, and this was a scene they'd rather not be involved in.

'I guess I understand that. But is that all you found out? To have got that far you must know a bit more about the man than just that.'

'Not a lot. In the last six weeks he has been paid a lot of money. I'm sure I don't need to spell out to you that that means he's part of a large network. Apart from that he's single, bisexual, fifty-one, has expensive tastes and is an expert in Islamic art.'

'It all helps. Thank you for what you've done.'

'Yes, well, Mr Mulligan, that is as far as we go. This sort of thing is best left to people properly equipped to handle it.' And he rang off.

Mulligan left the hotel and walked round the area, the north end of Bloomsbury, an odd mixture of late Victorian brick flats, tall terraced houses that looked almost Georgian, municipal housing built, he assumed, where the bombs had dropped, and one or two streets of much smaller terraced cottages. Purbeck Street was one of these. He noted number 14, took in its smartness, its air of good money carefully spent, and walked on. The road was up, but the work almost finished. A long trench had been filled in, partly remetalled. The machinery to complete the job was parked behind barriers; orange lights winked around it.

Not far away, in Marchmont Street, he found an Indian restaurant that looked the sort of place Roget might use: it was not cheap, and it was almost empty. He used the payphone inside.

'Mr Paul Roget?'

'Speaking.'

'Mr Roget, your name has been given to me as an expert in Ottoman art. I am about to conclude a deal for some faïence pottery which the owner claims to be sixteenth century, and I feel I need some expert advice. I'll pay a good consultancy fee of course. But before we get down to the real business I wonder if you'd like to have a meal with me, so I can put you in the picture. Are you free right now?'

'Well, actually I am, but . . .'

'I'm at the Star of India in Marchmont Street.'

'Really? Yes, I know it. But this is all a bit sudden, you know? What did you say your name was?'

'Mulligan, James. But my friends call me Buck.'

There was a long pause, then: 'You did say . . . Mulligan.'

'That's right.'

Mulligan heard the long, in-drawn sigh, then: 'Mr Mulligan, would I be right in thinking you were in Amsterdam a few days ago.'

'That's right.'

'I . . . I suppose I had better come round then.'

Poor man. Scared shitless already. The Dutchman must have warned him.

Mulligan took a table for two in the long narrow restaurant near the door and as far from the four other diners as he could. A dark, round-faced Bengali took his order for a whisky sour. The place was dimly lit with dull tasselled lamps on the tables and decorated with crimson wallpaper in carnation patterns: typical – but unfamiliar to Mulligan. He found it almost impossible to read the huge menu and could make no sense of the little he could make out.

The glass door chimed and a large tubby man dressed in a pale grey double-breasted suit with a floppily knotted bow tie pushed through the clicking bead strings, came immediately face to face with the American who rose to greet him.

'Mr Roget? I'm Mulligan. Come on and sit down. Drink? Gin and tonic? It's very good of you to come out at such short notice. I'm afraid you'll have to help me with the food, I'm quite ignorant when it comes to Indian – further east of course is a different matter.'

Roget was clearly disturbed, his eyes flinched back and forth from Mulligan's, his movements were over hasty. He took the proffered menu, fumbled for spectacles. 'Do you really want me to order for you? Are you sure?' Then he pushed it away. 'Oh, I can't go into the whole business of Indian cuisine . . . if you're agreeable I'll order a fixed selection of vegetable dishes, and leave it at that.'

'That's fine, perfectly okay.' Mulligan was soothing, accommodating.

Roget spoke to the waiter, turned back to Mulligan, snapped away his spectacles. 'All right, Mulligan. Don't let's mess about over this. I don't think you are interested in Turkish pots at all. If I read you right, you want me to help you with your enquiries. That's the right phrase, isn't it? But is there any reason why I should? I mean quite clearly you lack the authority to make an arrest and you do not have the sort of evidence that would incline the local plods to take an interest in me. If you had you would no doubt have kicked my door down instead of inveigling me out to eat curries.'

'Well, I guess that is true up to a point, Mr Roget. But I'm pretty sure if I presented the dossier I have put together regarding your movements in Amsterdam during March last as presented to me by Van Willet, and checked out with the proprietors of the Hotel Imperial, and handed over to H M Customs, Dover Collection, well, let's say I think there would be enough there for them to reopen that file on Miss Harriet Jones. And that could lead to a Bankers' Book Evidence Act summons to look into your financial affairs, and a search warrant too.'

Roget attempted bravado, but blustered: 'Then I suggest you do just that. And let them make fools of themselves.'

He fidgeted in his pocket, attempting to check that the Sony micro-recorder was functioning. This had arrived in the post, and later there had been a brief telephone call instructing him to use it to tape any meeting he might have with Mulligan. But he didn't know if he'd activated it properly: it was not the sort of gadget he handled easily.

'But would they be making fools of themselves? I mean, if they were round at your house right now, what would they find? I think I can guess. Much of the paraphernalia associated with breaking up quite large quantities of cocaine into sellable lots. Is that not right? These spicy wafers are very good. What are they called?'

'Poppadoms. Oh shit.' Roget pulled out a handkerchief, wiped his palms then his forehead, took a large mouthful from the tall glass of gin and tonic that had arrived at his elbow.

Mulligan was happy to let him sweat for a bit. The waiter returned with a large round tray filled with six or seven dishes.

'This looks grand, and smells marvellous. Tell me, what's the procedure now? Do we dig into a little of all of them at once, or take them one at a time?'

Roget shrugged petulantly. 'Just as you wish.'

'I suppose some are hotter than others. That rice looks wonderful, such colour. Certainly I'll have some of that. And what do we drink with the meal? I'm not a great beer man, and I fancy the flavourings are going to be a bit strong for wine.'

'Lassi is good. Aromatised buttermilk.'

'Fine. We'll try that.'

Roget made an effort, took a grip. 'Look, Mulligan. This won't do. Either you really do have something on me that can be made to stick, in which case, get on with it, or you haven't. In which case, piss off.' This was the line he had been told to take: find out what Mulligan had on him.

'Chick peas. With a lot of coriander. Delicious. I'm afraid, Roget, things are never that simple. Oh, sure, they are for the bobby round the corner at the precinct station. Or the Customs man on the bench at Dover or wherever. The guys who like to see powder on the table, score a few arrests, keep the statistics looking good. But that's not my ball game.'

'Actually I do think it's high time you told me a bit more about that.'

Mulligan shrugged, spooned *maahn dahl* on to his plate, then sipped the lassi. Head on one side, he savoured it. 'I see what you mean. The ideal accompaniment. Very refreshing. Our aim is to dismantle an entire drug syndicate from the little people at your level, the street sellers and distributors, right up to the financiers and principals at the top, all in one go, and put them all in the slammer at once. If not for good then as near to that as possible.' He paused, head on one side, large dark eyes serious but intimate too, with a half-smile whose intention one might, in other circumstances, have guessed to be seduction. 'But what I am engaged in right now is recruitment.'

'I'm not quite with you.'

'Oh, I think you understand.'

But Roget's face had gone pale again, his hand shook, and his spoon stammered on the edge of his plate. Apart from everything else he was now terrifyingly aware of the tiny tape winding through its cassette in the recesses of his pocket. Terrified because, of course, it was monitoring not only what Mulligan said, but his own reactions too. He put the spoon down, pulled in a long shuddering sigh. 'I don't think I want any more to eat. Do you mind if I have another gin and tonic?'

Mulligan signalled for the waiter.

'Listen, Mulligan . . . no, I won't call you Spike or even James – '

'Not Spike. Buck.'

'Listen, there is absolutely no way I am going to do that for you. And there's no way you can make me. It simply is not on.'

'Let me figure it out for you. First let's be positive, look at the plus side. I am not offering you the sort of deal the Brit police can offer – a reduced sentence in exchange for Queen's evidence. I am offering you complete immunity. And I am offering you money. And if at the end of the day we both agree the necessity, I am offering you protection for life. A new identity, a new start in some pleasant spot, with a nice climate, all your assets, and I mean all your assets, intact. Okay?'

'Hang on, I'm no legal expert. But isn't that illegal here?'

'Sure it is. But I am not an officer of the law, not in this country or any other. This is an intelligence operation. We gather and interpret information. We substantiate it so that it will eventually stand up in court, not only here but in all the other countries involved. But we see that as the second part of the process. First get it, legalise it later. Then we hand it over to the national police forces, and we agree with them all on how to co-ordinate things for maximum effect, then they all move together. But they make the arrests, they run the prosecutions. That's not our job. And as intelligence gatherers we have a freer hand. Our philosophy is – first get the facts, then look for ways of making them stand up in court. You will be assisting the first process in return for immunity from the second. Does that answer your question?'

Roget said nothing, drank from the new gin and tonic, pushed back his plate and fumbled for cigarettes. Mulligan's gold Zippo flared for him.

'Okay. Now let's look at the negative side. If you don't join the club, a lot of nasty things are going to happen.' He put down his fork and his right index finger tapped his left thumb. 'One. The local bobby kicks your door down and you do ten to life. Two' – index finger to index finger – 'he doesn't kick your door down, he puts you under surveillance, aims to catch all the guys you're selling on to, and makes a big effort to find out who's supplying you, who's paying you. And after a time your bosses catch on to this, because they are a very big outfit, with resources, and they have their eye on you . . . ah. That's it, isn't it, Paul?'

The expression in Roget's eyes resembled that of a steer in a stockyard as the queue begins to move.

'That is number three. You can't have out from an organisation like that. Or only on their say-so. Or feet first. Right? The moment they think you are a danger they'll off you. That's what really scares you. Well, I don't blame you. At all.' He leant back, warm eyes filled with sympathy.

Paul's tongue flickered across his lips. 'And they're not exactly going to offer me a bonus if I work for you.'

Mulligan shook his head. 'But they're not going to know about that. One thing we are very experienced in – we have to be, since our strategy depends on it – is running undercover agents. Generally speaking they do not get to be rumbled by the opposition. You'll see. If you agree to come in with us, I'll explain the procedures, we'll go over them, you can tailor them to fit your circumstances. And you'll see how, so long as you're not careless – and you won't be careless – how we're going to make this work.'

'And if I don't. If I refuse?'

'I just turn the information I have about your Amsterdam trip with Harriet Jones over to the Dover Collection, and what I know about your current operation to the precinct drug squad. With a prayer that they know how to look after you.'

Roget, like a bull now, rather than a steer, suffering sharp pain from barbed and well-lodged banderillas, tossed his head, ground out his cigarette. 'This is worse than fucking blackmail.'

'I wouldn't say so. There's carrot as well as stick. I said, we'll set you up at the end of the day, leave your assets intact.' Mulligan leant forward; his voice took on a soothing quality, honey and oil. 'Listen. How long do you imagine you can last? You're all shot to pieces. You are going to make mistakes, the police are going to rumble you. Your bosses are going to identify you as a liability. I had a private investigator on you and in two days he had your number. Now admittedly he was pointed in the right direction, but even so, that really is not good news for you. So really, Paul, I would like you to look on this not as blackmail, or something you are being forced into, but as an opportunity, perhaps the only opportunity that is likely to come your way to get out of this mess in one piece with a reasonable hope of making a fresh start. I think you'll come to look on this as the stroke of good luck you never expected, as light at the end of the tunnel.'

But Roget's eyes were dull again, filled with pain, and again he shook his head, but more slowly this time, expressing incredulity rather than frustration.

Mulligan pushed back his plate, dropped his napkin in front of it, signalled for the bill.

'I'm not pressing you. I'm not saying this is it, come in with us now or I go to the police. I can give you a day or two. I'll come back to you on Friday morning, and by then you'll be seeing things my way. I'll fix up a safe place for us to meet, and we can get the whole set-up sorted out. You use the British Library? Okay. Be there eleven o'clock, Friday morning, and we'll see you safe from there.' He scribbled a signature on an American Express chit, stood up, spilled pound coins from his palm on to the plate, held out his hand. Roget looked as if he might bite it. Mulligan shrugged. '*A bientôt*. Take care.'

Outside, he trotted briskly up the steps into the Brunswick Centre, turned left, dropped down the steps again on the north side into Handel Street. From the corner of Handel Street then up Hunter Street on to Tavistock Place. From there he could watch the intersection which Roget would have to cross if he took his quickest way home. At street level it was almost dark, though the sky above the silhouetted roofs still held a nacreous light. Birds arrowed along the top of the canyons, starlings on their way to roost. There was little traffic – taxis coming to and from the railway terminuses, and, at the top of Judd Street, an orange sports car.

Roget came to the corner a hundred or so yards away. His head was hunched forward, hands clasped behind his back; he had a lot to think about. Then he looked up at the crossing and Mulligan saw his round face, livid in the orange light from the lamps. The American hurried on up to the next intersection, Leigh Street which crosses the bottom of Purbeck Street. He was not too sure why he was doing this. Partly he felt he needed to know what Roget's first reactions to their conversation were, but also too he had an unverbalised desire to see the plump, neat, frightened man safely home. The sports car, a Lotus Esprit, turned into Leigh Street too, pulled into the kerb across the bottom of Purbeck Street and parked.

Mulligan felt a sudden frisson of alarm. Above the generalised traffic noises he heard a heavy engine turn over on a powerful battery, then diesel fired, caught, settled to a steady rhythm. It was an odd noise to hear close to, at seven o'clock on a late October evening, a noise one normally associated with work. A little uncertainly, suddenly very conscious that he was not armed, he moved down Leigh Street, towards the Lotus, and saw Roget on the other side of the road coming towards him, head still down, almost at the junction already. He quickened his step, but stayed on the south side of the street. Roget did not look up, did not see him, did not see anything very much. Entirely preoccupied with his thoughts, he swung round the familiar corner, and his right hand felt in his pocket for his latchkey.

It all happened very quickly. The diesel-powered road-roller, driven by a man in a black leather jacket with a stocking pulled over his face, was coming down the street towards Roget. It crushed one of the orange winking lights, and sent another skittering into the gutter. Two more men closed on Roget, who tried to run, but they held him, struck him in the neck and the kidneys with blackjacks. One of them dipped a hand into his pockets, came out with the micro-recorder. Mulligan saw that. Then they toppled him over on to his back in front of the steel-clad roller. For a moment it looked as if he might twist himself out from under it in time, but it trapped his leg and trundled on. The scream cut out, as if a switch had been tripped.

Mulligan, obeying deeply ingrained, almost instinctive beliefs about how large policemen should behave in this sort of crisis, almost reached him in time, but the killers had been very quick. They turned to face him now, one with a large Browning 9mm automatic, the other with blackjack raised to his shoulder. Behind them the roller reversed, exposed Roget's hideously crushed remains. Mulligan turned on his heel, almost ran back to Judd Street, turned north towards the terminuses and his hotel. The Lotus slipped up to him, held his pace for a moment then the driver gunned the engine and it roared away. Mulligan almost walked into a lampost. He held on to it, felt his head swim, and then he retched and vomited, heaving up his Indian meal. A siren, shrill with that fast moaning beat, cut a swathe through the evening noise, and Mulligan hurried on, away from it, but feeling in his pocket for the pen that would record most of the sports car's number.

Part Five

Waterloo

29

Giann' Arnolfini trotted briskly down worn narrow steps into the central courtyard of the palazzo in which he had his Torinese apartment. Half way down he buttoned his grey jacket across his black silk shirt against the near-frost: cold night air from the Bernese Oberland had settled like silt on the Piedmontese foothills. At the bottom he paused, felt in his pocket for cigarettes. This was a moment he wanted to prolong, to savour.

He snagged the blue head of a wax match on his thumbnail, cupped his hand – broad, with black hair reaching down the top joints of his fingers – inhaled fumes of saltpetre, black tobacco. He smoked for a moment then pulled from his trouser pocket a chunky key-ring. With swelling excitement he weighed it in his hand, flipped over the rectangular tag. It was enamelled orangey yellow, framed in silver, with the green, white and red stripes of his country's flag laid narrowly across the top. Against the yellow a black horse with its tail a panache behind it pranced above the elongated top stroke of a capital F which stretched across the one word: *Ferrari*.

Giann' moved into the middle of the courtyard. Infra-red released locks, tipped a balance, the door lifted, swung. And there it was.

A red two-door coupé, Pininfarina designed, five-litre Testarossa. Aluminium body, steel doors and cockpit, engine rear-mounted in front of the back axle and housed beneath red camcovers: hence the name – *Testa Rossa*, red head. With Bosch K-Jetronic fuel injection system, five-speed gearbox, Connolly leather interior, tinted glass, air-conditioning, the very best in in-car stereo systems, it was almost cheap at nearly two hundred million lire, eighty thousand pounds. And of course, like all Ferraris, it had a tubular chassis.

For a performance car it was big, the rear especially high

above the big wheels with the characteristic row of engine vents, but the eighteenth-century, skylighted stable gave it room enough. Giann' prowled slowly round it, occasionally letting his hand slip over the icy smoothness of the bodywork before coming to the driver's door. He chucked the cigarette, let himself in and sat in the deep bucket seat for a moment, anticipating the power that lay at his fingertips beneath the rows of buttons and switches, a power signalled by the dormant dials.

Four floors above, Jill Jack stirred in the huge, round, silk-sheeted bed, slowly became aware that she was alone and that the light that filtered past the half-opened shutters, through muslin lacy curtains, still held the gentleness of dawn. She twisted out of the foetal position and on to her back, though her thumb remained in her mouth. There were problems, she knew, something to be remembered about this morning, about the day, days, ahead which she had forgotten. Most mornings now were like this: she woke with a head loaded with loose lead that rolled it forward or to the side if she didn't make an effort to control it, and bleak black feelings of anxiety, panic even, filling her throat and upper torso.

She sat up, hands clutching thin, bare white shoulders, then ran her finger ends across her temples, scraping them back into her short black hair, and as she did her startlingly blue eyes fell on red overalls flung across the back of an upright gilded chair near the bed. A shield on the pocket, the prancing horse . . . Christ, it was coming back now. Ferrari. They were flying to a convention of Ferrari owners in . . . where was it? France. The other side of France. Biarritz. And all because Ernesto, Signor Prezz' Spezz', old Mr Cut-Price himself, had given Giann' a new Ferrari, something even better than the Lamborghini Miura, and he wanted to show it off.

She swung long legs, bruised at the top of her inner thighs, off the bed, and then suddenly sank forward again, elbows on knees, face in hands, as the despair welled back. She fought it for a moment then felt for the silvery foil card that lay in the bedside table drawer and broke out one of the small waxy suppositories which it housed. This was the moment of the day when she hated herself most, but she hated the waking panic, almost a form of vertigo, far more. She spread her legs, lifted one foot on to the bed and squeezed the bullet-shaped object against her anal sphincter. Resistance, then it slipped in and the moist muscle closed behind it ... easier than swallowing a paracetamol.

Outside, an engine fired, revved, settled back into a contented roar punctuated by the ticking of the electrically powered, electronically controlled pump that would supplement the conventional mechanical one until the engine was hot. Feeling a little better already, perhaps because drugs taken that way work quickly or just out of anticipation, she got to her feet, moved through the cool morning light to the tall window and looked down.

Dear Christ, yes, that is a nice car. But, oh dear, why the fuck couldn't the bastard, millionaire though presumably he was, afford a Teasmade, like the one her Mum and Dad had in their Byker's Wall flat in Newcastle? And who's this coming into the yard from the street? Young Giorgio, the kid brother of Ernesto and Giann'. She rather liked him – he still had an innocence that she too clung to, the innocence that said it was all to do with fun, having a good time, and not money, power, status. But the other man she had learnt to fear – Francesco Cellini, tall, thin with big eyes and a predatory nose.

The three men had no time for her or anything else but the cars they were creaming themselves over, for two more doors had lifted and tipped and two more Ferraris, identical to the first, were revealed. They were in ecstasy. They blew kisses through fingers and thumbs, slapped each other on the backs, swung each other about like kids. Soothed truly now by the morphine, Jill Jack turned from the window and headed for the huge *en suite* shower stall. Best to get through it and dressed before they came up, else they would all strip off and be in it with her. But tea, a nice cup of tea, would have been nice ...

After coffee and hot white rolls they were joined by two other girls – a Romanian with rich black hair whose schoolgirl French was about the same standard as Jill's but whom she disliked as somebody basically, deeply silly, and a tall anorexic Swede who said nothing but occasionally relieved Cellini of the necessity of fondling his private parts in public. They paired off and in convoy cruised round the Galerias before roaring down the boulevards and out into the suburbs.

The spin was short, though on it they clocked two hundred

kilometres an hour in thickening traffic, ended at a large complex of garages and workshops on an industrial estate. Burning rubber they halted outside large doors beneath a huge sign – Eat well with Mr Cut-Price! – and in front of a Ferrari transporter. Ernesto, as usual a lugubrious version of the bonhomous persona that grinned down from the hoarding, lurched heavily out of his silver Mercedes and padded over to them. Meanwhile mechanics in baseball caps and Ferrari overalls that were serious – the oil marks on them said so – took over the still sweating Testerossi, gunned the engines, drove them in turn up the ramp into the workshop. Four men in leather jackets, all with cold eyes and fingers that twitched near their shoulders, moved on to the corners of the access roads.

Ernesto was even more miserable than usual, Giann' higher. For a moment it seemed as if temper might flare between them, but Giann' took a grip on himself, and young Giorgio too, and they listened to their older brother with a seriousness which was clearly self-mocking, but still serious enough to keep him cool. He spoke for a long time, with much emphasis, much repetition, threatening, pleading, finally with heavily assumed resignation, and they nodded, agreed, patted his plump shoulders, clearly made solemn promises on their mother's grave, and sealed them with brisk fingers flickering in the sign of the Cross. 'Ace, king, queen, jack, ten,' Jill murmured to herself, remembering her father's Nonconformist parody of papist practice.

Torino airport next, and a chartered Lear jet to Biarritz. Meanwhile the transporter would drive through the day and the night across the Lombardy plain, through Provence and north of the Pyrenees, to arrive with time to spare for the mechanics to tune the cars for the first events of the next morning.

Well cushioned now by the morphine that the suppository continued to release through controlled dissolution into her bloodstream, and gently rocked too by iced vodka and caviare, Jill enjoyed the flight. The Alps gleamed with fresh snow, the massif of Mont Blanc filled an ovoid window for all of ten minutes, sank away to forested foothills and then the heaving landscape, autumn parched and terraced, of the tributaries of the Rhône. Aping the pose of an air hostess the Romanian girl served cocaine. The Swedish girl sighed, leant across to Jill, said, in a heavily accented whisper: 'After charlie he' – she indicated the big-nosed Cellini, next to her – 'always wants I should suck him off. It's so boring . . .'

Meanwhile Giann' weighed in with a long diatribe against the snobbery of all the fucking dukes and princes and English lords and bourgeois turds who would be at Biarritz, especially the ones who made a stupid fetish of driving the older models like the 500 Superfast and the 250 GTO with their wooden steering wheels and wire-spoke wheels which took half an hour to clean after you'd been through a puddle. Well, that lot would all get a shock when their transporter turned up with three brand-new Testerossi on board, they'd know they'd been properly shafted when they got on the formula two circuit at Brindos.

The base for the convention was a big motel at Chantaco, a hamlet south of St-Jean-de-Luz on the lower slopes of La Grande Rhune, a huge conical mountain shaped like a young girl's breast with a monastery for a nipple and a discreet funicular to get you there. There was access to the motorway that links San Sebastian in Spain with Biarritz, Bayonne and eventually Bordeaux in France, and beautiful views over undulating hillsides covered with pines and the deeply eaved red and green villas of the Basques. Below lay the port of St-Jean, low tamarisk-covered cliffs and the Bay of Biscay: sea mists and the switchback hills concealed the fact that much of it was built up in more or less random ribbon development. Behind the Rhune snow on the more distant peaks of the Pyrenees flashed back the last rays of a sun that set in the ocean.

The members of the club were content to keep fairly much to themselves on the first evening, settling into their respective chalets. This suited the Arnolfinis too, because of course their transporter had not trundled across the whole of the south of France and their chalets were conspicuous as almost the only ones that did not have Ferraris parked outside them. They went to bed early without any of the excesses that usually marked their nights. Indeed, for once Giann' made love to Jill as if she were his *fidanzata* rather than his whore: prolonging the experience until she simulated the orgasm his machismo

273

demanded, and then ejaculating on her tummy rather than inside her.

Dawn – pearly, fresh, misty, with the tang of salt and pine in the air – altered all that, because with it came the missing transporter. Out on the forecourt Giann' directed the unloading with as much noise as he could manage, even asking an Englishman with a 500 Superfast (still in the blue and white colours of the Ecurie Ecosse for which it had originally been raced) to get up and move it so the new Testerossi could be run off and parked exactly where they would appear at their most impressive. He took it in good part. 'Chaps who pitch in a bit later than the rest of us always want to make sure we all know their wheels have arrived,' he remarked.

He went on to explain that while the Arnolfini cars were indisputably the newest Ferraris, they were certainly not the most exclusive nor necessarily the best. Only forty-seven of the 250 GTO were ever built – the Shah had two, the Aga Khan one, Niarchos one, and their present owners were in the same league or near it.

Nevertheless the arrival of the Arnolfini cars did much to rebuild Giann's self-image: the thing was that while the club fell into heterogeneous groups which normally would find very little to say to each other, they were there because of one overriding common factor – a passion for the works of Enzo Ferrari. So the old money, headed by lean old gents in tweeds, casual sweaters, even plus-fours, and carrying names that occasionally predated Napoleon but included some pretty solid bourgeois ones too (there was a Mengele, a Courtauld, and a Guinness amongst them), joined with the new money (the heir to a post-war Marseilles construction firm, and an awfully decent chap who built ships in Osaka) in admiring the latest manifestations of their ageing hero's genius.

Particularly a Colombian, Mercurio Welser, the son of a senator reputed to be a coffee baron but everyone *knew* where the loot really came from, ignored his own 328 GTS Spyder, and made a particular point of coming over to Giann' and Giorgio Arnolfini and Francesco Cellini to beg from them the privilege of having a spin in these, the newest monsters. Giann' was not keen, but the club is a gentlemen's club and it has its unwritten rules: one of which is that you must have a darned good excuse to refuse a fellow member a go in your car.

At ten o'clock on the Saturday morning, the Colonel of Police arrived from Bayonne in a brand-new edition of the big Renault GT turbo with six outriders on two-litre BMW bikes. With an ever-crescendoing air-splitting thunder, beneath swirling clouds of exhaust, the Ferraris, nearly sixty of them, formed up behind him and he led them at a steady one hundred and forty kilometres an hour down the slip road and up on to the motorway. The northbound carriageway had been closed to traffic three minutes before they got on to it. This sounds excessively unctuous on the part of the authorities, but in fact caused little inconvenience to regular users. The distance the convoy had to cover was less than twenty kilometres, and as the last Ferrari whipped away it could be re-opened behind them: there was no way normal traffic could catch them before they reached the Brindos exit.

It was a short but exciting ride. Giann' surged ahead of the Renault almost immediately and held his Testarossa in the lead for three kilometres at speeds approaching one hundred and seventy miles an hour while Jill, well spaced out again, clung to his arm and sang with the glory of it, at the blurr of pines and hills and fields and villas, and the awful screaming roar. Then two more cars pulled level and surged past: first Giorgio with the Romanian girl, white-faced and clearly terrified, then a Swiss downhill ski champion in a racing Daytona, probably pushing one hundred and ninety, using eight thousand three hundred of its available eight thousand five hundred revs, enough anyway to stretch the road between them as if it were a white indiarubber-band.

Giann' laughed, but there were tiny beads of sweat on his temples: he allowed the revs to drop a little and two more cars swished past. He re-established bravado by first pinching Jill's inner thigh, then: 'Steer for me, *chica*,' and he fumbled out his cigarettes.

The circuit – ten kilometres of concrete strip undulating across the hillsides, with a vicious hairpin where the elbow touches the Nive and a wrong judgement can put you in it – puts a perimeter round the small airport that serves the area and a golf course whose fairways thread their way across the hills and round copses of pine. The pits had been opened, the pumps filled and the workshops manned as if for a full day's racing, which in effect it was, but a strictly private one. Not only police but a couple of coachloads of CRS armed with automatic rifles and full riot gear made sure of that. There were, after all, amongst the older members of the club, people whose wealth and political power demanded that they never went abroad without the sort of security that one associates with heads of state or major corporations.

The organisation, left in the hands of a man who had stage-managed royal weddings and a couple of World War II battles in his time, was immaculate: unobtrusive yet efficient. Cars roared off round the circuit in groups of a dozen or so matched for age and performance. Outright racing was discouraged, though occasionally, where it was understood a bet had been laid or an incautious boast called, this ageing but very dignified general would allow three or four to run three or four laps on their own.

Lunch was hampered specialities of the region: Arcachon oysters from up the coast; langoustines with mayonnaise; Béarnaise pâté de foie gras, not so rich as the Strasbourg variety but perhaps more subtle; yellow corn-fed chickens from the Landes; Bayonne ham; peaches marinated in red wine; and a big black Pyrenean sheep cheese whose diameter was the same as the steering wheel on a 500 Superfast and which alone would have cost a thousand francs at the Isturitz Carrefour. All this was eaten in a small pine wood on a hillock at the eastern end of the circuit furthest from the airfield and nearest the town of Bayonne, which lay below them and apparently surrounded by the watermeadows bordering the silvery meanders of the Nive. Again art or luck had contrived to hide most of the urban development from where they were: what they saw were the Vauban fortifications and the graceful twin spires of the cathedral. And it was during this lunch that the Colombian, Mercurio Welser, insinuated himself into the Arnolfini party.

Jill, in her red Ferrari overalls, was peeling a langoustine for Giann' when the shadow fell across her.

'Your cars are the sensation of the convention.' The voice was deep but mild, the accent a South American's attempt to make Spanish sound like Italian.

She looked up over her shoulder, flashing the smile of slightly uneven teeth which a few weeks ago had offered innocent excitement, but which already looked practised, studied. The big man, dressed in a crumpled grey suit with a dark blue shirt, stooped to his haunches, ignored her and handed a card across her to Giann'. He was much the same type as the Italian, but a little older, thinner, fitter, more deeply tanned.

'I was pleased with my 328 Spyder until I saw them. I hope you will let me drive them. I think this morning you said I might. My father – he is a senator, you know? – rather hoped I would find an opportunity to try one out. He is thinking of acquiring three or four, but has his doubts. He is a little old-fashioned and fears these new models with all their high technology might lack soul, *alegría, gracia*. I try to tell him that a car is a car is a machine. But . . .' He shrugged, pouted at the silliness of older men.

Later he repeated this line as an excuse to try all three cars. He was an experienced Ferrari driver, he said, and what he wanted to know, what his father wanted to hear, was that in spite of the fact that the cars were meant to be identical he could detect differences, a personality in each. This was true, he asserted, of the earlier series. Thus he held, briefly, the ignition keys of each in his hand, and presumably contrived to make wax impressions of them. The cars were, of course, protected electronically as well, but in the ambience of the convention these devices were left unactivated so mechanics could retune them and members sit in them.

That evening, the Saturday, the club went to Biarritz, to the Hôtel du Palais for their big banquet of the meeting, and during the following night Jill overdosed herself with morphine.

Jill Jack was falling apart. She was already dependent on morphine, had reached a stage where she would do anything to maintain or regain the spaced-out euphoria which alone made consciousness tolerable. And it was not just the craving, the depression that dragged her down, but the sense too that she had travelled in and down and away from the lively, showy, pert, almost hyperactive girl she had been barely a month before. The second night at the Chantaco Motel, filled with booze, coming down from a coke high, and bilious with the few mouthfuls she'd managed to eat from each of eight courses, she dragged herself out of Giann's bed and made it to the bathroom. There she was sick, and then she stayed there, *en prière* over the toilet bowl, shivering convulsively for half an hour or more, while he snored on next door.

At last she pulled herself up, looked with wild eyes deeply shadowed at her thin naked body in the full-length mirror. She realised that it had gone: the glamour, the glory. She was wretchedly thin now, not lean or slender. Her skin was blotched and dried in places with something that had begun to look like eczema and which paint would not conceal. She had two sore hangnails and without gel her short hair was lank. The one thing she had left to sell, the one thing that would buy the suppositories she depended on, was spent, used up. Giann' did not keep her for sex, nor even as a pet he could bully, though there was a lot of both. He had taken her on because she was desirable, an acquisition, like a Testarossa, something that set him apart, something that made men, and women, say: there goes Giann' Arnolfini – he always has the best. Well, he was not the most sensitive or perceptive of people and it might be a day or two before he woke up to the fact that her company was conferring on him a different sort of cachet, but when he did that would be it. Over. Out. Then what? She shuddered. Then, she supposed, it would be sex, sex only, brutally taken, degrading, and from someone like Cellini. The good life would be over.

What was to be done? She thought desperately of Bonnie Day, Muriel really, dear steady Muriel and Orlando Gardens, Clapham. All she had to do was clean herself up a bit, get some clothes on, call a taxi . . . but she felt so weak, so cold, so fucking awful. Exhausted. Flaked out. First, before she could do it, she'd have to sleep, she knew it. And there was only one way to get sleep . . . Fumbling in the bathroom cabinet she found the foil card and for the first time broke out one of the small waxy suppositories not at dawn but in the middle of the night.

A demon deep within her – the demon she had always had, that had driven her to wilful precosity even in infancy, that energised her wit and her sparkle – grinned now: this was what she had come to the bathroom for, all the rest had been talk, excuse, flannel to manoeuvre her to where she wanted to be, perched on a toilet seat with one foot on the edge of the bath, torpedoing herself.

Soon she felt warmer, easier, at peace with herself. She went back to bed and in the dark pulled her thin body like a cloak round the bent broad back of Giann', finding in it a totally spurious comfort. It had not been, she reflected, as the waves of Morpheus, red and velvety, surging to the rhythm of her own slowed breathing, carried her out into a warm sea of oblivion, it had not been a dull weekend . . .

It was not a serious overdose, but it left her confused, even stupid, in the morning. Angrily Giann' and the others left her behind to sleep it off while they took part in the Sunday morning treasure hunt. She still felt sick when they returned, and refused to go down with them to St-Jean-de-Luz for the seafood lunch at the Kaiku which was the last function of the convention. Members were bused to both meals: it would have been inappropriately ostentatious for them to bomb through the narrow streets of either resort in a convoy of fifty-plus Ferraris.

At about half past two, then, on the Sunday afternoon, Jill woke up out of a deep and tolerably healthy sleep, feeling a lot better, and in desperate need of a cup of tea. On the large forecourt in front of the chalets there were already three transporters loading up the cars whose owners preferred not to use them as ordinary tourers, or who had come impractically long distances. There was a lot of noise, a lot of exhaust, and a fair amount of general activity – servants, porters and mechanics all busily dismantling the weekend. She tried to escape from it all by going to the motel's salon, which had a panoramic view over the Côte Basque. She ordered tea, sat back in eau-de-nil leather and took stock of herself. There had been excitement, yes, and glamour, and glitz, but she realised too that there had been degradation and that she was perilously close to becoming a junkie. At three o'clock on a pleasant autumn afternoon, in reasonably normal surroundings and with not an Arnolfini in sight, this no longer seemed a clever thing to be.

She would be glad to get back to Bonnie/Muriel in Clapham, and she felt for the first time for some days that she really would be able to, really would be able to break out of this trap and get back to normal. Meanwhile there was the view to enjoy – a green civilised sweep of hills, pine-clad or with steep meadows dotted with freshly made haystacks, steep conical heaps of fodder piled round tall poles, three or four of them to each field. And over to the left she could see a corner of the harbour and the yacht basin of St-Jean with its long moles protecting it from the Atlantic surf beyond.

A mechanic appeared in front of her. He was, she said later, just like all the others, in oily Ferrari overalls, dark, good-looking, gold ID bracelet, not really much else to say. He spoke, she thought, Italian, but later she admitted that perhaps he said not *per favori* but *por favor* when he asked for the key to Giann's Testarossa, and perhaps he said *gracias* and not *grazie* when she went back to the chalet and gave it to him.

'But why not? Why should I not have done so,' she sobbed, again and again, 'he already had a key. He showed it to me. It was the same, but just didn't quite fit, quite work. A faulty one. So, what else should I have done?'

The transporter was found abandoned in a wood near the road to Cambo, the frontier post favoured by *poids lourds*, the trucks and containers that are routed away from the tourist crossings of Hendaye and Behobie. It was generally supposed, though never proved, that the three cars – for all three Arnolfini Testerossi had been hijacked – had been off-loaded and put inside three converted Navarra wine tankers returning empty to Pamplona. That is supposing that they were indeed smuggled into Spain at all: there was never any proof that that was the case.

The media were impressed with the way Giann' Arnolfini took it all. He displayed, according to one sheet, an almost English sangfroid, a quite remarkable readiness to accept that the cars had gone for ever, and that he would just have to live with their loss. He presumed, he said, that there were others available in Enzo's workshops.

What he concealed was the fact that for several days he lived in mortal fear that the cars might be recovered, might fall into the hands of the police. Or worse still that an inexperienced driver might crash one of them on a public highway. In either case it seemed likely that the full extent of his loss would be revealed: for all three cars shared the same secret – twenty-five kilos of ninety-three per cent pure cocaine, pumped into their tubular chassis. The plan had been simple enough. After the convention they were to be transported up the coast to Bordeaux, where documents had been prepared transferring ownership to Mermaid Pleasure, an English firm based at the south coast town of Lymington with offices in Southampton, where delivery was expected in ten days' time.

Giann' was convinced that Jill Jack had been part of the plot. He handed her over to Francesco Cellini, who saw to it that her morphine habit became dependency, and would remain so without qualified medical treatment. She soon ceased to offer any resistance at all to his demands, which went far beyond anything Giann' had ever required of her.

30

Harriet hated flying, so Lovejoy insisted that she took two little green happy pills – these and club class champers left her with tunnel vision, and a sense of near-weightlessness. At Brussels National Airport arrivals are fed into a glass rotunda of duty-free shops and cafés. A very long moving pavement perspectives almost to nothing and carries them to the terminals. At night, in driving rain, the blackness beyond the glass left her feeling that this was not an airport at all but perhaps a space station, that the 737 had been no ordinary jet but a space shuttle.

The silvery ripples of Lovejoy's head sank beneath her down an escalator, followed by the straw thatch, surely stitched there, of Myklades. She felt pressure in the small of her back.

'Come on, Harry, don't dawdle.' Rupert. And Albert Burke was somewhere behind him, checking out their tail. She felt warm, protected.

Grenscontrole, Grenzkontrolle, contrôle de frontière, border control. Wedged in the queue between Myklades and Rupert, nothing to fear really. Well, yes really, lots to fear, but two factors mitigated the terror: it had become chronic, a habit; and when it took the shape of outside authority, Passport Control, Customs, and she was in the company of these . . . gangsters (and almost always she was these days), the reflection always hovered at the back of her mind that they had a lot more to fear than she, and if they thought they were safe, then probably she was too.

And, of course, the glance that was given to her passport

was perfunctory, and their luggage, retrieved from one of the many carousels by Burke and Rupert, piled high on a trolley, glided untouched through the green channel. And then her stomach dipped, and the whole Dover thing flashed back at her in vivid recall, for there, behind barriers, was the Oriental, Malay or whatever, who, with his wife, had videoed her and Roget in Amsterdam, had been there too when Senior Investigation Officer Price had put his hand on her shoulder.

Wearing a peaked cap now, he came round the end of the barrier to meet them, a smile offering service hovering in his dark eyes. Myklades paused, acknowledged him, turned.

'Babalatchi will show us the way,' he said.

Harriet, her heart still beating faster than normal, hung back while Babalatchi and Burke loaded the baggage into the boots of large cars. Rupert came back to Harriet.

'Hector wants you to ride in the Cadillac with him, okay?'

'Why not?'

Babalatchi opened the door for her, and Myklades presently folded himself in, rather awkwardly, beside her. The other three men crowded into a BMW, Burke taking the front seat, riding shotgun, and with the Cadillac in front the cars swayed and dipped round concrete piers and down ramps out on to the motorway – a ribbon of light which again could have been strung across space for all she could see beyond it and the curtains of orange rain.

'You remember Babalatchi, then?' Myklades' voice, quiet, from the flickering shadows beside her. His lighter flared, the fragrance of Yeni Harman filled the small spaces between them.

'Yes.'

'Really, you know it is to him, or rather to his wife, Taminah's, skill with a video camera that I owe the ... privilege of knowing you.'

Motorway signs expanded above them, were gone. The place names were always doubled, Flemish echoing Walloon, one of them actually recalling that dreadful coach trip from Amsterdam: Gant – Gent. They looped round a spaghetti junction and the sign was for Mons – Bergen, Charleroi, and Paris.

'At the time it was of course the much-lamented Roget we were interested in. His operation, how well he ran it, what sort of risks he took, how well he would react to arrest. But when we played back the tapes it was you who appeared. You did very well. Very well indeed. We were all very impressed, and then Rupert identified you, told us who you were, that he knew you and so on. And we realised how useful you could be.'

Harriet did not like to be reminded of Paul, was only just learning to live with the awfulness of what had happened to him, at the hands, Rupert had explained of gangsters employed by San, the Chinese he had traded with in Rotterdam. Lovejoy's pills had helped her with that crisis too.

The big car surged on. Presently there were no more street lights just reflectors. There was almost no noise apart from the whisper of the wipers slicing sight out of darkness. She sensed rather than saw that the wide road cut a swathe through what looked like a large forest of big trees, beeches.

'Why are we coming here? Why do you need me?'

'For two reasons. First you will meet principal members of Crystal. They have been told about you, and have expressed a desire to meet you. I suspect that they wish to be convinced that you are not some sort of narc. You will bear that in mind, because if they are not convinced . . .'

Out of the darkness she felt his hand on her knee, suddenly squeezing, then digging like talons into the muscle.

'Ouch! Hey, don't do that.'

'Convince them.'

She was frightened, as well as hurt, and angry with herself and him that this was so, and she forgot to ask him what the second reason was.

In less than twenty minutes they left the motorway, and drove across what seemed in the darkness to be hilly, hedged fields. They slowed, entered a close of large detached houses, and finally pulled up outside high double gates made out of sheet metal and set in a ten-foot white wall topped with barbed wire. Gravel crackled, long streamers of weeping willow briefly caressed the hardtop, headlamps swung across lawns and cypresses and then over the front of a large two-storeyed white house with many windows, each with its pair of dark green shutters.

'Welcome to Sans Souci. I hope you enjoy your stay here. The other guests do not arrive until tomorrow. And we do not expect to begin work until after lunch. That leaves the morning free, when I would be grateful if you would accompany me on a walk over the surrounding countryside. I should like you to take pictures of the landscape, and occasionally of me. Until then, then.' He squeezed her knee again, but gently, added a soothing caress.

Inside, the house was a show-piece of modernism, the brutal modernism of the thirties combining futurism with art deco and Bauhaus functionalism. There was a sunburst clock in the hall, geometric patterns in the carpets and curtains, the curve of the banister on the stairs was supported on a simple zig-zag of white-painted metal. One felt a young Joan Fontaine or Ida Lupino might appear there, dressed in an Orry-Kelly gown created from sculptured drapes of shiny pearl-grey satin. Out of the general confusion of arrival a girl of about fifteen in a blue denim dress, who could have been the daughter of the Malays, led Harriet to a small but comfortable room on the upper floor. A little later her bags arrived, two Samsonites, as well as her photography kit, and then a toasted ham and cheese sandwich with a weak whisky and soda. It was half past eleven. Harriet ate the sandwich, unpacked as much as she had to, got into the bed, and sank the Scotch. For a few moments she listened to the rain on the window, then, aided by two more of Lovejoy's pills, white ones this time, slept.

She woke, at about seven, to the thick head and dry mouth the pills usually left her with, but no recollection of nightmares to dog her through the day, and a grey dawn with gusting wind and squalls. She went to the window to see what sort of landscape it was Myklades wanted to be photographed in. In the foreground the plain lawns with a couple of fir trees and a small cedar dropped not to a wall on this side but a high wire fence. There were insulators on the posts, which suggested alarm systems certainly, and possibly high voltage as well. It did not, however, cut off the view beyond.

Most of it was unexceptional: rolling agricultural land, much of it ploughed, some green with beet, some with winter wheat. It climbed, but with intermittent folds and hollows, to a long irregular ridge a little less than a mile away, but running on to the east before being lost in woodland. To her left a straight road followed higher ground, dipped out of sight, climbed again first to a cluster of substantial farm buildings then to a hotel or restaurant set at what was probably a crossroads.

Nothing extraordinary . . . except to the west, beyond the crossroads, a further quarter of a mile on there was another, larger cluster of buildings on the skyline, and a pyramid. Literally a perfectly triangular pyramid, big even at that distance and crowned with what had to be a substantial piece of statuary, though from here it looked like a pimple. She pulled out her biggest lens – only a 200 mm Rolleinor but mounted on one of her Canon SLR bodies it gave her the magnification and clarity of image she needed to see that it was not in fact a pyramid but a turfed cone, and that the structure on top was an enormous limestone plinth supporting a huge bronze lion.

Just as she held it in focus a gleam of early sunlight bled along the ridge, throwing the scattered buildings, the few trees and the giant mound into sudden and dramatic silhouette against the black clouds and squalls that the north wind still rolled in off a distant sea.

'Dear Lord,' she said aloud to herself, 'I know where we are. It has to be Waterloo.' And Myklades, she recalled, was a Napoleon freak.

'Mont-St-Jean,' he said. 'More properly it is the battlefield of Mont-St-Jean. That is the name of the rise in front. The village of Waterloo is a mile and a half away on the Brussels road.'

Wind gusted about him lifting the lank yellow hair so it looked like a bird's crest. With his hands thrust deeply inside the cape he had worn at Wrykin Heath, and gesturing with his head, swinging and stabbing with it as he talked, he looked again like a bird, a stork perhaps rather than the flamingo that had come to mind at Southampton.

'This is about as far forward as he came.'

In front of him the road dipped and climbed to the crest a half-mile away; behind him, a line of white farm buildings was strung along it, and painted on the gable walls so passing cars could read it coming from either direction, *Rôtisserie Belle Alliance*.

'Would you like a picture here?'

'Why not? He stood here, in the morning, and watched the troops deploy. Lancers, dragoons, cuirassiers and chasseurs.

The Guard in bearskins. Drums. Trumpets. They cheered of course as they went by and filed off down those ridges to the east, and further back behind the farm, to the west. The cannon came last. It was wet, heavy, sticky, you can feel what it was like.' He stooped, balled a tiny lump of the orange clay and tossed it away before putting his hands back in his pocket.

Vive l'Empereur. She used the 'Blad, firing from the waist, from below him, using a wider-angled lens than is usual for portraits, exaggerating the foreshortening. But no way was she going to make this thin pale man with his freckles and foxy colouring look like the Little Corporal, however broodily he posed. She realised she'd do a lot better with the tripod out, but was buggered if she'd mess around with that in this wind, and the backs of her hands already numb. At least the rain had gone and the clouds were white now and breaking up to the north over Brussels. But behind his head they were still black with drifting squalls beneath them. She slotted in the dark slide, gave the magazine a quarter-turn, released it, and replaced it with 400 ASA black and white. The face would be a white mask, the spectacles would carry reflections of Mont-St-Jean and the white clouds in front, the backdrop of storm clouds would be grainy but sharp.

'It started over there on our left. On his left. You see that farm, down there in the hollow at the foot of the slope. It not only protects the enemy's right, it's a salient, it threatens the flank of any central attack. So he decided to take that out first. It started at about eleven o'clock. Accounts differ.'

He set off across and down a long rolling slope of recently tilled land, skirting a copse of thorn and alder in a tiny combe to the west of the road. It did not bother him that they left a line of footprints across the greasy but friable surface, almost as conspicuous as if they had been on a snowfield. And of course he did not offer to carry her bag.

She found herself objecting too to the way the Allies were the enemy.

After a time they hit a track for farm machinery dividing the fields that led directly to the farm he was heading for. It was ditched and edged with coarse grass, and briars. She spotted a runner of field pansy still in bloom: tiny yellow and white flowers.

She had to trot a step or two to catch up.

'I should like a good picture of these buildings. Hougoumont, they are called. One from round here and one from inside the farmyard.'

She sized them up. A house, grey and ochre brick, stone corners, dark grey slate roof, and a large but off-centre double wooden door big enough to let a haycart into the yard beyond. Red-tiled barns on each side, and running away to the right a long orchard wall. Both barns and wall had slits in, the sort one sees in fortifications. A timeless setting – apart from the motorway thrusting through a cutting a couple of hundred yards away.

'Do you want to be in it?'

'No.'

No. *He* had not been here. Back there was as near to the fighting as he got.

'The resistance was formidable. Mainly from the enemy Guards. Napoleon's brother Jerome was in overall charge of the assault. It is arguable that the Bonapartist tendency to nepotism contributed to its failure. Jerome has been criticised for not blowing the place to pieces with his artillery, but it was not so easy as it looks. There was then an extensive screen of trees in front of the house . . .'

His lecture went on. Delivered in dry, guttural tones, it soon became a catalogue of slaughter rather than of heroism, of desperation rather than sacrifice. She shut it out, concentrated on problems of composition and detail: there was more sunlight now, shifting quickly as clouds sailed by above.

Inside the wide yard he asked for more pictures, and as she set them up the horrors went on. Every Frenchman who got in was hacked to death save one drummer-boy, Jerome's howitzers did eventually fire the house and the barns, and the wounded who had been put in them were left to burn because the defenders were too busy defending. And really it was just a farmyard, with tractors and a dung-heap, and its own little chapel. A labourer pottered about. A woman came from the house with a shopping bag, got into a middle-sized Audi and drove off. They ignored her and Myklades, immune to the presence of ghoulish visitors preying on the past of their humdrum livelihood.

'Where now?' she asked.

'To the top of *la butte*. You can imagine that the views are extensive. I have observed that you constantly change the magazines in your camera. This may compromise the other purpose of these photographs. And of your presence here.'

'Which is?'

Panting slightly, for they were now climbing a steep slope and had to hug a wire fence that separated ploughed land from beet, he explained: 'I wish your negatives to be indisputable proof that I was here at the same time as the people we have come to meet. I suspect that they will not allow a group photograph like the one I engineered at Wrykin Heath. But they are vain, and they will not object to being photographed separately, although they may ask you to change cameras. That should not be a problem if you keep your wits, and usually you do.'

He paused, hand on chest, then wiped spittle from the corner of his thin mouth. The cold wind banged about them. 'For I imagine if the negatives are kept uncut, and there are always pictures of me placed amongst pictures of them in what are identifiably the same surroundings, the effect will be the same. To prove to an outsider that we were all here together.'

'Yes. Yes, that will be so. I can do better. I can cut in pictures of a time and date watch.'

'Good. I see you have the idea.' The cold elusive smile came again, and again she was annoyed to find it felt like a reward, that it mattered to her that she pleased him.

He went on: 'There are strains in our little group, which could become serious and I should not like to be . . . denied.'

They struggled on. The whole area was deceptive: slopes were generally steeper than they looked, declivities deeper, and nothing quite straight. The only feature that maintained itself was the ridge she had seen from her bedroom window. 'He was mad to attack up these hills. Wasn't he?'

From in front of her he turned, and his eyes were icy again, though his cheeks were now rouged with the wind. He looked at her for a full ten seconds then muttered: 'Focking British.'

A long narrow flight of stone steps, mercifully railed but still vertiginously steep, climbed to the huge bronze lion, passant, regardant, one paw on a ball and weighing, the notices said, twenty-eight metric tons. British, she supposed, but before he could correct her, a new voice, husky, low but female, got in first.

'Ah, but you see this is a Belgian lion. Not British at all.'

She was shorter than Harriet, but not much, and older, quite a lot older. Her clothes were classic – a couturier scarf, a lightweight but rather long gaberdine coat, good boots, all in shades of beige and tan. She had a long thin nose, and lilac eyes which were sharp, intelligent.

Myklades turned at the sound of her voice. 'Lili.'

'Hector.'

They exchanged *baisers*, but without warmth, warily.

Myklades made introductions. 'Lili Brel, this is Harriet Jones. Harriet . . . Lili.'

'Not a British lion?'

'No. It was erected in 1830, shortly after the foundation of the Belgian state, and as a warning to the French: this far and no further. I know – because I am Belgian. In fact when Wellington saw it he remarked: "They have spoilt my battlefield." *My* battlefield! He was an arrogant man.' She turned back to Myklades. 'I should like a word or two, alone, before we return to the house. Perhaps over a coffee down below.'

Harriet realised two things: that this meeting had been arranged, and that Brel did not want to share it with her. 'I shall need at least a quarter of an hour here if I'm to make a proper go of this.'

'Good. We'll meet you in the Hôtel du Lion then. I have my car there and I can save you the walk back to Sans Souci.'

Harriet watched them negotiating the long flight of steep steps, Myklades in front, his hand up to keep the wind off his face. The woman behind, her gaberdine flapping. Suddenly the sun shone strongly and threw their shadows and that of the lion on its plinth out on to a ploughed field below. A curious effect, one which she quickly snapped using the Canon: the action conferred power over them, revived her *amour propre* which had been dented by the slightly dismissive way she had been treated. And of course she was fulfilling her new duties: to picture Myklades in the company of his confederates.

The picture took her attention away from the battlefield and on to the minor road from Braine-L'Alleud. Cruising along it up from the motorway was a small but impressive convoy: a large, white, new Rolls-Royce followed by two silver Mercs. As they glided towards the foot of the mound she had time to change her lens for the 200mm Rolleinor. Blown up the picture would pick up the registration numbers for she felt sure these

too were guests at Sans Souci. She was right. The big cars
threaded through the tiny complex of hotels, souvenir shops
with a rotunda containing dioramas of the battle. At the
crossroads on Mt-St-Jean they turned right, as she guessed
they would, dropped past La Haye Sainte, crossed the battlefield, and then dipped off the main Charleroi road at La Belle
Alliance, heading for Plancenoît. She smiled wryly at herself.
The master would be pleased – already she was doing well.

31

By two o'clock everything was in place. Rupert and Burke, with
ten men, had made Sans Souci secure: the motorway junctions
were watched, there was a man on top of La Butte du Lion with
a radiophone, any approach to Plancenoît would be monitored.
Indoors Feijoo did his sums in preparation for the finance
meeting next morning, Pedro and Jana went through a workout
and the post-workout inspection, Harriet checked her photographic equipment in the light of Hector's requirements. Dr
Lovejoy alone was at a loose end: none of his charges at the
moment needed his services, though he reckoned that as the
concentration under one roof of vicious personalities thickened
during the day and evening, he would be needed before long. In
the meantime he remained in his room and caught up with the
latest developments in the technology that had been the foundation of his reputation. On the table in front of him was Ivo
Pitanguy's comprehensive *Aesthetic Plastic Surgery of the Head and
Body*. It was huge, as big as a serious atlas, had cost him six
hundred Deutschmarks, was worth every pfennig.

At two o'clock then the first scheduled meeting, a sub-
committee reviewing security in Europe, assembled in the
library: Myklades, Lili Brel, and banker Antonio Pérez, Marquis of Boltana. They arranged themselves informally in
armchairs in front of a coal fire burning in a large yellow-tiled
fireplace. Everything in the room, limewood bookstacks,
square armchairs, cuboid occasional tables, was done in the
monumental modernism that characterised the whole house.
It all conferred importance on its users, but was functional,
that is to say comfortable, as well.

Boltana, big, silver-haired, fatter than his corseted waist admitted, rosy-faced, made a half-turn towards Lili Brel. His smile had gallantry in it, acknowledged her chic grooming, the beauty that remained in her lilac eyes and the neatness of her slim body. 'Hector,' he said, 'has kindly agreed that we should open the proceedings by listening to this.'

He placed a cassette recorder on the octagonal table at his elbow. 'Our engineers enhanced the sound quality when they transferred it from micro-tape, but in other respects it has not been tampered with.' He dabbed the play button.

What I am engaged in right now is recruitment.

I'm not quite with you.

Oh, I think you understand.

Boltana pressed another button and the tape whirred on. The player had an indexing facility. 'If you're interested you can play the whole tape, unedited, but for now I'm just giving you what I take to be the meat of it . . .'

I am offering you complete immunity. And I am offering you money. And if at the end of the day we both agree the necessity, I am offering you protection for life. A new identity, a new start in some pleasant spot, with a nice climate, and all your assets, and I mean all your assets, intact. Okay? . . .

Hang on. I'm no legal expert. But isn't that illegal here?

Sure it is . . . The bland, quiet, smooth voice drawled on. In the background the occasional chink of crockery, liquid trickling into a glass, the rasp of a lighter. Then close to, and resonant, Roget's voice again, a harsh, worried bark. *This is worse than fucking blackmail.*

In a salon on the other side of the house Harriet unpacked her photographic bag and began a routine check of what was in it, cleaning lenses and filters with Dust-Off and sable brushes, checking her stock and wondering if she could find a corner in a refrigerator to store it. On the kidney-shaped table there was a deco statuette in ivory and bronze depicting a tennis player, Suzanne Lenglen perhaps, performing an overhead smash.

The door clicked. A tall, lean girl with light brown high-lighted hair, large brown eyes, and a nose that was just a shade too small for what otherwise would have been a beautiful face, came in. She wore a baggy pale blue sweater over a lilac leotard, black tights, blue legwarmers. Her feet, which were large and long-toed, were bare.

'Hi,' she said. 'Do you mind if I share this room with you?' The accent was Texan or something like it, perhaps not quite so broadly Southern.

'Of course not.'

'I get kind of bored on my own, and there's nothing to see from my room upstairs but fields.'

So not then a Waterloo freak: which was a relief.

'You a pro photographer? I mean like with all that stuff, you must be?'

'That's right. Portraits mostly.'

'That's keen. Take one of me?'

'Why not?' Another opportunity to carry out the boss's instructions.

'Okay. How do you want me?'

Harriet laughed. 'Hang about. I don't just do snaps, you know. I like to give it a bit of thought, work out the best combination of film, camera, and so on. And it helps a lot to know a bit about the subject too.'

'Oh, right. I mean fine. My name's Jana Pensión. And you're Harriet Jones?'

'That's right. You can call me Harry if you like. And you're here with Don Pedro . . . ?

'That's right. I'm his physiotician. Physiotician to Don Pedro Mendoza y La Cerda, duque de Pastrana y príncipe de Eboli, no less. And a grade A asshole. I should know. I keep it clean for him . . .'

'Really?' Harriet offered an embarrassed little laugh. 'And what else does a physiotician do?'

'Keeps a guy fit. Left to himself he'd be a combo alckie and dopefiend. But he reckons he is the summit of genetic breeding and he aims to breed the ultimate best. To this end he is fixing to lay the only girl in the world with a pedigree to match his own, and he wants to be in good shape when the day, or night, arrives. Could be quite soon. I mean like this genetic miracle will be here this evening.'

'Really? Who on earth is she?'

'Europa Malatesta. Name doesn't mean a thing, does it? But there you are. Woman of mystery . . .'

*

Back in the library Boltana switched off the recorder, pushed himself back into his chair. 'Well. There we are then. I do think we have a problem here. Lili?'

She recrossed her legs – the nylon hissed – took a cigarette from a slim gold case, accepted a light from Boltana.

Then she smiled at Myklades. 'I think first it needs to be said that your organisation handled this business very well indeed.'

He shifted in his chair, wriggled his back, gave his shoulders a shake. 'Personally I think the means of disposing of the nuisance was unnecessarily . . . savage. But the people I put in charge of this side of things judged it necessary.'

Boltana circumcised a cigar, posed with it an inch from his mouth. 'Why? Why necessary.'

Again the shrug: '*Pour encourager les autres*. It was felt that a message to all our employees would be useful at this point in time. The easiest way to get it across was by making the removal of Roget dramatic enough to ensure generous cover in the popular media. On balance I think they were right.'

Brel tapped the end of her cigarette on a chrome ashtray fixed to a strap made of fine chainmail that hung across the broad square arm of her chair. 'I take their point. This man . . . Mulligan? Mulligan made a very seductive offer. Clearly we must feel confident that temptations of this sort are resisted. But it is surely equally clear that demonstrations of this sort, while fine in themselves, are not enough. They don't solve the problem, they don't eradicate the danger . . . You know I really can't emphasise enough how . . . all this is alien to me. You must forgive me if I seem over-anxious.'

Myklades dabbed a handkerchief to his forehead, edged his chair back from the fire. 'Not at all. We are all in a sense amateurs in all but the financial side of what we are doing. I am sure we all share your concern. Rollering Roget was not the only step we took. I have been to some trouble to find out what we can about this Eurac – '

'Well, Hector. Just what is immediately relevant, eh?'

Harriet was enjoying the session. She rarely took women, and when she did they were usually the wives of her clients: almost always middle-aged – fat trouts or skinny battle-axes. Jana was very different. She stripped off the bulky woollen. Her leotard was cut low but tightly, cradling small braless breasts, revealing lean shoulders and long firm arms which had the creamy warm brown colour, flecked with moles and freckles, of some species of wild mushroom. She swung herself about with a total lack of physical embarrassment, her movements fluid and expressive. Occasionally she guyed cheesecake, arched her back, tensing her buttocks and pouting, once the serious intensity of the competitive gymnast. Finally she sat on the table by the statuette of Lenglen, leant back on her forearms with her legs up in the air in the pose that swept the world on the Fonda tapes.

'You could always model, you know? Between jobs.'

'Yeah?'

'Certainly. I'll have to see how these shape up, but I think you're good. Not many models can carry off so much body exposure without either turning out to be the wrong shape in the wrong places, or they come across as beefy, butch. You look fine.'

Harriet was drawn to lean toughness in men – it was what got her with Rupert, and she was conscious that her own body was too soft: she wasn't fat, but she couldn't jog a mile or sprint for a bus. And what she had to admit to herself, and it was a self-realisation she could allow to emerge, since the presence that promoted it was, most of the time, not a presence but an image she could manipulate in her viewfinders, was that the sexual appeal of Jana's lean suppleness, her hard but unpronounced muscle, was enhanced not diluted by the fact that it was not accompanied by male threat, neither by the threat of the phallus itself nor by the male tendency to bully and hurt.

A tendency suddenly thrust upon them as Pedro burst open the door.

'Jana, I have been excluded, it seems, from a very important meeting. I am very angry, very upset. And you know what that does to my blood pressure. What are you doing on that table?'

'Having my picture taken.'

'So I see. Why? Who are you?'

'Pedro, this is Harriet Jones. The photographer. Harriet, this is my boss, Pedro Mendoza.'

'Ah. What are you doing here? Why do you use a Canon?

Everyone knows the Olympus range is better. I thought Rolleiflex was the large-format camera most men preferred. Or Leica.'

'Hey, put that down.'

Pedro ignored her, but let the Hasselblad drop back into the bag. 'Jana, that man, Myklades, is a shark, a shyster, he's swindling us, I'm sure. None of the others can see it. And I was most anxious to feel at ease this evening, to feel my best. What's to be done? What can you do?'

'If it's that bad, Pedro, perhaps you should see Lovejoy.'

'No. He's a quack. I don't want drugs.'

'Another workout? I'll put together a sequence that'll calm and relax you, make you feel better.'

'No. But damn it I think I've got it. A ride. That's it. Get hold of Babalatchi, get him to contact the stables at Papelotte and tell them to saddle up a couple of nags. You know the sort of thing.'

'Two?'

'Yes. You can come. I'll go and change.'

Harriet, angry at his intrusion, and suddenly oddly pained at the thought that Jana was being removed, said: 'Three. Make it three.'

Pedro turned at the door, frowned, then shrugged. 'Very well. But we should be quick. It will be dark in a couple of hours.'

'You really have done very well to find out all this.' Lili Brel leaned forward a little, back straight, head up but a little tilted, signalling the obvious question behind the compliment.

'Yes indeed.' Boltana's brassy bass echoed the theme, made the question explicit. 'It is almost as if you had penetrated that dreadful drab building in Rue Armengaud, had your own mole in place there.'

Myklades, warmed by their approval, but still wary, sat back deeply in his chair, let his sour little smile play on them both for a moment. 'Not exactly. But we have access to a source to which all Eurac files are available. The same source enables us to get what we want from the PNC too, the British Police National Computer.'

'You can access all that?' Lili frowned. 'Only security services have that sort of rating.'

'Precisely. I am talking of the Joint Computer Bureau, the facility that is shared by the MI5 and the MI6.'

An expression that was almost greedy flickered across Brel's face. 'You have unlimited access to the JCB?'

Myklades laughed. 'Oh no. But to files relevant to us, in short to cocaine, yes. That is in part the explanation of our success in identifying and either absorbing or closing rival firms. It is a very useful source, of course, but limited. And one can't always get what one wants from it as quickly or as certainly as one would like.'

His tone was dismissive now. He lit another cigarette, busied himself with it, closed the door. Brel and Boltana exchanged glances, hard, speculative. Finally a grimace and a pout signalled agreement to let it ride . . . for the moment.

'Right.' Brel was brisk again. 'What you have made quite clear is that this Mulligan's attempt to recruit Roget as an undercover agent was not an anomaly, the action of a maverick, but the implementation of what is institutionalised as part of Eurac's methodology. What he said on that tape is not pie in the sky, they do actually have the funding available to recruit and pay spies.'

'Actually, the funding will come, I believe, though by indirect routes, from the successes they achieve, from the fines and sequestrations of property they hope will arise from their successes. That was the way Centac was justified in America . . .'

'How they fund it is not – will not, I sincerely hope – be any concern of ours.' Boltana's laugh was a bark that carried threat.

'No indeed.' Lili's laugh was also dry. 'But clearly we are now faced with a new threat. One we must think carefully about and counter. We were very lucky with Roget – all right, not lucky, your procedures worked admirably – but things may not fall out so well next time. The point about a successfully placed undercover agent is that one does not recognise him as such until it is too late.' She paused. 'Him? Or her? Unless . . .'

'Unless?' Boltana leaned forward, a smile of something approaching delight as his own mind caught up with Brel's. Myklades too, holding his cigarette in the eastern fashion between index finger and thumb, tensed alertly, waiting.

'Unless their undercover agent is in reality . . . ours.'

Harriet blamed herself. She had been stupid to allow her anger at Pedro's boorish behaviour to get her into or rather *on to* this. *This* was an Arab filly, bright chestnut with a white blaze on her forehead and one white sock: skittish certainly, and adventurous, but well schooled too. But *this* was also gathering twilight, with cold squalls again swooping in from the north over a wickedly sloping hillside, part ploughed, part maize stubble, part unlifted beet, and sliced by narrow tracks paved with irregular cobble slabs, often cut to a depth of ten feet or more below the general level of the fields. Usually these cuttings were edged with elder, willow, hazel, chestnut, but sometimes these remnants of ancient double hedges had been completely cleared. Thus it was possible to go at full tilt up an incline and find that skills and determination one thought had been forgotten an age ago miraculously asserted themselves in micro-seconds and somehow one was still on the back of a snorting, jarred, frightened beast that had also had to make a swift choice – whether or not to take a sixteen-foot jump with an uncertain landing and an idiot on her back. Napoleon's cavalry had had the same problems.

Pedro, on a big black thoroughbred hunter, a gelding called Oberon, had known the sunken road was there, put the horse at it, cleared it with a yard to spare, and was now galloping in a wide circle above her, hurling great clods of deep orange earth into the air behind him. His antics became more weird and more precise, the circles tighter, and marked with fierce accelerations and sudden stops. He was shouting too in Spanish, reining the horse in fiercely then spurring and whipping it on.

Jana trotted up to Harriet. She rode well, western-style, on a palomino pony. The Centre d'Equitation at Papelotte provided the right gear for this: with American generals at Nato and diplomats at the EEC both in Brussels, there was plenty of demand.

'You all right?'

'I'm all right. No thanks to your bastard of a boss. And what's he doing now? He's murdering that horse, ruining him.'

'*Rejoneo*. Bullfighting on horseback. He fancies himself at it. Took it up this autumn on his *ganadería*. You plant like barbed darts in the bull's neck till it's almost dead with exhaustion and loss of blood, then you fail to kill it with a lance and some poor *péon* has to risk his life doing it for you with a dagger. Look. That's what he's pretending to do now.'

Pedro had dropped the reins and, sitting bolt upright with his arms bent above his head, spurred Oberon into a sudden gallop, then twisting his body from the waist to the side he clearly mimed launching the *rejones* at an invisible foe. Unfortunately he also startled a flock of larks out of the stubble. Oberon shied, dumped him.

'Whoops!'

'Oh dear.'

'Serves him right.'

Oberon was well schooled, good-natured. For all the bad treatment he had had, he came back to Pedro instead of obeying his instinct and heading for home. Pedro caught his reins, held them tight up under the horse's mouth and whipped him, hard and long on his neck and withers, until he stopped backing and rearing, until his proud head dropped, until he was shuddering from head to tail in the cold driving rain. Then Pedro gathered the reins again and swung back into the saddle.

'He had to do that. He'll say it was to teach the horse a lesson, but that's not the reason.'

'Because we saw it happen?'

'That's right.'

Harriet wriggled in her saddle. 'God, I'm going to be sore after this. I haven't ridden for years.'

'I might be able to help.'

'Okay.' She gathered up the reins, turned the Arab, pressed her into a trot. Together they hacked back to Papelotte through the rain and gloom of the battlefield.

32

Harriet lay on her front, on a big towel with her cheek on her forearm. She felt good: the sound of the rain drumming on the window, the deep heat from a lamp penetrating her sacroiliac, the physiotician's hands, firm and sure, probing, circling, pressing.

'Your muscles are definitely in spasm up here.'

'What does that mean?'

'Well, they're like clenched, you know?'

'But why?'

'Well, I think maybe you jarred your pelvis a bit roughly. Maybe pulled something a bit out of place. It's gone back now, but it's left stretched ligaments, this spot of muscle spasm. Nothing to worry about. You'd have got over it in a day or two anyway. But this will help.'

'It certainly feels as if it should.'

'Am I being a bit heavy? Hey, you're coming up quite rough and sore on the inside of your thighs. Saddle burn. If you ride in jeans you've got to do it western-style. I've got some cream.'

The hands went away, came back deliciously cool and soothing.

'God, that's nice.'

'Is it? How about this?' The hands moved up, kneading her rump, searching.

'Hey. Don't do that.'

'No?'

'No. I'm not that sort of girl.'

'No one is. Until they've tried.'

'Maybe. But not now, not yet. Okay?'

'Okay.'

The hands slipped back to the insides of her knees. Then went. Harriet sensed that the tall American girl had sat back on her calves away from her, then got to her feet. She heard the clink of enamel, a drawer being closed. All that equipment, even a personal computer like the one she used for her photo files. And just to keep one pompous, cruel, silly bastard of a man in tiptop condition. The moment had gone. She was relieved that Jana had not pressed her, had stopped so coolly – relieved, but just a touch sad too. For Harriet, anything, once. She felt perhaps she'd let herself down.

'You know, I think that's it. No more I can do now. If there's still any pain tomorrow and we get the chance, let me know.' A switch clicked and the heat from the lamp died.

Harriet turned over, sat up, pulling the cotton wrap she was wearing back over her knees. Their eyes met: Harriet's green, appealing, a sort of apology; Jana's amber, flecked with gold, expressionless but somehow intense.

'Thanks.'

'My pleasure,' said with a hint of dryness. 'You know your muscle tone is not as good as it should be,' but then the expression shifted, a frown of curiosity, and interest, head on one side.

'What is it?'

'Activity outside. I wonder what's going on?'

Apparently being fit meant your hearing was more acute too – Harriet could hear nothing but rain. Jana snapped out the light, pulled a gap in the long orange velvet curtains. Harriet stood behind her, looked over her shoulder. This room was on the opposite side of the house to hers, had a view over the flat lawns, through fir trees, past the weeping willow, to the high white wall and gate beyond. It was completely dark now but some light spilled from the house, especially from the entrance below and to their right. Three men in heavy, belted raincoats, dark trilbys, were coming up from the gate, two more crossed the gravel forecourt to meet them. The build and walk of one was familiar enough – Rupert. One of the ones coming towards him was big and thickset enough to be Burke. He held a radiophone to his ear, apparently spoke into it. The groups met, talked, looked about them. Rupert looked at his watch, spoke again, turned and nodded up towards the house. Instantly, magically, the whole area was lit from floodlights concealed in the trees and under the eaves. The rain became muslin shot with gold; the harsh emerald green of artificially lit grass, the bruised reds and browns of twin beds of late begonia plants flooded back. Burke pulled a pistol from his coat pocket, checked the magazine, snapped it back, put it away, and as he did the big sheet metal gates swung open.

Two huge circles of light that looked blinding even coming into all that light, and behind them five yards of cream and maroon Rolls-Royce, an almost unique Phantom III, with a Barker sedanca body sculpted in simple 1930s low relief. They watched it slip along over the gravel towrds the house, occasionally briefly hidden in part by the black trunks of trees, gleaming in the lights and the rain. Two of the men had fallen in on either side of it, were keeping pace, hands pocketed, raincoats swinging.

The big car swept on to the forecourt, took a wide turn and halted a yard from the steps. Rupert stepped to the passenger door, opened it, raised his hat. Then he offered his hand to a thin brown claw that had appeared in the opening, and helped from it a slight figure in a white raincoat and wide-brimmed white fedora. The man straightened, looked about, pulled the coat which he wore like a cloak thrown over his shoulders closer round him. Rupert helped him to the steps. Burke reappeared. From somewhere he had procured a huge umbrella, striped red and yellow, and it entirely shielded from view as well as rain the other occupant of the car. All they saw was a neat pair of ankles, classically perfect court shoes, then she too was gone.

'Well,' Harriet breathed, 'who were they?'

Jana turned back into the room, pushed past her. Her face had become a frozen mask, but two teeth bit into her bottom lip and indicated the force of the emotion that possessed her.

'Vehicles. Carriers. Transit camps in transit.'

'I'm not with you.'

'They aren't people. Not at any rate according to the Dook of Plaza-Toro. What we saw are the current hosts of the most perfect genes in the world. Most perfect as of now, that is.'

Harriet almost stamped her foot. 'Come on, Jana. Who are they?'

'They are Enrico Malatesta, and his granddaughter Europa. He is descended from a Roman senator's daughter who was raped by Alaric the Hun. To that, through her mother, she allies the genes of the Byzantine emperors. With a bit of Genghis Khan thrown in. She is, and I quote, the most perfectly bred female still capable of parturition, still able to hand on those precious genes, in the world.'

Her voice was very even, the western drawl giving it measure and lilt, and overlaying the gall that still spoilt it, just as gall in some newly killed animals spoils the flavour.

'And Plaza-Toro aims to marry her?'

'Yeah, I guess that too. But mainly he aims to fuck her, impregnate her with his genes. That way they'll make a baby that will be the ultimate tops. Jesus knows where the poor bugger is going to find anyone worthy of the resulting genes – that's a problem Pedro hasn't gotten round to facing yet. If it's a girl he'll probably fuck her himself. Look through any stock-breeder's handbook and you'll see incest is the name of the game.'

'You don't seem too happy with this situation.'

'Shee-it. It's nothing to do with me.'

'You can't want to marry him yourself.'

'Fuck off, Harry. You're full of shit.'

'No, but really!'

'Full of shit. Listen, Harry, I can do what I like with the guy. He's mine. All mine except for one thing – that rotten, stupid, shitty obsession of his. And do you know what he's worth? One hundred million bucks. And that's not counting the art, the collections, which maybe double up. And do you know what he's paying for those genes? Ten times that amount. Ten times. That's the tag Enrico has put on her. One thousand million bucks, in instalments, through to her twenty-first. And if he's paid up then he gets to creating the genetic masterpiece of all time. And I mean of all time. According to his theory, those genes don't just go back to Adam and Eve. They go back to the primeval ooze – '

A bleep, high, insistent.

'That's him. My master calls.' She dabbed a button on her wristwatch, killed the bleep. 'He's had a bath, too hot. In it he probably jerked himself off, and lost a few billion genes down the waste-pipe, he usually does. Or sodomised the help. And he's maybe had a snort, or two. Anyway, he's got his blood pressure back up after all, and he doesn't feel good, and he's nervous about meeting The Gene, long time no see, so maybe little Cinderella Jana can fix him so he feels like cool again. It's cocktails at eight, isn't it?'

But cocktails it was not. Very small glasses of Dom Pérignon in the drawing-room with opened Colchester oysters and limes cut into quarter-moons laid out on beds of crushed ice. Protocol ruled. Mendoza, Boltana, Myklades, Brel and Feijoo stayed within the curve of the kidney-shaped table. On the other side of the statuette of Lenglen, or whoever, stretched up on ivory tiptoe for the perfect smash, Harriet, Jana, Rupert, and Burke kept their awkward distance. Hovering between the two groups a tall lady in her late fifties with permed grey hair and wearing a long black gown kept a severe eye on what was going on. This was Madeleine Thuin, the housekeeper of Sans Souci. Babalatchi and Taminah, also in servile black, stood by the doors.

The men wore dinner jackets, the ladies gowns. Pedro's jacket was dark blue with black frogging and signified that amongst his many other accomplishments he was a member of one of the highest orders the Vatican bestows. Rupert wore his Military Cross and Falklands medals, Burke his Queen's Medal. Harriet was in her blue silk sheath with Granny Austen's pearls. Jana alone wore a short black dress, but it said Armani, and the emerald necklace and earclips she wore said even more.

Harriet murmured to Rupert: 'Isn't all this a hoot?'

'Why?' Even he seemed a touch subdued, not only on his best behaviour but watchful, wary.

'Well. I mean. What are they all, after all? A bunch of gangsters aping their betters.'

'Steady on, old girl.'

'What do you mean?'

'Whatever else they are, they are one's betters.'

This coming from the younger brother of a belted earl, albeit in the Irish peerage, seemed a bit over the top.

'Come on.'

'How do you measure *better*? By breeding? Many people do. By money? Most people do. By power? Possessions? Style? Education? Accomplishments? That's an area of personal taste, I suppose, but by many, many people's standards this lot has it, has it all.'

'But they're still a bunch of gangsters. I'm not being moral about it. I just think it's funny.'

'Well, don't let on. They do unfunny things to people who find them funny.'

She shuddered, suddenly had to fight a deep angst that still got to her when she remembered the reality of what she was doing. But Rupert had turned from her, his attention, and everyone else's, now on the big double doors, inlaid with black, orange and white woods and ivory in modern versions of classical key patterns.

'This is it. The big moment.'

The doors opened and there she was: Botticelli's Primavera, Europa Malatesta. The moment was hieratic, Byzantine:

clearly, whatever else, she was a sacred object, a fetish, an incarnate palladium. Beneath abundant hair, gold with not enough red in it to make it reddish gold, but enough to make 'blonde' an inadequate word, in which small diamonds and pearls winked like stars, a broad and unblemished forehead, white like snow with sun on it, dropped to a perfect nose, thin, quite long, separating sculptured cheekbones. Her mouth was firm, full, but not large, her chin small but not weak. But the greatest perfections of all were her eyes: an intense, cornflower blue, with lids pronounced but not heavy, they carried an expression of unassailable serenity that even when they smiled spoke of a soul that existed in a world where it contemplated the artifice of eternity, and faced with equanimity what is past, or passing, or to come.

Her tall slim figure was clothed in fluted ivory lawn, cut full enough to float on the warm air around her when she moved, and a diamond of some significance set in white gold nestled in the hollow between her collar-bones. Her fingers, long and pale but strong, held a jewelled purse and a small fan made from thin leaves of ivory.

Applause, a polite whispering of palms against palms, led by Madame Thuin, but spreading through almost all of them, rose, sustained itself for a moment or two, then fell away. As, if, thought Harriet, she were royalty – which, of course, apart from the fact that no kingdom as such acknowledged her sway, she was.

Jana, at Harriet's shoulder, uttered, between clenched teeth, one of the few words that can be spoken thus.

'Fuck.'

Behind Europa came her grandfather, Enrico Malatesta. He had once been a big man, perhaps a fat man. But now his skin hung on him as loosely as his clothes, his white hair lay lankly across a brown dome mottled like a diseased boletus. His face was dominated by a large and once aquiline but now decisively hooked nose that almost met a prognathous jaw. The unnatural jut of it was such that occasionally two brown fangs appeared, reaching up outside the thin top lip. As a face it was a ruin, but an imposing one, and the eyes, set between folds that fell away on either side of his face like scree on a fissured mountainside, gleamed with a watchful yet entirely self-possessed intelligence.

They moved into the room. Pedro took Europa's hand and kissed it, led her amongst them, performed introductions: it was all done very quietly, very coolly, without fuss. Behind them Dr Lovejoy closed the double doors. Whether he had come through them behind the Malatestas or whether he had arrived a little earlier Harriet could not be sure. But it seemed to her that the watchfulness – anxiety, even – in his eyes betrayed that he was there in a professional capacity. On Enrico's account? Presumably. But the old man looked very fit for his age, which, Rupert murmured, was going on eighty.

They dined formally at a long ovoid table whose furniture maintained the relentless art deco modernity of the whole house: the plates were square, buttercup yellow, broadly banded with gold leaf. Even the glasses were square inverted pyramids and not too easy to use. The food was bland, and the drink not lavish. On her left Dr Lovejoy, placed opposite the Malatestas, told Harriet that the house had been built and decorated in the early thirties for a Belgian arms manufacturer, and lovingly preserved in spite of changing fashions. On her right Rupert had worse news.

'Hector wants to come to your room tonight.'

'Why? What for?'

Rupert's grin was explicit.

'I'm not going to let him mess me about.'

'No? Well, anyway. I think you'd better let him in.'

'Why? Hell, Rupe. I don't mind Hector. In many ways he's got a lot going for him. But I really would rather not have him in bed with me.' She giggled: although the Malays had been mean with the shampoo, on top of a couple more of Lovejoy's little helpers it was having some effect. 'I'd much rather you dropped by.'

'Not tonight, Harry. Listen. They' – his grey eyes flitted briefly across the faces of Boltana, Brel, Malatesta – 'are checking you out. Promotion is, I understand, on the cards. And an especially important and dangerous job. Not dangerous to you, but it will put them to some extent in your power. So they really do want to believe you're one of us. And being seen to be Hector's mistress will help. A lot.'

'Rupe – ' She tried to inject a nursery gaiety into her voice,

305

kids pulling a fast one over the grown-ups. 'Rupe, I'm a humble sort of person. I'm quite happy to remain in the position to which God called me. Especially if going up means the ultimate sacrifice.'

'Sorry, Harry. In this sort of organisation, you go up or out. Maybe if you go up it has to be on your back. But if it's out, believe me, it's not only on your back, but feet first. *The* ultimate sacrifice.'

Gritting her teeth, and feeling again that sudden chill, Harriet resorted to displacement activity. The light, most of it from a starburst of intricately frosted glass set above their heads, was good, would have been merciless if it had been any brighter, and she found herself scanning, with an eye that was in its way as professional as Lovejoy's, the lovely face on the other side of the table.

Suddenly she frowned, then looked up and round the table, seeking out Jana. She had news for the American girl – news which might please her.

Europa's beauty was a paint job. Done with extraordinary skill, but nevertheless a mask. No saying what it hid, but certainly there were skin grafts on both sides of the finely shaped jaw-bone. Why? An accident . . . burns perhaps, lacerations from flying glass? That didn't seem right – those minuscule marks contouring the replaced area were too symmetrical. Disease? But wouldn't the same apply? Disease does not lay on its pits and scabs with a ruler. The face shifted as Europa moved and the light that shone on it too changed, and almost it seemed to Harriet that the marks were gone. Certainly a hugely successful paint job concealing the coachwork beneath. But unblemished, unmarked, perfect, Europa was not. How far and why she was spoiled remained a matter for conjecture, and presumably for Pedro to discover. Harriet, remembering the beating he had given his horse, wondered what he would do to Europa when he found out.

Later, back in her room, she took two more of Lovejoy's pills to allay the sudden panic that overwhelmed her at the thought of Myklades' approach. They worked quickly, produced a rush of euphoria and a distancing effect too. Lying on her bed in the darkness she felt her body relaxed and warm, but also as not quite her own, as something separate, away from her. The knock when it came was not peremptory, but firm enough to be heard over the wind that still gusted round the house.

She called: 'It's unlocked.' She reached across and put on the bedside lamp.

He was dressed in his silk dressing-gown, smelled of colognes, deodorants, had obviously showered.

He sat on the edge of the bed, covered her hand with his, which was, as usual, cold, then his head came forward towards hers. She turned, but let him kiss her neck, below her ear. His breath carried the stark odour of disinfectant mouthwashes, but the sourness still intruded.

He sighed, very deeply. 'They think you are my mistress.'

She said nothing. The implications were clear: 'They' clearly meant Crystal; it was important to him that she should at least maintain the deception.

'They have a plan for you. Rupert will talk to you tomorrow about it, late in the morning. I am not going to tell you what it is, but it will be a great help for all of us if you do it. There is no danger for you in it, but there is risk for us, for them. They will be placing a great deal of trust in you. Do you understand what I am saying?'

She lay back, with her eyes closed. She remembered how he had dug his nails into her thigh and said 'Convince them'. She heard in her head a playback of Rupert's voice: 'Sorry, Harry. In this sort of organisation, you go up or out. Maybe if you go up it has to be on your back. But if it's out, believe me, it's not only on your back, but feet first. *The* ultimate sacrifice.' Again she shuddered.

The pressure of his hand returned, but more firmly. Presently he turned out the light and she heard the rustle and sigh of silk. Then in the darkness the cold length of his body pressed against her side. She turned her back to him and let him fondle her breast. In the darkness the blemished pallor of his skin no longer mattered; she was surprised by the lean strength of his legs and arms and torso, was ambushed by a tremor of desire. She turned again to face him, put her head into the hollow of his shoulder, let her hand, her fingers run down his back. 'Be gentle,' she said.

But his response was not what she had expected; it remained cold, mechanical, and undefined. She remembered Wrykin Heath: what was it he had said: 'I rely on professionals for that sort of service.' Something like that. Well, sod him then. And she turned away, a little mortified now, lay on her front. He moved, more decisively this time, and she felt his weight along her back, and a stronger presence that he had yet managed. Soon she realised he was trying to bugger her and the hoarse murmur carried on his sour sterilised breath seemed to be trying to explain why, but clinically, without passion.

'I do it this way because it confers on me a more total possession. You know what I am talking about.' He pushed away at her in the darkness. 'It used to be a secret, almost a hermetic secret. This way the semen, and other cells too, pass into your very blood, become truly part of you. Biologically you will remain mine for life. From now until you die my garrison will patrol your veins. You will remember this should you ever seek to betray me . . .'

Yet he failed to penetrate her anus, although he did eventually achieve a sort of climax against her perineum. As he urged himself on towards the moment, she thought of Steve, her toy-boy assistant. *Turn your back, and he'll shaft you*, he had said. She thought too of Jana – certainly sex with the American girl would have been a lot more fun and probably less perverse than this. But there was also something theatrical about it all, something contrived. It was as if she had been asked to perform a part in a ritual. She remembered too (her career photographing British businessmen had made it all too clear) how men do believe in rituals: the Lord Mayor's Banquet, ringing the Lutine Bell, frock-coats and striped trousers in St Paul's, and the Masons. Most women, she thought – and certainly it was true for her – didn't give a fart for any of it.

Yet she felt a sort of pity for him, and some tenderness even, and when he left her she squeezed his hand.

She slept, woke in darkness but with wind and rain again beating across the fields outside. She recalled that out there, a-hundred-and-seventy-odd years ago, forty-five thousand men had been mutilated and slaughtered in a single day. When one remembered what men did to each other one could be grateful that what they got up to with women was no worse than it was.

33

Next morning at ten o'clock the finance committee assembled in the library: Myklades, Lili Brel, banker Antonio Pérez, Pedro Mendoza, and his financial adviser, Teseo Feijoo. They arranged themselves in much the same way as before – informally in the cuboid armchairs in front of the yellow-tiled fireplace.

Boltana again nodded his silver-haired dome towards Lili Brel. His smile now went beyond gallantry: he had spent a hour or so in her bed during the night, had rediscovered pleasures that had left him feeling warm towards her. Her slim well-toned body had hardly aged in twenty years, though clearly she had gained in experience. 'We thought, did we not,' he said, 'that you would open the proceedings with a summary of how things stand at the moment?'

'Marqués, Gentlemen.' She smoothed the wool of her Chanel skirt over her knees, straightened her back, let her cool eyes meet his for a second before offering a smile whose calculated politeness included all of them. Boltana had changed more than she had: she had found him fat and heavy.

She spoke quietly but quickly, with confidence – a delivery that made interruption an impertinence. Her voice was husky but not deep. 'I am afraid what I have to report is not going to make very pleasant listening. As you know we originally projected that in the first year Mendoza Holdings would make available to Crystal two hundred and fifty million of Swiss francs. We have been in full operation now for four months. Forward projection on the basis of those months indicates a very considerable shortfall is likely. Worst case, net profit for Crystal could be as little as fifty million. Being as optimistic as I reasonably can I cannot see any possibility of achieving more than seventy-five.'

She looked around them again. Boltana, massive and

relaxed, continued to exude bonhomie much as a *jamón serrano*, a ham cured from acorn-fed free-range pig, sweats salty meatiness. Feijoo too, small, lean, grey-faced with pitted skin, also appeared unmoved, though perhaps his habitual twitch, a reflex galvanised by some source beyond his control, was a little more pronounced. Mendoza, however, looked stormy, lowering, his cheeks flushed with sudden anger. The emotion accentuated the habitual sulky look that made him not quite so perfectly handsome as he imagined himself to be. Myklades drummed his long mottled fingers on the chair-arm. Behind their tinted spectacles, his cold eyes flicked from one corner of the room to another, avoided those of his colleagues.

Brel went on: 'I have prepared a digest which explains how I arrive at these conclusions.' She passed stiff grey paper with accounts perfectly tabulated and printed to each of them.

Mendoza put his to one side. 'Can't we take this as read? I mean, we all know Lili can do sums and I know very well that I cannot. I feel dizzy after two minutes of this sort of thing. Surely what we need to do is work out why this has happened and then a strategy for putting it right.'

Boltana looked at him over the half-lenses he had folded out and put on. 'Come, come, Pedro. Lili is not one to waste our time. I imagine her exposition will indicate precisely the sort of answers we should be looking for. Please proceed . . .'

She took less than ten minutes. When she had finished she sat back in the armchair, snapped open her Hermès crocodile bag which was tucked in beside her, lit a Dunhill. Blowing smoke into the air above her head, she said: 'There you are, then. Not good, eh?'

'No. No, decidedly not.' Pedro was white now, head up, back straight, fingers clutching the arms of his chair. 'What can I say to Enrico? He would be quite within his rights to call the whole thing off. This is only the third time I have met Europa, and this news is going to quite ruin the whole occasion. I am no financial genius – I pay people to do that sort of thinking for me – but it seems to me from what Lili has said, that Myklades has a lot to answer for, eh? What?'

Boltana re-established his authority as informal chair. 'Hector. What do you say? Nothing if you would rather not at this juncture, but after that I do think you have a right of reply.'

'Yes, yes. I had supposed that the Duke would seek to lay the blame at my door.' The cold eyes flicked round their faces then returned to the ceiling, where a light-fitting constructed from chrome and cone-shaped shades, black on the outside, orange inside, was set in a plaster starburst. 'And I concede he has some reason. Even he can see that the returns that we projected Ambrose Finance would make are not being met. Lili's breakdown has to some extent suggested the reasons for this. I would like to elaborate on them.'

Boltana circled the glowing end of his cigar in a gesture that clearly said: be our guest.

'First.' Myklades tapped one straightened thumb with the index finger of the other hand. 'You will recall that at our first meeting I quite confidently suggested that seed capital of fifty million of Swiss francs would be inadequate. And I have been proved right. We have had to use nearly eighty million, which is more than even I expected. Partly of course this has been due to the poor performance of the pound and the dollar against European hard currencies. When we first set this up the pound stood at 2.75. Today, in Brussels, it was trading against the Swiss franc at 2.33. Mrs Thatcher's economic policies have done us more harm than her much-vaunted campaign against drug abuse' – he allowed himself a sour smile – 'but a pre-election boom and victory for the good lady should do much to enhance the standing of sterling and the profitablility of our enterprise.

'Sterling accounts for fourteen per cent of the shortfall. We have had to spend more on Ambrose Finance than we expected. Because our conversion of Ambrose took place in the run-up to Big Bang we were unfortunately in a seller's market for almost everything we needed: office space, hardware, software, and people we can rely on. In this area too' – again the smile – 'Her Majesty's Government has not been helpful. Clever rogues with the right City background have been at a premium. When such people can name their own salaries and demand platinum hellos from legitimate concerns like BZW, and Merrill Lynch, it has not been easy to persuade the particular people we wanted to join us . . .

'Security and counter-surveillance have also been more costly than I expected, with regard both to salaries and equipment. However, I am sure you will agree that this is one area where it would be ... ah ... criminal to skimp. The Duke will be in no position to give anyone the benefit of his genes from inside a jail, at least, not personally – ' This too came with a smile, assumed to blunt the insult. It failed.

'D-d-damn it, Toñi, I can't let him get away with that ...' Pedro stammered with rage, was perhaps on the point of calling his man out.

And indeed Boltana sharpened up his normally smooth tones to rebuke Myklades. 'Come, Hector, that won't do. An apology is in order – '

'I did not intend to give offence, and I am sorry if I have. I wish to express as strongly as I can that money spent on our security is money well spent ...'

Brel was not the sort of person to offer the Belgian equivalent of 'Hear, hear, hear', but a more than usually emphatic nod of her head said as much.

Boltana was bland again. 'None of us dispute that. So much for unforeseen capital expenditure ... Yes?'

Pedro, not to be put down, had raised a finger.

'This item here. Mermaid Pleasure. You haven't explained why it was necesary to sink nearly nine million Swiss francs into that.'

'No I haven't. But I will when I have clarified the main reasons for these difficulties we are in. The shortfall is also very largely due to factors over which I have no control, or nothing like as much control as I should like. First. The Arnolfini-Scapino set up. Using models as couriers. That ridiculous and indeed disastrous caper with the Ferraris. Now all of this was wished on us by Malatesta. Perhaps he thought he was doing us a favour. Perhaps he thought he was doing his Mafioso friends a favour. All right. To some extent they were useful, it was useful to have a system in place, and running, one that we could develop. But all that has now outlived its usefulness.'

'Tío Toñi, Uncle. I don't see why I should stay to listen to this. Already he has insulted me, the lady I am engaged to marry, now he is about to include her grandfather. I would remind you that this is your family too.'

'Pedro!' Suddenly Boltana's voice was Olympian in its majesty. At the sound of it Brel smiled inwardly to herself, remembering something from long ago. Feijoo twitched, and glanced up out of apparent reverie, exposing the yellowish whites of his widened eyes. Boltana continued to growl like distant thunder. 'Pedro, you will not be so impertinent as to remind me of family duty. And I will remind you that we are not yet related, except as remote cousins, to the Malatestas. Please listen to what Hector has to say.'

Pedro's flush deepened. For a moment they thought he was going to get up and leave, but he stayed put, chewing angrily on a thumbnail.

'Yes?' Myklades looked round again, breathed in, went on. 'That whole . . . *routine* is an expensive risk. Frankly these people are cowboys. They get into scrapes I have no control over, they are involved in criminal activities that have nothing to do with our operation, they are simply not reliable. The Biarritz business was unforgiveable. Seventy-five kilos . . . gone, disappeared. Eleven million pounds on the street. Twenty-five million Swiss francs . . .' The tinted glasses tilted, again his eyes searched the corners of the ceiling, but this time the thin mouth stretched into a grin he was trying to suppress. '. . . But I can at least say that the loss of the Ferraris themselves is one that the Arnolfinis have agreed to carry, that at least will not be a charge on Ambrose or Crystal. However, packaging still seems to be a problem. Since using expensive motorcars as wrapping paper has come unstuck I suppose he will go back to packing product inside excessively pretty girls. Again, I could see the point if our customers actually got the benefit. To have your coke delivered prewrapped inside the cover girl from *Elle* – '

Boltana rumbled: 'Hector, stop making jokes.'

'All right. But believe me the use of models is ridiculous. They draw attention to themselves. They can only carry small amounts at a time . . .'

'But that surely is the point! One is caught, and what have we lost? The others get through.'

'No, Duke. One is, as you say, lost, and we have to neutralise her. One way or another. It is all added risk, expense. Anyway. Subject of course to your approval . . .' – said with sarcasm – 'I aim to run down that connection and replace it with something far safer, far more reliable, something far more in keeping with the size of our operation. Something, in short, capable of importing into the UK three or four tons of product a year. Safely, given the security I have built up with people like Bridge and Burke running it.'

'Mermaid Pleasure?'

'Yes, Marquis. Mermaid Pleasure.'

But Pedro was not so ready to listen: 'I really must protest. I think this must all be gone into most carefully. There are ways of doing these things. Traditional ways, tried and tested. Myklades is empire-building, getting into his hands a whole area that basically has nothing to do with him. We took him on to manage the financial end of things in the UK, and distribution, not the importation of the stuff. I do urge on you the necessity to be most circumspect before you agree to this quite radical alteration in the way things are done.'

'Certainly we will look at Hector's proposals very carefully. But I suspect he has not yet finished.'

'No, Marquis. I still have one last reason for our failure to achieve the targets we hoped for.'

'And that is?'

'Well – ' Myklades shrugged, spread his thin white palms. 'In my estimation at the bottom of all our trouble lies the agreement that was made with the Arias people in Barranquilla. In the first place it was not for enough product . . .'

'I don't have to put up with this.' Pedro levered his cigarette from its holder, stabbed out the end, stood up. 'I have been subjected to innuendo and insult. Now the most major contribution I made to this business, at very considerable personal risk to myself, is being called in question. Teseo, you will kindly see to it that you defend my interests properly throughout the rest of this abysmal meeting. Toñi, Lili.' He nodded a tiny bow to each of them and was gone.

Silence, then Boltana sighed deeply, shook his huge head. 'Really, you know, I don't think we need take all that too . . . Please, Hector, carry on.'

Myklades returned from the inner domain he had withdrawn to. 'I was saying. That agreement guaranteed us barely six months' supply. In spite of the slight shortfall in sales, we have already shifted three hundred kilos of what was bought, and we have not yet agreed a price or amount for the next six months. Worse than that, it now seems clear that the agreement alienated the largest rival grouping of Colombian suppliers. First poor Feijoo was beaten up by them . . . that was bad, very bad, but was clearly merely a warning. Since then it has become clear that they, and particularly I mean the Welser family, have done everything they can to make life difficult for us. Most notably they have made it a condition of continuing to supply San in Rotterdam that he should not deal with us. Other alternative supplies have dried up on us too. Once these people have decided to be a nuisance to us there is no saying how much damage they might do us – '

'I am sure you're right.' Brel's voice had a cutting edge. 'I received this morning confirmation that this is so.'

Boltana turned to her. 'You have?'

Again she resorted to her crocodile handbag. Her long pale hand came up with a small piece of computer printout. On it, reproduced clearly enough in tiny microdots, was a cutting from a newspaper with a picture. 'This came over the wire to my private office in Bern yesterday. I received it by the same means this morning. Not the least annoying thing about it is the fact that the people who sent it knew of my connection with you and knew where to find me.'

She passed it across the space that separated her from Boltana.

He pushed his lenses to the top of his nose. 'Spanish. I'll translate. Barranquilla. Second of November. Less than a week ago. El señor senator Don Guillermo Welser takes delivery of three new cars. Needless to say, they are the best . . .' He looked up, let the lenses drop back down his nose. 'Needless to say they are Arnolfini's missing Ferraris.'

Feijoo made one of his rare interventions. He snorted, suppressed what clearly would have been a laugh. Myklades reached across.

'May I?' He barely glanced at the cutting, perhaps already knew from Brel what to expect, but his tone too was now firm, signalled that what he was about to say was non-negotiable. 'As far as I am concerned this is the last straw. If this operation is to continue, if I am to remain part of it, then the Arnolfinis *and* the Colombian connection must be phased out.'

There was a long silence. The fire crackled and a flame spurted.

Boltana cleared phlegm from resonant passages. 'Can we do without Arias?'

Feijoo passed a white hand through receding wiry hair, then

swiftly it dived to the pocket of his black silk suit, flicked a Chesterfield into his mouth, and snapped his thin gold lighter at it.

'We can. It will take time to set up the alternatives. But they certainly do exist.'

Brel shifted. Nylon hissed as she recrossed her legs. 'If it will take time then we must keep Arias on line until we are ready to drop him.'

'Of course. And that is part of the strategy I am about to suggest.' Feijoo fidgeted. His eyes crinkled against the smoke from the cigarette he had left in his mouth so he could whip out a large silk handkerchief, wipe his hands on it and stuff it back in his top pocket. 'It goes like this. First, I think we, Pedro and I, should go back to Colombia and renegotiate the contract. Initially they wanted twenty-five dollars a gram. We agreed at sixteen. I think that was too little, and that is why there has been all this trouble. I think we should give them twenty-two – ' Both Myklades and Brel were showing signs of distress. Feijoo rushed on. 'This need only be a temporary measure. For a year perhaps, not more than eighteen months. During that time we will put in place better, cheaper sources of supply.'

Boltana was roughly sceptical. 'Poof. How? The Colombian barons control the major sources. No one has been able to bypass them for anything but the smallest amounts for a decade.'

Feijoo's head continued to twitch. 'But the situation is changing. Nothing lasts for ever.' He pushed himself back in his chair, pulled in smoke. 'As you know, product originates on many thousands of small plantations on the east side of the Andes, mainly on the upper slopes of the Amazon basin. The area, which is huge, half the size of Western Europe, crosses frontiers and runs in an enormous semicircle from Venezuela in the north to Bolivia in the south.' Now he was running, the need that had been troubling him receded. He stubbed out his cigarette, slowly, with exaggerated thoroughness, watching his fingers working at it as he did so, without allowing the operation to interrupt his flow.

'Generally speaking coca leaves are processed into pasta close to the plantations, often by the growers themselves, or at plants owned co-operatively by them. Then, for historical, economic and political reasons, most of this pasta is bought by Colombian syndicates like the one led by Arias, processed by them into cocaine hydrochloride, and sold directly by them in the user countries, or to syndicates like ourselves. What we have to do is break this chain, find a way of diverting substantial amounts of pasta away from the Colombians. The point is, it's there. Already the growers are producing more than the Colombians can handle. All we have to do is find a way in. It'll take time, which is the time we must buy by offering Arias his twenty-two dollar gram, but once it's set up the savings will be enormous.'

'Why has no one tried this before?' Brel was at her most incisive.

'Lack of motive, lack of resources. But mainly because the situation in the growing area is only now changing, and changing fast.'

'How so?'

'With the exploitation of the Amazon and Amazonia. The traffic to the borders of Peru and Colombia has expanded many times over in the recent five years or so. River traffic, air traffic, even road traffic with the Trans-Amazon Highway, are now running at very much higher levels, but the infrastructures are not in place, the controls, the policing. The few officials are overstretched and corrupt. It should be possible to set up a network of buyers and a processing factory without drawing too much attention, and then ship it, fly it, down the Amazon . . . and the capital outlay will be really very small. All we need to do, the most difficult thing to do, is to establish the right contacts in the area. When that is done the rest should be easy . . .'

Distantly they heard the crackle of a racing engine started and gunned, the tonic triad of its horns. Pedro signalling that his tantrum had not yet died away.

Boltana was impressed – with Feijoo. 'I think perhaps you and Hector have been working together in this. Pedro had better not know *that*. But yes. I can see some arrangement along these lines might solve our problems with Arias and the Arnolfinis too. But Pedro will hate going back to Colombia. That could be a problem, yes?'

'Not necessarily.' For a moment Feijoo was almost coy. 'If

he is assured that Immaculada Dalfinger will be there, he'll go.'

'Very well then.' Boltana smiled at all of them, a valedictory benediction. 'We shall have to think this over very carefully.' He heaved himself upright, then to his feet. 'We still have much to do. Formalisation of the marriage contract, then a little celebration with, I believe, photographs to be taken by the excellent Miss Jones. Am I right?'

'Yes. I imagine that by now Bridge will have finished explaining to her what we have in mind for her.' Brel also stood. 'I must say, Hector, I am very impressed with your Harriet. I think she will do very well for us. I intend to offer her a small piece of our enterprise, perhaps one-quarter of a per cent of turnover. I suppose there is no chance of your persuading her to marry you?'

Myklades' sour smile came again, and his accent was more than usually guttural. 'She is not, I am afraid, the marrying kind. But Harry will not let us down.' The double *r* rattled in his throat, claimed ownership. 'I wish I could feel so confident about the Duke in Colombia . . .'

Part Six

The Bogotá Contract

34

A small launch with a yellow funnel purred twenty nautical miles out of a small fishing port and down a long necklace of emerald keys that diminished in size as they curved away towards the horizon. Between these islets and the mainland the water was calm with a slow steady swell. Occasionally it shelved to green when sculpted ripples flickered beneath the shadow of the yacht, and shoals of enamelled fish swung away from it. Sponges floated dreamily and grey swellings indicated conches. Then the bottom dipped again to purple and indigo, the wake boiled white, even whiter than the snows on the Sierra that floated above a mauve mist behind them.

The wind blew from the east, black squalls rode on it in pursuit of the sun which occasionally they caught and blotted. The rain walked like ghosts of giants beneath the black clouds, but always a mile or two off, beyond the reef and the keys. The tide was ebbing and banks of grey and reddish-grey marl heaved clear beneath the mangroves. Flocks of small waders carved parabolas against the clouds before flattening into a wide swathe and settling with a short run on spindly legs, a quick flutter and adjustment of wings, to probe the wet surface with knitting-needle bills.

The rear of the boat, from the small deckhouse that served as a bridge to the stern sheets, was covered with a striped awning, and there most of the party sat. Three Guajiro Indians, descendants of the Tairona who had lived in the forested slopes of the Sierra, moved amongst them with drinks: spritzers made from California Chablis and Perrier, *tominis* concocted from rum, coconut water, bitters and limes. There were dishes of tiny wizened potatoes in fiery coriander sauce, thin wafers of dried fish. The Indians were dark, faintly Mongolian, and fat. When the party came aboard they had stood at the head of the gangplank with Winchester pump-action shotguns. An M6o machine-gun zipped up in heavy plastic was mounted on the small foredeck.

Pedro was throned in the stern sheets, his arms spread across the gleaming rail. The bad temper that had plagued him and everyone in contact with him since he had first realised that a return to Colombia was unavoidable was lifting. It seemed that he was not required to stay with his parents-in-law, and Immaculada Dalfinger was there to console him. Nearby Jana Pensión watched the tall, white-blonde model with wary admiration; Jorge Aguirre fondled the large dark girl he had been with nine months before at Carnival, who was now, he said, his fiancée; and below, in the one small stateroom, Feijoo played cards for low stakes with his old adversaries – fat Felipe with the fluky voice, and Desiderio Rapal, the ageing Salsa singer and Colombian film star: the beauties of the Caribbean had long ceased to interest them.

'There will,' Pedro announced, 'be fishing. I could use the exercise. Jana's workouts are fine, but they are substitutes for the real thing, the pitting of muscle, sinew and brain against those of a stronger, fleeter beast. Man is a hunter, and I blame many of the ills of civilisation on the fact that we are deprived of the need to exercise the skills evolution designed us for. Denying the genes always brings trouble.'

Immaculada sat facing him on a slatted bench. Her bare knees were splayed provocatively, her long, strong legs, perfectly hairless, stretched towards him. 'Have you done much game-fishing?' she asked. 'I am sure you have.' Her eyes, no longer masked, were a hard greenish grey like certain agates between lids slightly puffy; her voice was husky but not deep. She contrived, with every gesture and movement, every intonation, to suggest that she was taking Pedro very seriously: as someone of substance.

'Not game-fishing at sea since I was a boy. One of the last trips my dear father took me on was out of Key Largo. The man we hired had worked as a lad for the outfit Hemingway used. I have to say his account of poor Ernesto was not flattering. A clear case of the pen being mightier than the rod, eh?'

Immaculada's laugh had just the right quality of mannish, locker-room complicity. Behind her, leaning over the teak rail with cleats and eyelets in brass polished to flash like liquid gold in the sun, Jana Pensión winced, but admired the accomplished technique as well.

Flattered, Pedro went on: 'I was only fourteen at the time but managed to hold an eight-hundred-pound broadbill for three hours. It's the back it gets you in, you know, the back and the shoulders rather than the arms. I think Jana is quite happy about my back.'

'Your back's AOK.' She could not resist demonstrating title to his body. 'But your stamina might be in doubt: too many cigarettes, too much hard liquor in the last few days. And what-all else.'

'But, darling,' said Immaculada, 'your stamina is just fine.'

María Dolores, the large girl with tumbling locks of brownish-black hair who had been with them at Carnival and at the Bar de los Ruiseñores, seemed determined to make a friend of Jana. 'I know I'm overweight. You must tell me how to lose two, three kilos.'

Jana sized her up. The flame shorts were well-filled, an evenly tanned tyre of plumpness lapped the waistband beneath the short-cut shirt. In a decade the breasts could be an unsightly problem.

'Five. You should aim for five.'

'Oh dear. I suppose so.' Dolores pushed loose hair out of her eyes. 'But I am not as fat as Jorge. Not that it seems to bother him or get in the way. I mean some men, when they get bellies like that . . .'

Jana remembered that workout, on the lawn at the Arias house, way back in March. 'Jorge's in fair shape for his size. He's a strong man.'

Dolly made round eyes. 'He certainly is. He has to be. In Colombia the occupation of minder is a high-risk one. You need to be fit to survive in that profession. You are all here on business, I think.'

Jana's pale brown eyes widened but remained expressionless.

'Well, that must be the case. I know Don Felipe advises Don Octavio in some areas. And Desiderio Rapal owns two plants where *guarapo* is processed.'

'*Guarapo?*'

'Pasta. Coca pasta.'

Jana turned away, looked down the snowy wake past Pedro's head. It was now framed by wings of gulls that had latched on behind.

'I don't know anything about all that.'

'Oh, there's no need to be like that. Everyone's in the cocaine business here, everyone who is anyone.'

Only three keys remained in the chain and they could now see that the second to last, little more than a small brown coral nipple on the bosom of the deep, had been built on. Among the wave- and wind-smoothed roundnesses, unnaturally flat surfaces of basalt and concrete gleamed, tinted glass flashed as they circled towards a small sandy bay on the south side. They were clear of the mainland now, almost beyond the protection of the reef. The dark sea was running, the swell smacked the hull, sent small showers of spray across the deck. A hundred yards behind, the water broke, sliced by shards of flashing silver.

'Bonito or albacore,' cried Jorge, and then there was a sudden shout from the deck-hand up in the bow: '¡Delfines, delfines!'

They crowded to the side to see. Three dolphins, one smaller than the others, a family perhaps, curved up out of the waves, hunted the shoal of fish. Jorge stormed down the deck, vaulted up by the port-side lifeboat, dropped on to the foredeck. The launch swerved, and the roar of its turbines, far more powerful than the antique superstructure suggested, wound up into a roar that was almost a scream. Real sea now broke over and along her as she hit the swell full on, dowsing Jorge and the forward deck-hand and soaking the rest behind the deckhouse. Glasses scuttered and smashed.

On the foredeck Jorge tore the covers off the machine-gun, wrestled with a catch that held it fixed. Suddenly it was free, and he heaved it round. The muzzle searched for the dolphins, which were now on their leeward beam, still a hundred yards off but going in the same direction, still hunting the bonito, and unaware that they themselves were hunted. The gun barked, then clattered in a long burst, the brass hulls spewed past Jorge's thick shoulders, tracer arced across the purple water, and one of the dolphins, caught at the apogee of its leap, exploded in a crimson cloud.

The master of the ship, a black-bearded mestizo in a white

cap, throttled back and circled the debris. Within moments the bonito had turned on their predators, swarmed in, tails and fins thrashing in the stained water as they fought for the larger lumps. Jorge and Desiderio Rapal, up from the card game below, blazed away into the fracas using the pump-action shotguns; they were urged on by Dolly and fat Felipe, who jumped up and down beside them, hallooing and shaking their fists above their heads in triumph whenever one of the big fish was hit.

The noise was enormous and some moments passed before anyone noticed that the Guajiro in the bows was again leaping up and down and shouting: '¡*Tiburón, tiburón!*'

Pedro, who had so far maintained an Olympic detachment from all this, commented: 'I expected as much. The noise, the commotion, you know, as well as the smell of blood, always attracts them.' Yet he joined the rest on the other side to watch three black triangles scything purposefully in out of the ocean, between the two last keys. The master knew what was required of him. He swung his craft away from them in another wider turn that again brought some spray sheeting across the deck, letting the big sharks get into the boiling mess that was staining the sea with a widening pool of oily blood, and while he did, his mate, the largest of the Guajiros and marked with a large scar down one cheek which ended in a hole at the corner of his jaw where his ear had been, moved between the male guests offering green metal eggs from a heavy wooden box.

The yacht circled back, timing its return to the carnage just as the first of the sharks twisted its wicked mouth and white belly to take the top half of an already blasted dolphin, and as he did Jorge and Desiderio lobbed a bomb each towards him.

Everyone aft of the deckhouse ducked below the teak rail: the grenades were not the stun bombs used by commercial fishers who want bigger than bite-size pieces to take to market, but M26 frags. Several shards of razor-sharp metal whistled across the deck, or thudded into the gunwale, and one of them sliced the awning above Jana's head.

Felipe's high voice screamed like a banshee as they circled in for another strike. 'For Jesus' sake, take it wider this time, throw further.' His fat cheeks were streaked with blood: not his own but a shark's. They did, and the effect of the greater distance was instantly flattening, debilitating. With the far too close burst of the first two frags the whole incident had hit a high from which it now dropped like a leaky balloon. Although these grenades exploded less than fifty yards further off, the difference in the noise, the fact that none of the shrapnel reached them, turned the experience into a spectacle: the orgasm was over.

The yacht turned towards the island, its dark ochre rock now glowing in the light of the immense burning sun that reddened behind them. A handful of sooty terns mewed sweetly, moved in against the wind to roost on the windward side. The tide had turned and a pair of roseate spoonbills, their colour sharp against the grey marl, ran with delicate, quick, forward-running movements, took to the air, also homeward bound. And behind them a cloud of raucous gulls gathered over the fast-dispersing remnants of the massacre.

A finger of dressed rock stuck out into the bay, made a small pier just large enough for the yacht to berth at. Two more boats were pulled up on the sandy beach – a fishing boat about a third of the length of the yacht, and a small skiff. The Guajiros slung all the luggage – and there was a lot – on to the quay. Jorge stooped, used his free hand to unloop the hawsers, slung them thumping into the water. The engines deepened purposefully and the Guajiros hauled the trailing ropes on board as the launch backed slowly out into the bay. The mestizo master, who had not left his deckhouse at all, touched a finger to his cap, spun the wheel.

Jorge turned. His large, even teeth flashed beneath his thick moustache. 'Welcome to Cayo Retiro.'

Pedro took a step towards him. 'I take it we have been kidnapped.'

'Certainly not, Don Pedro. Certainly not. Cayo Retiro is a . . . retreat. A quiet place where you can talk, and reflect and discuss, and eventually agree. Don Octavio has put it at your disposal. It is, you will see, very comfortable. It is also very secure and very private, and there is no possibility of our being under any sort of surveillance at all. We shall have everything we need.'

'Except the means to leave.'

Jorge shrugged, smiled. 'The moment I can tell Don Octavio

on the radio that you are all in accord, satisfied mutually with the arrangements you have made, he will send back his boat.'

Steps cut from polished brown rock climbed and twisted to low doors of tinted glass set beneath a lintel of undressed coral, pitted and brown. Jorged directed a black box at them, pressed buttons, and a minor miracle unfolded like a flower at dusk. First a distant motor coughed, settled into an unobtrusive hum. Then lights began to glow – behind the glass doors themselves, but also in unexpected places right across the island. Surfaces that had looked like rock were suddenly lit from inside, others glowed as concealed floods illuminated them. Water tinkled and giant ferns, orchids, and more exotic flowers and plants appeared. There was music, Andean flutes accompanied by an ethereal tinkling and jangling. The eruption of man-made light was strong enough to chase back the last reflections of the sinking sun, and tropical night closed above them like a lid; only the horizon burned for a few moments more with the last of the day glow.

Doors sighed open. They followed Jorge up steps, dishevelled and exhausted, leaving wet footprints on the rock. Dolly was in front, and her flame blouse and shorts were patched with dampness that looked like blood. As she reached the top a large white bird suddenly rose from a crag above them and floated on ghostly pinions out into the velvet night. She shuddered and said: 'I'm frightened.'

Jorge took her hand, small and white in his large, black-furred paw.

'No need, *querida, mi alma*,' and he passed her through and the others after her.

Inside, the dwelling, part house, part cave, seemed to be made of tinted glass and black marble discreetly veined with quartz. The air was faintly musty, stale; but as they walked through, reactivated air-conditioning coped with it. Within five minutes it had reached an even temperature of seventy-two degrees Fahrenheit and smelled fresh.

The central room was virtually a round island set beneath a dome of glass and surrounded by water, just wide enough to step across but bridged too with slabs of marble. Its centre-piece was a circular marble table polished so deeply that its surface looked like black water. In the centre, a gold raft, about a foot long, propelled by gold oarsmen, and carrying at the front a gold man wearing a gold headdress, seemed to float. The man held up both hands, almost touching the wings of his mask, in a gesture of blessing. Around this table gold Tairona masks, armlets and a gold bracelet snake with emerald eyes had been set out on low marble pedestals, cunningly lit from concealed spots.

Pedro refused to be impressed. '*El Dorado*. The Golden Man. One knows the story. Servants? Is there no one here to take care of things?'

'No one at all.' Jorge was expansive. 'You see, that is what makes Cayo Retiro so ideal for our purposes. Everything is so well arranged there is no need for servants.'

Pedro was not convinced. 'I cannot believe the arrangements include devices to transport our baggage from the quay.'

In the end Jorge himself manhandled fifteen assorted bags to the top of the outside stairs and through the glass doors. There he left them, saying they could take what they wanted to their rooms as need arose. Most stayed where he had dumped them.

For the rest Cayo Retiro lived up to his promise. There was food in freezers, and a microwave to thaw and cook it. There was plenty to drink. On the ocean side of the complex there was a suite of conventionally furnished bedrooms and bathrooms. In other areas they found a library of paperbacks in Spanish and English, a video-player with a collection of feature films, gear for skindiving and snorkelling, and three sailboards.

Not long after sunrise Jana in a leotard slipped out of her room. The glass doors opened as she approached them, and the warm air from outside breathed around her like balm. She sprang from the steps on to the rocks, made her way above the main sandy beach towards a smaller one she had seen from the boat. Land crabs rattled away from her, and a sooty tern rose from a rounded-out hollow in the coarse shingle above the waterline. It hovered above her with its white swallow-tail dipped towards her and its black dagger of a beak, but then, as she moved on, it circled, came back to its clutch in time to stab at encroaching crabs.

The island narrowed, dipped towards a headland, and she could see both sides. To the north the sea sapphire black, flecked with ermine, the horizon a line as hard as glass beneath a sky that was empty. Tide and wind dragged it along the rocky edge so there was no surf, just a ceaseless turbulence growing here and there to sudden explosions of white that rose as high as twenty feet and seemed to hang for a second before crashing like spilled bricks. The southern side was serene, the water pale aquamarine above white sand, shading to greens before disappearing into a lilac mist that already lay between it and the mainland. A couple of hundred yards out, just in front of the mist, a white triangular sail, its apex tipped forward, glided above a board. The sail was white but in its centre flashed the El Dorado mask appliquéd in cloth of gold. The board swung, creaming foam beneath its tilted prow. As it came round, Jana recognised the plump tanned body of Dolly in a red swim-suit. Above and beyond it all the distant Sierra glinted beneath a vapour trail that sliced the sky in two and pointed the way to Bogotá.

On a crescent of sand as white and fine as cocaine Jana swung herself into the workout she had planned. She began with a slow warm-up of prancing steps, loosening circles and shake-outs, moved into a fierce mixture of modern dance and gymnastic exercise. She was soon sheeted with a sheen of sweat which the sand clung to. After twenty minutes she wanted to shift to stomach toners; she moved off the sand to a flat rock, but found that already it was too hot to lie on.

'Fucking Caribbean,' she said, stripped off her stained leotard, and charged into it. Gems burst beneath her heels like wings. She swam for ten minutes, fast and well, and for the most part on her back seeking to get to the muscles and sinews the hot rock had denied her, then she let the tide and swell drift her back in, until she lay on the wet sand with occasional wavelets still breaking over her thighs and back. A yard or two away sand flies danced ahead of the water, but where she was she was safe from them, and she shut her eyes.

Minutes passed. She dozed to the nudge and slap of the little waves; the caress of water trickled and slipped into grooves and crevices. Then for a moment, she thought a fly had dared the water, was scurrying down her spine between her shoulder-blades. She was about to flinch it away when she realised that it was not a fly, that the splash and gurgle of water had altered almost imperceptibly, that the temperature on her back had dropped as if a cloud had materialised in the clear sky. A deeper chill took hold of her; she could feel the goose pimples surface on her skin. She cursed herself, but soundlessly, for a stupid cunt to let herself be caught so, then rolled on her back, throwing her elbow across her eyes to shield them from the glare.

Long golden legs straddled her, soared in grotesque fore-shortening as if seen through a 28mm lens to a crotch made sexless by white sharkskin. Beyond, framed between the undersides of her small breasts, the face of Immaculada Dalfinger peered down at her. A smile lifted the corners of her mouth. She bent her knees, let her buttocks drop until they rested neatly and exactly in Jana's pelvic hollow, between her diaphragm and her mons veneris. The weight was a presence, but not oppressive. The smile lengthened, threatened to spread to the eyes.

'Did I frighten you?' She held a clenched fist above Jana's navel. The last teaspoonful of dry sand she had been holding trickled down, then briskly she brushed her palms together. 'You need not be frightened of me, you know.'

'No?' Jana eased herself up and back, so her elbows behind supported her and her face was lifted a little higher, a little nearer the other woman's, but she did it all carefully, not wishing now to dislodge her.

'No. My job is to keep Pedro happy for as long as they want him to stay.'

'I figured that was it.'

'It's not easy. He gets bored.'

'Certainly does.'

There were one or two moles on her skin but only one serious blemish: the sickle-shaped scar on her right breast. The wound left by her black-phase jaguar had not healed well.

'Jorge will keep him happy today, fishing.'

'Better make sure he gets a big one.'

Immaculada laughed, shared the offered complicity. 'We are friends, yes? We should trust each other a little.'

Their eyes – brown flecked with gold, and grey-green chalcedony – held each other's reflections for a moment, then Immaculada let her knees drop into the water on either side of Jana's waist. She squeezed gently, and let a second quiet laugh bubble in her throat.

Fifty yards away Dolly's sailboard skimmed past the tiny

headland that separated the two beaches, the triangular sail lurched as she touched shingle then tipped sideways out of sight.

35

'Listen,' said Felipe Cortazar, and his podgy ringed fingers pushed the table edge so his chair tipped, 'there are five groups buying *guarapo*, processing it, and distributing *perica* out of this country. Five groups – families if you like.' His voice fluked back into its falsetto register. '*¡Mierda!* Why am I telling you this? you know it already.'

Opposite him Feijoo sat slumped, his face set like a roosting bird's, a starling's perhaps, between raised shoulders, eyes glinting, alert, but the rest of him very relaxed. It was going well. He had conceded a lot, gone to twenty-five dollars a gram without a fight, but the other side knew that they now had to match his supplementary conditions if the deal was to go through.

Felipe sighed, let the chair drop forward with a dulled metallic ring on the stone floor. 'Five families, but two have bifurcated, one of them twice, so really eight groups. Two of those do what Don Octavio says, so in all we control three of them, but not the other five.' He shook his head so his jowls wobbled. 'About half of Colombian production we can answer for. Not the rest.'

'But,' said Feijoo, 'it is a cartel. You agree prices. You agree not to compete in the same market. Don Octavio already had the market we were trying to take off your hands. All we want is guarantees that it will stay like that. That the only product that gets in there is what we guarantee to buy off you.'

Felipe raised his eyes to heaven signifying deep irritation, a school-teacher faced with a recalcitrant dunce who will not learn his lesson.

Desiderio Rapal smiled sharkishly. 'Of course we guarantee no product of ours will reach your market, not directly from us.' He injected a pleading, wheedling note into his voice, like a mother coaxing a child to take unpalatable medicine. 'But we cannot speak for the others. Especially we cannot speak for the Welsers, who have caused you, and us, so much trouble. There has been bad blood between the Welsers and Arias, but things should be better now with Jorge's engagement to Dolly – '

'She is a Welser?' Feijoo frowned, touched a scar at the corner of his right eye, recalled the beating he had been given at the bullring.

'A niece. So not too important. Though her father is in the government. Still, it may help.'

He tossed the tune back to Felipe, who played it reedily, punching the air with his cigarette. 'And there is another factor. You have persuaded Don Octavio that there are advantages in selling to you for twenty-five dollars a gram what he can sell for three times as much . . .' Feijoo's head lifted, a sudden intake of breath expressed scoffing disbelief. Felipe smiled, turned his palm up. 'Give or take a dollar or two. It could become a habit. It could spread. You are not buying all he and his assoicates have for sale. You are not buying half of it. Less than twenty per cent. Suppose he is persuaded to sell for twenty-five or thirty to someone else. Say to our Italian friends in Marseilles. You cannot expect him to control where they distribute it. Or at what price.'

Feijoo let his eyes wander round the almost circular room. The walls were lined with polished black marble, and the curve was broken only by the heavy door. It was lit, this late in the morning, entirely through the small flat glass dome above their heads that matched the larger one in the central hall next door. Heaven knew how the air was kept fresh, everything looked hermetically sealed, secure. The only relief to the Spartan opulence was a large gold bowl in the centre of the table between them in which six small water-lilies floated, white-petalled lotuses, blushing to pink near the pointed tips, each one perfect in shape and structure.

He smiled, and his eyes returned to meet Felipe's. 'But you do it. You do it already. From San Francisco to São Paulo, from Sydney to Stockholm, the wholesale price, not the retail price but the wholesale price, has varied by no more than ten per cent at any given time over the last two years. How you do it I neither know nor care, but you do it, and you can go on doing it for us. And to help us believe that you will, we are suggesting you put fifty million in escrow. We suggest you use a bonded vault in Santa Cruz de Tenerife, and we'll set up lawyers there to hold the keys . . .'

'A vault? So. Fifty million in what?' Felipe's voice squeaked angrily like a chalk on slate.

'Gold bullion.'

Felipe threw up his hands, pushed back his chair so it screeched on the stone, slapped his hands together in disgust.

Feijoo cupped his pale hands round a Chesterfield and breathed blue smoke at him., 'You've got it. And in Tenerife too. Ex-Heathrow.'

Felipe swung back at him, prodded a thick finger. 'You know too much. You know a lot too much.'

Feijoo smiled. Then suddenly Felipe sneezed, then sneezed again, and again, a great storm of sneezes. Desiderio and Feijoo had to get up and hold him as the sneezes seemed to tear through his massive chest.

'I'm sorry, I'm sorry,' he wheezed and fluted at last. 'It's those fucking flowers. To some flowers I am allergic . . .'

'The important thing,' said Pedro, 'is to know when to strike, when to lodge the hook securely in the fish's jaw. And how hard to strike.'

'And how should I know that?' Immaculada rested her cheek against his upper arm, smiled up at him. She was sitting in a swivel chair set in the stern of the boat, holding the game rod in both hands with the butt still slotted in its socket in the deck. Pedro leant over her, an arm on each side of her head, also holding the rod.

'Instinct. The inborn, bred-in instinct of the natural hunter. Just as I know instinctively the precise moment at which a grouse will swerve, so I know precisely when to strike and how hard. It comes from a sort of empathy one has with the nobler beasts. One has it or one does not. I have it. Ah. Dolores. Thank you.' He took from her a glass that had already misted, sipped. 'Daiquiri. And almost as cold as it should be. Really, you know, it should numb your tongue, like cocaine. Give you frostbite.'

'So you can't taste how strong it is?' Jana did not wait for an answer but faced forward again, leaning out beyond the gunwale which sloped up to the roof of the deckhouse, became its lintel. It was really a very small boat: the cockpit they were in at the back was barely big enough to take the swivel chair, hold all the ancillary tackle and leave enough room for three more people to move around or even sit without rubbing knees. There was a little more space under cover, but most of it filled with the hatch that covered the engine. Beyond it Jorge sat on a swivelling stool with the small wheel in his huge hands.

From coldboxes and a basket Dolly prepared drinks, cracked lobster shells.

In front of them there was nothing but the dark sea and a horizon that seemed too close, on the port beam the last of the keys dropped astern. Behind it the sun flashed from the glass dome in the centre of Cayo Retiro.

'What,' said Jana, 'would happen if we jumped Jorge and took his boat back to the mainland. Thanks, Dolly, but I'd prefer just straight juice if there is any.'

Jorge turned, grinned luminously from the shadows. 'Felipe and Desiderio would chop up your friend Feijoo and use him for marlin bait. And anyway, you don't know how much gas we have on board. Maybe you'd run out before you made it.'

'The coastguards would pick us up.'

'We own the coastguards.'

'The navy?'

The three girls said it with him: 'We own the navy,' and they all laughed.

Dolly added: 'And my father owns the air force.'

Into the silence that fell Immaculada cried; 'Darling, it's pulling quite a bit more than it did. Does that mean I have caught a fish?'

Pedro grabbed as large a mouthful as the packed ice in the glass would allow, set it down, reached across her again, grasped the rod above her hands. 'Yes. Yes, there's something there. Steady now, steady. No. No, don't wind in, let it take line . . .' – some memory from twenty years ago stirred – 'give him line but make him work for it. Jorge. Throttle back.'

'I already did.'

'Darling, do I strike yet? I mean, what is striking? What am I meant to do?'

Dolly handed juice, crushed strawberry in colour, towards Jana, but missed complete contact so a spoonful was slopped

334

on to the American girl's knee before she could get a firm grip on the glass.

'Oh bother. I'm so sorry. I'm not quite myself on a boat, you know.'

'Don't worry, it's nothing. You looked pretty good on a sailboard this morning.' She looked up at Jorge's fiancée. The dark girl looked tired, preoccupied, pale beneath her rich tan. What's Jorge been doing to her, she wondered. There was a lot of savagery in Jorge, she reckoned, and not too much inhibition.

Dolly became aware of her attention, smiled wanly.

'Sailboarding isn't real compared with this. Don't you think this is fun?'

'It's okay. But I don't think Pedro really knows what he's doing.'

Pedro was getting excited again. 'There's a dip in the line. Wind in, reel in, fast, faster if you can.'

'Darling, I'm doing it as fast as I can.'

'He's swinging out now. To the left. Jorge, Jorge! To the left!'

Jorge spun the tiny wheel. The dipping line tautened, sang like a cello string and then dropped, flopped into the water, the life gone from it.

Pedro was beside himself. 'I said left. Why did you go the other way? We've lost him. Lost him straight away, right at the beginning. We could go all day and not get another. Why the devil did you go the wrong way?'

'Señor. You told me to go left. I went to the left. My left, the boat's left, even the fucking fish's left. But not your left.'

Pedro thumped the gunwale. 'I will not be spoken to like that. Take us back to the key. Immediately.'

'No.'

'Why not?'

'They can't work if we're fucking about under their feet all day. Dolly, *querida, mi alma*, give Don Pedro another drink. Bait up and chuck another line out.'

Immaculada built bridges over troubled waters. 'Darling, you take the chair this time. I'm sure you'll be a lot better at it than I am.'

'Yes. That would perhaps be better.'

The sweet smells of diesel, shellfish and rum drifted round

the cockpit. The benches the women sat on vibrated seductively with the throb of the engine. Jana and Immaculada sat together on one side, Immaculada with a long bare arm draped round Jana's shoulders, Jana with her hand on Immaculada's knee. Dolly sat opposite, looking back to the diminishing chain of keys. Her largish teeth chewed constantly on her bottom lip, picked up carmine lipstick from it, and the hand that gripped the gunwale was clenched so the knuckles showed white. Occasionally she offered the other two a shy but distracted smile across the untidy tackle. Jana thought: Dolly has a deep anxiety problem – I ought to know why.

Feijoo said: 'Look, tying this angle up is something we have to let lawyers do when we get back to the mainland. The next thing we have to talk about is payment. At present financial instruments are passing directly between Berkeley Key bank on Tortola and your accounts in Switzerland, Liechtenstein and Bogotá. We feel that this leaves us a bit overexposed, especially the Bogotá link – '

Felipe fluted, and his gold rings flashed as he waved a podgy finger. 'That is not negotiable. We made it clear from the start that some sums must be paid in hard currencies directly into our Bogotá banks. We have many people, many very important people, in the government, in DAS, the secret service and so on, leaders of the conservatives, who have to be paid, and paid in Yen, Deutschmarks or Swiss francs. All right? You can understand this? Yes?'

'Sure. Sure I understand it.' Feijoo smiled yellowly. 'But there has to be a better cutout, cutouts cost, and at twenty-five dollars a gram I think you should carry that cost.'

Rapal shrugged. 'We've covered a lot of ground. Before we take this one on I need a break. I need a leak and a sandwich.' He stood up, fetched his jacket off the back of his chair, draped it over his shoulder.

'Okay. Why not?' Felipe raised his bulk, then dragged out his handkerchief to dab eyes that had begun to run again. He squeaked: 'And let's take those fucking flowers.'

Feijoo leant forward, took the large bowl in both hands. It was beaten into dimples like copper, but being gold, was heavy. Its bottom was raised into a shallow dome, and as he

336

lifted it something clattered on to the table top from underneath it.

'What is that?'

A round black disc, about two inches across and half an inch thick.

'That,' said Feijoo, 'has to be a bug.'

They all looked at it as if it might bite, could be poisonous, and then, with eyes carefully emptied of emotion or meaning, at each other.

Rapal cupped his thin claws round a Senior Service, snapped a lighter, breathed smoke. 'It was,' he sighed, 'the idea of Dolores Welser that we should have flowers in here.'

Two o'clock and the sea was flat, oily, bloomed violet shot with gold where the sun caught the rolling rises of its heave, embroidered with patches of yellow weed. The engine idled, only an occasional touch on the wheel needed to keep her head to the swell, prevent her from wallowing beam on. It was hot now and they had all stripped off what few clothes they had been wearing and all were, to varying degrees and through various means, high.

Jana now sat in the fishing chair, tilted back, legs spread to the sun, letting it swing with the motion. Behind her shades her eyes were open, and her ears alert. She had had only fruit juice, and eaten nothing, and yet she was buzzing – on anticipation. Perhaps hunger, the sea, sun and sky combined to promote a steady flow of adrenalin and other more complicated substances to make her vibrate with certainty that something was going to happen.

Behind her, in a litter of plastic glasses and lobster-shell shards, three fish, all of them substantial but none of them noteworthy, slithered wetly on the boards in sea and slime and their own velvety crimson blood. Their jaws were torn: they had been clumsily gaffed. The last, a tarpon, was still alive, gasped soundlessly, and occasionally banged its silvery tail. For a brief moment it had been beautiful, haloing itself in sun-struck spray as it leapt six feet in a despairing attempt to wrench the hook from its lip.

Jorge had shouted, disgust in his voice: '*Sabalo*, Jewfish. Lousy eating, chuck him back.' But there were no scales on board and Pedro would not relinquish his conquests until he had had them weighed and photographed.

Dolly was draped along the upholstered bench that ran the short space between the stern and the point where the rail climbed. She was twisted so her cheek was pillowed on one elbow while the other arm hung loosely over the side, almost to the water, which occasionally reached up to give her fingers a sloppy kiss. She had been sick when Jorge gaffed the first fish, a small marlin, and spilled its still palpitating intestine. Now her eyes, tormented with foreboding, searched the deep. Occasionally huge jellyfish drifted by, a foot or so beneath the surface, blisters filled with mucus, eyes that would not blink.

Under the deckhouse canopy Pedro sat cross-legged on the convex engine casing, holding a plastic glass in both hands above his ankles. It was about half filled with a yellowish clear liquor, and occasionally he sipped it. At first he had shuddered at its bitterness, now he seemed not to notice the taste. His eyes had the far-away unfocused look of someone who is walking through landscapes of the mind.

Immaculada knelt behind and above him, holding his temples between the palms of her hands. Her voice murmured dreamily: 'A giant ball of golden fire, a crater in the hillside, a lake. A god had come. So every year, at the time the meteor struck, they made a god of their king, their *cacique*. They smeared their bodies with red achiote, and they put on feathers, gold ornaments and emeralds. Around the rim of the crater they lit fires. Then they went to their *cacique* and painted his naked body with resin . . .' Slowly she began to caress Pedro, ran her hands down his back, across his shoulders, pushed them beneath his arms to circle his chest and stomach. 'Then they poured gold-dust over him, and the dust stuck to the resin . . . *El Dorado*, the Golden Man.'

Jana refused to turn, to watch, but she listened, and she remembered how Immaculada had poured white sand down her back, into her navel, and she wondered what the liquor was that Immaculada gave Pedro, what she would have to do to find out.

'And they led him to the edge of the crater, where a raft made of balsa logs covered with gold beaten to airy thinness waited for him, and he came towards it, the Golden One, moving through clouds of incense. Musicians raised gold trumpets . . .'

Perceptibly the wind freshened, and swinging her chair Jana could see the afternoon storms climbing over the edge of the horizon.

Jorge sat across the driver's seat with his knees up and his head back. Occasionally his heavy breathing developed into something between a snarl and a snore, and once he came stumbling and swinging into the cockpit and pissed long and loudly over the gunwale, into the sea.

A bleep, repeated. Jorge's hand groped for a handset.

'¡Dígame! ¿Don Felipe? Sí Aquí. Seguro . . . ¿Qué? Seguro. Sí. Horrible, horrororsa, sí. No . . . Adiós.' He replaced the handset, twisted with his arm over the back of the seat and looked down and back but over them all, said nothing. His face was dark, in deep shade against the brilliance of burning sky and sea beyond the windscreen, yet Jana felt sure that his eyes grew moist, liquid. Then he shook his head and sniffed, then sighed. They waited. All three women, with their heads up, watched him; only Pedro remained as he had been, unmoved, his dream of gilded godhead unbroken.

Dolly cleared her throat. Her face was even paler, and deep purple shadows had formed round her wide brown eyes. Her voice trembled. '¿Querido? ¿Qué? ¿Qué pasa? Is anything wrong? What's happened?'

Jorge threw back his head, exposed his thick throat and they could see the vein in it throb, then he bellowed, loud and long, a terrible bellow of pain such as one hears from a badly fought bull, and out of the bellow words began to form. '¡Querida! ¡Mi alma! . . . My darling, my soul.' Then he flung his heavy, strong naked leg over the seat, and hoisted himself after it, tumbling, then staggering across the yard or two that separated him from Dolores, and the whole boat dipped with him, drifted across the swell and tipped him on to her. Together they collapsed onto the deck and there, with the dead and dying fish slithered against them, he struggled to take her; nor did she appear to resist, but the boat dipped and rose, water splashed across the gunwale, dowsing all of them, and Pedro and Immaculada tumbled sideways off the engine casing. Jana grabbed handholds, climbed her way across them, and the horizon swung up and then sickeningly down again as another

339

long barrow of a wave hauled them over its ridge and down the other side. She got to the wheel and forced the head of the boat round again, into the rising breeze and the swell, then turned her head over her shoulder.

Immaculada swore a steady stream of obscenity that seemed to be directed at Jorge. Blood trickled steadily from Pedro's cheek and mouth, and he appeared to be crying. Beyond them she could see Jorge's hairy buttocks rising and falling, could see Dolly's long and perfectly painted nails tearing down his back and sides. The tarpon slapped her thigh with its tail and died. Jana turned back, her eyes flashed across the controls, she found the throttle, the engine roared and the boat surged forward, like a thoroughbred from a starting stall, its flat snout of a bow hitting each crest and thudding into the trough beyond.

'I think we've got this about right now. Of course we'll have to find a law firm in Panama that we can mutually trust . . .' Feijoo tipped his head, and this time it was not his habitual twitch. 'I think I can hear the boat.'

Through the silence they could hear a buzz like a distant mosquito.

'You could be right.' Felipe pushed back his chair so it squeaked to echo his voice. 'Let's go and see.'

They reached the glass doors just as it sliced through the channel between the two keys. The first squall of the afternoon was moving in from the east, a purple bruise on the sapphire sea. The boat's bow carved combs of foam out of calmer water, and the aerial on the deckhouse roof whipped in the air as it swung into a steeper turn towards the tiny jetty.

In flat dead water Jana put it through one hundred and eighty degrees, cut the motors back at just the right speed to counter the impetus that now carried it in reverse. It backed on to the jetty as the first waves it had thrown up swirled on to the white sand.

Before it touched, Dolores threw herself across the narrowing gap. Barefoot but back in her red swimsuit she raced up the jetty, leapt on to the sand on the far side, and, almost before they could realise where she was heading or why, she reached the sailboard she had beached in the morning, thrust it into the water, swung herself on to it and hauled up herself and the sail in one flowing movement. The board slid forward against the tiny wavelets, carried only by the force of her initial launch, and slowed almost to a standstill, then the sail shuddered as it drifted beyond the lee of the house, shuddered then filled, and she bent her body like a bow and let the sail belly, and they could see her dark head framed against the appliquéd gold mask.

Yet Jorge had time. He loped up the steps, pushed through the three men at the top, hammered on the glass door which was slow to respond, and was out again in a moment brandishing an M60 machine-gun, the twin of the one on the launch that had brought them to Cayo Retiro. For all his size and strength it was a cumbersome thing for him to handle, and the belt of ammunition he had slung over his shoulder slipped so he had to hoist it again and loop it over his head.

He ran past the end of the jetty just as the sailboard was about level with it, and then on over the rocks, heading for the small point that separated the two beaches. He slithered, stumbled, almost lost his footing, but kept pace with her, for although the wind was quickening more and more as she got further out, it blew diagonally across the small bay, carried her across the point rather than away from it. He had as much time as he needed, time to unsling the belt, release the safety catches, load and aim. The clatter was deafening, reverberated across the island, sent terns and waders swirling into the sky behind them. Tracer arced upwards from Jorge's shuddering body, then as he got control swooped down, cut across the sail and the girl's body, hesitated and swung back again. During a particle of time the sail held the storm of metal and torn tissue then spilled into the sea.

He went on firing until the belt was used up, disintegrating into clips which flew from him with the brass hulls of the cartridges, until the board had been shattered into shards of unidentifiable glass fibre. When he was finished he stood for a moment, then he swung the gun behind him and heaved it out into the water. They heard him, a long-drawn-out wail: '¡Querida! ¡Mi alma!' fading and breaking up at last into moaning sobs as he sank to a crouch, clutching his face in his hands.

Rapal lit a cigarette, rasped behind cupped hands. 'And too we must not forget the Welsers stole seventy-five kilos plus those fucking Ferraris.' He breathed blue smoke across spaces already polluted with cordite.

Felipe Cortazar pulled out a handkerchief, wiped his face, his neck. He cleared his throat, and his voice ricocheted into its usual whine. 'We still have work to do. If we are to be ready to go to Bogotá the day after tomorrow we had better get on with it.'

Pedro, climbing the steps ahead of Jana and Immaculada, lifted his head and forced his eyes to focus. 'Bogotá,' he said, 'is not an agreeable city. Really, it is not. You know?'

36

The pilot of the *Conquest* made a small detour, offered them a view of Lake Guatavita, a small tarn, a glinting eye at the bottom of a steep-sided crater whose sides were covered in what looked like coarse grass and scrub. The surrounding countryside was moor, grass, a few woods, terraced fields. It looked cold and bleak.

'As is often the case,' said Pedro, 'the legend, the myth surpasses reality.' He looked pale, still wore a plaster on his cheek covering the cut he had received when Jorge allowed the boat to wallow across the swell. 'Amazing to think the whole business of El Dorado, the extraordinary expeditions, the massacres, the treks through jungles and across deserts, right to the Orinoco and the Amazon, all took place because of that squalid little lake.'

Sobered, he had assumed the persona which he believed was his real self: distinguished leader of society, knowledgeable, intelligent. At such times his inclination to tell people what they already knew or had no wish to know became even more pronounced. 'The irony is that the Chibcha had no gold of their own. They traded it for salt, of which they had a lot, and for emeralds. Of course none of the Conquistadores believed that. A culture that was ready to cover its leaders in gold-dust and then make them wash it off in a lake, would, they reasoned, have a surplus of the stuff, an inexhaustible source . . .'

He must, thought Jana, have got hold of a Baedeker or a Fodor.

The plane dipped towards mountains, passed quite close and not far above a huge statue of Christ, entered cloud again, and suddenly rows of orange airline lights appeared in front of them, hung in the mist like a jewel, receded in an isosceles triangle to a control tower labelled in lit letters *El Dorado*.

Freeways circled the city and carried them away from it up steep hills through meadows where huge mushroom-coloured cows grazed, and then down avenues of eucalyptus trees. The cold mist thickened into rain offering only occasional glimpses of the vast sprawl below, of skyscrapers, churches, parks and squares laid out on a grid with its main arteries already marked by necklaces of light. Although the swift fall of night had not yet begun it was dark not with the shadow of the mountains but with a black smog that rendered toxic an atmosphere already rarefied and deficient in oxygen.

Iron gates swung open, guards in paramilitary uniforms smacked the butts of their machine-carbines in salute. The drive was paved with stone and meandered through gardens of yellow and red roses to a three-storeyed house, pale pink beneath brown tiles and with a six-pillared colonnade covering the middle third of its frontage. Top-hatted footmen in red greatcoats were ready for them with huge umbrellas. Rosy light from a huge Venetian lantern reached into the ghostly rain, and the mountain air was scented with rose and spiced with eucalyptus.

They were welcomed inside by Jorge Aguirre, who had left Cayo Retiro ahead of them – unable, he had said, to remain in the place where the love of his life had died by his own hand. A helicopter had winched him away from them during the night. In fact he had gone on ahead to brief Don Octavio and his associates about the sort of deal that was emerging. He led them across huge oriental carpets whose deep blue glowed like lapis lazuli into a colonnaded reception room where coffee steamed in eighteenth-century porcelain and sweetmeats and *petits fours*, Rémy Martin and Dom Pérignon had been laid out for them. Beyond the windows on one side orchids wept silently beneath the rain; on the other a disc as white and round as the Host, dipped between the genuflecting mountains.

'Certain arrangements have been made and we hope you will approve them,' Jorge announced. 'At nine o'clock, Don Octavio proposes to introduce Don Pedro to three of his principal associates in the library where the broad outlines of this historic contract will be agreed. At half past ten Doña Serena and Don Octavio invite you to share a simple supper with them. Afterwards we have the Boccherini Quintet of Cartagena who will perform works by Boccherini and Mozart.'

Delicately he shelled a tiny egg-custard sweet from its paper case and popped it beneath his large black moustache.

'Tomorrow we check out the small print starting at ten and finishing by four in the afternoon. Our secretariat will then prepare copies which the principals will be able to initial at an evening reception tomorrow night.' He grinned, dropped the polite precision. 'Okay?'

Pedro looked at Feijoo. Feijoo shrugged, removed a crumb of sugar from the corner of his mouth. The silver rain whispered to the windows tales from the velvety blackness beyond. Pedro cleared his throat, spoke firmly. Jana recognised the tone he used when laying on the line his ancient name, his dukedom, his right to the courtesy title of prince, and his personal assets worth a hundred million dollars.

'Teseo takes care of this sort of thing for me. I shall be happy to attend the signing ceremony tomorrow night. Until then . . .'

Felipe Cortazar interrupted, his falsetto slicing the air like an electric saw. 'Ah. But I am afraid Don Octavio is most insistent that you should be present throughout these deliberations. It is a matter of impressing upon his associates your personal commitment. Naturally they have the highest respect for your person, your status, your reputation as a man of honour, and they insist you should be witness to everything. I assure you a successful outcome depends upon it.'

Jorge's smile became even broader. 'The fact is of course, my dear Duke, they are fucking snobs.'

In the bustle that followed, Immaculada reached out a thin white hand. Jana responded to its pressure and followed, certain that behind her Pedro's jaw had tightened as he bit back the request or order he was too proud to make. Immaculada led her down a service corridor to a yard behind the house. There were several cars there and she chose a flame-red Porsche which she drove with the nonchalant ease of a young housewife taking the Mini to the supermarket. It took her only ten minutes to get back into town. She turned off Carrera Séptima near the bullring, swung down a ramp into the basement carpark of the Olympic Towers. She needed plastic to raise the barriers, to activate the lift, and keys as well as plastic to release the catches on her fifteenth-floor front door.

The apartment was furnished and decorated in white with touches of arterial red and gold. The carpets were covered with long-haired Angora goat rugs, the deep low chairs in cream-coloured vellum. There was a log fire, gas-ignited, but real logs that gave off spicy smells as the crackling blue flames took hold.

Immaculada dropped to her haunches in front of a lacquered cabinet. From it she took a gold disc, six inches in diameter, and a small gold box. Slowly, delicately, she spooned out a tiny pyramid of snowy powder, and cut it into four lines across the disc using a thin blue steel blade.

'Do you take coke?'

'Not often.'

'Nor do I. Not much, then. Enough, eh? Then we'll have a shower and I'll lend you some decent clothes and we'll go out. It's a mean city but a lot of fun. I'll show you.'

Nothing much on the first line. But the second brought a cool, electric rush. The flames in the fireplace, the shimmering gold, the rain outside that streaked the black window, and Immaculada's voice which had the roughness of velvet pushed against the nap, whirled inside her head.

Later Immaculada sat in front of the fire and Jana knelt behind her to comb out her hair. As she pushed the gold-mounted tortoiseshell teeth round the small nacrous ear, feeling the firmness of the skull soften as they passed into the nape of the neck, as she watched how the wet hair divided into neat lines and ended precisely over the first obvious vertebra where white shoulders angled in, she suffered a brief pang of longing.

'First we'll go to the Tequendama. There are always airline pilots there. It's quite close.'

Her feet, shod in emerald-green high-heeled shoes whose lizard-skin facets sparkled, rattled down steps into the street. She wore black-phase jaguar, like Napoleón, a long coat that glowed and was cut full so it swung with her movements. On anyone less tall it would have looked bulky. Sheer black stockings disappeared beneath its hem, were anchored, Jana knew, to the black suspenders which were the only other garment Immaculada wore, apart from jewellery: an emerald necklace and pendant emerald ear-rings mounted in platinum. She trailed behind her an odour of musk.

She flinked across Carrera Séptima dodging the ancient buses and Jana followed. She was wearing a soft black leather coat over a miniskirted black dress which was tighter than she would have liked although she was a couple of inches shorter than Immaculada. But Immaculada had been admiring. 'It's muscle you know. You are very strong.'

In one of the hotel's quieter bars they sat at the counter, drank fruit juice and, heads touching, planned. 'The two men behind us are British Caledonian. They are really rather nice, but they have very little money. Qantas are the easiest because they get drunk very quickly, but they are also the most boring. Sometimes too they vomit. Ideally, we want to find a loner, but that is rare, they stick together, and men on their own are wary of girls in pairs. But we will see what we can do. Ah. I think already we are in luck.'

'I'm sure you two little girls will let me buy you a drink.' He was a big man, very big. He had a crew cut, a red face that glistened, a red jacket and loud plaid trousers. In spite of these the most noticeable things about him were his hands. These too were huge but looked like a baby's – they were podgy, the red skin on them looked blown-up. He ordered champagne and they moved to a low table set in a dark alcove. Distantly Sinatra did it his way.

'My friends call me Matt. I sure hope we can be friends. I sell tractors. I've just sold a lot of tractors and right now I'm looking for a good time. They told me before I came not to go out after dark looking for one but wait right here and let it come to me, and hell, I think they were right. Isn't it hot in here? Wouldn't you like to take off that coat?'

Immaculada's fingers found a fastening, then returned to

deep pockets. She allowed the pelts to shift and then drew them close again.

'Holy shit.'

'I'd rather take it off in your room,' she murmured.

Matt pulled out a huge handkerchief and wiped his face.

'I'd reckoned . . . on having me a steak first, something to eat.'

'There's room service. Have them send up a steak. Why not?'

He ran his tongue round his lips, pulled them back in a snarl that showed crevices between his teeth and gums.

'I've had a tiring trip, you know? I'm not so sure I can manage . . . handle . . . take on board . . .'

'Two of us? That's all right. My friend only likes to watch anyway. It's the only way she manages to come. Playing with herself while she watches. Isn't that right?'

Jana managed to nod.

Immaculada stood, smiled. 'Let's go up then. What number? And let's take the bottle with us.'

As Jana closed the door behind them, Immaculada swept off her coat and slung it into a yellow silk chair, flung herself on to the bed, which was still covered in yellow box-pleated satin. She bounced, landed on her knees, stuck her bottom in the air, peered round her arm.

'Come on then, Matt. Come on.'

'Jesus,' croaked Matt. 'Jesus. I knew tonight I was going to get laid, but I never reckoned it would be so soon.'

She wriggled sideways across the bed so her feet, still in emerald lizard-skin shoes, hung over the edge, sunk on to her elbows and her back arched up like a roller-coaster track to the curve of her bum then the line swooped down the backs of her legs to the inside of her knees.

'Let's just hang on a moment. I mean, let's finish that bottle.'

'Come on, Matt. I'm ready for it now, I mean, Matt, you make me feel cheap hanging around like this. Carmen is ready too, aren't you, honey?'

Through clenched teeth Jana squeezed the words: 'Certainly am. But perhaps he can't get it up . . .?'

'Shit, woman. I got no problem there. Look. Look at this.'

'No, Matt. We can see you got no problem there. Let me

347

help you off with those things. These pants of yours, they're very smart. And I like the fancy clocks on your socks.'

'Hey, you speak darned good American, Carmen.'

'Well, I studied there for a time. Now come on, Matt, she's waiting, why don't you get on with it?'

'You mean like she is now – you know, doggy-fashion?'

'That's the way we like it.'

He moved in and the bed creaked very slightly as Immaculada shifted so her bottom moved in and dropped a little. The tractor salesman splayed his legs to adjust to the new angle, and reached forward, putting his blown-up hands on either side of her as though he were unwilling to touch her with any part except his large and fully tumescent prick, which quested like a blind snout beneath the broad curve of his belly. Behind him Jana worked quickly; he heard something snap, but had no idea that it was a surgical glove. He came close, and again Immaculada eluded him, and he moved further off balance, knees now pressing on the edge of the bed, his own enormous bottom covered with a fine down of ginger hairs arched up, and at that moment it happened.

Jana reaching from behind gathered his balls and some of his prick into her gloved hand, and her thumb probed for his anus. For a moment it felt cool and damp.

The agony bit. He leapt upwards, swinging round and blindly smashing out at her, but she ducked and squirmed under his arm, then he had to grasp his crotch as the burn steadily rose in terrible intensity. He looked at his hands and found them covered with a fibrous orange and greenish slime. His mouth opened for the scream he had so far suppressed.

Immaculada shouted: 'Cold water. Lots of cold water, shower it and go on showering in cold water until the pain wears off. If you're quick, you'll come to no harm, but if you linger . . .' Already he had gone, lurching blindly into the bathroom.

'Right, come on. Cash only. No cards, no traveller's cheques, just the cash.' Briskly, she went through pockets, shook out his wallet, found a billfold. Jana stripped off the glove, rinsed her hand in the wash-basin. Within a minute they were ready to go.

At the door Jana turned and called out: 'Matt. You'll be okay. No need to think of a doctor or anything like that. What

348

you got on you is a paste of mashed chilli, grated ginger, and lime juice. Is all. Ciao.'

They stood for a moment on the sidewalk, heads on each other's shoulders, embracing tightly and rocking with laughter, then Immaculada took Jana's hand, and half skipping, half running they swung down Carrera Séptima. Modern blocks soared between the nineteenth-century apartments with wrought-iron bars on the windows, sculptured or stuccoed entrances. The streets were not crowded. Indian women wrapped in heavy dark ruanas lingered on the corners, shielding dishevelled children from the cold, and calling plaintively: 'Marlboro, Marrl-borro.' Jana was not sure if they were begging for cigarettes or trying to sell them. They ducked into a rapido-burger, ordered burgers with chilli sauce, and that set them giggling again. Immaculada totted up the take.

'Two hundred and twenty-five dollars. Two thousand pesos. That's really not bad, you know. Mostly they rely on plastic, keep fifty dollars mugger's fee, that's the going rate. The really city-wise ones even get the desk clerk to pay the whore off when she leaves and charge it, to avoid getting rolled. Matt'll be wiser next time. I wonder who he was selling tractors to? We should have found out.'

She bit into her burger; the tip of her tongue curled errant sauce back into the corner of her plum-painted mouth.

'Why? Why should we have found that out?'

'The coke barons handle the imports of agricultural machinery as part of their Yankee operation. They buy all the leading makes at the factory gates, that's how they convert the dollars they want to use here. The laugh is that there is a government subsidy for importers of tractors. No, whoever Matt sells for is not going to be popular with Don Octavio. Come on. We've got our stake. Let's see what happens.'

They sauntered on down Séptima. Although most shops were closed there were still a few open, and of course bars, discos, nightclubs and restaurants. Salsa and Caribbean music echoed out of alleys or from ghetto-blasters. Urchins and teenagers hovered, eyes bloodshot with malnutrition or dope – in amost every group reefers were handed round. They begged, offered girls or boys, dope or *perica*, were poised to pounce on a purse too loosely held, or grab a wallet exposed as a fare

349

paid off his taxi. Some offered leather goods, twisted-silver-wire trinkets, Sacred Hearts, posters of popular singers including Desiderio Rapal, from spread blankets. They did not expect to make sales: their wares were bait to trap the attention of the unwary, who would find themselves bundled into a doorway, tripped, or just jostled and their pockets picked or briskly emptied at knife-point.

The two women passed through unscathed, almost the only people who actually walked down the sidewalks rather than scuttling from cars or taxis. Why were they left alone? Perhaps because Immaculada was known – known as someone who could retaliate swiftly and mercilessly; perhaps because in spite of her finery the street recognised one of its own.

Shortly she cut across the avenue and threaded them amongst a concentration of older blocks where the life seemed noisier, warmer, in spite of the fog that rolled out of the mountains and often lay a foot or so deep across the paving so men and women appeared to float on amputated legs above it.

Here there were beautiful people: transvestites of both sexes, the men peacocking it in sequinned gowns, with fur stoles and outrageously high heels that set off their calves and made their bottoms swing with bravura and allure; the women middle-aged and fat, in double-breasted suits and two-toned shoes, using their own obesity to mock the grossness of the successful bourgeois.

Immaculada pressed a buzzer by a narrow door covered with wrought iron, spoke briefly into a microphone, locks clicked, and the door opened. A narrow staircase, painted in crimson gloss that held together cracked plaster, dropped them to a basement. A huge black dressed in jeans with a T-shirt that read 'US MARINES' displayed teeth filed to points, offered Immaculada five, opened another door.

The large room, also painted in red gloss, was packed, and, apart from a brightly lit pocket-handkerchief of a stage at the far end, almost impenetrably dark apart from the glow of joints and occasionally the flare of a lighter or match beneath tin foil. There was a bar, but serving only half-litres of rum and Coca-Cola. Many of the clientele were in some sort of disguise, possibly to add fantasy to the ambience, more probably to preserve anonymity: they wore face paint, false beards, eye patches, even nylon stocking-masks. There was music, deafening, although at that moment attempting to provide suitable accompaniment for the act taking place on the stage.

This consisted of a girl, completely naked apart from body paint patterned to suggest bright green tropical foliage and flowers, and a very large snake. It was olive brown with black ovoid spots on its back and points of white along its sides. Its body was thicker than the girl's arms. It had already circled her neck, reappeared under one arm, had made a turn round her waist, and, tongue-flickering like black lightning, was now heading south over her stomach.

Space was made at a table and bottles of Coca-Cola with straws were put in front of them.

The lady on the stage placed one foot on a spangled stool. In her right hand she had a short black wand. The snake lost interest in her navel and took a right turn towards the new angle at her waist, so she tapped its nose. The soprano sax which had been wailing in the conventional pattern of snake-charming music, switched on top register and the drummer added in a slow crescendo on his largest cymbal.

A chair was squeezed between Jana and Immaculada, who had opened her fur and pushed it back off her shoulders so the top part of her body gleamed whitely in the reflected glow from the stage and the emeralds bounced some of it back. A long leg, jeans ending in shin-high Gucci boots, swung past Jana's face, and a lean dark man climbed down between them. His face swung very close to Jana's and she saw that one side was conventionally handsome in a Hispanic way, that the other was strawberry coloured and strawberry pitted, probably by a burn. Then she squawked, loudly, but the sax was squawking too.

Twisting in the cramped space his left hand had found and cupped her breast through the black crêpe de Chine of the dress, and his right hand had dabbed her, she found later, across the border between the aureole of her nipple and the white skin around it, with the end of his cigarette. Two or three sparks flew and the pungency of burning silk hit her nostrils with the pain, then in the dark she saw the cigarette glow green beneath dark eyes that dared her to react.

On the stage the re-routed anaconda was at last getting its head under the lady's crotch and heading up the back of her thigh to reappear over the top of her raised leg. At fifteen feet it was only a baby.

The man with the cigarette had his face close now to Immaculada's ear, and his left hand was clenched round her right wrist, holding it clamped to the table.

The drummer smashed his cymbals, the lady threw her arms up in a stagey gesture of achievement, and . . . blackout. But just as it came the man ground out his cigarette on the back of Immaculada's wrist. When the lights came up – dim ones, very dim but not just over the stage – he had gone.

'Who the fuck was that?' Jana was deeply angry, but frightened too. Not least because Immaculada looked uncharacteristically cowed.

'Police.'

'Shit. What sort?'

'DAS. Political. I've got to think. Think out what to do.'

She chewed her lip, nursed her wrist, occasionally glanced around with a wild look in her eyes, then she pulled the fur back round her and stood up.

'Come on. We have to go.'

Already the streets looked emptier, colder. Newspaper gusted about, most of the beggars and street arabs had gone, only the old remained over steaming gratings or outside bars. Safe in the taxi Jana was still angry, and the fear was receding.

'What fucking right does a shit have to do a thing like that?' She had pulled down the top of her dress, was trying to establish the extent to which she had been damaged.

'You saw the burn on his face.'

'So?'

'Five years ago Toñi Rey was in the riot squad, in uniform, and a student got him, square on the shoulder with a petrol bomb. Not often they blow on that sort of impact but that one did. A girl did it and so it was done properly. Ever since, he likes to burn women, just a little, whenever he thinks he can get away with it.'

'Screw him. But why do we have to go home? What did he say that makes that so much a necessity? I liked that joint. It was keen. Neat. We've hardly spent any of our loot . . .'

'Shut up a moment, Jana, I have to think.'

The American girl pulled away, stared out of the window.

'Shit. Look at that.'

Coming down Septima towards them, pushing through the black cloud of diesel smoke it was itself creating, a tank. The turret was open. Helmeted and goggled like a death's head a soldier sat, exposed from his waist up, clutching a machine-carbine.

Immaculada said nothing. Jana glanced across at her. She sat very straight, still nursed her burnt wrist. Again Jana felt a spasm of feeling, a desire to reach out and offer comfort.

Back in the white apartment, Immaculada took off her make-up, made and drank coffee, changed into a plain black denim trouser-suit, a yellow polyvinyl raincoat.

'I have to go out. See some people.'

'Can't I come too?'

'No. You must stay here and wait for me. If I'm not back by midday, and if the streets are quiet, then take a taxi back to the Arias house, and forget about me.'

'What the fuck's going on? What do you mean, if the streets are quiet? Forget about you? I'm coming with you.'

'No, you're not. The people I have to see would not let me near them if I came with someone. They could even decide to kill us.'

'Then I'm going back to the Arias house right now.'

'No. Don't do that. Listen. You saw the tank. You saw how the streets emptied. It's like a sort of unofficial curfew. It's not safe until daylight. Please stay here.' She was pleading now. 'I'll be okay. I know what I'm doing. I should be back before dawn, but don't worry if I'm not.' She brushed Jana's lips with her own and was gone.

For an hour Jana wandered about the apartment, trying to kill time. She flicked on a television, got a choice of *Bonanza* and *Miami Vice*, turned it off. In a bathroom cabinet she found a lot of pills and capsules. Most of them were unfamiliar and she didn't feel like experimenting on her own. Right at the back, probably not touched for years, a bottle of 8mg Librium. She took four and a glass of orange juice and felt a bit better. Amongst the CDs there was a Julio Iglesias record. She lay on cushions and Angora rugs, put a log or two on the fire, almost slept.

At midnight she heard the squeal and rattle of tracked vehicles, turned out the lights, drew the blind, looked out. Four tanks were parking in the piazza in front of the bullring.

It looked as if some of the floodlights inside were on, and troops were debus-ing from combat-painted vehicles parked by the main entrance. Nearer to the Olympic Towers riot police erected barricades, sealed off the approaches. Jana shivered, suddenly felt frightened, uncharacteristically lonely. She redrew the blinds, put one of the lights back on, and prodded the scented logs. 'Immaculada,' she murmured, 'Immaculada, I wish you were back.'

The city lightened with a false dawn, the sky reflecting a sun still cut off by mountains, and police sirens wailed. She went to the window again. Two black armoured Mercedes vans, windowless apart from armoured windscreens, swung out of Séptima, came round the piazza and parked by the entrance. Their escort of bikes, and a police jeep with flashing light and banshee siren, peeled away from them. Beams were unlocked, lifted down, the double steel doors pulled open. The people inside were tumbled out like bales of awkwardly shaped goods. Only two tried to struggle. They were clubbed with carbine butts, and even from the fifteenth storey in a bad light Jana could see the sudden rush of blood down a young man's face. None wore a yellow vinyl mac.

In the next hour three more convoys arrived. In all Jana saw about two hundred people herded into the bullring. Then a sliver of white gold edged above Montserrate, grew into the disc of the Chibcha sun. Warmth flooded through the window, and the streets below steamed white. Ignoring what was happening in front of the bullring an old man appeared and took down the shutters round a kiosk that sold bubble-gum and cheap newspapers.

37

Immaculada looked pale and tired but otherwise unharmed. The two women held each other for a moment then Jana gave way. 'I've been really frightened – really frightened, you know? You read about this sort of thing, see newscasts, but they don't tell you what it feels like. What is going on? Is it a revolution or what?'

'No. Not yet. Just a purge. Listen, I want a drink and a bath, and I'll tell you some of it.'

'I thought purges was something the Commies did. Like Castro in Cuba, and those new guys in Nicaragua. Anyway, what have you got to do with it all? Why did you have to go out? I'll fix you a drink, draw a tub, but I want to know.'

Her head floating in scented steam Immaculada began to talk.

'Toñi Rey told me. A round-up of the left. There were some he wanted me to warn. Problem was, why. I mean, he could have been serious, really wanted these particular ones warned, or perhaps he just wanted me to lead DAS to them . . .'

'I don't get all this. Not at all. How come you know these Lefties? It's not your scene, no way is it your scene.'

'Listen, have you heard of *Sendero Luminoso?*'

'Luminous sidewalk? What sort of shit is that?'

'Shining Path. It's no sort of shit.'

'It sounds like shit. Captain Marvel shit. You know, I really don't understand any of this. You're talking like some sort of Leftie yourself.'

'Listen, Jana. You want to get places, you want to know about this sort of thing.'

'All right. Go on.'

'The old revolutions failed. Arbenz in Guatemala, Allende in Chile. The Sandinistas can't win. But there's a new force now. Organising the peasants across borders, really getting to the Indians, and the workers too, a proper base in the millions down there at the bottom of the heap. And Shining Path is right there, has nothing to do with the old Left, the old liberals, the professors and doctors and dentists and social workers; they're real, and they're going for broke, and because they have millions and you can't cut down millions, put them in bullrings and shoot them, they'll win. One day. Okay. In Peru and Bolivia they're called Shining Path. Here they're called *El Jardin en Flor*, the Flowering Garden.'

She lay back. With the paint and the grime coming off, and the tension leaking out of her body, she looked softer, more vulnerable and older too.

'I know some of these people. I know them from way back. I keep in touch, they keep in touch with me. With my connections I can be useful to them.'

'But why? Why keep in touch, why be useful?'

'Jana. You've not been listening.' She pulled her shoulders out of the water again. The scar left by Napoleón's claw glowed fiercely. She spoke slowly. 'One day these people are going to win. And when they do they're going to make a very clean sweep. They will kill. On the same scale the right kills now. That's never happened before in the Americas.'

'You can get out. Surely you'll want to get out.'

'Maybe. Perhaps not. Perhaps it won't be that easy. I don't want to be a boat person, an exile. So I keep in with them. And there are other reasons too. They need things. They need things now. Arms. Transport. Things that cost. It's a growth area. And they have things to sell too.'

'Like what?'

'Pot and coke do grow on trees. That's a fact. But what makes them grow? Who plants, who harvests? Peasants, Indians who join the Flowering Garden because Flowering Garden breaks their legs if they don't, and pays them double for their crop if they do. Do you begin to understand it all now?'

'I'm getting there.'

'Sure you are. One day they'll win and I think tonight I got it right. Got to them enough to make them feel warm about me, but without overexposing them to DAS. And now I want to go to bed. With you. And sleep.'

She stood up and the fragrant water slid off her. Her body had lost its white look, looked fresh and innocent. Jana wrapped her in a hot towel.

Jana discovered satisfactions she had never before experienced. She learnt too how to generate them: from then on a woman who shared her bed could expect a good time. Knowledge is power. Later they slept unbothered by the gunfire that reverberated round the drum of the bullring, of the chants, shouts, screams, the clatter of horses' hooves, the pop of CS gas canisters, the thunder of water-cannon. The sun climbed steeply to an almost exact zenith and plunged back. When Jana next looked out of the window, on her way back from the bathroom, it was as if nothing had happened at all. The buses swung round the square and picked up office workers on their way home and the old man sold afternoon editions of papers that announced that the security police had swooped in a successful operation on the homes of known terrorists, had uncovered caches of Soviet and Cuban weapons and made many arrests. A Marxist, atheist plot had been defused thanks to the viligance, professionalism and integrity of the forces of law and order.

For a time they lay facing each other, eyes entwined and fingers too, then Immaculada yawned and stretched.

'Soon time to take you back. Back to your prince.'

Jana giggled. 'Not quite.'

'What?'

'Mine.'

'Yet. You're working on it.'

Jana turned on her back to avoid Immaculada's eyes. 'There's a thing or two you could tell me. I mean – you had him pretty well eating out of your hand.'

'You want to know what I was giving him?'

'Yes. I mean like he really believed he was the El Dorado guy, and all covered in gold, when you told him he was, and he'd taken that stuff.'

'Well, I'll tell you. It's yagé. That's the Indian name. Some tribes call it ayuahuaska. It's tricky stuff. You can only get it from twigs of a vine that grows on the eastern side of the mountains, down towards the rivers, lower than coca. And you need quite a lot, and it has to be fresh. You boil it up, for just the right length of time, two hours, the wood only, no leaves, make an infusion. And then you have to use it in twenty-four hours, though I've found if you freeze it when you've made it, it'll keep.'

'And it acts like peyote.'

'A bit. But stronger. And, as you saw, with a little practice you can control the hallucinations, that is if the subject knows a bit about what you're talking about, and you help him a bit in other ways. That way you can give him a really good trip, or, if you want, a bad one.'

'So where can I get some? Supposing I'm not in small-jet range of the jungle?'

'You can't. But there are others that work as well or better. A powder you take like snuff or *perica*, and it's stable.' She pushed long legs out from under the cover, stood, and stretched again. 'I'm going to have a shit and a shower. See if

357

you can make my coffee machine work.' From the bathroom she called: 'There's one other thing.'

'Yes?'

'These hallucinogens are tricky in other ways. Give a guy an overdose and he can have fatal convulsions. So until you know how he's going to react or how strong a particular brew is, you want to have an antidote handy.'

'Which is?'

'Any anti-convulsant sedative. Barbs are fine.'

In the scarlet Porsche again Immaculada said: 'Your prince snorts a good bit.'

'Certainly does.'

'More than is good for him?'

'Sometimes, three times since I've been on the payroll, he's got into a state with it, nervy, paranoid, difficult.'

'What do you do then?'

'Give him a shot of morphine. He doesn't know what it is, but it calms him down again.'

Immaculada took the car between two trucks like a bird, then let her hand drop on to Jana's thigh.

'Honey, you'll get your prince. Remember me when you do.'

Men in black ties, women in long dresses, gathered in the reception rooms. Amongst them strutted a scarlet cardinal with a purple monsignor in tow. Waiters served the champagne, whisky-sodas, rum punches, and again there were tiny potatoes like wizened shrunken heads in hot coriander dip. At the end of the largest room there was a colonnaded semicircular alcove lit dramatically, framing a dais and an ormulu-mounted Empire table topped with rose marble. On it were four large folders bound in red leather tooled with gold leaf, and two gold pens set in jade pen-holders. Somewhere a quartet enlarged by a double bass fiddled away: pom, pom-pom, pom-pom-pom-pom-pom-pom – a little night music.

Pedro was sufficiently beside himself actually to approach Jana rather than wait for her to come to him.

'Where the devil have you been? I've never been so bored in my life. I have a nasty pain in my neck, just here, you know what boredom does to me. It really has been dreadful. And the music. The wretched viola's D-string is nearly a quarter-tone flat. Just listen to it. Your dress has got a hole in it. You ought to change it ... It looks like a burn. I suppose you've been smoking pot. Well, I wish to hell I'd been able to find some ...' He paused, looked at her with eyes that looked momentarily bereaved, puzzled, though his voice was as peremptory as always. 'Please find your way to my room as soon as this is all over. My neck!' He moved away, then turned back. 'By the way, I haven't seen Dalfinger since we arrived yesterday. You don't know what's become of her, do you?'

The animated gabble of those who seek to impress those whom they know will not be easily impressed surged up around her beneath the blue layers of cigar smoke that drifted into the chandeliers, sucked up by the heat of the countless bulbs. Mozart chugged on gamely. She took a glass of passing Dom Pérignon and looked around to see who else was there apart from Pedro she might talk to and located fat Felipe Cortazar, with, inevitably, Desi Rapal at his shoulder. And they were, yes, sharing a joke with Feijoo: suddenly the Guatemalan's yellow teeth flashed and she heard his nervy staccato laugh cutting through the general noise. Truly the final meeting must have gone well enough for both sides to make a tolerable show that they were pleased. Then Feijoo's head jerked and she realised he was not at ease, was surreptitiously scanning the crowd – though whether anxiously for a friend or warily for an enemy, she could not tell.

A flunkey, in powdered wig, cut-away red coat and white vellum breeches appeared on the low dais, banged a silver-mounted staff on the floor. Through the crowd six old men converged upon the platform. They were large, overweight, corseted, immaculately suited, wore extremely expensive watches and heavy rings. They all had white hair, in two cases not their own. Their skin glowed with good living, the charisma that protein, good booze and limited exercise taken on boats or ski-slopes provides. And they all now assumed expressions of serious preoccupation as they greeted each other round the marble table, murmuring to each other without smiling, fishing for spectacles, surreptitiously wiping their hands on large handkerchiefs. From amongst them Don Octavio emerged, came to the edge of the step, and won a sort of silence, even from Mozart.

He spoke briefly, with carefully coached dignity, of the momentousness of the occasion, of the pride it gave him, of the far-reaching consequences, of the benefit that would accrue to all concerned. He was sure they were all aware that they were about to witness an historic agreement, involving many millions, even billions of dollars over the coming years, between a group of Colombian businessmen and a European consortium, an agreement that would bring stability and security to an area of trading that had always been problematic. He asked them all now to welcome Señor Don Pedro Mendoza, Duke of Pastrana and Prince of Eboli, who was there to represent their new European partners.

The applause was nicely judged, carefully modulated: not a spattering, but not vulgarly effusive either. Pedro looked young, vulnerable, a chick amongst vultures. The speech went on. It was indeed a source of great satisfaction that under the more liberal regime provided by the new government it was possible to celebrate an occasion like this in such an open way. It was good to see at least two ministers had felt able to attend . . .

A large man, leonine, but a lion showing signs of mange and age, approached Jana, offered her a cigarette from a platinum case crusted with yellow diamonds, which, of course, she refused.

'I am looking for my daughter,' he said. His voice was deep, throaty, yet there was intensity there too.

Jana waited.

'María Dolores. Known as Dolly. Perhaps you can help.'

Jana felt this like a blow. Whoever he was, however powerful, she felt she should not be seen with him.

'I don't think so.'

'Perhaps not now. But do take my card, get in touch.'

She looked at the card: Senator Guillermo Welser, addresses in Bogotá and Cartagena.

'I can pay you whatever you want.' The lion's gaze passed over the crowd. 'As well, better than any of these.'

As he padded away she shredded the card to confetti, dropped the pieces.

Frightened now Jana looked about her, picked up suddenly and quite close to her, but partly hidden in a side alcove, her friend and lover Immaculada Dalfinger. She moved towards her, hoping for reassurance, even advice on how to handle Welser's menacing intervention. Dalfinger's back was to her,

her head thrust down exposing the nape of her neck, so she could talk into the ear of a man smaller than herself, but standing very close. The conversation was brief, serious; then round the model's shoulder, white like a dove's wing, Jana saw the man beyond nod, his hand flash through his grey wiry hair, and his head jerk, unmistakably. It was Feijoo. Jana bit her lip, puzzled now as well as frightened. In all the time they had been together or near each other on both trips, she doubted she had seen the Guatemalan businessman and the tall Colombian model exchange more than ten words of conventional courtesy. What were they up to? What was going on? She felt suddenly cold and a little angry – not as much in Immaculada's confidence as she had supposed, and excluded from the help she needed.

Again applause. Gold pens were passed from hand to hand. Feijoo moved out of the alcove, and Jana took a step towards it, but a strong presence, heavy, threatened at her shoulder, barred the way. Jorge Aguirre, monstrous in a black tie whose droop echoed that of his huge moustache, grinned down at her with teeth that flashed like a predator's. Tall and tough though she was, the solidness behind his white shirt and crimson cummerbund felt like the back of a bus relentlessly pushing her back, a bus in the hands of a homicidal madman.

'I think just now you spoke to the man who should have become my father-in-law.'

'He did not tell me he was Dolly's father.'

'I think he did. It would grieve him terribly to know how she died.' The big head shook in psychopathic mockery of grief. 'It would grieve me terribly if he knew. I think you know what I might do to someone who seemed likely to tell him.'

She kept outwardly cool; inwardly the terror she already felt was screwed up a notch or two more.

'Do I?'

His voice took on a hot throatiness she had heard in it before. 'If it was a woman I would cut off her breasts.' He smiled, pulled open his tuxedo so she could see the Astra Magnum in its fancy holster. 'And rape her. With this. Then, because she had said too much, I would leave her with a necktie. Do you know what that is?'

Pale now, she nodded. She knew. Her throat would be cut up under her chin and her tongue pulled through the gash to

361

hang there like a tie. Again she tried to pass him but he moved to block her. And Immaculada had gone.

Laughter from the dais. Don Octavio held up one of the leather-bound folders, high above his head in both hands, and, to the loudest applause yet, the Boccherini Quintet of Cartagena struck up a brisk martial rhythm. 'Non Piú Andrai', from *The Marriage of Figaro*. Presently several people began to clap in time, but on the dais ceremony still ruled. Solemnly Pedro shook hands with Octavio, then allowed himself to be embraced. He was also required to kiss the cheeks of his mother-in-law, Doña Serena, who had appeared at her husband's side. She was dressed in a black sheath and her emeralds were enormous. Her eyes were perfectly expressionless.

'A marvellous woman,' murmured Jorge. 'So brave, she has suffered so much.'

Jana glanced at him, saw that he was in the grip of a feverish excitement. She shuddered. No wonder Pedro could not stand Colombia. No wonder South Americans from other countries reverse two letters and call it Locombia – the country of madness.

Part Seven

Harriet in Paris

38

Réaxions, *Iris Publications, Rue du Fossé aux Loups, Wolvengracht,
Bruxelles, Brussel*

Dear Mr Mulligan:

As I am sure you know, the multi-language news magazine Réaxions
has recently been launched simultaneously in Flemish, French, Dutch
and German. Next month we plan to add English and Spanish to the
list.

An integral part of the policy and philosophy of Réaxions is support
for a pan-European police force equipped to deal with international
crime, particularly drugs and terrorism, and to this end we are planning
a series of articles about the relevant agencies that are already in place.
In this context we should be grateful if you could grant us an in-depth
interview relating to your past career with Centac and your current role
with Eurac.

The format of the interview will be a 'profile' and will include a full-
page portrait photograph, with perhaps smaller pictures of you carrying
out daily routines.

The photographer will be Harriet Jones, who can be reached at 36
Witham Square, London SE1. Her telephone number is 01–582 4511,
and she is hoping to hear from you soon.

Please be assured of my deep respect

Rodolphe Montoyer
Features Editor

Bait? Certainly. But bait that had to be taken. Mulligan
dialled the London number.

Her tone was cool, professional. She spoke slowly, her voice
pitched low. Yes, she had been commissioned by *Réaxions*; yes,
she'd love to come to Paris – if she was to take pictures of him
actually at work, she would have to, wouldn't she? She

preferred not to fly, could he meet her at the Gare du Nord, 6.35 in the evening, tomorrow? Why not.

The strike was why not. A pink handout, left on the table of the Buffet-Brasserie at the Gare du Nord, explained. How the CFDT, the FO, CFTC, FMC, and FGAAC had called it in order to *améliorer le service ferroviaire*. When the *cheminots* go on strike, the users of the *chemin* are immediately inconvenienced, it said. Too right, thought Mulligan, and balled the paper, slung it at the feet of the plump glossy waiter who moved between the tables.

The strike was collapsing: but with rolling stock stuck in the wrong places the 6.35 from Brussels was forty-five minutes *en retard*.

Late trains thicken crowds. People come on time to mingle with those already trapped by the delays. Units of the CRS, stretched and nervy from Arab terrorist attacks, pushed their way through, always in threes: two in front with revolvers, truncheons, radios and one behind, forage cap pulled like a widow's peak between his eyebrows, eyes swivelling exactly to echo the tracking muzzle of his automatic rifle.

A sudden commotion, a nervous swirl in the crowd as people urgently distanced themselves from its epicentre: a drunk, a big man with a huge belly, donkey jacket riding up his back, trousers slipping to reveal most of his immense bum. Too much for the two ordinary police, one man, one woman, so the CRS moved in to help. Bellowing, with bloodied face, he clutched his balls, went quickly, not quietly.

The waiter came by again, scooped up Mulligan's cup, wiped the table. He whistled the sort of jaunty tune that stays popular in France no matter what the rest of the world listens to. Beyond his back Mulligan saw windows angled like a snake's forehead, like those on a big aeroplane, of a huge diesel. They slipped towards him through the darkness and the light towards the end of the *quai* bounced off them. He looked at his watch, did up his coat, straightened so he could see better through and above the crowds, but did not get up. He wanted to see her before she saw him.

Like water released from a pool by a child on a beach, the passengers slipped through the bottleneck of the barrier, merged with the crowd, became part of the eddies and currents heading for taxi ranks, the Métro. But a few particles drifted to a stop, became visible as they put down cases, stretched necks, looked about.

Dressed in a rich green corduroy waisted jacket, over a full rust-coloured woollen skirt and boots, she stood for a moment, like a tall nervous bird. Her crest of red-gold hair glinted in the dull light, her head flicked to one side then the other. Two bags, one soft, knobbly, scuffed, photographic, the other chic, a soft Samsonite, hung from her shoulders left one hand free while the other steadied the straps. Uncertainly she nibbled a gloved thumb. Then, tall as she was, she saw him framed by the huge window, saw his round grey pelt of a head rise as he realised she had seen and recognised him. Her mouth creased with amused petulance at the way he had hidden himself from her.

He came up to her through the crowd with an easy grace surprising in such a big man, took her hand.

'Harriet Jones? I'm James Mulligan.'

There was a moment of awkwardness that followed smiles too open as if already they were old friends, even more.

Then he said: 'Let's be practical. Do you have a hotel?'

'Not actually booked.'

'Do you have one in mind?'

'Not really.'

'Would you object if I suggest something cheap, anonymous, near at hand?'

She liked the sound of his voice. It was deep, had a pleasant Southern drawl, was firm, decisive, beneath the surface politeness.

'If it's not too primitive.'

'Not primitive at all. I've checked it out.'

He began to head off, and she resisted now, irritated at his confidence, at the ease with which he had taken command, so she stood firm, head up, eyes distant.

'Sorry. Anything the matter?'

She shrugged, self-mocking. 'Just. . .Paris. You know?'

He looked up too. Huge cast-iron pillars made slender by their height – the conceit of nineteenth-century engineers to stretch metal to do what was beyond marble and point the conceit by moulding them like classical columns – soared above the orange globes into fastnesses of gloom broken by the gleam of the glass beyond.

'Of course. And think what it was like in the age of steam. All those clouds billowing about and the noise – it was built for that.'

'Yes, well. I do remember that, actually. From when I was five.' Again she was a touch irritated that he had appropriated her moment. 'Come on. Where's this hotel?'

But she was pleased enough to follow his broad back through the swirling crowd, the hurrying faces, preoccupied with delight, despair, complacence and boredom. Pleased enough too that he had taken off her shoulders the wearisome business of deciding where to stay.

The Paris-Liège, two-star, turned out to be a bare two minutes away, in Rue St-Quentin, and was decent enough: a narrow entrance, steps up into a foyer that spread a little but not much behind the shops that fronted the street. A tall Arab recognised Mulligan, handed him a key. The lift was almost too small and she resented the intimacy it forced on them. It took them up five floors, and as it stopped she firmly took the key from his hand.

He smiled. 'Supper? I take it you don't want to do any serious photography until tomorrow. But we could have a bite together.'

'Why not? I'll be down again in. . .half an hour. All right?'

He grinned. 'An hour if you like.'

The room was tolerable: two beds, one double, one single, covered in dark blue candlewick, curtains to the floor in the same material. She put her bags on the single bed. Beyond a tiny balcony fenced with curly cast-iron, the canyon of the street dropped away to lit shop-windows, scurrying pedestrians, traffic noisily shunted by the lights. To the left the grey neo-classic façade of the station blocked off the end. Paris. She bit her thumb, anxiety, fear even, creased her brow, but she shrugged it off, turned back into the room, began to make it her own.

She unpacked briskly, set up a silver-mounted travelling mirror on the narrow desk, hung two dresses in the tiny wardrobe. She took off her jacket, inspected the bathroom that lay behind a door glazed with frosted glass. It was minute: a tiny shower-stall, blue tiles, a wash-basin and a loo, no bath, not even a bidet. She thought Mulligan might have done better. She decided not to shower, washed instead, then stretched out on the double bed, smoked.

There were two pictures, both posterlike prints of lithographs. One war pretentious, an overblown iris in white and orange on a brown background with 'Klizia' written across the top, and 'modern art expo' across the bottom. 'Klizia' bothered her: it meant nothing, was faintly and unpleasantly suggestive, as indeed was the treatment of the flower. The other picture was better: a lady in a white dress with beige hem and ribbons sat in a director's chair against a background of yellows and blues – sand, beach tents, sea and sky.

Harriet crushed out her cigarette, stood up, smoothed her skirt, sat in front of her mirror and began to brush her hair, slowly, rhythmically, trying to counter the waves of anxiety that kept sweeping over her as soon as she failed to find any displacing activity. In the end, sooner than she had intended, she put on her jacket, checked out a small handbag for cigarettes, lighter, money and so on, and then unzipped her camera bag. From it she took what looked like an Olympus compact in a soft leather purse with a wrist strap. It was small enough to fit in the palm of her hand. In fact the body had been skilfully adapted to take a miniature micro-recorder, much like the one Roget had been given. The leather case was soft enough for her to activate it without taking it out.

She checked the cassette and the back-up in her bag. Provided she could get a minute or two on her own to turn the first cassette over, and then to change them, she could record for up to four hours.

She returned to the foyer in only a little more than the half-hour she had asked for. Unfolding himself from the low leatherette bench by a tired yucca plant as she came out of the lift, Mulligan said: 'Look, I think we have to talk. But for reasons that will be obvious to you I'd like to do it on the move. So let's combine it with a walkabout, and give you a chance to see gay Paree again. When were you last here?'

Already they were out in the street, heading back up to the station.

'Five years ago, actually.'

'You'll notice changes.'

He headed straight for the Métro, handing her a yellow ticket as they descended the tiled steps. She remembered how it's cheaper to buy Métro tickets in *carnets* of ten or more. At the bottom of the escalator a busker, young, dark, in sneakers, threadbare jeans and anorak, blew a maudlin tenor sax and on the platform the vendors of ethnic leather and copper jewellery packed away their stalls.

The carriage was almost empty – two black youths, sharp, streetwise, bantered at each other in clipped throw-away argot. Mulligan sat opposite her, leaned forward, elbows on knees which almost touched hers, spoke almost directly to her ear.

'Right, where do we begin?'

In the palm of her hand she activated the concealed recorder, but doubted its ability to pick their voices up against the racket of the train.

'I'm not sure I know what you mean.'

'Come on, Miss Jones. Come on!'

'No, really. And you can call me Harriet. Or Harry if you like.'

'Fine. And I'm James or Buck but never Jimmy. Okay? But let's not mess about. You're not here to take my picture.'

'I'm not?'

'No, ma'am. You could be here on Mr Myklades' account. To pick my brains about how well Eurac is functioning against him, to feed me misinformation or possibly both. You could also be here on your own account. Clearly that is what you'd like me to believe. Right?'

This was altogether too direct for comfort. Her eyes flinched away. *Pour votre sécurité vous ne devez pas . . .* For your safety you should do this, you shouldn't do that. Certainly it would be foolish to open this particular door too soon. *Gare de l'Est. Strasbourg St-Denis. Correspondances pour Lignes 8 et 9.*

'But one question we do have to clear up first is why. I mean, why are you doing it? What's in it for you, Harry?'

'A photographer's fee. Rather a good one in this instance. Five hundred plus expenses. Since I'm not paying I do think I could have done better than the Paris-Liège. . .'

'Don't give me crap. What's in it for you, Harry?'

She pulled back; her eyes met his across the increased distance, and flicked away again. Suddenly she shuddered.

'I'm frightened.'

'What of?'

'Prison, I suppose.'

'You expect them to be caught?'

She nodded, dumbly.

'And you want to be on the right side when that happens.'

'That's right.'

'Why aren't you even more frightened of them than of prison? Do you know what they would do to you if you turned Queen's evidence? It would not be pretty or quick. Definitely neither.'

'But they don't know where I am. They think I'm in Brussels. Photographing Rodolphe Montoyer, the editor of *Réaxions*. He's an old chum, and I got him to write to me commissioning me to portrait him, and then to write to you. He didn't ask me what was going on. He likes me. He just did it. . .'

'Bullshit.'

She looked over his shoulder. *Les places numerotées sont réservées par priorité. . .aux mutilés de guerre, aux aveugles civiles, aux femmes enceintes et aux personnes accompagnées d'enfant âgé de moins de quatre ans. . .* Typical French males, putting war wounded before the blind, and everyone in front of pregnant women and women with small children.

'It's not bullshit. And it's not just that I want to keep out of prison. I want them to be caught.'

'Why? Because they're naughty boys and ought to be punished?'

She twisted away from his sarcasm, but came back defiantly.

'Yes. Something like that.'

The expression on his face was insulting, deliberately so. For a moment she was torn by desire to please and hatred for what felt like bullying.

The train decelerated and the grin softened the handsome mouth again. 'Les Halles,' he said, and got up. 'We'll get out here. If you haven't been in Paris for five years you'll notice some changes.'

They left the station by stairs that went down not up, and into a concourse filled with stalls: boutiques, bric-à-brac, antiques, which widened into a much larger hall, a huge place beneath a high wide roof supported on soaring white concrete pillars. Much of it was in shades of white – polished marble floors, pearly walls – and there were long arcades of shops, supported by structures woven out of colossal tubular blue beams. The shops were grand with gilt, brass and even gold leaf, gay with modish Christmas decorations. There was a five-screen cinema: the biggest queue was for *Alien – Le Retour*.

In spite of everything that was going on between them, Harriet wanted to stop and look, even regretted that the camera she held was not really a camera, but Mulligan strode on so that, tall though she was, it was difficult to keep up. They passed the Botticelli shoe shop and climbed a long staircase through an area that was not yet finished or filled, an area where the shaping of the concrete stood out more clearly, revealed references to medieval vaulting, reminiscences of cathedral architecture, but much of it fantasised by the miracle of reinforced concrete into spaces and shapes the Gothic architects must have dreamed of but could not achieve in mere stone. A cathedral then, a place to worship the God of the twenty-first century whose Name will not be Jah but Capital.

Out in the cold December air a sky with clouds and moonlight lit a wilderness of building machinery, boarded walls, fingers of black steel feeling for the light from the concrete in which they were embedded: when Harriet had stood here last she had been on the edge of the biggest man-made hole in the world. It was filled now, but only, for the most part, to a messy chaos at street level. What they had been in was merely the crypt of what was to come.

He strode off down a sweeping circus of older houses. She trotted behind, aware of the squeaky clatter of her heels on the flags.

'I prefer my version. Of your story,' he said.

'That I'm being planted on you by Hector? Why?'

'Hector!' The sarcasm was there again.

'Why not? I know him quite well now. And in spite of everything. . .he's got a sort of. . .I mean he thinks of himself as a sort of businessman, and in a way I do too, and he has flair. . .'

'He's a fucking murderer.'

She stopped. He went on. She refused, determined not to let him dictate every move. They skirted the site again – on one side pillars of aluminium latticework promised further architectural fantasies, on the other in a brightly lit rôtisserie, deep red leather banquettes, globe lights, ferns and brass, chefs in tall hats supervised rows and rows of turning chickens although there was not a single customer in sight.

He came back to her, head on one side and thrust forward a little, hands deep in the pockets of his coat.

She held her ground. 'He's not a murderer. I'm sure he's not. He's really quite gentle.'

'He flattened your friend Roget. Under a road-roller.'

Suddenly she felt dizzy and sick, as she had when she had heard the first report of it on Captial Radio.

'But he didn't! The people he used to buy cocaine from in Amsterdam did that. A Chinese called San.'

He looked down at her for a moment, then nodded his head. 'Yes. Yes. They'd have to tell you something like that.' And he was off again, and she had almost to scamper to catch up with him.

'Supposing, supposing that was true and I believed it, that would be all the more reason for me to come to you. Out of fear, out of a wish to see them all locked up.'

'But Hector has flair.' Again he mocked her. 'He's a sort of businessman. He's – '

'Oh, damn you!' It was a shout, almost a scream, and she stopped again. 'I'm here, aren't I? That's what matters, isn't it? It doesn't matter why I'm here, does it?'

'I think it does.' But he walked a little more slowly now, and for a time in silence. She remembered the recorder (how long had it been running?), suddenly realised the danger: it recorded Mulligan, but it recorded her too. She would have to be very careful not to say anything that would anger them. . .

The thought forced from her a desperate, quavering sigh. It was all too much, too frightening, too fucking complicated. She stumbled on a broken pavingstone, but recovered before he could help her. For a moment she looked up, above and beyond him. Set in the wrack of unfinished building, plant and cranes, a church rose up beneath a bright and aureoled three-quarter moon – a beached sea monster from another age: big, black, medieval, with a large rose window, flying buttresses, and a stub of a tower at one end.

'Look, James. Please. I mean it. I do want out. I really do.' Her breath caught in the middle of 'really'.

'I guess you do. I mean, who wouldn't, in your situation?' He strode on, but she caught his head flicking over his shoulders as if he were checking who was behind them, although the streets were almost deserted. They came to another complex of shops, brightly lit, but closing – Délirium-Désir, filled with black plastic and leather, Burger King, Whoppers, like Leicester Square, begonias with fleshy leaves gangrenous in the streetlights, then suddenly Mulligan took a swift turn to the right and they almost ran into a youth in a red corduroy jacket, eating a beefburger. Immediately he stuck out a hand and whined: '*Un franc, m'sieur, m'dame un franc.*'

Head on one side Mulligan looked down at him, grimaced, and turned again, back the way they had come, leaving the youth behind them.

'What do you do for Myklades? What part do you play in the action? I mean, let's be clear about this: he has a very big operation running, buying cocaine, marketing it, banking the profits. What part in that process do you play?'

'Nothing. None.'

'Come on.' The way he always drew out the 'o-o-on' was not pleasant. 'What *do* you do for him, then? Suck him off?'

She stopped and screamed at him: 'Piss off, Mulligan. You're full of shit.' Then to dam the hysteria that swelled like a balloon in her chest she had to bite her lip almost till it bled.

'Yes. I guess you do. I mean, you are part of the entourage, the gang. You do *something* for him.'

'Listen. I've. . .introduced him to people. Business people. That sort of thing.'

'Uh-uh. Be more specific. What sort of businesses?'

'Banking, finance.'

'Ah-ah. I think I get the scene. Sir Alec Greene?'

'Yes. And others too.'

'The real nobs. Chaps you can really trust, won't let a chap down. In the City. Give his financial operation class, standing. A reference from the chair of City and Wessex carries clout. Of course, Myklades had that brush with the Department of Trade. And he wants to be able to make markets, move through the arena freely, and he needs credibility for that. Yes, yes, it makes sense. Of a sort. And you're a piece of that part of his strategy.' He paused. 'But he likes having you around too. I mean, who wouldn't? And you don't have anything to do with the coke itself?'

'No.'

'Just the odd toot now and then. On the house. But you do know that's what it's all about.'

'Yes. And actually I don't touch the stuff.'

'Why not? Say, that is something.' He stopped. Another huge square opened in front of them, dominated by a tall thin tower, brilliantly floodlit. Long, thin spear-shaped windows soared to huge gargoyles on the very top corners, peered out over Paris, dared whoever to cross the river and attack the ancient city. At its foot a carousel – gold, silver, thousands of mirrors, unicorns and chariots – and, again, no one near it apart from a woman police officer in a long mac with a cowboy hat, but narrow-brimmed. She murmured into a radio. Mulligan glanced at her, moved on, then his head came up again. 'I know where we'll go.'

To a restaurant, Harriet hoped, a bar at least. She was hungry, tired, needed a drink, a pee, and a chance to check the recorder. But no, he loped on, across the Place du Châtelet. She was glad to leave the Châtelet. Towers like that disturbed her, provoked a mental tic that said phallus, in response to a childish memory. . . Trees, a wide road, then the sky opened above them and suddenly there was traffic streaming towards them, away from them, over a bridge. To the right, floodlit and reflected in the black water, the Palais de Justice, long and huge, threatened them from beneath square, pointed towers. To the left, above black buildings, the twin massifs of Notre Dame, also lit.

'So actually you have nothing to do with the process itself. But you know about it. And right now you are doing the right thing and coming to the authorities.' He stopped. 'Why come to me, to Eurac, and not to your community policeman?'

She looked over the iron parapet at the inky water. It swirled slowly, glinted like fresh tar. This was the big one, the one they had guessed he would be bound to ask. She took a deep breath. They wanted to be sure she got this one right, they wanted to feel certain Mulligan was convinced by her answer.

'I was at Lowndes Square. I engineered the invitation from Sir Alec. It was easy to guess how he would react to having his door kicked in, and he played up perfectly, without any prompting. He had no idea he was being used, which was why he did it so well. Anyway. I was there. I saw you there. I saw Tyler there and that dull Customs man. I read the newspapers after. Above all I heard Rupert and Hector talking, crowing, bragging about it. And one thing came quite clear. Not only did they fear you, Eurac, but they clearly had nothing to fear from the local plod. And not just because he is a plod, but because someone there, some plod, maybe even that man Tyler – no one can be as stupid as he allowed himself to seem – was feeding them information, keeping them always one step ahead of the game. So I came to you. I came to you because they'd know within hours if I went anywhere else.'

She looked up at him. Moonlight and streetlight illuminated his face, which suddenly beamed as if blessed. Outrageously, he winked, tapped the side of his short but well-shaped nose, and then, for the first time since they had shaken hands at the Gare du Nord, he touched her. He kissed the ball of his index finger and dabbed her mouth with it, letting it linger, cool and dry, for just a second. Then he took her elbow, hurried her on.

'Yeah, I guess that figures.' Again the glance over his shoulder as they came towards the end of the bridge. She tried to turn too, and caught, she thought, just a glimpse of a red jacket a hundred yards behind them.

The buildings that closed about them as they left the river were huge, not ornate, suggested granite in their hard-edged severity rather than limestone. Windows were barred, and the gates of foliated cast iron left few chinks through which to peer, looked as if the giants who had locked them had thrown away the keys.

'Okay. For the time being I take you at your face value.' They swung round two sharp corners.

Three high pointed arches rimmed with ranks of angels, seven semicircles, then banks of saints. The rose window. Then slender columns that soar as finely as those at the Gare du Nord but whose function is not load bearing but to bewitch the eye into seeing, not vast tons of stone stacked block upon block, but grace and earth-defying lightness.

'She's good, isn't she? Notre Dame.' Giving 'dame' its English pronounciation. And again the sudden pressure on her elbow, as he moved her into shifting shadows beneath trees whose leaves rustled like aspens. A moustachioed giant on a horse loomed above them with a bragging grandeur quite at odds with the feminine majesty behind them. Charlemagne leading one of the more crowded pages in *Astérix*, a band of warriors with axes, horned helmets, more moustaches. And here too there was a portakabin, a paling fence and all the plant of a building site.

'Listen. I want you to go back to your room now. . .' They were in almost complete darkness squeezed between the plinth of the statuary and the side of the hut. 'And meet me tomorrow on Platform Two at the Gare St-Lazare at twenty-five past nine. Have you got that? Okay. Ciao, see you then.'

He stepped out of the darkness and grabbed the youth in the red corduroy jacket, who had just reached the corner of the hut – grabbed him with one arm across his neck, the other twisting his right arm into the small of his back. Then he pushed and swung him away, in a practised movement that left him holding the youth's hand and wrist in his own two hands. His powerful leg came up, found a lodging in the youth's waist and he flapped the arm in the sort of movement one gives a heavy rug, out on the lawn, shaking the dust out. There was a dull snap, like wet wood, and the boy screamed.

Mulligan was off, loping away between the clifflike buildings, coat flapping in pools of light. Harriet, hand to her face, fingers spread, fought back her own scream. The youth staggered to his feet, and his expression shifted to one of pleading appeal. She shook her head at him and turned, ran too, after Mulligan. But when she got to the corner he had gone.

39

She ran across the river on to the Rive Gauche, found the St-Michel Métro: on Ligne 4, Direction – Porte de Clignancourt, she could get back to Gare du Nord without a change. But of course now she had no ticket, and the ticket office was shut. Wretchedly she scouted through her bag, found the five francs that would serve, got through the automatic barriers, all new since her last visit, and down to the platform.

She didn't like it now, not on her own. The long tiled tunnels, the smell of warm urine and *pommes frites,* the journey endless in spite of the frightening racket and speed of the train, the men who came and went, strap-hung above her when they could have sat at a distance, eyed her bag, eyed her legs. And as the train surged, braked, jolted to a stop, surged, whined and rattled on, she became aware of other needs again: hunger, thirst, a pee, and one that went deeper. She was frightened, confused, in a hideous fix. She wanted the daddy she could still call back from memories of infancy, the one who gave advice and help she could not understand but in a tone that implied that the world was rational, that if you took a little trouble things worked out as you wanted them to. The daddy she'd known as a big man before she grew to be almost as tall as he, the daddy whose wisdom she had not doubted before he became a pompous fart who drank too much.

At last. Escalators, stairs, the open air again, busyness, the narrower streets, the no-nonsense façade of the big station, the restaurants still full, and the seafood stalls still open with mussels and oysters on beds of crushed ice. God, I'm hungry. But I can't face a restaurant on my own.

There was a sandwich stall, run by Arabs. What a confusion of choice – not merguez, those spicy sausages filled with wood-chips, certainly not a plastic frankfurter. What, then? Something solid. Large, fatty. The man in front of her ordered a Tunisian Sandwich. It was big, a load of stuff heaped into a baguette – she'd have one. And a can of Coke. And yes, damn it, a paper cone of *frites* too. Deftly the Arab, dark stubble, eyes that raped her, wrapped the lot into sheets of white paper, slapped back some change from the fifty-franc note she gave him.

The Paris-Liège, yes, but what was the number of her room? The man at the desk recognised her, said nothing but handed her the key: 528. The fifth floor, the tiny lift, the door opposite the lift, one of those awkward locks set in a sort of brass protruding button, cannot make the damn thing work, and the corridor dark but for one safety light that glowed at the far end. . .

The warning messages flashed through her mind with the speed of a pulsing cursor: she had left a light on, she always did; this was not the sort of hotel where chambermaids came in to turn down the sheets. . .then as she fumbled for the switch, the arm came from behind, and the hand locked over her mouth, expertly clenched it shut.

She reached behind, twisted, tried to put a distance between the warm hardness of his chest and her back, rummaged for a place to hurt him, his balls perhaps. She hesitated and the light snapped on.

Blinking through tears of rage, pain and fear, she found she was looking at a card held in front of her face. She shook her head, managed to read: *Before you say a word make sure the recorder is OFF*.

He breathed in her ear: 'You understand?'

She nodded.

'Where is it?'

She wriggled her immobilised right hand. He released it. She brought the camera, still in its soft leather case, into view, pressed the button through the leather.

'Is that it?'

She nodded, and at last he let her go, slipping the wrist strap off her wrist as he did so.

'Mulligan, you unspeakable sod, that's my supper.'

The package had tumbled to the floor, unwrapped itself, left a smear of chilli sauce on her skirt as it went. There they had trodden on it, made a pulp of paper, bread, sauce, tinned tuna, olives, a green chilli pepper, carrot. . .and the cone of chips too had rolled away shedding its load over the carpet.

Harriet began to cry, like a child.

'You need a drink.'

'I need a pee,' she gasped through the sobs, and fled into the tiny shower-room .

She took her time, got the crying under control, examined her neck for marks, combed her hair, sponged her skirt. When she came out he was sitting in the chair in the corner, by the window, in front of the wardrobe, legs stretched out, hand in the pockets of his coat which he had not taken off. On the table between the beds he had laid out what was redeemable of her food and tidied the rest into the small tin bin. The camera case was open on the bed, the recorder out, exposed. He had left on only one light, the small strip above the single bed. It gave the room a cosy, intimate look.

A half-smile warmed his face, quizzical, friendly, designed to reassure.

'A drink? Maybe we can persuade the concierge to get something in.' He nodded towards the phone.

'Actually there's a half-litre of Scotch in the wardrobe.'

'Just the job. Glenlivet. Duty-free. Why not the full allowance? Too bulky, greedy too.' He cracked the metal seal in the screw top. 'Water? Half and half? No ice I'm afraid.' He fixed two drinks using the tooth mugs from the shower-room.

She sat on the single bed, up near the pillow, drank half straight away. Then picked at the food. 'Ugh. It's cold. I thought it would be warm, but it's fridge cold.'

'Tasty though.' The tone continued chatty, conciliatory, commiserating.

However, with the whisky warming her, settling her, the anger flared back. 'Right, then. Before I call the management and get you thrown out you'd better tell me what you're playing at.'

'Recruitment, dear Harry, recruitment.' He leaned forward cradling his glass between his knees, head on one side in what she would come to recognise was a characteristic posture. 'And before, out there, well, clearing the ground.'

'I still don't know what you mean.'

'No? Okay. You were fired at me. Let's not bullshit each other about that. Spiderman fired you at me, he would not have let you within a hundred miles of me otherwise. You flew to Brussels this morning with Rupert Bridge. He took you to the *Réaxions* office. You were, no doubt, well briefed there, but they put a tail on you when you left, on the train, and they kept you under surveillance right through until I dealt with that back at Notre Dame – '

'Did you have to be as brutal as that?'

'He'll mend. And they instructed you to record as much as you could that went on between us. Neat arrangment that, but, as you'll learn, we can do better. Okay, why – why all this bother? To hear what I might tell you? No. You were meant to be telling them that anyway. But to check out just how fair you were playing with them, check out just how far I was trusting you. They need to think I trust you.' His voice hardened. 'And I need them to think I trust you.' He relaxed again. 'Which was why we played out that little charade out there for the benefit of your dinky little toy, and anyone else who might be around. I think we did quite well. I think you did very well.'

'Really.'

'With luck when they get to play it back, and get to hear a report from our friend in the red jacket, they'll believe I'm beginning to trust you, and they won't know about this little chat we're having now.'

'No?'

'No.'

'I can tell them all about it.'

'I don't think you will. Freshen your drink?'

'All right.'

'I should try to eat a bit more. It's really not so awful, and the *frites* are okay.'

He moved about, a large man trained out of any clumsiness he might have had, refilled their glasses. 'Have you finished with that? Sure? Okay, I'll trash it.' A tidy man too, a man who did not like mess. 'Smoke?' He offered her a Marlboro which she accepted and his Zippo flared for her.

'What do you mean, *recruit me?* And why are you so sure I won't tell them about now?'

'I said just now that I want Spiderman to think I trust you. But the irony is I do have to trust you. I have to know whose side you're on, and it has to be my side. The goodies. Right?'

'And suppose I were not a goodie already, how would you propose to make me one?'

He pointed a finger. 'No bullshitting, remember? None of this "I'm shopping my friends because they've been naughty and teacher ought to smack them" – right? Because as of now you are not a goodie. You are a cocaine smuggler, and you run with cocaine dealers. Right?' He sat back, smoked too. 'But I aim to get you to want to be a goodie. First, if you step out of line, I shop you. Okay they offed Roget, but I still got enough out of him, and out of Van Willet, to fill in the gaps the Dover Collection missed out on, and if I give it to them they'll reopen your file and bust you. That's for starters.

'But I can do better than that. These people are evil. They really are. They did off Roget. I saw them do it. Listen – Rupert Bridge, the Honourable, was there, he actually came along to watch. That's the sort of "gentle" man he is. Well, there's a lot more like that I'll tell you tomorrow out at St-Cloud. We have some quite hairy files out there, make quite scary reading. The point I am making, Harry, is this. Anyone who tangles with a mob like that is in deadly danger. Not only are they evil, they are paranoid with it. If they think you are double-dealing they will do far nastier things to you than they did to Roget. . .'

She stubbed out her cigarette, pushed a pillow up under her head, pulled her feet on to the bed and her knees in. Semifoetal, he said to himself – she feels insecure.

'You're not exactly selling the idea of being on your side,' she said.

'No? But this is the point. *I can shop you to them.* I can feed them misinformation. I can let them know that I know something about them they'd rather I didn't know, and I can let them think that I learned it from you. . .Are you with me?'

Her eyes glowed from tired sockets in a white face. 'You wouldn't do that. I don't believe you could.'

'You'd better believe it, Harry. Look. The situation I am talking about is one in which I will have come to believe that you are after all, through and through, on their side. Now, the day I believe that of you, then as far as I am concerned you are worth. . .nothing.' He snapped his finger. 'I treat you then just as I treat them now. They are an evil, ugly mob who I am going to take down, lock up, and, where I can get away with it, put down. Like vermin. And you might not even know when you've crossed that line in my mind, because I'll go on using you, for as long as I can, then. . .out. I shop you, let them do what I might not have the heart to do myself.'

His body swung forward again. 'And that brings me to point number three. I am going to win. And if I don't it will be because they take out a contract on me and some operator is clever enough to pull it off. And then Eurac will just slot another Galahad into my place. And so on. We are going to win. Hopefully with me in charge. But that is the scenario. The empire Myklades is a part of is going to come down and it's going to bring down an awful lot with it. There's going to be debris.' (He said 'd'b-ree'.) 'Human debris. And if you're on the wrong side of the fence when that happens, you're going to be part of it. Now, you may not believe we're big enough to do this right now, and that's another reason why you're coming to St-Cloud tomorrow. I aim to impress you, and I will, I aim to make you believe we're winning, and you will.'

She turned on her back, head back, chin up, eyes half-closed. There was a long moment of silence, and down below the traffic surged.

'Is that it?'

'That's it.'

She sighed again. 'You'd better tell me just what it is you want me to do.'

'You're on board?' Too quick, too eager – mentally he kicked himself.

She gave the tiniest of shrugs. 'Maybe. Can I have another cigarette?'

He came across, lingered a moment after he had lit it, then squeezed her shoulder. She smiled up at him, wanly. He fixed them both another drink.

'I really am sorry there's no ice,' he said.

'I really am sorry this is such a cruddy hotel.'

'Come o-o-on. It's not that bad.'

'What next?'

'Are you on board? Have you joined the Mulligan fan club?'

'I don't know. It's beginning to feel as if I might have.'

'Cheer up. It's meant to feel good, joining the goodies.'

'Is it?'

'Okay. Let's get one or two things clear.' He sat down again, leant forward, the tumbler held in his hands across his knees. 'They want me to think that they think you only went as far as Brussels to take pictures of that Montoyer guy. So what am I supposed to believe you are telling them about why you are staying longer?'

'That Montoyer has fixed me up a commission in Paris. So I can stay here, be in Paris for at least two more days.'

'Right. And for this double bluff to work you must actually have an intro to someone here – I would expect them to expect you to bring back pics of some Parisian notable. So, who he? Who have they fixed up?'

'Dr Guy Lovejoy. International quack to the mega-rich. Very glam. Very much a *Réaxions* type. He'll be at the Inter-Continentale on Thursday at eleven in the morning.'

'But that won't be all. When you go between those classy lamp-standards in the Rue Castiglione, you won't just be going to a photo session. They'll be debriefing you on what we've been up to, and they'll be doing it right. We are certainly going to have to get our act together very, very well indeed if it's going to stick.'

He thought for a moment, elbows on his knees, round face framed by the palms of his large hands, the cigarette still lodged between the fingers of his right hand. Then he straightened, laughed again and stubbed it out. 'You know something? All this has a very familiar feel. The same twists and turns, the same elaboration, and finally the same evil wit, as the Lowndes Square business. Who puts these things together? Bridges? Myklades himself? Both?'

She shrugged, shook her head signifying uncertainty rather than disagreement. 'Both, I think. They. . .seem to enjoy the way their minds work. Rupe gets a real buzz from Myklades, but I think it's reciprocated too.'

'Yeah. And that brings me to another point. Trust that cousin of yours like you'd trust. . .a rabid mongoose. You put a foot wrong and he'll strike.' He paused for a moment, looked into his glass, swilled the end of his drink round the bottom, then looked up, spoke with the forceful sincerity Americans use when they really expect you to believe them whether or not they are telling the truth. 'Harry, I want you to know my first consideration right now is to save your pretty neck, keep you alive and in there – partly, I'll be honest, so you can get to be a real help. But too because. . .well, I don't like to see pretty things broken. Right? There's one more each in this bottle, should be just enough, and not too much. . .'

'You have it. I don't want any more.'

'Nor do I. Then I think we should turn in. Can I borrow your toothbrush?'

'Mulligan. You're not staying here.'

'Not the whole night. I'll slip away in time to get to St-Lazare by a different route. But I can't go home, because they'll have that staked out and I don't want them to know when I get there. And I'm not going to risk bumming around the streets finding another place. No, this will do fine. Don't worry. You move to the big bed, I'll take that one. . .No buts, that's the one I take, it's nearer the door – '

'If you think there might be visitors you stay. But no

toothbrush sharing – I mean it.' Said jokily, and, he reckoned to warn him off any closer intimacy.

But in the night, in the darkness, she began to cry.

'What's the matter?'

She brought the weeping under control, blew her nose. 'I'm frightened. I'm not really a wimp but I am just terribly frightened.'

'Well, I guess I can understand that.'

'Mulligan. Buck. It's not a lot of comfort saying that.'

He said nothing, lay on his back, listened to her breathing, listened to the struggle she went through to get it under control, then the rhythms of tiredness and Scotch took over, and finally sleep. He guessed he'd turned down some sort of invitation and he hoped he had not done further injury to her self-image by doing so. Maybe they'd get round to something of the sort later. If the relationship developed. At that moment he did not want to add complications to an already very complicated situation: he was not, finally, totally hard. He did not want to feel about her, for instance, in the same way as she did about Roget. He did not want to weep for her, however inwardly.

Eventually he slept too, but lightly. At six o'clock his watch buzzed him awake. He dressed, and slipped away.

40

The dismal train journey through the suburbs of Paris on a cold grey day, cemeteries, the brutality of La Défense, rain streaming down the windows, Mulligan pushing her by the elbow up the steep climb then along Rue Armengaud, the surly guards, the blank hideousness of what seemed to be the quintessence of police stations everywhere – all turned out to be an apt prelude for a day that was mostly horrible.

For a moment or two Harriet felt Anton Suk might be some sort of relief: he was lean, well-built, dressed in designer denims, with red shoes and a red belt. He was beginning to go bald but had style, energy, commitment. He spoke English fluently but with a quite marked accent and occasional lapses of idiom and grammar. Clearly Mulligan liked him and she was prepared to. But what he showed her was horrid and frightening.

Eurac 4 had enormous amounts of information on what was code-named the Web, all computer stored, cross-referenced and subject to the latest Pathfinder technology. At one point the tall lean Czech dabbed keys and to Harriet's horror her own name bled across the screen with a list of twelve entry numbers. He accessed three of them: the Dover Collection Report, followed by a summary of Mulligan's interview with Van Willet, and then a transcript of his fatal confrontation with Roget. She took the point: they had enough new information to give Senior Investigation Officer Price all he needed to reopen the file on her.

Mulligan did not spare her in other ways either. After lunch, which he insisted on taking at a small and very ordinary *café et brasserie* up the road, he took her back to his own office. It was little more than a cubicle – cream painted, a filing cabinet, a small table, two chairs and a view past a big block of flats on the other side of the railway line across to the Bois de Boulogne and the Eiffel Tower. He slid out one of the drawers, pulled out a folder, spilled glossy colour prints, eight by ten, across the desk top.

They were hideous, portrayed in harsh, unmitigated, flashlit detail what had happened to Roget. One forearm alone had escaped massive mutilation; one hand, the left, with his thin gold watch still intact on the wrist, still, somehow, in spite of everything, very much Roget.

She choked, gasped: 'Why are you showing me this?'

'Because your people did it.'

'It's not true.'

He told her the whole story: how he had got Tyler to pick her file off the PNC, how that had led him to Van Willet and so to Roget.

'I still don't believe you. If you could get within a mile of proving it, you'd lock them up. You'd have to, for murder. But if you can't convince a jury, why should I feel convinced?' She grasped another straw. 'If you're telling me the truth, then they killed him because they thought you were successfully turning him. It was your fault. And now you have the. . .now, even after that, you are awful enough to ask me to do the same.'

He turned on her, the charm of his smile entirely compromised into a sardonic leer. 'But you forget. You've been fired at me. It's not my idea that you should be here now.'

'I still don't believe Rupert killed Paul. You're just saying all that, showing me these horrible pictures to get me on your side. But I am already. . .' Her voice fluked into an almost plaintive whine.

He shrugged. 'So you say.'

But after that she began to volunteer information: odd snippets she had gleaned through overheard conversations, she said, things she'd pieced together. 'They tell me very little openly, directly. The idea is that if things do fall apart it will be very difficult to prove that I knew about cocaine, knew that cocaine was at the centre of it. . .'

By three o'clock the obvious question could not remain unasked: 'You know so much, why don't you just arrest us all?' He explained. While most of it was substantiated fact a lot still would not hold up in court. Much of it was a question of making connections: good defence lawyers would claim they were arbitrary, And anyway positive action, arrests, were not Eurac's responsibility: all they could do was present the national forces involved with all the evidence and help them co-ordinate an operation. Lowndes Square had effectively halted co-operation with Floor Five at New Scotland Yard, and even with New Fetter Lane. 'It won't last for ever, but right now we've a long haul rebuilding those particular bridges.' It was also entirely Eurac's responsibility to decide at what point they should pass on their findings; and again, after Lowndes Square, they were going to hold back until they had reached higher levels of certainty. That was another lesson that had been learnt.

But the main reason was that most of the evidence was circumstantial, and much of it, particularly the financial side of it, very complex, and not all of it legally obtained.

'Where did it come from then?'

'Anton hacks. He can hack into anything.'

Suk smiled back. 'Oh yes. No trouble, no sweating. I do just a little burglary here and there, the electronic sort of course, I pick my way into secret places. . .'

Mulligan laughed. 'Hacking Anton. Hacking not picking.'

The Czech bridled: 'Oh my God, James, I do nothing so brutal as *hack*, I pick. Pick, pick, pick.'

'All of which is all very well. But what we need is powder on the table, something no jury can refuse to acknowledge. That was what Tyler thought he was getting and what we thought we were offering him, though I suspected things weren't right from the start.' At this point his voice throbbed with seriousness, sincerity again, and he reached across the desk, folded his palm around her wrist. 'Ultimately, Harry, that's what this is all about. That's what, one day, you'll be able to give us. Not the whole scenario, but just that one vital piece of information: coke, cash, and Spiderman all in the same place at the same time. And when you do, you walk away free. I promise you. With a new identity if you like, but free and with whatever sort of money you need to set yourself up again in a new life.'

As the afternoon wore on these moments of intimacy, of sincerity, of offered hope, arrived more frequently. She suspected their good faith, but welcomed them nevertheless. Frequently she qualified what she had to say: 'They told me I could tell you this,' or 'This may not be true – I think this was made up especially for you.' He insisted that it did not matter: much could be learnt from thinking about what lay behind these allowed leaks or pieces of misinformation.

Then at last, just as it got dark enough for the metal tower to be placed only by the red light on its tip but before the illuminations re-revealed it, he turned on her. 'And what don't they want me to know? What did they tell you you must not on any account tell me?'

She blanched, felt her heart lurch although she had been waiting for it. He banged the table, came round behind her, suddenly fixed his strong fingers into the hollows between scapula and clavicle, dug with them, made them hurt.

'There isn't anything. I promise you. I'm answering everything you ask me. Buck. I'm on your side. Really!' The pressure increased. She tried to wrench free, but the grip tightened, began to burn. 'Don't. Please don't. There's no need to hurt me.'

'No?'

'No, no.' She let out a long shuddering sigh. 'Oh, no Buck,

no, no there isn't.' She felt the fingers relax, become soft, caressing, and she let her head drop back against his arm.

'Well?'

'You know I said I knew Rupe was going to Newcastle, in the north of England, to buy a share in a leisure airfield. And I thought that was just part of all the finance side, laundering coke-users' money through joyrides, and plane chartering and so on, they never really had – '

'Right.'

'Well, he's also going to buy a helicopter-freight firm. Chinooks, made redundant for carrying people since the North Sea oil-rig crash. And I think it's to do with some new scheme they're putting together to get cocaine into the country in bulk, instead of small amounts. . .'

He pushed her away, and a slow smile lit his serious eyes. 'Tell me about that. All about that. How you heard it, what makes you sure it's something they really would not want me to know about.'

She did, and did it well – well enough for him to feel that if it was some sort of hoax, then at least she was in part being hoaxed as well.

He took her back, in a taxi this time, to his flat in Rue Lamarck. It was a warm, easy, pleasant place to be after Rue Armenguad. He opened Veuve Clicquot, deftly sliced and rolled slivers of smoked salmon, found a small pot of Beluga caviare. In spite of everything she could still mock him. 'Who do you think you are: James Bond?' But she enjoyed the attentive luxury.

He put her on a low but large white hide sofa, and when she perched at one end with her arm on the back and her knees pulled in beneath her he placed himself in an armchair beyond her easiest angle of vision.

'Tell me. Who's running you?' he asked suddenly.

'Running me?'

'Who's your control?'

'I'm still not with you.'

'Don't you read spy stories? Deighton, le Carré, that sort of thing?'

'No.' She sighed, relaxed a little, let her head and neck rest on the back of the sofa. 'Should I? Why should I?'

'No reason.' He offered a little laugh, warming, intimate, leaned forward and refilled her glass. 'What I'm getting at is this. In spook terminology you are a field agent. Someone operating on enemy territory. Such people always have a control, an officer in charge of running them, someone they report to, go to for advice, someone who sustains them in the very lonely and dangerous business they are in. Someone too who knows and understands them, who can interpret and evaluate the information the spy, the spook, the double agent brings back. So. Who does all this for you? By the way, before you answer, don't worry about this place. It's bug-proof. Our colleagues in the Troisième guarantee that. So?'

'All right.' She drew in breath, let it out slowly, turned her head so their eyes met. 'Cousin Rupert fills that bill. He briefed me. You know I met him in Brussels on the way here. That was the last checkout.'

'And you report to him tomorrow at the Inter-Continentale? For what in the spook trade they call debriefing?'

'Yes.'

'While you take pictures of Lovejoy?'

After this the tension continued to dissipate. Harriet was tired, very tired, but with the warmth, the food, the drink, the weariness was melting into a pleasant drowsiness. Music leaked from inconspicuous speakers – anodyne but not mind-less, a piece for cello and orchestra by Max Bruch. Mulligan busied himself with a slow easy skill in the open-plan kitchen end of his split-level room putting together the makings of an omelette and a green salad. He carved a baguette into chunks, slashed them with garlic butter, put them into an oven.

He opened a second bottle, said: 'Of course I shall make a pass before you leave.'

'Of course. I'd wonder why if you didn't.'

'Don't tell me now what the answer will be. I'm only mentioning it now so it won't be an embarrassment later, give you time to make up your mind about it.' He poured, looked at her over the rim of the glass. 'You're very beautiful.'

'I know. So you can cut out all that crap. It's not necessary.'

He grinned – suddenly, very openly, like an adolescent given a racing bike for his birthday, a swish camera, a promise.

A little shy Harriet got up, moved about the room, found four small clay biscuit-fired pots on a shelf, decorated with free-style brush-strokes, apparently representing snakes. 'These are pretty.'

'Hopi indian ware. Really a bit pseud. You know, for tourists. They used to have cactuses in them, but it was silly to try to pack those up so I chucked the plants, kept the pots. Do you like black olives?'

'Yes. If they're pseud, why do you keep them?'

'My son gave them to me.'

Of course. At his age there would have to be a family, one family at least behind him, somewhere. But there had been bitterness in his voice – no, not bitterness, sadness – so she moved away from the pots, sought to change the subject.

'Do you know what fucks me up most about what's been happening to me?' she said.

'No.'

'It's the pills Lovejoy has been giving me. Lovejoy's little capsules. I wish I knew what he was filling me up with.'

'Difficult to say. Obviously he's using the classic up and downer combinations, sometimes simultaneously, sometimes alternating them. Tranks and maybe opiates set against speed and coke. Or, more probably, allied synthetics.'

'It scares me when I'm far enough away from it. Trouble is, at the time they work.'

Suddenly he was professional again. 'I don't think you should worry too much. The danger is dependency, addiction. And I don't see how addiction is going to be useful to them. If they turn you into a junkie you become a liability. The very nature of what they are asking you to be means that they have to let you run free, and it's no use hoping that you'll be dependent on them for the next fix. No, I think they just aim to keep you feeling euphoric when you're in their company. And of course Lovejoy is a typical doctor. . .'

'Yes?'

'Yes. Most doctors are a touch power-crazy. Occasionally you get one who goes over the top, likes to feel everyone around him is behaving the way they do because he's pulling the strings. Doctor Cornelius with Coppélia, Pygmalion and Galatea. You get the scene.'

'Policemen, of course, are not a bit like that.'

'Not at all.' He laughed, was suddenly behind her, pushing a gentle kiss behind her ear, his arm around her chest, his broad hand on her ribcage careful not to find her breast too soon. She let her body lean back against him, found him as solid as a tree.

She stayed, seduced not by passion or lust but by the security and comfort he had on offer: a respite from the deep anxiety that plagued her, anxiety that occasionally screeched like chalk on slate, like an ambulance wail, screeched up into panic – a respite more human than Lovejoy's chemical panaceas.

In bed he was very, very good. For an hour or so they simply lay there, smoked, occasionally drank. They talked about nothing very much in particular: places they had both been to, anecdotes from unproblematic periods of their lives, discovered shared tastes in books or music, occasionally disagreed but with bantering good humour. And occasionally they traded kisses and then caresses that admitted first the possibility then the imperative of passion. And he waited – waited until the need to take him into her could not be denied a moment longer. Once there he was strong and urgent, but still controlled, made their bodies play music together until she came like a cup filled with wine until it flows over and he followed her.

For a time she slept in his arms, that loveliest of sleeps. But after an hour or so he stirred, left her, perhaps to go to the lavatory. Left in a darkness that was after all strange if not alien the fears flooded back. When she felt him beside her again she turned away. He pulled himself against her, stroked her arm, but she shrugged herself on to her front with her cheek in the pillow away from him.

'Do you really think they killed Paul? Roget?'

'Sure. Sure they did.'

Silently she began to weep. That he could say that, without qualification, mitigation or offered comfort, betrayed what had, after all, been only a moment.

41

'Is she going to be any use at all?'

'Oh, sure. Bound to be. I reckon we'll find everything she told us will check out.'

'My God, James. Of course it will.' The tall Czech drew out the vowels of 'God' and 'course'. He rarely raised his voice for emphasis, instead had this habit of dragging words out when he wanted to weight them. 'Their who-o-o-le purpose at this stage is to convince you that you can trust her. The question is, can you?'

'No. No, of course not.' Mulligan was brisk, firm.

'Well, James I am glad to hear you say that. I feared. . .I mean she is an attractive woman.'

'Sure is, Anton.' This time he flashed the Czech the brazen smile that males use to signal to other males that they know just how attractive a certain female is.

'But she won't pull the flannel in your eyes.'

'Fuck off, Anton.'

The Czech pouted, grinned, swung his swivel chair back to the keyboard and screen he was working at. It was set in a horseshoe console – one of eight similar cells spread out down the long windowless computer room at Interpol. He tapped in titles, codes, swung back again.

'So. What have we gained?'

'In terms of pure gain, not a lot. Some information about Rupert Bridge which we can give Tyler. That was about it.'

'No, James, you are wrong.'

'Sorry. Did I miss something?'

'You certainly did. I think your mind yesterday was after all somewhat distracted by her. . .charms.'

'Oh. Really? Oh, sure, she talked. But most of it we already knew.'

'All of it we already knew. Except the Bridge-Newcastle business. And that, precisely, is what is so significant.'

'How come?'

'Really, James, I think fucking a nice lady has fucked up your lateral thinking capability. Look. She is part of a very large organisation. Comparable in scale with a medium-size national retail chain store. Or since supermarkets deal in many products a better analogy would be a chain of petrol stations. Now. The amount of statistical and factual data that clusters round a set-up of that size is enormous. An employee, even one near the top, is never going to be in command of more than a very tiny percentage of it without access to records. Similarly, a hostile organisation trying to penetrate it from outside will, at the outset at any rate, only appropriate a very small amount of all the relevant data.' He tapped away. Graphs unravelled across the screen in three colours. He nodded his round balding head at it. 'You know what this tells me?'

'Anton, you know I'm computer illiterate. Stop bullshitting me.'

'It tells me that the overlap between what we just happen to know about the Web and what Miss Jones told us cannot rationally be discarded as contingent or coincidental.' A six-figure number flashed in the right-hand corner of his screen. 'The chances of that being the case are more than eight hundred thousand to one.'

Mulligan straightened above the video terminal, rubbed the small of his back, gritted his teeth. The fact was that the night had left him in a euphoric, expansive mood, above all relaxed, at ease with the world – the edge of resolve, normally kept keen by a more or less permanent combination of resentment, hate, anger, and frustration, had been dulled. Bit by bit Suk was honing it back to its lethal sharpness.

'Okay. So she was telling us what they told her to tell us, and she did it by the book. . .'

'Absolutely. But that's not all.'

'Go on. Spell it out.'

'Can't you see it, James? When they briefed her they knew already precisely what we know. Bar one, every single item she gave us is already logged in here. . .' and he rapped the edge of the console. 'They have accessed us. It is statistically, rationally, the only possible explanation.'

'Shit. Jesus.' Mulligan took a turn round the room, came back, smashed his fist in his palm. 'But that means we can't move without them knowing. That means that they monitored the Lowndes Square operation not through the British PNC or CEDRIC as we suspected but through us. . .'

'It doesn't mean that, James. Be rational. If they've hacked into us, they could have hacked in elsewhere too. But you're right too: it certainly does mean that as things stand we can't move without them knowing about it.'

'As things stand?'

'Yes. But from now on I can run the two data systems side by side and keep one of them locked in. I shall have to decide on a day-by-day basis what goes only on the locked-in system, what I keep from them. Incidentally this will not only improve our security, it will also give me a basis from which to run a marked banknote routine. We must work out something that will really make them react. Plant it first here then there in the system. When the reaction comes then we have a clue as to how they're getting in. . .You're with me?'

'Of course.' The post-coital euphoria had quite gone. 'Right. Listen. I have to go and think this all through. . .'

'Hang on. There's one more thing.'

'There is?'

'Jones told you she's to portrait Lovejoy this morning. In the Inter-Continentale. And that she'll be debriefed there. Yes?'

'Yes. And she's carrying a radio bug. A van outside is picking it up and recording what happens. I don't expect to get much out of it but it will be a sort of test for her, and when she reveals it to them it'll prove to them that I trust her and that they can go on trusting her too.'

'Very clever. But at the moment it's Lovejoy I'm interested in. Have a look at this.' Suk stooped over a briefcase beside his chair, pulled out a glossy magazine. *Réaxions 3*. On the cover a romantic, soft-focused picture of a man who would have been handsome if his eyes had not been too close together and his mouth sulky, and a woman who was beautiful, but in a contrived, lifeless way. He read: MENDOZA-MALATESTA: NUPTIALS IN 1990.

'Jones is credited with that picture.'

'So? We know she does commissions for that rag.'

'Yes. But read the cover story.'

Mulligan took the glossy large-format magazine, built like *Harper's* or *Vogue*. *Réaxions* purported to be a news magazine, and there was news in it, culled and summarised from Europe's leading dailies, but the choice of what to include, and the slant with which it was presented, echoed the content of the feature and opinion pages. It was an organ of the New Right, of the New Enlightenment – against organised labour, against state ownership, for the economics of the unfettered market. In places it went into areas Mulligan found distasteful: Europe for the Europeans, not only blacks out, but Yanks too. There was also self-conscious elitism, cultural snobbery, insistence on traditional values in art, design, even in food, drink and clothes, and a constantly reiterated demand that Europe should return to classical, Renaissance, pre-modern standards. Moveover, it seemed that the great families of Europe, whose more stylish members were often mentioned, and always with uncritical flattery, were the natural custodians of these standards.

The central feature in this issue celebrated the engagement of Pedro Mendoza, Duke of Pastrana and Prince of Eboli, to Europa Malatesta, the granddaughter of Enrico, who could also call himself Prince and Duke if he chose to, but who preferred to be remembered as Mussolini's private aide and confidant. . .More pictures and again attributed to Harriet Jones. And they had been taken at Sans Souci, the house owned by a Belgian company that Tyler had linked to Myklades, whose housekeeper was the sister of Mrs Milland who had brought twenty litres of pure spring water all the way from Lourdes to Knightsbridge. Among the many guests present were the financier Madame Lili Brel, the international osteopath and surgeon Guy Lovejoy . . .

Suk waited until Mulligan lowered the magazine. 'Okay. Did Jones mention this assignment to you? No? She'd say because it had nothing to do with Myklades. But Lovejoy she talked about. And he's the link, he and she, between this mob of very, very rich fascists in their Belgian hideaway making a dynastic marriage, and Myklades, Ambrose and cocaine. Really a coincidence this time? Or something more. Listen,

James.' Suk swung back, and his small dark eyes were now hard, searching. 'One thing has always bothered me about the Web. You know what it is.'

'Where the money's going. What it's for. You're obsessed with that.' It was something about Suk that annoyed Mulligan at times. It was a distraction, an irrelevance, got in the way of Eurac's chartered aim: to bust major European drug rings. Suk's excuse was that bad money was used for bad ends.

Suk went on: 'Well this could be the clue. Listen: for forty years Enrico Malatesta has lived for one thing. . .'

Harriet, with a bloom on her not even Rupert's skills had been able to confer, took a taxi from Mulligan's apartment, picked up her things from the Paris-Liège and went on to the Inter-Continentale. Circling Vendôme, with the tyres purring over the flat cobbles, and the Ministry of Justice standing guard over Van Cleef and Arpel, Boucheron and Verny, she knew she was crossing the divide between different worlds. The commissionaire, a top-hatted giant in a coat that really was old gold, opened the door for her, while Buttons carried her bags across the tesselated pavement and between the gorgeous candelabras of ormolu, copper, polished steel and white marble that add magnificence to the honey-coloured arcades of Rue Castiglione.

Inside, more marble, walls done in pale yellowish ochre with just a hint of mustard in it, mirrors, gilt, and an overall evenness of warmth that carried on its breath expensive fragrances promising good things to eat, and the company of the rich. Buttons took her to the second floor, along wide corridors, lit by candelabras and small chandeliers, through deep carpets on which Thai and Cambodian maids piled clean sheets and shook out immaculate ones. A discreet knock and she heard Rupert's voice call: 'Come!'

'Harry, darling!'

'Rupe, dear.'

Myklades was there too, and Lovejoy. Myklades angled himself out of a deep sofa whose upholstery matched the walls, took her hand, and touched his cheek against hers. As always she had to repress a shudder at the clammy softness of his skin, at the hint of poison on his breath. As always too she felt the pull of the man, the grasping energy that dragged all but the most solidly anchored of personalities towards him, like scattered iron filings. He put his hand on her shoulder. She knew he was reclaiming possession after her jaunt away from the clan.

'Harriet, our harrier.' As always the *h's* were very slightly guttural. 'Returned to the lure. Rupert will see what quarry you have trussed for us. Unfortunately, I have business elsewhere.' The pressure became a shade stronger. His eyes seemed to bore into hers from behind the tinted Dior spectacles. 'You look. . .as if you had a good time. Don't worry. I am not jealous. A touch envious perhaps. There's a difference. I really am most truly sorry I can't stop now, really I should not be here at all, but I did wish to see for myself that our *yarak* is safely back on her block.'

'Yarak, Hector?'

'Armenian, my dear: for a keen falcon. Take care.' He kissed her again – not expecting or requiring a response, but to set a seal on her return.

He headed for the door. Rupert caught Harriet's eye as he went. His raised brows and pouted mouth expressed amused surprise and congratulation too. Clearly he felt she had risen in Myklades' esteem. Perhaps they had not expected her to come back; perhaps extending the falconry imagery, they had thought she might 'carry'.

Lovejoy rose. He was wearing a Pierre Cardin tracksuit, Nike jogging shoes, exuded good health and healthy bonhomie. His handshake was discreetly rough. He made sure it hurt. Not much, but it hurt. 'Dear Harry. I trust you have a film in your camera? The commission from *Réaxions* is perfectly above board.'

Harriet sought to compose herself by resorting to her profession. She unzipped her bag, took out a light-meter.

Rupert, his elbow on the mantelpiece, watched, his thin mouth twisted into a cruel grin. 'While you work we can talk?'

'Oh yes, certainly.'

She stood in the middle of the room eyes flitting over it, settling on one point then another, searching out backgrounds for Lovejoy's glossy tan. The same yellows and golds as everywhere else: not the ideal colour to set him against.

It was a big room, with big furniture, armchairs to go with

the sofa Lovejoy now lounged on, watching her with narrowed, professional eyes; two high double doors, white with ormolu handles; high windows that looked out on the black limbs of the chestnuts in the Tuileries. Two or three leaves remained, eighteen carat, to set off their sinuous grace.

Camera? The 'Blad. Almost she wished she'd brought something with an even larger format – she'd need to be cunning with the background, bleach out some of the colour, not to lose the warmth on his cheek-bones. She wondered if he'd object to a little powder.

'Right,' Rupert drawled. 'You met Mulligan, he took you to that nasty little hotel, you went for a walk, and separated at Notre Dame, where he did poor Emile a quite nasty mischief. Perhaps one day he'll meet me down a dark street and we'll see just how professional at that sort of thing he is. A long walk and a long talk. What about?'

Harriet pulled out her tripod, extended the legs. 'It's on the tape. In my bag. Do you want it now?'

He shrugged. 'Later will do. Then you went back to the hotel. Did he fuck you there?'

'Damn.' Suddenly she found she could not get the thread on the post of her Leitz ball and socket to tie with the matrix in the top of the tripod. She had realised too that Rupert's response to her apparently transparent sexual infidelity might not be as mature as Hector's had been. She straightened, tapped the chunky metal joint in her left palm, unconsciously strengthening her psyche with its cunningly engineered and familiar perfection.

'I went back alone. I didn't see him again until the morning. He told me to meet him at the Gare St-Lazare. It's on the tape.' Mulligan had sworn to her that there was no chance at all that they knew he had returned to the Paris-Liège.

'And he took you to Interpol, and the Eurac wing in Interpol. Is that on tape too?'

'No. Visitors have to leave cameras and bags at the desk. It was a pity really that the recorder was hidden in a camera. If it had not been, if it had been strapped to me, then. . .' She shrugged, smiled. Mulligan had enjoyed putting that one together. Judging from the genuine colour that spread up Rupert's sinewy neck, he had been right.

She squatted over her bag again, rummaged, came up with

the 'Blad, and two magazines, still in their cartons, but she came up too quickly, felt a moment of dizziness, and fumbled. Instinctively she held on to the camera, dropped one of the magazines.

'Damn again. Fingers and thumbs today, I'm afraid. I'm not usually so clumsy.'

'It's been a very stressful time for you.' Lovejoy, his voice as seductive as brown honey.

'Yes, yes it has.' She stooped again, managed to scoop up the errant box and put it all down on one of the tables, a round one set on a single fluted pillar above three claw and ball feet. To her consternation it tipped very slightly, and she had to gather them up again and look for something more stable. She made it to an armchair close to Lovejoy and put camera and magazines on a low marble top between them.

She widened her eyes, the way one does when one is tired, seeking for cool air on normally unexposed eyeball. None of the air in that place was cool.

'And I haven't slept a lot. Perhaps I could have a cup of coffee?'

'Of course.' Lovejoy snaked out a long arm for the phone. 'It'll be here in a moment.'

Self-consciously relaxed though he was, his hard eyes continued to watch her with a deep but disinterested intensity while she continued to try to get her act together.

Rupert took it up again. 'Why did he take you to Eurac, to Interpol?'

'The aim was, he said, to impress me. To convince me that he was going to win, close you down. Put you all in prison.'

'"You." Why *you*? Aren't you going to go to prison too?'

Harriet attempted gaiety. 'Come on, Rupe. Stop being such a bully. That was the point, you see. Because I was so impressed, I changed sides. I am now working for him, spying on you, and when finally the combined police forces of Europe sweep on you all, I shall be a hero person. There. I think if it's possible to draw the drape a fraction, cut down the outside light which is a bit cool – '

'There are some things one should not joke about.' Rupert came off the mantelpiece, jabbed his finger at her. 'If anything at all like the scenario you have outlined occurred you would be a hero person in several different places at once. And they would not all have died at the same time.'

Lovejoy cut into what was beginning to sound like the sort of vicious quarrel only consanguinity can sanction. 'Oh, come, Bridge. Harriet is under very considerable stress, has had a very trying time.' He went on: 'I'm sure she acquitted herself admirably. Ah, here is the coffee we asked for.'

The oriental maid put a tray on the low table in front of him, sketched a curtsy and went. He sat up, busied himself with the porcelain. 'Sugar, cream? Very wise. But I do not advise too much. See: it is strong. Very good it smells, but too much may make you, as the French say, *nerveuse*. Perhaps I should have asked for *décaffiné?*'

'It's just fine. Do you mind if I smoke?'

'I don't advise it. I don't advise anyone I know to smoke. But please feel free.'

She fumbled in her bag, not her photographic one, came up with a Marlboro and a lighter: the larger sort of disposable. It gave a spark, but would not light.

'Oh damn. I don't seem able to get anything right today.'

'And I'm afraid neither of us can help you. Let me ring for a replacement.'

'No, no, really.' She offered a half-laugh. 'You're quite right, it's a nasty habit.' She put the cigarettes away, left the lighter standing on the table.

Her cousin moved in again. 'Acquitted herself admirably, I'm sure. But on whose behalf? We should be frank about her situation: it is impossible. Ultimately, in a situation like hers, she can serve only herself. We must convince her, and ourselves, that our interests mesh with hers more efficiently than do Eurac's. But she must convince us that she believes this too. You are right, Lovejoy. Harry must be under a lot of stress. Mulligan has been at pains to hijack her from under our noses. It is in our interests that he should think he has succeeded. How can Harry persuade us that Mulligan thinks she is his without at the same time sowing seeds of doubt that it might indeed be so?'

The doctor glanced across the coffee-cup that he was just about to drink from. 'Poor Harriet. No chance at all of doing that if you bully her so. She looked so well, so relaxed, when she came in. Now look at her. That's what your imitation of

Torquemada has achieved. Harry, do you have any of the pills I gave you here? No? Well, try these. Nothing drastic, happy-pills really. Take them with your coffee eh? Why not?'

She took them, little green ones, reassuringly similar to Librium. And the effect was much the same. Quite quickly she found she could manipulate her machinery accurately and efficiently, felt at last she was making the right decisions about light, colour, depth of focus.

Rupert too appeared to relax: was content while she worked to lead her through a straightforward account of her day at Eurac, only occasionally throwing in a query, or asking for her reactions to what she had seen. She left out the photographs of Roget. She began to experience a pleasant glow, was conscious of the possibility that her colour had come back, and realised that she didn't give a damn if it had.

'Feeling better, Harriet? Certainly you look a lot better,' said Lovejoy.

'Actually, I am. Jolly effic. . .' She was going to attempt 'efficacious', but thought better of it. 'Jolly good, those pills.' She giggled. 'I suppose they're some sort of truth drug. . .?' And she giggled again, peered down into her viewfinder, clicked, cranked the handle.

Rupert, eyes narrowed, chose that moment to pounce. 'I suppose that the recording device Mulligan gave you is not in that camera. But I do wonder where it is. It would be silly to break up all your equipment in order to find it. Silly to make you take off your clothes in case it is strapped to you.'

'No. No, please don't do anything like that. It's in that fucking lighter,' she said, and, over-relaxed as she was, a giggle began to swell beneath her breast-bone. 'And it's a transmitter, not a recorder. I've been trying to think of a way of telling you it was there, but since you've brought it up, well. . .' She leaned towards it. 'If you're there, Mulligan, well then, they've rumbled us, sorry. Really sorry. Over and out, okay?'

Lovejoy picked up the heavy glass ashtray. He glanced at Rupert who nodded. Lovejoy placed the lighter on the table, and smashed the ashtray on to it, and then smashed it again. Out of the casing it bled tiny printed circuits and a couple of batteries, fingernail-sized discs.

Quiet laughter welled and spilled between them, all three of them. Lovejoy handed Harriet a handkerchief, and she flopped back in a deep armchair, dabbing at the corners of her eyes, and let the laughter flow.

Through it she heard Rupert say: 'That's fine, good. Now we can get down to work and you can tell me just how dangerous Mulligan really is. Should we waste him? Why not?'

For a moment she thought she might be sick, felt sure her face had gone ashen again, but somehow retained a sort of control in spite of everything. 'Oh no, oh dear me no.' Her voice sounded strange, distant, beyond the rushing of blood in her ears, but light, cool. 'He's not the one you. . .we have to fear at Eurac. The man you've really got to get off our backs is the computer whizz they've got there. Suk. Anton Suk. . .'

She thought she was saving Buck Mulligan's life.

Part Eight

Treasons, Stratagems, and Spoils

42

A day later, fine particles of snow gusted across the Plaza de España, Madrid, swirling like tormented clouds of chiffon through the light of the tall streetlamps, eddying like sand round the ankles of the few pedestrians. Teseo Feijoo paused on the top step of the Hotel El Príncipe, frowned angrily at the sting of the tiny flakes on his face, pulled his head into his collar. Then he gritted his teeth and scampered the short distance across the square, beneath the grandiose monument to Cervantes and Don Quixote, and into the portals of the Banco de Corpus Cristi. The big brown stone-faced building was not quite dark – in the deserted public hall dim lights illuminated long high counters and simulated marble pillars, and up on the third floor large windows, tall unshuttered rectangles, glowed more brightly.

The guards, grey-uniformed *policía armada* with scarlet bands round their peaked hats, and machine-carbines in their black-gloved hands, accepted his hastily muttered password, pushed back one side of the huge doors – nineteenth-century iron, glazed with engraved glass, reinforced with stainless steel bars. On the other side a tall male secretary, beautifully suited in very dark blue, briefly touched his hand, welcomed him, asked him to follow. The door clicked solidly shut behind him.

By the time they reached the third floor Feijoo was glad to surrender his topcoat and scarf. He tweaked his handkerchief a millimetre further from the top of his breast pocket, smoothed his greyish wiry hair with grey hands, set off across the wide acres of Aubusson that separated him from the big desk and chairs in front of the windows. An eighteenth-century grandee in silks eyed him aloofly from his gilded frame. Boltana, behind his desk, was scarcely more welcoming, waved him into a chair without speaking. Opposite him Myklades and Brel barely acknowledged him.

Lili Brel was talking, prodding at a copy of *Réaxions 3* with a perfectly manicured but very angry finger. '. . .I don't care what you say, this was a gross blunder. This links me, and you' – she stabbed at Boltana – 'to Myklades and the whole London operation. We made it a particular condition of the Plancenoît meeting that any public record of it should exclude Hector – '

'But there is no mention of me.' Hector's voice, normally rough, almost whined. 'There is no indication that I was there.'

'Don't pretend to be obtuse. Those photographs are ascribed to Jones. Eurac knows very well that Jones is part of you. They also know very well that Lovejoy is too. Hector, they are not fools. Right now they will be looking into this with all the technology at their disposal, will be trying to find the links between Ambrose and Mendoza Holdings, perhaps between Mendoza Holdings and Crystal.'

'Lili, I am sure they will find nothing.' Boltana's voice was balm. 'You have been far too clever for even the possibility to arise. . .'

'Am I any more clever than that man Suk? Why should I be? No. This simply will not do. That ascription of those pictures to Jones is a blunder, a very gross blunder. And it is the sort of thing that must not be allowed to happen again – '

Myklades stiffened, his face basically pale but blotched with bright patches of vermilion. 'It was not a blunder. It was a slip. The merest detail – '

'It was a blunder and it was sloppy.'

'Lili, Hector, we really must drop this now. We are not here to discuss this. We are here to listen to Señor Feijoo. Teseo. My dear chap. I am sorry. . .Please, forgive us. We are – you may find it hard to believe, but we are ready to listen to you.'

Feijoo straightened, pushed on glasses, pulled a folder from his document case. He scanned his audience: Boltana beaming robustly from the far side of the desk: Myklades, foxy behind his tinted spectacles; Brel, immaculate as ever, the expression on her face still angry but offering him her attention.

He cleared his throat. 'You already know the outline of the new deal we have struck with the Arias syndicate. I won't pretend it's satisfactory, nor that it was pleasant dealing with them: all along it was clear that they were convinced that they were bargaining from strength. We finally agreed to buy three tons a year at twenty-five dollars a gram and the only guarantee at all that was on offer was that they would deliver ninety-three per cent pure *perica* in shipments of one hundred and forty-four kilos at times specified by us to coincide with the Prezz' Spezz' pick-ups at the Santa María shrimp-processing rig. That's the deal as it stands and I assure you it is the very best on offer from Arias. He still reckons he's shaving two dollars a gram out of consideration for his son-in-law, and because he respects our operation in the UK, and financial standing.'

Myklades' long pale freckled fingers were drumming on the arm of his chair; his large but pinched nose swung like the questing beak of a wader.

'It won't do, you know,' he said. 'At that price our profit margins are slashed and there is no chance of meeting Malatesta's requirements, no chance the Duke will get together his bride price on schedule.'

Brel was still irritable. 'The bride price is not really important, Hector, you know that. Its main purpose is to tie Pedro into the scheme of things, keep him there as the front man of Mendoza Holdings. Enrico will grumble, but he'll be happy to take what we can give him.'

Myklades shrugged. 'All right. But the Duke will blame me. . .'

Boltana's deep voice was more soothing. 'It doesn't matter a lot who Pedro blames, so long as he continues to believe in what he is doing. But Teseo has not finished. You have more to tell us, I think.'

'Yes, Marqués.' The Guatemalan pushed his palms over his hair again, recrossed his legs, but still could not suppress the nervous sideways twitch. 'You commissioned me to get the best new deal I could from Arias, while exploring the possibility of finding a new source of supply. Events in Colombia have convinced me that this step is even more important than we thought. The feud between the Arias and Welser clans has escalated. It is no longer a commercial war, it is taking on the characteristics of a blood feud.'

Boltana sighed. 'If that is the case, then we must detach ourselves from Arias as quickly as possible. The Welsers will strike at him through any means they can, and we will be caught up. No doubt of it.'

Brel shifted, and her sharp head thrust towards Feijoo. 'How much do the Welsers know about the current operation?'

Feijoo fidgeted, considered, answered: 'Very little. Dolores Welser was in place, it now seems certain, not as a means of forging a truce through a marriage between the two clans, but in order to penetrate the Arias group as a spy. It would not have been necessary to use her in this way, put her at risk, if they knew about the deal in any sort of detail.'

'The Ferraris. They knew about the Ferraris.' Myklades smiled his thin smile as he said this, pleased perhaps to remind them that far grosser failures in security had occurred than the one Brel had tried to hold him responsible for.

'They were tipped off by the Mafia. There was resentment there that Malatesta was using the Arnolfinis to the exclusion of other Genoese families.'

'So it should hold up for a time. Unless the Welsers find some other way in.'

'I think so, Miss Brel. But only for a time. Which brings me to the second part of my report. I have, in accord with your instructions, discovered an alternative source of product.'

'Ah, aha.' Boltana waved his cigar. 'Please go on.'

'All right. But first there is one very important factor, consideration, which has to be cleared up.' Feijoo pulled out Chesterfields, his thin gold gas lighter, but his fingers continued to fiddle with them, occasionally flicking the catch on the lighter, occasionally pulling a cigarette half clear of the pack then pushing it back.

'And that is?'

'Arms, Marqués. Arms. The suppliers I am talking about do not want cash. They want arms. The right arms – nothing very sophisticated is required, nothing very expensive, not beyond the level of ground-to-air missiles. The rest is small arms, machine-guns, mortars, grenades, booby traps, the sort of thing that can be easily handled in forest and mountain. There. I think you must be comprehending the thrust of my proposal. Ideally, if we could barter the sort of arms these people want in exchange for the coca pasta they could produce if the incentive was fully there, we could do without Arias and the Colombians. No problem. And get our *perica* for about half what we are now paying.'

Traffic grumbled below. Nearer at hand a less mechanical but hardly more human rumble and snort. Boltana was laughing.

'My dear Teseo, I wonder if you appreciate the irony, the absurdity of what you are suggesting?'

A touch of colour burned in the Guatemalan's cheek-bones, emphasising them, hinting at the Indian element in his genetic make-up.

'Absurdity, Marqués?'

'Spell it out, Lili.'

'I think, Teseo, what is amusing Toñi is the idea that Crystal should be financed by guerrillas, and that they should be aided with arms in return.'

'What is so strange? For decades the Shan tribesmen and the Nationalist Chinese warlords have bought arms with opium. The Mujahadin get rockets, missiles, mortars the same way.'

The voice rumbled again, still jovial. 'Teseo, the Mujahadin are fighting Russians. The Shan tribesmen and the Chinese private armies are bulwarks of freedom against the red hordes of China and Vietnam. But the people you want us to deal with call themselves Marxist-Leninist. Maoist.'

Feijoo grimaced. 'Same difference.'

'Well, yes. But Enrico Malatesta believes himself to be not only a man with a mission, but a man of principle too. Nevertheless' – Boltana shifted hugely in his square chair, and a strong pink finger prodded the air, swung between Myklades and Feijoo – 'I don't reject what you are suggesting. And clearly you've given the matter some thought. For instance I imagine you have an arms supplier in mind?'

Myklades nodded. 'Kapp-Duxbury. We already have a substantial holding.'

'Oh dear me yes. That might do very nicely.' The jovial laughter continued to rumble. 'What do you say, Lili?'

'I don't like it at all. I don't like it one bit. Up to now both the CIA and InterCom have kept away from us. Off our backs. There is some sympathy for our aims. That will be lost when they find out that we are arming Communists. And . . . you will have to persuade Enrico.'

'Or simply not tell him. Keep him in the dark. Don't worry about Enrico. I'll handle him.'

The Inter-City thundered through the flat lands. North of Grantham broken snow lay like rags on the listless fields. But inside, the train was warm, and in its scruffy, grubby way cosy. Rupert, with his toughened steel document case on his lap, did his homework; the Kapp-Duxbury file. Rupert Bridge had his failings, but indolence, in spite of the foregrounded hedonism of his lifestyle, was not one of them.

His connection with Kapp-Duxbury had begun three years earlier, after his brief experience trading on the floor of the London Mineral Market. The tale that he had been barred for racial remarks about the Jewboys who had it sewn up concealed the truth: he had stuck one of them with a load of bauxite at just the right moment, and he had not been forgiven – the man still owed two million because of the deal. Left jobless, Rupert cashed in on the value of his army career and joined Kapp-Duxbury as a salesperson. For over a hundred years Kapp-Duxbury had see-sawed between huge success and near-bankruptcy, and Rupert joined near the bottom of a downward curve.

In 1883 Chas. Duxbury, a Birmingham munitions manufacturer, invited Johann Kapp, a Swedish inventor to come to England with his patented and entirely reliable percussion detonator. The firm thrived, accumulated capital in truly vast amounts. Exploiting the arms race that was a substantial cause of the First World War they followed Vickers to Tyneside and made floating weapons systems, capable of hurling high-explosive shells twenty miles or more with considerable accuracy. It was a peaking competitve market and it nearly ruined them. Old man Duxbury switched to tanks in time but the real saviour was the Kapp light machine-gun of 1918; the first hand-held quick-firing automatic carbine, and the last expression of Johann Kapp's ageing genius. Going through several modifications it rivalled the Sterling or Sten gun, the Thomson sub-machine-gun, and, in its heavier versions, the Belgian Bren.

The Kapp gun was a cushion: research and development were wound down, reinvestment hardly went beyond factory maintenance and new cars for the executives. K-D was not prepared for the inventiveness of a Siberian peasant called Mikhail Timofeyovich Kalashnikov. The AK 47 won wars. Deprived of the opportunity to buy or even manufacture them under licence, those Western firms that had maintained and kept in place research and development facilities came up with their own versions: the FN FAL 7.62, the Armalite AR 18, the M 16. None did as well, and in Vietnam Americans threw away their M 16s if they could get their hands on a genuine AK, but the manufacturers were laughing all the way to the bank. Not, however, K-D, which continued to live off the fat and later the seed potatoes provided by its most famous product.

Governments in Pre-Thatcherite Britain did not allow companies like Kapp-Duxbury to go to the wall. Wilson's government bought fifty-one per cent of the shares and invested huge sums developing a new range of ground-to-ground and ground-to-air missile launchers. These were extremely effective, simple to use, and precisely the weapons the War Department, or rather the Ministry of Defence, had been asking for. Just the thing for the hundred and one brush-fire and bush wars against insurgents that a disintegrating empire had been fighting from Suez to Cyprus to Malaya. It was called the Nutcracker precisely because it is a better way of cracking nuts than saturation bombing from Boeings.

But by 1974, when the Nutcracker range came into production, most of those wars had been won, and most of the empire had been lost, and by 1979 the new technology was well over the horizon and so was Mrs Thatcher. The new technology meant weapon systems again; not Dreadnoughts this time but complex (and vulnerable) computerised clusters of hard- and software with multi-faceted capacity, spawned by information and communication systems and way beyond the more primitive resources of K-D. One illiterate can load, aim, and fire a Nutcracker (though two can do it quicker) and take out a Chinook gunship or an armoured car. This makes it the ideal weapon for all the Paddies, Micks, wogs, wops and dagos from Manila to Timbuctoo who are stupid enough not to like the governments a wise providence has given them.

Which is why Mrs Thatcher does not like it. Production was finally stopped in 1983, several warehouses on Tyneside were allocated, and the unsold stock mothballed. A year later the government stockbrokers began quietly to sell K-D, thereby privately privatising it, and in 1985 it was announced that K-D need not expect any further government contracts in the foreseeable future. Within a year, a cluster of nominee buyers had gained control – none of them unconnected with Ambrose Finance.

The Inter-City slipped through one of those forgotten northern towns, Doncaster or Selby, with its neglected municipal architecture proudly if incongruously imitating the Gothic glories of Siena or Bologna, and the problem Rupert addressed himself to was how to get Nutcracker out of those warehouses.

The problem was the end-user certificate system. Arms cannot be sold abroad without an export licence, and an export licence is not forthcoming without an end-user certificate. This has to be provided by the buyer and declares that s/he will use the arms her/himself and not sell them on. And an end-user certificate is only worth the paper it is written on if it is signed by a ruling government that has Mrs Thatcher's seal of approval. And not many of the Nutcracker's potentially willing buyers were governments, yet, and those that were almost always needed Nutcrackers to combat insurgents that had Mrs Thatcher's or Mr Reagan's not always clandestine support.

The arms trade, like that in drugs, exposes the deep and ineradicable hypocrisy which underlies all free-marketry and the so-called philosophy of the New Enlightenment: if the unmediated market is the best way of deciding what sort of medical care or education should be available, why should it not also decide the production and sale of fun drugs and not so fun weaponry?

But now as the train rushed on through a landscape made bleaker not so much by snow flurries as by the sight of lifting gear that no longer turned, steel plants whose furnaces had been put out, and, on the peripheries of the towns, high streets where one in every three shops was boarded up, help, unexpected but not coincidental, was nearer than Rupert supposed.

'Ah, Bridge, old chap. Mind if I join you? Seat not taken?'

This being the first class Rupert was sitting at a quite commodious table, in a single seat on one side of the open-plan carriage. The similar seat opposite him was empty. He looked up, found at his shoulder the tall but featureless character with round large spectacles, large ears, and his head set permanently at a quizzical angle who had apparently been in charge of the boat whose gunmen had shot up *Snowstorm 1*.

'Do you have to make a point of jumping up through trapdoors? No, by all means take a pew. The chap who was using it got out at Doncaster.'

'I know. He was keeping it warm for me.'

'I can believe it. I should have recognised the smell coming off him. Well, what do you want?'

'Very little. Indeed, I am a bearer of gifts rather than requests. My main aim is to see for myself how you're doin', how you're bearin' up under the strain of the frightfully duplicitous life you lead. I must say you're looking pretty chipper.'

'Sod off or come to the point.'

The tall man sighed. 'They tell me personable charm is one of Rupert's assets. I wish just once you'd find it in your heart to let me sample it. However. Perhaps this will please you. The end-user you want will go through. There was a little problem with some tin-pot Hitler in the FCO, but we got round it. Frankly he didn't believe the cover-story, said it had been used too often.'

'The Israeli bit?'

'Lord no. No one believes that. Except hopefully investigative journalists and maverick members of parliament. No, he argued that if a quarter of the arms that were supposed to be destined for Unitá in Angola ever got there they would have pushed the Cubans into the sea a decade ago. He's got a point.'

'What made him change his mind?'

The tall man tapped the side of his nose. 'We have our methods. There. That's about all. I thought you'd like to know all was well before you actually got down to brass tacks with old Chas. Duxbury. And as I said, I like to drop by for a chat every now and then, satisfy myself that you're shaping up as well as your reports suggest. Oh yes. One other thing – '

But the cushion of air pushed in front of an oncoming express banged past the window, and the bugle call of its two-tone horn rode above the racket.

'. . .One other thing.' The tall man leant a little closer.

'We've evaluated your comments on the chap you're bothered about at Eurac, and we do tend to agree that a spot of the old XPD might be in order. Certainly he seems pretty sea-green, and we don't have the clout to have him shunted elsewhere. However. . .'

'Yes?'

'Well. We do rather think the outfit your loyalties are ostensibly committed to is at the least as well equipped to cope as we are. And if you're not too clumsy about it we'll see the Frogs don't pursue their enquiries too diligently. Fair enough?'

Chimes and an ethnic voice announced the imminent appearance of Durham.

'Which, old boy, is as far as my ticket takes me.'

'Thank Christ. Some gift that turned out to be.'

'*Dona ferentes?* What a boon a classical education is. Helps one to keep a sense of proportion.'

Charles Duxbury III was overweight, insecure, and, because he could no longer afford coke, a drunk. He lived in the huge neo-Gothic mansion his grandfather had built out of granite and the profits from using sub-standard steel plate on battle-ships. It was set in shabby neglected parkland. A mile or so away a thick grey wall, tumbled about in places, snaked across the bleak snowy fells, disappeared behind a plantation of regimented fir. Standing in a tall window of leaded diamonds Charles thumped Rupert's shoulder. 'Reassuring to think we still have something between us and the kilted Pict, eh? Eh? What do you say, Bridge?'

Behind them, his wife, a thin, tired mad-looking lady called Agnes sighed audibly over the coffee-cups she was attempting to cope with. She was – her genteel Kelvinside accent betrayed it – Scottish.

'Peh noo attention, Mr Bridge. He always says the-at.'

'Only if you're in the room, dear. Which, I have to say, you shouldn't be.'

'Why not, pray? You told me we were to have coffee in here.'

'I said *we* – that is me and young Rupert – would. I didn't mean you too. Now push off, there's a dear. Business.'

'Ah. Now Eh understand why the decanters have been left

out. Well, don't make yoursel' stupid with it, that's all. Eh shall be in the drawing-room if you want me.'

An hour later.

'Now let's see if I've got this straight, old chum.' Cut crystal chimed against cut crystal, and liquid gurgled yet again. 'Damn it, it's only burn water, eh? Peat bog and sheep piss, another little drop won't do us any harm. Eh? No? Why not? It's damn good stuff I can tell you, cost a fortune, liquid gold. Where were we?'

Tea-time and outside it was very nearly dark. The wind had risen with dusk and sudden sharp gusts of cold air eddied round Rupert's ankles. Over the years Castle Duxbury had been neglected.

'You say you can get us a contract, a buyer for twelve hundred Nutcrackers, plus twenty-four thousand rockets for the use of, and two thousand Kapp guns, the K-D nines, plus a million rounds for the use of, which, I have to tell you is jolly good news. But. BUT. The end-user certificate comes from Israel, because you've got a chum in the right place there. Am I getting this right?'

Rupert suppressed a sigh. 'Yes, Charles. Spot on.'

'And the chaps in the FCO, and the Department of Trade and Industry, and the good old MoD – sod the lot of them for what they've done to Kapp-Duxbury – know damn well that Israel has no more use for Nutcrackers and Kapp guns than it has for peashooters and elastic catapults. But they all think that the whole thing is a wheeze to get our products to Unitá in Angola and that we are really being paid by South Africa. And that suits them all very well, because Mrs T likes Unitá, but can't give them the overt support she would like to because (a) they're rebels, and (b) they're just the long arm of President Botha who no one is allowed to like these days, though he was always a good customer of ours. Cheers. Are you sure you won't have a drop more?' Charles Duxbury III leant forward out of the cracked leather of his armchair, and went on: 'But they're not really going to Unitá at all, are they?' He tapped the side of his nose with a podgy finger.

'No.'

'Of course not. And know how I know that?'

'Because it's a scam we tried two years ago and it didn't come off.'

417

'Ah. You remember.'

'Yes.' Which was not surprising, because it had been Rupert's brainchild.

'So where are they going?'

'Best not to know, old chum, if you don't have to. Just so long as we can set up the documentation that will get it all out of the country, that's what counts.'

'Ho. Hum. And what about the gelt. I take it that's real? All kosher and above board, I hope? Not funny money . . . I mean I don't think I could recommend the board to accept a banker's draft drawn on the Royal and Loyal Bank of Andorra or whatever.'

Rupert set down the empty Waterford tumbler he had been cradling and reached a wallet out of his inside pocket. From it he took a pale blue slip of paper.

'I think you'll find this is a negotiable financial instrument.'

'City and Wessex. Finsbury Square Branch. Pay Bearer. Three hundred and twenty-five thousand pounds – '

'Ten per cent deposit, give or take a bob or two. Earnest of our good intentions.'

'Rupert, if this clears, it will do very nicely.'

'Yes, Charles. And here's a little something for you personally. Show how we appreciate what you're doing.'

He hauled his case on to his knees, unlocked it, pulled out a cube of sealed silver foil, each side about three inches long.

'Open it carefully. It might crumble.'

'Oh Jesus.' Suddenly Duxbury's voice was a croak, and a sweat had broken out across his wide forehead. 'If that's what I think it is, I don't think I can. You do it.'

Rupert put his case on the floor, leaned round and lifted a low occasional gate-leg table into place between them. On it was a small silver salver. On that he placed the cube, and then, using a mother-of-pearl-mounted penknife, he slit it open, peeling back the foil. The cube was white, pure white, and in the firelight it glittered.

'Five hundred grams,' he said. 'At today's prices just about exactly the one per cent personal sweetener you deserve.' The grin which could still be engaging suddenly split his face. 'Coke to Newcastle, eh?'

43

Feijoo, equipped with credentials which described him as the representative of a Mexican firm marketing a low-tech device for extracting and processing rubber, travelled by fits and starts towards a rendezvous in the upper reaches of the Amazon, to a spot not far from where the borders of Colombia, Brazil and Peru all meet. The three cases that went with him carried the components of a Nutcracker elaborately labelled to suggest that they would prove invaluable to latex collectors, and their passage through Customs halls was eased in the usual ways.

His progress up a chain of contacts within the Flowering Garden movement took him through a town called Pasto high up in the Andes and near the Peruvian border. The slight, nervy Guatemalan hated it. The cold thin air brought on an attack of asthma such as he had not experienced since adolescence, and outside the well-run Swiss hotel most of the people lived in sod-roofed huts. Leprosy seemed to be endemic.

Nothing happened for three days. On the third, driven by boredom, he went to a free filmshow in a small adobe hall. It was sponsored by the Reformed Evangelical Church of Dallas, Texas. Surrounded by landless peasants whose only luxury seemed to be chewing coca leaves – certainly none had ever enjoyed a hot bath – he watched a film about a pastor in Bogotá who ran a co-operative brick factory. The ascetic evangelist exuded hostility to life even when he fondled children. His distraught neurotic eyes signalled fanaticism without fire or energy. The message was clear: wherever you find true social progress, there you will find the true church. The projectionist threaded up a second film and Feijoo left.

Back at the hotel the porter told him he would be met in the post office the following morning.

He stood there, at the appointed time, and nothing happened. He read the text of a poster showing a jack-booted, goose-stepping soldier. It proclaimed '*¡Campesinos!* Your army is fighting for your welfare. Crime degrades a man and he cannot live with himself. Work elevates him towards God. Co-operate with the police and the military. *They only need your information!*' Feijoo read this three times.

'Tea? I can't take anything stronger, I'm afraid. It's the altitude, you see, sends up the blood pressure.' Herr Schindler poured. The fragrance of jasmine. Feijoo feared it would reactivate the asthma, and his head responded to the thought with its galvanic rightwards twitch.

The German ran the local soft-drink factory, made a habit of inviting foreign visitors for tea and an informed chat about the local flora and fauna. He had a thin ravaged face, sharp nose, down-curving mouth.

'I used to be tough as nails. But a doctor here gave me an injection of iodine which upset my whole metabolism. If I eat anything with salt my feet swell up.'

He showed Feijoo volumes of pressed flowers and leaves, cases of beetles and butterflies nailed through their chests with steel pins.

'The llama dung beetle is interesting, don't you think? Quite a rarity since the *campesinos* do just about everything you can imagine with the stuff except eat it themselves. Poor bastards probably even resort to that at times.' He looked up, held Feijoo's eyes through round steel-rimmed spectacles. 'Of course all this is nothing to what you can expect on the Putumayo. Watch out for a big grasshopper, a powerful aphrodisiac: if it lands on you and you can't get a woman right away you will die. I have seen men running round jacking off from contact only. Your cases have gone on ahead of you. You should make for Leticia.'

Feijoo took a taxi, a smart Chevvy, the two hundred miles back down the Inter-American to Cali. The fat, brown, jolly, cigar-smoking mestizo who drove reckoned they could do it in three hours – in time to make the connection by air to Leticia. And the rate at which the big spongy car wound in the thin tarmacked thread in spite of the fact that it roller-coasted over icy passes at ten thousand feet, hairpinned into steamy forest basins at five, convinced Feijoo for a time that it might be on.

But there were delays: twenty miles from Cali, they ran into a long tailback behind an army checkpoint. Beyond it a village burned: black smoke drifted across the gorges, was sliced by ear-thrashing rotors of a dark green Chinook. Soldiers in combat gear, M16s cradled across their forearms, patrolled the street in carefully spaced formations; from an armoured car a podgy, sandy-haired, scarlet-faced American directed them through a radio from beneath a round, peaked cap. Bodies, pigs, a donkey, and three *macheteros* had been pulled off the road and dumped outside the one small *supermercado*. One of the *macheteros* stirred and a soldier shot off a sharp burst from his carbine, reduced his head to a mess that looked like crushed water-melon.

Feijoo missed his connection and had to spend a night in Cali. He booked into the Americana, walked out into the velvety dusk of a town that always buzzes between the crags that surround it – one with an enormous statue of the risen Christ, the other with a megalithic Calvary of three giant crosses. Street-wise blacks offered girls and cocaine, lovely women tall and lean with rumps like milk chocolate squeezed into tight skirts or cut-down jeans sauntered in pairs down the arcades and sidewalks, drank Coke (the real thing) from cans through straws; smaller girls, Indians, but pretty too, sold oxidised filigree silver charms, Chiclets, and Marlboros. Feijoo ate well off steak and allowed himself to be serviced by a girl whose lithe body had a pelt of fine, almost invisible dark fur, but who could do marvellous things with her tongue.

In the morning he caught the DC8 to Leticia, leaving the huge jagged escarpment of the snow-capped Andes behind in a violet haze, flying out over the undulating deep-piled carpet of the rain forest, laced with lazy brown waterways. In the plane young men played loud tape recorders, drank, fondled girls, goosed the stewardess. Two of them got on to the flight deck where – and, with only a woven cotton curtain between, Feijoo could hear them – they joshed the pilot, who was clearly a chum, and tried to persuade him to let them have a go.

Glad to get back to earth safely, Feijoo was, nevertheless, not happy to be in Leticia. A trading station between Peruvian Iquitos upstream and Brazilian Manaus downstream, the stream being the Amazon itself, it is one of the hubs of the drug network sucking in coca leaf and pasta from the forest hinterland, processing and trading it on by plane, truck and boat back up to Cali and Popayán. Feijoo feared that someone from among the pilots of the small amphibious planes that buzzed in hourly, the gunmen with agate eyes who rode shotgun for them, the smooth plump buyers who sat in the shady cafés, might recognise him from Barranquilla or Bogotá. He knew that if Arias knew where he was, he would be killed.

In Leticia then he kept an even lower profile than usual, staying in the German-run Alemanos, which is clean, cheap, and the nearest one can get to a quiet hotel. Schindler had recommended it and thereby signalled that it was where the next contact would be made. But quiet it was not. Outside youngsters bombed about the few paved streets on Hondas and Suzukis with gleaming ghetto-blasters steadied on their hips, scattering broadcast ear-shattering helpings of Salsa and Reggae.

Afflicted now with a severe head-cold and deep travel fatigue, Feijoo skipped lunch, pulled the blinds in his room, dropped a couple of mandies and managed to sleep.

He woke in cooler darkness though outside the cacophony of music, diesel generators and motor scooters was as relentless as ever. Nevertheless he sensed that someone was in the room with him. Without, he thought, visibly stirring, his fingers, beneath his pillow, curled round the butt of his small Beretta. The movement provoked a low, husky laugh. Clearly any attempt to come up shooting would risk having his head blown off. He very slowly withdrew the hand so whoever it was could see it, turned on his back, and opened his eyes.

The light that filtered past the slats of the blinds and the mosquito netting was coloured, broken and moving. It gave the small room a sub-aqueous, dreamlike appearance at odds with the racket beyond but very much in keeping with the alternately lit and silhouetted figure, slender, tall, of Immaculada Dalfinger.

'Welcome to Leticia, Teseo.'

'Oh yes. Sure. Thanks.'

She had changed, and, to Feijoo's way of thinking, not for the better. He had always feared her style, her cutting edge like that of a much sharpened kitchen devil worn down to a sliver of slightly serrated steel, but he had felt at home with her metropolitan pallor, the whiff of evil, of city gases that came off her. But she was browner now, her muscle tone firmer, and her naturally bleached blonde hair was scraped back off her forehead in a way that drew attention to the slope of her face, the height of her cheek-bones: there was Indian blood there in spite of her name, which was one of the oldest in Colombia. She wore a simple cream-coloured linen dress and thin thonged sandals, very different from the avant-garde fashions she affected in Barranquilla and Bogotá.

'Listen. You must stay in this room until dawn tomorrow. I've brought you a sandwich and a beer, so there's no need for you to go out. Set your alarm for an hour before dawn; that's five o'clock, and get down to the port by half five. A couple of hundred metres upstream from where the boats to Manaus tie up you'll see there's a little marina for planes, amphibians. Third one in, a white Cessna with a blue tail-fin, you just get in and wait. Right?' She got up, smoothed the dress with long brown fingers. The nails that had been long and always painted were cut square and unvarnished. She paused at the door. 'Hey, Teseo. Can you put that Nutcracker thing together? And make it work? Because we can't.'

And with that she was gone.

Sunrise less than a thousand feet above the Amazon forest: a sea of nacrous mist, through which the taller trees loomed, blushed, turned to gold, and suddenly the small plane had an elongated shadow that rushed away from them, perhaps thrown as much as a mile. The mist rose, was sliced by the floats, shredded by the props. The temperature in the tiny cabin dropped, and Feijoo felt icy panic grip: the pilot, a thin, dark man with shaven head and a quarter-inch of stubble, seemed to be flying on a compass bearing, nothing else.

Dalfinger turned from the co-pilot seat, grinned at Feijoo in one of the two passenger seats behind. 'Don't worry, he knows the way, don't you darling?' And she nibbled at the man's ear, which carried a small gold ring. 'And there are no mountains, not for three hundred miles.'

There might, thought Feijoo, be other aircraft. Worse dangers had not occurred to him until, a moment or so later, Dalfinger turned again.

'It's because of the mist that we fly at this time of day. The air force has Mirages with sidewinder missiles. We keep low and they don't pick us up on their radar, and in the mist they can't see us.'

Twenty minutes later it began to thin. The Cessna followed a wide, meandering brown river at such a low altitude that it was like driving down an avenue with trees on either side. Suddenly and for no reason at all that Feijoo could see the pilot throttled back, dropped them on to the surface. Above the increased engine noise, the roar of water beneath the floats, he shouted, in American English: 'Nothing to fear now but crocs. Hit a croc, lose a float.'

Indians, small, well proportioned, their skin the healthy colour of creamy coffee or chocolate, welcomed them. They wore strings of white porcelain beads round their necks and kept their genitals in simple cotton pouches, white or yellow. They left the pilot behind, slashing branches and huge plantain leaves to cover the Cessna – whether as camouflage or to keep the interior cool, Feijoo could not say. The Indians took Feijoo and Dalfinger down a track that was well worn, well marked, but three times petered out in thickets and then rediscovered itself before it reached their *maloca*. Their gait was not graceful, but a speedy, jerky sort of near-run, which soon left Feijoo breathless, clutching his chest, and mopping his forehead with a sopping handkerchief. A thorn penetrated the open leatherwork of his fancy shoe, and his wild cotton jacket was plastered to his back. When they had to wait for him, the Indians ignored him, chewed coca, conversed in smooth bird-like voices. Dalfinger smiled vaguely as though she could hear distant music.

The approach to the *maloca* was signalled by a sudden clearing in the forest: trees had been felled, and – a crisp blackness on the surface showed it – burnt. Suddenly they were in a garden, a plantation but there was none of the tidiness of organised furrows: bright green manioc – plants three to five feet high with leaves like lupin leaves, and through their tubers providing staple starch – were interplanted with chilis, pineapple, banana, sugar cane, cashew nuts. Women moved through it with what seemed like sinuous laziness, but in fact was a serious labour of weeding, clearing, tying up, tending, harvesting. Small naked children helped or played quietly; babies clung to their mothers' necks, or slept in wicker carriers on their backs. The women were bare-breasted but wore simple full skirts of brightly coloured trade cotton. In a similar space behind the *maloca* Feijoo could see a plantation of slim, graceful bushes with creamy white flowers, small pointed leaves – the pruned bushes of *Erythroxylum coca*, but there was this difference: they were planted in neat straight rows. Cash crops are grown in straight lines but what you grow for yourself interprets the lie of the land.

From outside, the *maloca,* set above its gently sloping gardens, resembled the few truly traditional wooden peasant chalets that remain in the wilder parts of the Bernese Oberland. It was, however, bigger: from a roof-tree thirty feet high neatly layered thatch fell steeply to eaves that were only a metre or so from the ground. The huge triangle of the end wall was similarly thatched to the lintel of the narrow but high doorway; below that level it was covered with squared-off sheets of bark that had been painted in elaborate patterns, derived from yagé-induced visions.

Inside, the effect was of cosy grandeur, domestic majesty. The trunks of six forest giants, the main supports of the roof timbers, soared into a smoky darkness shot with thin beams of light, a darkness filled with objects stored at all levels to the thatch itself: boxes, cradles, baby bouncers made from basketry; spears, bows, arrows, blow-pipes fashioned from bamboos and brightly ornamented with tufts of macaw and toucan feathers; musical instruments, long clay trumpets also oddly reminiscent of alpenhorns, bamboo panpipes, drums; and on the lowest levels of all pots and pans made from clay, mixed with the enamel dishes, knives, shotguns, and machetes that the Indians had traded for coca leaves.

Below the level of about five and a half feet the floor was relatively clear, though, at the back, beyond a partially drawn basketwork screen, Feijoo could see three women mashing manioc roots in big clay vessels. Nearer there were benches and stools set out in neat semicircles, what looked like a fat dugout canoe but was in fact the receptacle cassava beer was fermented in, and further in, but round the edges, hearths and hammocks. A forked pole supported coca and tobacco pouches, ankle rattles, and decorated gourd maraccas. The *maloca* smelt of smoke, dung, fermentation, and Feijoo hated it.

In this dusty but sun-flecked gloom the three rectangular steel cases that had disappeared from his hotel in Pasto while he was taking tea and pumpernickel with Herr Schindler looked like objects from outer space – magical blocks placed there by the mysterious aliens of *2001, A Space Odyssey*. Surrounded by head-shrinking, drug-crazed cannibals, they comforted him, spoke of technology, of civilisation, of the rational intellect that over the centuries had pulled itself up and out of this hot, dark, seething mess into the bright clean world of IBM, Star Wars, microchips and thermonuclear power. There was a connection between the two worlds – one had grown out of the other, he knew that – but they were as widely separated from each other as the mess of powdered coca leaves these pygmies so relentlessly chewed is separated from the pure white crystals he then, at that moment, so desperately craved.

'Paco. Paco? Are you here?' Immaculada's call was hardly more than a whisper, but at the far end one of the women, lit by the bright square of the women's entrance, looked up over her shoulder from the pan she was working on, smiled, shook long black hair from her face, went back to whatever she was doing.

Nearer, twisted creeper squeaked on wood, a hammock swung, and a long smooth dark leg felt for the beaten earth of the floor.

Paco was tall for an Indian, as tall as Feijoo, but at first sight not very different from the rest of the tribe. Like them he wore nothing but a genital pouch, but instead of the two or three strands of surfer's beads twisted round his neck he had six or seven. As he moved forward a shaft of sunlight fell across short-cropped dusty black hair, a wide brow, Oriental eyes, straight but spreading nose and a firm mouth drawn like a hunter's bow. It was a face more than typical of his tribe, it was its essence: symmetrical, handsome, and above all lit with eyes that shone with intelligence and confidence.

He embraced Immaculada warmly, turned to Feijoo. He spoke in the sing-song Spanish he had learnt at mission school. The Father had baptised him Paco, after St Francis, who, like him, talked to the birds.

'They tell me you can work that toy.' His head jerked towards the boxes glowing ghostly and silver behind him. 'Is that so?'

Feijoo, who had been put through a crash course on Nutcracker Assembly and Deployment at Skrape the week before he left, nodded. But it seemed an aeon ago and he doubted he remembered it all.

When he had finished, and he was fairly sure he had got it right, Paco hoisted the long, awkward stove-pipe of a launcher across his narrow but well-muscled shoulders, and his two brothers carried the bandoliers, each holding six missiles, cigar-shaped bombs with fins.

Paco grinned. 'If this works, you have a deal. ¡Vámonos, chicos!'

Two hours later, after the walk back to the river where they found the Cessna pilot asleep in his cockpit, smelling of rum but with an AK 47 across his knee, and then a trip in three dugout canoes, and finally another walk, they came to a second *maloca*.

It had been partly destroyed by fire. As they approached, the Indians fell silent, looked grim. Many of the plants in the garden had been uprooted, and a haze of sour smoke hung over the broken roof-tree, the gaping hole in the roof. Inside they found three rows of bodies, loosely wrapped in cotton shrouds, or covered with basket-work screens that had been pulled down. There were twenty of them, men, women and children. In the very centre of the *maloca* there were four soldiers, tied with thongs to the centre posts, young lads, dressed in combat-splashed denims and jungle boots. They looked tired, frightened. All of them were mestizo, one was part black.

Paco explained, 'It was a war party, you cannot call it anything else. The government will say that these Indians, a family from whom my mother came, so they are my cousins, were trading coca, which is now meant to be illegal. In fact probably they were not trading enough coca for the dealers back in Leticia. We are not greedy. We grow enough for our own use and to trade for a few machetes, a bale or two of cotton every now and then. And a few bags of leaves each year get us those. Don't worry, you will be paid. Not with Indian-grown coca, but from the big plantations in Peru and Bolivia. High-altitude coca, which is far stronger. But we will see it gets down through the forest to the Great River for you.

'Anyway, for whatever reason, the army sent in a war party

427

to destroy these people . . . I will not show you the bodies. The women have been raped, sometimes with instruments. The children have been mutilated, disembowelled, the men castrated. The soldiers came up the river in powerboats and all but these four went back the same way. Unfortunately for them these found some of this.' His hand reached to a decorated and beaded pouch that still hung from a beam up in the roof. He opened it, spread a fine purple powder on his palm. 'It is a very powerful hallucinogenic, psychotropic, and is normally only used under the strict control of the shaman who prepared it. These overdosed themselves and fell into catatonic trances. The sergeant who was in charge, an American, believed they had poisoned themselves. So he simply left them behind. We know all this because we were there, in the forest, watching. We three. There was nothing we could do but watch.'

He pointed to his brothers, who were crouching now as if weighed down by the bandoliers. One looked up, spoke. Even in the birdsong of their language he sounded impatient. Paco straightened, sighed. 'He's right. We must get on with it. See how well your toy works.'

The four soldiers watched them go with blank uncomprehending eyes.

They moved back down the garden to the furthest point away from what had become a shed, a shell, a shambles, the furthest point at which they still had a clear view of it.

'We'll use the incendiary sort.'

Feijoo, making adjustments for range, said: 'Tell your brothers to keep clear of the back. Of the exhaust.'

Paco did, stooped to one knee, sighted, squeezed the trigger which was mounted below the pipe.

There was a whoosh like a sudden tornado, and the acrid stinging smell of burning propellant. The missile, guided by the infrared beam, looped twice in the air and passed precisely through the oblong doorway, three hundred yards away. A heartbeat, then the whole fabric of timber and thatch bellied out and upwards and blossomed into an enormous flower of flame.

Back in the Cessna, flying now through the mists of dusk, Immaculada turned to Feijoo.

'Is Jana, Jana Pensión, still with you, still with El Señorito?'

'Yes.'

'Send this to her when you get back to Leticia.' She handed him the pouch containing the purple powder that had betrayed the soldiers. 'Tell her I will write to her when I know how it can be wisely used.'

44

Some things mark you for life, and the Protestant Sunday is one of them. This thought relentlessly asserted itself in Mulligan's mind on average forty-eight times a year, usually at about the moment his Rowenta gold-filter coffee machine gave a brief sigh, an aromatic sputter, signifying that it was almost through. Not even the smell of fresh coffee could do more than lift the edge of gloom that descended with it. Not even the fact that he was an atheist in a Catholic city renowned for its hedonism could mitigate the long hours of boredom spiked with tremors of guilt that lay ahead: for although the mythology of WASP-land would have you believe otherwise, the French take Sunday pretty seriously too.

The steady toll of the bells of Sacré Cœur bleeding sanctimonious religiosity across La Butte de Montmartre bore witness to that. And after Mass, celebrations, yes, but strictly *en famille*. In the restaurants tables are pushed together to accommodate a dozen or more at once, and small children in frothy dresses or straitjacketed in awkward suits trade kisses for sweetmeats with geriatrics wheeled out for the occasion. A French Sunday may be fun for them, but not for a middle-aged single male whose Sunday soul has been marked for life by Quaker Meetings and Bible readings.

Mulligan pulled up a blind, poured coffee into a big French breakfast bowl, added milk, *demi-écrémé* – he wasn't going to go mad with the cholesterol, not even on a Sunday – dipped the horn of the first of three croissants, and bit it off. He sat back and tried to persuade himself that the view was worth looking at.

It stretched ten miles or more, but on a cold grey morning in early January was not even impressive, let alone beautiful.

Looking north and east from La Butte it was shredded for the first mile or so with the railways and marshalling yards running out of the Gare du Nord and the Gare de l'Est with cemeteries between, then factories, suburbs and the woods round Coubron.

He snapped on a Bartok quartet, folded out the *Herald Tribune*. Later perhaps he'd make a real Sunday of it, try to make an impression on *The Name of the Rose*, which had so far proved impenetrable. That's what Sundays were for: the Quaker Meeting and the Bible reading replaced by self-improvement, by a serious attempt to remind himself that a long time ago he had received a good liberal education in the Humanities, and that Cultured with a capital C was something he had once claimed to be.

It was a relief when, an hour or so later, the phone burbled.

'James?'

Even with just the one word of inflection, the accent, were unmistakable.

'Anton?'

'Yes. James, I have to see you. And very quick.'

'Sure. Why not? Come right over.'

'It's not so simple as that.'

'Oh?' Mulligan visualised the tall Czech, his face creased in the dark worried frown which was only occasionally relieved by the blessing of a sudden smile – open, warm, offering.

'I can't explain over the phone, but it should be, I think, somewhere anonymous. What, James, I am trying to say is this. Right now I am in a public phone box. I am sure, absolutely sure, that I am under surveillance. I want to be able to get back into my car and drive to meet you, but without it being known that that is where I am going. If I start driving up Rue Lamarck they'll guess where I am directed. Headed. And they may well try to stop me.'

'Can't this wait until tomorrow? I mean at St-Cloud we can talk.'

'No. We must meet now. It is very urgent. Oh my God.'

'What is it?'

'James. You don't have a car.'

'No.'

'And the Métro is still on strike. All right. We'll do it like this. I'll meet you on Boul' de Rochechouart, outside the

Anvers Métro, there's a little park, Place d'Anvers . . . Okay? In half an hour.'

Ten minutes after Suk's call Mulligan set out. He paused at the street entrance to his block of flats – three of them only in a square modern house at odds with the terraced tenements that dropped down the steep hill to the north. People were coming off the railed belvederes, down the short wide steps from the huge eyesore above – eyesore to Mulligan at any rate, especially when it advertised its function as one of the most popular churches in Paris. And climbing them too. The last Mass of the morning was just over; in a moment or two the main service of the day, Sung Eucharist, would start. The clangour of bells washed all other sounds out of a sky that was black, pregnant with snow.

He buttoned his coat against the bite of icy air, made the short climb to the top, the circuit round the front of the church, and then dropped down more stairs to the funicular. It was, of course – but one could easily forget the fact – run by the Métro, and therefore closed. Three pickets fought off the anger of a small crowd of worshippers and tourists who were quickly shedding any charity Mass might have instilled.

The only way down was on foot, a steep descent by flights of stone stairs through the Villette gardens and the Place St-Pierre. A glance at his watch showed he might not make Anton's half-hour. Almost he ran through Rue Steinkerque – the haberdashery shops were shut but he had to swerve and dodge as the other churches nearby filled and emptied. Panting slightly he paused on the boulevard. Plane trees soared naked apart from a few black seed-cases like tiny chain-and-ball flails; the green pagodas were still fly-posted with raucous support for the strike and the pre-Christmas student demonstrations against Chirac's proposed education reforms. Up the road behind him three tourist coaches from abroad were parked in a small cluster of backpackers.

On the far side, separated from Mulligan by four lanes of traffic as well as the central division, there was a small square set back from the boulevard, more plane trees and acacias too, and, parked up against cast-iron railings, a 2CV, painted maroon and glossy black, facing him. Anton's car. Mulligan made it to the middle, raised his hand in a wave, was about to shout. Anton's round head, beneath the flat cap he always wore out of doors, turned towards him.

What happened next remained totally clear in Mulligan's mind, totally accessible, for he had trained himself to go over and over any terrifying or traumatic experience until it was etched as if with acid on the plates of his mind. Only that way could he be sure to overcome the anaesthetising amnesia induced by shock.

A tall man dressed in a dark topcoat approached the 2CV head-on walking down the wide pavement. He had a thin narrow face, a large nose. He stooped. Anton pushed up the horizontal flap of his window. No one knows what the stranger said. Perhaps (for it transpired later – much later, since the remains were not easily identified – that he was a businessman from Poitiers) he was asking the way. Or the time.

The noise – part scream, part roar – came from behind Mulligan, and, in his memory, lasted for much longer than the second or so it took for the rocket to smash into the 2CV. It penetrated the bonnet and exploded against the engine under Anton's feet, not far below the stranger's stooping head. The blast took off one of the cuboid headlamps perched on the mudguard, fired it like a cannonball into the stomach of an elderly lady. She died two days later. The steering wheel and instrument panel, gear and brake linkages tore Anton and the stranger apart in one merciless split second. A moment later the petrol tank blevvied, sent a searing blast of hot air banging across the carriageway smacking Mulligan on to his back in the fine gravel the boules players use in summer.

Responding to the training he had been given when he first joined the FBI twenty years earlier, Mulligan rolled on to his front, covered his head with his arms, pulled in his knees and waited. Waited for his diaphragm to regain control of his respiration, for his eardrums to recover enough to retune to the noises around, waited to see if the killers were satisfied with what they had done or whether they had realised their mistake, that they had fired too soon, waited in all for about one and a half minutes. By then his ears had recovered enough to detect the crunch of gravel, the screams of the injured distanced by numbness, and the guinea-pig yelp of police cars. He pulled himself to his feet, dusted himself, pushed his way through the gathering crowd back up Rochechouart to Pigalle where he caught a taxi home. His shaking legs were beyond attempting the ascent of La Butte de Montmartre unaided. He fumbled with his latchkey and a few flakes of snow drifted out of the stillness of the sky.

Two days later the snow in Witham Square fell heavy, large-flaked, warm. It lay like a duvet across the dog-fouled grass of the garden in the middle, simulated the swags of ornamental blossom that would grace the two black-boughed cherry trees at Easter. In the street it was already churned to slush.

Harriet paid off her taxi, stood, tall, thinner than she had been, sheathed in Russian sable, and swayed slightly as she fished in her purse for her keys. She looked about her. Her cheek-bones were more pronounced, her face whiter: possibly through art, fashion – pallor was the new look, and it set off the grandeur of her hair, swept back now into a coiled pile of red gold behind her small white ears. Emeralds glinted in the lobes. She looked around and her high-arched nose wrinkled in amused disdain. An address south of the river, however upwardly mobile that particular square, would very soon be a thing of the past.

At the top of her three steps, with the first key already in place, she caught the movement, twenty yards away, in the doorway of the corner shop. Her first reaction was to operate the locks as quickly as possible, get in, away from a possible predator. It flashed through her mind that two locks left a girl more vulnerable on her doorstep. Then she realised who it was.

He gave her time to take him in: the cropped grey hair, the height, the neat topcoat, and as he came nearer, the large eyes, smiling, the neat but generous mouth, above all the confidence, the certainty with which he did things.

He stopped, head on one side, looked up.

'You'll ask me in?'

'Of course.' She smiled too, but her heart lurched.

He went in front of her into the narrow hall, waited while she reset the locks, and then as she tried to brush past him caught her cheek in his large palm and kissed her lips coolly, briefly. Helped by the spaced-out distance Lovejoy's pills put between her real self and the outside world, she consciously chose not to respond with overt enthusiasm, nor to be a coquette and deny him.

'Have you eaten?'

'Yes.'

'Coffee, then.'

He followed her down a short flight of narrow stairs into the crowded kitchen. She flicked on spotlights, pointed him to a high-backed chair, withdrew to the far end of the narrow room where she was hedged in by shelves, work-surfaces, cupboards, appliances.

She was, she thought, reading his thoughts. 'It's all a bit of a mess.'

'Oh, I don't know.' In fact he was worried about the small espresso coffee pot she had unscrewed, emptying old grounds into a plastic bag. He hoped she would not overload it: he wanted the taste of coffee, not the hit.

'Take your coat off, why don't you? And let's have a brandy? There's some on the shelf there. You pour it, and please, Buck' – she turned to him now, full on, her green eyes wide and tired, her bottom lip trembling – 'don't be mean with it. Or anything else for that matter.' She shrugged out of the sable, and let it drop over the back of the other chair. She was dressed in a short black watered-silk dress with very thin straps. Her shoulders looked thin, white, vulnerable. Manipulatively she added: 'Please?'

'Okay.' He laughed, found two tumblers, half filled them. 'Cheers.'

In bed at least he kept his promise. He had made love to no one but himself during the three years that had passed since his wife and children had left him, left his obsessive preoccupation with his work for Centac. The reality again of shared bodies and shared ecstasies after so long a time was again the ambush it had been in Rue Lamarck. There was no denying his need, and she welcomed it.

Greyness before dawn, but the streets on the other side of the terrace already grubby with busyness, found him, still naked, smoking a Marlboro and looking out through her narrow sash window at the tiny gardens, the blackened houses. A cat stalked a pigeon across the thick snow, crouched, lashed its tail; the pigeon took note, flapped up to a leaning wall. The cat retrieved *amour propre* by shaking snow from his paw then

434

swiftly licked his long tummy. Mulligan thought: maybe I'll get more lucky. Bloody better. Yet there was tenderness in his eyes, even the anxiety of not yet satiated desire, as he looked back at her coiled beneath the duvet, one arm circling the crown of glorious hair, spilt like treasure across the pillow.

She stirred, stretched out long white arms above the cover, long toes peeped at the other end. She held it for a second, then let her head drop back again. She smiled – a slow, open smile of untrammelled pleasure.

'Good morning, lover.'

'Hi.'

'Give us a gasper.' He did and she caught his arm, made him kiss her. 'Do you know how to make tea?'

'Of course.'

'My hero. You can do *anything*.'

He pulled on pants, shirt, trousers, padded down to the kitchen.

She joined him there, wrapped in blue and green cotton, just as he was putting the mugs on the table. He sat opposite her and his eyes were serious.

'They tried to kill me, you know?'

She flinched, and the softness of gratified desire began to leak from her face.

He went on: 'You know, I thought I was more use to them alive. With you monitoring me one way, a conduit of misinformation to the authorities, and supersnake keeping an eye on me the other, making sure every move I took was reported back. I reckoned I was just about irreplaceable. I guess I was wrong.'

Her voice sharpened, but she tried to match his sarcasm with throwaway nonchalance. 'You've got it wrong, you know? They fired when they did, even though that poor man was there, precisely because they didn't want to kill you.'

'They? Who?' He reached across, grasped her thin wrist. 'Three people died. Others were mutilated.'

Her eyes filled, her lip trembled.

He pressed home the advantage. 'They were nice people. Good.'

'You're not being . . . you're not being fair.' She let out a long sobbing sigh, wiped her eyes on her sleeve, pulled her legs and feet in under her, curled into herself.

He resisted the temptation to hit her, merely tightened his grip, let the silence lengthen so the inanity of what she had said became stark.

'Why? Why did it happen?'

She disengaged her hand, pushed long fingers through her hair again, shook her head. 'Oh Christ, I don't know what really happened. But there was a sudden scare, a big crisis, very quick, you were about to find out something they didn't want you to know. Don't ask me what. Please. I honestly do not know.'

'Tell me something they don't want me to know. Go on.'

'It's not easy. It really is not easy. They don't trust me. Any more than you do. I really get to know very little of what is going on. Except what they want me to know.'

'I'll tell you what I want to know. I want to know about Plancenoît. Waterloo. Who was there and why. When you took those pics of Mendoza and Europa Malatesta.'

'Oh shit.'

'Go on.'

She patched together a version, admitted that Rupert had been there, had inveigled her then into becoming the double agent they would fire at Mulligan, at Eurac.

'That's not what I want to know. I want to know what Anton might have put together. What he may have come across once he started following out the lead that connected you, and therefore Myklades with Mendoza, the Malatestas and that Brel woman.'

'I don't know. I honestly do not know. They met a lot. In twos, threes, more formally I believe in the afternoon and the following morning . . .'

'And Myklades was there. He was there too. Wasn't he?' His face was white now, eyes narrowed, fists clenched. Suddenly he looked very dangerous and she was frightened.

'Yes, yes he was.' Her eyes, deep-shadowed now, met his across the table, flinched away. A tear formed, rolled, she sniffed and reached across, held on to his fingers, clinging. 'Buck, James. That really is something they did not want you to know. And that frightens me. Look after me.'

'You should have told me before. Anton might still be alive if you had.'

'Don't.' She turned away again, the tears flowing faster.

Almost brutally he shredded a Kleenex from its carton, handed it to her, refused her any more comfort than that. 'Tell me now. Everything you can remember about Plancenoît.'

It took her an hour but added very little to what he already knew or had guessed. It remained a matter of supposition only that Ambrose and Myklades on one side, and Brel and Boltana on the other, were linked in any criminal way. She kept back the one important thing – Crystal – but made a lot of the business of Pedro and Malatesta, of Jana Pensión, made of the whole anecdote a smokescreen to conceal the rest. He thought she was susceptible to the glitz of it all, the ancient names, the wealth, the strangely *built* quality of Europa's beauty, the romance of the long engagement, and the ill-concealed jealousy of the American girl. He was bored by it, thought less of her because she seemed excited by it all, but let her run on in the hope she'd release some further nugget of important information.

'. . . I had one really fine-grain negative that really caught those scars, and I got a doctor chum to check them out. And he said he thought it had to be an operation to correct a prognathous jaw, but done in infancy. You see, it's usually done in late adolescence when it can happen inside the mouth and leave no scars. Anyway I sent Jana the photo and told her what he had said . . .'

'Okay, okay. That's enough of all that. It's not relevant. I can see two possible reasons that might explain why suddenly they felt they had to kill Suk.' He stood up, moved restlessly about the tiny kitchen. 'Because of the mistake of crediting you with those pictures, he was establishing the link between these people and Ambrose. And that had to be stopped.' He paused, thought, remembered. Suk's obsession with what the money was for. Bad money used for bad purposes. Inexplicably he shuddered, shook his head. 'And somehow they knew he was getting close. Which leads me to the second reason. Somehow everything we do at Eurac, everything anyway that gets routinely logged on the computers, gets back, gets back to Ambrose, Myklades, whoever . . . And it's possible Anton had rumbled the how of that. That would be a prime motive for offing him.'

He was back close to her, standing above her, and suddenly she wrapped her arms about his waist, pushed her head into

437

his stomach seeking comfort, forgiveness perhaps. 'But there's another reason too,' she said.

He felt a leap of excitement inside: was she really about to tell him something that would break the whole business open?

She was crying again, gasping to speak. 'They asked me . . . who I thought was most dangerous in Eurac . . . where the danger there to them lay. Buck . . . I didn't want them to kill you. I told them Suk.'

It took an hour to convince her, and himself, that it was unlikely Suk had been killed on her say-so and then to reestablish enough rapport between them to make it possible for him to come back to her. Eventually though he let himself out of the house, stood at the top of the steps, buttoned his coat, peeled on gloves, looked quickly and expertly over the small square, the slush, the rounded edges of heavy snow in the still unblemished garden, heard the slipping drip and rustle of it as it thawed from the cherry trees. Most of the parked cars had gone, gone to work; there were one or two new ones in their places. His sensitive, actor's mouth hardened into a thin smile.

Without waiting to be asked he opened the passenger door of the red Sierra, slipped in beside Tyler.

'Take us round a couple of blocks and then park. No call for Madame to see me with you.'

Tyler found a slot outside a red-brick Victorian primary school, the playground almost filled with portakabin temporary classrooms. A few mothers who had dropped their children twenty minutes earlier gossiped outside the high, heavy-duty chain-link fence. All sorts – fat and floppy, rangy and stylish, homely and street-wise, black and white. Women's world, Mulligan thought, kids to school, gossip, shopping, housework, it has its own rhythms, an unforced pace – crazy that most of them want to get out of it, to be . . . like Harriet.

'I could bust you, you know that? Maybe I should bust you,' Tyler said.

Mulligan sighed, offered his Marlboros across, snapped his Zippo for both of them. He coughed on the fumes, wound down the window.

'I've thought about doing the same for you. But since you've opened that can of worms you can have first dip. What have you got on me?'

'Let's start with consorting with known criminals and their associates. You just spent the night balling Spiderman's tart.'

'Come on, Tyler. No need to needle me. Don't be cheap.'

Tyler pushed back his cheese cutter cap, unbuttoned his big coat, wriggled into the upholstery. 'How about murder? Accessory before and after.'

'What the fuck are you talking about?'

'Paul Roget. Stomach contents scraped off the tarmac of Purbeck Street revealed a small amount of freshly ingested vegetable curry. Nearest curry house, Star of India, Marchmont Street, knew Roget, fairly frequent customer, had your signature on an American Express chit . . . One witness, a cleaning lady, on her way to London University Senate House, saw you fifty yards away when the roller rolled. Apparently you didn't do a lot to stop what happened. And the Sûreté put you not a hundred miles from Place d'Anvers when that rocket struck, day before yesterday. Your turn.'

Mulligan thought, took his time, spoke carefully. 'There's a snake, a supersnake. You were the only person this side of the Channel who knew I was going after Roget, who knew I had pulled the Harriet Jones file off the PNC computer . . . Listen, it's even possible Suk went to you for information about Ambrose and you tipped them off that he was getting close. Your turn.'

One of the mothers peeled away from the group outside the school gates: dark chocolate legs beneath a short fur-trimmed suede coat. Tyler sighed. 'Lovely . . . Listen. There is another explanation. You know you told us to keep an eye on Rupert Bridge, check out why he was going to Newcastle?'

'Yes.'

'Well. Let me say in the first place that while he did wine and dine directors of both a leisure airfield and a fleet of freight helicopters, he also went to Kapp-Duxbury, the weapons manufacturer he used to work for. Unfortunately we were just watching, not listening, so we don't know what went on. Still. All very interesting. Not least because it was a K-D Nutcracker blew your mate apart. Could be coincidence. Lots of Arab groups have them courtesy the Ayatollah and the official story is one of them did it to protest Interpol's new involvement with terrorism ... That's all by the way.' He wriggled, belched. 'Sorry, kippers for breakfast, could be a problem until lunch-time. Anyway. On the way to Newcastle, Bridge had a short conversation with someone else. We checked him out. Guess who.'

Mulligan shrugged.

'A spook. MI6.'

For a moment Mulligan felt he would not be able to bear the reaction he felt, but through the cold sweat that leaked into the nape of his neck and down his spine, through the nausea and the sudden dizziness he heard in recall and on playback 'Spider' Dayton's prophecy of how and why Eurac would fail: ... *And if you succeed, if you really get to the top or near it, then Eurac will run into the jaws of the same fucking monster that screwed Centac. You get that high, you hit politics. You hit politics, you run into the CIA. Or whatever front the CIA has over there. Troisième Bureau. SIS. That's what killed Centac. If Eurac works it'll kill Eurac too. The folk in pairs like Mormons, dressed like Mormons in pin-striped vests, and like Mormons fucking sure that they are right and everyone else is wrong ...*

They'll screw you. The moment you point a finger at some Warlord who fights Commies with arms bought with heroin, they'll screw you. The moment some Southern cone president says 'My democratically elected government will crumble and let the reds in if you go further down this track,' they'll shaft you. You know that. Better dead than red ... fine, I go along with that ...

He fought it all, digging his nails into his thighs, came out of it. 'So?'

Tyler sighed again. 'They're not the piss-artists they're cracked up to be. The fact they showed themselves there, to us, was on purpose, a warning.'

'So we close ourselves down. Back off. *Finis.*'

'As I understand it the form is we go softly, softly until we can legitimately say either we had it wrong, or there will never be the evidence needed for a conviction and then we shelve it. The form then is that we get a very hefty pat on the back for doing so well, and we're put on another job.'

Mulligan reached for the door.

Tyler reached across, put a strong hand on his wrist. 'It doesn't have to be like that. Listen. We. Eurac. Floor Five at NSY. We've got a hell of a lot against this mob. They are, after all, amateurs, and with illusions of grandeur. I reckon we can go on and on and on until a few of them, and I mean the ones at the top, get really busted for good, and there's so much already on record that no one up there is going to be able to say you should have stopped, there was the cutout.'

Mulligan pushed a hand across his brow, looked out at the now deserted shabby street with its smirched slush, drab brick. Distantly raised children's voices sang: *The Lord of the Dance is He*. With his Quaker-Shaker background he abhorred the sentimental words that have been pushed over the tune he sang as a little boy: *'Tis a gift to be simple, 'tis a gift to be free* . . . Was a civilisation that could do that worth worrying about? 'Go on then. Convince me. But first find me a coffee I can drink.'

Tyler let out the clutch, and the car pulled away from the kerb. Mulligan knew Tyler was an emotional man, but nevertheless he was surprised when he felt the pressure of the English detective's hand momentarily squeezing his knee. He smiled, sidelong, and caught the grin that was on Tyler's face too.

45

Towards evening, with darkness falling swiftly over the wet, dirty city, Tyler drove Mulligan down the sweeping greasy terraces of Chelsea and West Kensington into the narrower, humbler roads that lie behind Hammersmith. They parked beneath a streetlamp in front of a terraced Edwardian cottage – a front door with a porch, a tiny bay window, another above it, and a new dormer knocked in the low roof above that. Sleet slanted across the orange light, but inside the car Mulligan felt hot, tired, flaccid. They had spent the day talking: in pubs, in a drinking club, in the car. They had smoked too much, drunk more than Mulligan liked under circumstances where he couldn't go to bed and sleep it off, and eaten really awful food. But at least trust, even a sort of friendship beyond the buddy-bonhomie of a shared profession, had developed.

Tyler stretched as much as the cramped space around them would allow, loosened his belt and belched. 'Pardon me. Better out than in. Listen, time you met Arthur Lord. Used to be a copper, worked with the Fraud Squad, got pissed off with it. Decided they were all either wankers or bent. Joined the anti-terrorist section, got his legs blown off by the Provos. Now uses the expertise he picked up on the Fraud Squad as a freelance consultant on the outside. That's his cover. In fact he's a computer whizz on a par with your mate Suk. He's hacked into Ambrose for us, and I want you to hear it from him how it works. Or how he thinks it works. One thing though. He's a very thorough sort of person, suffers from a touch of the anal retentives, so don't be surprised if I seem to bully him to make him let go. Okay?'

'Who pays him?'

'We do, for this. Slush funds. Other jobs he does for the press, for people who want to know something about a company or group of companies before they put money in, that sort of thing. He does all right. And he's not bent. He uses illegal methods, purely electronic, but definitely on the side of the angels. He'd be a very rich man if he wasn't.'

They were let in by a small plump woman, with bright dark eyes, dressed in a twinset and skirt with a quiet check. The hall had an old-fashioned hatstand and floral wallpaper but was bright. The house smelled of cleaning agents, cabbage, and dog. Through the sitting-room door Mulligan could see a small white Scottish terrier watching TV.

'Hullo, Rex, Arthur's up in his den. Is he expecting you?'

Tyler kissed her cheek and patted her arms. 'I said we might call.'

'Go on up then.'

They climbed stairs made even narrower by the chair-lift that had been fixed into the wall, then steps with a second chair-lift, and knocked on a plank door. The room they entered covered the area of the house so was quite large, but low-roofed except in the middle. It was painted starkly white, the furniture was functional and minimal, and the whole place would have been dominated by the working tools of Lord's trade – three video terminals, telephone, a radio and television, two modems, and steel cabinets that were large, blank, and locked. There was a lot of computer printout around, and a bookcase of reference books – all relating to finance, company law, and kindred subjects. Would have been dominated by these things had Lord not turned out to be one of the largest men Mulligan had ever met, with his legs on he would have been a good four inches taller than him. He had a huge head, nearly bald, glasses, tweed jacket, and a resonant voice, for Lord was not thin, but big-boned, big-chested. He moved a large pipe to his left hand, and his handshake, offered over the table, was all right.

'Sit yourself down, why don't you? Drink? Tea? Coffee?' His voice was almost accentless: educated but with no upper-class honk or quack.

With relief Mulligan heard Tyler refuse, for both of them, but Lord insisted and actually buzzed his wife on an intercom.

'Arthur, you know why we're here. All you know about Ambrose. But' – he looked at his watch – 'James has a plane to catch.'

But Lord would not be hurried. He swung the chair (and Mulligan could see the stumps of his legs cut off just above the knee), and reached a pipe down from a shelf. Very deliberately he filled it with Black Sobranie. Then he lit it with Swan Vesta matches, three of them. Finally he pulled a heap of documents from the end of the table so they were under his nose, slipped out a microfiche and slotted it into a VDU.

'Ambrose . . . (puff), on the face of it . . . (puff), straight-forward company (puff). Directors real people, with real addresses, though tend (puff) to be semi-accommodation addresses (puff), one of them that Lowndes Square place (puff) you visited. Arbuthnot and Sebourg accountants. Billings solicitors. Big firms, big reputations – all right both have been employed by and defended dodgy firms in the past, but that's part of what being an accountant and a solicitor is about.' The third match hit the ashtray, the pipe was at last going well and the delivery accelerated too. 'Well capitalised, half a million, so that makes it look reasonable, shows creditors owners have seen fit to put something in the kitty. Shareholdings mostly registered in names of nominees in Isle of Man, Jersey, Liechtenstein. That gives it a whiff of excitement, but on the other hand the commercial and banking references are solid. If City and Wessex says you're good for three million at a time, then you are. Address is right. Not too flashy, not too up-market, but solid . . .

'What do they do? They trade. Trade with other companies'

spare cash on all the London markets. A lot of it seems to go through firms like Barclays de Zoete Wedd, and Citex-Bauer-kredit, which is to City and Wessex what BZW is to Barclays. And that's right in the open, entirely scrutable, clean. With firms like that it has to be. But also they trade through tame dealers inside the Black Box, the markets where members trade with each other on their own account as principals. Minerals, currency, Eurobonds, futures. There are three guys at Ambrose who hold seats in these markets and they have accounts with others who buy and sell for them. And in that area it's very difficult indeed to get solid evidence of fraud or misuse of funds or whatever . . .'

But Tyler was looking at his watch again. 'Arthur. Please. The barest outline, how it works . . . all right. ALL RIGHT. Not how it works but a workable hypothesis, how you think it might be working. Just so James gets the broad picture, all right?'

An inward smile briefly moved across the expanses of Lord's face, a smile that distanced him from the bullying tone that was creeping into Tyler's voice. 'Perhaps a diagram, a visual aid would help.' He produced a large sheet of paper, spread it across the table, a flow chart, nicely coloured, circles and broad arrows, and all through his exposition prodded it with a thin gold ball-point. But first he let them look at it for a moment while he fingered more dark tobacco from his tin.

'The first interesting thing is that all the companies whose financial surpluses Ambrose claims to be recycling to the benefit of all are either selling services, or are businesses where very large sums in actual cash change hands as a matter of routine – '

Mulligan asked: 'How many companies altogether are involved?'

'At the last count, forty-two. In the area I'm going to talk about first, eighteen. The point about actual cash is obvious: video-game parlours, a small chain of independent bookmak-ers, and then of course people tend to pay cash, even in quite large sums, when buying and selling second-hand cars and boats. There's a chain of shops, each one tiny, buying and selling gold at discounted prices . . . you get the picture. Growth industry, they are in fact part of Thatcher's Victorian-isation of our virtues: they fulfil the function of pawnshops.'

Lord's spectacles glinted, checking that a wry point had been taken. Then he went back to his chart.

'Drug syndicates, as you very well know, have always faced two problems. Keeping the flow of money separate from the movement of the drug, so they can't be tied together, and coping with very large volumes of hard cash. People tend not to want to write cheques when they buy their fixes. Right? So a distributor takes delivery of a kilo and splits it into ounces for his street dealers. He also takes delivery of, say, a set of twelve mint-condition Victorian sovereigns. Or better still several small items of jewellery which, because of its uniqueness, has a notional, fluctuating value over and above its value as real metal and gems. Right. He inherited these from his Granny, or found them in the attic, and having distributed his ounces, he takes them to the high street gold shop and sells them. He's paid.

'Meanwhile the ouncer has been selling his ounces, he keeps his cut, and goes to the gold shop and buys an item of jewellery, or a sovereign. The money he pays, which of course is far more proportionally than the shopkeeper paid the distributor for the same piece of gold, is passed up the line from the gold shop to Ambrose. Meanwhile, the next time the ouncer takes delivery from the distributor he gives him back the gold trinket. Which the distributor, with all the other gold trinkets from all his other ouncers, again flogs back to the gold shop, and so on. The only person who has to keep his books straight and open is the gold-shopkeeper, and he's making maybe fifty or a hundred similar transactions a week, most of them legitimate. He records these transactions in exactly the same way as the rest – he has bought items from anonymous vendors who just walk into his shop, and sold them likewise for a nice profit.

'Right? Now similar transactions can be managed with bets on the horses, especially if you've got a time stamp that's set ten minutes slow: the distributor always wins; the ouncers always pick losers ... and pay cash. And the bookmaker passes the profits for reinvestment to Ambrose. Again betting slips are anonymous, numbered only, so the same two people can pass thirty slips a day each if they need to. Similarly the same cycling of cash can be done through a video-game parlour, a second-hand car dealer and so on. All right, I know what you're going to ask: where does Ambrose pass its profits? Why don't the owners of the bookmakers and the gold shops and the video-game parlours beef when they won't get profits from Ambrose? Let's just deal with the second one first.

'In the first place Ambrose does quite often make a small return on the money it invests or speculates to the source companies. And sometimes it says, just as any commodity dealer, futures dealer, is entitled to, sorry old boy but this one came unstuck and you lost. But the main point is that all these little chains of seedy gold shops, backstreet car dealers and so on are run at street level by franchised managers who do as they're told. Remember: they may, if they bother to think about it, suspect that they're part of a laundering operation, but they never, never, come in contact with the cocaine at all, so there really is nothing they can be caught on. The only danger is if they get greedy and start fiddling their VAT or tax returns too obviously ... but even then they're not really exposing their owners or Ambrose. And their owners? Well, obviously they are our old friends the offshore companies with nominee directors, *id est* Hector Myklades and associates. Come!'

A knock on the door. Mrs Lord, smiling benevolently, distributed enormous mugs of mud-coloured fluid, put down a plate of custard creams. Lord restuffed his pipe.

'Thank you, dear. But that's only the down-market side of the whole operation. Having looked at all the figures I can get hold of I would guess, and it is very much guesswork, that at this level there are something like thirty distributors out there each running say twenty ouncers who each shift ten, twenty grams a week, probably taking say a couple of grand and keeping five hundred. An educated guess would put the turnover in this sector at something like sixty million a year with a gross profit right at the end of the line of say thirty-five or forty million. And you're talking about users, I would guess, who never spend more than fifty quid a week on their habit – lower-paid professionals, upwardly mobile skilled workers who want to impress, get a bit of glamour in their lives down on those Wimpey estates in the suburbs, youngsters in the XR 3 set who want to get an edge over their peers, right down to inner-city crack users. At this level it's not that different from coke rings I've helped you bust in the past, just bigger.'

446

'XR 3s?'

Tyler filled in. 'Souped-up Ford Escorts, customised trims, that sort of thing. Car of choice amongst the pre-yuppies.'

Lord swung his chair round, paddled it with his hands to a keyboard at the other end of the table. Mulligan realised that once he was in it he probably stayed in it, perhaps for hours on end. Anything he could want was in reach. He dabbed in commands, and new sets of diagrams and graphs scrolled across the screen as he talked. The pipe too got fairly continuous attention, and the delivery remained slow. Tyler fidgeted, but Mulligan was riveted. It was all new to him.

'But the up-market end is something else, believe me. What we have is a cluster of companies, some part legitimate, I would guess, but with one or two employees subverted, others entirely existing as fronts but all sharing one common factor: they purport to sell services. Take this one, Monte Bello Consultants. It sells advice on how to manipulate the media. Present them with a public relations problem and they will give you an hour of their time coming up with a tailor-made, personalised strategy designed to fit your requirements. And they'll charge you five hundred quid. That makes you an ouncer. But staffed, if that's the word, by a loose group of men and women in advertising, PR, publishing, who get paid fat consultancy fees, retainers, even straight salaries. They're the distributors. Busy little number that, lot of coke sniffed in that milieu. What else? Head-hunters. Business consultants. Financial advisers. Promoting and marketing "invisibles", as they are now called, transmitting data and information, trading shadows, ideas, fantasies.

'Look, I'll show you the sort of thing I mean.' The chair moved again, the pipe set down, he brought both huge hands to play on another keyboard. 'Bavarian Water Board embarks on a capital project, a dam in the Alps. Issues Eurobonds to raise one hundred million Deutschmarks. Twelve per cent coupon redeemable in five years. Worth buying a few? Worth selling what you've got? Depends on interest rates elsewhere, rates of inflation, and so on. Large number of imponderables. You go to the New City Advice Bureau and you'll find a neat, warm, slick office and a video terminal like this. They'll tap in the information and get you a pretty picture predicting different yield curves for different sets of putative circumstances and you go away knowing just how much your Bavarian Euro-bonds are going to be worth if Kinnock wins an election or the Ayatollah closes the Gulf. Well, you think you do. And you've parted with a lot of money for the information. But what have you bought? Air, thin air. Nothing substantial at all.

'They've got correspondence courses on their books, travel agents. Beautician and health clinics. All selling either air, or time – time which once it's gone, a week on a health farm, a holiday in Wales, is virtually unredeemable, it's impossible to prove that what you say you paid for during that week or month or fortnight wasn't real, didn't happen.

'So. This is what I reckon happens. Again, at this up-market end you have distributors like that poor chap Roget, passing not ounces now but more probably a hundred grams at a time down the chain. The distributor is paid by a consultancy for his input of expertise; the retailer buys expertise from the consultancy. Of course they switch it all about: one particular distributor's retailers won't use his consultancy, they won't be tied in any traceable way . . .'

'But isn't this terribly complicated? I mean the whole thing must take an awful lot of organising.'

Lord looked over the top of his spectacles. 'Young man. We're talking about a marketing organisation vertically integrated from point of supply to consumer, turning over three hundred million a year, making a trading profit of two hundred million. There's plenty of slack there to be taken up by the very best and latest in hardware, software and people with the expertise to use it. It's no different from Sainsbury's. Have you seen the investment they've made in electronics? And not even Sainsbury's has profit margins like these chaps. And the beauty of it is that only a very few people indeed on the financial side need even suspect that cocaine is at the bottom of it. Like the high street gold dealer, your man at the New City Advice Bureau may wonder occasionally at the amounts people are prepared to spend for financial advice, but that's as far as it will go. And as long as the same faces don't crop up too often – and remember he's doing legitimate business too and he can't tell the difference – what questions is he going to ask? And that's another of the beauties of it all: in many cases the legit sides of the business pay a lot of the salaries, while the hidden coke side keeps them profitable and therefore legal.

'But the best scam of all, for servicing the distributors and retailers at this top end of the market, which I reckon accounts for most of the two hundred and forty million turnover not handled by the high street cash movers, is the Designer Living Card. It's a credit card whose retailers must be purveyors of the unique, the desirable, the beautiful, the best. I quote the publicity which is put out by a firm called Good Life Promotions. Tied in is a company called Leisure for the Discerning, which runs a mail order firm where you pay your bills only on your Designer Living Card account. Now the beauty of this is that it can use cheques right from the bottom up, it gets right past the pitfall of every big-time drug syndicate that ever existed in the past: the problem of warehouses filled with currency. You know all about that, you worked for Centac, you had a poke at Sicilia-Falcon, the Tijuana connection. Right. While I get this going again . . .' – he meant the pipe – 'Rex can tell you about Luxury Din-Dins, Chipping Kemble. You're not drinking your coffee.'

Tyler put himself into the light shed by an Anglepoise lamp. 'Couple of faggots out in a Cotswold village not far from Oxford. Prepared frozen gourmet meals, kept them in big freezers in their garage. The very best. Beluga caviare, Dom Pérignon, salmon from the Severn, grouse from Scotland, it was all there, really the sort of meals that if you had say twelve coming to dinner you wouldn't be a bit surprised to get a bill for a grand. Large very posh clientele all over one of the richest areas of rural England. Dial a dinner for a naked lunch. And' – sudden emphasis – 'clients paid for the coke with their Designer Living Cards, which they were using for other things as well, and settled up monthly. And Designer Living settled with Luxury Din-Dins . . .'

'But they should be collecting, what, five per cent? Not seventy-five.'

'Ah yes. But Luxury Din-Dins also hold Designer Living Cards which they use to buy their salmon and cases of Dom Pérignon, and so on. And in amongst it all they also buy air: advice, holidays. It's all so fucking legit the only way you can bust it is by finding powder on the table.'

'And you did?'

'Yes. We did. But not enough. Hundred grams. Faggot A said he's bought it in a pub in Bristol. He'll do five years, most of it comfortable. The rest is all hypothesis, unprovable as things stand. We just know it's like the way I've said it is because Arthur had already rumbled the Designer Living Card – Ambrose connection, and the rest makes sense. But it's going to be fucking difficult to prove. And not least because what we do know for certain Arthur has found out by strictly illegit means, and if it got to court untreated I'd be out without a pension, and the villains would walk with damages for wrongful arrest.'

Mulligan attempted the coffee. It was horrible. 'I still can't get over how big it all is. Don't credit cards have to be supported by a major bank?'

'Certainly. And there's an interesting point there.' Lord nodded approval at the manly way Mulligan was coping with the drink, and went on: 'DLC pre-existed all this, they were backed by Nat-West and tied in to Access. Then Ambrose and associates acquired it, and shifted the whole thing over to the Banco de Corpus Cristi. Bit of a fuss having a British card backed by a continental bank, but City and Wessex got in on the act and smoothed it all through. And the point is it is a prosperous business in its own right. I would reckon less than fifty per cent of its turnover is coke-related, and that actually means only about five per cent of the paperwork. And it's going to be virtually impossible to disentangle that five per cent from the rest, even if we went in with complete authority to turn the whole thing out from top to bottom. Look at this. It's actually a part of Paul Roget's account with them. Rex asked for it and they gave it to him without batting an eyelid, he didn't even have to go before a beak, and it ties in with Roget's bank accounts.'

Another blue microfiche. 'Dealer in Oriental *objets d'art*, right? Good Life Promotions come to him with a wheeze for the Leisure for the Discerning mail-order catalogue. A limited set of reproductions of Persian miniatures from the fourteenth century. Here's the actual catalogue. Look at the copy, the pictures. Beautiful. New process, guaranteed indistinguishable from the originals. A harem of lovely houris in various stages of undress. Nubian eunuchs with scimitars, almond blossom, and sweetmeats. Vision of Islamic paradise, but it's Art too. Genuine gold leaf on the frames. Right? First they paid Roget five thousand guineas consultancy fee. Then they gave him a hundred and fifty thousand to go out and buy the originals. He bought them in Amsterdam from a gallery that is owned by a firm that ties in with Ambrose in ways I won't bore you with now – the point is that the originals were already in-house, already belonged to Ambrose, Iris, whatever. They pay Roget fifteen thousand commission, and they've shifted a hundred and fifty out of the country perfectly legitimately. And all over the country their ouncers can now buy a set of ten framed prints, limited edition, new process, virtually indistinguishable, blah, blah, for a thousand guineas a throw. And on top of that there are quite a few punters out there who really do buy them. And on paper there's no way of telling one from the other. I tell you one thing though.'

'What's that?'

'There's a creative imagination out there who is having a whale of a time dreaming up scams like this. You can sense a giggle there, a whiff of malicious enjoyment. And a very astute financial brain. Or two. But you know all that already. And that's really about it. I can go on for hours but basically repeating myself.'

Tyler sighed. 'Buck, there you are. That's the Ambrose connection, the picture so far. Arthur, many thanks, old chum, but Buck really does have a plane to catch.'

'Glad to be of help, any time, anything you think I can do, just ask.'

Mulligan leant forward. 'Actually I think there might be. We've a security problem. Certainly at Eurac with the PNC. Everything I log is leaking. Someone, somehow, is monitoring everything I do, everything I report. Could this be done by hacking, by the sort of methods you used to get all this on Ambrose?'

Lord peered at him through a new fog of smoke. 'The short answer is no. Oh, sure, the PNC and no doubt Interpol too are vulnerable at pretty low levels of access. No one thinks twice about pulling the life history of some petty crook via his car-number and the DVLC at Swansea, or whatever. And higher up you could do it here and there, once or twice. But you'd have to be very careful because every access is logged, at the top four people have to approve and so on. It's very secure. It has to be. To get a steady, reliable, day-to-day account, illegally, of what you put in would not be possible.'

'Okay. But supposing the security services had a mole in the Web, who was in fact a double agent, whose final allegiance was in fact to the Web?'

'That, young man, could be a very different kettle of fish. All the major European security services have access to just about everything, but here, in Britain, with less fuss and red tape than anywhere else. Both Germany and France, for instance, have quite stringent safeguards. But here MI5 and MI6 can slot into almost anything through a thing called the Joint Computer Bureau. And in specific areas the access is easy and very quick.'

'They are?'

'Need you ask? Terrorism, obviously. Arms. Serious money. Drugs.'

Tyler took Mulligan back to Heathrow and his flight to Paris. On the way he asked: 'Where are you heading now?'

'Zurich.'

'Why? Hang on. I can guess. That girl who got involved with the Arnolfinis and knocked the head off of one of them. Was she smuggling coke for them?'

'No. But as I understand it her mate was.'

'What do you expect to get out of it?'

Mulligan shrugged. 'Who knows? But right now it's really burning inside me. Because of Anton, you know. And anything I can find, anything that turns up, I'm chasing. Right?'

For several minutes Mulligan watched the high lamps of the M4 swing rhythmically by.

Tyler asked: 'Do you think we'll ever get to the top? For certain? Do you think we will get to them? Knock any of them off?'

'Sure. Sure we will. Or die in the attempt.' Mulligan remembered the flare of searing light and the blast in Place d'Anvers, Tyler the mess that had been Roget, and like children they both suddenly shuddered, involuntarily and together.

Then Tyler laughed, high and brazen and thumped the horn of the car. 'Fucking sure we will.'

46

Kloten airport keys you in to Switzerland: it is tidy, elegant, efficient. The buildings seen from the plane are grey, stylish, the cement rendered successfully to look like stone. Mulligan, who had stayed the night at one of the airport hotels before catching the first flight in the morning, was met airside by Commissioner Barlach, who shared most of Kloten's characteristics. He whisked him effortlessly through halls with silvery-grey, charcoal-grey, and stainless steel interiors. Moving out by unorthodox routes they caught a glimpse of the spectacular departure area with its terracotta walls and ancient flying machines, real ones not models, suspended above split-level concourses linked by gleaming escalators.

But Zurich itself seemed messy, with no perceptible centre that Mulligan could see, sprawled over low hills, the buildings for the most part faced with a dead off-white stucco. The black BMW dropped them at the Reiterstrasse police headquarters and Barlach made one of his few remarks of the short journey, gesturing towards a very ordinary, nondescript hotel on the other side of the street, the Pension Bahnpost.

'She was holed up in there. Handy for us really.'

In his office – well furnished, indeed by the standards of European police forces, as Mulligan had come to know them, sumptuous – he added, while shrugging off his grey checked overcoat and peeling off black leather gloves: 'I should suggest you see her straight away. We shan't be able to hold her beyond tomorrow morning. She killed the man. She says so.' He shrugged. 'But she has a very good lawyer here – the other side don't want any scandal so they're not disputing her statement. Self-defence. All the Italian examining magistrate wants is an undertaking she'll appear in Turin when they're ready for her; with that undertaking he's prepared not to press charges. A sergeant will take you to her.'

Mulligan was shown into a small but pleasant room: the bright patterns on the curtains, the picture on the wall of a sunny Alpine meadow, would not have disgraced a cheap but honest hostel. A tall girl, dressed in a short black woollen dress over black woollen tights, was sitting at the dressing-table reading a paperback. She had straight blonde hair well cut to half-way down her neck, scraped back from her forehead and held behind her ears by enamelled clips shaped like butterflies. She wore pink-rimmed spectacles, large, round, and at first sight she did not strike Mulligan as a beauty. But the face had character – good bones, large striking blue eyes, and a mouth that was full and well shaped although there was no paint on it. Her chin was square, solid, almost large. And her body was something else: she was tall, very fit, with not an ounce of superfluous fat on her though she was by no means skinny. In a swimsuit, he guessed, she would look like a goddess.

'Bonnie Day?'

The look she gave him said that he was a fool or impertinent.

He laughed. 'Okay. Of course you are. My name's James Mulligan. I'm American. But I work for a European drug enforcement agency connected with Interpol. And I'd like to ask you a few questions if I may. You've made a very full statement already, and I don't think there's any question of my asking you to incriminate yourself any furth – '

'Ah'm innit to ma tummy-burron aw-ready, is whit you're telling me. Goo ahead. If Ah don wanna answer Ah'll jes' shurrup.'

He tried a grin on her but she rejected it for the forgery it obviously was. He swung in the only other chair in the room, cell, and sat near her but not too close, then produced a pocket-sized micro-recorder and set it up between them on the dressing-table.

'Here's a promise,' he said. 'You can wipe it clean, if you feel you've said more than you want . . .'

She shrugged. 'Ye've probably gor'another in yer pawcket.'

'No. The point I'm trying to make is this: it's not you I'm after at all. You've got enough on your plate. But you've been . . . in touch with people, villains, who I am very interested in – in fact I want to see them where they belong, behind bars, and I think you can help me.'

She gave a short, bitter laugh and her head twisted away in disgust.

'Put the boggers in prison? What bluddy guid wou' tha' do?'

'She meant a lot to you, didn't she? This Jill Jack.' His voice had taken on an unctuous tone which he himself heard as false: like a vicar or a social worker.

She flared back at him. 'Yer. She fuckin' did. An' yer nee'n't ger'any soft ideas aboot it neither. We wasna lezzies, or any stoopid thing like tha'. She wor my mate. Tha's all. No, it's not all. It's everything . . .'

Her voice caught but she recovered quickly and talked. Later, with some difficulty because of her accent, which of course he did not attempt to reproduce, he made an edited transcript, cutting out her repetitions and the few times when he had had to prompt her or delve for more detail.

It started back in September – well that's not long ago is it, but it seems like yonks. We were in Turin, doing a gig modelling like these gold coins and medallions – they were real right enough, they needed a small army to move them about the place . . . All right. Well we got a call from this agency, Clouds it's called, off Oxford Street, the address is in my diary, they took it off me, you'll have to ask them . . .

We've been on their books since they opened, but they got us no work at all until this one. The client was Good Life Promotions, and they aimed to flog this gold stuff through a mail-order catalogue that goes out to Designer Living cardholders. Yes, one of their guys came out with us – Buckingham he said his name was, and he liked to be called Duke. And he was a right bastard – he got us into it in the first place I reckon.

Well, it was a good job, we were all set to enjoy it, Turin's always a good place to work, they really are pros – we did a spell there back in the spring, just freelancing and managed three weeks there before the work dried up and we had to come home. Tell the truth, after that we hit a lean patch, very lean, almost through to September, and then all we got was a really flaky job at Southampton Boat Show . . . But there was a stroke of luck there, see, this photographer she's a really great pro, she was there on a commission . . . Okay, I'll keep to the point.

Anyway. It was all going very well the first morning's work, but that evening, late afternoon really, this Duke character said we had to have supper at this ultra-smart restaurant, but really you know it was just like the smarter sorts of spaghetti houses in London, and meet this guy Giann' Arnolfini, who was like a friend of Duke's.

Well, first sight and all that he was all right, you know? I mean he was a bit on the tubby side the way most wops are – not many of them like Roberto Rossellini, are there? But very smooth manners, and obviously loaded up to here, the Gucci shoes, the Rolex Presidential, and this real whizz of a car, Lamborghini Miura, named after famous fighting bulls he said, and had this bull badge on it. Anyway, he took us out to this like villa up in the mountains north of the city, and there was a party sort of grew up during the evening. Well, it was really heavy I can tell you, lot of coke being snorted, and pills being dropped, but champers too, and nice things to eat, and this fantastic scenery, the mountains, and all that scene, you know?

But it was all right, really. I mean some of the blokes came on a bit, but they generally backed off if you told them you weren't in the mood, but one didn't, and he got real stroppy, but then Giann' came along and smacked him about a bit, and in the end it was all right.

Yes, well, I have to admit, we did stay the night. I mean I wasn't bothered, but Jill got a bit high, I think they did get some coke into her, well yes, they did, and she, yes, she definitely did end up in bed with this Arnolfini guy, and there was quite a scene in the morning, because this other guy, the one who'd got really randy over her, found her in Giann's room, and there was another guy there too, but he'd just come in for something, but the randy guy, whose name was, yes, that's right, Francesco Cellini, got the idea she's dossed down with not one guy but two so he was even more pissed off than when she'd turned him down.

So next day we went over to Verona, you know, shots with these medals in front of Juliet's house, all that scene, and that went okay, but this Giann' he took us there and he kept hanging around, and I could see he was now really hung up about Jill, and she seemed to fancy him so come the evening, when he said have supper and that, I like backed off, and went back to the hotel and went to bed with a book. I read a lot.

Well, she showed up about noon which was cutting it a bit fine, because check-in time was 1.45 and we started to pack, and then Duke showed up. And he had like these four parcels, done up posh like from a posh shop, and he said they were chocolates, but cut a long story short, two of them were coke and we had to leave them in the toilet of this burger joint called Scapino near Covent Garden and there'd be a grand each for us if we did, and he said it was all for Giann', and Jill ought to do it because Giann' had been so nice to her. Neither of us wanted to touch it, and wouldn't have, but he threatened us first with cutting us off from work, then with having a razor job done on our faces . . . So we did it, and got through, no hassle, and sure enough there was a grand for each of us.

Next two or three days Jill seemed poorly, like she had a funny sort of cold: sweaty, runny nose, peeling a lot, but her temperature was subnormal and she seemed sort of high too, in a laid-back sort of way. Well, I was a proper narna about it and never twigged, even though she said she was taking a medicine for it that Giann' had given her. They were suppositories, done up in foil, you have to like pinch them out of the foil, and no label. I said it was disgusting sticking things up your bum, and didn't want to know. She said continentals always dosed themselves that way and it was the best way. I didn't argue. I should have.

Anyway just about when they ran out he rang her and asked her to go back to Turin and she came back after being away just over a week, but she only stayed two days. She'd brought back another two kilos of coke with her, and she was shoving those suppositories things up her bum again, and I rumbled them this time, had it out with her about them and she said like they were morphine and she felt good while she was on them, and rotten off them, and I could piss off. We had another big row about it and she said she was going back to Turin and Giann'. And I said he was abusing her, just making her mule his coke for him, and the Customs would rumble her coming back and forth all the time, and that would be the end of her. But she said this time Giann' wanted her to go back, because he'd got a new car, a Ferrari this time, and there was going to be like a sort of rally of Ferrari owners in France and he wanted her along with him. I didn't like it. I didn't want her to go. We had a bit of a row about it, and she went. I mean like when she said I was just jealous, then there was nothing to do but shut up.

Well, I expect you read about what happened next in the papers, I mean really you probably know more about it than what was in the papers, being with Interpol and all that, but anyway Giann' and a couple of other Italians had their Ferraris nicked – it was really quite a laugh, wasn't it? I mean, some joker just ran them up on a transporter and they were never seen again. There were pictures of Jill and Giann' in the papers, she in red Ferrari overalls, and all that scene . . .

Anyway I heard nothing more until a week – no, it's still less than that, just four days ago.

She actually rang me up and said she was in a terrible fix and could I possbily come and help her. She sounded awful, druggy, but hysterical too. She said Giann' had ditched her, and she was shacked up with this Cellini character, and she just managed to give me the address before she was cut off. Well, I did what anyone would do and got myself back to Turin just as quick as I could, and a taxi to this swank apartment in a new luxury block. I just walked in and rang the bell. What else could I do? And this fat old – well, you know, quite old – lady dressed in black opened the door and I pushed in. She was the cleaner, and she seemed quite pleased to see me when she realised I was English, like Jill, and just why was clear soon enough. Because I found Jill in a bedroom . . .

She was in a terrible state. Pathetic – no, worse. You can't . . . I can't really . . . I'm sorry. Well, she was just huddled up on this bed with a sheet over her, sucking her thumb and she was in a terrible way. She was thin to start with, I mean like Ethiopian thin, hadn't eaten properly for ten days. And she had spots and scabs, and bruises too. And she couldn't speak, not properly, but she just cried and cried. So anyway, I thought well, I have to get some clothes on her, and clean her up like, and there weren't any of her things in that room I could see, so I started looking about. It was a big apartment, and very lux, but an awful mess too. Dirty clothes, and glasses, and food uneaten. The cleaning lady by the way had pushed off. I don't know why. How should I know? Maybe she realised she'd be in trouble for letting me in, so she went. Anyway I was in the bathroom when the latchkey started clicking, the bathroom was like off the hall, and I heard it straight away.

They came straight in, Cellini and two of his mates, and they were drunk or high or something, but they didn't stop to use the bathroom. They went straight in, and went to the bedroom where Jill was. I could hear her sobbing and crying, and they were laughing and then one of them, Cellini I suppose, bellowed at her and I think he hit her. I just flitted about the place trying to find a weapon, found a big knife in the kitchen, nothing better . . .

But I didn't have to use it, which was just as well 'cos I don't think I could have. They'd all taken off most of their clothes and just dumped them like on the floor, over the backs of chairs. And one of the men was holding Jill, and the other was doing it to her, and Cellini was standing watching and doing it to himself. And one of them had had a gun stuck in the waistband of his trousers, I suppose, anyway it was just sitting there on top of these clothes. And of course it was Cellini who saw me first and came at me so I just picked it up. It was a big thing, a revolver, you know? Anyway all I had to do, all I could do really was yank on the trigger, and I did, it was a long hard pull but I could feel it was working. I could hear it clicking inside and then it went off. And took off the top of his head.

That's it really.

*

'Was she any use to you?' Commissioner Barlach, grey eyes like granite, looked up at Mulligan, across his large handsome desk. Big hands, strong fingers rolled an old-fashioned ebony ruler slowly up and down the leather-mounted blotter.

'I think so.'

Mulligan hid his disappointment. He had hoped that Bonnie would be acquirable, up for sale, that a trade might have been possible – get you off the murder rap, and you do a little undercover work for us . . . But it clearly was not on. For a start she wasn't going to get done for murder. She'd be home, in Clapham, on bail, within twenty-four hours.

Barlach understood all that. The smile he gave his ebony ruler was almost a sneer.

Mulligan, without waiting to be asked, lowered himself into a black leather chair, the leather fastened with brass studs. It was more comfortable than it looked.

'Why did she come here, to Zurich?'

Barlach's eyes met his, across the desk. He shrugged, a tiny movement. 'She panicked, took a taxi to the airport. The first plane she could get on was to Kloten.'

'What happened to the other girl?'

'She's in a Turin hospital. Morphine dependency. Malnutrition.'

For a moment or two they listened to the traffic noises. They seemed very even, no car horns or police whistles. The Swiss respect silent conventions – like traffic lights.

'This one, Miss Day, says you've got a diary of hers. She mentioned a name or two, and couldn't remember the addresses. Could I . . . ?'

Barlach's fingers left the ebony ruler, pressed a button.

Mulligan noted the address of Clouds and then turned to the other things Barlach had had sent up. Bonnie's passport in the name Bonnie Day, and credit cards. But her driving licence was made out to Muriel Clegg. With a name like that Bonnie Day really did seem like a good idea. He wondered what Jill Jack's real name was.

And of course there was her portfolio. No aspiring model moves an inch without her portfolio. It was much like a conventional album, but a bigger format, and with floppy covers. She looked good in it, sometimes of course virtually

459

unrecognisable. And three pictures included the pert, heart-shaped, mischievous face of a shorter girl with big blue eyes and dark hair whose appeal was at first sight even more striking. One showed Jill Jack – for clearly that was who she was – wearing a gold medallion which Bonnie held beneath her chin so the reflection off the gold lit Jill Jack's long white throat. A red background glowed behind them. What was striking, powerful even, was the expression in their eyes – clearly they were delighted with each other.

There was another picture which caught the same resonance between them.

This time they were on a dais, beneath what looked like canvas. They were wearing Guernsey sweaters over short shorts. And behind them, blurred but not so blurred that he was unrecognisable, Hector Myklades.

'Jesus,' said Mulligan. 'I have to go back to her and ask who took this picture, and when and why.'

This time Barlach's shrug said: 'Be my guest.'

After a second interview with Bonnie, Mulligan checked into the Pension Bahnpost across the road, and sat in the room they gave him, played back the tape and sat and thought about it for an hour or more. Then he made a lot of phone calls, and then did some more thinking. When Bonnie was released the following day he was waiting for her at the airport. He intercepted her in the check-in queue at the BA desk.

'Miss Day?'

'It's you agin. Wha' y' want wi me now?'

'You've got half an hour to spare. Could we talk for a few minutes?' He led her to an empty black leather bench beneath a suspended flying machine, scarlet with scalloped dragon wings. 'You really hate these people, and what they did to Jill Jack, don't you?'

She said nothing – compressed her mouth into a scoffing line. But her eyes were cold, calculating.

'And I think you could help me. Help me see they're properly dealt with. Would you let me talk to you about it? Tell you what I have in mind?'

She shrugged. 'Y' can talk. Burr Ah don' wanna miss m' ple-an.'

47

The brief ritual of the photocall drew to a close.

'Sir, señor, do you think you could move just a little to your left, and raise your head?'

'Why?'

'Because, sir, your spectacles would then reflect the crest of the mountain opposite.'

Pedro frowned, pushed mirrored shades with white doeskin sidepieces on to his forehead, revealed eyes whose whites were jaundiced, set in purple sockets. Those there who knew him were taken aback: in a year he had aged ten. His speech was slurred.

'You are meant to be taking pictures of me. And Signorina Malatesta. Not the landscape.'

His eyes, narrowed now against the fierce light that blasted off the snow, raked through one hundred and eighty degrees taking in the huge bowl that lay beneath him, then lifted to reverse the movement, netting this time the broken, irregularly serrated edge of the mountain cirque that enclosed it. He paused on the high clean line in the middle, where the mountain crest became for a moment a straight unbroken edge, a knife blade held against the deep blue throat of the sky. The Wildstrubel. To the left the line swooped, then soared again to a chunkier ridge, almost a peak, the Steghorn. It was as if he owned it all – indeed, for three days, he did.

He leaned forward on his sticks, head jutting slightly. The cameras whirred and clicked.

'Would the signorina like to come down, move in a little bit closer?'

'Of course.' Her voice was gentle but confident, conferring a favour but firm. Her skis whispered, hissed to a standstill precisely one metre from his. A paparazzo from Milan sighed at the elegance of it. Whether or not this lot could properly be called royals was a matter the popular arbiters of such points would argue in the sheets his pictures would illustrate, but certainly they could ski. Properly. And not all the royals he came into the mountains to photograph every year were that able. Europa did not fall over. She was not a bean-pole. She was not given to simpering giggles or braying laughs. She was as good as Queen Sofia, had style. Where had she been hidden for twenty years? Why?

'A little closer perhaps?'

'You'd like me to put an arm round her?'

'Si, señor. After all, if this holiday is to celebrate your engagement . . .'

'No. We are not film stars . . .'

'No, señor. Certainly you are not. But the English . . .'

'They are a circus. We are not. And we are celebrating an engagement not a marriage.'

One of the journalists glanced down the long drop of the nursery slope they were on. A quarter of a mile away and below them stood a two-storeyed building, white with a red roof, elegant wrought-iron balconies in front of shuttered windows, terraces with tables and chairs, awnings and parasols. On one side a recent annexe had been built on, concrete and glass but as stylish as the rest, housing a heated swimming pool. Chunkily rounded gold letters spelled it out across the cornice: HOTEL KAISERALP.

'Under one roof.' It was said drily: the impertinence was apparent.

Boltana, fearing a scene, intervened. His anorak and salopette were white – to minimise his bulk. 'It is a private party. Friends and close relatives. Neither the Malatestas nor Señor Mendoza wish to be bothered once this session is over.' He glanced at his watch. 'May I remind you that your cable car leaves in ten minutes and there will be no facilities to accommodate anyone who is not on our guest list.'

Another voice, that of a tall girl in a leather coat. She wore round rose-tinted shades and blonde hair peeped beneath the edge of the Angora cap she wore. 'It is true then that you have booked the whole hotel?'

Boltana maintained a geniality they responded to; tired of Pedro's surliness most of the twenty or so newspersons and photographers drew round him. Yet he hesitated: her English had been accented and it took him a moment to work out what she had said. 'For three days, yes.'

'And all the slopes and the pistes?'

'Yes. Even the cable car will only run when we need it and its passengers will be vetted by our people at Unter dem Birg.'

'Could you put a figure on how much this has cost?'

'Certainly not. But we look forward to reading your newspapers' estimates. It will be interesting to see to what extent fantasy outstrips reality. Now, gentlemen. Ladies . . .' He began to shepherd them down the slope.

From where they had been hovering above, four or five skiers swooped down: Brel in a sable hat and an umber suit that could hardly have been padded at all, Lovejoy in scarlet with a scarlet hat, flapping ear-pieces and scarlet Cé-Bé goggles. Behind them two guards in black, with black mirrored shades and short-cropped hair fanned out to stations on the wings of the group. Illegal guns bulged beneath zipped pockets, and only a fool or someone who had been paid not to see them could have ignored them. But there were no Swiss police within five miles. Why should there be?

'Well, that went off all right,' Lovejoy's voice was pitched to mark a closure, the end of an argument.

Pedro was petulant. 'It wasn't necessary. And one of them was insolent.'

'Oh, I'm sure it was necessary,' Lovejoy drawled. 'Toñi is always right about these things. No possibility of keeping an occasion like this hidden. They were bound to get wind of it, so give them their crumbs and then kick them out.'

Europa too sounded edgy, the polished aloofness she had shown the press now dropped. 'I don't like being photographed without the chance of vetting the results. You know that.'

Lovejoy was reassuring. 'You looked magnificent.'

Brel intervened, her quiet voice cool, incisive. 'Nevertheless I am puzzled by one of them. The tall girl in the leather coat. I have not seen her in the pack before, and she handled her camera like an amateur. You should check her out.'

Pedro swung his head to and fro, bent his neck back then forward, rubbed the nape. 'This sort of thing always gives me a headache. Where's Jana?'

*

The big red gondola whirred and clanked, tipped over the edge of a sheer precipice with a drop of at least two hundred feet to scree, snow and the first firs below. Choughs sailed up from the ledges: small crows with yellow beaks, they mewed and cackled as if they had never seen it before. Further rock faces slipped by curtained by greenish frozen waterfalls that looked like clusters of stalactites. Inside the car they speculated. The cost. The privacy. Why? What for? Orgies, opined one. Druggy parties. The Duke looked a mess, was clearly overdrawn healthwise. Someone recalled that a month or so ago an associate of Mendoza's, Teseo Feijoo, had been busted leaving Madrid airport with half a gram of cocaine. A bail-bond set at half a million pesetas had to be deposited before he was allowed to go on to Miami.

A French journalist with a cassette recorder, tall with thin, lank dark hair and a pockmarked face shook his head. 'Drugs certainly. Orgies perhaps. But business too. That's the real reason, the only reason for spending that sort of money to be on your own ... I can smell it.' He sniffed noisily. 'The loveliest smell in the world ... serious money. That's what it's about. And that's the real story. Not this bullshit about an engagement.'

'Oil?'

'I don't think so. How about stardust. Stardust for ... arms? Mendoza's first wife belonged to a coke clan.'

Bonnie Day looked back up the lines of looping cable. At that moment a hang-glider, boldly blazoned in harsh black and white, launched out and began a long climbing sweep on thermals from the warm valley below. Black goggles on a white helmet lent a death's head look to the pilot, and she shivered.

Then she spoke to the journalist with the cassette recorder. 'You know, they can't have built that hotel up there just using these cars. There must be another way up.'

'Sure there is. Over the Ammertenpass. It's a gap that lies to the west of the Wildstrubel, used by the farmers when they bring the cattle up to summer pasture. Not recommended in winter, but at the turn of the century they got carts over it in the summer. You ever done any hill-walking?'

'Lots. You?'

He shrugged. 'Some.'

*

464

Up at the Kaiseralp, they gathered on a terrace for coffee and schnapps. Their eyes tracked the hang-glider, soaring beyond the edge of the escarpment, hardly circling at all, his climb marked only by his diminishing size.

'One assumes,' Pedro remarked, 'that he is one of ours. I mean one hopes he isn't some sort of spy, or one of those evil jackals from the newspapers.'

Jana, chin tilted up on the tips of her forefingers sounded almost dreamy. 'He sure knows what he's doing.'

Pedro was annoyed. 'Really?'

'Really. I've done some hang-gliding, you know? That guy knows what he's doing.'

Malatesta, wrapped in silver furs, tapped the ferrule of the cane he held with both claws between his knees. 'He certainly does, my dear. He came third in the Luftwaffe championships last year.'

'So he really is one of ours.'

'Very much so.' Malatesta sounded smug, proprietorial. 'Walther von Sachs. An admirable young man, and living proof that the spirit of the Teutonic Knights is not a thing of the past. He will demonstrate his mettle in two months' time. You'll see.'

'Nevertheless. If he were one of that noisome pack it would be interesting to take him out. There's not much wind. A thousand metres would you say? A bit more? I'd use my HK 91 with small mark ammunition.' Having established albeit an illusory ascendancy over the distant figure that was drawing far too much attention away from himself, Pedro smiled, stood. 'The snow is good, and I don't intend to waste it for a moment longer.' He stretched a hand towards Europa. 'Coming?'

'Of course.' The grey Botticelli eyes looked up at him, narrowed against the glare. 'I'm longing to have a go at the black-rated piste. They say it's quite a run. Miss Pensión?'

Pedro was abrupt. 'Jana may well be the best thing on wings yet to come out of Tulsa, but she is a novice at skiing. I'm afraid it's still the nursery slope for her.' He stooped, poured a shot of kirsch into his coffee, drank it off.

Jana countered: 'You start in on the hard stuff at this time of day and you'll not even make it to the nursery slope.'

Lovejoy, still in his scarlet ski-suit, was more gallant, offered to teach her on the nursery slope above the hotel. A drag-lift took them to the top. Below them they saw Lili Brel fastening the toes of her boots into langlauf bindings, then she was off striding across the snow, body thrown forward, punting herself along on the tall sticks the cross-country skiers use, head up, skirts swinging.

'Admirable,' breathed Lovejoy. 'Such flair.'

Jana was cross. 'She looks like she was from another century.'

'That may be no bad thing. It often seems to me that one of the things we have lost is the art of doing nice things beautifully.'

'Stuff. She's too studied. Too much in love with her own self-image. Okay. Show me how to get down this slope . . . beautifully.'

'Right. You have already learnt the snowplough stop, and by weighting the lower ski you can turn into the hill and use gravity to slow you down. The next thing is the traverse with parallel skis. Stand across the fall-line. Good. Skis parallel and almost touching, uphill edges digging into the snow, the uphill tip just a little in front, it leads the way. Good. Now swing your knees into the slope and twist so your body from the waist to the shoulders faces downhill. Weight on the lower foot. Once you are moving in this position and you want to stop you simply add weight to the downhill foot and lean out more from the slope. You will turn into it and come to a standstill. Right. Now watch.'

He slid away from her, arms up, sticks dangling, his mellifluous, George Sanders voice talking it through again, exaggerating the stance so almost it looked comic. But he was graceful too, and the control was perfect.

'Now you follow, doing precisely the same.'

She did, and she had it right, she knew it, and knew too she was hooked. For now, for the first time, she sensed and plumbed the whole art of it, how pressure, balance, angles, gravity, the quality of the snow, are variables at any given moment in an equation which is always essentially the same, and whose resolution can be made to achieve the maximum of effect with the minimum of effort. There was a lot still to learn but she knew it could be learnt: it was all there in that effortless glide across the fall-line, the hiss of the snow beneath her skis, the gentle stop as she narrowed the angle into the slope.

'Bravo. Now next time you must do a full turn at the end of the traverse, so you can go back across the slope. To do that, you must first slow as you did by weighting the lower ski, then moving into snowplough you shift all your weight on to the uphill foot. This will bring you down and round, through the fall-line and back facing the other way. As soon as you have completed the turn the skis become parallel and touching again, and you are traversing the other way, uphill ski leading, knees into the slope, torso out . . . Like this.'

'Hang on. It's very hot, you know?' Already she had taken off her anorak, was down to salopette and a jumper beneath it, but sweat glistened in the nape of her neck beneath her curly hair, and her shades had steamed up. 'Nobody told me it could be hot on a ski-slope. Pardon me.' She unclipped the straps of the salopette, let the bib fall, then elbows raised pulled off the jumper. Lovejoy's tongue flickered across his lips as he saw her creamy skin, small but very full breasts, the nipples darkly aureoled and suddenly erect in the air which was chill in spite of the direct heat of the sun.

'Nothing to pardon. Believe me, you are very beautiful. And . . .'

Hands on hips clutching her sticks, body part twisted to face him, she eyed him for a moment from beneath her pushed-up shades, squinting against the glare. 'And . . . ?'

He shrugged. 'You have . . . a bloom on you. And I am a doctor, have some experience – '

'I guess you think I'm pregnant.'

He shrugged.

She pulled up the bib of the salopette, refastened the straps. 'And you could be right. Now show me how to do this turn.'

She followed, did as he had said, felt a moment of panic at the point when she was facing straight down the hill, albeit with speed well throttled back by the snowplough, but nevertheless the downhill ski slipped away, and . . . 'Shee-it.'

His broad, short-fingered hand, clad only in pierced driving gloves, gripped her bare upper arm, dug for the muscle. Her dark eyes blazed, and she wrenched herself out of his grasp.

'How the fuck do I get up on my own?'

'Well, my dear, that too is a lesson that has to be learnt. Skis parallel across the fall-line. Take the sticks by their

467

middles in the uphill hand, put the downhill hand on their tops and . . . heave.'

She tried, but her skis slipped from under her.

'Let me give you a hand.'

'No sir, I said no.'

'You should not always refuse help, you know. I can help you with the other matter too, if you like.'

'Abort me, Dr Lovejoy? Piss off.' And she pushed herself upright, on her own.

'My knee hurts. Quite badly. I suppose at my age I should not attempt a professional level of performance.'

'Nothing to do with your age. If you had made a professional preparation you would have been all right. I can't feel any swelling. You don't squawk when I probe. A little heat should sort it out.'

Jana rolled in a lamp, adjusted it. Pedro, swathed in towelling, lying back on the soft black leather adjustable couch that now went with them wherever practicable, watched her firm lithe movements, felt confused by the aura of well-being that flowed from her, like a young thoroughbred mare in the peak of condition. Really – and it was a thought that came quite frequently as he got to know Europa better – there was no reason why his genes, like those of Sherpa his stallion, should not be spread around wherever they could do most good . . .

Outside, the mountains disappeared behind a whiteout that turned grey, black. Inside, her long brown bare feet and the casters of the lamp made no sound on the thick carpeting. She moved back behind him, continued to knead his neck.

'I was all right at Gstaad. In January.'

'At Gstaad you had no one to impress but yourself. Today, I expect, you pushed yourself.'

This was true, though not the whole truth. At Gstaad Pedro had not felt demeaned by a tumble: his monarch was there, and had tumbled more than once. But at Kaiseralp, in front of Europa, he had attempted to buck the natural consequences of a too ambitious wide-parallel when he had failed to get sufficient edge on the ice crust. Instead of letting the fall happen he had fought it, and twisted his knee. But not that

468

badly. Not badly at all: a fact of which both Jana and he were well aware.

After a time he sat up straight, shook his head. 'That does feel better, both the knee and the tension.' He turned, looked up at her from dulled but anxious eyes set in sockets that were brownish purple. 'So you recommend a workout. Get me in better shape for tomorrow?'

She shrugged. 'It's a long time since you did a full hour. But I don't see that a few suppleness exercises will do anything but good.'

'Right.' He threw off the towel, swung legs to the floor, stood and stretched, flexed muscles, from fingers and toes to buttocks and stomach.

Jana moved to the cassette player thinking: he still fancies himself, can't see what's happening, the liver spots, the varicose veins, a slackness of skin where the muscle tone has gone. She slotted in Brandenburg Two, the high trumpet one, in a James Last-like version. Up-market from Springsteen and the Stones, faster too.

'Oka-a-a-y. We'll loosen up, warm up. On your heels, on your toes, knees bend, heels . . . toes . . . knees. Heels . . . toes . . . knees. Now. Cross-over hip swing, leg as high as possible, belt-level you should manage, alternate legs. Right, now use that table, thigh abduction, and adduction, back and forward, make them swing. Fine, fine, two, three, four. Right. Now we'll try some lunges with hip extension and knee flexion. Feet apart, lunge forward, back leg straight, flex the other knee, return to position one and . . . repeat. Lunges front and side, front, side, front – '

'Oh my God.'

'What's the matter?'

'My knee.'

'Your knee?'

'Yes, for Christ's sake, my knee.'

'Okay, okay, I thought the way you were going on you'd had a heart spasm. The knee's troubling you? Giving some discomfort?'

'Red hot poniards. I think it's the cartilege, you know?' He was hopping up and down in his jockey shorts, holding it.

She snapped Bach-Last off, put a lean hard arm round him,

led him back to the couch. 'Is it really *that* bad? I mean THAT bad?'

Again the pleading anguished look.

Sadistically she offered: 'A doctor, perhaps. Lovejoy? I mean if it's that *bad*.'

'Don't fool with me.' The Duke recalled that she was the retainer, he the boss.

'Okay. Lie back, then. Let me get it ready.'

Nurse Pensión squinted over the point of a needle. 'Are you going down to supper? I think you should. And if you do, you'd better be able to be sociable.'

'And if my knee is still hurting later . . . ?'

'We'll have the other half. Now let's see if you can make me a nice big vein . . .' She squirted a drop through the eye, pinched his flesh. It all went in as easy as a poor man into heaven.

48

The snow fell on the thin skin of ice the evening freeze had formed. On the terrace at nine o'clock the next morning Europa was ecstatic, clapped her hands with glee. 'Oh, we're so lucky,' she explained, 'to get deep powder on ice already, as if it were spring.' Then she frowned, bit her lip, looked up at the sky, where a thin haze was quickly clearing to deepest blue. In a moment or two the sun would nudge a rim over the Schedelsgrätli edge and the powder would begin to thicken. 'Why isn't he here? Why can't he get up?'

Jana glanced across the table at her, over her bowl of thick chocolate. 'What's so great about powder on ice then?'

'Oh, it's the very best. Believe me.'

'I'd like to try it.'

'Oh, it's not for novices.'

Jana raised an eyebrow, waited. Waited for three-quarters of an hour.

Europa prattled: about Fabergé, Alfred Brendel, the merits of bringing one's own tea with one when one travelled. Then she balled her fist and banged it on the table. 'Oh, why doesn't he come? I suppose he's with the other men. Business.

Sometimes I think he works too hard. Aren't you supposed to look after him? Don't you think he works too hard?'

'I don't think he works too hard. In fact he doesn't work that much at all. I'd say he was still having trouble with his knee. But say, why the worry? The snow's still here.'

'But it's changing all the time. Every minute, every second. It's thickening, becoming porridgy.'

'Well, okay. Get out on it. Don't wait for him. I'll come with you.'

Europa frowned, bit her lip, nodded towards the snowmobiles parked on the other side of the low wall. 'Can you drive one of those?'

'Sure I can.' Not sure, but she'd have a darned good try. 'Get your skis and all that together then.'

There was no problem about the snowmobile: a two-stroke engine, one forward gear, press-button ignition. It was a fun vehicle to drive, Jana decided, as she took them down a winding track of snow already flattened by a plough, across the undulating fields of drifted whiteness to the foot of a chairlift a mile away, on the lowest slopes of the Steghorn.

Europa creamed her porcelain skin, dragged a cornflower-blue sweat-band over her blonde hair, pulled down her shades. 'I wish you could come up with me.'

'Sure. You can give me some lessons when you're bored, and by this afternoon maybe I'll be able to.'

'It's not as easy as that.'

Jana shrugged, watched the girl's easy, confident progress on skis through a gate manned by a surly operator and on to a lift, acknowledged her wave as she was carried up and away, then looked round over the great bowl of snow below and the semicircle of peaks, ridges and escarpments above. It all looked empty at first sight, but bit by bit she picked up isolated specks of movement, activity. Nearest was the scarlet figure of Lovejoy swinging elegantly down the piste in a series of linked turns that drove the powder swirling around his knees. Much further away, silhouetted on the crag to the left of the hotel that marked the end of the escarpment above the valley below and the cable car, two black figures like ants kept watch. Casting back along the line she picked up two more, assumed they were placed at intervals right the way round. Then furthest of all, way out over the abyss of the valley, again using its thermals, the black and white hang-glider began to soar, steadily climbing until it broke into the clear sky above the distant range of mountains.

Momentarily she envied him, the emptiness, the space, the power to move in a third dimension that not even the pilot of a plane, committed always to move forward, feels as strongly as the hang-glider pilot. He was good, too, was high enough now to take another five hundred feet from the wind which, at ten thousand, blew a steady unchanging comet tail off the summit ridge of the Wildstrubel. Then he drifted below it, came in from the valley, across the bowl of Kaiseralp. Well, she was working at it, at getting the freedom and power to do as she liked for the rest of her life: she'd get all the hang-gliding she could use before long, and learn to ski as good as Europa. Better.

Skis hissed beside her. Lovejoy pushed up his goggles. 'What's happened to your señorito this morning?'

She shrugged, all expression carefully drained from her eyes. 'How should I know? He's not *my* señorito. He's hers.' She nodded up the slope. A bright-blue speck had just come into view right at the top.

'Oh, come on. Right now he's yours. By beddy-times last night he'd had too much snow, and I don't mean this stuff. And not just snow. He was snow-balling. You know what I mean. Cocaine and morphine together. I know what I'm talking about, it's what I give my cancer patients.'

'Listen, Doctor, what Pedro does to himself is not my business. Okay? I'm paid to pick up the pieces and stick him together again. How Humpty-Dumpty falls is up to him.'

'I understood Humpty-Dumpty was pushed. But by whom? Great unsolved mystery, yes?'

'And no way is he mine.'

He lifted his ski-stick towards her tummy. 'No?'

'I don't know what you're talking about.' Suddenly she was angry. 'Listen. If you think he's been balling me, you're mighty mistaken. I'd rather be balled by King Kong.' Momentarily she smiled, remembering just who it was. 'Much rather, I guess. Here she comes.'

As the angle of the slope flattened, Europa came out of linked step-turns and managed a *wedel*, keeping the points of the skis always in the fall-line and swinging the tails in a series of arcs about the points, maintaining speed without loss of control. She was thus able to end with a ferocious hockey stop that arced powder across them.

After lunch, with the snow thickening, and slower, Europa took Jana back to the nursery slope, turned out to be a better teacher than Lovejoy had been. A couple of hours later Jana announced that she was bushed, had had enough. She'd gone a long way in the time, had mastered side-slipping and stem-turns: she found side-slipping boring, but conceded that she could understand how it might be a useful technique on a steep and narrow slope. Outside the hotel they snapped off skis, hoisted them into the rack by the terrace, loosened their boots, and Europa pulled off her sweat-band, shook out her spun-gold hair.

'Coffee?' she asked.

'I'd rather have a swim. I'm all sweaty. Anyway, I've had as much coffee as I allow myself.'

Their styles were as different in the pool as they were everywhere else. Jana went in in a shallow dive, and did two lengths in a racing crawl that was as smooth and sleek as a sea-lion; Europa climbed to the top board, poised for a full minute, head bowed, hands clasped loosely in front of the cutaway crotch of her white sharkskin swimsuit. Then up went her arms, she extended herself on tiptoe, took one bouncing step, jack-knifed at the apogee of her rise and swallow-dived down. The surface plopped as she broke it, scarcely disturbed enough for the waves to reach the sides. As her head broke the surface she rolled on to her back and with feet fluttering coasted to the side.

'Wow, that was great!' said Jana.

'My instructor said I dive to Olympic standards.'

'You must have a raft of medals.'

'Oh, Grandpapa has never let me compete.'

'Why not?'

'It's something Malatestas just don't do.'

'Bullshit.'

Later they lay on towels spread on the warm honeycombed slabs that edged the pool. Sunlight, direct and reflected off the snowfields outside, played over the gently moving water, reflected back off the ceiling and sent shifting patterns like marbling across their bodies: the one lean, hard, tanned to a deep cream, the other less muscled, and a pure warm white. But not unblemished.

'You know, you're just about perfect. Too good for Pedro.'

'Oh no, I'm not perfect. But Pedro is. He's good-looking, and so clever, and so . . . oh, just utterly distinguished.'

Jana bit her lip, kept her voice level. 'Nevertheless, it must have come as a shock when they told you you were to marry him. I mean, had you ever met him when they told you that?'

'No, I hadn't. But really I had met hardly anyone at all. And it wasn't a shock. You see, Jana, people like us never marry for love; from very early on I knew I would marry whomever Grandpapa thought best. So it was wonderful when he decided on Pedro. And now I do know him a bit, well, it will be for love as well. I only feel it's such a shame about his first wife – sometimes I feel guilty a little that so much happiness is coming to me as a result of that terrible accident. And you know what makes it so wonderful is that it all comes after so much pain and unhappiness, it's like the end of a fairy tale.'

'I can't believe your childhood was painful, unhappy.'

'Oh, but it was. You see I wasn't always as beautiful as this.' The tinkling laugh she gave, Jana judged to be inane.

'Come on.'

'No, it's really true. I was born an ugly duckling . . .'

'That I can't believe.'

'I suppose not. Not now.' She turned on her side, resting on one elbow. Her large blue eyes were limpid, and serious. 'Jana, are we friends?'

'Yes. If you want to be.'

'If we're friends we must always tell each other the truth. Is that right?'

Jana found it quite irritatingly difficult to resist crossing her fingers. 'Of course.'

'Then tell me: am I really beautiful? They all tell me I am. Grandpapa. Pedro. Guy of course more than all the others. But he would. They all would. But is it true?'

Jana laughed, relieved not to have to lie. 'It's true. It really is absolutely true.' She let her eyes travel slowly over the whole of the body in front of her and made sure that the other girl knew what she was doing – from the crown of slightly waved gold hair, a nimbus against the bright snowglare, down over the delicately sculpted shoulders, the soft swell of her breasts, over the costume whose pure coarse whiteness served to accentuate the soft warm whiteness of her skin (and here a memory of Dalfinger stirred – at Retiro Cay the Colombian had worn bikini pants made from the same material), the long line of her leg beginning where the fabric was cut away over her hip-bone, swooping down to relish the softnesses of her inner thighs, the long curves to small knees carved from polished alabaster. At last she reached out a strong brown hand, cupped Europa's cheek and ear, and smoothed her temple with her thumb.

'You're beautiful. Just perfect. You really are.'

'Oh, thank you.' Europa caught Jana's wrist. 'That's so nice too.' She pressed the other girl's hand more tightly into her cheek. 'Nobody much touches me like that. One of the nurses . . . when I cried. But she was ugly. And you're beautiful. Too.'

'No. Not like you.' Jana sat up, took Europa's face in both hands, held her, let the tiny lap of water, the shimmering reflections, the humid warmth of the spaces around them, soothe out the tensions she felt: it was a struggle not to check out the clues she had been offered – why did Europa not like being alone with Dr Guy Lovejoy; why was he, more than the others, at pains to tell her she was beautiful; and the pain, the unhappiness, and the only affection she has experienced from an ugly nurse . . . It all chimed with the original clue, the one provided by Harriet Jones. She gave her head a tiny shake, told herself that she already knew the answers, and that soon Europa would tell her the details, just let it happen. The temptation was there too to let her fingers map out the filigree of silver scars the shadowless light revealed, but that also she resisted. The fairyland Europa lived in denied their existence, and Jana planned to let her live there a little longer, perhaps for ever.

49

Through the early months of the year Pedro liked to keep on the move: chasing out the devils of darkness and short days with whatever distractions whatever continent he was in could offer. He could of course have gone to the southern hemisphere, but preferred not to. 'One should not,' he would say, 'deny the seasons. Their immutable rhythms are an essential part of our natures.' What he called to himself his court, what the gossip columns called his circus, went with him.

After a fortnight in the Bernese Oberland, ending with the three days at Kaiseralp, he announced that he had had enough of skiing, his knee was still not quite right, the Veneto was the place to be. That year Easter would be earlier, following the late one of the year before, which meant that pre-Lent Carnival fell this time in the third week of February; the mild winter had left more migratory water-fowl than usual in the delta of the Piave and the marshes to the west of the Venice Lagoon: Pedro took a villa on the Brenta with wide grassy lawns, huge cedars and plane trees, within easy reach of both, and passed the days leading up to Shrove Tuesday shooting duck out of opalescent skies.

On the last Saturday before Lent Lili Brel closed her Bern office for a week and arrived at the villa. Two hours before dawn on the Sunday a quite large convoy including Malatesta's ancient sedanca Rolls, Pedro's new Rolls Bentley, and smaller vehicles with secretaries, gun-handlers and so on, sped fifty kilometres or more through the industrial squalor of Mestre, past the closed campsites and Marco Polo Airport, across the fens to the less polluted marshes in the east. They were promised better sport here than they had had so far.

The shooters, five of them, clambered down from the canal bank into squat black punts. Pedro had to be helped – his knee still bothered him – and presently they were poled and oared

476

out between banks of sedge and brown frosted grasses into the white banks of lightening mist. When they were gone Jana let herself out of one of the smaller cars, and, dressed in a quilted tracksuit, set off down a narrow causeway that ran above the marsh. A little later Brel, dressed in suede edged with Tibetan snow leopard with a cap made from the same fur, got down from the Rolls Bentley. Her man came from the rear with her two rangy Irish wolfhounds, handed her the leads.

Dawn brought an icy breeze out of Carinthia and the Julian Alps, and to the north and west the long escarpment of snow-clad peaks, low on the horizon, caught the sun and briefly flashed it back as brilliantly as if from glass. To the south and west the square tower of Torcello floated amongst tree-tops above a bank of mist that still lingered, and beyond it the leaning campanile of Burano. Nearer, but still quite tiny, the punts, now widely scattered, pushed through reeds and sedge into patches of open water towards the shooting barrels, hides made out of oak-staved hogsheads sunk into the shallow lagoon. The boatmen put out wooden decoys and live tethered ducks that swam in tiny circles, quacking plaintively in what surely should be warning notes but which would soon attract flights of mallard, pintails and widgeon. The shooters clambered awkwardly out of the punts and into the barrels.

As the mist lifted, Brel could see the American girl half a mile away, not jogging, but running with the easy lope of the very fit beneath a tiny cloud of breath vapour that went with her. Already she had reached the end of the causeway, was now heading back the way she had come. Brel's mouth pressed into a tight little smile, and she slipped the leashes on her big grey dogs.

Jana of course saw them coming, and they in turn saw her. When thirty yards still separated them the wolfhounds hesitated, puzzled that the quarry had not turned to flee, circled aimlessly for a moment, and then, as she came up with them, fell in behind and followed her, at a slower lope than before, with their noses to the ground. Lili pouted secretly to herself, produced a silver whistle, blew a silent blast. The dogs' heads came up, they overtook Jana, broke into a full run again, and returned to their mistress, who patted them, slipped treats into the corners of their chocolate-brown mouths, released them.

Jana approached, stopped, stood arms akimbo, legs astride across the path.

Lili spoke first. 'I'm sorry if my dogs bothered you.'

'The fuck you are.' Jana's normally brownish cheeks were flushed to a peachy glow, and not just by the cold, or her run.

'Well, you knew how to cope.' Lili, who had made it her business to know all that could be known about the American girl, recalled that some of her childhood had been spent on a farm in New Mexico. No doubt there had been dogs, real dogs, on it. 'Do you want to go on with your run? I'm not sure I would advise overexertion.'

'Why not?' Still truculent.

Lili turned back towards the cars, more or less forced Jana to come up to her shoulder, fall in step with her. A flight of widgeon, with blue secondaries, the males with russet heads, carved an arcing parabola over their heads against the shot-silk of the rising mist, swept in on the open water to feed. Gunfire crackled, and they dropped out of the sky like weighted paper bags.

'Why not? Why shouldn't I run as much as I darn well want to.'

'Lovejoy tells me you're pregnant.'

'Shee-it. What fucking right has he to tell you that?'

'You have professional ethics in mind? Not Guy's strong suit. But in fact of course you are not his patient, so the most you can accuse him of is indiscretion. He also tells me that you are giving Pedro opiates. Other things too no doubt. No. Don't stop. Don't try to ignore me or be rude.'

Jana caught up again. 'What the fuck do you want?'

Brel swung on her heel, faced her. For a moment she tapped real chamois leather against her lips as if considering giving an answer. Then she gave the tiniest shake of her head. 'Perhaps later. But let me tell you this, Miss Pensión: I know what *you* want. And you won't get it on your own.' She turned again. 'Pedro's punt seems to be returning. He will say his knee is troubling him, but it could be he needs . . . a fix?'

'Neither. Von Sachs has outshot him. Just as at Kaiseralp he outskied him and upstaged him with his hang-gliding.'

'I expect you're right . . . Oh dear. There's that woman again.' They were back amongst the cars. As anomalous as a pit-pony amongst thoroughbreds there was now a pale blue

Renault 4. A leggy blonde girl in a long leather coat stood behind it, snapped them with a Pentax. In the passenger seat was a man . . . not old, sallow-faced, you couldn't see more.

'Who are they?'

'Paparazzi, I suppose. But very persistent. They must be seen to.'

Jana heard the steel in the older woman's voice, and respected it.

In the afternoon of that Sunday the circus moved to a palace in Venice itself and Boltana flew in from Madrid to join them.

'You are quite the most beautiful woman I have ever had.'

Jana Pensión looked at her reflection in the huge, ornately framed mirror that faced her four feet away. She saw streaked and highlighted hair, cut fairly short but curly and full; a good brow above dark amber eyes, a nose whose relative insignificance was not evident full face, a mouth subtly painted to appear more generous than it was; lean cream-coloured shoulders, breasts firm and full – she was still not used to them thus – with erect brown nipples; a long, lean torso with a deep-navelled flat tummy.

Probably he was right.

A tanned hand, darker than her skin, plump but large and strong, came into view, the fingers climbed her ribs, the palm cupped a breast; middle finger and thumb rolled the nipple between them. She felt the prick inside her thicken and she responded by tightening her pelvic floor, and she heard him swallow and grunt with increased pleasure. She pressed in with her knees on his waist. Certainly he was fat, and overweight – she was glad he liked to have her on top of him – but there was still good tone there.

'You're okay yourself, you know?' She looked down and her eyes met his.

Boltana's widened in self-mocking disparagement. 'Come, come. There is no need to lie to an elderly gentleman like myself. Fat, out of condition . . . already you are being kind, there is no need to be sycophantic.'

She allowed herself a smile, let her weight increase the

pressure where it meant pleasure for her, and rocked her pelvis. 'At least you can do it. You know what you're doing.'

'And my nephew does not.'

She frowned 'Are you asking – or telling me?'

'Making an informed guess. It would be interesting to know if I have it right.'

'Oh, I guess you're right. He's still conventionally fit, but he has an awful lot of bad habits, and they're beginning to tell. But I wouldn't let him do it to me anyway. Never have.'

'Why not?'

She laughed. 'I don't have to spell it out, do I? I mean like if he managed just for once to get it up in a normal sort of way he'd make a big deal of it like he was doing her a favour like no girl has had since the Annunciation. And he'd believe it. No, thank you, sir.'

Boltana laughed too – a rumble from his deep chest, which she felt as a mild vibration as well as heard. She rocked on, slowly exaggerating the movement, and felt him thicken and harden even more inside her. For all he was fat and nearly old, now it was well up it was big, a real presence. Suddenly she felt she really was enjoying herself, knew that if he hung on she could bring herself to an orgasm – something that, before him, had almost never happened with men.

He recognised this too, felt the heat and the tumescence, did not want to disappoint her. He made sure that he did not, watched her carefully as she came a little further forward, pressing down on to the well-padded pelvic bone, marked the tiny drops of sweat forming between her swinging breasts, the quivering of her lips, the tightening of the sinews in her neck. Then her head came up and the long shuddering sigh seemed to come right from where he could feel the spasm, right through her long body, and the dark creamy skin above her breasts blushed like the ripe side of an apricot. And as she came down, sinking him into her even deeper than before, so he felt the hard muscle of the cervix, he let himself go too.

His chest rumbled with pleasure as it happened. Before Jana it had been a long time since the actual moments of emission had been so unforced, so effortless.

'Lili tells me you're pregnant.'

Jana, still naked, still in front of a mirror – but this one smaller, hung above a Seicento wall table – halted the rhythmic flow of a silver-backed brush through her hair, lowered her arms, turned back to him. 'So?'

Propped up now amongst cushions and bolsters, sipping chilled dry white wine, Boltana peered over his half-lenses. He made a fetish at moments like this of not trying to conceal the depredations of age and good living. He was a long way still from senile decay, and the silvery thinning waves of hair across the big dome of a head, the glossy weightiness of broad fat shoulders, the grey hair that made masculine a chest that would not have disgraced a Buddha, would appear, he rightly judged, repulsive only to ignorant girls indoctrinated with sexual standards set by advertisers and film-makers. He had feared that Jana Pensión might bring to these the even more stringent ones of a person who believed the body is a temple, but . . . apparently, not.

'And not by my nephew?'

'Certainly not. Like I said: he's degenerate. Can't do it.'

'Surely . . . with that Colombian girl. Dalfinger?'

'No way. He tripped with her. On mesc and yagé. But no sex. Listen. I don't think he bothers with it much any more, but I reckon he's always had problems where ladies are concerned.'

'So. You'd have me believe I'm the lucky man.'

'You are.'

'How flattering. At my age. But could he . . . is there any way he could be made to believe he is the father?'

'Sure.'

The rumble again. 'I won't ask how.'

'No secret. I used to jerk him off, but in a way that made believe it was clinical, therapy. Training him up to the mark for the big event with the Gene. Right? Well, he already believes I kept the sperm, froze it. I can make him think I've used it. You know?'

Boltana's tongue paid a fleeting visit to the outside world, he wriggled his massive buttocks deeper into goosedown, sighed, sipped his wine.

Eventually he said: 'You should, you know, do whatever Lili says. She has our best interests at heart.'

'Yes?' The brush stopped, the arms came down, in the

mirror he could see how her breasts settled back on her ribcage, and he noted the careful lack of expression in her eyes.

'I think so.'

She sat quite motionless for a moment and he let his gaze travel down her back, relishing its thin brown toughness, the swelling curves below her waist, the natal cleft. Outside, the wind gusted down across the Canale di San Marco, and the tall shutters rattled. Presently she resumed brushing.

The next night the town was wild with the wind. Starting in the frozen Steppes it had howled up the Danube, shed a degree or two over Slovenia and merged with the swoop from the north of a frontal system that had started way out west, over Iceland. Already it was gusting snow and tumbling yellow spume balls off the surface of the Lagoon. Where water lay in sheets across the flags in the lee of buildings it froze. Most of the streetlights, apart from the grand cast standards in the Piazza, were suspended on wires across the narrow alleys, and they tossed like the tormented, flinging shadows across the shopfronts, swinging them up and down the peeling walls, the shuttered casements.

The wind shredded the flames off torches hurling gouts of burning tar into the faces of those who followed, shredded the macabre fantastic costumes too, as bands of revellers surged from bar to bar. Four huge fireworks, each a burst of a million stars, exploded above San Giorgio Maggiore and rode the wind weirdly, holding their shape but sailing briskly above the Giudecca before fading. The organisers called it a night, tarpaulined the rest, and the musicians in the Piazza packed up their instruments, went home or sought out the bars that did not already have their own bands.

On the colonnaded steps of the Teatro La Fenice Pedro's circus gathered about him as the audience streamed away from a performance of *Un Ballo in Maschera*. With difficulty he clutched his gold cloak about him, held on his jewelled and plumed hat. His mother had been a member of a cadet branch of the Bourbons and he had not felt it inappropriate for him to appear in Carnival costume as the Sun King. Winter brutally disagreed. Next to him, in garb as unsuitable if more stylish and less presumptive, Europa appeared as Venus in Botticelli's

Venus and Mars, though with the added embellishments of a diamond tiara and the pear-shaped five-carat pendant, loupe-clean and colourless, that had been his birthday gift to her the month before.

A crowd, much smaller than he had expected – and, considering the indignities the weather was forcing on him, he was grateful for it – lingered while he tried to strike natural but not foolish poses for the few paparazzi who had remained out in the storm.

Among them a tall girl in Harlequin outfit made a show of using her Pentax, called above the wind to her companion: 'What would those stones be worth if they were real?'

'Of course they're real. They're the realest thing about her.'

At that moment several things happened at once. Somebody wrapped Europa in a long purple velvet cloak, hurried her not to the gondola that had been booked but to a closed *motoscafo*, and Pedro, after a moment of indecision, followed. Through the gap they had left, two masked men clothed like executioners in skin-fitting black leather and led by a very tall figure in a Darth Vader costume from *Star Wars* surged down the steps and into the small group of photographers, With precision and competence they singled out the tall Harlequin, bundled her over the nearest narrow hump-backed bridge, and down a dark alley up which the snow-laden wind howled. The men in black leather held her, Darth Vader ripped the black cap and mask off her head, straight blonde hair tumbled down, blue eyes burned at him with hatred but the mouth opened to scream. He tore off her ruff, stuffed it into her mouth, and then hit her across the face four times forehand, backhand, with his studded, gauntleted fist.

From inside the mask the voice came – human, in English but accented Germanically. 'The Signorina Malatesta does not want you to appear near her again. Understand? Next time it will be much worse.'

The men dropped her, she fell to her knees. One of them swung her camera in an easy curve over her head and into the narrow spumy canal beyond.

Later a velvet black-phase jaguar cat looked down from one of the smaller rooms at the back of the palace and into the colonnaded square that lay behind it. Below, louche figures, dressed and partially dressed in travesty or with epicene elegance, capered in mock and not so mock simulations of copulation, occasionally standing back to make obscene and beckoning gestures up at the windows above them. A door clicked, and the cat, expecting Boltana, did not turn. But it was a simulacrum of St Teresa of Avila who appeared – white hood above brown habit, rope-soled shoes on fine-boned feet which floated across worn but still beautiful Turkish rugs to join the cat at the window. Her face was a mask, skilfully moulded in imitation of Bernini's portrayal of the saint in ecstasy, and recalling, as Bernini does, the Medusa heads of antiquity.

'You chose not to have supper,' the saint said.

'Frankly lobster and sucking pig are a turn-off as far as I'm concerned. Listen. What are those characters down there up to?'

The saint looked past her shoulder. '*I pederasti*. They're waiting for Pedro, I'm afraid. They've come to expect his company when he's in Venice.'

'Shit. You know it's a wonder I manage to keep him in as good shape as I do.'

The saint was dry. 'No one doubts the value of the services you do him. Listen. I think we should talk.'

'Maybe. But you shouldn't have sicked your dogs on me. You know, if they had come on, come at me, I would have killed them. And that would have been a pity. What do you want?'

'How would you have done it? By catching their front legs and forcing them apart? Ugly. And while you did it to one, the other – '

'No. By using this.' The cat spread her hand. A small aerosol, much like the ventilator asthmatics use, lay in her palm. 'Nerve gas. But a very strong one. It's silly to train in public areas without one. Come on . . . Sister. What do you want?'

'Reverend Mother would be more appropriate. Let's discuss what I want later. First I have to convince you that you cannot get what you want on your own.'

'I'm not doing so badly. But go on, you can try. Hey. Here he comes.'

The *pederasti* were mopping and mowing, made elaborate

courtesies and rococo bows, whichever their fantastic costumes dictated, to a lean but limping figure who had appeared amongst them, wrapped now in a long black coat spangled wizard-wise with arcane symbols. As they led him away amongst torches that flared in the wind, the two or three who took up the rear turned, and repeated the obscene gestures they had made before, but in derisive triumph now.

'You know, that's the happiest I've ever seen him look? Crazy. You're right. I could use some help. Mother. But you have to convince me that by getting what I want I help you. Otherwise, I won't trust you, nor you me, and no deal. Okay?'

'Of course. You are quite right.' The saint spoke slowly now, and for the first time as an equal speaking to an equal. She pulled the heavy drapes across the casements, but during the next hour or so the wind gusted through cracks and occasionally they stirred. Once even the rugs lifted with the draught. It was an old palace, in need of refurbishment.

From that evening on, the conflicting interests, the inner contradictions that had always existed within Crystal, and those within what Eurac called the Web, began to tear them apart.

Part Nine

The Kaiseralp Contract

50

'Giann', I have to say I am very frightened.' Signor Prezz' Spezz' pushed back his plate. Of the three Imbottini Delizia – rolled slices of veal stuffed with pounded white truffle, ham, mozzarella cheese – he had eaten only half of one.

Giann' Arnolfini, whose appetite remained robust, looked up, waggled an empty fork, spoke with his mouth full. 'You are more of an old woman than ever, Ernesto. You know that?'

The older man, his face ashen, his hand trembling, sighed, wiped his brown lips with his napkin, drank water. At his feet Eyck, his small long-haired terrier, yapped and whined, sensed that the master had finished, waited for the plate to be put down for him.

Giann' tapped the edge of his plate with his knife. 'You know this is no different from any of the other moves. There's no reason for it to go wrong. No reason at all.'

'Gi-i-i-ann'.' He drew the word out into a whine that matched his dog's. 'There is again one hundred and forty-four kilos with my name and face wrapped round each one of them . . . it's a crazy routine, crazy to keep doing it the same way. But that's not why I am frightened.'

He pushed back his chair, balled his napkin, stood at the window with a toothpick shielded behind the palm of his left hand. The dog leapt into his place, seized one of the veal rolls and took it to the tiled floor, sent a silver fork slithering and chiming after him.

'You shouldn't let your dog do things like that. It's disgusting. Why are you frightened then?'

Ernesto looked down through the huge pane of glass and shivered. Sea mist, thickening to drizzle, pushed icy fingers through the lean black cypresses; the sea beyond, glimpsed through shreds of it, was gunmetal grey and merged into it so it was difficult to say where one ended and the other began.

The great city, climbing the hills on the other side of the curving bay, looked dull, bleak. A foghorn on the lighthouse at the end of the long mole boomed mournfully beneath its circling light. Like a ghost ship, floating somewhere between sea and sky, a medium-sized refrigerated cargo ship slipped by, and into the roads. The black beetle of the pilot launch scuttled across the surface towards it.

'Here she comes. *Gelada Fini*.'

Giann' spooned and forked a generous helping of Insalata Buca Lapi on his plate, salad with Gorgonzola crumbled into it. 'Eh? I'm waiting. Why the terror just now, this time, today?'

'At the Yacht Club, this morning, an hour ago . . . no one talked to me. No one at all. I was a pariah, Giann'. A leper.'

'Maybe you didn't bathe this morning. Maybe they smelled the fear on you.' But there was now a note of uncertainty in Giann's voice. To be snubbed, ignored, at the Yacht Club was bad news: after the Ferrari episode the Arnolfinis had had to put up with some bantering, but it had been good-natured, even admiring: a family who could lose three Testerossi without appearing unduly worried, was a family to respect. And then when Cellini was wasted in his own apartment and Bonnie Day got off, they assumed the Arnolfinis had come up with a particularly slick way of dealing with a guy who had stolen your girl. But this was different: if the bankers, the merchants, the brokers of Genoa didn't want to know them any more, they could very well be in big trouble.

Ernesto sighed, ignored the sarcasm. 'Giann'. Listen. These people Enrico has working for him in England are not our people. They don't know our ways. They offend people. They are too big. They are too greedy . . .' He was fumbling for words, groping to frame concepts he understood very well, concepts that were a deep part of his culture, too deep for easy verbalising: neither his education nor what little reading he had done gave him words like 'hubris' or 'over-reaching'; but he knew very well what he felt. 'They turn people who should be good friends, people you have to work with, people who have their pride, who have their position in the world, into bad enemies. Not just here in Genoa, but in London too, New York . . . You know what they are saying?'

'You're going to tell me anyway.' Growing anxiety was making Giann' outwardly sulky.

'That these people want the whole of Britain to themselves, that they have even betrayed people who would not come in with them or give up . . . That's too greedy, Giann', that can't end well. And they've upset the Colombians too. We always got on well with Arias, we did not make the mistakes the Philadelphia families made . . . Oh Holy Mother, Holy Mother of God, sweet Jesus, Maria, Joseph, Holy Mother, my pills Giann', quick, my heart pills. Holy Mary, pray for us now and at the hour of our . . .'

He stumbled away from the window clutching at his chest, groping towards the sideboard. His face, pale before, was now livid, his lips mauve. Giann' pushed over his own chair to get to him, helped him down into another, found the pills in his pocket, poured water. He rang the bell, then turned back to his brother, stood behind him, held his forehead in the palm of his hand, tried to soothe his shoulder. Slowly the gasping breath came under control, a little real colour came back to the flaccid, mournful jowls.

'It's all right. I think. I think it's going to be all right. The pain, already it's not so bad . . .'

'Okay, Ernesto, okay. But what brought that on? I'll tell you. You worry too much, you get into a state . . .'

'No, Giann' . . . Look. Look out of the window.'

Giann' peered down through the mist. The freighter had turned, stem on, its high stern towards them, its Panamanian flag hanging limply from the staff, a haze of vapour above the stack that carried the stencilled caricature of his brother, and the monogrammed letters PS. And under its lee, clustered beyond the chute of permanently pumped water from its leaky bilges, four smart cruisers, high-bowed, armed with heavy machine-guns, flagged with the green, white and red tricolour, nudged against jute fenders. He did not need binoculars to read the lettering on their hulls, he knew they were Customs launches and the Port Police.

Behind him Eyck leapt up for the last of Ernesto's veal delicacies, and somewhere in the rooms below a doorbell peeled.

Almost a year of ever-increasing prosperity for Danny had brought changes to the Santa María shrimp-processing rig. The bridge, which had been a dismal place of rust, blistering paint, and consoles from which one set of technology had been ripped and another botched into place, had become a wide, airy, shaded room that made the most of the three walls of glass, with the panes angled in from overhanging eaves. First Danny had scrubbed it out, then rehoused and neatened the controls of the diesel generators and the shrimp-sterilising and freezing equipment, finally he had decorated it with pastel-coloured paintwork and tasteful wallpapers representing bamboo thickets. On the wall that was not glazed he had carefully mounted a collection of stuffed tropical birds he had picked up for a song on a flying visit to San Juan on Puerto Rico. These he had cleaned and refurbished, perched or hung them on nylon filaments amongst the hugely flowering fuschias he had bought on a later trip.

Suited in off-white linen, perched on a chrome and black leather barstool with one elbow on the wide ledge that ran all the way round beneath the windows, with a tall glass of crushed ice, rum and tropical fruits, he listened to quadro-phonic James Last and watched the still distant bows of a freighter as she slowly took on substance through the lilac shimmering heat haze of midday. Drawing on his past as a deckhand he put it at about four thousand tons, general cargo, and with its stubby thick funnel and superstructure amidships, kingposts fore and aft, at least thirty years old. Nothing like the quite reasonably smart (even by his exacting standards) pair of reefers that made up the Prezz' Spezz' fleet which dropped in, in turn, once every six weeks to pick up shrimps – shrimps and coke. The last, the *Gelada Fini*, had called three weeks ago and would, he reckoned, be docking at Genoa just about then.

He had got that little problem beaten too: had tidied up the procedures so he was able to pack the flood of plastic bags that arrived once a fortnight into Prezz' Spezz' cartons without getting into a mess or a panic, without too overtly involving any of his crew. Moreover, without being greedy, he had suggested a substantial increment from his employers for his pains. They had promptly agreed a new salary structure, and, witness the comforts with which he had surrounded himself, he was now doing very well. Indeed, the British community in Tortola looked forward to his visits, he had a regular girlfriend, a mulatto in Road Town, and the very helpful manager of the Berkeley's Key Bank was helping him to buy a nice little property on Peter Island with a thirty-four-foot sloop to go with it.

Danny reckoned he could complete the three years they had contracted him for, and then that would be it: retirement at forty to a tropical paradise and an income of forty grand a year for life. Bloody marvellous.

The creamy bow wave beneath the prow of the freighter diminished until the thick satiny turquoise swell, shot with yellow weed, was almost unbroken, and at the same time her configuration shifted as she slowly turned beam on. Yes, the superstructure and funnel were exactly midships, and beneath them on the black, rust-streaked hull, the words: *La Bruja del Mar, Colón*. This fat old tub a sea-witch? Well, why not? The only witch Danny had ever known had been a blowsy, evil old woman with huge legs who terrorised the small Hampshire village where he was born. Even above James Last he heard the drawn-out honk of her hooter, and a few minutes later he saw they were putting down a motor-skiff. Danny finished his drink, pushed through the storm doors out into the heavy humid heat, on to the gantries, ladders and catwalks which took him down to the little floating pier where the shrimp boats tied up.

Two hours later they had not solved the problem of how to shift a container that purported to carry twenty-five tons of copper ingots, ex the London Mineral Market warehouse in Rotterdam, via Tel Aviv, out of the hold of *La Bruja* and on to the platform of the Santa María. It was a question of the relative heights involved, the obstructions and protuberances that projected from the rig at a variety of levels, and the consequent unwillingness of the master of the freighter to lay her alongside. He was a tall, skeletal man, with jaundiced skin, of indeterminate race, who spoke Spanish with an impenetrable South American lisp and very little English. Danny, however, kept his head and with the aid of a pocket calculator and several sheets of exercise paper managed to work out that something might be done at high tide in three hours' time if in the meantime they used oxyacetylene equipment to sheer off an angular structure of girders and pipes that stuck out from one corner and which had no doubt served some purpose when the rig was drilling for oil, but now seemed expendable.

Throughout the afternoon a team of three – two from the boat, and the other one of Danny's Mexicans who had worked in the demolition industry in Mexico City before the earthquake cost him his job – worked under Danny's direction. Slice by slice lumps of hot metal splashed hissing into the oily water below until at last what was left buckled under its own weight and collapsed with the biggest splash of all. It had been hot, tedious, noisy, dangerous work, and they were all in evil tempers when it was finished. They had been bothered too by the regular appearance, high above them, of a small pleasure plane, a Beechcraft, that circled overhead, its engines buzzing like a mosquito. Clearly it was there to see what was going on, there was no other possible reason for its repeated presence, and that made both Danny and the master even more nervous and irritable.

At about six o'clock, with the sun dipping towards a clear western horizon but with a big black bank of cloud crowned with anvil shapes climbing the sky in the east, Danny declared it would work, they were ready. They were back on his refurbished bridge and the master went immediately over to a large, ornate but functional barometer that Danny had picked up in a Road Town chandler's. He tapped it, marked the arrowed hand's jerk to the left, said: '*Con este tiempo, no vale.*'

The swell was rising and not just with the tide. The wind had begun to gust; the whole operation could take an hour at least, and by then they could be in the middle of a storm or worse. Danny, big, strong, anxious and angry, took him by the lapels and shook him. He felt like a bag of bones.

'You tell your fucking mate to get your fucking boat alongside in ten minutes or I'll drop you in the water. Right?'

It took twenty. With huge piles of cumulus gold and red where they reflected the setting sun, purple and black beneath where squalls already cruised towards them, with the wind whipping spray off the rises of the swell, *La Bruja* nudged the biggest fenders the Santa María could put out, and Danny crossed his fingers as he felt the whole rig shudder. The lifting gear was already over the opened hatch to the rear of the superstructure, powered winches began to turn and the top of the container slowly rose into the black square. At the moment it was level with the fairings of the hatch, they all heard it – the scream of a supersonic jet hitting their ears without warning at the top of its pitch and volume.

It was a Dassault Mirage, its wings vertical, the lower tip scarcely more than ten feet above the wave crests, hurtling in a wide semi-circle round them at about, Danny reckoned, a distance of a full nautical mile. It was white, like a sea bird, silhouetted against the squalls, catching the last of the sun and so brightly lit that for a moment they could see how the markings on its upper wing surfaces had been masked. Then the wings flattened and it climbed almost to the zenith, turned in a high roller-coasting loop away from them so it was little more than a speck, but, just when they thought it had gone, it swooped back down towards them. At three miles it was back over the sea, and they saw the flash of the white slug under its lean belly as it dropped clear and ignited, then the wings in full dart-like configuration again against the blackness and it was gone again up, way up, away. But not the missile, the Exocet. Danny had time to listen to ten bars of the James Last Orchestra playing *In the Mood* before it struck. Time to wish it had been Glenn Miller.

It passed between the piers of the rig and hit *La Bruja* on the beam between the superstructure and the stern, exploded in the space beneath the suspended container. Steel-melting temperatures were achieved in less than three seconds, fifty armed and fuelled Nutcracker missiles detonated almost simultaneously, and the already white-hot sides of the ship ballooned outwards. The nearest piers supporting the rig buckled and twisted like burning snakes, and the whole platform toppled into the inferno the ship had become. A mushroom cloud, not atomic, but big enough, climbed into the stormy sky.

There were no survivors.

At Boa Vista, sixty miles down the Amazon and in Brazil, Feijoo met up again with Paco, the Tukanoan Indian shaman he had met on a tributary of the Putumayo five weeks before, and was introduced to a trader, some of whose ancestors were Indians from Portuguese Goa, and agreed with him in principle the terms under which plastic barrels filled with pasta but described as palm oil would be shipped downriver to Manaus. He then made the mistake of returning upriver to the airport of Tabatinga. The problem was that, having spent one day on a paddle steamer going downstream, he decided he preferred just the one-day trip back and then the flight to another five days on board. It was a mistake because by then his trail had been picked up, and the tiny airport was watched, as indeed was the larger one back over the border in nearby Leticia.

Unaware of the danger he was now in he waited for an hour in the airport lounge, relaxed with a beer, watched the brown, scantily clad Brazilians turn the departure areas and bar into an improvised dance hall with spoons, glasses, bottles and a couple of guitars. Not long before departure a young man, neat in white short-sleeved shirt with dark well-pressed trousers, came over to him and asked to see his passport again. Just a routine check. He flipped over the pages of the green booklet, appeared to examine the visas, handed it back with a smile that was reassuring and deferential. Only then did Feijoo see that the left side of the man's face was blotched with a large, ugly, strawberry-coloured burn mark.

Two hours later he was in Manaus after a spectacular flight down five hundred miles of river and swamps, forest and cattle country to the confluence of the Río Negro and the muddy Solimóes. He booked into the São Francisco, on the Avenida 7 de Setembro, took a swim in the small but clean swimming pool, changed, and took a taxi downtown to a bar on the edge of the red light district. There, in an ambience of sawdust, peeling paper, smells of urine and vomit, badgered by strangely endowed women to sample favours that promised originality if nothing else, he located and introduced himself to Gerónimo Carrión.

Carrión was tall, had a streaked beard, black and grey, masking a cadaverous face, wore a grubby linen suit whose sleeves were too short and exposed thin but arthritically lumpy wrists. Feijoo, always nervy, and by now suffering deep fatigue from nearly two months of not always comfortable travel, of constant danger, and difficult negotiations, found him worse than disconcerting. His chill presence in that bar galvanised not only the Guatemalan's habitual twitch, but also a horrid feeling of deep angst.

Carrión was *un cocinero*, a cook – a man who knew how to use potassium permanganate to oxidise out from the pasta the unwanted alkaloids, make toluol, the balsam of the tolú tree, work as a solvent, and hydrochloric acid fix the cocaine alkaloid into a stable crystalline salt – who could do all this and keep the balance right, not too sharp, not soapy . . . and Carrión was even better than your average run-of-the-mill *cocinero*: he had set up plants to do it, factories, not just kitchen stuff but on an almost industrial scale – gleaming vats, stainless steel flasks, producing *perica* of pharmaceutical quality, large, lambent, rocklike crystals, one hundred per cent pure. Just such a factory had he had in a Philadelphia suburb, processing pasta imported by a syndicate operating out of the Guajiro Peninsula of Colombia, betrayed by Arias and his colleagues, busted by the DEA and Centac in 1983 . . . Carrión had skipped a two-million-dollar bail-bond, was now down to his last ten grand, was looking for work.

It took Feijoo an hour, more than an hour, to convince him that work was what he had to offer. The trouble was that Carrión had been offered work often enough before, and always he turned it down. Before he touched it he had to believe that the project would be professionally run on a substantial scale, that it would not be undercapitalised, that it would be safe – both from the law and from the Colombians who were now his enemies – that the sources of pasta were reliable, and that the pasta would be of a minimum guaranteed quality and so on. He had a husky, dry light voice that was difficult to hear in the racket of the bar, and he spat frequently into the debris on the floor. Feijoo at first thought it was phlegm sloughed by coke sniffing, but later decided that Carrión was consumptive.

He achieved some sort of a deal at last – at any rate a promise to go on talking, at a different time and place, for a second meeting the following day. It was an appointment Feijoo was destined not to keep.

As he unlocked the door to his room in the São Francisco the light by the bed snapped on before he could find the main switch. Jorge Aguirre, large and robust, was slouched across the one armchair.

He pulled himself to his feet, lumbered towards Feijoo,

closed the small Guatemalan's shoulders in his huge paws and kissed him briefly on each cheek. 'Teseo, amigo. I am so sorry, I really am very sorry.'

Feijoo felt the harshness of his big moustache, smelt the rum on his breath.

'Sit down, why don't you? Have a drink.'

Ice chimed in a tall tumbler, rum then Coca-Cola followed. Feijoo took it in hands that were already clammy, shaking.

'Drink up, there's a good fellow.'

Round and through the transparent distorting cylinder, over the horizon of brown clear fluid with its bobbing slice of green lime and clicking cubes of ice, Feijoo saw Aguirre's jacket part, then the big Astra Magnum levelled. His dying brain registered the shattering glass, the explosion of liquor, but not the noise. He was dead before it reached him.

51

The Gates Lear crossed the barrier of the Jura Mountains at ten thousand feet, well below the commercial airlanes, lost height sharply over the Bielersee, and began the short run up the valley of the Aar towards Bern. Below, the valleys were green and lush with the new growth of spring, big mushroom-coloured cows drifted across flowery meadows, and the larches and birches were hazed with pale but brilliant green. Even the endless industrial estates of tidy drab factories looked a touch less drab than usual. Yet in front of and above the small plane the massive northern faces of the Bernese Oberland were still sheeted with snow.

The PA system chimed, Avon calling, and the pilot murmured in a voice as smooth as Swiss chocolate: 'ETA at Bern airport just five minutes away. The temperature there is a pleasant sixteen degrees Celsius with hazy sunshine. I'm afraid the descent will be quite sharp so some auricular discomfort may be experienced. Please return to your seats and fasten your safety belts.'

'Shit. That was quick.' Rupert Bridge, sitting naked on the toilet in the tiny cubicle at the back of the plane, tightened his grip on Harriet's waist, and she, with her long white arms hanging down over his shoulders, pulled her chest closer into his, accelerated the rotation of her pelvis.

'Come on, come on, come *o-o-o-on*.'

She was riding a cocaine-high as powerful as any she had ever experienced, and any doubts about what she was doing had been burned off like paint beneath a blow torch. At that moment her brain was an ultra-finely tuned seeker and receiver of sensory stimulus, her body the machine tooled up to satisfy it. Her knees pressed on either side of his narrow waist but the pedestal was low and her long feet were firmly flat on the floor of the plane. Through their tender soles she could feel the increased vibration of the reversed engines, she could weight them, lift her spread bottom and swing herself round on him in spiralling circles. Then the wheels thudded and rumbled, the sudden deceleration made the knot their bodies were tied into lurch forward across the tiny space so she felt the door cold on her shoulder-blades, and the release came with a shriek of surprise and then whooping laughter.

But dressing was a scramble, with no time for a proper wash, with Albert Burke where they had left him in the passenger area bullishly smirking at that day's edition of the *Sun*, and awareness that outside Immigration and Customs officials were impatient to service them and the plane. By the time the three of them were ready to disembark Harriet felt she had stepped off cloud nine without a parachute. She stood at the top of the four fold-down steps and looked over the airfield. It was tiny: a squat control tower, portakabin offices, a row of hangars with light aircraft parked in front of them; low hills and no sign of the mountains.

'It's a touch squalid, isn't it?'

She felt no better in Hector's coffee-coloured Mercedes, which Pablo had driven out for them. The road angled round the airfield, through a drab mixture of industrialised agriculture and scattered concrete suburb. Presently it skirted a steep hillside, shared it with villas that pretended to be chalets, and a railway line. They passed a Migros supermarket that looked like a supermarket anywhere.

Rupert tapped out a number on the Vodaphone. The conversation was brief and one-sided.

'He's not in a good mood, I'm afraid. Wants you to see him

as soon as we get to the hotel. The psoriasis is back and he's due to meet Crystal at half two.'

'Oh shit.'

'And when the meeting's over it's back to the airport and a chopper up to Kaiseralp.'

Briefly they were on an urban clearway, then cobbles with oily green and cream trams. They skirted a river in a gorge and beyond it, ghettoed by the ox-bow, spires and domes, blocks of ancient buildings faced in the nineteenth-century stonework that signalled the burgeoning hegemony of commerce all over Europe. Presently they crossed the river.

'You know, sometimes you all make me feel like . . . a tart.' She said it with a forced laugh, intending to make a joke of it.

Hector's needs turned out to be closer to those of a small boy who has been plagued with bullies in the playground and incomprehensible nonsense from teacher than those of a cross tycoon: he was not looking for a slave he could shout at, but comfort and explanation. Still, Harriet reflected, this too is a role tarts are required to play. Tarts, secretaries, *mothers*. She dabbed his scabbed and suppurating back with cortisone ointment in a coal-tar base, listened to his litany of woe, looked over his shoulder at a view across the Aar which was advertised by the very name of the hotel they were in as beautiful but was filled by a cast-iron viaduct of no particular distinction. Beyond it lay a wooden suburb that could have been in Bonn or Prague or anywhere.

At least his welcome had been almost affectionate – relieved at any rate. 'My *yarak*,' he had cried, clasping both her hands in his cold fingers, head on one side almost smiling at her through his tinted glasses. 'My haggard. Always I fear you will not come to. You rake out, I know you do, but in the end you return, you wait on.'

She knew by now that a haggard is an adult hawk caught in the wild, but she couldn't resist saying that she certainly felt haggard, knew she looked a mess.

'My dear, you look fine as always, and once we are at Kaiseralp it will be a holiday for you. But first you see my focking spots are back, and before I go out I beg you to anoint them for me.' And so she did, and listened to him moan.

Everything, it seemed, was going wrong. Old sources of

product had failed, new ones had failed to materialise. The first half of the established route down which cocaine moved had been lost, the rest of it was clearly in serious danger. Reserves of capital to replace lost product and replace the means by which it could be moved into Britain were appallingly low. It was not just a question of a cutback in profits – profitability itself was a question. And almost worst of all, Teseo Feijoo had disappeared. Gone. Vanished. And that was serious, could be very serious indeed. He concluded: 'But at least it would seem that your friend Mulligan is not at the bottom of it all.'

Her finger, poised above his sacroiliac, hesitated then dabbed on. 'How can you be so sure of that?'

'Only one of these catastrophes is the result of police action, and even there there is no reason to suspect his intervention. The police in Genoa could have moved at any time: it was not evidence they required but motivation. For the rest, our Colombian colleagues' – he made the word sound like a bitter insult – 'are to blame. But it remains a mystery. How they knew. How did they know . . .?'

'What?'

But he shook his head, fell silent. She dabbed and smoothed on. 'I suppose all this is the reason why the psoriasis is back.'

'I told you. It is genetic.' His voice pitched higher, became more emphatic. 'It is not my fault.'

She let her finger linger, made a wide, soothing sweep with it. He brooded, head hunched forward, so she felt a tremor of tenderness over the sparse gingery hairs that climbed from the nape of his scrawny neck into the thatch of implanted yellow. Then the muscles tightened and the head jerked up.

'Mulligan has taken leave of absence. You know that?'

'No.' She felt her headache get worse. She should not have let Rupert give her coke on the plane, not let him . . . Oh Christ, why not? It had been a laugh – oh dear me no, more than a laugh, it had been a gas.

'Did you know Mulligan was on leave?' His voice was shrill again.

She made an effort 'Is he? I'm not surprised. He was upset, you know? That man Suk was a friend. What you did upset him – '

'I did not do it. I told you that. That I told you to tell him.'

'All right. But I'm not surprised Buck . . . Mulligan is pissed off, has gone on holiday.'

'Oh no.' Suddenly he swung round at her, caught her wrist. 'Oh no. People like Mulligan do not go on holiday. Never. He's working outside the framework, he must be. Why? How? What's he up to? Eh?'

She pulled away, rubbed her wrist. 'I don't know. And – '

'I know. I must not hurt you, I must not be rough, I must not do this or that . . .' The whine was now sardonic. 'But you must please listen. What does Mulligan think he can achieve, how does he think he can achieve anything, outside Eurac? What does he think he's playing at? Please. You must find out. Get in touch. Let me know.' He stood up, reached for his shirt. 'But now it's two o'clock and I have a meeting at half past. And at five we go out to Kaiseralp. Have you had lunch?'

Now he asks me. 'I had a ham sandwich on the plane.' She giggled at the memory.

'Good.'

He pulled on his shirt, white with a blue pin-stripe. On the bed was a dark blue suit pin-striped in white. Christ, thought Harriet, he's trying to look like an English City gent. Perhaps because he remembers that I told him in Southampton he should look continental, he thinks that here he should look British. Too late to do anything about it now.

He knotted a tie. Royal Air Force, for Christ's sake. 'But you must tell us what Mulligan is up to.'

A three-minute walk across Casinoplatz and Theaterplatz took him into Marktgasse and Lili Brel's offices, which were above the Bauercreditbank and opposite the new Bern office of the Banco de Corpus Cristi. She had the top floor of what had been the town mansion of a seventeenth-century burgher but refaced outside and rebuilt inside several times since. A small boardroom that overlooked the discreet charm of one of the most laid-back financial and commercial sectors in Europe was conventional apart from the large Miró that hung over the marble fireplace. In the rear a small suite of offices housed a personally trained staff of five, three women and two men, who monitored the various operations she was running. Outside, the brass plate announced CommConsol (Bern), AG. A smaller one beneath it had one word only: Crystal.

Malatesta had already taken the seat at the head of the table. He sat slumped in a grey suit made of thick worsted that made him look like a large doll a child has dressed in real clothes. But his eyes, set in a face seamed and pitted like ancient granite and much the same colour, glinted with malevolent intelligence. Brel and Boltana were on either side of him facing each other. Myklades hesitated, wished not to seem to be making an ally of one over the other, took the seat furthest away, opposite the ancient European.

Malatesta spoke for ten minutes. His voice rattled like gravel shaken in a sieve, occasionally rose to a complaining whine. Crystal's coffers were almost empty at precisely the moment when he had expected them to be full. A lot of expensive but sound groundwork had been done, the Movement was now poised. Elections were pending in the United Kingdom, Spain, Italy, and Portugal. It was vitally important to keep up the pressure in France. There were very many smaller calls on their resources: one example amongst many was that Crystal had been asked, through discreet channels, to help with Barbie's defence in Lyon. And poor Kurt in Austria was by no means yet entirely out of trouble even though they had done much to finance adequate media support for him abroad as well as at home.

Just as important, and just as expensive, was the ideological warfare they had been waging for five years. Already their orchestrated campaign in the media had developed an atmosphere that was congenial to the principles of National Socialism: the economics of the New Enlightenment, new research in genetics, race, and sociobiology, much of it financed by Crystal, the reinterpretation of the years 1920–1945 as a crusade against Communism betrayed by American and British fellow travellers and Jews – all these had contributed to re-establishing the intellectual respectability of what they believed. It was no longer interpreted as an act of intellectual terrorism if a TV or newspaper commentator espoused or propagated these principles.

But they were now on the threshold of the next phase, of re-creating the mass movement without which no real political power was possible. As they knew very well there was a three-pronged strategy for this and each prong was going to cost – cost millions – and that was the reason why he and his associates had gone to Boltana, and eventually Mendoza, and out of many months of secret discussions devised the means by which Crystal would be fuelled with coke money.

The old man lent forward, nose and huge chin stretched out, curtains of loose skin hanging beneath, and the collar of his jacket rose behind his neck almost to ears whose lobes were also stretched and droopy. 'One. Through channels like our satellite TV company, Star Charge, and acquisition by Iris Publications of organs with mass appeal we will achieve in the working classes and petty bourgeoisie the shift in thinking that we have already created in the intelligentsia. This sort of shift has already taken place, without our help, in the media with mass appeal, particularly in the cheaper press, in the English-speaking world – proof, if we needed it, that we are working with the current of history, not against it. With the sort of financial backing that can buy newspapers and TV networks we can do the same in the heartlands of Europe.'

He sighed wheezily, not out of emotion but to reoxygenate blood thinned by the effort all this was costing him. 'Two. We have to finance and restructure the existing parties of the Right so that they are ready to harness this resurgence of popular fascism and give it political reality. This, of course, is not an aim in Britain or America, partly because the current American and British governments are already perceived to be the political expression of this ideology. Of course this is not so: they merely reflect some useful aspects of it. More import-ant, we have learnt the lessons of history, know that in those countries more can be achieved through entryism, through the infiltration of the Conservative and Republican parties by determined, politically motivated men and women, than through the creation of mass parties. In Europe, however, mass parties have been organised in the past and will be again, but only if they are properly funded.'

He shifted his frail body back, his chin sank to his chest, his thin brown fingers wiped spittle from the corners of his thin down-turned lips. Boltana also shifted, turned his big head slightly away from the old man, contrived to conceal a yawn. The corners of Brel's mouth lifted in a tiny but sympathetic smile. They had both heard it all before, at length. It was admirable in a way that the old man could do it, hold it all together in his mind, keep the message, the admonitions, the exhortations to do better clear and fluent: but he had had a lot of practice, was doing it by heart. Myklades alone listened intently. He was not a member of the Crystal board, was only occasionally allowed to be present at the deliberations of its inner cabal. His eyes behind the tinted Dior spectacles remained totally expressionless though unblinkingly alert. Whether it meant anything at all to him, whether or not the sounding board of his own vanity and ambition resonated to this message, was a secret he kept to himself

The voice rattled on. 'The third prong of our strategy is to attack the opposition by whatever clandestine means we can. We have already made effective use of infiltration of social democratic parties especially in Germany, of *agents provocateurs* to stir up suspicion and fear of the Left in Britain and France and Spain. We have resorted to assassination when no other way of removing a menace could be found, most notably in Scandinavia. By financing movements like the Guerrilleros de Cristo Rey, and the Ulster Protestants, we have made sure that the consensus politics of the liberal and left centre are constantly revealed to be impotent in the face of permanent crisis.

'But the time is now upon us when we must launch the series of spectacular events that we have planned for so long, which will alert the common man and woman to the new factor that has entered the political equation, a force that declares that the deep pride every truly human, truly Aryan man and woman can have in the power of their race and nation need no longer be denied . . .' The beaked nose and chin came up again out of the shoulders which dropped away, and the collar too quested sharply to right and left as he reached for this peroration, then suddenly shrank back again, and the voice died to a hoarse whisper. 'The first of these . . . will take place . . . in a few days' time. It alone will cost three million Swiss francs . . .' – the hands twisted upwards, the fingers bent clawlike over the palms – '. . . and I am not sure the money is there.'

Lili Brel looked at the tiny gold watch on her slender wrist., and again the detached smile lit her pale eyes. 'Well, some of it will be.' She stood, smoothed her Chanel skirt, moved to the big window. The three men followed her. At the end of the street, much of it a pedestrian precinct beneath a tiled roof with an almost pagoda-like sweep, the gold fingers on the big dial of the Zytgloggeturm reached three o'clock. Chimes and glockenspiel music spilled out over the subdued noise of the traffic. From under an arch in the stone arcade across the way a small procession emerged into the lemon light of the hazy spring sun: two dark-suited men each carrying two steel and chrome cases, two men in dark blue uniforms, peaked caps, boots, with heavy revolvers on their hips on either side and very slightly behind. A policeman on a two-litre BMW watched and murmured into his radio. They skirted the small, prettily gilded fountain in the middle of the road and passed out of the view of the watchers above, into the arcade again.

Lili sighed. 'Seven hundred thousand five hundred and eighty-six Swiss francs. The net contribution of Mendoza Holdings to the account of Crystal this week.'

Boltana breathed: 'The interface. Minimum of paperwork. No traceable electronic fund transfer, just good old hard cash, transferred from the numbered account of one Swiss bank to another.'

Brel's smile became a subdued laugh. 'They tell me it's the same notes each time: they keep a stock in the Banco de Corpus Cristi . . . Oh. Oh no.'

She turned from the window, a little paler than before. Boltana murmured: 'Lili?'

She touched his hand. 'Later.'

Malatesta blew his hooked beak of a nose: 'Nevertheless. Three months ago it took four men and eight cases. I want to know how you propose to halt what is beginning to look like an unfortunate trend.'

They moved back to the table, took their places again.

'Well,' said Brel, already recovered from whatever it was had bothered her, 'the first step is already in train. Senator Arias, and many other Ariases, arrive this evening, as you know. What we have to decide are the parameters of the deal we are going to try and put together this time.'

Boltana rumbled: 'Hector, I think the ball is in your court.'

Myklades squinted up at the Miró, black blobs on a deep crimson background, with flashes of bright, carefully contoured colour. It looked like the essence of a bad dream, but erotic too. He took off his spectacles, cleaned them, and speculated. For Brel to hang it in her boardroom it must be pricey. But why? Perhaps Harriet would know. He felt a tremor of anguish deep in the cold recesses of his heart at the thought of his haggard, his falcon . . .

He replaced the spectacles, sighed, cleared his throat. 'I suppose so. In a sense. But I must disclaim responsibility for what has happened. And at the same time I must warn you not to minimise the consequences. We have lost' – he tapped his fingers – 'thirteen million pounds sterling with the confiscation of the *Gelada Fini*'s cargo; eight hundred and forty-four thousand pounds sterling worth of Kapp-Duxbury arms, which would have ultimately realised for us, in about August this year, cocaine worth ninety million pounds. Plus a shrimp-processing rig which, quite apart from its usefulness, earned us legitimate money too. Worst of all, since Teseo Feijoo cannot be found, we must suppose that the alternative source of product he was negotiating will fail us.'

He shifted in his seat, pulled a sheet of paper from an inside pocket, unfolded it, but did not refer to it. His pale eyes continued to search the Miró for meaning, but his voice droned on, guttural, breathy.

'In spite of all this and as a result of careful forward planning, and the establishment of secure stockpiles of prod-uct, we can keep the operation running at a reduced rate until the end of August, and we expect to bank with Mendoza Holdings the sort of sums you have just seen moved across the street below. But by August thirty-first we will be dead. Unless we can, after all, rebuild bridges with Arias.

'The questions are: how much do we buy, and what are we now prepared to pay? First. How much? I spoke just now of how we are now operating at a reduced level of activity. This is creating, inevitably, a vacuum in the market which other suppliers now reemerge to fill. If, in September, we wish to regain what slice of the market we may have lost, I think we must be prepared to embark on a brief campaign, say up to Christmas, of selling large amounts of product at a reduced price, possibly even a heavily reduced price . . .'

He droned on for five more minutes, came to his conclusion. 'To re-establish a money flow equivalent to that we had in January, to regain lost ground, we must, therefore, ask Arias to come up with one and a half tons by the end of August.

How much you will pay for this, and by what means, are for you to decide. That is not my concern.'

He refolded his sheet of paper, and his long pale freckled fingers came back into view holding a muted orange pack of Yeni Harman. He lit one, and Brel's nostrils twitched at the fragrance of the very best Bafra tobacco.

She looked round the table, tapped its surface with a gold pencil. 'Two points. First. Hector Myklades is in error to disclaim responsibility for what has happened. It was he who argued so cogently at Plancenoît that we should move away from Arias. I would guess that most of the trouble we are now in arises precisely from that decision. And second. If Arias asks for the price before or on delivery, and of course he will, then we have some very serious thinking to do . . .'

Boltana rumbled: 'Lili. You know very well that I will not cross bridges in advance. We will not discuss how we will pay until we know what we will pay. For that reason you must come to Kaiseralp with us – '

'No. You can speak to me here on this.' She tapped what looked like an ordinary if stylishly modern handset. 'It's a radiophone with variable frequencies and a scrambler.'

'Come, Lili. What nonsense is this?'

'Outside, just now, the girl who we used to think was a paparazzo was watching the money transfer. I have asked you before to check her out and no one has. Perhaps now Bridge is here' – she nodded at Hector – 'something will be done. But in the meantime I am sticking to the rule I insisted on when all this started. I will not be seen to associate with cocaine pedlars. Neither wholesale, nor' – and the smile she offered Myklades was not soft – 'retail.'

52

Towards dusk, on the same day, a privately owned DC 8 touched down, like the Gates Lear, at Bern airport. Two silver-grey Mercedes 500 SEL, a Volkswagen minibus, and an unconverted VW van were waiting for it in the tiny parking area outside the terminal. Bern airport could well be the smallest in the world for a capital city and this convoy had effectively blocked public access to it for half an hour. No one minded a lot. The last of the charter planes that arrive during the day had been cleared an hour before; the private individuals and members of the flying club who are the main users of the field have their own parking places.

Nor were the Customs or police much bothered. The arrivals owned companies in Switzerland. They were on a short visit that would take them up to a private resort in the Bernese Oberland, and then back out again. If they had drugs with them, gems, even arms, these would stay with them, and leave with them: so long as they remained insulated from the regions they passed through what they had with them was their business and not that of the Swiss authorities. The philosophy that makes Switzerland still the best though by no means the cheapest place to have a truly private bank account wrapped the new arrivals as invisibly and as effectively as Athene's cloak protected Odysseus.

Even so the travellers were not at ease. There is still something about Europe that tends to abash visitors from the New World, even when they are as wealthy as even the wealthiest Europeans, even though their European surname, traced in direct descent, goes back to pre-Columbian times. And so, as the N6 motorway gently unravelled in front of them, Octavio Arias de Quesada and his wife Serena came to a rare truce in the war of attrition that gave their relationship structure and meaning, and joined together in finding that the landscape was similar to that round Bogotá, that the incidence of roadworks was almost as high.

The shadows were lengthening over the steeply terraced vineyards of Spiez, halfway up the southern shore of the Thunersee, when the convoy switched to the relatively minor road that climbs the Kander valley past Reichenbach where Holmes and Moriarty tumbled to everlasting fame. At Frutigen, the small but busy little town that services the two valleys that debouch there, they followed the signs for Adelboden – 'Noble Earth'. With no railway, and only a single road which at times has to tunnel into the mountainside, and at other times is a single track hugging the cliff face beneath avalanche barriers, Adelboden is the least spoilt of the Bernese Oberland resorts. Not that the Arias entourage ever saw it.

A mile short of the village, and in gathering gloom, the

convoy swung left, was presently churning dung-streaked slush along a winding narrow road that skirted pine-edged meadows, threaded across and back over a stream that the melting snow had turned into a storming torrent. Everywhere there were signs of the first real thaw of spring: big cows with swinging udders and clanging bells hung from broad worn leather straps meandered reluctantly back to the barns where they had spent the winter; though the new grass had not yet sprouted, the meadows themselves were only rarely streaked with snow, and in odd tussocks close to the fences the first tiny Alpine daffodils with swept-back outer corollas caught the last gleams of the sun as it dipped behind the western massif.

The road climbed and headlights swung restlessly over larger patches of snow, briefly illuminated deeply eaved wooden farmhouses and denser woods of tall firs, until at last they reached the cable-car station which services Kaiserlap. As the convoy slid into the carpark Octavio murmured: 'Well. We have come to the right place.'

Serena yawned, simulated curiosity. Knowing that it would not be easy to get a drink between Bern and the Kaiserlap Hotel, she had dosed herself with Valium before the aircraft touched down. 'Why do you say that?'

'That's Malatesta's car.'

Again the feelings of inadequacy, the certainty that whatever he did here, on this side of the ocean, would somehow be upstaged, brought actual bile into Octavio's throat. He got out, massive in furs, felt the rasp of pure but chilly air on his chest and quickly lit a cigar. Around him, they assembled: plump Felipe Cortazar, his shrill-voiced financial adviser, a maid for Serena, two valets, four bodyguards, and four drivers who also doubled as minders. They were already stamping the ground against the sudden cold, banging gloved hands, and the vapour of their breaths faded above their heads.

Arias toyed with the idea of ordering one of his thugs to kick in the elegantly sculpted rear panel of the sedanca body of Malatesta's ancient Rolls but thought better of it. A small group of men had appeared at the top of the railed steps that led into the cable-car station. In the centre of it Rupert Bridge pressed Albert Burke's elbow. 'He's brought a small army with him. That's really not very friendly, you know?'

Arias shifted his cigar into his left hand and took his wife's thin elbow. '*Vámonos, querida.* But we stop five yards short of those steps and make the bastards come down to us. Right?'

But even this gesture was lost, for just as they reached that point a photo flash seared their eyes, coming from beneath the giant tilted wheel round which the moving part of the cable-car machinery ran. She was quick, very quick. Long-legged, her leather coat flapping behind her like wings, she reached the safety of her pale blue Renault 4 before the fastest of the Colombians could reach her. The engine was running and in gear. A sallow-faced man behind the wheel slipped the clutch as she tumbled into the back seat, and they were gone, spewing slush and sheets of icy water, down the hill, into the gloom of the woods.

Arias was furious, swore in Spanish, then English. 'Who the fuck was that?'

Rupert achieved suavity. 'Just a newspaper. Not important. We know who it is and we'll see it goes no further.' He chewed his bottom lip. 'We'll see to it.'

'Teseo Feijoo is not here, then?' Arias grinned knowingly, remained standing in one of the small boardrooms that had been set aside on the first floor for the serious business of the weekend. His heavy hands rested on the back of an upright chair and his eyes drifted past Boltana's head, their attention momentarily caught by the black and white hang-glider drifting across the top corner of the big picture window. It soared and circled, brilliant against the blue of the morning sky above the sharp line of the Wildstrubel, but much closer.

Behind him Felipe Cortazar's voice fluted: 'Who are we dealing with, then?'

Boltana smiled, a fat cat offered cream. 'You? You will be talking about the details to my associate Hector Myklades.' He gestured behind him and the tall Armenian, his neck still wretchedly raw with scabs and lesions, moved forward. 'But first I think – don't you – that there are some aspects of all this that can only be settled between principals.'

Arias flinched. His head moved to the side, sought support.

'All right. If you insist. But Felipe stays here too.'

'No. We'll sort out the broad outlines eyeball to eyeball, just the two of us.' The smile was still there, but not in the voice or in the eyes. 'When we've done that – and I don't see that it need take more than an hour or so – then Hector and your man can check out the details.'

For all he felt psyched by the ambience, Arias was no weakling. He recognised the challenge, welcomed it. Stripped of all protocol, denied access to the mystifying world of hi-tech data-systems and the rest, this would be a very straightforward business, as simple as a pair of bar bullies Chinese wrestling. At the worst no more taxing than a poker game. There'd be some skill in it no doubt, the ritual of a slow start while each probed the other's resources, of bluff and assumed concession concealing the sudden pounce, but that had always been what made real business interesting, exciting, the way it used to be before the smartasses moved out of the woodwork of business schools.

He grinned back. His large hand stroked the morning smoothness of the cheek permanently tanned by equatorial sun and good living to the colour of best calf's liver, thick fingers squeezed his bottom lip. He shrugged.

'Okay.' He half turned his big head, jerked it. '*Fuera*. Be on call.'

Felipe shuffled out. Myklades paused at the door.

'I'll be in my room, Marqués, when you want me.' He dabbed his neck with a handkerchief.

Boltana swung a chair out from the big oval table, sat, let a limp leather document holder slap on to the surface in front of him, unzipped it and pulled out three large sheets of thick cream paper, satin finished, bound with red tape. He cleared his throat. 'The agreement you signed with my nephew in Bogotá five months ago. Right?'

Arias nodded. Boltana slowly tore the sheets in half, then tried to compound the gesture by tearing them again, but the paper was now too thick. Arias smiled to himself, wriggled his big buttocks into the leather of his chair, put his elbows on the table. It was a trivial thing, certainly, but already this Spanish grandee, this head of one of Europe's largest banks, had overreached himself.

Serena Arias clad in eau-de-nil silk pyjamas drifted through airy spaces, past giant windows that looked out on to sunlit snowfields sculpted by the winds into unblemished rises and slopes like Saharan sand-hills. Beyond, the rock broke through: grey or the colour of dark honey, and climbed to the peaks and escarpments above. In two places where the snow clung to the slopes of smoother combes spidery pylons linked by looping cables carried chairlifts out of sight beyond the lower bluffs and salients.

She moved on through public rooms where a cleaner polished tables or a footman cleared coffee-cups and the debris of breakfast. They watched her with mute curiosity. The Hotel Kaiseralp is not small, and though the combined parties amounted to nearly thirty people they were easily lost in its spaces – those who were not already out, heading for the slopes, or taking up watchful positions from vantage points that overlooked the floor of the cirque, and the cable car.

In one room the pungency of harsh uncut Virginian stabbed at her nostrils: Felipe Cortazar stumbled to his feet. She paused, head on one side, and listened. Beyond the high panelled door behind him she caught the rumble of her husband's voice. She nodded sagely to herself and floated away again, back the way she had come, but then on and down the curving stairs carpeted in crimson with iron and ormolu banisters. From a large reception area she peered through doors with bevelled glass panels, past ferns and yucca plants, to a bar, but at just gone ten o'clock the spaces beyond the counter were still caged in metal. Wearily she addressed herself again to the climb back.

Back in her room Serena sat for a moment at her dressing-table, pushed a silver-backed brush through her thinning hennaed hair, retouched her full but permanently scowling lips, smoothed more foundation into the wrinkles round her cold green eyes. She looked, she knew, fifteen years older than she was, and it didn't really bother her: not as long as the fire, the anger, and the intelligence still looked back at her from her mirror. Not so long as she could still see there a distant recollection of the daughter she had lost.

A shadow, lilac-coloured in the sunlight, floated across the fine lawn curtains, and then below her on the terrace she heard the scrape of metal chairs pushed back and voices raised. A two-stroke engine fired, purred. Then another. She got up again and looked down, out and across the snow dunes. Two glossy crimson snowmobiles broke away from the building, towing sledges with skis. On the first two figures she could not identify. On the second her son-in-law and his new fiancée. The shadow tracked out across the snow after them. Serena, her eyes screwed up against the glare, sought out of the sky the hang-glider, swooping back again after its soaring flight above the chasms of the valley beyond the escarpment. Its arrowed dragon wings drummed in its slipstream; the helmeted goggled pilot swung below, his body sheathed in a padded cocoon against the cold.

She fantasised him into a bird of prey, swooping towards the second crimson snowmobile, a crushable scuttling bug. Talons and a cutlass of a beak shredded muscle and purple offal out of torn bodies like the condors she had once known, high in the Andes, long ago.

'Have you ever been in a chairlift like this before?'

'No.'

'Well, just fall back into it as the edge of the seat hits your behind, let it scoop you up.'

Cables purred and metal clanked, the double chair swooped, caught them, lurched up.

'Shit. I nearly dropped my sticks.'

'But you didn't.'

'What happens at the top?'

'It drops you at the top of a short slope and you have to ski off. If you don't the people behind run into you.' Harriet glanced back. Pedro and Europa. Fairy prince and princess. Except they seemed to have less and less to say to each other. The chairs climbed on above gullies and morasses, then followed the serrated edge of a ridge. The deepest parts of the snow-filled declivities were marked with twisting black lines in which brown water gleamed.

Jana too looked back. 'Can they hear us?'

'No.'

'Listen. I have to thank you. For sending those photos of her royal whatsit. They're checking out just like you said they would. And it's not just her face, you know. I got sometime on my own with her when we were here last. At the swimming pool. Boy, did they put her through hell. I mean when she was little. She told me a bit about it.'

'Still. She's lovely now.'

'Sure. But man-made. Hey. Will you just look at that? That guy is good.'

The hang-glider slipped down the air above them, cut a wide swathe above the cables, then dipped, banked, and arced beneath them.

'Listen. That was something. It may not have looked much but he came a lot closer than he should have and then risked a stall to turn so sharp. He's good, and crazy with it.'

Harriet shivered. 'Gives me the creeps though.'

'Yeah. I know what you mean. Weird. Never says a word, just looms up on you and gives it you straight from those hard blue eyes. Looks like this is where we get off.'

At the top, with the Oberland spread about them, crags and massifs jutting up out of indigo haze for twenty, forty miles around them, and the glacier of the Wildstrubel glistening almost on a level with them on their left, they paused for a moment, taking it all in.

Pedro joined them, pointed out and named, with some inaccuracy, the more notable peaks that could be seen, then he and Europa pushed off and began the descent, weaving back and forth, crossing and recrossing each other's tracks. Harriet and Jana followed, but slowly, and with occasional tumbles. Halfway down they stopped. Below them, at the start of the chairlift, where the snowmobiles were parked, the hang-glider had finished dismantling his craft, and put on skis just as Pedro and Europa came up with him. A moment or two, then, as if a chemical reaction had taken place, as if molecules had separated into atoms which recombined in response to some law of nature, Pedro climbed into one of the snowmobiles, while Europa and Walther von Sachs, the pilot in whom, according to Malatesta, the spirit of the Teutonic Knights still lived, made for the chairlift.

They came up with Jana and Harriet, only moments after they had got to the bottom of the piste.

Jana asked: 'What happened to Pedro then? It's not his knee, is it? He'll be needing some physio if it is.'

Europa pushed up her goggles, shook spun gold out of her cornflower eyes. 'No, not his knee. He doesn't like the snow. It's melting. Too thick, he says. And also some danger of avalanche. But Walther doesn't mind.' She turned to the tall, strong-looking German, still in the close-fitting rubberised suit he'd worn when hang-gliding. It was white, with flame-shaped black stripes. 'You don't, do you?'

He barely shook his head, his face still goggled and reflecting the snowscape above a blond moustache which was all you could really see of him, then he turned and headed back to the lift.

Jana sighed. 'Nevertheless, I'd better go and see to his highness.'

'Yes, would you?' Europa smiled. 'Take the snowmobile. We'll ski back.'

As they unloaded their skis at the hotel Jana suddenly straightened, threw her hand across her eyes against the glare, and bit her lip.

'What is it?'

'New arrival.'

Two or three hundred yards off, a man was striding down the path of trodden snow from the cable-car station. In a black loose-fitting greatcoat that flapped about him, and moon boots, he was big, burly, dark-haired, tanned.

'He's not one of our people. So I suppose he must be Colombian.'

'Yeah. I know him. Jorge Aguirre – and bad news, let me tell you. Bad news.' She turned to Harriet, put her hand on the English girl's shoulder. Their eyes met and held for a moment. 'Listen. You did me a good turn. Let me do you one. Things, you know? All this. It's all falling apart. It's gone. Right in the centre. Like a big tree with rot in the middle of it. I'm not telling you any more, but believe me I know. Get yourself a chute and work out where you're going to fall. Okay?' She squeezed, smiled, turned. 'Hi there, Georgie. You look fit.'

53

'You have not been taking many photographs.'

'No.'

'Why not?'

'A Colombian hoodlum told me to take my camera back to my room when I came out with it.'

'Fock him. He had no business to do that. Bloddy liberty. I want photographs as usual. Of me, with them if possible, all of them, the Colombians as well, and if not then on the same strip of negative. Ouch. I will not look pretty in them, but there will be no mistaking me in this condition. It's bad, eh?'

'Much worse than yesterday. Does this stuff do any good at all?'

'It brings temporary relief. Lovejoy says it's the best around.'

'Your skin's cracking on the backs of your knees, on your heels – '

'And on the soles. Sometimes it is painful to walk.'

'Turn round.'

'I can do the rest.'

'You might as well let me.'

He turned. Harriet had been on her knees to do the backs of his thin legs; now she looked up at him and briefly he took her cheeks in his hands. Normally cold and clammy, they felt hot and dry. She could not resist a shudder, had to pull back.

He sighed, looked at his palms. 'Stigmata, eh? And you are my Mary Magdalene anointing me with precious ointment. Not so precious though. It costs only three pounds a tube.' The sigh came again, with a hint of desperation. 'How can anything so cheap be any use? I am keeping you indoors. You should be out skiing.'

'I had a good run this morning. Now it's slush on top. The skin's even cracking in here.' She ran her finger down the tightening groove of his groin into the mat of foxy pubic hair.

He sighed again, added a guttural, rueful laugh, which ended as an apologetic snigger. 'Either stop. Or go on. You know what I mean. I don't mean . . . focking, just . . .'

She felt the tremor of pity spiced with angst he could sometimes inspire in her. She kept her voice even. 'All right. You lie on the bed, I'll sit beside you.'

He did as she suggested, but went on: 'Mulligan is in Adelboden. Did you know that? Has he been in touch with you? No. But this is interesting. A woman, apparently a photographic journalist, has been bothering the Mendozas for two months. Burke went down to check her out and found her talking to Mulligan. There. Does he always recruit photographers? There would be a sort of logic in it if he did. You are doing that well. Quite well.'

She was pleased he had mentioned Mulligan. It was nice to think of him while she did what Myklades wanted. With the thought of both men in mind at once she could not suppress a tiny giggle. 'Mary Magdalene was a tart too, wasn't she?'

He caught her free hand. 'You are not my tart, Harry. You are my *yarak*.'

Later, dressed in his silk gown and smoking a Yeni Harman, Myklades sighed. 'Mulligan, you know, is the least of our worries. It is becoming clearer and clearer that there is a real traitor in the camp. Someone revealed our plans to find a second source of product to Arias. And there has been at least one other major leak. Who? One person or two? Working together or independently? Perhaps Mulligan knows. Perhaps you should see him again soon, perhaps you should see him here. See what you can find out. Not today, tomorrow perhaps, or the day after, when I have worked out the right approach. All right?'

A door or so away, Jorge Aguirre used a long handle geared to a ratchet to wind an awning down over the balcony of Serena's room, fixed it back into its bracket, turned back into the now shady room. Silver gleamed from looking-glass frames, from the backs of brushes and combs; the subdued light still glowed on cut-glass bottles of perfume and cologne. Serena Arias, still in eau-de-nil silk pyjamas, sat curled up but high on the bolsters at the end of the satin-covered bed, peered up at him over the tall glass of rum and lime he had given her.

'That's better. Thank you. Well?'

Jorge's even white teeth flashed down at her in a grin, and with thumb and finger he smoothed his heavy black moustache. 'I caught up with him in Manaus. Brazil. He was setting up a deal with a *cocinero*, Gerónimo Carrión – remember him?'

She nodded. 'And?'

The grin became broader, and he tapped the bulge in his left armpit.

'Both of them?'

'Sí, señora. And no bodies.' He shrugged. 'The piranhas of the Amazon are very ecological about waste . . .'

She nodded slowly and one painted fingernail traced the contour of her top lip. 'But that was, must have been, some weeks ago. Where have you been since?'

'The records office at LA. The Spanish archives at Simancas.'

'And?'

His face darkened, cloudy with suppressed anger and pity. He swung a chair into the bedside, sat on it, took her hand. 'Doña Serena. It is bad news. Both stories check out.'

Stillness spread from her across the room, then she sighed. 'Are you sure?'

'Sí, señora. In both places I hired professionals to look for me.' He let go of her hand, reached to the floor, came up with a box-like briefcase. 'I have photocopies of all the documents, and transcripts of the Spanish ones. They are not easy to read in the originals – '

'Just tell me the gist. I'll read them later. Start with the Spanish.'

'Sí, Doña Serena. There are five documents. The first is a deposition made to the Inquisitorial Tribunal in Jaen in 1497 in which a certain Don Jésus Arranda, formerly Joshua Ben Suleiman, successfully defended himself against the crime of *Marrania*, or secret Judaism. The second is a contract relating to the marriage between Anna-Maria Arranda, the second daughter of Jésus Arranda and Don Primero La Cerda, Conde de Pastrana. His daughter married the Mendoza who became the first Duke. The man who was your son-in-law when your celestial daughter was alive, has Jewish blood. He's a Kike. But that's not all.'

'Go on. The police department in Los Angeles.'

'Again our informant's information was accurate. The file is stored on computer but I was able to get a printout with surprising ease. I felt that the way had been prepared for me by someone who had influence. The file is in the form of a report made by William Nulty, detective lieutenant in Homicide. It has an appendix which includes sworn statements from witnesses. The gardener, Ángel Ortega, amongst others, records that there was a terrible row between Mendoza and Octavia, but he alone is specific about some of the things said.

You see, he was the only one there who understood Spanish. You remember, Mendoza never denied the quarrel, but said it was about Octavia's extravagance, and that he bitterly regretted it . . .?'

She was lying back now, chin in the air, the loose prematurely wrinkled skin momentarily tightened, eyes closed. She raised a hand. 'I remember. Go on.'

'Ángel says that in his hearing there was no mention of money at all. But that she attacked him. They had never made love. She had found out why not, why he had not been able. Forgive me, Doña Serena, that I should utter this filth to you. But she had discovered that her husband is a *maricón*, a pervert, he does it only with boys. A Jew and a pervert.'

The silence again. It was as if the thin, worn, raddled woman on the bed had gone into a coma. Jorge waited, leaned back now, thumbs in his belt, legs splayed. Head on one side he could hear distant noises: the clank of a ski-lift, the buzz of a snowmobile, the drip and slip of melting snow. Then his ear tuned to something else: a minute rustling, rhythmic, fast, in time with the tiny rise and fall of her pigeon chest.

The clawlike fingers clenched and relaxed. 'What else?'

He decided to be brisk, cut corners. 'The helicopter that buzzed her car was Mendoza's, and he was the pilot. This has significance. At the inquest the jury were instructed that no identification of the helicopter had been made. So, between Nulty's report, which included Angel Ortega's statement, and the inquest, decisions were made to protect Mendoza. I had a private dick trace Nulty and ask him about this: he said, why not. Mendoza claimed he was following Octavia to try to persuade her to return, to ask her forgiveness. There was no way he could see Mendoza had deliberately caused the accident . . .'

'But he did.'

'Sure he did. Always I said so. I have said so always.'

'Yes, Jorge, you have.' She opened her eyes. 'You're a good boy.'

'So, shall I waste the bastard?' He touched the Astra Magnum nestling between his thick arm and huge chest.

She sighed. 'Not yet, Jorge, not yet.'

'Doña Serena, why not? Please!'

'Wait, wait.' She reached for her drink, finished it, handed him the glass. No question but that he was doing the right thing by getting up and refilling it. 'Did you find out any more about who gave us these leads?'

'No.' He dropped ice on to the bottom of the glass. 'It's someone close to Mendoza, and possibly someone who has an in into police networks. They certainly were ready for me in LA.'

'Could be the photographer woman. Jones.'

'Don't know her.' The pleading in his voice became more pronounced. 'Listen. Why don't I kill him now?'

She gave a short bitter laugh. 'Because Don Octavio believes his udder still has a few million in it waiting to be milked.'

Jorge shrugged stoically, handed her the refilled glass.

'It's going to be a few million more than we expected.' The voice seemed to rumble out of the huge back that almost filled the lower part of the tall window. Above it the afternoon sunlight flashed from the needles and crags to the east of the Steghorn, and, reflected, glowed translucently along the crust of ice that was forming over the shadowed snowfields below. Boltana turned, sucked smoke from his cigar, let it billow round his glossy head, uttered a short bark of a laugh into the radiophone handset he was holding. 'There's some good news too, but I'll tell you the main outlines first. He won't shift less than two tons, and he won't take less than thirty dollars a gram. Those two factors are not negotiable; the details may be.'

Brel's voice, made strangely featureless by scrambling devices, murmured in his ear as she read off the data her brain was programmed to produce without effort. 'Ninety million Swiss francs. How? When?'

'Well . . . he wants ten now, before we leave. An instantly negotiable financial instrument.'

'Dollars.'

Boltana sighed. 'Yes.'

Brel was brisk. 'That we can do. On the Tortola account. It'll take a telephone call or two, a little readjustment, but basically no problem.'

'EFT to a Panama account? He wants it cleared before we leave.'

'Certainly. No problem. And the next payment?'

'He wants us to charter a banana boat, ex-Santa Marta, approximately twentieth July. It'll be clear of the Caribbean and well out of Mirage range forty-eight hours later. He suggests we put an agent on board to check out the cargo, and if we approve it then we pay up the next thirty. If he doesn't get it within six hours the boat turns back. Our boat. His crew. Hector says that won't do but the details are negotiable and he and Cortazar are working on them. Incidentally' – Boltana put an edge on his voice – 'Poor Teseo is no longer available.'

He let the silence lengthen, waited. Brel broke it. 'Oh?'

Boltana's massive head shifted into a still noble profile: like that of one of the older and more competent Roman emperors. 'Aguirre found him in Manaus on the Amazon and killed him.' He sighed. 'I'm sorry, but it is not a surprise after four weeks' silence. And in a way it was his own fault. It was a harebrained scheme.' He allowed Feijoo's memory a brief half-minute of silence. 'But it remains a mystery how he found him so soon, how they knew who he was dealing with.' Boltana sighed. 'Anyway. Final payment, the remaining twenty as soon as the boat enters European waters.'

'So. All of it. The full sixty million US dollars up front before we see a penny return.'

'That's right, Lili. But remember it will fetch three hundred and twenty million pounds sterling at current prices. And even if Hector follows his loss-leader policy until January on say the first two hundred and fifty keys, we should still clear a net profit – a net profit of not less than one hundred and fifty by the end of next year. And. And Arias has promised that if we can make this deal stick, our third attempt, he'll continue to trade on the same basis.'

'That's all very well. But if Hector is to continue to make regular substantial payments to Crystal, with no further reduction in the flow, he cannot possibly find ninety in Swiss francs by the third week of July, a total of one hundred and fifty by the middle of August.'

'Yes. He said that. And he reminded me that Ambrose cannot raise its turnover without more product to sell.'

Brel would not let go. 'And Enrico won't postpone. He's too old, has too little time left. Like Moses he's seen the Promised Land and he wants to get down there.'

In spite of everything Boltana laughed with something like good humour. 'I doubt if that's a comparison Enrico would find amusing. Nevertheless he may have to hang around on the top of Pisgah for a few months longer.'

'He won't wear that, I promise you. He'll cancel the engagement, pull Europa out. And that will make Pedro think again about the whole business. Especially now he doesn't have Feijoo to handle things for him. In fact as it is I can see him ditching Mendoza Holdings (Tortola) without Teseo to manage it. And if he does that we become very exposed.'

Boltana glowered, bottom lip thrust out, cigar clenched between podgy fingers on the arm of the chair: he had taken the point. After a moment or two he sucked in smoke again, grunted. 'All right. BCC will have to put out a bridging loan. You'll have to fix it, Lili, check out what the overall shortfall is, then talk to me about ways of doing it. Naturally it will have to be very well hidden. It's immaterial whether it's to MHT or Crystal, just so long as my shareholders can't track it down.' He relaxed a little. 'Right, now the good news. Arias wants arms. Under the counter. I offered him the whole of K-D, but he thought that was more than he needed. But he is prepared to shave fifteen dollars if we can meet a shopping list he'll give us. As I understand it K-D can manage most of it and K-D's connections in the arms world should look after the rest. Hector and young Rupert will have to look after that side of it.'

There was a pause. Brel's voice, when it came back, was dry. 'I'm surprised that people who can deploy Exocets at will need the sort of thing Kapp-Duxbury can provide.'

'There are two sides to that. In the first place Arias has convinced me that it was not he who Exoceted the rig. It was the Welsers. Someone had leaked to them not only the rig move, but the precise time when the K-D arms were to arrive. I believe him. There's a Welser in the Defence Ministry. The second side is this: the Colombian conservatives want to step up the dirty war against the guerrillas. The official police and counter-insurgency forces can't cope without going beyond the bounds set by the wets in the US Congress, which funds and arms them. So they're reorganising volunteer paramilitary cadres along SS lines, death squads and so on, but operating in the mountains and jungles as well as in the agricultural and urban areas. It's these we will be equipping now, not the other side.'

Brel laughed quietly, distantly. 'Well, that at any rate will warm whatever functions inside Enrico in place of a heart.'

'Quite. So there you have it. Over the next day or two Hector and Cortazar thrash out the details, and you and I look at the financing side of it. And of course, the day after tomorrow, Walther von Sachs inaugurates Enrico's final stage with his firework display.'

Again a longish silence at the other end. Then: 'You know, Toñi, that is a desperately silly plan.'

'I know, Lili, I know. But Enrico has not much time left, Lovejoy has made that clear, and he wants to leave his mark, his thumbprint on history.'

Boltana glanced at the end of his cigar, discarded it. Behind him the Steghorn disappeared behind wreaths of cloud, and snow began to fall. The weather changes suddenly in the mountains, even in spring.

54

The next day, after lunch, Rupert set off with Harriet round the perimeter of the névé basin on Nordic touring skis: he had learnt the technique during his tour with the SAS, and she, with some experience of langlauf as well as downhill, had picked it up under his instruction during the morning. The new snow, deep powder on a thin icy crust, produced ideal conditions, and with the early sun masked by haze held its texture well into the day in spite of the lateness of the season. The setting was magnificent and she began to use it as an excuse to take photographs: with her 200 mm Rolleinor and using high-definition ASA 25 in the brilliant light, she was, she hoped, getting shots of people even at quite considerable distances which would still blow up into identifiable likenesses. Meanwhile she prattled on about what bliss it was to take landscape for a change, and not to have to worry about its vanity, or whether it would pay.

Suddenly, when they were almost at the furthest point possible from the hotel, right in amongst the ice-fall debris beneath the Steghorn, and actually above the top of the black-graded piste they had been on the day before, Rupert's bleeper chirped. He dug a radiophone out of his rucksack, tapped a couple of buttons, put the earpiece up under his balaclava: Harriet could hear only his side of the conversation, which was monosyllabic. After a minute or two he pulled out the Kummerly and Frey 1:25,000 map of the area, spread it over the snow in front of him, squatted, and began making specific, precise instructions, stabbing at the map with his finger as he did so. At last he snapped back the aerial, put the RT away, but left out the map. He looked up at her, pushed back his snow goggles, revealed a grin that she now knew well. It meant mischief, wildness, adventure. It could also portend malice, cruelty.

'Intruders.'

'I thought it wasn't possible, except by the cable car. Or helicopter.'

'Well, it is. But there's only one way over, and that's by the Ammertenpass.'

'Which is where?'

'Can't see it from here. Look, see that big crag . . .' He pointed down the wall of heights to a peak that marked the corner at which the cirque turned into ninety degrees, then dabbed the map. 'We're here, this is that crag, you can see it's five kilometres away and not really a lot higher than we are. It's the lowest feature in the whole cirque. Well, that's the Ammertenspitz, and the col, the pass, is even lower and tucked in behind that bluff that sticks out a bit. And that line of red dashes means a mountain path – suitable, in summer, for walkers.'

'And?'

'Two of them. Well kitted out, with mountaineering skis – small, light, with skins to allow for uphill walking.'

'Ski mountaineers. On a perfectly legitimate jaunt. Leave them alone.'

'If that's what they are we will. They'll just walk and ski through, we'll give them a coffee at the hotel, and put them on the cable car.'

'But you don't think it's going to be like that. Why not?'

'Because on all the routes they could have used there are signs saying the cable car is not functioning. All right, they may have missed them, but mountain skiers are cautious people, get themselves properly genned up. All right, they heard that the car is working, but only for us, and they felt this was a touch OTT and decided to go on their hike and trust to our decency to let them down once they made it. All right. But we have to check them out, be sure that that is how it is.'

'And how will you do that? I mean, they'll just say that they're bona fide ski mountaineers, whether they are or not.'

The grin again. 'First, we let them know we've seen them. And if they react by going to ground then we know they're up to no good.'

'I suppose they've only been seen from the hotel so far.'

'Oh dear me no. We have a couple of chaps hidden on the col they went over.'

'Well, why didn't they stop them, just tell them to go back?'

'We have to know what they're up to.'

'What do we do now? I mean us. You and me.'

'There's a hut down there right in the middle of the névé and about a hundred and fifty metres from the track they're on. We're going to go down to it. On the way we'll be very conspicuous on the snowfields and they'll see that we're across their path. If they hide then, or try to go back, we'll know they're up to no good. The quickest and safest way down is on the piste – do you think you can handle it on these skis?'

'Yes, if you don't make a downhill race of it.' She packed camera and lens away into their soft cases and these back into her rucksack.

But the unfamiliarity of the bindings, with heels free for walking, the extra purchase she had to get off the front part of her foot to do a basic swing, caught her out as soon as she developed any speed, and dumped her a couple of times. Impatient, he hurtled on ahead, using the most beautiful of all ski turns, the Telemark, kneeling first on one knee then the other, creating a cloud of powder that went with him, swirling about his lowered shoulders, all the way down the one-kilometre run.

At the bottom she found him talking to the surly man who operated the lift. He skied back to her, explained: 'I'm closing the lift and sending him home. We don't want locals watching us for the next hour or so. Anyway, no one's come out this afternoon. Afraid of avalanche, apparently.'

'Aren't you?'

Rupert squinted up at the Wildstrubel and the sun just edging along the high, distant edge. 'This is the most direct sunlight this bit gets all day, until just before sunset, so there are no sudden, extreme shifts of temperature. That's why the snow has stayed so good. Over there though the slopes are steeper, they get four hours of sun on a clear morning, and up on the corner on the Ammerten it'll be sudden shade, well, in places, from now on. That's where avalanche'll come, if anywhere.'

'That's where these people are.'

'Yes, and another reason for supposing they are not bona fide snow tourers. If they were they'd keep away from an area like that at this time of year.'

The hut they were heading for was about half a mile away across undulating snowfields, but mostly downhill. The smooth wind-sculpted shapes, many of them quite steep, like huge white whales petrified just as they arched their backs for a dive, were astonishingly beautiful. As they neared the hut a couple of small birds flew ahead of them, stopping when they got too far in front, flying on as they caught up. They were white with black primaries, and black in the middle of their tails. They gave harsh chinking calls, but also sang twitteringly as they flew.

'What are they?'

'Snow buntings perhaps. I saw them in Norway. But I think this is south of their range, so perhaps they're snow finches. Not easy to tell them apart. Hey, look. There's a bird of a different feather.'

Harriet followed his outflung arm, pointing north, past the hotel, up into the sky over the abysm of the deep valley beyond. Scarcely more than a dot at the distance, the black and white hang-glider spiralled slowly up the thermals.

'Walther von Sachs.'

'He gives me the creeps. What's he doing here apart from flying that thing?'

'Protégé of Enrico's. Enrico is paying him to do a really amazing stunt in a day or two. Meanwhile, at this moment in time, he's helping us.'

'Watching intruders?'

'That's right.'

Harriet shuddered, remembered the tall fair German she had been introduced to at supper two nights earlier. He was altogether too much: an Identikit Teuton, the ultimate Hun. He even had duelling scars on his cheeks, framing his blond moustache, and he had been a bore too, said little, ate little, drank water, went to bed early.

'I don't like him.'

'He's all right, and bloody good at flying those things. Good in a Star-fighter too. Flies in the West German equivalent of our Red Arrows.'

The hut was small, buried in snow almost to its deep eaves on three sides, but on the downward northern side the door had been dug out. Inside there was one room with wattle byres fencing off cupboard-like spaces under the sloping roof. Although it was clean it smelled of sheep: centuries of sheep.

Rupert lit an oil lamp. 'Another fortnight or so and they'll be up here – they actually do come over the Ammertenpass for the spring lambing and summer pasture.' He shrugged out of his rucksack, unpacked the RT, map, a pair of Zeiss binoculars, and, to Harriet's horror, the four parts of the collapsible version of the Kapp submachine-gun, which he briskly slotted together, ending up by smacking in the curved magazine that distinguished it from the similar Sten.

'You're not going to use that?'

The grin again. 'If I have to. Not the weapon of choice in these conditions, but the best available.'

They moved out and round to the south side of the hut, Harriet with her camera, Rupert with radio, gun and glasses. He stood for a moment, with arm upflung against the glare, then activated the RT. While he talked Harriet searched over the ground where the intruders were meant to be, using her lens to get a little magnification and greater sharpness of image. From where they were now they could see the col, a scoop at the end of the almost straight edge of the arête. Just below it there was a relatively flat area of impacted snow or ice that caught the sun although it was all on the north face, but then the slope steepened, rock appeared in spurs, and for the next winding mile or so the path was in deep blue and purple shadow.

Rupert spoke briskly, his usual lazy drawl forgotten. 'Gone to ground. Bert says they must have seen us and they've taken cover. But they can't move up or down without becoming visible. And he's now pretty sure he knows who they are. They're meant to be journalists, though Bert checked them out in Adelboden yesterday and the girl doesn't have the right credentials . . .'

'Girl?'

He shrugged. 'Makes no difference, does it?'

'I suppose not.'

'It could be serious. Your mate Mulligan's in the area and was seen with the girl – '

'He's not my mate – '

'Anyway, we shall find out.' He turned back to the mountains, methodically scanned the area, vector by imaginary vector.

'They must have good glasses back at the hotel, to have seen them at that distance.'

'Telescope. So guests can watch climbers in the summer. And you forget, we've got two men up on the col behind them, and they're in touch with Bert too. But our intruders are certainly keeping out of sight now, out of sight of everybody. Still, we have our secret weapon. Watch this. Walther is jolly good.'

She turned back, looked up into the hazy blue sky above the low roof of the hut. Black against it the triangle of the hang-glider was arrowing in on a course that took it straight over them and straight towards the arête, the Ammertengrat, the long summit ridge to the left of the col. Without thermals, it was losing height.

'He's going to crash, isn't he?'

The shadow floated over them, a second behind the glider.

'No. Watch.'

As the snowfields climbed into the rock faces above, the glider climbed with them, and as the slopes steepened, its climb accelerated.

'There's always an updraught along mountain faces, known as marginal lift, the more precipitious, the fiercer it is. What he's doing is called "scratching", going as close as he can to make the most of it. Not recommended for novices, because there's always turbulence at the top. He'll regain enough height to get him back across the névé to the thermal over the hotel, and then back to the big ones over the valley. That way with the wind coming off the Wildstrubel he can go on for ever. And at this point he's got a better view of the area than any of us.'

The RT bleeped. The excitement in Rupert's voice was screwed up another turn when he put it down.

'Yes. Walther saw them. And they saw him. Apparently they'd made themselves a snow shelter, looked as if they meant to hole up until dusk, so certainly they are up to no good. But they've given up now and are heading back to the col.'

'Thank God for that.'

'No, Harry. I keep telling you. We need to know what they're up to.'

'So?'

'I've told our two chaps on the col to show themselves as they get back up, show their guns, fire a shot or two if necessary, drive them back in. We'll go up the path to meet them.'

He put on a comic German accent. 'We haf ways of making them talk. Don't worry: quite nice ways from Lovejoy's black bag. Though I expect Walther can come up with something less civilised if those don't work. The first kilometre is very straightforward, we can ski-walk it.'

But it was of course up a gradient the whole way, and though gentle for the most part, Harriet soon found she could not keep up. But she followed doggedly in his tracks, pausing every now and then to search through the shadowed rock and ice and snow in the corner of the cirque in front, while she got back her breath. She was aware of deeply conflicting emotions. On the one side a heart heavy with apprehension for the intruders, on the other the excitement of the hunt gripped her throat. It had been like this the first times riding out to hounds: apprehension of the kill spoiling the flavour of the hunt. Well blooded, she had soon got over that.

Half an hour later, from a hundred yards in front of her, Rupert called: 'There they are. I can see them.'

Pushing with arms that already felt leaden, she heaved herself up to him.

'On the top of the salient, the spur. Just where it begins to flatten into that icefield. Just inside the shadow, probably they don't want to expose themselves.'

She followed his finger, still could see nothing.

'Here, take the glasses. One in something dark, brown or even dark blue, looks like rock and perhaps it's meant to, the other in a white anorak and salopette.'

'Got them.'

'See? Practically camouflaged. Daft for mountain skiers.'

No way of identifying them at this distance, and with both in snow goggles. But could one of them, the one in dark clothing, possibly be Mulligan? Christ. Oh dear Lord, let it not be. Then, as she watched, they began to move, onwards, upwards, on to the two hundred yards of sunlit ice that separated them from the watershed.

Rupert barked at the RT, and two figures silhouetted black against the sky beyond appeared, right on the lowest point of the col. The intruders froze, closed up, turned and began scampering, slithering, slipping and clambering back down the path they had just climbed.

'That's it, they're ours.'

Rupert pushed on his sticks, surged forward. As he did, the hang-glider swooped lower over them than before, cutting across the corner from one mountain face to the other. They heard Von Sachs shout, a high bugle-like call of triumph, and saw his right arm flung out palm down, in salute. Rupert fisted the air in reply.

As they climbed further into the cirque Harriet began to understand the lie of the corner they were approaching. The angle dominated by the Ammertenspitz to the right of the col was filled with the ice plateau which sloped gently for about six hundred feet and it was on the inside edge of this, up against the rock faces, that the quarry were now slithering down. Shortly the ice would give way to a long ridge that came out from the corner, bisecting the angle, dropping away into the névé below. At the top this ridge was broken with rock and ice falls, rocky spurs and deep gullies.

At the lower levels the slopes had been gentle, but the path now took them into the first really steep, really broken country they had had to deal with. It also took them out of the sunlight, but the effort of the climb left Harriet unaware of the drop in temperature. In ten more minutes they were on the shoulder.

Three visible poles showed how the path dropped briefly below them then climbed and traversed a very steep slope before coming back above them. Very little rock showed through anywhere: the slopes, even where almost vertical, were sheeted in snow and ice. Only where rockbands with overhangs jutted out near the top was there any appreciable amount of grey or ochre stone. Black dots spiralled in front of these and she could hear the plaintive high-pitched cackle of the choughs, occasionally graced with haunting trills. And now they had stopped moving, she felt the bite in the air, and the gloom of deep shadow contrasted with the glaring snowfields they had left.

'What now?'

'We wait here. Make use of what Wellington called the visual ridge, let them come round that gully, and take them as they come up to us. It's quite possible that with their attention on Walther and the lads on the col, they didn't see us move away from the hut, so as well as having height on our side we'll surprise them too.'

He unslung the Kapp gun.

'What do you mean, take them?'

'Well, initially, stand up suddenly and say: "Hands up". And if they behave, that'll be it.'

'You're really enjoying this, aren't you?'

The grin again. 'Yes. Haven't had such a buzz since Wireless Ridge. Aren't you?'

'No. I'm cold. How much longer, do you think?'

'Five minutes. They've had shorter to come, and downhill, but very tricky country and probably scared shitless by every shadow.'

But it was longer than that, nearer fifteen. Time for Harriet to watch the drip on an icicle, which must have been in the sun an hour or so earlier, diminish, hesitate, cease. The hang-glider circled in slow tight spirals, or made curving swoops from one rock or ice face to the next. The comparison was obvious but unavoidable. 'He's like a vulture. The sort they call Egyptian. I've seen them in the Pyrenees.'

Rupert laughed. 'He wouldn't be flattered. He fancies himself as some sort of eagle. You know what classy Krauts are like.'

'Is he classy then?' The English obsession – one supposes Scott and his men whiled away blizzards talking about class.

'Probably not, though likes to think he is. Bit of a tharg if not an actual narg. His dad was an *Oberstürmführer* in the SS. Served in the Ukraine. Neither a rank nor a posting Krauts with real clout took.' The RT bleeper chirped again. Again the conversation was brief. Rupert put the handset away, picked up the Kapp gun, gave a turn of the strap round his left elbow. 'And that was him. Whatever else, Walther is bloody good at his job. They stopped at the bivouac they left before. He reckons they had a long chinwag, even an argie-bargie, but now they're on the way down again. Listen. In case anything untoward happens, I mean like they actually manage to get away, could you try to get a snap or two of them?'

'Oh Christ, yes.' Suddenly aware that her professionalism was about to be used and tested, and grateful to have something real to do, she busied herself with buckles and zips, got her light-weight Pentax and Rolleinor zoom lined up, realised that the ASA 25 was now going to be far too slow in this dimmer light, especially if people were moving, and it seemed likely they would be, swapped the body for a Canon loaded with Tri-X.

She was ready just in time.

They were hurrying now, walking not skiing, using the tracks they had already been over twice, and which were firm with the freeze, across the slope with a drop of about three hundred feet below them, walking on a narrow ledge cut into the mountainside. Their short skis together with other impedimenta were now strapped to their backs, they had crampons on their boots and were using ice-axes as walking-sticks. The one in the darker gear, it was dark brown, paused at the end of the ledge, waited for the one in white to catch up. He said something and the voice that replied was high, female. At about a hundred and fifty yards' distance and a hundred feet or so above them it was not possible to hear what they said in spite of the clear air and echoing faces, but a woman she was.

Harriet shivered with sick anticipation, put the viewfinder to her eye, adjusted aperture and focus. With grainy film she probably wouldn't get much of a result, and anyway both were kitted up with snow hoods and goggles, but just as she pressed the button the figure in white pulled her goggles off, demisted them in the cold air, pushed back her hood and shook out fair hair. She had round-lensed spectacles beneath the goggles, and her face was slightly scarred. Both she and the man looked up at the hang-glider, now soaring on the marginal lift above them. Harriet felt suddenly sure that was not the first time she had had that face in her viewfinder, but could not remember when or put a name to it. She fired off two more frames.

Rupert whispered, and she felt his thigh press against hers. 'That's bloody noisy.'

'It's the SLR mirror. Nothing to be done about it. It's not really as loud as you might think.' Hopelessly she wondered whether she ought to tell him she might be able to work out, recall who the girl was, but doubted if she could without her files.

Across the gully, the quarry started the descent into still precipitously sleep but now broken rock and ice fall which gave them and the path the chance to hairpin down to the bottom. Soon they were out of easy sight, and there was no chance of more photographs without exposing too much silhouette above the skyline. Harriet and Rupert lay with their backs against the snow wall, facing out over the névé, gazing up into the long tongue of the glacier that climbed two thousand feet to the rock steps and flutings that mark the summit ridge of the Wildstrubel, with its comet-tail of snow vapour. After seven or eight minutes, they heard, through the distant cackle of the choughs and the single-toned moan of the wind, the chink of crampons, the voices.

'They're nearly here.' Rupert pulled off heavy snow mittens, and his brown fingers, which she knew so well, moved relentlessly to a familiar programme, peeled on supple black-leather gloves. *Savagery beyond the call of duty. Load of Argies.* Suddenly she felt sure he was going to kill them.

She turned, scrambled to the snow crest. 'Go back, please, go back while you can.'

She had a momentary glimpse of upturned goggles halfway up her side of the gully, reflecting the arête behind her head, mouths open in astonishment or fear, then Rupert's hand caught her shoulder and swung her back down and away, slithering into the snow.

'He roared: 'You stupid cunt.' Then: 'Stop. You must stop. Come up here, and you won't get hurt. Turn round and come up or I will fire.'

She heard the crampons screech on ice and rock, scrambling

for footholds, saw him lift the Kapp gun, but he levelled it, did not point it down, fired off maybe half the magazine across their heads into the snow and ice above and beyond them. The sound of it, like blows about the ear from an angry teacher, ricocheted back and forth between the two faces, amongst the crags and spurs for perhaps twenty seconds more, then silence, only the choughs swirled higher and higher, cackling frantically. Harriet clawed her way back on to the ridge in time to hear a voice, male, calling: 'All right. We're coming up, don't shoot . . .' – in time to see and hear it happen.

There was a muffled detonation, like an underground explosion, and cracks ran like lightning across the wind-impacted snow just above her eye level, on the slope of the gully opposite her. For a heartbeat nothing happened, then the whole wall beneath the fifty-yard-long crack began to slip. For a moment it held together and she had the horrid illusion, as her eyes remained fixed on the falling wall, that she was soaring. Then it began to break up into smaller slabs and rolling boulders of snow, and suddenly she was hit by the wind, a great gust of air displaced from the bottom of the gully and curling up to the lip of the ridge. It caught her head like an uppercut delivered by a giant and threw her five yards back into the snow behind her. Down below it also hit Bonnie Day and her companion, caught them about halfway down the slope below her and opposite the one the slab avalanche had dropped from, gave them lift which held them for a moment above the maelstrom of exploding snow and ice that was filling the gully below them, ripped away a bag, a ski, a hat, goggles, sent them spinning up above the swirling snow, but could not save them, possibly even killed them with its blast before the rising flood engulfed them.

The ball of air, at war with itself and with succeeding blasts as more and more snow displaced more and more air below, hurtled on and up, but von Sachs had seen it coming, had put himself into a long side-slip which had already taken him low down over the névé. He swung back, but had lost too much height, was forced to land three or four hundred yards north, back towards the hotel. The ungainly movement, legs thrust forward in their cocoon, the wings pushed up to act as air brakes, forced the comparison back. Just so do the bigger vultures look. He shrugged out of harness, folded his wings. Far in the distance the whine of snowmobiles began a slow crescendo.

Towards six o'clock, two days later, Mulligan waited for Harriet in the jolly dining-room of the Bear Hotel, Adelboden. It had an unstudied perfection he still relished after four days: panelling in seasoned varnished pine, a division down the middle separating the drinkers from the serious eaters, lights bright but not harsh, and round the sides benched alcoves that lent privacy to their users without cutting them off from the rest. It was old-fashioned but not consciously so – perhaps only in Switzerland and some corners of Eastern Europe is this still achieved: newspapers rolled on polished batons and thrust away in deep pigeonholes, waitresses capped and aproned, waiters with stiff shirts beneath their black jackets.

And it was popular too. Outside, the town was empty: the one street scrubbed and washed after the thaw, the window of Hari-Sport opposite in disarray as the ski gear was taken out and the mountain walking, climbing, tennis and riding gear took its place, everything drawing breath between the two seasons. But it seemed any tourists there were were in the Bear, and local shopkeepers, a group of ski-instructors in blue and yellow still, landlords of chalets all there to eat a celebratory dinner, drink beer and schnapps, let themselves go after five months of hard labour.

Mulligan, of course, sat in a corner, from which he had a clear view of all the exits and entrances, saw her before she saw him. She was wearing a chocolate-coloured cord suit with big lapels and a very full skirt, boots, and a patterned angora tammie which she pulled off as she sat, shaking out her hair as she did so. He had been hard on her the last time they met, unfairly hard after a good night in Witham Square, now she was brisk, business-like, closing off situations where he might be able to hurt her. She let him order her a large white coffee, let him light her cigarette with the gold Zippo, came straight to the point.

'They want you to know that they have agreed to buy a single consignment from Arias of two tons. That it will arrive in England in one single shipment at the end of July or beginning of August. That is true, okay? Later I'll be telling you where and how, and presumably that will not be true.' She blew smoke steadily into the air above her head. 'They want me to find out what you're up to, why you're no longer logging your reports on the Interpol computers, what you've been doing here. I should warn you they know a bit about that, they've had you under surveillance, so whatever you tell me had better fit what they already know.'

He leant back, spread his big frame along the bench, eyed her with an expression that carried a lot of male superiority in it. For a moment she hated him for it. 'Why I'm not logging everything on the computer is obvious. Suk knew you'd cracked it. He'd already opened a new file with entries only he knew. I think he'd got pretty close to you all, he couldn't conceal the lines he was following, only the conclusions he was coming to, you found that out and . . . that was it.' He leant forward. 'I'll tell you what I've been doing here if you tell me something first.'

'Yes?'

'A French journalist and a press photographer left here two days ago. They intended to cross the Ammertenpass into Kaiseralp. They were professionals, believed that considering who had taken the hotel, and who had turned up, there had to be a very good story. I lent them some very sophisticated listening devices. I want to know what happened to them.'

She told him.

When she had finished he sat back again, and let out a long wretched sigh. He looked suddenly older. 'Accident then. When the bodies surface in the thaw, there'll be nothing to show that anyone knew they'd been caught in it. Happens every year. Major avalanches in the area every day at this time of year. Only strangers silly enough to get caught . . .'

Suddenly Harriet's head struck across the table at him. 'You bastard. You set them – her, because it was a girl – set them up. You let them go up there, knowing the sort of opposition, knowing the sort of security . . . What the fuck is the difference between you and them, Mulligan? You should ask yourself that some time.'

'I couldn't have stopped her. She'd already taken amazing risks in the last few months and got away with them – '

'Why? For Christ's sake, why?'

'She had her reasons. Very good reasons. She has a friend, her mate, a really best friend who's now in a psychiatric hospital back on Tyneside where they came from. Paranoid schizophrenia, almost certainly irreversible. She sits in a corner of a padded cell, in a straitjacket, and wets herself. Your lot made her like that.'

'You could have stopped her.'

'No. I don't think so.'

He stubbed out his cigarette, looked around, suddenly wary, aware that a change had come over the big room. There was still laughter and cheeriness at the peripheries, but a near-silence was spreading out from the tables that had a view of a television set placed high up on a bracket above the bar.

Birch trees – silvered trunks, branches and leaf stems a rich glossy brown, buds swelling, pinpoints of brilliant green bursting through cases as bright as beetles' carapaces. Cunning lens work got a star or two out of raindrops, pointed up the message – spring, rebirth, reconciliation – then panned back and back so a long imposing wall could unravel across the small screen. Zoom in again. The wall inscribed, not largely with gilded letters, but filled with words done small but cut deep, graffiti that no detergent could wash out.

'Do you really want to watch this?' Mulligan touched the back of Harriet's hand. 'They've shown it at every news break on the hour since it happened this morning.'

'Yes. Just a minute. Wait, and I'll tell you why.'

Mulligan's eyes, not a TV camera, dwelt briefly on Harriet's face: her hair was shorter than it used to be, he thought, not so rich, scraped back under a band, white forehead lined and grooved between the eyebrows as she thrust her head forward to concentrate on the high, distant screen. Cheeks – one bruised, the other rouged in a vain attempt to balance the bruise, indeed far more make-up everywhere than she usually wore. Her eyelids were green like the birch buds, her lips not too carefully painted with Indian red. He panned down to her hands on the tablecloth in front of them, nails painted to match but chipped and the white skin lined over the knuckles. Christ, she's aged.

The commentary, in German, dragged his eyes back to the screen. A large wooden cross. There were stirring cloudscapes in the sky behind it; the camera lingered on them. Mulligan's eyes flinched away again.

Harriet touched his hand, forced him back to the small screen over the counter. Low steps, a brutal arcade of granite or concrete, men and women in black, black suits, black dresses, others in dark military uniforms. Flags dipped, then the camera panned up to the sky again and a group of white and black Starfighters swooped over in close formation, performed a slow roll, a salute. The camera followed, tracked back towards the ceremony, then suddenly jerked away, up again, zoomed out reminding the viewer that it was after all placed a good distance away, zoomed in again to pick up a single Starfighter this time, hurtling back, far lower than before, skimming the firs, on a course that would take it only feet above the cross. Against the blackness of the sky you could see the flashes below its wings as the four sidewinder missiles ignited, then the picture lurched, zoomed in and out, the commentator's voice rose to a pitch that wasn't far off a scream, and the screen filled with the concourse in front of the wall, just as the first missile burst there.

One of the ski-instructors, short but burly, with close-cropped grey hair and an angry face, stood up, scraped his chair, went across to the set, reached up and pulled the power-plug. Two or three people applauded, most with some relief went back to their drinks, their celebrations. A few remained quiet, thoughtful, but not for long. You can't blame them, Mulligan thought to himself. You can't expect the Swiss to get involved, with anything really. He himself hated to be reminded: his father had been one of the first into Belsen, and he had come back a broken man. That's what the Holocaust had done to Mulligan: turned the man he worshipped, as only a ten-year-old boy can worship a good father, into a nightmare-ridden alcoholic whom his mother left, taking James with her, when he was twelve.

'Why did you want me to see that again?'

She spoke slowly, with deliberation, quietly. 'Walther von Sachs, the man who did that, who ejected and got away, no one knows where to, is the man I was telling you about. The man who piloted the hang-glider and hunted down those poor people on the Ammertenpass. Shooting up that ceremony at the extermination camp, at which the German armed forces

539

were making an act of contrition for their part in the Holocaust, is to be the first of a programme of similar stunts
designed to show that the spirit of National Socialism is alive
and well. I know because Malatesta gave him a hero's send-
off last night in the ballroom of the Kaiseralp, in front of a
huge swastika flag. It was horrible, really horrible, he was
demented . . . little ugly old man, raving and ranting and
spitting. He almost had a fit and Lovejoy had to give him an
injection. I thought you should know.'

Her cigarette hissed in her coffee. She stood, squeezed past
tables and chairs, was gone.

Part Ten

Rupert

55

Rupert trotted up stairs, pushed through glass doors into a dimly lit but spacious gallery whose inner wall of curved glass looked down and out on to a marketplace. Red leather benches rimmed a shallow circular pit. Young men, sharp in suits, one or two with jackets off, showed tension in contrasting ways: some chattered, nervy, lively (they're the ones who've had a sniff before coming on the floor, thought Rupert); others sat with legs stretched out, affected nonchalance, but prepared themselves with deep breathing, mantras, charms and prayers.

Behind them the spaces began to fill with small groups, teams of two or three, with pads and pens, some women, smart, hard; some had radiotelephone handsets with stalk aerials, others filled the telephone booths behind. Rupert remembered the electricity building up a voltage big enough to sustain a five-minute discharge, and his palms prickled with sweat. He grinned at the memory, pulled the handkerchief from his top pocket, wiped his hands, pushed it back, just as he always had when he too had been, briefly, a dealer on the floor of the London Mineral Market.

The big clock on the wall flicked on towards twelve-thirty, a large sign, black on white, signified that bauxite was to be traded, a tall, grey man with bifocals took his place at a lectern, and down to Rupert's right drifting into the middle of one of the teams came the bulky but sharp figure of Sam Dorf. He was older than almost everyone else there, his suit a pale grey instead of the usual pinstripe. The corners of his puckish mouth lifted in anticipation of the action, and his eyes, not large, but bright, flickered round the arena. He caught sight of Rupert above him, lifted a podgy finger and the smile broadened a trifle.

A bell rang, a short sharp blast. Dealing began quietly enough, the dealers on the floor testing, probing, but built to a feverish climax of shouting, waving, of clerks moving up behind the dealers, orders screamed from the phone booths. Eyes narrowed in calculation, or widened suddenly with determination above mouths which snarled or bellowed, and glanced more and more often upwards, drawn compulsively to the relentless clock. Rupert saw Dorf, suddenly anxious, move forward with a gesture, a nod, then the big man relaxed, the smile was back just as the bell rang again, at precisely twelve-thirty-five. He looked up, eyebrows raised, and tipped his hand in a gesture that had nothing arcane about it, mouthed: 'Drink?' Rupert nodded, trotted back down the stairs in time to meet him as he came off the floor.

Corridors in textured ochre paint, marbled halls with show-cases filled with luxury toiletries, and cast-iron, teak-banistered staircases brought them to the other side of Plantation House and to a restaurant with some style. At the central horseshoe bar Rupert ordered large gins and tonic, turned to enjoy the most striking feature of the place, a collection of oils from, he judged, the twenties and thirties, chosen to capture the hectic hedonism of the era. There were very few customers, and since Rupert got virtually no change from a fiver it was easy to guess why.

'Cheers.' Dorf raised his tumbler. 'I think I've found the chap you need. We're to meet him at one, but I thought I'd take the opportunity to have a word with you first.'

'That's fine. There's something else I want to broach with you too.'

'You first.'

'We need a secure wharf and a warehouse in Rotterdam.'

Dorf's deep laugh boomed richly across the spaces around them. 'I trust you're not asking me to lend you the key to the LMM facility there.'

'No, of course not. But I know you do a lot through Rotterdam, so I felt you could point me in the right direction.'

'Be more specific. What sort of security are you looking for?'

'Basically longshoremen who aren't too good at arithmetic.'

The laugh again. 'Considering your earlier requirements, that figures. I must say I'm impressed. I thought the commodity you trade in came wrapped in latex and stuffed in popsies. A touch surprised too.'

'Why?' Rupert tried to keep the edge out of his voice.

544

'Well, Ambrose. They seem to be going through a slack period there. Volume of business they've put my way recently but a shadow of what it used to be.'

Rupert ran a finger round the rim of his glass, weighed up how much he could say to Dorf. 'We've had our difficulties. Of supply mainly. That's what all this . . . is about. Big shipment, get things moving again.'

'Ah, that's all right then. I was just worried that for some reason unbeknownst to me I was no longer flavour of the month with them, that they'd gone over to Brand X for my part of the weekly wash. That's fine then.' He looked at his watch. 'Better make tracks if we're to be at Simpson's by one.'

'Not eating here then?'

'Lord, no. Wallace is one of the old brigade. Not his style. Semi-retired now. Doesn't come up more than once a week, mainly to get away from his family I believe, has a nice place out in the country near Chelmsford, but after fifty years broking ships, can't keep away. But he's not in the mainstream any more, doesn't care a toss about how he makes an extra bean or two, and he's greedy, which all adds up to why I think he's your man.'

'And what's the line you've given him about me?'

'Well, he says he's not curious – which is a lie, of course. He wants to know, but without it ever being provable that he knew. I emphasised the absolute necessity of keeping to a strict timetable and I rather think he's got it into his head that you're shifting something perishable or living. Bengalis. Tamils. That sort of thing.'

They hurried through sheeting rain beneath big black umbrellas, down Lombard Street, threaded a brief warren of alleys and yards. Simpson's, never Rupert's favourite place, seemed even more awful than usual: the smell of beer, grilled meat, onions, soured with that of heavily soaked serge; the crowd, red-faced and raucous, even more dense than usual, storm-driven into a log-jam four deep behind the bars.

'Pissing down, all over the sodding country. Thought I'd tool over to Lords this pip emma – no chance.'

'Covers still on at Wimblers too.'

'Listen, what I want to know is, is Felicity putting it about in a general way or is she just sleeping with that shit Julian? I mean I could invest in some muffins and call in on her place

545

about teatime if I thought there was a halfway chance she'd drop them for me. Ideal way of spending a wet afternoon.'

'No chance, old boy. Felicity never puts it out without a noggin or two under her belt, and she don't booze before sundown. Know that for a fact, I've tried.'

'Actually, thought we'd try the Norwegian fjords this year. Bloody good election and I think we can now lash out on a bigger boat. Do some real sailing, some real fishing.'

A man once tall, now stooped as if the weight of wool on his back was too much, like chain-mail on a valetudinarian horse-soldier, his eyes hidden by drooping eyelids and his nose pitted like a strawberry, waved at them in the vexed way lollipop ladies use at school crossings. Dorf and Bridge squeezed past benches like old church pews, pushed at the meaty backs that bulged out in their path, diverted carelessly placed umbrellas whose handles threatened to castrate them. Rupert briefly gripped a leaden white hand, got rid of it as soon as he could.

'Haven't seen you here before, have I?'

'Probably not.'

'Didn't think so.' The voice jabbered, like the first Kapp guns, good on short bursts, tended to give up quite soon. 'Stick to what they do best, shall we? Loin chops. Braised onions. Bubble and squeak. House red.' The waitress, Irish-Cockney, was brisk and jolly, treated Wallace like an old but favoured cocker spaniel. 'Count the City lunches on one hand I've had anywhere else. Cheap, you see. Quality too. And old. That's good. I like old things. See those racks? They're for top hats. You want a couple of small tubs in the first week of August. Ro-ros? Reefers? GCs?'

'I beg your pardon?'

'Young sir, there's no need to. Each to his last, and the jargon of his trade . . . Cheers.'

The house red turned out to be a sensible Rioja.

'A ro-ro is a boat you roll on and roll off containers on wheels. The *Herald of Free Enterprise* was a big ro-ro. I imagine you want something a bit smaller and without a free car-wash thrown in . . .' The laugh that came with this was more like a Bofors than a Kapp gun. A reefer turned out to be refrigerated, from frozen for fish and meat through to chill for fruit, and GC was general cargo. Feeling a touch underbriefed, Rupert plumped for GCs. An hour and three bottles of Rioja later,

Wallace came to what he termed the nub. 'The commissions are all laid down. But if you want this done as discreetly as I think you do, and with utter, utter, utter reliability, as to dates and so forth, here's the number of my City and Wessex account and I'll see' – a bushy eyebrow, grey and straggly, levitated – 'a sweetener there in a day or two. A thou?'

'Five hundred.'

'Young sir. No need to be bloody parsimonious. You've come to the wrong man if you mean to be.'

Rupert sucked in breath and decided he was bored. 'Oh shit, yes. A grand.'

Three days later Chelmsford Chartering of Cook House, Bergamot Lane, EC, confirmed that on 2nd August next the eight-hundred-ton general cargo *Byker Lass* would dock at the Kapp-Duxbury wharf Wallsend on a four-day charter, Wallsend to Rotterdam and back, and that *La Demoiselle des Pieux*, a coaster of similar size, would be available on a three-day charter Rotterdam to Cork Harbour from the third. The client was Mr John Smith of Wimbledon and the fact that Wallace had let the charter go through to a clearly fictional character was the service that had earned him his sweetener.

During the next three weeks Rupert continued to work as Myklades' chief of staff, and on the whole made a better job of it than Soult did for Napoleon in the run-up to Waterloo. However, like his avatar's, Myklades' resources were impossibly stretched. He now had to work to a circumscribed budget: it was huge, representing most of the loan the Banco de Corpus Cristi had put at the disposal of Mendoza Holdings (Tortola) – huge but final: there would be no more.

More and more devolved on Rupert. Again he finalised extremely complicated negotiations between Kapp-Duxbury and an Israeli shipping agent. He found and booked for a week a suitable small wharf and warehouse at the east end of the Rotterdam docks, and arranged for two tons of Sol-Methrine B, a designer pesticide developed to deal with *Bemisia tabaca*, the white fly that attacks cotton, manufactured in Düsseldorf under licence from Sol-Chem (Haifa), to be deposited there. He also ordered shipments of four tons of Manganox, trade name for a Swiss-made catalyst used in the manufacture of high-heat-resistant insulators made by a firm with factories in Gateshead and Cork.

The other main components of a plan he and Myklades had been putting together for nearly a year, ever since they had decided that the Arnolfini-Scapino move should be run down, were a communication system and a small fleet of yachtsmen. For the first he had invoked the Old Boys' Act and bought, for a quarter of a million pounds, the components of a communication system not normally commercially available, and, using Designer Living Card files, found an out-of-work Oxford-based post-doc, with a coke habit he couldn't afford, to instal it. DLC accounts also revealed boat-owners whose lifestyles exceeded their incomes, and they too had been lined up and waiting for some time.

And finally it seemed he was the only person available whose loyalty was not in question and who had the capabilities to check out the cargo at its point of departure.

In the second half of July he flew out to Barranquilla, arrived in a white crumpled suit, with jet-lag and documents that proclaimed he was a roving reporter for the international news magazine *Réaxions*. At Barranquilla he caught a Flota de Velocidad bus down the coast to Santa Marta, where he checked out from a discreet distance the presence of a seventeen-thousand-ton reefer called *San Fermín* berthed at Wharf Three in the northern corner of the port beyond the huge IDEMA grain silos. Hot beyond belief yet buffeted by the Madwoman, La Loca, the wind from the Sierra that makes a salt-pan of your back, he checked that she was actually taking on board twenty-kilo cardboard cases of green bananas labelled Turbana Colombia and that no one as far as he could see was taking any untoward sort of interest in what was going on apart from himself.

In the evening he made his way to a small café behind the waterfront called El Palacio de las Frutas and ordered a *crema de guanabana*, which turned out to be the most pleasant non-alcoholic drink he had ever tasted – made, he later learnt, from the custard pear and milk. He looked round the dim white-washed room decorated with an ancient Coca-Cola poster – *la chispa de la vida*, the spark of life – and a coloured print of Bolivar, wondered if there was an escape route should he need it through the small yard beyond, lit by two bare bulbs and curtained with flowering creepers. Large moths buffeted and banged between the two areas. Presently a small dark boy sidled away from the pinball machine and asked him for a cigarette. Rupert shook out a Piel Roja, lit it. The boy nodded slowly to himself, studied the burning end of the cheap cigarette, sucked on it, and then melted away behind the smoke into the alley beyond.

Ten minutes later the crackling purr of a very powerful racing engine filled the narrow spaces between the concrete tenements that lined the street. A door clunked and Jorge Aguirre came round the front of the car, stood in the doorway and beamed, flashing big teeth beneath his glossy black moustache, arms spread so the heavy red leather holster in his armpit was clearly visible.

'*Mi amigo*,' he crowed, '*Ruper-r-r-rto, buen amigote mío*, forgive the silly charade, *los jefes*, the bosses, insisted on it.' Rupert had risen and the huge Colombian took him in his arms in the warmest possible way, running his big, broad, hairy hands down his trunk from armpits to waistband. The moustache was like a hearth-brush on his cheek, and the odours of sweat, dark tobacco and Spanish cologne filled his nostrils. With some distaste Rupert considered the possibility that Jorge was what people like Rupert still insist on calling 'queer' – all very well to use the false bonhomie that went with the occasion to frisk him, but really he was making rather a meal of it.

Rupert did not frighten easily – indeed, what he normally felt in circumstances where ordinary people are frightened was an intense nervous excitement sweetened by hilarity; but in circumstances over which he had no control whatever, and which might justifiably be considered exceptionally dangerous, something a little more akin to a normal human response took over. The car was so customised it was impossible to say what it had started out as, but Rupert reckoned that the engine was a four-litre V12 that had probably begun life on a racing track. During the next three hours he did occasionally sweat a little, gritted his teeth, and once actually made a grab for the crash handle above his head. Jorge acknowledged this one unstudied movement by grinning hugely and massively slapping Rupert's thigh. He also, for the remaining hour or so, drove a little more circumspectly: not out of consideration for his passenger, but because he had achieved what he had been looking for – a reaction.

Also perhaps because what had been a tolerably new, tolerably well-engineered main road, the Troncal de Caribe which links Cartagena in the west with Barranquilla, Santa Marta, and finally Río Hacha, halfway up the Guajiro peninsula in the east, gave way to narrow roads, not always metalled, often pitted and rutted. Occasionally, even, the sump of the big powerful car clanged on rock or earth and the concussions as the heavy tyres thudded in and out of potholes made the independent wishbones, coil springs and anti-roll bar feel like the shock absorbers on an MG Midget.

On Aguirre's skill Rupert made shifting judgements, which eventually panned out as definite pluses. The big Colombian smoked cigarettes taken from a pewter and mother-of-pearl case, sat back in the big bucket seat in an S-shaped attitude that suggested total relaxation apart from the alert perpendicular of his big bull neck, talked incessantly: about the amazing time they had had at Kaiseralp; about the extraordinary cultivation, generosity, magnanimity of the splendid people he and Rupert worked for, Boltana and Arias, Mendoza and Myklades. But all the time his fingertips played along the rim of the steering wheel, eased the gear stick and dabbed at the switch controls with the unflustered and precise reactions of a brain surgeon coping with a cranial haemorrhage. They covered three hundred and fifty kilometres, in total darkness beyond the sweep of the headlamps, in under three hours. Rupert decided that he would avoid a fight with Aguirre on anything but the most unequal terms.

They arrived at a *finca* on the north-eastern tip of the Guajiro peninsula shortly before midnight, were welcomed by a tall man in a white jacket over an open black silk shirt, with a once handsome face now ravined and pitted and a voice which carried at its back the broken twang professional singers often have. 'Señor Desiderio Rapal, call him Desi,' Aguirre announced, 'and a very good friend of *los jefes*. Indeed, practically a chief himself now, eh?' and he slapped Rapal on the shoulder.

Rapal ignored him. 'Meester Bridge, we have a very busy day ahead of us. If we are to be ready by five in the afternoon we will have to start at eight in the morning. I think we should get some sleep while we can.'

At seven a plump boy in T-shirt and cut-down jeans woke him with *tinto y taco*, strong black coffee and cold tortilla fried into brittle biscuit. He pulled back shutters on to a bleak white landscape of cactus and starved maize, of white walls made from piled boulders, and white dust. But the land tipped down neglected terraces to a cove and the sea below – flat nacrous silk shot with turquoise beneath a white-gold haze. An old man with white stubble over brown skin beneath a broken straw hat came up a winding path with a stick across his shoulders. From the ends two iguanas hung upside down, still writhing, their legs lashed together with wire.

An hour later Rapal and Aguirre led Rupert through the *finca*, which was expensively furnished with a grotesque miscellany of European antiques, heavy black rough-hewn peasant-style tables and presses, and the latest in chrome cylinders and black leather. There were a lot of pictures of Desiderio framed in silver or gilt: photographs, posters, and one large oil, in the company of popes and presidents, mafiosi and bullfighters. Finally a moving bookcase revealed tiled stairs that took them to a lower level and a very businesslike steel door.

Rapal drawled: 'The local colonel of police insists on it. If it's ever discovered it's well enough hidden for him to be able to claim he could not find it.'

Beyond the door was a large laboratory, a small factory that lay beneath the entire *finca*. A corridor ran down one side, one wall glazed, with glass doors opening into a chain of linked work areas, the other white rough-hewn rock. Each sector marked a stage in the process that converts *basuko*, dried cocaine base, into pure white crystals. The caked, cinnamon-coloured powder was stored in what looked like tea chests, crates lined with foil. There were ten of these, empty, stacked in the first room and one a quarter full. Rapal murmured: 'It has not been easy to organise this, you know. Usually we don't handle more than five hundred keys at a time. But we've managed.'

The succeeding chambers contained sacks of potassium permanganate, glass and stainless steel vats of solvents and acids, retorts, cylindrical cauldrons with pressure-clamped lids that reminded Rupert of the institutional kitchens, modern, clean and functional, of army depots in Aldershot and Winchester. He recalled that the cant term for the sort of place he was now in was *cocina*, kitchen. But the smells were chemical, volatile, brought a nostalgic pang to the man who had once, in a distant age of innocence, glued together the tiny parts of Airfix kits to make models of dinosaurs and Polaris submarines. The last area was the largest, dominated by two stainless steel hoppers, each linked by a belt to huge rolls of heavy-duty plastic bags on one side and heat-sealing clamps on the other. Four persons, sexless and anonymous in white surgical overalls with caps and gauze masks, stood ready.

Rapal leered at him. '*Una muestra*, a sample, before we start, yes?'

'All right. But I shall want to run the tests on each batch.'

'There is no test as good as *una muestra*.'

Rupert shrugged. Rapal pushed open the glass door. It was even cooler inside than it had been in the corridor. He led Rupert and Aguirre past the sheathed zombielike figures of the technicians, climbed six metal steps on to a short low catwalk that ran behind the hoppers. He lifted a lid. Beneath harsh bright lights the white crystalline powder glittered like the spring powder of Kaiseralp in the early morning sun. He handed Rupert a metal rod with a hollow cylinder on the end. The rod was about two feet long, the cylinder three inches with a diameter of less than one.

'Give it a good stir. Go as deep as you like.'

Rupert did just that. One of the technicians took the scoop from him, smoothed off the surplus, tamped down the contents, tipped them carefully on to the tray of a set of Ohaus electronic scales. The weight, measured in micrograms, and flashed up digitally in pulsing magenta, correlated exactly with the volume of the inside of the cylinder. The technician took a smaller measure, tipped it into a petri dish, slotted it into a small table-top machine. Again readings from spectroscopic analysis confirmed pure cocaine hydrochloride. Finally, using a laboratory scalpel, he drew out three thin lines on a glass plate and handed it to Rupert with a three-inch piece of glass tubing.

Rapal was right. There is no test as good as *una muestra*, no substitute for the cool fever of a pure angel-dust high.

'And the next.'

They moved to the second hopper and repeated the procedure.

'Each hopper,' said Rapal, 'contains one hundred kilos, pharmaceutical quality . . . As pure as Snow White before the Seven Dwarfs got to her.'

Step on it once, street price fifteen million pounds.

'. . . and it takes half an hour to empty and fill fifty two-kilo plastic bags. Allow an extra couple of hours or so for refilling the hoppers, retesting each batch, and we should be able to get our two tons packaged by three o'clock this afternoon.'

Three perhaps four hundred million pounds. Rupert, still on cloud nine from the two heavy lines of pure he'd taken, looked back down the shopfloor of the most profitable factory in the world. Its owners and their clients could tumble governments, destroy cultures, finance genocide. And really it was rather small, low-key, could have been an aspirin factory.

He realised they were waiting. Grinning slightly, working out that in the next six hours or so he was going to have to cope with eighteen more lines of pure if he was to do the job properly – and that that was more than enough to kill, so he'd have to space them, take say four more but at random, so they wouldn't know when he was going to use his nose, when he was going to allow the weight test and the spectroscopic analysis to be enough – he gave them the nod. Rapal thumbed buttons, a motor somewhere began to thrum, the belt rolled, and the first two bags spread their openings beneath the hoppers. They were stencilled – *Sol-Methrine B* in large letters, and in smaller script *Sol-Chem (Düsseldorf) AG*.

Outside, at noon, the sun blazed from a brassy sky, glittered like shards of razor-sharp glass along the ripples of the sea. Inland, behind the *finca*, four skeletal goats gave up the search along the bottom of a dried-up *rambla* for clumps of low thorny scrub with tiny brilliant blue flowers, huddled with the Indian boy who watched them beneath an overhang of crumbling white conglomerate, nudged and butted each other for the shade. A thermometer, supposing there were one there, would have pushed above a hundred, and even the insects and lizards took a siesta. Only the generators that powered the machinery in the plant carved out of the rock beneath hummed steadily on.

At about three o'clock there was a pause. At the end of the assembly line Rapal said: 'There. That's the good stuff. And now you want four hundred kilos of rubbish, yes?'

Rupert nodded. 'Just so long as it passes the standard c-c-c-crude tests for the presence of some c-c-cocaine hydroch-ch-chloride.' He wiped his hands on his handkerchief, tried to twist the grin off his face.

The hoppers were refilled from thick hessian sacks with a wet, grey, clotted sludge. Rapal commented: 'Virtually useless, well trampled on, twenty per cent and the fools let the humidity get out of control.'

'Just the job.' Rupert giggled. 'And quite rightly in plain wrappers.'

For the bags were now unmarked.

The day burned itself out. Imperceptibly a pale lilac haze blunted the fierceness of the glare, the white light off the water shifted to yellow, purple shadows spread like stains, a goat bell jingled and gravel skittered beneath dainty black hooves. And out in the mist a mournful one-note bellow, such as one might imagine a bereaved whale might make, heralded the slow disclosure of the high black prow, the three ochre king-posts, the superstructure and smokestack of the *San Fermín*. The bolero beat of her engines drummed dully across the lambent spaces, white foam briefly churned below her stem as one prop reversed, and her long rust-streaked hull swung broadside on. Anchor chains rattled like heavy gravel tipped down chutes, the long sad boom came again, and a cloud of pink flamingos from a salt marsh on the other side of the headland spiralled broadly up above the mist, swung in a huge arc around the sky, necks in flattened *s*'s, legs trailing.

A small JCB with lifting attachments trundled, one by one, four pattens, each loaded with two hundred and fifty stencilled bags, and then one with two hundred plain bags, down a prepared track to the makeshift jetty it had helped to build; a small lighter, flat-bottomed, round-prowed, chugged them out to the reefer. Rupert and Aguirre went with them, watched the labelled bags stowed into a small cube container in the forward hold.

'Lot of boats carry this sort of container these days: used for anything from four tons of video-tape recorders to unenriched uranium ore. Anything that everyone wants kept secure.'

The locking devices were simple, involved two magnetic pegs, two sets of resettable six-figure combinations.

Aguirre set one, pocketed his peg, grinned at Rupert. 'One number you never forget, eh? The date of your mother's birthday.'

Rupert grinned back, inanely high, but dabbed in the first six digits of his army number.

Up on the bridge the captain logged a halt to pump out water ballast at Chicken Point, Punto de Gallinas, before proceeding into the Gulf of Venezuela and the port of Maracaibo, where he would take on chilled beef, frozen shrimps, coffee, and two tons of Sol-Methrine A pesticide, manufactured there at the Solchem petro-plant under licence from the parent firm Solchem (Haifa). It was packed in two-kilo bags and stacked on top of the unlabelled low-grade cocaine.

56

Two days later, at one o'clock in the afternoon, Rupert arrived back at Heathrow. At the bench, he was turned out, rubbed down, and even had his rectum searched by a doctor whom Senior Investigation Officer Philip Seton jokingly referred to as Dr Goldfinger. He tried a little bluster in his 'officer and gentleman' style, but was told it would get him nowhere. Since the Hayward case had broken, well-spoken young sirs with regimental ties were flavour of the month. He was of course clean, and so it was something of a shock when, instead of releasing him, Seton led him to a star interview room. There, on the desk, was a foil-wrapped cube, the twin of the one he had taken to Duxbury of K-D more than six months earlier. And behind the table sat the tall but unremarkable man – unremarkable apart from the fact that his head seemed permanently if quizzically set on one side – whom he had last seen on the train to Newcastle.

'Oh Christ. I might have guessed.'

'Quite so, old chap. Take a pew, won't you? I'm afraid it seems they found this in your baggage.' He poked the silvery cube.

'They did not.'

'No? Well, let's conduct this conversation as if they had. Do sit down, there's a good chap.'

Rupert did as he was told. The tall man leaned towards him, beamed. 'Let's get straight to the point. They're a lot closer to you than they should be, you know?'

'Who?'

'Mulligan and Tyler. Eurac and the NDIU – Floor Five at Scotland Yard. And closer to Crystal, which is what bothers me. Apparently that man Suk was putting stuff on a protected file at Interpol which even we didn't have access to, and some bright lad there has cracked his entry codes. Embarrassing, very.'

'So. What do you want me to do about it?'

'Well, first let's recap. As you know, Myklades will shortly receive his two tons. He'll sell them, pass the take on to Ambrose, Mendoza Holdings, and so to Crystal – hopefully through his usual channels, which we now have fairly well broken. Now it's vital to our operation that no one moves against Myklades until the money reaches Crystal. For one thing's for sure: if Myklades goes first, then all the doors between him and Crystal will be slammed shut, locked and the keys thrown away. Are you with me?'

'Of course. But surely you've got the clout to blow the whistle on Mulligan and Tyler?'

'No can do, old chap. In the first place Myklades has to think they're on to him. He's feeding them disinformation through that Jones girl, your kissing cousin. I must say she has a lot of talent, we might recruit her one day . . . where was I? Yes. Myklades expects reaction from that, that he can monitor. He won't feel secure unless he sees police action against him which he's in control of, and if he don't feel secure then he'll abort.'

'Tell Mulligan and Tyler to go softly, softly. Incorporate them.'

'No, no. The Old Bill hates that sort of thing. One of them will blow it, if not now then one day, especially if we come unstuck and fail to get to Crystal. Write their memoirs, you know? No. The way we must do it is let them run, but bugger them about a bit if they seem to be doing well. That'll be part of your job. Let us know if you feel really threatened, and we'll put the boot in. There's another thing first, though. Little waste disposal job, the sort of thing you're so good at. One of Myklades' distributors has been rumbled and we rather think he might cough on the DLC-Ambrose connection rather more prematurely than we want. So he'll have to be taken out.'

'Do I have to?'

The tall nondescript man smiled his Cheshire cat smile, touched the half-kilo cube in front of him. 'Oh yes, I think so. Don't you? I'll give you the details. Chap operates in Oxford, and that's another factor. Down the chain there's a cabinet minister's brat involved, and possibly a Royal . . .'

Outside at last, Rupert sat for a minute or so in his Lotus in the long-term carpark and thought about it. Then he drove carefully within the speed limits towards central London, eye on the rear-view mirror, turned off the M4 at the Chiswick flyover, parked at Gunnersbury station beneath the IBM Building. He bought a ticket for Richmond, boarded the train as soon as the flood of homeward-bound commuters getting off allowed him to, then himself got off as it began to move from the station. At the ticket barrier he flashed not the ticket he had bought but a Greater London railcard. He turned right at the top of the stairs, and right again at the end of the bridge. This took him on to a long tarmacked footpath running above the railway line, into a small leafy enclave of streets set between the motorway, the railway and Chiswick High Street. A large grey Victorian house, detached, with big bay windows, stood between smaller Edwardian villas. He climbed a boxed-in red-painted staircase to the first floor and opened the door, which was secured with a voice-reading device. He had to recite 'Mary had a little lamb whose fleece was white as snow.' Burke's joke.

He went straight to the phone set on a low table in the hall and dialled a number.

'Bert? Rupert. They turned me out at Heathrow. No problem, I was clean, but there might be surveillance on me. I'm at Grosvenor Road. Two hours? Can't you be quicker than that? No? All right then. The gents on the green at nineteen-thirty hours, then the church, then the Red Lion. See you.'

The large four-roomed flat smelt stale and musty, unused. He pushed up sash windows, checked through the net curtains the still steady flow of commuters, realised any attempt he could make to see if his metaphorical tail was clean would be futile, remembered the state of his actual arse, had a bath. The bathroom was tiny, at the back of the house, had a gas-heater that stank of partially burnt fumes and dropped crumbs of black stuff into the sink. The walls had once been painted in white and blue gloss in a design that suggested hard-edged Picasso, or possibly Hittite goddess figures, but the paint was peeling. Later, with a weak gin and tonic taken from the fridge in the kitchen and a tape of *The Yeomen of the Guard* on the ancient music centre, he was able to relax for an hour or so.

At twenty-five past seven he let himself out, turned left, headed for Turnham Green. The evening sun was warm on his back, there was a strong smell of roses, honeysuckle and nicotiana on the evening air. Domestic London at its best. 'I have a song to sing-o, Sing me your song-o,' he warbled to himself.

On the green the gents was open, the church was locked. He used the gents, stayed in one of the cubicles for a full five minutes, read graffiti, wondered if the long scrawled tale of what Ron would let you do to him if you turned up here at eight o'clock on Tuesdays was true. He walked three times round the church, sat in the porch for another five minutes and then made his way down to the riverside pub Burke had designated.

A chic conversion job had been done on it: it was now split-level with an upstairs reached by a spiral staircase, and with little low windows overlooking the river. The burly ex-police-man was sitting by one of these nursing a pint glass of bitter. He looked sour, angry even; his small dark eyes glittered, his heavy knuckles were white. Worst of all he looked totally out of place. The bars were busy, but there were no women, the men were dressed brightly or outrageously, and the noise level was high.

'I'm sorry,' he said. 'It's wicked the way a place can change in six months. Six months ago this was an honest pub, I swear it. Now look at it. Knocking-shop for a load of faggots.'

'I'll get myself a drink.'

He too ordered bitter. The barman flirted. 'Ooh, that's the second tonight, we are all butch all of a sudden.' Rupert looked round. Everyone else was drinking lager – draught Fosters, judging by the posters featuring Paul Hogan.

Back upstairs Burke was brisk. 'You're clean. No one getting up your arse, which is more than I can say for anyone else here. But where are your wheels?'

'In the carpark at Gunnersbury. The Lotus.'

'Right. If they were following you they'll have bugged it by now. Give me the keys. I'll see it's moved in a day or two. Now listen. Hector's got a job for you to do in Oxford, before you come down to Swaythe. Waste disposal ... Nothing dramatic – bloke wants to top himself and needs some help, if you catch my drift. The address is 36 Exeter Gardens and it's off the Banbury Road, guy called Derek Caill – '

'I remember. We had him on an induction course at Skrape. Nasty little creep, punk, red hair, could use a mouthwash. What's he been up to? Fingers in the till?'

'Worse. He packed in the punk modus vivendi six months back. Upwardly mobile, far too conspicuously so, recently traded a new XR 3 for a Toyota MR 2, that sort of thing. Anyway, got disgruntled apparently that we weren't shunting enough product his way, couldn't live with this supply problem we've been having and went back to Scapino for a top-up . . .'

'Little blighter! Right, he'll have to go. But I hope Hector isn't going to make a habit of using me for this sort of job. I'm only an amateur, gifted perhaps, and I'd much rather he went back to using a proper pro firm.'

'Quite. And this one is by no means straightforward. You see the problem is . . .' Burke's face came closer so their cheeks almost touched and he put a massive red hand over Rupert's leaner stronger one while he explained. The barman below, polishing glasses, looked up, felt touched. Love, he thought, can bloom in the most unlikely bosoms.

Bert, thought Rupert at about ten o'clock the next morning, was right. Life never is that simple. He was standing now on the top floor of a house similar to the one he had left in Grosvenor Road but even larger. Again the staircase, which was rather fine with good solid banisters ending with a polished sphere on top of a square column, had been boxed in leaving one front door on each landing, and the one on the top was very firmly fastened. Which of course was as it should be. The course at Skrape included a lecture from an ex-copper, a mate of Burke's, who gave the recruits a sound drilling on how to make domestic premises secure. There was, however, a frosted glass panel with a narrow lintel overlooking the stairwell.

He returned forty minutes later with a plank of solid timber four feet long, one end of which was sawn off on a diagonal, a quality glass-cutter, a tube of Bostik No. 1, and a suction-plunger – a cone of black rubber mounted on a stick such as is used to unblock drains.

He placed the plank across the stairwell, the diagonally sawn-off end resting on the lintel below the pane of glass, the other on the banister rail where it levelled out at the top of the stairs. He swung himself out on to it. Somewhere down below someone started playing a recording of the Kreutzer Sonata. At this moment he really began to enjoy himself. Adrenalin and other juices were pumping into his bloodstream, building up a high as good as a coke one: he was perched over a thirty-foot drop facing one minute's work with inadequate tools and the certainty that the slightest mistake, a tiny moment of bad luck, would drop him into the hall below, or, if fate took a different turn, into the deepest shit. An insect buzzed against the skylight above him, traffic murmured in the distance, and then, much closer but below, a door catch clicked.

He eased his shoulder, loosened the holster that held the 9mm Browning he had found under the floorboards at Grosvenor Road.

A young woman appeared on the landing below, coaxed a shopping bag, a folded pushchair and a two-year-old infant out of the flat after her. She didn't look up. Why should she? She had never had reason to before, though the darkness of the stairwell with the light blocked from the skylight by Rupert's body might well have prompted her to. It took her a long time, a hell of a long time, to get her little convoy down and out.

A worm of mental discomfort squirmed like the onset of a tooth abscess during the process. Really it was a bit much that he, Rupert, was doing chores of this sort. Hector was over-stretched, no doubt of it; the whiff of eccentricity that had always hung about the whole operation and given it the spiky flavour Rupert enjoyed, was going sour, rancid, like an over-ripe Stilton . . .

But when she had gone, and he was alone again with the

insect, and the traffic noise and the Kreutzer Sonata (adulterous lovers hurrying towards each other, towards shared climax), the worm was forgotten and he worked quickly and precisely.

First he fastened the sucker to the corner of the glass nearest to the end of the plank. Then he scored a large curve enclosing the corner, and straight lines down the edges of the corner keeping just inside the putty. Then he took a deep breath and, holding the handle of the plunger firmly in one hand, rapped smartly round the outside of the curve. The exhilaration experienced as the pear-shaped piece of glass held by the plunger came free was sublime.

He wriggled his thighs along the plank, swung his legs over the banister, and the plank slipped. There was a moment of silence, then it crashed on to the tiles thirty feet below. He felt the racket must have disturbed the readers in the Bodleian, a mile away, but his first thought was *Fuck you, Hector.* Certainly the noise got to the music lover. The Kreutzer ecstasy was terminated precociously, another door lower down clicked open. Rupert straightened his tie, his Royal Buff Caps tie, dried his palms on his handkerchief, fastened the middle button of his jacket and trotted down the stairs. On the first landing a tall thin man was looking up at him. His lank black hair only partially concealed incipient baldness; he wore jeans and a Brasenose College sweatshirt.

Rupert nodded at him as he passed. 'Dropped my plank.'
'Oh.'
As Rupert passed on the way back up he said: 'Terrible crash it made,' and went back into his flat. Presently the music began again.

57

At about the time Rupert arrived in Oxford a bronzed and more relaxed-looking Mulligan was paying off his taxi in Dacre Street. New Scotland Yard is wearing green tulle again this year, he thought, looking up at the skirt of green net at third-floor level, set to catch debris from the repairs being carried out higher up. Looks like an over-fat ballerina in a green frock.

He crossed the road in front of the revolving stainless steel sign.

The grey foyer was busy, filled with big men in heavy dark suits, with big shiny black shoes, moving in and out with the busy purposefulness of tanks. For once Mulligan almost became part of his surroundings: only the cut of his light-weight black raincoat, the stylishness of his footwear, the continental layering of his grey hair, betrayed someone who was not an English copper.

He peered over the high counter top. 'James Mulligan to see Rex Tyler, Floor Five.'

The uniformed WPC behind the counter was beautiful: big brown eyes, swags of pinned up black hair. The neck and shoulders of a discus thrower stretched the white shirt; the robust thighs of a distance runner gave perfect contours to the black skirt, police black which people still insist on calling blue.

'Mr Tyler will be down in a moment. Would you care to take a seat?'

Mulligan turned away, found he was looking at a bright gas-flame in a glass case, a penned book of remembrance: A. Jacob . . .

Not enough, even with the grey marble walls and the black leather banquettes, to lift the atmosphere of overcrowding, penny-pinching, things done on the cheap that he always felt when he came here. He recalled how Tyler had told him the building had been wished on them when they moved out of Whitehall, a job-lot the government or somebody was stuck with, not custom-built but something they had tried to adapt, ended up by adjusting to. And now it was all falling apart, was virtually having to be rebuilt from top to bottom.

'Buck, great to see you, great you're here. Sorry I've kept you waiting, I'm getting you fixed up with a pass, I promise you, but the mills of the ADC's office grind exceeding slow. Christ, you're looking well.'

'I'm surprised they even let me over the threshold.'

Tyler, grey with tiredness but high on the big one, driven by the certainty that they were going to crack it this time, no matter what the expense of energy and spirit, took his elbow and hurried him to the lift. 'Thing of the past. Forgiven if not forgotten. Bridges entirely in place again. Have you heard the latest? From Eurac, I mean?' He fingered the button marked five.

'No. I've been out on my own for two weeks.'

'Well, they cracked Suk's secret file. Five days ago.'

'Hey, that's great. Was it good news, what had he got on it?'

'I'll tell you, I'll give you the digest, just hang on a moment . . .'

The doors slid open on to off-white walls that had once been white, and the sort of grey carpet that's meant to clean the dirt off the soles of your shoes before you get off it.

Tyler slammed back a door, narrowly missed knocking over another WPC carrying a pile of box files, swept into the long open-plan office which fills most of the fifth floor. A wall of noise hit them.

He swung himself into an office chair behind a large but very plain desk, waved at an upright chair on the other side. 'Take a pew. I must say Arthur Lord did you proud on this. They asked him to have a go and, bingo, he did it. Give him a bell some time and tell him you appreciate his efforts, eh?'

'Of course I will.'

Suddenly the head of steam was lost, the energy had leaked away, and they sat there looking at each other across the desk piled high with files, papers, littered with pens, rubberbands, paperclips.

'Coffee?'

'Is it from one of those machines?'

'Yes.'

'Does it dispense Coke?'

'Yes.'

'I'd rather have a Coke.' Mulligan stretched, looked out and over the big long office, one hundred and fifty square feet of it. It was busier than an ants' nest. Typewriters and telexes clattered. Phones rang, men and women, some in uniform, most not, moved about from desk to desk. Data slithered across the screens of video computer terminals. It was noisy, overcrowded, dirty, and a lot too many people were smoking. Mulligan felt for his Marlboros, his Zippo.

Tyler set down plastic beakers. 'Well, anyway, we're okay.'

'We are?'

'Basically Suk's file checked out or chimed with a lot that

Arthur had turned up, and a lot we were uncovering by legitimate means. The upshot is the top brass here had a meeting day before yesterday, lawyers in too from the DPP – Department of Public Prosecutions, not a mile away from your DAs – and the result is that they accept that we really have located a monster, that the Web and Spiderman are objectively real not just figments of our imagination, and we are now under orders to go for them. I wish you'd been there. Why weren't you? Where were you?'

'Sorry. I was fishing. For salmon. Norway.'

There was a pause. Statements of this sort are rarely heard on Floor Five.

Tyler drank, grimaced, went on: 'Two extra goodies. You're reinstated as someone who uses Lifebuoy and is nice to know. You are our official link to Eurac, Interpol, and all police stations east of Dover. Good?'

'Good. And?'

'Well, you know the set-up. Rival agencies. Customs and Excise. Regional drug squads. It's accepted now that an operation of this sort has to have an overall boss . . . and I've been elected. And the codename is, wait for it, Snowdrop.'

'That is great. Really great.' Mulligan meant it, was relieved that he would not have to accommodate to someone else, but had misgivings. Tyler, he knew, was a maverick, an individualist, was known as such. This was a hot, very hot potato. The thinking must have been: if hands are going to be burnt, let them be his.

Tyler pressed on: 'Okay. What we need now is a date and a place. For the drop. Everything else hangs on that. We've got fraud squads and Customs and Excise wearing their VAT hat, which means no warrants needed, ready to go for DLC, Ambrose and assorted other companies, but we can't touch them until Spiderman has powder on his table for obvious reasons. So. Make with the girlfriend – '

Mulligan frowned, showed irritation. 'Not my girlfriend.'

'Come on. Don't tell me you never had your leg over. Has she got a line yet on where and when this two tons arrive?'

'I'm meeting her tomorrow.' He sensed Tyler's disappointment, hurried on. 'And listen. When I do I want none of your lot around. The meeting has to be absolutely clean. Not just because of her, but because the other side will be watching, and if they see a load of plods trampling the ground for a mile around they'll . . . well, they might kill her. Worse still they might abort.'

'All right. All right.' Again the sudden loss of energy, then: 'We have to go to Oxford.'

'We do?'

'Yep. I've been keeping this till I'd told you the latest from St-Cloud. The regional drug squad at Oxford have pulled in a very tasty villain, who is coming apart at the seams and wants to talk. Coming?'

'What do you think?' He was already stubbing out the cigarette.

'That's my boy. If you had a hat I'd tell you to grab it,' crowed Tyler, reaching for his. 'There's a fast mobile and a driver waiting for us in Broadway.'

Not the fastest mobile in the world, but fast enough and very comfortable – a Daimler four-litre Sovereign in police livery, which meant traffic got out of the way when drivers saw it in their rear-view mirrors. Yet even before Westway lifted them up above the peeling paint and cracked stucco of Bayswater and Notting Hill and the wide windscreen was filled with big white clouds rolling through a blue sky, Tyler had filled in the details.

'NatWest Fraud Office alerted us first. Manager of their branch in Headington, North Oxford, didn't like the smell coming off one of his accounts, a Derek Caill. Six weeks ago banked five grand plus or minus in cash, then again three weeks ago. There's more to it than that – a connection with Ambrose Finance of the sort Lord told us to keep an eye open for, and of course he's a DL cardholder. Anyway. The NatWest Fraud Office alerted the Oxford Regional Drug Squad and they kept an eye on this Caill, and of course were passing everything back to us as it came in. Well, it became clear he had two sources. One was well organised, drops made before they told him where to pick them up, that sort of thing, had all the look and feel of Spiderman's operation, but of course they've found ways of making the cashflow look all right, so that didn't fit with these ten grand in notes and coin. But then the silly bastard made another pick-up from our old friends at Scapino, much in the way of the old routines they used to run. Incidentally, there's a lot more activity there than there used to be, and we plan to turn them over too when the balloon goes up. But I'm pretty sure they don't have a lot to do with Spiderman and Ambrose any more.'

'So what do you think this Caill was up to?'

'Well, I think it's fairly easy to put together. I must say the NatWest bank manager is being very helpful, but under the Drug Trafficking Offences Act 1986 he is obliged to be more positively forthcoming than used to be the case. We'll be seeing him later. But it looks as though for whatever reason Caill was not getting the turnover from Spiderman that he was used to, so he went back to Scapino to top up his cashflow.'

Mulligan smiled grimly but with self-satisfaction.

'What's tickling you?' Tyler asked.

'I'll tell you in a minute.' He looked out of the window. Fields, factory farming, trees intermittent now amongst the industrial estates and the Wimpey homes. Uxbridge. He was slightly annoyed he'd betrayed any emotion, but there was something important to him in all this.

'Anyway, they kept very close surveillance on him, and they must have a fucking good team there. They identified three ouncers – the wife of a research scientist who'd joined Maggie's Army so they needed the income, a college servant, and a rep for a firm called Monbella Graphics. And by yesterday afternoon they felt there was so much angel-dust blowing about they had to act, they'd be in trouble if they didn't, so we gave them the go-ahead and they fingered all four. They're all in the Oxford nick and the Beak there will remand them in custody for a week. That's the scenario as of now. Anyway, you sly old bastard, what were you grinning about just now? Things beginning to go all right at last, is that it?'

'Something like that.'

'It was all a bit flaky for a time, wasn't it? First Lowndes Square, then Suk blown up, and none of us speaking to you. You must have felt very isolated. Then that girl in the Alps. Is that why you took off to Norway?'

'Yes. Yes it was.'

'Say no more, 'nuff said.'

And now Mulligan really warmed to Tyler more than ever before, for he sensed Tyler's appreciation of what had happened to him. In more ways than one he had been responsible for Suk's death, and Bonnie Day's. Jones could go too. He had needed a total and unscheduled break to sort out where he stood, had taken it, cut off all communication with the outside world and thought the thing through. Finally it had been von Sachs' missile attack that had made him hang on in there: Anton would have insisted. Six people had been killed in the attack and twenty-eight seriously injured. Peanuts. Compared with. Nevertheless. And Suk, whose parents were members of the Czech Communist Party, had been born in another place – Treblinka – and his mother had died there. Suk – who knew that evil money is used for evil ends.

'Hullo. What's this?'

The driver, a young good-looking constable in black-epau-letted short-sleeved white shirt, was handing the radiophone handset with his left hand back between the front seats towards Tyler.

'Oxford on the other end. Want a word with you, sir.'

The message was short, provoked a vicious response. 'The fucking idiots. The stupid imbeciles.' He handed the phone back, turned to Mulligan, ground a cigarette end into the ashtray on the armrest between them as if it were a poisonous insect. 'Know what they've done? Only let him out on bail. Solicitor from London. One hundred thousand pounds bank-er's draft and a solid assurance that his client was prepared to help the police in their enquiries. And the bench let him go.'

Mulligan's lips tightened. 'Get his home address. And let's get there. Quick, eh?'

The driver responded without waiting to be told, and beneath the banshee wail of the siren took them up to a hundred and twenty for the last fifteen miles of the motorway. It took them less than a quarter of an hour to get halfway down the Banbury road into Oxford, and they were there ahead of the local police, but only just.

Lacking Rupert's initiative, or any motive to be quiet, it took two burly constables two noisy minutes with a fire-axe to get through Caill's front door defences, but as they stood aside the silence that met Mulligan, Tyler, and a uniformed inspec-tor was like a wall. You develop an instinct, thought Mulligan, about rooms where there's a stiff. Especially if the end has been violent. Not that this one looked violent. The decor and furnishings, expensive, overblown, obscene, with joky posters and photomontages in stainless steel satin-finish frames, huge artificial flowers simulating giant poppies, the best and latest in consumer durables, were all undisturbed.

Derek Caill was not to be disturbed either. Dressed in a modishly baggy black suit, his red hair swept back off his forehead, his round spectacles awry across his spotty face, he was curled up on a red leather hide sofa with his thumb in his mouth.

Up under the big sash windows there was a rectangular white table mounted on white metal legs. On it there were a few papers, a paperback *Prick Up Your Ears* left open but turned jacket side up, and the Amstrad PCW 8256. The screen was alive, the cursor still pulsed at the end of the message.

Sod the police. Sod Scapino's for getting me into this. I've had a good run and I'm taking the easy way. No problems. No need to cut me up, it's Nembutal and Scotch, Nembies rule, OK?

Mulligan felt Tyler's presence at his shoulder.

'I'm not taking that too seriously,' Tyler said.

'I should bloody hope not. Selfers don't write joky notes. But why in particular?'

'There's been a break-in. And very recent. Piece of glass sliced out of the bathroom window, overlooking the stairwell, and stuck back with glue that's still giving off vapour. Clever job though. Thirty-foot drop and no visible means of support.'

The awful joke was unavoidable. 'Spiderman.'

The laughter that came was spiked with hysteria, and not as easily controlled as the Oxford policemen thought it should be.

58

Harriet's mother – like most women of her age and caste – had had to conceal from the world both her intellectuality and her sensuality. The repression of both had been incomplete and they surfaced at unlikely times and in unlikely places. Once, when taking Harriet to Salisbury at the age of thirteen to be kitted out with a new school uniform, she had paused in the Close, looked up at the spire and said: 'Really, it's just a phallic symbol, you know?'

Thirty-five years younger than her mother, learning far more from her peers than from the nuns at the weekly-boarding convent school for girls she had been going to, Harriet of course knew exactly what was meant, yet was amazed to hear it from Mama. And she never forgot the occasion. Indeed, it had made such an impression that it created an ineradicable mental tic: for the rest of her life whenever she saw a spire or a free-standing column the memory was tripped. As it had been that night in Paris in front of the Châtelet.

And never more cogently than when she came to the Tower at Swaythe, known also as the Campanile Folly. Built in 1902 out of brick on a steel-reinforced concrete frame, it is an imitation of the campanile of St Mark's in Venice. This was not mere whimsy: the aim of the entrepreneurial construction millionaire who caused it to be built was to persuade the City of Venice to use the new technique of reinforced concrete in the rebuilding of their tower, which had fallen down in July of that year, and to give his firm the contract. This he did not get: but Hampshire was left with the Tower at Swaythe.

At two hundred and fifty feet, it is seventy feet shorter than its model, but from a distance the resemblance is exact. Hardly narrowing at all, the fluted brickwork, pierced down one corner with small arched windows that mark the staircase that supplements the lift whose shaft runs up the centre, soars to a cornice beneath sixteen arched windows, four filling each side, then a block which houses the lifting mechanism: the glans, if that's the way your mind runs when you see a tower. Finally a pyramidal prepucal roof is topped not with an angel but a gilded globe.

Close to, though, it has a tatty look, the brickwork needs repointing, the cornice, entablatures and balustrades at the top are roughly moulded concrete not carved stone, and it is set on a bleak moor where patches of thin grass survive the encroachments of etiolated heather and scraggy gorse. It is serviced by a narrow, unfenced tarmacked track.

But inside, at the top, in the suite of rooms that enclose the lift shaft, a transformation had begun when Mermaid Pleasure acquired it in 1983, and had then been taken further by the new owners, a holding company registered on Sark with nominee directors.

A week after she first entered this suite, Harriet met Mulligan a few miles away, at the Beaulieu Road Station Hotel, at four o'clock, and for the first ten minutes or so could talk of nothing else.

'It really is quite fantastic, you know? There it is, sticking up out of a clump of scraggy pubic gorse like the prick of Gog or Magog, or the Old Man of Cerne – from a distance, you know, you feel you can reach out your hand and wank it. That blob on top is like a bead of golden come . . .'

Mulligan wondered, not for the first time, just what sort of shit Lovejoy was giving her. Also, looking around the garden they were in, a mixture of ancient orchard and modern children's playground with the railway line fifty yards away behind stabling and a high hedge, he was worried about what the other two couples who were there, and their kids, might make of this sort of talk. Her voice was more shrill than it had been, carried further.

'. . . but inside, at the top, it's another thing all together. You know, I went up it when I was a kid, and Hec . . . they have transformed it.'

'Oh yes?'

'First the lift. It used to crank and creak and take ages, now it's one of those high-speed ones. But it's the top . . . Well, the views always were terrific. Almost in front there are the Needles like broken teeth sticking out of the sea and, you know, they look small and below you, as if you were in an aeroplane. And then the Isle of Wight and, you know, you can see the sea the other side of it for quite a way, certainly beyond Freshwater Bay. And up the Solent, beyond Lymington to Fawley and Gosforth . . . and on the other side of Christchurch Bay, Hengistbury Head and way beyond over Bournemouth to Poole Harbour – '

'In short the ideal place from which to oversee the whole operation.'

She giggled, put her long thin fingers over his hand. 'That's precisely what he thought you'd think, what he wants you to think.' She sensed his doubt and her eyes hardened, her lips compressed into a thin line, then she shook her head and turned away. 'Yes. Really. He's going to stay there all through it all watching his forty-footers, one called *Ambrosiana*, the other called *Designed Discernment*, competing all through Cowes

Week. He'll have guests. Sir Alec Greene. A junior minister at the Department of Trade called Charles Bosham. Even Uncle Geoff might turn up. You see? The Lowndes Square bit all over again if you do try to drop in. I say, are we going to get any tea?'

He looked round the garden, peered into the pleasant-looking conservatory behind them, looking for the waitress who had taken his order. When he looked back Harriet's eyes were fixed, the pupils contracted, staring, emerald chips. She is, he thought, a lot thinner than she was four months ago, even paler. Her hair, once so glorious, was scraped back off her forehead, was streaked with fairer colouring so it looked tawny rather than red-gold. Lean, and, he sensed, tougher, as though she had looked deeply into herself and her situation and come to certain irreversible decisions about it all.

'It would,' she said, 'be altogether too obvious, wouldn't it? A control post, a headquarters, perched like that up above the marinas and the yacht basins, and even the wharfs where the Customs launches are moored. No. It's a bait, it really is. To lure your resources down here with all this show while the real thing is mounted on the other side, the other end of the country. Where it will be done discreetly, quietly, successfully. A bait, but such an obvious one that he doesn't expect you to take it.'

He drummed his fingers on the table for a moment, looked out past apple trees already laden with swelling fruit, past pines to undulating heath just beginning to haze with purple. It was warm, very warm when the sun shone past heavy cloud, but the light wind bore a prescient chill when it did not.

'Okay then, so where does it come in?'

She leant back. Her eyes narrowed, the shrillness left her voice and she spoke with quiet determination. 'No, Buck Mulligan, it's not as easy as that any more. I know where it's coming in, I really do. But before I tell you I want guarantees. Yes, I know, I remember all you've said about what you can do to me if I rat on you, let you down, but quite simply that's not enough. I've spent a lot of time thinking this through, and one thing I'm now fixed on is this. When this is all over, however it turns out – and I'm covered in other areas too, against all eventualities I think – however it turns out I am going to walk away from it as though none of it happened.

571

And I mean walk away. None of this reduced-sentence-in-an-open-prison shit. Right?'

The growing uneasiness he had been experiencing bloomed into something colder, nearer dread. He thought of Tyler. He thought of how things had changed. And every moment that he hesitated he knew weakened whatever hope he might have had of convincing her. Fortunately the waitress appeared with a tray and all the paraphernalia of an English cream tea.

'There's gateau-s too,' she chirruped, 'Black Forest, Chocolate Fudge Cake, Strawberry with Fresh Cream – shall I bring the trolley?'

By the time she'd gone he reckoned he had thought it through. As Harriet poured tea he began: 'I can no longer do that. I think you realise that. This is, at the moment, entirely a British operation. And under British law criminal co-operation with the police can do no more than pray for, beg for, but certainly not demand, clemency, leniency. This entire case is going to end up in British courts and I can't make promises.'

She nodded quite furiously as he said all this, and took him up where he left off. 'But that's not all, is it? In this absurd country it's illegal to run an undercover agent who is herself carrying out criminal, indictable offences . . .' – and now she spaced the words very deliberately indeed – 'and police officers who do, get sent to jail. That's for starters, Buck. But going on from there, I have a very clear picture of the routines you've been running for the last eight months. Of the extent to which you have gone way beyond the law, not only in England, but in France, Switzerland, Italy, to get what you want. Right?'

For a moment he tried to brazen it out. 'Come on. What judge in what country, faced with the enormity of the crimes committed by Crystal and all its associates, is going to fail to sympathise with my motives . . .'

But she was shaking her head again. 'That sort of cop-out gets by in storybooks. But in real life how much of what Crystal is, is ever going to get into the open, let alone the courts? Do you really think you'll ever get people like Boltana, Mendoza, the Malatestas in dock? No. You know you won't. And that's why you've been carrying on the way you have, trying to harm them, damage them by basically and provably illegal means. Means which, if anything like the whole story

even begins to get aired, will put you in the dock as sure as
. . .' – frantically she searched for an image and found it in the
orchard – 'as sure as God made little green apples.'

Suddenly, with only the briefest warning on its two-tone
horn, an Inter-City train, Weymouth to Waterloo, blasted
through the tiny station on the other side of the hedge. As the
silence flooded back he felt, almost heard, the beat of his heart.

'You're attempting to threaten me, blackmail me.'

For a moment there was a real, terrible anger in her eyes,
and a purplish tinge appeared in her face near the corners of
her painted mouth.

'Okay, okay, I take the point. So what do I have to do?' he
said.

She breathed in deeply, getting the sudden rush of emotion
under control. 'The first thing is to stay alive. Convince Hector
that you are sufficiently harmless, indeed even useful, for it to
be an unnecessary extra burden on his resources to order your
murder.'

'How do I do that?'

'Act, be seen to act, on the false information I'm about to
give you.'

'Which is?'

'That two tons of cocaine are arriving in Rotterdam on the
third of August, will be shipped on in a coaster to a rendezvous
off the south-east tip of Ireland, where a Spanish wine freighter
takes them on board. They'll be landed at Bristol on the eighth
of August.'

'And how do I make sure he knows that the NDIU and the
other relevant agencies are acting on this information?'

'Just make sure they act. Convincingly. Burke has mates in
the right places. They're waiting to see you go into action. In
Bristol.'

'All right. Is there any more tea?' He waited while she went
through the appropriate rituals. 'Okay. Where does the real
drop take place?'

'The NDIU will get, at the end of the day, two tons of
cocaine. And a lot of villains. You will have set back Crystal a
long, long way. I can promise you they will be financially back
to square one. Right?'

'Yes.'

'But you don't get Hector or me or Rupert. We walk away. That's the deal.'

'Shit.'

He stood up so smartly that she had to dive to save the crockery. He stormed round the garden, the playground, the orchard with its ancient apple trees, and she sat there and waited.

He came back. He was brusque, dismissive. 'All right. Where? When?'

'Newcastle. On the third a boat called the *Byker Lass*, carrying a mixed cargo including two tons of a chemical called Manganox, leaves Rotterdam for Newcastle. She's due to dock midday on the fifth at Wallsend.'

'Right.' He pulled back the chair he had been sitting on, made its metal feet screech on the stone floor, sat on it again. 'If that works out, I'll do my best for you. There's going to be one hell of a shambles; there always is when the doors are kicked down for the big bust, and that may get in the way; on the other hand it may help. But don't get the idea I'm too bothered by your threats. All right, you could embarrass me, cause me a lot of hassle, but if I help you walk away it's because . . . Well, I just don't want to see you rot in jail, and because you've been a real help, shown yourself to be basically a goodie. Right? The others I won't say the same for. We're pretty sure Bridge killed a guy two days ago, did you know that? And he put away Bonnie Day and that French journalist, and incidentally that must all make you reconsider the possibility he killed Roget . . .'

Her eyes remained cold, refused to flinch.

He went on: 'There's one more thing though. We have to arrange a way of talking to each other if either of us needs to. We have to have a number we can both ring, leave messages on for both of us to pick up and answer. Look. A lot could depend on this. I might need a vital piece of information; you might need to tell me where you're going, what stones you don't want us to lift so you can hide under them. And anyway, you're meant to tell me more details about this fake Bristol drop, remember?'

She thought about this for a long time, nibbling at a scone, apparently watching the white-rumped house martins swooping between the pines. At last her fist closed over a paper serviette. 'There's an answering machine on my phone at Witham Square. I am still in business as a photographer, you know? I still occasionally ring to see what's there – '

'That's ideal.' He was brusque now. 'From tomorrow there'll be a live listener on the other end as well as the machine to make sure whatever you say gets to me as quickly as possible. And if I have a message for you, then when you ring they'll give it to you. So try if you can to ring at least once a day.'

'You think of everything.'

'I try. If you're going to come out of this free and in one piece, I must.' At last he leaned a little closer and his finger moved towards her mouth, offering an intimacy he had so far denied her. But her face flinched away.

He sighed, looked at his watch. 'The slow train that gets me back to Southampton will be here in five minutes.'

'And I have to get back to the Prick of Swaythe.' Suddenly she caught his thick, strong wrist in her long white fingers. 'Buck. Get the Bristol thing right. That's serious, you know? If they don't think you're going for Bristol, then they'll off you.'

He freed his hand. 'They can try. Okay then. Take care. You that way, I this . . . as the poet said. We meet at Philippi. He said that too.'

As she moved away he called: 'And the name of the boat that's bringing it to Rotterdam?'

She turned: 'The *San Fermín*.'

Two hours later he was in the foyer of New Scotland Yard again, having used the train's Vodaphone to summary for Tyler what he had learnt, and, yes, she was there again, the athletic WPC. She'd caught the sun somewhere, sun or wind – fuck-all sun in this crazy country. There was just a hazing of dark hair on her top lip and strands hung down in front of her ears, and more on her forearms the way some Italian girls, some Spanish . . .

Mulligan went on thinking about her as Tyler again led him down drab busy corridors, up in the lift and out again.

'We've checked out that Tower. The ADC's unhappy about it. Spiderman rented it for Cowes Week. Last year and the year before Fujippon took it. It's a stylish place big corporations like to hire, particularly during Cowes. And two years ago Fujippon insisted on a lot of electronics so they could monitor the Jap entry in the Admiral's Cup. My feeling is that your young lady has it right: it's a blind, it's too obvious by half: to try to smuggle two tons of cocaine into the south of England during Cowes Week would be absurd, megalomaniac, Napoleonic. And really' – and he said this without a smile – 'the ADC is not willing to authorise yet again kicking down a door behind which the likes of Sir Alec Greene might be lurking. You know, I really do think we have to go for Tyneside and make a convincing gesture in the south-west. I mean one thing's for sure. If your girlfriend hasn't got it right she's up the creek for fifteen years; so she's got it right.'

They'd reached his desk again. Tyler again obtained cups of coffee and Coke. 'Newcastle looks good. Myklades already has a small-plane airstrip there, and those Chinook choppers. K-D are there and I think we should bust Duxbury – after all we're pretty sure he has a habit to keep up . . .'

But one word had set off a train of thought in Mulligan's head. Napoleon. Myklades was a Napoleon freak, that was for sure. From way back, Mulligan now drew on his own memory banks. The Corsican corporal had had his charm for him too when, as a rather withdrawn adolescent in St Louis, boxed in on one side by the very wealthy but strict Quaker uncle and aunt who had taken over his upbringing after his mother had tired of coping with him, and on the other by peers of crass philistinism who could not see beyond the American dream of the Eisenhower years, he had retreated for a time into heroes and hero-worship. Napoleon succeeded by the feint to the left or the right, he forced his opponents to weaken the centre. Lightning marches reconstituted his own centre and the columns blasted through before the divided enemy could regroup . . .

'. . . I haven't checked out the *San Fermín*, yet. Hang on.' Tyler picked up the phone but the call was just to the other end of the long noisy room. A man in a navy-blue blazer, brass buttons, not part of a uniform but suggesting the nautical, raised a thumb to him as they both replaced their handsets. 'Price. Used to be at Dover, in fact he was the guy who pulled Jones a year ago, now on the Customs desk here. They've got all the shipping news on tap. You'll have to handle Rotterdam carefully if you're to stop them busting the *San Fermín* themselves. By the way, we've settled on Oxford for the operations room.'

'Why?'

'First, it's where we can hold Bridge if we get him. Second, the offices of the Designer Living Card and Leisure for the Discerning are there. Third, it has good communications to the west, the north, and even if need be to the south. Agreed?'

Mulligan thought of Brussels in June 1815, but before he could answer found he was looking up into the cold eyes of the man who had ordered Harriet's body search at Dover. Little Hitler she had called him, and she could be right. And here he was, handing Tyler a printout.

Tyler, with the enthusiasm, the energy, the exaltation seeping back into his voice, recited: '*San Fermín*. Seventeen-thousand-five-hundred-ton reefer, registered Panama, on charter to another Panamanian company, sailed ten days ago from Maracaibo, due Rotterdam day after tomorrow, the third of August. Mixed cargo, food and chemicals. Chemicals. W'hae, I like it, I like it. Buck. It all fits. We have a date for the showdown, the last round-up, its the OK Corral at last . . .'

On the way out, as he got to the foyer and saw the open triangle of roads outside, the patch of green, the big polished metal sign all suddenly blessed with strong sunlight, Mulligan felt a sudden surge of excitement, of confidence. Without checking his stride he swung right round the glass cabinet with its gas flame of remembrance, back to the high reception counter. She was still there.

'What's your name?'

Her eyes were big and very dark brown, but not in the least cow-like. They narrowed warily, ready for impertinence or rebuke, ready to fight her corner. He liked that.

'WPC Porter.'

'First name?'

'Beatrice.' She blushed very, very slightly. 'I prefer Bea.'

'I'm not sure I do. WPC Porter, Miss Beatrice Porter, I suppose you're qualified to drive in the line of duty?'

'Yes, Mr Mulligan.'
'We must see what we can do for you.'

59

The Dutch Customs officer was called like Holland's greatest painter, Van Rijn – but here the similarity ended. Van Rijn was tall, blond, and had the huge broad toucan beak of a nose that a lot of famous Dutchmen have had, and people of Dutch extraction: John Updike, Art Garfunkel, John Gielgud. Perched eighty feet above the neighbouring wharf, in the cramped cabin of a crane, he talked Mulligan through the arrival and docking of the *San Fermín*.

'Right. My colleagues will be almost the first to leave the boat. They boarded her two hours ago near the mouth of the Nieuwe Waterweg. They will have gone through the holds and checked what they could see there against the manifests. They will have queried the chief officer on any matter that looked wrong to them. They will have paid no attention to goods remaining on board, scheduled for a destination beyond here. Of course, they have powers similar to those enjoyed by our British colleagues to search without warning, to insist on containers being opened and so forth. But they use them rarely, and only when they have had an indication that such action might be rewarded. Like our colleagues too we are understaffed and overworked. Over a hundred vessels dock in Rotterdam every working day, never mind the leisure craft that filter in and out of our waterways and leak into the commercial areas or use them as short cuts. They will not have checked the crew nor the crew's quarters, this not being normal practice. Crew who leave the ship are checked at the dock gates. Here they come now.'

Two men in dark, vaguely nautical uniforms, with soft briefcases under their arms, descended the short railed gangplank to the quay. Almost immediately they disappeareed in the litter of containers, stacks of timber, cranes and rails that lay alongside the long low warehouse, built in old brown brick with black corrugated roofing. A logo made of intertwined OVW for Otto Van Wijk was stencilled at intervals along it and on three huge cranes, one of which, mounted on six sets of bogies, now trundled down rails to service the *San Fermín*.

'I guess the next hour or so will be pretty boring. Watching five hundred tons of green bananas off-loaded . . .'

Boring and uncomfortable. The cabin was entirely functional, which meant that since the enormous crane was operated by only one man, there was only one seat – metal and plastic, very thinly padded – and the rest of the space was taken up with a bank of controls: levers, wheels, dials and push-buttons. Van Rijn sat in the seat, Mulligan, head thrust forward and down by the low ceiling, was squeezed in behind him with a wall-mounted fire extinguisher pushing into his back. It was stuffy too, the fitful early August sunshine very warm when it came, fermenting the slow build-up of body gases that all too quickly compounded the smells of oil and warm plastic that were already there.

For a time there was interest of a sort outside. High up as they were, they had a huge view of the world's busiest waterway: a slowly curving stretch of steel-grey water with just a hint of oily green in it, three or four hundred metres wide edged with apparently endless quays, forested with cranes and lifting gear, stacked with containers, lined with big boats from every major port in the world. Half a mile upstream the slender column of the Euromast, altogether more stylishly shaped than the Post Office Tower in London, marked the beginning of the city, giant high-rises, office blocks, parks filled with poplars, and, just before the curve of the river took it out of sight, the flattened steel arcs of the Verl Willemsbrug spanning the Maas, the Meuse.

But the romance was not obvious: containerisation has shut it into boxes. And the boats were drab, many of them seemingly rusty hulks, cluttered with gear, streaked with the greasy grime of diesel fuel, any grace at bow or stern where the flow of water still dictates the line defeated by the cost-effective geometry of the rest. The *San Fermín* was no different, and the eight-hundred-ton coaster *Byker Lass*, already tied up at the OVW wharf, looked even more squalid. At thirty years old, with high wide prow designed to buck the choppiness of the North Sea and a low superstructure that seemed to cower as far back from the high fo'c'sle as possible, one felt that if she were cast off and allowed to drift like a crewless *Marie Céleste*, she'd waddle back to Tyneside out of sheer habit.

Mulligan liked the barges though: not for their long narrow sleekness slicing through the water, gunwales only inches above the surface, but for the little bungalows perched on the sterns, with lacy curtains, potted plants, and washing strung out to dry. One of them, flying a Swiss flag and inscribed *Jungfrau von Delemont*, Basel, occupied the last of Otto Van Wijk's berths and was unloading pattens of what looked like two-kilo grey bags filled with some chemical . . . Using binoculars Mulligan deciphered the stencilled stamp on them: the one word *Manganox* written in red, circled in blue.

Van Rijn's radio bleeped. Mulligan waited, listened to a Dutch dialect which sounded so like some sort of swallowed-back nasal English that it was infuriating to find it remained incomprehensible.

'My colleagues have seen the manifests. The shipment is very mixed and not all of it by any means destined to be unloaded here. One item is very suspect, however, though a circumstantial story explains it.'

'Something to do with Manganox?' Mulligan's mind leapt, but was wrong-footed.

Van Rijn frowned. 'No. A chemical called Sol-Methrine A. There are two tons of it. Apparently it is a pesticide, inert as a white powder, done up in two-kilo bags, destined for Mersin on the south coast of Turkey, but . . .'

'Go on, go on – they're off-loading it here.' This time the jump was well judged.

'That's right.'

'And the circumstantial story?'

'An outbreak of whitefly in the Turkish cotton crop is predicted. The aphids mutate quickly, so there are several types of Sol-Methrine. Sol-Methrine A was ordered from the plant in Venezuela. But now it is decided that Sol-Methrine B, made in Düsseldorf, is what is required. So the *San Fermín* drops its Sol-Methrine A to be warehoused here, and picks up the Sol-Methrine B which, with the Manganox, was part of the cargo of that Swiss barge.'

'So, so far we have documentation for two two-ton parcels of Sol-Methrine, and four tons of Manganox, all done up in two-kilo plastic bags. What is Manganox?'

'It's a catalyst developed by a Swiss chemical firm which is used in the production of heat-resistant insulators used in nuclear power reactors.'

'And where's it going?'

'We don't know for certain, and my colleagues did not ask since there was no call to and you have asked us not to alert them to our attentions. But previous shipments have gone to Tyneside and Cork in Ireland. In both places there are factories making these insulators. The interesting factor is that Otto Van Wijk does not usually handle it.'

'You've got an awful lot of this at your fingertips.'

Van Rijn looked doubtfully at his hands.

'I mean, you know a lot about all this in advance.'

'Ah, I understand, you were speaking in idioms.' A slight blush crept up the fair Dutchman's neck; whether from embarrassment or pleasure it was difficult to say. 'Yes, of course, we have constantly updated reference banks on the cargoes that go through the port so we can spot any unusual or inexplicable movement. And you briefed us in advance so it was not difficult to identify and reacquaint oneself with the relevant data.'

Mulligan watched a further hundred or so twenty-kilo cardboard boxes of Turbana bananas dropped on the quay and forklifted into the warehouse, realised his leg had gone to sleep.

'Tell me if anything interesting happens.' Hobbling, he moved out of the cabin, through the big steel box that housed the powerful winches, out on to a catwalk on the other side. The air was fresher here: at least it moved and an imaginative effort could find the tang of the sea at the back of the combination of diesel and the stagnant water from a nearby dock basin. He massaged his leg for a moment through overalls put on to lend credence to the story that they were maintenance engineers, felt for cigarettes and cursed when he realised he had left them in his jacket pocket back at the Customs House.

It was, he realised, all a lot too hairy, all far too likely to go the way Myklades had planned; likely that, Napoleon-like, he was feinting between left, centre and right. And the implication was that the cocaine was headed somewhere quite different from any of the three putative destinations. It was even possible, though they would be right in the shit if it were so, that this whole *San Fermín* business was a feint.

Tyler's hunch that the north-east of England was the destination had received confirmations. Two days earlier, up on the Northumbrian fells, Duxbury had crumbled. It had had its amusing side, according to Tyler. As soon as the police identified themselves as members of the regional drug squad Agnes Duxbury, thin, mad, had declared in her posh Scottish accent that she had been about to ring them anyway. She led them straight to the library, to the 'secret' drawer in her husband's desk. 'Eh mek noo doot this is the muck you'll be looking for,' and revealed three hundred grams of cocaine wrapped in foil that had clearly held much more, perhaps as much as half a kilo. 'The silly wee man was tekking far too much, it was doing him noo good at all.'

Down at the Newcastle nick Duxbury had talked and talked, and amongst it all came the news that Rupert had been in the area a lot in recent months, and that the leisure airstrip was also now being used by the small firm using war-surplus Chinooks to fast-move freight about the north-east. The assumption to be made was obvious enough. The *Byker Lass*, having dropped two containers of Nutcrackers, Kapp guns, and munitions for the use of at Rotterdam for onward shipment to Israel, all perfectly legitimate and properly documented, was to return with the cocaine which would be winched off her at sea at night and 'coptered back into Northumbria, dropped in one of the more deserted areas and warehoused. But was this the assumption Myklades wanted them to make? Was this the bluff, and the information he had wanted Harriet to pass on that it was to be landed at Bristol a double bluff?

Still longing for a cigarette Mulligan ducked back into the engine housing, squeezed back into the cabin on the other side.

'Listen, without making waves, do you think your people could find out what boat is picking up the Manganox scheduled for Cork?'

'Making waves? Ah, you mean causing undue turbulence. We'll try. Meanwhile I was about to call you – we have two visitors just arrived on the wharf who might interest you.'

Fine-tuning his binoculars, the first man Mulligan saw was

big, with huge shoulders, a good head of black hair. He turned, revealing a reddish face filled with bonhomie and a large black moustache, to talk to the man behind him. And now Mulligan's interest blossomed into that greatest of satisfactions that is founded in part on relief: as when with a new lover one feels and knows she has come, that one has held on long enough. Precisely focused as he strode along the narrow walk between gunwale and the open hold was Rupert Bridge, neat in a well-cut grey suit with two vents, a narrow-brimmed brown derby pulled over his forehead (the one he wore when he went racing), but still completely unmistakable.

'The date of one's mother's birthday,' Aguirre murmured, slipping the magnetic post he had carried for nearly three weeks into its slot.

'Yes, indeed,' said Rupert, and dabbed the first six digits of his army number.

Aguirre straightened, rubbed the small of his back with huge palms, cast a slow look around them at the bleak red ribbed walls, like the inside of a cartoon whale, and up into the rectangle of sky above them. Then he stooped, lifted the beam their open sesames had released. Still on their four pattens the one thousand packets lay, exactly as they had left them at Punto Gallinas, the most northern point of the southern cone, seven thousand miles away.

'*¿Una muestra?* Make sure there has been no deterioration? It is not possible, the temperature has been a constant eight degrees. You saw the bananas. Still green. But you are welcome.' A shrug, the huge palms spread.

Rupert waived the offer.

'Then you authorise the EFT of twenty million US dollars to our account in the Berkeley's Key Bank and we can move on to the next stage. There is a telex in Otto's office.'

'Sorry, old chum, you've got that wrong. EFT only authorised when the goods are off this boat. Them's me orders.'

'*¡Mierda. Hijo de puta!*' Aguirre crashed his palms together.

'Come on, old sport. The shipment from Kapp-Duxbury is in your hands. Play fair. You can't expect to hold both shipments, and the money.'

'*Hostia*, I have to go make a phone call. I can do it from the bridge.'

583

While he was gone Rupert looked round the almost empty hold. It now held just two tons of Sol-Methrine A from Maracaibo stacked on four pattens. At the bottom of each stack lay a quarter of a ton of unmarked, spoilt, positively trampled cocaine of no great value. But in the secure container they had both just opened two tons of virgin pure untrodden snow, worth four hundred million on the street if the current price trend continued, sealed in bags marked Sol-Methrine B. He felt pretty sure he knew what the purpose of Aguirre's phone call would be, and he grinned to himself as excitement began to mount in his stomach and chest and he felt his scrotum tighten with it. He pulled out his handkerchief and dried the palms of his hands, and the glee he felt suddenly bubbled up in a laugh.

Presently Aguirre returned. 'It's okay. You relock your side, I leave mine open, and you authorise the EFT as soon as she sails.'

'No. You could get back on board after she's sailed and relock your side too. No EFT until I've seen this parcel off the boat. Them's me orders.'

Silence spread across the cavernous space around them. Beyond, the busyness of the world's largest port buzzed on. Aguirre's hand moved slowly towards his left armpit and Rupert did not flinch, maintained his pose, shoulders against a stanchion, feet lightly crossed, head bent forward. Aguirre's hand reappeared holding a wallet, from which he took a thin gold tooth pick. He worked at his teeth for a full two minutes. Then:

'Can we talk about this?'

Rupert lifted his head, straightened his knees, said clearly but very quietly: 'We can talk.'

Somewhere behind him a rat that had been deprived of a home by the removal of the bananas, and been hiding in a bilge hole, made a break for it, scuttled round the perimeter of the hold, found nothing to its liking, and returned to the bilge.

Perched above them but beyond the sight-line so they could not actually see into the bottom of the hold, Mulligan and Van Rijn speculated: Olympians directing the affairs of those below. Mulligan rejected the comparison – to be so confident so early was to invite a slap if not retribution from whatever forces do shape our lives.

'They're a long time down there.'

'I suppose when you are transferring ownership of goods worth three to four hundred million pounds you take trouble checking them.'

'Maybe.'

The radio bleeped, again the incomprehensible babel of English sounds. Finally Van Rijn interpreted: 'Another boat, a coaster like the *Byker Lass*, is due this evening after the barge has cast off. She is *La Demoiselle des Pieux*, registered in Le Havre, owned by a small company that is really her master and his wife. They are to take on a mixed cargo including bananas, of course, and two tons of Manganox. Sailing for Cork Harbour. And again Chelmsford Chartering of Bergamot Lane had a hand in drawing up the contracts.'

'Right.' Mulligan straightened as far as the low roof would allow, rubbed his back. 'I think it's time I made a report back to base. You've got to keep your line open here so I'll go back to the Customs House to do it. Just let me check out I have it right: this, as we understand it is the official version of what's happening. The *San Fermín* is dropping two tons of Sol-Methrine A, picking up the K-D assignment and two tons of Sol-Methrine B. She sails for the eastern Mediterranean, Mersin and Haifa, when?'

'Eighteen hundred hours. And she has a scheduled stop at Bordeaux the day after tomorrow.'

'Right. The *Byker Lass* sails with bananas and two tons of Manganox at nineteen hundred, ETA at Wallsend the day after tomorrow at noon. That's giving her forty-one hours for the trip. Isn't that rather long?'

'No, not really. She's an old boat and with the estuaries it's all of seven hundred kilometres.' He thought for a moment 'Okay. She could do it in less, but you must remember it costs more in harbour dues and so on to keep a boat idle on a wharf than just chugging at reduced speed at sea. If her next pick-up won't be ready at Wallsend or wherever she'll loiter at sea rather than in harbour. That's very much normal practice.'

'Okay, I take the point. And the . . . what did you say the name was?'

'*La Demoiselle des Pieux*. She leaves an hour after the *Byker*

Lass, and is due Cork about the same time, noon the day after tomorrow . . . At last. Here come your friends.'

First Bridge then Aguirre swung legs over the fairing that ran round the hold, and again Bridge pulled out a large handkerchief and wiped his palms. The two men laughed at something, then bounced down the gangway on to the quay. Aguirre looked up at the crane above them, not the one Van Rijn and Mulligan were in, and made a circular motion with his hand above his head. The derrick swung, a hoist slowly dropped into the hold. Mulligan waited, and the two men on the quay waited too. Shortly the first patten came into view. Two-kilo bags, each labelled Sol-Methrine A, presumably two hundred and fifty of them.

'Whoof. That's it then. That's the most I've ever seen in one place at one time. Not even Sicilia-Falcon kept that much together at once – not anyway when we busted him. Okay, I'll be off. You'll log everything that goes on and comes off?'

'Of course.'

Down on the quay Aguirre dropped an arm round Bridge's shoulders and with head bent close to his ear, shepherded him into the warehouse.

Part Eleven

Snowdrop

60

'Been a splendid day, old chap, really have enjoyed it.'

Sir Alec Greene held out a hand as big as a ham. Myklades took it, and his pink glasses reflected the landscape beyond the banker's head: the tops of sick-looking gorse-bushes, the rumps of two brown ponies with leggy foals, the distant trees.

'It was good you were here on a day *Citeewax* did well. Showed my two a clean pair of feet.'

'*CiteeWEX*. But not well enough, eh? That's what your computer said – what was it, Harry? Must get it right when I see the skipper this evening.'

Harriet, at Myklades' shoulder, lifted her head, offered – she hoped, for the last time that day – her social smile, pushed fingers through the hair above her ears. 'Um, let me see. Wasn't it that she should have put on sail earlier as she approached the Berthon buoy?'

'That was it. Give old Robbie a rollicking about that, eh?'

Yet the big heavy man lingered, one hand on the top of the door his chauffeur held open for him. 'Must say I got a better feel of it all up here, than I do down there. Better company too. Tell the truth they're a toffee-nosed lot down there.'

From inside the big white Rolls his blowsy wife called: 'Really, Alec, how can you say such things? HRH was quite charming to me yesterday when I complimented him on his reading of the lesson at the church service. Come on, we'll be late for the Royal Yacht Squadron ball. You're not coming then, Harry?'

'Not this year, Lady Greene. We've got a big party coming tomorrow and I have to get things straight for Hector.'

'Jolly good, then. Who did you say was coming?'

'I don't think I did actually . . . but we're hoping Uncle Geoff – '

'Lord Slaker. I see. Well, come on, Alec, I really don't want to be too late for this one.'

'Yes, dear, of course.' Sir Alec cast a lingering longing look up the two hundred and fifty feet of the Campanile Folly, silhouetted against the drama of scurrying grey beneath a higher swirl of white mares' tails, but eventually lowered his massive behind on to white hide.

'Perhaps City and Wessex might take the lease next year.'

From nearby Burke grunted: 'For Cowes Week the Tower's booked through to 1993, isn't that right, sir?'

Myklades' thin lips stretched into a grin.

The chauffeur let the door clunk. As the Rolls whispered away, Burke followed it for ten yards or so then as it gathered speed raised his hand in what looked like a brief salute but was in fact a signal to the minders in the copse at the end of the track that the last of that day's guests had gone.

Myklades put his white, freckled hand on Harriet's shoulder, turned her back beneath the stuccoed entablature of the door, into the satin-finished steel of the modern lift.

'As usual, my dear, you did well.' His grin softened, became a plea, as if he feared rejection. He kneaded the hollow inside her collar-bone.

Coming out of the lift she moved straight into the big room that filled the south side of the Tower, pushed open panels in the double-glazing that ran the whole length behind the slender arches and balustrade that crudely echoed the Campanile of St Mark's.

'Poof! That man's cigars. And his wife's perfume. I don't know which is worse. I'm sure she could afford something better.'

'On some bodies even the best smells cheap.'

'I suppose so.' She gathered an armful of wilting sweet peas and gypsophilia from a large majolica pot, dropped them into a black plastic rubbish bag, began to gather together the nineteenth-century Royal Copenhagen tea-cups and plates.

'You don't mind doing this?'

'Of course not.'

'You know I want no one up here I can't trust. You, Rupert, Burke. Those flowers looked all right to me.'

'But by tomorrow they would have looked tatty. I'll get some more in the morning.'

He frowned now and his voice took on an edge. 'Tomorrow there is no need. You know that.'

But he was speaking to her back as she moved through a door that opened into the service area of the suite on the north-west side. He could hear her loading the Trice dishwasher.

'There's no need tomorrow. Or the day after. You know that,' he repeated when she came back.

She stood for a moment in one of the open spaces, hands clutching the edges of the glazing, head back, fighting the vertigo she always felt when she did this in spite of the waist-high balustrade. It was worth it, if only you could force back the spasm of panic. People who say vertigo makes you want to jump don't have real vertigo: just a suppressed desire for suicide. Real vertigo forces you into the wall furthest from the edge. She remembered Bonnie Day and the French journalist edging down the icefield at the top of the Ammertenpass and shuddered.

'Hector. Could I have one of your nice cigarettes, please?'

'Of course.'

She breathed in the aromatic smoke, held it, felt steadied. The view certainly was impossibly magnificent. To the left Gosport and Portsmouth were a black line that twinkled where the five o'clock sun picked on a sheet of glass or metal eighteen miles away, giving an outer edge to the Solent – deep blues, greens, flecked with white, studded with sails that skimmed like bugs on the surface of a pond, movements meaningless to the onlooker but purposeful to the bugs themselves. Off the tall slender stacks of Fawley where two flares burned waste gases a supertanker edged round the Calshot Spit in the controversial lane that was banned this year to all yachts.

Across the water Egypt Point, East Cowes, and the Royal Yacht Squadron marked the northernmost tip of the island that climbed behind them through the woodland of Parkhurst Forest to the chalk down beyond. Much nearer, and way down in the shallow wooded valley below, so it seemed they were almost on top of it though it was a good mile and half away, the town of Lymington clung to its estuary on the mainland beneath her. She could see both marinas and the little car ferry just now chugging in from the island, in time to take

Greene's Rolls back to Yarmouth. Then across the water again the land rose to the cliffs of Alum Bay, the Needles and the indigo of deep water beyond.

She shifted, drew on the perfect cigarette, let the smoke trickle through flared nostrils, marked how, now she was looking into the sun, the sea took on a steely glitter in front of Hengistbury Head; how, inside it, Christchurch Harbour, also with its marinas, shone like a polished silver tray in front of the conurbation of Bournemouth and Poole. But such was the height and position of the Tower she could see beyond Bournemouth to a glint of water in Poole Harbour and the sweep of the coast round to the purple hills of Purbeck above Swanage. In the middle, like a spider walking on water, an exploratory oil-rig. All in all they could see, from where they were, about twenty-five of the forty-five miles of mainland coastline between Swanage in the west and Gosport in the east, had an unbroken view of the Isle of Wight from East Cowes to the Needles. Above all, an awful lot of sea.

'I said: there's no need for flowers tomorrow.'

She fought back a vertigo that now had more to do with her situation than the fact that she was nearly two hundred feet above ground and four hundred above the sea a half-mile away, turned and stubbed out the Yeni Harman.

'Hector, I know there won't be any guests tomorrow. But we have told plenty of people there will be. So far we have had guests every day and every day I have gone to Lymington to buy fresh flowers, fresh fish and bread and so on. Okay? So tomorrow I will act just as I always do. And I will do it on Wednesday too.'

'Do you really suppose someone will notice whether you go or not?'

'If they are watching, yes. If they are watching they will notice any aberration, any alteration in the habits we have already developed in the last four days.'

He shrugged, still petulant, looked at his watch. 'Rupert should have rung by now.'

Harriet bit her lip. 'I'll fix you a drink.'

'Not strong. Red vermouth and water.'

But she had already mouthed the words in sardonic anticipation as she turned towards the drinks cabinet. For herself she poured a very large gin with not a lot of Slim-Line tonic.

The lift door whispered and Burke came in. 'Well done, darling, I'll have a bottled light ale, if I may,' and he patted her rump. She wasn't at all sure she was going to be able to put up with Burke so much on top of them all through the next two days.

Five hours later she was pretty well drunk, lying back but with her feet pulled under her in an armchair covered in a new chintz she'd chosen in the Winchester Laura Ashley a month earlier because it echoed the near-abstractions of the Miró on the wall opposite her. Drunk and frightened. She hated this time of day, or night, in the Tower. When it was built the Admiralty had insisted that it should show no light at night, and the regulation was still in force. This meant a total blackout which should have given a sense of insulation, but it made her feel that they were suspended like Coyote in the Road-Runner cartoons when he's gone over a cliff and hangs there before dropping.

The fact that Myklades and Rupert were arguing did not help. It had never happened before.

'It was focking stupid to hang around in Amsterdam with that psychopath.'

'Hector, I was not hanging around.'

'We have to do business with scorpions. But why socialise after?'

'Hector. You told me to keep him sweet. He'd never been there before. He wanted to see Rokin, what goes on there. I got him to take on a few drinks, found him one of the less tatty houses and left him there. All right? That's all.'

Harriet staggered to her feet, peered at them through tunnel vision, swayed. 'Well anyway, Rupe, I'm damned glad to see you, if no one else is. And now I'm going to bed . . .'

Somewhere, almost off-camera as it were, Burke loomed. 'Sir, I think you should look at the weather forecast.'

'Well?'

'It's already blowing up out in Biscay, force seven south of Ushant. The forecast for tomorrow night through to Wednesday simply is not good.'

'Focking English weather. Is this serious?'

'Don't know yet, sir. Simply do not know. But it could be.'

Harriet remembered a sea-shanty from nursery thirty years

ago. 'From Ushant to Scilly 'tis thirty-five leagues,' she sang. 'Or twenty-five? Or forty-five. I'm going to bed.'

In the morning, down Lymington High Street, it certainly was blowing, and the wind carried warm rain on it too, which at least kept down the crowds that plague the place through Cowes Week and most of August. It was almost possible to buy bread and fresh fruit without being pushed off the pavements by the yellow wellie brigade or having to queue for more than five minutes in each shop.

Not, thought Harriet, light-headed now on the little yellow helpers Lovejoy gave her to lift the morning hangover, that many of them are actually in yellow wellies. This year's look seems to be fishermen's smocks worn to just below the crotch, hiding tiny shorts and leaving exposed yards of hairy leg ending in flip-flops or espadrilles. At times like this she could understand Hector's hatred of most manifestations of the British way of life, though, thanks to the pills – not tranks but Apisate, sustained-release amphetamine supplemented with Vitamin B – she wasn't really too bothered about hating anyone, though she did feel irritated when people got in her way. She was conscious that the pills made her want to hurry – perhaps, as soon as it opened, she'd drop into the Angel for the first G and T of the day, to calm her down. Meanwhile she had three big men to look after and there was still a four-pound sea bass in the fishmonger's – wrap it up in foil with butter, fennel and a bayleaf or two, and Bob's your uncle. And if she was quick she might still be able to pick up a couple of dozen Beaulieu River oysters at the new seafood boutique in the little alley that runs down to the quay . . .

She tuned in on the muttered conversation in the queue behind her but without looking round.

'Ralph says they can't come tonight, making an early start in the morning.' A female voice.

'Ralph, an early start? How early is early?'

'Well, that's just what I said. And do you know what Phyllis answered? Three o'clock in the morning. Three hundred hours ack emma.'

'But that's Ralph's bedtime. What's he getting up then for?'

'That's just what I said. And she had a totally unconvincing story about wanting to snap St Catherine's Point at dawn. But do you know what I think . . .'

The voice dropped to a whisper and Harriet lost it until it surfaced with the man. 'Golly. Do you really think so? I must say Ralph always has been a bit of a card and I was wondering where he'd got the loot from to buy a new Sadler 32. Well, jolly good luck to him, that's what I say.'

'Well, that's what I said too.'

Sweating slightly and chuckling too, Harriet came out into the spitting rain, looked up at the black on white clock face on the square church tower, twenty past ten, turned left and hurried on down the hill past the Angel and rows of small shops set in pleasant Georgian cottages and town houses, down the hill to the quay. Glimpsed through the gaps between the houses, the island loomed grey beneath racing clouds. She wondered how many similar conversations were going on all over the south coast, how many times the same memorable lumps of flotsam would bump into each other in the eddy and flow of marina gossip, whether it was possible for one person, one outsider, to hear the same sort of thing often enough to make something of it . . .

In all of this she was, of course, following her usual routine of resorting to displacement activity in the run-up to a moment of decision or danger. But there was no way she could postpone the moment any longer and, timing her arrival at precisely ten-twenty-five, she swung into the small florist's at the top of the cobbled traffic-free hill. Three people in front of her. Then two, then . . .

'Oh, I say, I have a most urgent phone call to make, you know, do you think I could possibly use your phone?'

The middle-aged woman in a green nylon overall with the embroidered Interflora badge grinned conspiratorially and said with heavy emphasis and a thick Hampshire accent: 'Of course, dear. It's not something we normally allow, but being as you're such a regular customer . . .'

Ten minutes later, having placed her order of gladioli and dahlias for delivery to the Tower before lunch (Hector had rebelled against the delicacy of sweet peas), and relieved to have found no instructions or requests from Mulligan, she came out again into sudden sunshine, hot and steamy after the squall, the cobbles giving off the dusty, faintly sulphurous smell of warm dry stone suddenly rained on. After all then not the Angel for her G and T but the pub on the quay, where she could sit outside, take stock, watch the world go by.

It annoyed her, as it always did, that she had to go to the bar and get the drink herself – one day perhaps European civilisation would reach these shores and waiter service would be a normal option – but once she had it, a triple in a tall glass with lots of ice and a slice of lemon bobbing prettily, she was prepared to relax and enjoy what was going on. The worst of the morning had been dealt with. In so far as she understood the schedule nothing much anxiety-producing was on the horizon until nightfall.

In front of her, yachts were puttering under power out of the smaller of the two marinas, heading for the Solent and stations from which they could watch the first day of the Royal Yacht Squadron races; to her left a low wooded headland carried road and railway down to the Yarmouth ferry . . .

'Well met by daylight, proud Harry.'

She squinted up into the sun.

'Rupe. Take a pew. Why is everyone spouting the Bard at me these days? Still, as you say, well met – what's the news with you?'

He frowned, swung a leg over the bench, sat opposite her. He also had a gin and tonic, but smaller, in a wineglass. 'Spouting the Bard? Who could that be? Not Hector, for sure. Racine or Goethe but not the Bard.'

Aware that booze and speed had lured her into precisely the sort of mistake she must not make during the next twenty-four hours or so, she sought quickly to change the subject. 'Sweet coz, what brings you into this neck of the woods?'

'You really. Mermaid Pleasure is my excuse.' He gestured with a flick of his head towards a new block of holiday apartments built in maroon-coloured brick. The style suggested the past, declared the modishly new. A brass mermaid combed her hair to the left of the entrance, and a dark blue and gold Renault Trafic van with the same trademark was parked outside. It had a large CB-type aerial. 'I told Hector I'd spend the morning checking out the drop points, but really I was hoping to get a word with you on your own.'

'Civil of you, I'm sure, but why?'

Elbow on the table, he chewed the ball of his thumb for a

moment, then caught her eye and held it. His own, a stony blue which set off his black eyebrows and hair, were serious. The skin round them was unusually dark, and suddenly she realised he was very tired or under a lot of strain, or both.

He touched her hand with one finger. 'Party's over, Harry.'

The sudden chill she felt was like a crab. This echoed exactly what Jana Pensión had said to her. 'Are you sure?'

'Oh yes. Quite sure.' He swung his finger round the rim of the glass, and a hint of a grin flickered. 'Thought you should know. I mean since it was me got you in in the first place.'

'So?'

'Well. If I were you, I'd close that account in Berkeley's Key and shift the assets into something a bit more liquid. Bearer bonds. Have them mailed to an accommodation address. You see, it'll take a week or so for the full extent of what's happening to get around, but when it does you're quite likely to find that account frozen. BK is owned by the Banco de Corpus Cristi, is one of its assets, and it's well on the cards BCC could go bust. Or at any rate cease to trade while the fuzz sort out the clean loot from the dirty.'

'Oh shit . . . I don't know how. Oh, Rupe. Is it really as bad as that?'

'Yes. How, is easy. Look, here's the address of a mate of mine who trades Eurobonds. He's nothing to do with Ambrose or Hector or anything like that. Just send him a cheque on your Tortola account, tell him I told you to, and as soon as he's cleared it he'll buy for you. Leave it to him to choose what, but tell him he's not to trade on your account, just buy and post the bonds when he's got them. Make it poste restante, PTT, Cibeles, Madrid. There you are. He won't let you down. Now you can do something for me.'

She shuddered. 'There had to be a catch.'

'No catch, Harry. Just one of several forms of insurance I'm taking out too. Also a sign of trust between us, and a guarantee for you that I'm not trying to pull a fast one by telling you to get those bonds. Here.'

From his inside pocket he pulled a washleather drawstring bag. 'You're going to the post office anyway. Put these in an unregistered Jiffy-bag, fill in a green Customs slip saying they are a present worth fifty quid, and send them to yourself, poste restante Amsterdam this time. There is some risk, but not a lot. Just that Customs might take a closer look. But one in a hundred, if that. Now. When all this is over I'll get in touch and we'll go together and pick them up, flog them, and you can have ten per cent for your pains. But if anything . . . well, you know, happens to me, well then they're yours. All right?'

'Oh God, I feel awful.'

'No you don't.' He looked at his watch, finished his drink. 'I must dash. Pecker up, Harry. Remember, at bottom you're as tough as old boots.'

He swung his legs back over the bench, pecked her cheek, walked briskly back to the Mermaid Pleasure van, waved, and was gone.

The temptation was not to be resisted. She loosened the string, tipped the contents of the bag into her palm. She let only a few stones, five or six, trickle out, just enough to be sure. They were dull, uncut, unpolished litle grey pebbles, that yet held the light and threw it back. And they were not really all that small. What the fuck's Rupert up to now? She wondered. But soon realised that even if her brain had been functioning sweetly on all six cylinders she'd never work it out. Then the sun went in and rain once more splashed, large-dropped, on to the table, on to her palm among the stones. She tipped them back and sat for a moment, heard as in a dream the train that trundled across the low bridge towards the ferry, the restless shimmering cackle of tackle clattering against aluminium masts in the marina, the distant mewing of gulls . . . Bastard post office is half a mile away, she thought, back up opposite the church.

She was back at the top of the Tower by a quarter past twelve having contrived to do everything Rupert had suggested – save that she committed only half her assets in the Berkeley's Key Bank to the licensed dealer whose address he had given her, and she had wrapped two of the largest stones in a tissue and pushed it into the bottom of her bag, where it lay amongst the rest of the debris there: more tissues, hairpins, the wrapper off a Swiss truffle that dated back to Adelboden.

'Where have you been? You have been far too long.' Myklades stooped to grind out a half-finished cigarette as she came through the lift door. 'Raking off still, after all this time – damn it, it won't do.'

'I don't think I have been any longer than I was yesterday –'

'A full half-hour more – '

'Anyway, look: I've got a splendid fish for lunch – '

'Fock your fish!'

'Hector please. What's the matter?'

'Your focking British weather is the matter.'

'But the sun's out again. It's a bit blowy I know, but – '

He clawed her upper arm so it hurt and pulled her to the window, pointed west. 'There, look at that.'

An arc of black cloud hung along the horizon, apparently above but in fact beyond the Isle of Purbeck and curving round right out to sea. At the distance it did not look all that much, its base still a good thirty, possibly forty miles away, but clearly it marked a front, a very strong front indeed. There would be strong winds and squalls in front of it, gales behind.

'We had three yorts coming up from the west you know?' (*Yorts* for yachts.) 'Two out of Falmouth who left ahead of the storm and have now put into Plymouth, and one from Plymouth which has stayed put. If they don't get through in time either we have to improvise or we lose sixty million sterling.' He banged his forehead with his palm, and shouted: 'I hate improvisation.'

'Don't blame the weather on me.' She pulled away, rubbed her arm, gathered up her shopping and headed for the tiny kitchen. As she got there the door on the other, western side of the lift shaft swung open and she heard the clatter of a printer, the babble of a radio weather forecast.

Doors banged, there was more shouting, and then, as if someone had tripped a switch, the light levels dropped by half and rain clattered on the glass wall. Still only a passing squall, cavalry reconnaissance ahead of the massed phalanxes of the real storm that already looked a great deal nearer. Harriet went into the tiny bathroom that lay beyond the kitchen, found the happy pills, the tranks, the Benzos Lovejoy recommended when things were getting quite deeply out of hand, took three with gin. Back in the kitchen she picked up the heaviest of the kitchen devils and hacked the head off the sea bass.

Seven o'clock and the wind was hitting the top of the Tower as if it were a punch-ball mounted on a stiffly coiled spring. Back in the kitchen again, watching a Calor gas flame push steam through coffee, she murmured to Rupert: 'It seems you were right. This is beginning to feel like *Götterdämmerung* on a bad night.' Her speech was slow but not slurred. Behind her he held her waist between his palms. 'Rupert. Why don't we just walk away? Take the lift, press G for ground. Get back to earth. We've cashed in whatever chips we had, haven't we?'

'No, Harry.' He spoke quickly, hardly more than a whisper, but each word weighted. 'You don't walk away from people like Hector. You have to wait until they tell you to go. And you part on as good terms as possible. I told you that before. Remember?'

He turned back into the main room and presently she followed with the coffee. Myklades was sitting at one end of the dining-table with two telephones at his elbow, scattered papers in front of him, computer printout, much of it in narrow strips torn off the Telex. He looked up at her, paused in mid-sentence, leant back so his tinted glasses flashed. There was, so far, no sign of the psoriasis which she had been expecting and dreading hourly. His thin lips twisted into a grin that was almost triumphant. He is, she thought, rising to the occasion.

'The weather,' he crowed, 'is not going to be a problem for much longer. Racing this afternoon was cancelled and the Admiral's Cup offshore race tomorrow has been postponed until Thursday, so we postpone till Thursday too. All our people have been informed. No problem, you see? What do the sea faring nations do when faced with a storm?' He spaced the words: 'They . . . ride . . . it . . . out. Although they are not on horses but in boats, they ride it out. I shall do the same.'

She set down the coffee. Burke and Rupert, both pale and tired, reached for it. God or the weather gave the Tower another shake, but a friendly one, as if agreeing. Harriet momentarily caught Rupert's eye, lifted her eyebrows. He shrugged, pouted and grinned. Then with the most minute of movements shook his head.

Blind to all this Myklades went on: 'We'll . . . ride it out, no problem. Meanwhile, my friends, we still have work to do,' and he tapped the table with his pen.

61

Two o'clock in the morning. High-speed wipers sliced half-moons of darkness out of the silvery opacity of the windscreen. A blue and white illuminated motorway sign loomed and was gone: London twenty-five. For a moment, from where Mulligan was sitting behind the driver, it made a silhouette of WPC Porter's head. Her ear, which was small considering she was a big girl, carried a tiny gold sleeper.

Next to him Tyler stretched as far as he was able and yawned. 'There was a nutter,' he said, 'who went to his trick-cyclist and complained that whatever happened to him, whatever he saw or heard, always made him think of tits. Try this, said the quack: windscreen-wipers. Tits, said the nutter. Come on, said the quack. Like this, said the nutter.' And moving his head from side to side in time with the wipers Tyler made a hissing kiss with each movement which quite resembled the noise they made.

'That is the most awful joke I ever heard.' Mulligan felt suddenly warm with embarrassment: he knew Tyler had told the story as an oblique comment on Porter's presence, would never have told it in the normal run of things. Of course she suppressed any reaction.

He referred back to the last radio message they had had. 'So exactly who is in the Tower of Swaythe as of now?'

Tyler yawned again. 'Your girlfriend – '

'Tyler, off my back.'

'Right. Miss Jones. Spiderman. Burke and Bridge. Burke drove Bridge out today, towards Christchurch, and somehow dropped him, and we lost him. He came back in a taxi. The surveillance skills down there are not as good as they should be, not as good as Oxford's.'

'That's all?'

'As far as we know. Burke has six minders based at Swaythe;

they take shifts two at a time to watch the Tower, but they don't go in.'

'I don't know much about Burke.'

'Ex-copper. Superintendent, Met drug squad. Flying Squad before that. Got slung off that and fined for going into another police area without permission – of course the Sweeneys all had a whipround for him, that was the way they did things in those days. I'm talking about ten years ago before the clean-up. Then rebuilt his reputation with the drug squad, seemed to be doing well, but then a couple of close colleagues of his got nicked by the Customs, for aiding and abetting an airside rip-off. They got off at the Old Bailey. Juries don't like convicting police. But Burke never quite got back to be flavour of the month after that so about two years ago he took early retirement and a silver handshake. Good copper, but bent.'

The big car, another Daimler Sovereign, roared on at a steady ton.

'He'll walk away from all this, you know,' Tyler went on.

'He will?'

'Sure. He's running a security firm. Called Burke Castle. Small firm, retained exclusively by DLC. He'll say he was in the servant's hall the whole time, doing the job he was paid for. One thing though.'

'Yes?'

'If it comes to rough stuff at the end of the day, he's handy with a shooter.'

'I'll remember that.' End of Motorway – 5 miles. Mulligan reflected: there was an unguarded chumminess in Tyler's voice when he spoke of Burke. Nothing so clannish as the Met. Worse than Masons, and most of them were. 'You won't be sorry if he gets clear.'

'No.'

He looked at his watch again, illuminating the digital face with a press-button, and leaned forward. 'You still reckon we'll be at . . . where is it, by dawn?'

'Sheerness. Yes, Mr Mulligan.' Her eyes didn't shift from the powerful beams, warped with silver rain like Lurex.

'They go in at dawn.'

'Yes, Mr Mulligan. We'll be there with twenty minutes to spare.' Nice voice, good manner. Respectful, but not to be put upon.

He sat back, shut his eyes, tried to sleep. He was very tired. It had been a sod of a day, spent sitting around the Oxford ops room, while other people got on with it. No satisfaction in it, just waiting, tension, frustration followed by one of those ghastly pub suppers the Brits seemed to think were so great, scampi and chips from a plastic basket and too much 'real' ale. Then just as they were all thinking of bed the call from the Port of London Collection, a conference with no one in the right frame of mind, and – inevitably, as far as Mulligan was concerned – the wrong decision taken.

Along with a lot of other small ships the *Byker Lass* had come in at dusk off the direct Rotterdam – Tynemouth shipping lane into the Thames Estuary, was hove-to a nautical mile or so inside the Nore Light, riding out the worst of the storm. In territorial waters. And the original order had been that she should be busted as soon as she was off the high seas, and kept under surveillance as soon as she was in 'copter range of the mainland.

'But,' Mulligan had argued, 'that decision was made when we thought she wouldn't show up until she was off Tynemouth. She's where she is now not to land coke, but to shelter from a force eleven gale.'

They'd paid no attention, and he shifted awkwardly at the memory of it, so his shoe nudged Tyler's ankle.

'This car ain't big enough for the both of us,' Tyler grumbled in a bad imitation of a Texas accent.

Everyone there had had a good reason for moving straight away. Customs said they'd be over a barrel if they let her go now and lost her. And anyway, the standing order was bust her if she got inside the twelve-mile limit. Only the heavy seas and the concentration of shipping the storm had brought to the estuary were making them hold their hand until first light. And without a doubt, behind them all, looking over their shoulders, nudging them in the ribs, was the sniggering ghost of the Lowndes Square fiasco. The internal enquiry had been firm in blaming Tyler and Seton for at least not checking the jerry cans of holy water at Heathrow when they had the chance. The outcome then was that here they were, swooping down off Westway into Marylebone at half past two in the morning, hoping to be at Sheerness by four.

And they would be. She drove well, in spite of the driving

rain – it certainly was a bitch of a night, pity the poor sailors
. . . The wide streets linked to make the inner ring road
whisked by at a steady sixty now, Madame Tussaud's and the
Planetarium . . .

Tyler sat up suddenly. 'Got to take a leak. The Kirkman
Place nick please, miss.'

'One-way systems, sir. There's the railway stations,
Euston . . .'

'The nick.' Almost he shouted. 'Put on the hooter and go
down Tottenham Court Road.'

She did as she was told. The siren wailed, the blue light
swivelled across the façades of the big shops, Maples and
Heals, a couple of taxis swerved out of their way, and they
swung into a short cul-de-sac. Tyler, coat smacking about his
knees, hand pressing his hat down over his big head, flapped
like a bat out of hell into the lit doorway. Porter immediately
swung the big car through a neat three-pointer so she was
ready to go. Mulligan reflected, she's efficient, no fool, knows
her job.

'Here he comes. Mad bugger,' he said. And yes she laughed
– a warm sound but brief and very much under her breath. He
wished he could see her face, her expression. Tyler paused on
the kerb, pulled up his zip, and launched himself back in.

'You should have gone too. Wise man when he can, fool
when he must. I was stationed here once. Always remember,
silly thing, bloke parking on the meter there and I nipped in
ahead of him. Stupid thing to do in front of the Bill, he said. I
am the Bill, I said. Of course, you fucking would be, he said.
So I fingered him for insulting behaviour. Not really, but I
could. She's still afloat, you know, still off the Nore. Thought
I'd just check, while I was at it.'

'You could have done that from in here.'

'Sure. But I don't like to appear over-anxious.'

Back on the ring road, the big stations, St Pancras and
King's Cross, then suddenly, as if the wicked witch had waved
her wand, the Portland stone and the glitzy architecture of the
big TV and film companies were gone, the tyres rumbled on
uneven road surfaces against a tatty backdrop of boarded-up
shops, crumbling tenements, drab council flats. Mulligan tried
again for a position in which a catnap might occur.

The day, though generally bad, had produced at least one

plus. The raid on Scapino went like clockwork. They pulled four kilos of thirty per cent pure, a couple of illegal handguns, and an illegal from Naples had cracked straight away, been caught out in a couple of contradictions and implicated Ricardo. It was the first time this had happened. In the past there had always been someone there prepared to take the rap and protect the boss, but this time his luck had run out.

And the outcome was that like most bullies Ricardo turned out to be what Tyler called a fruit bonbon: hard shell, soft centre. The interrogating officer had rummaged around for a bit in the nastier corners of the big Italian's mind, had got a reaction over Caill's murder, but not quite the one he expected, changed tack and said: 'Oh, we know you had nothing to do with topping Caill. Bridge did him in because he's been taking snow from you instead of Mr Spiderman, and that's why you're here now. Part of the same process. Bridge tipped us off you were broking coke again so here we are.'

Ricardo had blasphemed about Bridge for a minute or so, and then: 'He fucking shopped me? Then I'll fucking shop him . . .' and he proceeded to do so. By five o'clock all his dealings with Bridge from the previous July through to Christmas were on record and sworn to.

'Which,' said Tyler, when the Oxford CDI had argued that they should move on the Tower or wherever and pull Bridge in, 'is all very well, and will make great corroborative evidence. But in itself it's not enough. Think of the Hon. Rupert Bridge in dock in his striped tie with his cut-glass accent, his Falklands gong, versus that untidy wop. No contest. Tranmere Rovers away to Spurs.'

A brief glimpse of the Tower of London over on the right, then the brick and concrete box at Wapping looking not unlike the reactor housing of a nuclear power station. Appropriately enough, the wasteland they now entered blossomed evilly with aerosolled slogans proclaiming racial war and neo-Nazi aspirations. Mulligan on the edge of sleep hallucinated a stagnant pond exhaling fumes he identified with the emissions from gas chambers – and two brilliant insects, metallic green and gold, long-bellied, hovered above it on Crystal wings, copulated and dropped eggs from arcing ovipositors into the ooze below.

He woke with a convulsive jerk to the bright lights of a

spaghetti junction. A huge tower block soared above it, thirty storeys, linked by bridges to its independent lift shaft.

Tyler murmured: 'Balfron Tower. First time I nearly jacked in being a copper was when I got here five minutes after a young woman had jumped from near the top with two babies in her arms. They don't let families live there any more – '

Bea Porter spoke – the first time without being spoken to first: 'They still jump though,' and she took them down a slipway, out of the streaming darkness into the orange tube of the Blackwall Tunnel. In the time it took to get up on to the further bank of the river Mulligan dropped off again, but this time it was like going over a cliff into a black abyss.

Three hours later, aching in every joint and with the vile stench of vomit clogging his sinuses, he stood, just, at the rail of the *Byker Lass* and accepted with gratitude the push Tyler gave him from behind, propelling him safely off the top of the Jacob's ladder he'd been climbing from the pitching Customs and Excise launch below. Not far below, ten feet perhaps, but quite enough. He grabbed a stanchion, wiped his mouth on the back of his hand, fought back the dizziness and nausea, looked out and around. Huge waves, solidly grey, heaving to fifteen feet or more, swept by, but randomly it seemed, not in the long rhythmic lines of an ocean swell, their crests whipped to a soapy spume by a wind which too was gusty and irregular, the flailings of a punch-drunk giant.

On one side the view was dominated by the huge stacks, cooling towers, containers of the refineries and power stations on the Isle of Grain, the vapour and flame coming off them shredded by the gale, the sickly first light of a lemon-coloured sun glinting like shiny eczema off the blobs of the spherical tanks. On the other, just sea it seemed, heaving and inimical, dotted with boats similar to the one he was on, and like her using the ten-mile-wide estuary to weather the storm, just sea but edged to the north with the smudgy line of the low conurbation that links Southend with Shoeburyness.

But at least the rain had gone, just low bruise-coloured cloud hurrying across the sky as if desperate not to be left behind by the massed armies that had gone before. Two white gulls rode the wind, holding their stations with minute adjustments of their pinions, livid against the sky, till first one then the other slipped and angled down towards the wave-crests, allowing themselves to be driven for a quarter of a mile before soaring again, minute white specks now . . .

'Come on, Buck, it's here, you know. They've found it.'

Swinging from stanchion to rail, across decking that swirled with greasy water, he made it to a point amidships from which he could look down into the second of the two holds, and for a moment the dizziness gripped again. He shook it off.

It was shallower than he had expected, twelve feet perhaps, and filled at one end with cardboard boxes of bananas. In spite of the straps and ropes that were meant to hold them in place several had broken free, slid and slipped through the three inches or so of greasy water that swung across the floor, disintegrating with each blow as the heave of the sea smashed them against the rusty walls.

At the other end, and immediately beneath him, there was a stack of grey plastic bags, marked with red on blue *Manganox*, and it was here three men in dark blue Guernseys with shoulder pads had been working, carefully lifting down one corner of the stack, bag by bag, trying not to destabilise the whole pile, until near the bottom they had found what they were looking for, a layer of similar bags but unmarked. It was precisely as Van Rijn had said it would be. Just as Mulligan looked over the fairing one of the officers lifted the first of the plain bags, very carefully in both hands, and swayed through the mess around him to the steel rungs that would bring him back to the deck. There was a broad grin on his face.

Five minutes later it lay on a chipped Formica table in the master's tiny cabin. Using a penknife Mr Perkins, a senior investigation officer from Sheerness, cut a small square out of the top of it, levered up a tiny pyramid of greyish white powder on the end of the blade and tipped it into a round glass dish. This he passed to one of his juniors, who tipped about half of what he had been given into a test-tube, added liquor from a phial, snapped a lighter beneath it. It turned blue.

'W'haie,' crowed Tyler from the other side of the table, and dug Mulligan in the ribs with his elbow. 'W'hae. No error this time – we have charlie.'

The Customs men now swung into a well-rehearsed and familiar routine. A declaration was read to the master, a large morose Dutchman, approaching sixty at least, smelling of gin, bewildered and tearful, still in long woolly underwear beneath an oilskin. He was told that his boat had been impounded and would be towed into port as soon as the tug standing by could get a line on board. All hands not immediately concerned with the running of the ship were confined to quarters, no hands were to enter the cargo areas, and so on . . . In almost no time at all the little cabin had emptied, apart from one Customs officer, and Mulligan and Tyler, who sat on fixed stools with rotating tops facing each other beneath a swinging lamp with the bag between them.

'Come on, Buck, come on. Don't let a little seasickness get you down, we've done it. Powder on the table at last and a series of links that make a chain right back to Spiderman . . . Come on, crack your miserable face, give us a smile – we've done it.'

But Mulligan shook his round head, pushed the balls of his palms into his eyes, tried to force back the sick headache that was welling up there. Away from the sea and the wind the smells were getting to him now, the gin, the vomit that still hung around him, warm oil . . .

'It's not right, Rex. It's not right.'

'What do you mean, it's not right? It's fucking right. It turned blue. It's charlie, the test says so. Oh, for Christ's sake, don't be such a miserable sod, you get on my tits sometimes, you really do.'

Mulligan suddenly felt a surge of strong emotions which surprised him with its force and its colour: it was darn close to hate. He shouted: 'Tyler, it's all wrong, and now listen to me, will you?' Gripping the sides of the table he forced himself to swallow rising bile. 'Just listen to me.'

Tyler was sulky, but agreed to listen.

'When I was with Van Rijn we were both certain the coke was in the bags marked Sol-Methrine A. That were replaced with the Sol-Methrine B . . .'

'And you were fucking wrong! After you'd gone, these plain bags came out of the hold. The Sol-Methrine switch was a hoax, a blind . . . we've agreed all that and yesterday the Dutch Customs checked the Sol-Methrine A in the warehouse and that's what it is. Fucking pesticide.'

'Oh, shut up and listen. It still does not add up . . . For a start there's less than a quarter of the weight we were told to expect – '

'Oh, come on! Informers always exaggerate, you know that – '

'Tyler. If you won't hear me out I'm going to break your neck. Next. This stuff was going to be lifted off by Chinook helicopters. Now that always did seem pretty far-fetched, but that master, Van Hoch, is in the clear. If ever I saw an innocent, that's he. He's heart-broken . . .'

'But we know all that. It's the chief officer. He checked in the unmarked bags. They're not on the manifest, and he knows it, so he's the bent one, we've been through this – '

'And Van Hoch was going to let him open the hatches tomorrow night and watch a sizeable chunk of his cargo winched into the dark by choppers?'

'Mickey Finn in his gin?' But there was at last a note of doubt in Tyler's voice.

Sick scorn in Mulligan's voice matched the taste in his throat. 'And the two deck-hands? And the other two hundred unmarked bags now on *La Demoiselle des Pieux* heading for Cork? Okay, okay. I know we read those as the decoy, for Bristol via a Spanish wine tanker – '

'That was your girlfriend told us that.'

'There's too much unanswered, too many loose ends, too much that's wrong.'

'There always is. You know that. But the straight fact of the matter is this. That fucking bag has charlie in it, cocaine hydrochloride, the test said so, and there are ninety-nine two-kilo bags out there like it, and that makes it one of the biggest cocaine hauls this side of the Atlantic ever.'

They listened to the throb of the engines, the swing of the lamp changed direction as the boat turned beam on to the sea and they felt her shudder from stern to stern as the waves crashed into her. Then Mulligan reached for the bag. Perhaps Tyler thought he was just afraid the new movement might spill it on to the floor, but he cradled it for a moment between his palms, then thrust in his little finger, hooked out powder.

'Look at it. It's dull, flaky, damp.' And before they could stop him, Tyler and the Customs officer, he pushed it into his nose, first one nostril, then the other, and sniffed it up, noisily, heavily.

The boat came round, the noise levels dropped, she was heading for Sheerness, no longer under her own power, but behind a tug.

Tyler was white now, livid with rage. 'I can lock you up for that, you know. I fucking ought to lock you up.'

Mulligan pushed back on his palms, round pale face in the air, and waited. Nothing. No euphoria. A clearing of his head, yes. The vice that had begun to grip his forehead perceptibly loosened. That was all. That and a cold numbness in his nose, all through his nasal passages, on the back of his tongue. Then a sudden loosening of mucus so he had to pull out a handkerchief already streaked with vomit, and spew it up.

Coughing he spluttered: 'Tyler. Rex. That is shit. It really is. There's fuck-all charlie there – there may be some Novocaine, but the rest is shit. I swear it.'

Tyler was astounded, bewildered, shocked to his core. 'You mean you know? You actually know?'

Mulligan, recovering, let his big head slump wearily on to his chest. 'I know, Rex. Oh yes. I know.'

There was a long silence, then Tyler shook his head in continuing disapproval, disbelief. 'All right. Let's hear your version of the scenario.'

'I'd like a coffee or something. No. Tea.'

Tyler jerked his head at the Customs officer: 'Go on. See what you can find. Oh, for Christ's sake, he won't touch the muck again, just do as I say. Right.'

'Right. Bear with me, Rex. I haven't thought this all through yet, much of it's coming off the top of my head.' He breathed in deeply, through his mouth, fighting off the smells. 'I think both Newcastle and Cork–Bristol are decoys. Elaborate ones, expensive – even shit like this costs a bob or two, especially half a ton of it if that's how much there is. But put together to hold us down, and slow us up, even make us think we've won while the real shipment gets in somewhere else. Don't ask me where or how, because I don't know. But I'll bet it's a lot nearer the Tower of Swaythe than Tyneside. And I'm sure you'll find the knot that ties Chelmsford Chartering to Ambrose comes undone in your hands as soon as you put any pull on it. Ah, thanks.' A big enamel mug had arrived at his elbow. The liquid was orange, almost like tomato soup, and was very sweet, made with a lot of condensed milk. Mulligan had never tasted anything like it. 'I wonder if you could find me a couple of aspirin?'

'I'm not convinced.'

'Okay, okay. Listen, I'm not asking you not to treat this seriously, you must obviously follow it right through. But really, you know, this has to be a decoy. And another thing.'

'What's that?'

'Spiderman can't have been expecting this bust until noon today when this tub was due off Tynemouth. So already we're six, seven hours upon him. My guess is he was planning to land the real shipment at about the time he was expecting you to bust this one. Okay. Treat this seriously, of course. But don't think we've won yet. We've got to keep going, work out where the real shipment is. Christ, I'm just going round in circles, I'm too fucking tired.'

There was a knock on the cabin door. 'Mr Perkins would like you to see something he's found in the chief officer's cabin.'

Wearily they followed the young Customs officer down a short corridor and into a cubicle containing a bunk, a wardrobe and a small table. On the table there was a video terminal with a keyboard in front of it and on the screen a series of entries. Each one was dated, timed and had a nautical position, longitude and latitude marked at three-hourly intervals, with a descriptive comment: speed and direction in knots, then hove-to off the Nore. Only the last one was different: *0453 Customs and Excise launch alongside. Want to come aboard, it's a bust* and on the last letter the cursor still pulsed.

Tyler asked: 'What is it? Some sort of electronic log?'

'That's what we thought at first. But we've never seen anything like it before and it seemed a bit sophisticated for a tub like this. The chief, who's a nasty little rat if ever there was one, refused to say a dickybird about it so we had a closer look.'

'Well?'

'Well. It really is quite amazing. It's tied into the transmitter – the chief acts as the wireless officer as well, that's quite usual on small boats like this, and he must have organised that. But there's a scrambler on it, and also a bag of electronic tricks which we're pretty sure is some sort of timed frequency-hopping device. In short, I think it must be his way of reporting back to Mr Big, and probably of getting messages from him too. He'll have just had to type up whatever he wanted to say, press another key, the message gets encrypted by the scrambler and out it goes, but never twice in the same frequency. I don't know what you've got here, Tyler, but whatever it is, it's big. Very big.'

Distantly a ship hooted, was answered closer to by the *Byker Lass*'s siren, then a shout echoed down the corridor: 'Coming into Sheerness, sir.'

Tyler stretched, hands in the small of his back, face grey with tiredness. 'We'd better get back to Oxford, and we can bring them up-to-date on the way. I'll leave this little lot in your capable hands,' he told Perkins, 'but you must report back anything significant that turns up as it happens. Meanwhile I'll organise an expert to come in and look at this bag of tricks.'

Back in the Daimler Mulligan dozed again, while Tyler spoke endlessly on the radiophone and WPC Porter took them, still at a steady ton wherever she could, back up the M2 and A2 into London, and as he dozed he filtered through his mind an endless array of facts and memories from the previous twelve months. He knew he was searching for something, and he knew that the processes which were going on in his skull were beyond his conscious control. They were, nevertheless, directed: by something for which instinct is a totally inadequate word, by something in touch with the deepest impulses of his mind – sex, guilt, the desire to be the victor, the survivor in the struggle with Spiderman, the need to fulfil himself as a hunter. But also as a pattern-maker, as a mind that could find or impose some sort of order on the maelstrom of passion and fact, of memory and pain.

And through it all Bonnie Day, tall, elegant, tough, with Muriel Clegg's Tyneside accent, emerged again and again, a deeply troubling *revenante*, and he could not understand why. He pushed her down, as if she were a kitten he was trying to drown, refused to accept her relevance, blamed her reappearance on a tic of unassuaged guilt that he had not kept her from her crazy doomed attempt to bug the Kaiseralp Hotel. But it was not that one brief meeting he had had with her in Abelboden that kept recurring, but the earlier, longer interview in Zurich, and somehow she was there, not alone, but with Harriet too. The whole thing was getting nightmarish, painful beyond bearing, so he felt at times he had to reach up and grasp the sound of the car, the continuing rumble of Tyler's voice, drag himself out of dream into a world that was harsh and unforgiving, but at least, on the surface, rational. A world, moreover, that included Beatrice Porter.

Who, at Tyler's request, had put on the radio, a southern local station, to get the eight o'clock news. All the Brits ever talk about is the weather. 'Today's programme at Cowes has been abandoned, and the Champagne Mumm Admiral's Cup offshore event in Christchurch Bay postponed until tomorrow, weather permitting. The organisers hope to include some of today's lost events . . .'

Boats, yachts, racing. The connection. Bonnie Day and Jill Jack in a photograph, a photograph in Bonnie Day's portfolio that he had seen in Commissioner Barlach's office in Zurich, a photograph taken by Harriet Jones. And in the background Hector Myklades talking to a salesman for a cellular radiophone system. And all in a marquee at Southampton Boat Show . . . Suddenly he was wide awake.

'Rex. The phone, please.' He dabbed numbers, listened to the clicking of electronic gates opening, then a beep. Speak now. 'Harry? Listen. Get this right and I'll make it right for you. What was Myklades doing at Southampton Boat Show in September a year ago? That's all. Just tell me what he was there for.' He tried to inject warmth, bonhomie, into his voice. 'Speak soon, see you. Take care.' And then regretted it – in his own ear he had sounded as genuine as a second-hand car dealer, but it was too late, it was on the tape.

Suddenly as they came over the rise of Shooters Hill and east London was momentarily spread beneath them Mulligan's mind made one more leap. Thinking of Harriet he heard her voice again from Beaulieu Road: 'You don't get Hector or me or Rupert . . .' The absurdity of this, the grossness, had shocked him at the time, but he had put it down to the bonding, the sexual bond that tied her to both of them. But there was a far simpler explanation. She was bugged, knew she was bugged, had put in the request to impress her listeners. And if that was the case then the *Byker Lass* absolutely had to be a decoy, a feint. She absolutely could not have told him the truth about the drop if Spiderman was listening.

He sat up, wide awake and suddenly scared. 'Listen. You've bust the big drop – do you still believe that?'

'I do. Yes.'

'Does that mean the raids on Ambrose, DLC and the rest are going ahead?'

Tyler looked at his watch. 'Twenty minutes ago they went in.'

'Shit. Oh, fucking Christ, I think we've blown it.'

62

'Get up. Now.'

'Oh God, do I have to?' Some dream, some happy dream, she knew it had been happy, but it was gone . . . She turned on to her back, looked up into Myklades' face. It was very close to hers, she could smell the sourness. It was very pale too, the lips mauve, a pencilled line when he wasn't shouting, and under his chin, in the crevices of loose skin in his neck, small patches of pink. 'Oh yes. All right then. But what's the matter.'

'Make coffee. Properly. With milk. And hot croissants. None of your British excrement, and bring it to the control room. For all of us. As quickly as you can.'

'All right.' She held her head, waited for him to go, looked at her watch, five past five. Christ, she thought, I feel awful.

Ten minutes later she carried a tray into the control room. Using the microwave she'd carried out his orders exactly, yet for a moment or two they ignored her. She set the tray on the wide ledge under the north-facing window and looked out. Grey light, not much, cloud and a heavy gale so she could still feel the sickening swing of the Tower beneath her feet. From this side all she could see was an undulating plain of forest, some of it broad-leaf, most of it coniferous, broken by large areas of heath and grass. There were towns, villages, roads hidden in the folds, but, apart from the spire of Lyndhurst church on a hill ten miles away, she couldn't see them. Two ponies and two foals huddled two hundred feet below in a patch of shabby gorse, and a couple of crows let themselves be swept by the wind until they were black dots a quarter of a mile away, when they angled their pinions, dropped into the tops of a stand of wind-thrashed pines.

She turned. The entire wall facing her, which was the north wall of the lift shaft, was filled with small video screens, thirty of them. Beneath them, slightly tilted, and curved into a convex crescent, banks of keyboards. There were also dials, digital displays, and microphones on stalks. The three men were seated inside the horns of the crescent. Only three of the screens were lit.

She put down the tray. Myklades swung round and grabbed her wrist. His hand felt like a cold claw. He hauled her in, so she was wedged between him and Rupert, and thrust with his other hand up towards the most central of the lit screens.

At the top, underlined and centred, the words *Byker Lass*. Then eight or nine entries, each beginning with a time and a position.

'Read the last one. Aloud.'

'Five stroke eight. Oh four five three. Position unchanged. Customs and Excise launch alongside. Want to come aboard, it's a bust.' The cursor still throbbed on the *t* of bust. 'Well, that's okay, isn't it? I mean that's what you wanted them to do.'

'Yes. But not so soon. It was all carefully timed. This should have happened just as the last elements of the real shipment were coming safely ashore. On the new schedule that would have been 2 p.m. Tomorrow. They have caught up a minimum of thirty hours.'

'How long before they realise?'

'That's the problem. We don't know. We don't know how stupid they are.'

She moved around them for the next three hours or so, making more coffee, grabbing a bath in the one small bathroom and then having to get out of it when Burke needed to use the lavatory – 'Sorry, love, morning coffee always sets things moving a bit quick with me, I'm used to tea' – and all the time she struggled to make her own assessment of the situation, her situation.

And for most of the time the three of them, Myklades, Burke and Rupert, went over the same ground again and again with the manic obsessiveness which afflicts people who need to know but can only guess: the premature busting of the *Byker*

Lass would not present problems until the Customs and Excise spotted that the coke was rubbish; they would do the simple field test on the spot and that would detect the presence of cocaine – there was no reason to expect a detailed lab report until noon at the earliest, possibly not until the next day if they were really lucky. However, she heard Rupert admit that the gear in question didn't look good – grey, sludgy – and if there was an officer in the team who had experience of the good stuff, and surely there would be, he would be asking for a quick lab report.

The other problem was Hazel, which was what the communication system was called. Their man on the *Byker Lass*, the chief officer, had been instructed to throw his terminal overboard when the boat entered territorial waters off Tynemouth. There was a possibility he might have had the sense to attempt this before the Customs came on board off Sheerness, but they all had to admit it was unlikely – the bust had taken place at first light, and surprise had been almost complete. Rupert asserted that the chief officer would have had time to tap out the message that still pulsed on their screen, no more. They were lucky he had done as much.

'What can they learn from his terminal?' Myklades asked.

'Very little. The chaps on the receiving end are instructed to delete from its memory any messages they receive from us as soon as they've had them, and anyway in this case we haven't sent any. There was no point in trying to slow up his arrival at Tynemouth because we were behind schedule since we don't own the master, Dutchman Van Hoch. And we knew the storm was delaying her anyway. No, the problem as I see it is simply this: just that they now know we're using Hazel.'

'What about the chief officer? Is he safe?'

'Oh, absolutely. I suppose he might identify me if asked to. But I only met him once, three weeks ago, and that was in a pretty dark and grotty pub in Amsterdam. For the rest all he knew was that he had to allow on board one hundred unlabelled bags not mentioned in the manifest, operate Hazel according to instructions, and chuck it overboard at the appropriate time.'

And so it went on. And to Harriet's ear it didn't sound good. She definitely had the feeling that they were whistling in the dark.

Worse was to come. At ten past nine Burke suddenly squawked: 'Hector, I've got Ambrose on the blower. All right, they know they're not meant to know you're here but it's serious, bloody serious. They've been raided . . .'

The noise that came out of Myklades' throat resembled most the drawn-out caw of a carrion crow suddenly deprived of the carcase it is feeding on, and was followed by a crash. Harriet glanced back into the main room and saw, with a sudden surge of bitterness, that he had swept the majolica pot to the floor: it had been left to her by Granny Austen, was sixteenth century, the twin of one in the Wallace Collection, and she had brought it to the Tower because like the Laura Ashley Post-Impressionist chintz it went well with the Miró.

At which point Harriet made a decision. 'I'm going down to Lymington. Can I get anyone anything?'

Myklades swung on her. 'We don't need anything. Why are you going?'

'I'm going because I can't stand the thought of being cooped up here for the next twelve hours listening to you three talking yourselves into nervous breakdowns. Because I want fresh air, I want to be on the ground. I want to be amongst normal people doing normal things for a few hours. Right? Just don't try to stop me.'

The pleading, hurt look came back into his eyes, red-rimmed now behind his tinted spectacles. 'But you will come back, my *yarak*. You will come back?'

'Of course, Hector. In time to cook your lunch.' And swiftly, like a hen pecking at grain, her lips dabbed his cheek. Already it felt hot.

But when she came back a couple of hours later she found the mood had shifted again, to one of excited euphoria. Thinking it through they had decided that the raids on Ambrose, DLC, and Leisure for the Discerning were a good sign.

'You see, my *yarak*, they are not so stupid, one hopes, to imagine that we would go through with the move after they raided them. We would abort. So. They must imagine that they have the shipment, that the *Byker Lass* is the real thing . . . It worked, it worked you see? The feint worked.'

'But won't these raids harm you, harm us? At least cause problems.'

'No. No problems. The financial side is sealed off from product, from cocaine. And each rung in the hierarchy is sealed off from the one above and below. Come here and sit beside me . . .'

He pulled the chair she was heading for closer and took her wrist.

'In the first place our lawyers are already on the scene. But more important we know these plods have not touched the cocaine side of it at all. The only people who have anything to do at all with Ambrose and the rest who know that cocaine is part of the scheme of things are the distributors and street dealers. No more of them have been touched yet.'

She knew a little about how it was all organised. 'But won't they be able to pick them off the DLC records?'

'Harr-ee.' He drew out the syllables. Suddenly she realised he was high. On what? Coke? He hardly ever touched it. Some sort of speed then, something Lovejoy had fixed him up with for times of crisis. Or maybe just straight megalomania: certainly he was pleased with himself. 'Harr-ee, there are eight hundred and twenty-three thousand DLC cardholders and twenty-five thousand seven hundred retailers. Amongst all those a mere twelve hundred handle or trade cocaine. All the transactions are computerised, the clerks in DLC, Leisure for the Discerning, Good Life Promotions and Ambrose too are simply following routines. Of course at places in the chain there are functionaries who are encouraged to make manipulations . . . but even they do not know why and it will be very difficult to identify them. We have been prepared for these eventualities, you know? Isn't that so, Bert? Rupert?'

She felt a sudden wave of sick despair and self-loathing flood over her as she looked from one to the other and realised that on the face of it at any rate they really did believe they were going to win. Then she shrugged, went to the kitchen, washed her hands before preparing their lunch. What I have done, I have done.

'Mermaid Pleasure.'

Mulligan loomed over the desk Tyler was sitting at so that from below it looked as if his domed grey head was brushing the acoustic tiles of the low ceiling.

Tyler sighed, dragged his big hands down his grey cheeks, looked up at him. 'I know all about Mermaid Pleasure. It's the firm that owns the Tower at Swaythe. Spiderman's rented it through Leisure for the Discerning.' He lit the next cigarette from the stub of the old one. The joints of the first and middle fingers of both hands had shifted from orange to brown in twenty-four hours.

'No,' said Mulligan. 'He owns it. He owns Mermaid Pleasure. He bought it a year ago.'

'How do you know?'

'Jones just told me.'

'It's not tied in with the rest.' Tyler screwed up his face and thought. 'It's a registered retailer with the Designer Living Card, but then it would be. But it's not on Ambrose's books.'

'Which means he bought it not as part of his laundering operation, but for some other reason.'

'Christ, I think I'm with you.' He reached for a phone. 'I'll get someone straight down to Companies Registration Office, and Arthur Lord can have a look too. Where's its main office?'

'Southampton. But softly, softly there.'

'Of course. And just now we need a break.'

'Why? Particularly?'

'The Ambrose operation, which shouldn't have happened yet anyway, has gone sour on us.' He explained: solicitors, headed by Billings, had moved like crack troops held in reserve to plug a gap in the line. Behind them the big guns were already being trundled up: the next morning a High Court judge would hear arguments in chambers, and unless police barristers and lawyers from the DPP came up with something really substantial he would issue an injunction ordering the return of books and records so all three companies could continue legitimate trading. 'What we need before ten tomorrow is powder on the table. If we get that and can tie it in – and at the moment the only way we're likely to be able to do that is through the way the *Byker Lass* was chartered – we might just stand a chance of keeping a foot in the door.'

An hour later, nearly noon. Tyler slammed back in his chair, and shouted across the Snowdrop Operations room: 'Mulligan. Buck, come here. It's cracking, it's crumbling, oh for Christ's sake, the sod's gone to sleep. Someone wake him up.'

619

On the other side of the room Mulligan batted away the hand that was shaking his shoulder, threw a look of hate back at Tyler, went to a machine, drew off a beaker of Coca-Cola. 'Okay. What now?'

'Hazel. The man from Hazel who actually installed the system in the Tower for Mermaid Pleasure. He's been under our noses all the time, right here in Oxford. And you know what?'

'What?'

'That Miranda Payne we busted, who was retailing for Caill, it's her husband. He's in an interview room downstairs waiting for us. And of course he's shit-scared.'

'He would be, wouldn't he?'

'Right, Mr Payne. At this point in time it would be ingenuous of me not to admit that the charge of possession of a prohibited substance against you might not be pressed, and things might go a lot more easily for Mrs Payne, whose position is of course far more serious than yours, if you co-operate fully in our enquiries.'

Archie Payne, gangly, awkward even when sitting down, pushed his big hands through his mop of auburn hair. 'Oh, absolutely, er, o-o-officer. I mean, I know we are in an almighty fix, and anything, anything at all . . .'

'My name's Tyler. Now, Mr Payne, we are not experts at all, and Hazel looks very hi-tech to us. Just tell us what it can do, why Mermaid Pleasure had it installed, that sort of thing, but keep it simple. Right?'

'Well, basically, it's a lock-on-lock-off system, with encrypting facility, and computerised frequency hopping matrixed to –'

'Simple, Mr Payne. Hi-tech-wise we are illiterates. Perhaps you could start by telling us why Hazel. Chairman's daughter called Hazel?'

'Lord no.' Archie managed a boyish laugh. The sort of noise doting mums like to hear from seventeen-year-olds, it sounded incongruous coming from someone as old as Archie.

And that, thought Mulligan, is probably what's wrong with him – he never grew up. Problem shared by a lot of English public school boys for whom life has been one long disappointment after those glorious afternoons playing rugby football and those glorious nights buggering their compliant juniors . . .

'. . . short for Hazelhen, which is a poor cousin of the Ptarmigan – birds, you know? Ptarmigan is a weapons system developed by Plessey for NATO. T-t-t-terribly hush hush, and right on the cutting edge of communications technology, real state-of-the-art stuff. Well, not all of it's hush-hush, and using that part of the work that's been published, we thought we could put together a system that businesses who do a lot of talking to themselves might like, a system that in the normal run of things couldn't be broken into, eavesdropped on. Are you with me?'

'*We*, Mr Payne?'

'Yes, basically in the first instance I and a chum, we both parted company with Varsity Specials a year ago, and another chum who had worked for Plessey . . .'

'You got all this off the ground and functioning in only a year? Where did the capital come from?'

'C-c-c-company called Ambrose Finance . . .'

'And could you, with the right equipment, break into the system Mermaid Pleasure are using?'

'Well, no. I mean, that is rather the whole p-p-point of the thing, isn't it? Wouldn't have done our job properly if I could. But if I could get my hands on part of the system, see how they've set the co-ordinates – '

'You mean if we could get you the hardware off one of the boats – would that do?'

'Yes. Yes, I think so. I'd then have to set up a duplicate of their master system, but we've got all the specifications at the office, and the hardware out at the Abingdon factory . . .'

'How long would it take?'

'On my own a week, ten days.'

'Listen, my son. We'll get help. Those colleagues of yours you mentioned, and a set of the hardware from one of the boats, and you crack it in twenty-four hours right? That is if you want to see Mrs Payne before the year 2000.'

That was a mistake. For Archie recent events had suggested that what had begun to look like a life-sentence of sexual teasing, terrible rows, and constant nagging might be commuted.

Tyler rushed on: 'And as far as your own spot of trouble goes, I'm sure we'll be able to recommend a suspended sentence.'

*

Two o'clock, still the same day, a day whose dawn had found Mulligan heaving scampi, chips, real ale over the side of a Customs and Excise launch and into the Thames Estuary. Back in the first floor ops room of the Oxford nick, with the usual babel of clattering printers, out-of-date typewriters, bleeping computer terminals, and brisk chatter all round them, Tyler ran his finger down a long sheet of printout and read off whatever he thought was relevant: 'Mermaid Pleasure. Registered in Sark. Solicitors . . . blah, blah, registered office in UK, Ogle Street, Southampton, blah, blah, now here we are. They own several yachts of varying sizes, three, no, four high-powered cruisers, all available for short-term charter, self-catering apartments at Brighton, Buckler's Hard, Lymington, Keyhaven, Christchurch, Poole, ships' chandlers at the same marinas . . . Christ, where did they get all this stuff? This has to be it. This is the infrastructure they had to have to bring in two tons at one go. And you know one thing I'm bloody sure of now?'

'What?'

'Unless we get our skates on we run a very serious risk of being in the wrong place at the wrong time. We ought to be down there in bloody Hampshire, not sitting on our arses up here.'

Late afternoon and the view was magnificent. To the east the last big cloud systems of the storm were stacked marble bolsters piled on granite, beneath which the last squalls marched in columns across Portsmouth and Portdown, all lit as if for Eisenstein or Orson Welles by a sun which shone from almost clear skies in the west. Across the Solent every rain-washed feature of the island stood out with harsh clarity, the Needles shone like blocks of snow rather than rotten teeth and the sea was deepest, purest ultramarine flecked with charging white horses that crashed against headlands and sea walls, fountained foam above the nearby housetops.

'It still looks pretty rough to me,' said Harriet.

'Twenty minutes to high tide. With the ebb running against it it'll get a lot quieter. Wind's down to force five, backing south. I don't think we're going to have much trouble. Tomorrow they reckon is going to be perfect sailing weather.

Are there any more of those muffins?' Rupert lifted the lid of a silver muffin-dish. 'Lord knows when I'll eat again.'

Passing behind him she stroked his cheek then, with a quick glance towards the control room, brought her lips close to his ear. 'Do you have to go through with this?'

'Yup. Once it's all safely in the warehouse it'll be up to sales and distribution, which is not really my pigeon. We can just tell Hector we're going off on a long holiday, he won't need us till it's time to start putting together the next shipment, and so on. Blah, blah. And when it all falls apart we'll already be a long way off, and with luck he won't suspect me anyway.'

'It really is falling apart?'

'It really is. And not just because of these hiccups. The real dangers are far more serious and far less obvious.'

Feeling better she straightened, moved towards the kitchen, almost bumped into Burke. 'Shit, you gave me a fright. What's the matter?'

Weaselly mouth twisted beneath sharp nose, piggy eyes screwed up, big hands thrust into his jacket pockets – the big ex-policeman was disturbed.

'They've closed the Oxford ops room,' he said.

'Well, isn't that good news? Doesn't it mean that they think they've done their bit with the *Byker Lass*?'

'No, miss. I don't think so. I don't think that's likely at all. There's just a chance they're going west, to Bristol. If we get confirmation of that then we might begin looking on the bright side. But until then . . .' He looked at his watch. 'Don't be too long finishing your tea, young sir, it's almost time we were off.'

Twenty minutes later Harriet watched Burke's black Ford Sierra trundling down the track across the heath, apparently with only him in it, but, she knew, with Rupert in a coffin-like compartment under the rear seat. At the main road they turned right – for Christchurch, Bournemouth, Hurn airport. Possibly she would not see Rupert again. Possibly, in spite of his reassurance, the two words she had offered in answer to Mulligan's question had been enough. Well, she thought, Rupert has always looked after himself. He'll just have to do extra well in the next twenty-four hours or so, and she turned away, killing the dagger-thrust of guilt not with drugs but by an act of will.

From the control room Myklades called. His voice was

throaty, constricted. She went in. He was sitting in the middle one of the three chairs looking up at the thirty screens. He was – and somehow she had known he would be – naked, and the flickering green light played over his pallid skin blotched with the rising plaques of psoriasis.

'I can't leave here. I must watch them all. All the time. Did Burke tell you they have left Oxford?'

'Yes.'

'Where have they gone?' He swung the chair round, grabbed her wrist. 'Where have they gone? Eh?'

'I don't know, Hector. How should I know?'

'And you see what it has done to me?'

She went to the tiny bathroom, found a tube of Dr Lovejoy's ointment. Back in the control room she began to dab the scales on his back.

Without taking his eyes off the screens he said: 'It was the weather, the rain the night before. It cost him three hours. With those three hours he would have broken the British before Blücher arrived. You know what I am talking about?'

'Napoleon and the Battle of Mont-St-Jean.'

'And your focking English weather has cost me not three hours but twenty-four. Of course, he was betrayed too.'

'And you think you have been. There's not a lot of ointment here so I'm using it as sparingly as I can.'

'You and Rupert. You are very close. Always whispering in corners. I will kill both of you if you have betrayed me.'

Behind his back she bit her lip savagely, forced herself to stay calm, played her last card. 'And risk losing all those pictures I've taken of you with Crystal? They're your insurance, but they're mine too.'

Burke, who was adept in such things, lost his tail in a multi-storey car park in the centre of Bournemouth, and dropped Rupert off at Hurn airport, five miles away, only an hour after leaving the Tower. There a man called Jimmy filed a flight plan, flew him in a war-surplus Chinook twin-rotor helicopter along the coast to Shoreham. On the way they passed over the Tower but resisted the temptation to buzz it. From Shoreham Rupert took a taxi to Brighton marina. There from a public telephone box he rang a London number. On the way he had decided that, after all, things were a bit flaky and he might just as well activate his last piece of insurance. Then at the Mermaid Pleasure office he picked up the two youths who, that night and the next day, were to be his donkeys, do the heavy work for him.

They were dressed in the uniform of the Viking Vigilants, dark blue denim jackets and jeans with shield-shaped shoulder flashes carrying two V's with exaggerated serifs interlaced in such a way that they suggested, none too subtly, swastikas. To join the Viking Vigilants you have to be under twenty-five, unemployed, fit, and have a criminal record. The organisation exists to help young lads who have had a brush or two with the law to regain their pride through learning basic maritime skills, life-saving, and so on, but it also instils a strong sense of group loyalty and insists on self-discipline, physical toughness, and unquestioning obedience to the organisation's officers. It is a charity, and at that time was largely financed by tax-effective subventions from Mermaid Pleasure.

These two knew Rupert well: he had picked them himself from a troop he had given lectures to on the skills he had learnt with the SAS, and he had taken them on a three-day self-subsisting hike through the New Forest during which they had illegally shot deer with a cross bow. Later, satisfied that they were the right stuff, he had put them through a brief spell of training which had consisted mainly of throwing bags weighing two kilos from one boat and catching them on another at a mean rate of three bags a minute.

From pontoon seven on the West Jetty they boarded the pride of the Mermaid Pleasure fleet, a Riva 60 Corsaro, powered by twin MAN engines with a total capacity of thirteen hundred horsepower, and plenty of room below to accommodate four crew in sybaritic comfort or two hundred and fifty two-kilo bags of cocaine. She was called *Snowstorm II*. At 1800 precisely they cast off and puttered out in low gear from beneath the first of the chalk cliffs that rise east of Brighton. Clear of the Western Breakwater they turned right, starboard, and bucking the still strong westerly swell that threw occasional swags of sea across the bows, headed towards Plymouth, two hundred miles away. That at any rate is what the Mermaid Pleasure books said: *Snowstorm II* had been chartered by Mr and Mrs Paddy O'Reilly for a trip from Plymouth to

Wexford and back with the hope of a bit of shark-fishing on the way. Deposit paid on a DLC card.

She was a sleek, fast cruiser with a steeply raked bow that stood high out of the water, twin sets of controls so she could be navigated either from inside the cabin from behind windscreens as acutely angled as those on a Ferrari, or from the exposed cockpit above, and of all of the toys Myklades had given Rupert to play with, this was just about his favourite.

At midnight, in seas that were still too high for comfort, he rendez-voused with the *San Fermín* five nautical miles east of the EC2 navigation beacon which lies almost exactly at the point of no return between St Catherine's Point, the most southerly tip of the Isle of Wight, and La Pointe de Barfleur on the Cherbourg peninsula. There, and not easily, with one or two quite hairy moments, and one or two quite nasty bangs against the jute fenders the skipper of the *San Fermín* had considerably lowered to water level, he took on five parcels, each holding fifty bags labelled Sol-Methrine B (Sol-Chem AG Düsseldorf). The operation took thirty-five minutes, ten more than he had planned, and the next boat, a Neptunus 133 power cruiser, was already standing off and waiting.

By 0230 hours, only half an hour behind optimum schedule and well within the critical margins he had set, the remaining ton had been lowered on to two more power cruisers. Using an Aldis lamp – total radio silence had been observed throughout – he signalled congratulations and best wishes to the other three craft and then each turned and headed northwards on widely different bearings to complete what was the most difficult and dangerous phase of the operation. The *San Fermín* offered one blast on the mournful siren Rupert had first heard off Punto de Gallinas in the Caribbean and she too moved on, but south-west by west for Ushant, Bordeaux and the Med. He tapped a signal on his Hazel terminal, and forty miles away in the Tower Myklades authorised EFT of the final payment to Arias. Mendoza Holdings moved a further ten million dollars into the red.

An hour later, and at very first light, with the Isle of Wight a very distant smudge on his northern horizon, and the dawn a very distant promise to the east, he picked up the silhouette that his radar had already promised of a thirty-two-foot sloop, hove-to under a single fluttering jib. He laid *Snowstorm II* on her beam, twenty feet off.

He hailed: 'Ralph! Everything okay?'

'Rupe? Yes, we're okay, but it's a bit more rough than we expected. Phyllis has been sick as a dog.'

'Never mind, we'll manage. Right, if you're ready. I'm going to lay her alongside.'

The manoeuvre stretched his seamanship to its limits, and he had to wonder if the skippers of the other three cruisers were up to it. Silly to worry now, though, the die was cast, there was to be no turning back now. As the fenders touched, with far more of a bump than he would have liked, and with water slopping up to deck level between them, one of his Viking Vigilants leapt down into the cockpit of the sloop. Moments later his second lad dropped the first of fifty bags into his waiting hands.

Back in the Tower Myklades, huddled now in a towelling wrap, with Burke at his side, sat in front of the monitors and watched through the dawn as one by one they lit up, twenty of them. Cursors flickered across each and spelled out the message: a codename and the single letter A. Twenty yachts had each taken on fifty two-kilo bags and were now moving slowly into the sea spaces they would share with hundreds of similar yachts as the Royal Yacht Squadron regatta at last got underway in the Solent, at the same time as the Admiral's Cup offshore Olympic Triangle to the west in Christchurch Bay.

63

Two hours later and ten miles away at the South Hampshire divisional headquarters, Lyndhurst, Archie Payne reckoned he'd cracked Hazel – that is, he had worked out the frequency-hopping sequence the Tower was using, and of course he had the same decrypting box. He was, in his boyish way, pretty chuffed about it: 'You see I have done the work on this one,' he kept saying.

The overall picture had become much clearer. Myklades'

presence in the Tower, Mermaid Pleasure, and now the fact that messages were coming into Hazel from at least sixteen different sources, all pointed to the same conclusion. The shipment had been split, was being brought in on small boats, presumably to several different ports of entry. But all they were getting was a series of single words followed by the letters of the alphabet in sequence, *a*, *b*, and now *c*. The messages were far too short for there to be any hope of getting a fix on them – all Payne could say was that they were getting just perceptibly stronger, that the assumption to be made was that the sources were getting closer.

'And that,' said Mulligan, 'is all you are going to get unless something goes wrong. Clearly it's all going to plan: as each boat passes an agreed position it simply confirms that it's on schedule.'

'So what do we do?' Tyler banged his fist into his palm with the rhythmic insistence of a disturbed head-banging infant. In seventy-two hours he had slept for perhaps six, was coming very close now to the end of his tether, his brain clearly refusing to function properly. 'There are literally thousands of boats out there, and, counting the island ones, a dozen marinas and yacht havens within radio distance of the Tower . . .'

Mulligan had slept more. At fifty years old, ten years older than Tyler, his system simply gave in at a certain point and forced sleep on him no matter how he resisted it; he had also refused the Benzedrine the police surgeon had on offer. The result was that at ten o'clock the previous evening he fell asleep on his feet, was helped down to the basement and lodged in a cell where he got a full eight hours undisturbed, had had a proper breakfast of ham and eggs, and was feeling altogether a lot sharper than Tyler.

'We're going at it the wrong way round, aren't we? Look, we're pretty sure they're using Mermaid Pleasure facilities. These are what you should be checking out. The apartments they've got. Who's renting them? Have any been kept empty? I mean that would be significant at this time of year, wouldn't it? Same with the boats they charter. What you want is a really detailed breakdown of the whole set-up, not just what you can get off an advertising brochure.'

'You're right. Of course you are. But where are we going to get all that from in the time we've got? And without making waves? That's the problem, isn't it? They're such clever bastards they're sure to have at least one contingency plan to fall back on as soon as they sense we're on to them. Kick down the doors at the Mermaid Pleasure office in Southampton and they'll pull up the drawbridge everywhere else . . .'

'Look, it's just gone eight. The office won't be open yet. If you can find a way of picking up at least one person who works there before he or she gets there, so they can just phone in and say they've got a cold or whatever . . .'

'How the fuck are we going to do that?'

'Jesus, Tyler, I don't know, but for Christ's sake try . . .'

WPC Porter looked up from the stack of printout she had been scanning at a nearby desk. 'The address is Clifton House. That suggests an office block. There might be some sort of reception desk. Or perhaps a business that opens earlier in the same premises. What I'm getting at is there might be someone there who can identify a Mermaid Pleasure employee before they actually get into the office . . .'

'You're right. It's a bloody long shot, but it's worth a try. Anything at this stage is worth a try. Get a local, get a set of fast wheels, get moving . . .'

At nine-forty-five a plump dark girl called Sandra, seventeen years old but unfazed at being kidnapped by the police on the pavement outside Clifton House, in fact bubbling with excitement at it all, was rushed to the resited Snowdrop operations room, eleven miles away. She was only a filing clerk on a Youth Opportunity Scheme, helped out with the typing and so on, but she had been there six months, and she knew an awful lot about Mermaid Pleasure. Your first job, much like your first lover, excites curiosity in a way subsequent ones may not.

Twelve noon, and the first of the screens went dark on the message 'Mission accomplished'. Up in the Tower Burke popped a bottle of Mumm champagne. Down in Lymington marina Ralph did likewise, and toasted his wife Phyllis across the narrow table in their new Sadler 32. His T-shirt was dark with sweat, his eyes ringed with tiredness: twelve hours at sea followed by the effort of carting four black plastic rubbish bags, two at a time, not to the Mermaid Pleasure apartments across the quay but up the lane that leads to the yacht club and into a small cottage opposite an upmarket ships' chandlers. He made as if they weighed only a quarter of what they actually did, and the effort left him as limp as the dishcloth his wife Phyllis now used to wipe up the froth that had bubbled over.

The euphoria in the Tower was more frenetic, mined with labryinthine tunnels of deceit. The big reception room was huge with sunshine; below it, half a mile away, the Solent was brilliant as the big yachts heeled on their beam ends round the Berthon buoy, spilled out their jazzy spinnakers for the run back to Cowes with a force-four wind and the tide behind them, the water that deepest blue that is almost black and the foam sculpted by speed into rococo curlicues whiter than snow. And around and beyond them the smaller boats, all shapes, sizes and types, spectators, sightseers, were scattered across the seascape in shifting constellations whose patterns seemed random, though dictated by wind and perhaps also by their crews' desire for lunch in calmer waters.

'Which are ours? Can you tell?' Harriet mimicked the excitement of a small girl to hide the panic she felt, jigged up and down at Burke's elbow, so the shampoo in her glass slopped on her wrist. She gulped what was left and pleaded: 'Come on, Bert, give us a go.'

It was the big binoculars he was using that she wanted, but he held on, swept round to the west to Christchurch Bay six miles away where nearly forty yachts, the best of their size in the world, were just finishing the thirty-mile inshore race in the Admiral's Cup series, and they too were surrounded by a cloud of sails, triangular chips of enamel at this distance.

A sourness in the air, not entirely from the coal-tar base of the cortisone ointment, and Myklades was at her shoulder. 'Four more have checked in, two at Buckler's Hard, another at Lymington, and one at Keyhaven. It's going very well.'

'It certainly is.' Burke handed the binoculars to his master. 'Though I'm a little worried about the Christchurch Harbour end – with this wind the Admiral's Cup race is finishing earlier than we expected, and it's quite on the cards there won't be as much traffic out there as we would have liked when the tail-enders come in, in an hour or so.'

'Do you think we should reroute them?'

'It's an option to bear in mind. Oh and look, sir, as far as I understand these things, which isn't that far, I reckon *Ambrosiana* is doing better than she did on Tuesday.'

Harriet swore. 'Oh, come on, give us a go.'

Myklades handed her the glasses. 'Certainly I do not understand these things. It is a ridiculous sport where the first over the line at the end is almost never the winner, when you need a computer to work out a ridiculous point system ... You are all most mistaken if you think I care in the least how my focking yorts do.' He swallowed his champagne in a gulp, poured himself more, then grinned as broadly as Harriet had ever seen him grin over the rim of the glass. 'But this pleases me.' He gesticulated widely, included the sunshine, the distant boats, the large and vibrant Miró, the whole ambience of the Tower. 'This is magnificent. This is what I wanted. I have planned this for a year, I have gambled millions on it, and it is working. And there is more good news too. I have just heard from Billings. The judge in chambers has given the police forty-eight hours to make copies of what documents they might think they need, and then they are to get out and let us continue to trade. And trade we focking will, now we have something to trade with ...'

He turned on his heel, slopped the second glass down his tilted throat, swept back into his control room. Presently they heard him shout: 'Three more are in, three more. We are nearly halfway home.'

'Oh, damn it, I wish I could see one, just one, and know that that was what I was looking at. It really is rather tremendous, isn't it, Bert? I mean it is pretty huge, four hundred million pounds' worth, tacking and chugging into those little toy marinas amongst all the other little toys.'

'Here we are, miss, if I'm not mistaken. Black hull, not many black hulls, and with like a red Japanese sun on her big front sail. *Fujippon III*. She raced two years ago in that big competition. The Nips who put the electronics in here ran her, and we got her cheap for Mermaid Pleasure only a month or so ago ... crewed by three commodity brokers with expensive lifestyles.'

'Yes, I've got her, standing off Hurst Castle and heading I suppose for that funny little estuary with the slipway ...'

'Keyhaven, miss. That's the one.'

'They're pulling in the spinnaker, coming in under power. So, what's she carrying?'

'Same as all the rest, miss, one hundred kilos, fifty bags, twenty million quid's worth.'

'Aren't you afraid one of them will just put on all the sail it can and beetle off never to be seen again?'

'Not at all, miss. For a start each skipper who gets through gets a hundred grand on top of the hundred they've already had, and then of course each one knows what the consequences will be.'

'Oh?'

'Well, in the second place, as it were, we'll catch them in the end, but before that they'll suffer a grievous loss, a very grievous loss, a kid, maybe, or a close relation, a girlfriend, that sort of thing. Mr Myklades has a good hold on all of them.'

'But that's horrible!' She kept her voice down, glanced over his shoulder towards the control room.

'Can't say I like it myself, miss, and I assure you I have nothing to do with that side of things. Mr Bridge looks after that side.' He brightened his voice, sought to recapture the cheeriness of the earlier moment. 'And I very much doubt if it will come to anything like that at all. Now if you'll excuse me, miss, I ought to be back in there with him. I wonder if we could possibly trouble you for some more of those excellent sandwiches, like you provided yesterday . . . nothing like the old bubbly and a bit of excitement for giving you an appetite. Smoked salmon, weren't they? I thought so. Had them at my niece's wedding.'

Tyler, clutching a sheaf of printout, stormed across the big stuffy room to the windows where Mulligan was seeking some relief from it all in a pleasantly pastoral scene of fields, woods, a golf-course, ponies, only marginally ruined by the steady stream of holiday traffic that had piled up in front of the police station.

'We're getting the picture. It's becoming clearer every moment. They reckon they may have spotted two lots so far, one at Christchurch, the other in Lymington. The routine the same in both places: yacht comes in, ties up at a Mermaid

Pleasure berth. These are always situated with easy access to the Mermaid Pleasure apartments, so all the mule has to do is carry the gear in off his boat and dump it. As far as we can tell there's no one there to receive it – they just dump it, lock up and that's it.'

'So it'll be picked up later . . .'

'That's it. Presumably when the whole lot's ashore, someone will come round and pick it up. Sandra says they've got four Renault Trafic vans that go round the apartments on a regular basis, servicing them, collecting rubbish, restocking the freezers, that sort of thing. They've also got a warehouse on an industrial estate just outside Christchurch, leased from a firm called Woolingham Storage, owns a lot of warehouses all over the south . . .'

'So you reckon that's where it'll end up.'

'Looks like it.'

'Hey, Rex, I believe we're winning.' He aimed a punch at the Englishman's shoulder, and turned his own to take one back.

'I think we might be, I think we might. Only problem though is the usual one, Customs and fucking Excise. They want to pull at least one of those apartments right now, are shit-scared they're going to lose a haul . . .'

'But Christ, Tyler, they mustn't do that!'

'I told them, Buck, I told them.'

'That's the whole point of the way Spiderman's doing it. Two tons he could drop off in a container at Southampton. But if it went wrong he'd lose the lot. But this way it's all split up at the time it's most vulnerable, on entry. He loses one – what, one-tenth, one-twentieth? – and he's still laughing. It's also clear too that with Hazel he'll be able to warn the others. Look. They absolutely must not move until it's all come together again.'

'I've told them all that. Trouble is they just can't believe it's two tons we're looking at, two thousand kilos. The most they've ever had in one go before is a hundred . . .'

The alarm on Rupert's Swiss Corum watch bleeped him into wakefulness. Twelve-thirty. He turned over on the narrow bunk bed, listened to the sounds around him. In the next room the murmur of voices, Clint and Dean, his two Viking Vigilants, endlessly playing Pontoon for pennies, apparently their only resource when there was nothing else to do. Then beyond that very little: footsteps crunching on gravel, the braying voices of people of his class and caste as they entered the pub across the way. He swung his bare legs to the floor, padded on bare feet, stooped to peer through the tiny square panes of the cottage window.

He was looking across a steep slope, part gravelled, part paved, part laid out in flowerbeds at a row of terraced cottages that stepped up the slope from the Beaulieu River below to a tiny museum and hotel at the top. The cottages opposite were also part of the hotel, and had been converted into tiny low-ceilinged bars. The cottage he was in was similar but had been modernised as one of the most exclusive and expensive of the properties Mermaid Pleasure handled for private owners. It was not the furnishings or appointments that made it so, but the situation: this was Buckler's Hard, once a slipway where ships of the line were built for Nelson's fleet, now one of the smallest, most private and exclusive of the south coast marinas.

The window was bayed. By crouching a little and pushing his body into the curve, he could get a good view of the hard itself, a slipway, a quay, and down river pontoons with berths for perhaps thirty boats, mostly, at this moment unoccupied. On the other side oaks and mountain ash, the berries just beginning to blush, climbed to a low bluff, and at that moment the tall mainmast of a fifty-foot ketch, under two jibs and power, slid between him and the trees. She was the largest of the boats they'd used and one of the very few that was under charter from Mermaid Pleasure, rather than privately owned. He watched her slip into the berth next to *Snowstorm II*, then he moved to the tiny bathroom at the back of the cottage.

From here the view was rather different, looked out on to a service road, outhouses, the old outside lavatories converted into storage sheds, dustbins, and a field of Friesians with grubby backsides. Presently he recognised the portly figure of the man who had been chief officer on the requisitioned cruise ship he had sailed to the Falklands on five years ago, a large-waisted man in shorts, with thick hairy legs beneath a head that would have been an asset to a bishop. He was followed by two other men and three girls, all toting cylindrical canvas bags which the girls, nubile and scantily clad, were obviously finding too heavy.

They stopped at the back gate of the cottage next door, looked around them with obvious terror to try to see if they had been observed while the big man undid a brass padlock on the ex-lavatory. With some grunting and gasping the bags were swung into it. Then the entire party went through the house, and emerged on the other side, only moments later, but utterly transformed. The bishop had his arms round two of the girls, one of the younger men was singing 'O Sole Mio' with grandiose gestures, the other was goosing the third girl with ardour, and jaunting thus they crossed the slipway and disappeared into the pub. Obviously they had shed quite a weight off their minds with the bags, which, thought Rupert – and his mouth set in a hard thin smile – is rather ironic.

He banged on the door of the other bedroom. 'Come on, lads. We leave in ten minutes.'

A quarter of an hour later he backed a big dark blue Renault Trafic van, the high-roofed 1.8 version, with gold mermaids on its sides and the MP logo, down the service road. Dean and Clint briskly unpacked the grey plastic bags from the canvas carriers and stacked them up at the front of the freight area behind the driver's seat. There were one hundred and fifty of them, for the ketch was the third and last of the Buckler's Hard drops, then both climbed in beside him.

'What the fuck is Sol-Methrine anyway, chief?'

'Pesticide. Kills those nasty little whiteflies that ruin your dad's fruit bushes.'

'And what you got this stovepipe thing in the back for? K-D it's got written on it.'

'Mind your own fucking business.'

A mistake. Their silence told him that.

Rupert improvised. 'Actually it's underwater surveillance equipment. In case any silly bugger drops a pack in the drink.'

'Where now, boss?'

'Lymington, then Keyhaven.' He pulled a microphone mounted on a coiled metal stalk above the windscreen in under his chin, dabbed buttons. 'Control, control, do you read me?'

Myklades' voice, guttural, breathy. 'Freightman, we read you.'

'Pick-up A completed. Require your clearance to proceed to B on schedule.'

'Freightman, you have clearance.'

Rupert pushed back the microphone, switched off the radio, returned the transmitter to a new frequency. Up in the Tower, which they could actually see as they breasted the slope above the hard, a red-brick phallus four miles away sticking up into the cloud palaces of the windy sky, Myklades or Burke would be doing the same.

Lymington went all right, they took on another two hundred bags, but at Keyhaven came the first sign that not everything might work out just as Rupert intended. The pick-up point here was another converted and modernised cottage, painted white this time with black-framed windows, a slate roof, and a tiny brass cannon, the sort that used to be used to start yacht races, mounted on a plinth amongst the hollyhocks and geraniums in the garden. It overlooked the little creek, muddy now with the tide ebbing and dunlin and oyster-catchers scouting and probing along the flats, and with just one boat tied up to the little jetty, the black-hulled sloop that had raced for the Japanese in the Admiral's Cup two years ago. There was no sign of life on her, but Rupert was worried. She should have got out again on the tide – that was the plan in this particular instance.

'Wait.'

Leaving the two lads behind him he dropped onto gravel, fingered out a key, let himself into the cottage. It was cool and dark, black-painted beams hung with horse brasses contrasted with rough-cast walls painted white. There were pictures, silhouettes of nineteenth-century yachts painted on glass, framed in pearwood, and on the big black table, just as there should have been, one hundred plastic bags.

Only it wasn't right. They had been stacked on a rectangular base of twenty-five bags, four deep, and one bag in one corner was clearly missing. It didn't take Rupert long to spot it: it was on an armchair in front of the fireplace – an armchair upholstered in black cord which threw up the grey plastic, and the blue and red stencil. And the splash of grey powder that leaked from the gash across the swollen belly of the bag. Grey powder, very fine, like cement. It was a mule-kick to the stomach.

Rupert contemplated it for at least four minutes, legs astride, right elbow on the palm of his left hand, right index finger caressing his right cheek. Then he shrugged, and a Muslim would have read the gesture correctly: *Inshallah*.

He strode back out into the brilliant sunlight, banged open the door of the Trafic.

'Out.' Dean and Clint tumbled out. 'Get lost.' They did.

He reached into the glove compartment set in the driver's door and pulled out the 9mm Browning he had kept near him since Grosvenor Road in Chiswick, thrust it into his waistband, and trotted down the sloping path to the jetty.

He leapt into the cockpit of the yacht, heard the scuffle of feet slithering in panic below him. Using the rails he dropped down the companionway into the galley, and his feet did not touch the steep steps.

His eyes flickered over it all, the microwave, the tiny stainless steel sink, the cupboards, the standard in-board mini-computer that monitored the boat's systems, came to rest on the Hazel video terminal.

One line of script lay across it: 'Bags labelled: Sol-Methrine B ex-Düsseldorf.'

Again he paused and thought, but with his right hand close to the butt of the Browning, and he could hear as he thought, but did not let it bother him, the panic-spiced sibilance of frantic whispers beyond the veneered door in front of him.

'Right then,' he called at last. 'You can come out and tell me all about it. Jeremy, Adrian and Nigel, isn't it?'

Jeremy was a rotund, prematurely balding blond with protuberant blue eyes; Adrian was tall, had to duck his mophead to get under the transom; Nigel was clearly Jewish and the only one who smiled. All three broked foreign currency in the City.

'You carried the gear up into the cottage, and then one of you said a little toot won't do us any harm. Right?'

Jeremy pointed a finger at Nigel, who smiled and said: 'It was Adrian's idea.'

'Which, of course,' Rupert went on, 'was dead contrary to the rules, as you well knew.' His anger was burning now, was an imperative as great as the need to know. He loosed off a shell into the vaguely nautical but ornate brass lamp that swung over the big bed behind them, a bed that curved into a point where the headboard should have been, echoing the shape of the bow. The lamp exploded, and all three men hit the very little available floor-space in a tangle that was ludicrous.

'So one of you slit open the bag. And you found . . . well, not charlie, that's for sure. Right?'

They nodded.

'So then you followed instructions, at last, having broken several of them, and tapped in a message to Control. Control came back to you asking for what was written on the bags. And the message that is on the screen now, was your answer. Did you then press the "send" button?'

Jeremy nodded, though Nigel would have preferred him not to.

'Then,' said Rupert, and he let the anger burn momentarily bright like a very short fuse, 'what you have done is irretrievable and so are you.'

And he shot each of them quickly, accurately, and cleanly in the head.

Back in the van he switched on the RT link to the Tower.

64

Up there, ten minutes earlier, the brief exchange with *Fujippon III* had caused an abrupt shift from euphoria destabilised by angst, to one of menace and dread. Myklades had thought it through.

'This cannot happen. The safety procedures were impregnable. There were, in the *San Fermín*, two tons of Sol-Methrine B from Düsseldorf, and two tons of cocaine in identically labelled bags. It is not possible that the Colombians can have switched them. The secure container was opened and checked by Rupert and Aguirre in Rotterdam. Then closed again, but only by Rupert. Only he could have opened it last night. It is not possible for the two loads to have been switched except with his connivance . . . I think the man is a focking traitor.'

'It's possible, sir, that there is some other explanation.'

'Occam's Razor says that this is the most likely. Any other would have to be impossibly involved and complicated. How many of our yorts are still at sea?'

'Seven. Two more for Lymington, and the five for Christchurch Harbour, two for the Mudeford marina, and three for the quays on the Avon.'

'Put them all on standby for twenty minutes.'

Burke again swept the distant bay with his binoculars. 'The racing is finished there. There are already far fewer boats than there were. They will be very exposed.'

'All right. Tell them to proceed towards the Solent as if to watch the racing there. Then they can return to their berths in Lymington and Christchurch Harbour, towards nightfall if necessary. So. When is Freightman due at Keyhaven?'

'Now.'

'When you have put those boats on standby, make contact with him. It will be interesting to see if he has anything to say.' He turned to Harriet who was now standing by the big open windows. 'You look pale. As well you might. If I have been betrayed, and if I think you are part of the plot, I will throw you out of that window.' He laughed harshly. 'It will be a little like a medieval witch trial. If you are a male hawk, trained and steady, you will make a circle or two and come back. If not . . .'

She lifted her head, hand at white throat, cried: 'Hector, I am not a traitor. I'm not. You know I can't be. Remember, you made me yours . . .' It was a lousy performance, though the terror was genuine enough.

'Nevertheless, we shall see.' He swung back into the control room.

She followed, stood in the doorway, elbow high up on the post, her cheek resting on her palm. Burke busied himself at successive keyboards and new messages unwound across the screens that were still lit. Myklades hovered behind him, checking, occasionally pointing out the odd error Burke made. Presently a red light began to flash, but to the side, near a more conventional RT, the sort of appliance one sees at the headquarters of large taxi fleets. Myklades leaned across to it, flicked a switch, turned a dial.

Immediately they heard Rupert's voice: nervy, abrasive, the

flat twang more pronounced than ever as if he were speaking through clenched teeth.

'Freightman to Control.'

'Come in, Freightman.'

'Freightman at point C. There is a red emergency here. Here.'

The repeated last word signified that he was changing the frequency on which he was transmitting according to a pre-arranged sequence. Myklades turned a dial, kept up with him.

'Product at pick-up point appears to be Sol-Methrine B. B.' Again the retuning. 'A grey, cementlike powder.'

Myklades grinned showing yellowish teeth, and nodded his head. 'Freightman. Board the boat immediately. Ascertain situation there. There.'

There was a longish pause, say twenty seconds. Harriet suddenly realised why: the order was loaded, Rupert had not foreseen it, did not have the time he needed to evaluate its significance.

Then: 'Control? The boat has gone. You remember because it reached here after the tide had begun to ebb we decided it should put to sea as soon as the drop had been made. Made.'

Myklades pushed his long freckled fingers through his yellow hair, and the snarl he gave the ceiling stretched his face into something skull-like.

'Control to Freightman: situation needs further evaluation. Proceed here immediately for further discussion. Over and out.' The emphasis on the last word was heavy, and he threw the switch that cut them off, turned to Burke who had been following the whole conversation, his eyes more weaselly now than piggy, alert with a predator's intelligence.

'Well?'

'It's not true. We know they were there fifteen minutes ago. If they had sailed then they would have got out. But not since. Not unless the tide is doing something freakish. But even if they had they would still be in sight and they are not. We can't actually see into the creek but we can see all the channels that feed it east of Hurst Castle, the headland that protects the cove, and I can assure you *Fujippon III* has not come out of Keyhaven.'

'So.' Myklades spun on his heel, came up to Harriet and snapped his fingers beneath her nose. 'So. The Honourable

Rupert Bridge is a liar and Occam was right. When two hypotheses carry the same weight the simpler one is more likely to be correct. The razor to cut a traitor's throat.'

The interchange between *Fujippon III* and the Tower had been carried out entirely on the Hazel system and had begun half an hour earlier. It consisted of four messages from the boat and three from the Tower, and had ended with the one Rupert had seen still flashing on the screen when he boarded the boat. The effect ten miles away, at the Lyndhurst-based Snowdrop operations room, had been galvanising. After the early euphorias induced by Sandra's revelations about Mermaid Pleasure, it had all soured on them again. One of the parties who had been observed landing luggage at the new luxury apartment at Lymington Quay had been identified from the German Zöll plates of their big new Mercedes as the West German Ambassador, accompanied by his Head of Chancellery with their wives and children. Not even the Customs and Excise officer wanted to bust them. Checks on two other apartments that looked likely drop points also revealed occupiers of unimpeachable respectability. Again the ghost of Lowndes Square was grinning over their shoulders.

But Hazel now looked as if she might at last deliver. In the first place the second message from the boat had actually used the word 'cocaine'. In the second it clearly indicated that something had gone very badly wrong for Spiderman. And thirdly it had gone on long enough, albeit on shifting frequencies, for the technicians who had largely taken over from Archie Payne now that he had the system running, to get, if not a fix, then at least a bearing on where it was coming from. This passed through Keyhaven, and since the content of the messages suggested that the senders were both on or very close to dry land, the team immediately decided that Keyhaven was where the boat was. There was an added significance to this. No property belonging to Mermaid Pleasure was sited there, and so they had not put it under surveillance.

Tyler swung on Sandra, who was still ebullient, still achieving near-complete recall whenever they had a question for her, but who, because Tyler had shouted at her when she tended to prattle irrelevancies, had decided only to speak when spoken to.

'Keyhaven. What's Mermaid Pleasure got there?'

'Nothing. I told you.'

'Shit. Must have.'

Bea Porter looked up, her serious eyes assessed him, found him wanting, then she turned to Sandra. Her voice was always quiet, rather deep, and at times carried just the hint of an accent. Italian perhaps. 'You've told us about the properties Mermaid Pleasure owns. Do they lease any others?'

'No. Not lease. Not actually lease.'

All three of them, Mulligan, Tyler, and Porter, froze for a moment at the hint of something incomplete, unsaid. Both men began, but Porter, suddenly peremptory, silenced them, turned back to Sandra.

'No, of course not. Not lease. But perhaps you, they, act as agent for certain properties?'

'Oh ye-es. Definitely, and they cause more hassle than the rest put together. You see, you've got a landlord to deal with as well as a tenant and . . .'

'What sort of properties? Privately owned they'd be smaller than the apartment blocks.'

'Oh ye-es. That's right. Like cottages most of them. But always like close to the water's edge, and with names like, you know, the Smuggler's Haunt, and the Fisherman's Rest. There's a lot of them. At Buckler's Hard there's a couple. At Lymington up the road from our apartments. And at Keyhaven, and at Mudeford in Christchurch Harbour . . .'

Tyler could hold it in no longer: 'We've been watching the wrong fucking places. You could have told us this, you know.'

'Language. You never asked me. I could of said you never fucking asked me, but I didn't, did I?'

The Customs and Excise chief who had been hovering behind now intervened. 'Tyler, you're in overall charge of this operation. But I want you to record right now my expressed advice to you that we have to go in now. We know there's cocaine in the area, even if we're still not quite sure where. We know Bridge is out there and we have a warrant out for him, we are obliged to execute that warrant. We know the operation is being masterminded from the Tower at Swaythe. I shall record my objections in the strongest terms if we do not.'

'Powder on the table, so kick the doors down. Okay. But let's go carefully. Seal off the Tower. Get some marksmen in, Bridge is a killer and Burke can use a gun if he chooses to. Come on. We're going down too. It's been a long haul and I want to see the end of it.'

The first of two mobiles, a Rover 3500 in police livery, reached Keyhaven just as Rupert was about to leave. But instead of crossing the narrow bridge, it drove on to the top of the slipway above the jetty. Parked up by the cottage on the other side of what was now a muddy creek, the Trafic was almost hidden from it by bramble bushes. Rupert watched two officers in shirt-sleeves get out, put on their peaked hats with chequered bands, trot down to the jetty with their black radios slapping their broad thighs. Only one went into the boat. Rupert counted five. Let him find the bodies, then move at the maximum moment of distraction. He saw the officer still on the jetty respond to a shout, he supposed, from below, let in the clutch and came out gently, crossed the bridge behind them, hoped they would be too preoccupied with the shambles on the boat to notice him.

Whether they did or not he never knew, but a second mobile entering the tiny village in front of him certainly did. He saw the sudden white-faced glare of the number two in the passenger seat, saw the driver reach for his handmike as they passed, saw them in his rear-view mirror starting to make the turn before a bend in the road cut them off.

What to do? Wait and see. No point in trying to gun away from them – they've got more power, more manoeuvrability. Here they come. But staying behind. Why? Because they're pretty sure I'm an armed killer. Following instructions. Don't lose me, but don't move until they've got a roadblock in place in front of me, with shooters. Well, we can play that game for quite a long time, while I work something out.

He swung off the road into a country lane and embarked on a deliberately confused course that he hoped would keep the plods guessing, but at the same time it kept him moving in a zig-zagging way round the Tower, never closer than two miles, never further than four. At one point a farm tractor held him up for half a mile, and the police car came in behind him, but still made no move. This was hairy. If the tractor kept there long enough, they'd have time to set up a block ahead of it, but at last it turned into a field and the lane in front was still clear.

After ten minutes or so of this Rupert made his decision. There was absolutely no way he could tell how far Myklades had rumbled the depth to which he had been shafted. But shafted he was and by now he must know it. So, either way, he was caught, the game was just about all up. What had Harry said: it all feels a bit like *Götterdämmerung* here. Valhalla on fire. Not a show one would want to miss. Grinning again the Honourable Rupert Bridge took the left turn that would bring him soonest to the Tower, conscious that if the opportunity arose he had ample means for making a notable contribution to the fireworks.

'Yes, Derek. I've got that. Yes. Yes. Repeat that. Yes. Just a sec.' Cradling the black phone between his jowl and his collar Burke felt for a handerkerchief and wiped his broad but receding feline brow. His right hand continued to write in shorthand across the scribble pad in front of him. He pushed the handkerchief away. 'Go on, Derek. Right. Yes. Yes, I agree with you, it certainly looks like it. Right. Okay. Yes, go home, tell the lads they're all to go to their homes as quickly as they can but quietly. Then hang on in there. Hopefully I'll be in touch in a few days, and I'm sure there'll be enough in the Burke Castle account to pay you off, if it comes to that. Anyway, that's it for now. You're a good lad, Derek – I'll see you clear, never you fear, old son. Love to the missus.' And he hung up. Held his low forehead for a moment, pulled his hand down his long nose that started so broadly, ended with a point. Then he tore off the top sheet from the pad.

'Well?' Myklades snarled from a face that was blotched with scarlet again, the scarlet of the guelder berries in the copse below. 'Remember my forefathers decapitated bringers of bad news.'

'Get your hatchet then.' Burke glanced at the sheet, crumpled it, binned it. 'The police have occupied the village of Swaythe. That's what it looks like. There are eight mobiles, an ops van, a couple of minibuses. All in all about fifty men. And they've got shooters.'

Once more Harriet heard the long serrated wail which, high-pitched though it was, seemed to come from deep in the Armenian's chest. Then, swearing blasphemously and obscenely, he stormed out of the control room and round the big front room, sweeping ornaments, glasses, and bottles to the floor. At last he came back but held now a large automatic, silver-plated, which he levelled straight at Harriet's forehead. 'You. You and your whoreson cousin have done this. True Britons both. I have given you millions. I have given you a real life. I have even sealed you both to me with my seed. Yet you do this to me. Only the English could do this. Only the focking English are capable of this sort of perfidy. Beneath your smiling faces and your easy manners, you are self-seekers all, carrion-eaters, feeding off the maggoty leavings of lions.' He lowered the gun, put it on the console, and almost she fainted. He came across to her, took her face in his hands. 'My haggard, but no *yarak*. A bird of passage and now you want to be on your way again. Well, we shall see, we shall see.' Suddenly he forced a kiss on her, from lips that were hot again and scaly, then he shuddered and drew back. 'You kiss like Judas. Like the whore you are.'

Then he stood back and smashed her across the face, forehand and backhand, so the little diamond in his gold ring tore her cheek and lip. He watched her slip to the floor cradling her head in her arms, between her knees, then he turned to Burke. 'Activate Charleroi.'

Burke's face was expressionless yet pulsed with energy like a cornered fox's mask, whiskers trembling, eyes alert, calculating. 'I don't advise that, sir. It's not a scheme I ever approved. Very dangerous, almost certain to fail.'

Myklades reached for his gun. 'Do it.'

Burke shrugged, swung round on his revolving stool, picked up the phone again, dabbed numbers. 'Jimmy? Bert here. The boss says activate Charleroi. Good luck. You're going to need it.' He swivelled back to Myklades. 'Fifteen minutes.'

'That long?'

'He has to file his flight plan.'

'Right.' Myklades looked up at the seven screens that still glowed. 'Tell them to abort. Even though they are carrying excrement.'

'I was going to anyway.' Burke turned back to the keyboards. One button on each carried the single word. He tapped it seven times to the seven boats that were still running downwind with the pack towards the Solent. On each screen the message scrolled: 'Abort. Wait at least five minutes and no more than thirty for repeat confirmation signal. On receipt of confirmation signal, and not before, activate abort procedures.'

Harriet raised her blood- and tear-streaked face, looked round. 'Where's he gone, Bert? What's he doing?'

Burke shrugged. 'Packing?'

'Charleroi?'

'The ultimate fallback. The contingency plan we use when everything has gone as wrong as it possibly can. Don't know why he called it that.'

'I do. It's the road Napoleon fled by when he knew he had lost Waterloo.'

She pulled herself unsteadily to her feet, pulled herself along the wall of the tiny corridor that led to the bedrooms that filled most of the east side.

Myklades had already stripped. He was standing in front of the small dressing-table, one leg up on the stool, leaning forward, trying to push something into his anus. His eyes red-rimmed behind awry spectacles caught hers in the mirror, then flinched away, filled with the hurt that still sometimes touched her. 'I can't get it in. It's two focking flabby.'

'Let me.'

It was a condom, apparently filled with cotton wool, but not packed tightly.

'What's in it?'

'Diamonds. Go on. Push. It has to go right in. Past the sphincter.'

'Doesn't it hurt? I'm afraid my nails might tear . . .'

'Go on.'

The resistance gave and the hole swallowed the pack.

He stood up, rubbed his scrawny pimpled buttocks, reached for his pants, then a body belt. Moving quickly, he began to fill it – with documents, two passports, credit cards, ten gold Krugerrand. He buckled it, said: 'You should pack too. A passport at least you cannot do without.'

She frowned. 'How . . .?'

'Helicopter. It will be here in ten minutes.'

She shook her head. 'I'm not coming with you. Not off here. Into a helicopter.'

'But you have to. The photographs. The negatives. They are almost the only asset I have left of any real value.'

Tearful but determined. 'I'm not coming.'

He was buttoning a shirt, the green one she had made him wear at Southampton nearly a year ago, with the HM monogram. 'Then give me the negatives.'

'I can't. They're not here. You know that.'

'Then you have to come with me. Focking tie.'

'Let me.' He raised his chin and she knotted it for him neatly. Gold and brown acanthus pattern from Liberty. 'Your poor neck. It's no use, Hector. Just now you were angry, beat me, threatened me with that beastly gun, and now you've remembered that I might still be some use so you are trying to be nice. It won't do.'

He pulled on trousers, socks, shoes, exactly the ones he had used before. 'Maybe. But you betrayed me. See, that is the truth. How much? Enough. A word or two to Mulligan, not much but the right words. So if things went wrong here he'd get you orf. I am not stupid, you know?' He pulled on the French belted jacket. 'There . . . What's that noise?'

Police sirens, ambulance too perhaps, yelped and wailed.

He moved swiftly back to the big room, to the glass wall that overlooked an undulating plain of grass and gorse, then scrub, finally the sea. The wind was dropping, the sea looked grey, tired but still restless, the sunlight was intermittent, the Needles had resumed their usual grubby greyness. There were still whole flotillas of boats in the Solent though far fewer in Christchurch Bay.

Across the grass, still a good quarter of a mile away, came the Trafic van, black and gold, bucking and weaving over the uneven ground like a light-tormented bug, and behind but fanned out on either side two police cars, keeping a distance, not closing, but with headlights on and blue beacons flashing. A third was closing from the right at an angle that would bring them up to the foot of the Tower together.

'Is it Rupe?'

'Yes. My gun. Where is it? Let me kill him.'

He was gone for only a moment or two but in that time Rupert slewed the van across the entrance to the Tower, bringing its acutely angled nose within feet of the fenders of the car that had been coming from the side. Using the opened driver's door as cover he loosed off three shots which starred the police car's windscreen, killed the driver.

Then very coolly, but briskly and precisely, he adjusted the angle of the Trafic so the front fenders of the two vehicles touched, and the rear corner of the van lay against the wall of the tower, enclosing the entrance.

At this point the other two police cars also backed off, and Myklades, leaning over the concrete balustrade, fired twice at Rupert, below him. He missed, one whined away off the side of the van. Rupert reached inside and presently Burke appeared at Myklades' elbow.

'He's on the RT. Says he reckoned you've activated Charleroi and that you'd better let him in or else he'll blow you out of the sky.'

'How?'

'He has a Nutcracker in there.'

'Tell him Harriet will be coming with me. His' – and he spat the words – 'kissing cousin.' He seized Harriet with his left hand, clawing into her upper arm, and pushed the muzzle of the gun into the nape of her neck.

Five, ten seconds of sudden silence, then out of it crescendoing demonically the thrashing clatter of a large twin-rotor helicopter. But before it could blot out all other noise, both Harriet and Myklades heard the beginning of Burke's answer. 'He says fuck Harriet she must have told them about Mermaid Pleasure, open the door . . .'

The noise became pandemonium, the wind from the rotors smashed through the Tower like a demented bully, its shape blocked out the sun, a ladder snaked down towards the balcony, and Myklades released Harriet's arm but kept the gun muzzle in her neck as he groped for it.

Then several things happened almost simultaneously. A police marksman got a bead on Rupert's ankle, under the van, and shot his foot off. He realised the game was up, and released a K-D Nutcracker ground-to-air missile straight up vertically above him, and Burke, ex-Superintendent Burke, knocked off Myklades' head with one shot from the police-issue .38 Smith and Wesson he had somehow contrived to keep in his possession. The Chinook, repainted white, shredded under the impact of the missile. One rotor, cast free, spiralled into the sky like a child's toy. Most of the rest, spewing blazing oil and fuel, smashed straight down on top of its destroyer. With it it carried most of Myklades' body – his hand had grasped the ladder rung in an unbreakable grip at the moment of the bullet's impact. Presently the explosion of the Trafic's fuel tank and two unused Nutcracker missiles completed the holocaust.

Silence fell like a healing mantle and through it Burke moved. First he picked up Harriet. She was moaning, obviously in very deep shock, but physically undamaged, although her face was streaked with blood and bits of Myklades' head. He carried her into her room, put her on the bed and covered her with as many blankets as he could find. He went into the control room and pressed again the abort buttons on the seven remaining keyboards. He then put his gun down on the table in front of the door to the lift, sat and thought for a moment. Finally he threw a master switch, and the screens went blank, their memories erased.

During the last three minutes of all this the telephone had been ringing. Ears numbed by the explosions had been deaf to it.

'Burke here. You'll have to speak up, all that left me a bit hard of hearing. Tyler? Yes, I'll release the door. There's no one here now but me and the woman Jones. She's in shock but not I think otherwise hurt. Okay? Now, I'm opening the door. Oh, come on, Rex. I'm not going to do anything stupid. I'm just a security guard. You know that.'

Tyler, Mulligan, Porter, and a police surgeon came out of the lift. Tyler and Mulligan moved round the four sides of the Tower, through all the rooms, with the abstracted attention of tourists visiting a museum dedicated to a realm of human knowledge about which they are almost entirely ignorant. The police surgeon and Bea Porter attended to Harriet – the doctor gave her an injection, the policewoman very gently and carefully, and murmuring words of comfort not all of them in English, cleaned her up.

Tyler confronted his ex-colleague. 'Of course I have to arrest you, Burke.'

'Of course you do, Mr Tyler. But on what charge?'

'Several. But mainly aiding and abetting a conspiracy to import prohibited substances. Manslaughter too, from the look of things.'

Burke smiled his weaselly smile. 'I stand to be corrected on this one, Rex. But I think you'll find all the substances in question will turn out to be a pesticide. A . . . pest . . . i . . . cide. The homicide was in defence of a lady who was about to be dropped two hundred feet. What you can get me on, though, is unlawful possession of a gun.' He pointed to his Smith and Wesson.

'Fuck you, Bert.'

'Rex, you can try.'

Ambulance men contrived to get Harriet down the lift in a stretcher. Mulligan, left for a moment with WPC Porter, said: 'There's something about your accent. The way you speak English.'

Suddenly relieved by something so totally unimportant, inconsequential, she was tricked into a laugh. Her big brown eyes widened, her generous mouth opened over strong teeth. 'My grandparents were tally-anns. We still speak it at home.'

'Italians?'

'Hairdressers and purveyors of home-made ice-cream.'

'And Porter? The name . . . Porter.'

'Portinari.'

Mulligan rolled the words off his tongue, giving them a full, exaggerated Italian pronunciation: 'Beatrice Portinari . . .' He looked at her for a long moment, thought, thought again, and turned away.

During the afternoon the seven yachts tacked back through Christchurch Bay. On the way, in obedience to the abort signal, they dropped their cargoes overboard. Five of them dropped one hundred kilos each of Sol-Methrine B (Sol-Chem AG Düsseldorf). In the coming months the eco-systems of the bay collapsed: this had little economic effect – the local fishermen went out into the Channel for their catches. There were fewer local mussels and lobsters, and the small boys who fished for crabs off the sea wall with hookless lines baited with

650

bacon rind found that nothing was biting. By the following spring the area had recovered.

Two of the boats dropped cocaine in similarly labelled bags. It had been Bridge's plan that he would deliver Sol-Methrine to the warehouse Mermaid Pleasure had leased from Woolingham Enterprises and stack it with one hundred bags, two hundred kilos, of cocaine in the front. By this simple stratagem he had hoped at least to buy time to get out of Myklades' reach, and at best to convince him that he too had been tricked by Aguirre and the Colombians. Meanwhile ninety per cent of the original cocaine he had seen loaded on to the *San Fermín* would remain on it and in the possession of the Arias syndicate. For all this he had been paid by Arias, through Aguirre, four million pounds, much of it already converted to gems bought in Amsterdam.

The skipper of one of the yachts carrying real cocaine could not resist the temptation and kept back two kilos. Prices rose during the autumn and he was able to sell them outright for three hundred thousand pounds.

The cocaine that was dropped in the sea had less effect on the environment than the pesticide — in fact no noticeable effect at all.

It was of course an embarrassment to the NDIU and Tyler in particular that yet again no cocaine at all was intercepted as a result of these operations. However, enough of the whole Web came apart in the aftermath, enough cocaine was found still moving at the lower ends of the chain, and enough frightened people came forward. Arrests were made. It was discovered that two of the market-makers in Ambrose had been disguising coke receipts and coke payments by the simple expedient of using a time-date stamp set a week slow. Thus they could study the markets in their own time and forge transactions which exactly fitted the way they had moved. They could say, for example, to a distributor like Roget that they had bought and sold futures in foreign currencies for him over a week and made him a very substantial profit. And anyone looking into the transactions would have found they echoed the way that market had moved. On a larger scale but by the same method they made the coke profits of Myklades' companies look like the result of successful speculation, profits which could then be passed through offshore companies to Mendoza Holdings. It is of course very difficult indeed to get a time-date stamp that is wrong. But it can be done . . . if you have to hand the sort of starter capital Myklades had had.

One other consequence of the immediate lack of powder on the table was that Mulligan had no difficulty in securing the very early release of Harriet Jones.

65

Four weeks later, in the first week of September, Harriet returned to Amsterdam. She arrived in more style this time, from Provence where she had been recovering in her parents' converted farmhouse, travelling in a first-class sleeper. She still preferred not to fly unless she had to.

The wide square of the Dam was filled with golden sunlight, the usual tourists and buskers. There were, as before, Buddhist mendicants, *Hare Krishna, hare Krishna, hare, hare, hare Rama*, and a hundred or so backpackers and inter-railers pretending they knew where to go.

She knew: to the post office where her passport was all she needed to reclaim Rupert's diamonds. And Van Willet was the obvious person to take them to.

In his bright shop with its theatrical contrast between work and seduction, between the benches where stones were cut, ground and polished, and the sales area with its low soft leather seats and carefully focused lights, he welcomed her effusively but threw in a moment of memory for . . . 'Poor Roget. I knew he was up to no good. I did what I could to help him but . . .' A massive shrug. He had put on more weight in eighteen months.

Then he tipped the stones across a spread piece of chamois leather and was suddenly silent. He screwed up his right eye-socket, pushed a loupe glass into it, stirred the little heap with a pair of tweezers.

'You want me to buy them?'

'Yes.'

'I want to know . . . their provenance. Proof of your title to them.'

She gave him documents Rupert had left in an envelope in his room at the Tower, addressed to her. And a copy of his death certificate.

'I'll check these out. Come back in the morning.'

She stayed in gilded luxury in the Hotel Europe, dined on the pills her parents' French doctor had prescribed. Lovejoy himself could not have done more.

She left Van Willet's shop in the morning with a banker's draft worth a quarter of a million pounds. This, with the Eurobonds to be collected in Madrid, left her with nearly six hundred grand. In a sad sort of way she was pleased.

In the flower market she bought a large bunch of bronze chrysanthemums. She carried them to Rembrandtsplein and laid them in front of the small statue in the middle. For Paul. Paul Roget. As she turned away, she realised Mulligan had come up behind her.

'I'd like to say thank you. For Mermaid Pleasure. And sorry. Well, for lots of things.' He explained: she was still under surveillance – Eurac had heard she was in Amsterdam. He wanted to see her.

Over coffee in a brown bar she asked: 'Can you tell me what Rupe was up to? Where he got these diamonds from?'

Mulligan stirred sugar into the top of a cappuccino. 'The diamonds. That's easy. Can't prove it. Arias, the Colombians, you know, paid him with them – and a lot more too, I daresay, if we could find it – to make some sort of switch in the cargo so they kept the cocaine and Myklades, Crystal, got pesticide. Of course he could do whatever the fuck he liked.'

She frowned, puzzled by his sudden anger. 'Why? How?'

'Because he was working for, well . . . the secret service. MI whatsit. As well. And if you're working for them you can do whatever you goddamn like. You know it's worse here in that respect than it is in America? If you're a spook, you're a god.'

'Hec . . . Myklades knew about that.'

'Sure he did. But I bet he didn't know Bridge was recruited first by security and only second by Myklades. But don't get the idea he was some sort of spy martyr – '

'No. I wouldn't think that of Rupert. Can I have a cigarette?' How many had he lit for her? Surely this was the last. 'But why the spooks? I mean why the spooks versus Crystal.

Aren't we on the same side? European civilisation. Freedom. All that?'

She said it flippantly, but, and at last and for the first time, he really began to hate her: for he knew that if she ever thought about such things at all, this was what she thought. Still, for the sake of the record, to keep things straight, he marshalled what he had made out of it all.

'Crystal, the people they were fronting for and funding, the whole shoot, is a nostalgia trip. Down Memory Lane. And right now European capitalism needs it like a hole in the head. They were rocking the boat. I mean, for Christ's sake, rocketing a memorial service at an extermination camp? They were half a century behind the times. No doubt there will be a time again for something like Crystal, but not now. Europe's booming, and pushing back the frontiers of socialism in every area. Privatisation. Anti-union laws. Repatriation of immigrant workers. We're fascist already. And the anti-Semitism? Crazy. Look at Israel. Whose side do you think they're on? But the odd thing is this. In spite of the spooks, at the end of the day nobody pulled down Crystal. It imploded. Like a star. Collapsed on itself. Its inner contradictions, which is no more to say than the conflicting interests of its parts, destroyed it. It self-destructed, became a black hole. There's a sort of hope still in that, you know?'

She didn't, but she smiled. 'Listen. I've a load of negatives left. Photos of Myklades which are meant to tie him in with Crystal. You can have them if you want.'

'Are you trying to be a goodie after all?'

'Sort of.'

'Forget them as far as I'm concerned. They won't lead to any convictions. But they could embarrass. They could be an asset. For you.'

Presently he leant across the table, caught her chin in his hand and kissed her. He stood, buttoned his coat. 'I am sorry.'

'Why?'

'I used you.' And he went. Leaving her with the bill. She could afford it.

66

Pedro Mendoza y La Cerda, duque de Pastrana y príncipe de Eboli, stood naked in the unglazed, high-arched window of a Moorish tower. His skin was pallid and spotted, his body thin, wasted, his pale eyes bloodshot and luminously set in dark sockets. The once rich brown hair that had curled so robustly lay lank and unkempt to the prominent vertebra between his sharp-edged shoulder-blades. From the shadows behind him a strong brown hand offered a small round box. In the fingers of his right hand he took a large pinch of purple snuff, spread it on the back of his left hand, then snorted.

He remained rigid and his eyes burned, fixed on a rocky ledge a hundred metres or so away. There was a tiny cave behind it, and it was littered with droppings, small bones, fur. Presently a small eagle, brown-backed, with gold eyes, gold cere above an agate beak, gold talons, the leading edge of its scapulars edged with white and a black band across its white tail, launched itself into the freedom of the air, and as it soared in ever-widening circles its bright cold eyes flickered over the domain that lay spread below. Under the influence of the hallucinatory snuff Pedro believed he was that bird, and since the land it flew over had been his since childhood, it was not difficult for him to believe that his soul had flown from his mouth and entered it, that his soul saw through the bird's eyes.

First there was the palace itself, a series of interlinked courtyards following the line of the ridge it was set on, and enclosed below by battlemented fortifications. It was smaller than the Alhambra, but not much. Orange-trees with green fruit just yellowing nodded over sunlit pools where golden carp hung suspended in umber depths. Tiny fountains offered liquid tintinnabulations in cloisters of slender columns.

The pinions tilted, carried the bird up and behind the palace over fastnesses of rock and scree where shreds of snow still clung above etiolated pines, and the sea gleamed like molten lead beneath a dark horizon fifty miles away. Round he came again and rolling valleys unfolded beneath him. Wheatfields blackened beneath white plumes of smoke from burning stubble; herds of black bulls roamed idly through parklike forests of ilex and cork; topped-out olives, gnarled and grey, marched in strictly regimented phalanxes that scoffed at the unevenness of the ground, marched with squared-off citrus-groves whose night-dark leaves enshrined the glowing brightness of unripened fruit.

Between him and all this black swifts on their long way south swirled and swooped for midges, bright-blue rollers lolloped over the plantations, and jewelled bee-eaters collected on the telephone wires whose posts marked the twisting white road that climbed into the Sierra from the plain below.

A Peugeot 501 Estate, peacock-blue, air-conditioned, took the sharper bends and steeper slopes with untested ease, surged on, left the vegas behind, parted a bank of smoke from the stubble – from inside, Lili Brel could see the orange flames licking beneath it – entered the forest. Black monsters with black-tipped horns, broad heads dropping to noses narrower than those on conventional cattle, huge sleek shoulders, narrow rumps bearing a brand-mark formed from a P and an M, looked up at the passing car. She looked at her immaculate fingernails and remembered the dogs that had sweated out the sun of a Californian spring on the other side of the world, eighteen months ago. They too had signalled Pedro's obsession with breeding.

The eagle, Bonelli's Eagle, *Hieraaetus fasciatus* – so called because its spread tail with its banded end recalls the Roman bundle of rods that was carried before magistrates, the *fasces* that became the symbol of the Fascists – narrowed the sweep of its flight so it came back, back over the central garden of the palace. A long pool elegantly scalloped suggested a sinuousness appropriate to Paradise, to the Garden of Eden that Islamic gardens recall. There were exotic potted shrubs and small trees; goldfinches, bullfinches and canaries sang from suspended cages.

Here at one end of the pool sat a woman fit, like Eve, to queen it in any earthly paradise. Jana Pensión's skin was now quite deeply bronzed, she had let her hair grow a little, bound it with a gold fillet that matched her sandals. Her loose green cotton dress enhanced the beauty of a woman pregnant and near her term, who has eaten all the right things, done all the right exercises. On her lap, her long brown wrists curved round the swollen womb and her fingers flickered deliberately over her sewing. She was, as women brought up on smallholdings in Oklahoma still do when pregnant, stitching together a quilt for her baby's cot. The hexagonal shapes were, however, cut from finer fabrics than her mother had had to hand twenty-six years before.

Thirty yards away, at the other end of the pool, two men faced each other across a marble table set in exquisitely wrought iron: Boltana and Giorgio Vasari.

In a year and a half Vasari had hardly changed: less hair, more fat, and liverish eyes set in purple rings that still left one with the inaccurate impression of a man terminally ill. His grey suit looked as if he had been sleeping in it ever since, and his open-necked white shirt was grubby with ball-point fluid stains, sweat, and travel. Boltana, on the other hand, had lost weight, was in better tone than he had been for twenty years, wore a dark blue Aertex shirt, pale grey slacks and dark blue canvas shoes. The glow on his skin came from health as well as good living, and almost matched Jana's in its perfection. Occasionally, across the pool, through bird- and burbling water-song, she could hear their voices: Boltana spoke in Spanish, Vasari in Italian, but they understood each other perfectly.

Vasari's mission was clear: the engagement settlement he had drawn up between Pedro Mendoza and the Malatestas had not been met by Mendoza. The marriage was off: it was time to invoke penalty clauses, claim large sums of money, some property, and a Velázquez that had been held in escrow in New York.

Boltana, on his side, aimed to show that the party of the second part was guilty of fraudulent misrepresentation. And he believed he had the documents to prove it. He unlocked a steel case covered with crocodile skin and pulled out a file about an inch and a half thick. The red plastic cover looked new, was printed across the centre with the words *Europa Malatesta*, and in the bottom right-hand corner, one above the

657

other, *Prof. Reinaldo Pacelli, Dr Guy Lovejoy*. But inside the first page had an old worn look, was covered by fine handwriting, a strong twentieth-century italic, the once black ink now faded to a deep sepia but still legible.

Boltana gave the Italian time to skim through what was obviously a preamble, then turned the page. Vasari reached for the glass of liquid gold at his elbow, drank half of it, grimaced, wiped his mouth. Pale fino, the very driest in the world, didn't sit agreeably on his stomach, though he admired, and just now needed, its unfortified strength. He chewed a couple of manzanilla olives, spat the pits into the pool. A carp drifted towards them, glittered, sank.

Jana stitched on, a grim little smile playing on her lips as she inwardly recalled what Vasari was now looking at as Boltana turned the next three pages. On each, in the harsh colour-printing of photographs taken twenty years ago in flashlight, the colours even further distorted by time, a sequence unfolded of a naked female baby about three months old taken from every angle and with close-ups. She had a deeply cleft hare-lip, a jaw that even at that age was prognathous. Her eyes were almost invisible beneath heavy upper lids that gave her a Mongolian look, and her ears were only partly formed without the outer whorls. So it went on. The tiny shoulders folded in like a bird's but over a hollow chest, the stomach was already scarred where an emergency operation had corrected a pyloric stenosis, thin membranes linked the toes.

Boltana said: 'Enrico has toes like that, you know? And the same malformation of the chest. And of course his jaw . . . It all bears out entirely Catedrático Pacelli's diagnosis that these conditions were caused by genetic dysfunction . . .'

A car horn and Jana put aside her sewing, moved to the open unglazed arch set between cascades of the soft blue flowers of a Cape leadwort creeper, and looked down the fifty feet of undressed rockface, brilliant with ferns and streaked with mosses, to a small courtyard below. As she did, the microscopic dot of the eagle above her tipped its wings, swept smooth on a bowbend that brought him wide-circling and lower. She watched the passenger get out of the Peugeot, saw the chauffeur take cases from beneath the tailgate. Then she turned and walked the length of the pool.

For a moment she looked over Boltana's shoulder. The photograph mounted on the page now open showed the upper left dorsal torso of an eight-year-old. A grim thick line of black stitching held together a wound that circled the scapula.

'Toñi, Lili Brel has arrived – '

'Good.' He grinned up at her, eyes creased against the sunlight behind her. He turned back to the Milanese lawyer. 'You see, Giorgio, it is not simply a matter of deception: Pedro's doctors are also quite convinced that in large measure these revelations about Europa's genetic lesions contributed very significantly to his present mental condition, and we have been advised that an action for damages on these grounds . . .'

When Vasari left, he bore back to Malatesta the news that while he might or might not win a court case against the Mendozas, what was certain was that Europa's medical history would enter the public domain if he tried.

'Duchesa, Marqués,' said Brel, when he had gone. 'First, I have to report that I am no longer connected at all with Crystal. I have given notice of my resignation to Enrico and he has accepted it. There is virtually no money left in its accounts. I found it quite hard to meet the small expense of my last disbursement . . .'

Boltana rumbled: 'Idle curiosity prompts me to ask what that may have been.'

'A wreath for poor Rudi Hess. Now. We still have some pretty hard work ahead of us if we're going to save the BCC, without ruining Mendoza Holdings. As you know, Mendoza Holdings owes BCC nearly two billion Swiss francs, which moneys it disbursed to Arias for the two tons of cocaine he stole back, and to Ambrose in London against the time when Hector would have been able to realise the proceeds of the sale of the cocaine. Following events in England, there is now no possibility whatsoever of that debt being paid in the way we expected. So unless we do something pretty clever and pretty soon, either BCC or MH goes to the wall.'

She opened her case, spread papers across the table from which Europa's file had been cleared, looked over her spectacles at Boltana and Pensión, who were now sitting across one of the corners of the table. Boltana's large hard rested on the

American girl's thinner, smaller wrist and his fingers reached forward to play with the simple gold band on her ring finger.

Brel cleared her throat. 'If the strategy I've prepared is to work, then I must be sure of two things. One. That the validity of Miss Pensión's marriage to Pedro will not be challenged. Two, that the paternity of the child she is carrying, that the official paternity of the child, will likewise remain unimpeached.'

Boltana rumbled jovially again. 'Lili. Your precise use of language has always been not the least of the reasons why it is such a delight to work with you. That the validity of the marriage *could* be challenged, on the grounds that poor Pedro was not in possession of his right mind when he entered into it, is something we shall all have to live with for the rest of our lives. But the Malatestas are the only people who are likely to want to challenge it, when it is made public, and I think what Vasari has seen today will shut them up for good. As to the paternity of the Duchesa's child, I think I am the only person who might want to challenge that . . . and I am sure you are about to give me very good reasons why I should not.'

'Good.' She offered them both a smile that said more than her smiles usually did: there was irony and complicity in it. 'In that case I think we should be able to move to the next step quite quickly, which is to get Pedro declared legally as well as clinically insane. After that I propose to set up a trust, a regency, to manage Pedro's affairs in his name and on his behalf and that of his putative heir. Until this debt is cleared there is no question of the Marqués having a seat on it, as clearly he will be subject to a conflict of interests. However, the Duchesa – '

'Back off, Lili. Call me Jana like you always did, okay?'

'Well . . . I'll try, but you know I do tend to be a little old-fashioned in these things. Anyway, you will be a principal member of this trust as wife and mother of the two most interested persons. I shall be its chairperson. Once all this is in place, and I don't think it should take too long, I would advise in the first place the sale of Villa Mendoza in California, and of its very considerable art collection. Yes, Duch . . . Jana?'

'Two things. One. If it's at all possible, I'd like to keep Sherpa. The stallion, you know?'

Brel recalled how she had seen the Duchess watching She.pa cover the mare in heat that had been brought to him. She realised now just how wrong her interpretation of the physiotician's reaction had been. 'I'm sure that can be arranged.'

'Two. Harriet. Harriet Jones has in her possession several strips of negative, uncut, with time and date fixes, which indicate that Myklades was in our company on several occasions in the last year or so. She concedes that they would be of little use to the police, but thinks they might be of interest to the press. She wants five hundred thousand Swiss francs, and I think she should be paid.'

Outside, as the afternoon wore on and the purple shadows lengthened in the dried grasses of the meadows under the oaks, the eagle's eye was held by one particular silhouette that signalled to its simple brain the possibility of ecstatic satisfactions. The sweep of its soaring narrowed and it began to drop. The last two hundred feet it took like a stone, then rose again with a red-legged partridge in its claws. Up in the tower, in the darkness of his room, stretched on his fetid palette, Pedro stirred and shared the wild bird's bliss.

That night, in the privacy of her own room, and feeling deliciously relaxed after running through the Jane Fonda exercises for pregnant women, Jana slit open a packet that had arrived for her from Peru, by the evening post. As she expected it contained a further fifty grams of the hallucinogenic powder the Indians use when they want to share the lives of their spirit animals – not much mystery in all this when the powder, which is a powerful drug, is administered by someone with a shaman's powers of suggestion and when the animal and its habitat are intimately understood by the recipient. But there was also a long letter from Immaculada Dalfinger which did contain bad news.

The gist was straightforward enough. Dalfinger had been in close contact with a member of the Arias family: a council of its senior members had concluded that they had exhausted the possibility of extracting any further blood money from the Mendoza family; it was now time to exact the final revenge on Pedro and his heirs and settle the account that had opened when he had effectively murdered Octavia Arias. (That he had done so was not in dispute. It was known that she had discovered that his blood was tainted and that he liked buggering young boys.) Jorge Aguirre had begged for the honour of this task, and the council had commissioned him to carry it out.

Jana, duchesa de Pastrana y principesa de Eboli, gave the matter some thought, but no more than the first woman to claim those titles would have done. Then she found paper and pen and wrote in Spanish more correct than her American English:

Senator Don Guillermo Welser

Señor
We met at a reception in Bogotá last December at which you asked me if I knew anything at all about the disappearance of your daughter María Dolores Welser. At the time we were enjoying the hospitality of your daughter's murderers and fear constrained me from telling you what I knew.

But I now feel able to tell you that the actual killer was Jorge Aguirre, and that the circumstances of your daughter's death were as follows . . .

A Selected List of Fiction Available from Mandarin

While every effort is made to keep prices low, it is sometimes necessary to increase prices at short notice. Mandarin Paperbacks reserves the right to show new retail prices on covers which may differ from those previously advertised in the text or elsewhere.

The prices shown below were correct at the time of going to press.

All these books are available at your bookshop or newsagent, or can be ordered direct from the address below. Just tick the titles you want and fill in the form below.

Cash Sales Department, PO Box 5, Rushden, Northants NN10 6YX.
Fax: 0933 410321 : Phone 0933 410511.

Please send cheque, payable to 'Reed Book Services Ltd.', or postal order for purchase price quoted and allow the following for postage and packing:

£1.00 for the first book, 50p for the second; **FREE POSTAGE AND PACKING FOR THREE BOOKS OR MORE PER ORDER.**

NAME (Block letters) ....

ADDRESS ....

....

☐ I enclose my remittance for ....

☐ I wish to pay by Access/Visa Card Number

Expiry Date

Signature ....

Please quote our reference: MAND